DnDoggos

Get the Party Started

written and illustrated by
Scout Underhill

colors by
Liana Sposto

FEIWEL AND FRIENDS
New York

A Feiwel and Friends Book
An imprint of Macmillan Publishing Group, LLC
120 Broadway, New York, NY 10271 • mackids.com

Our books may be purchased in bulk for promotional, educational,
or business use. Please contact your local bookseller or the Macmillan
Corporate and Premium Sales Department at (800) 221-7945 ext. 5442
or by email at MacmillanSpecialMarkets@macmillan.com.

Library of Congress Control Number: 2023937719

First edition, 2024
Book design by Sharismar Rodriguez and Lisa Vega
Scout used Adobe Photoshop and dog cuddles, and Liana used
Clip Studio Paint and a 13" Wacom Cintiq for the colors.
Feiwel and Friends logo designed by Filomena Tuosto
Printed in China by RR Donnelley Asia Printing Solutions Ltd.,
Dongguan City, Guangdong Province

ISBN 978-1-250-83434-8 (paperback)
1 3 5 7 9 10 8 6 4 2

ISBN 978-1-250-83435-5 (hardcover)
1 3 5 7 9 10 8 6 4 2

To all my dogs past, present, and future—
thank you for keeping me alive.
—Scout

To Scout—
thank you for the adventure (so far)!!
—Liana

Welcome to DnDoggos!
Here you can meet the party!

Tonka (he/him)

Tonka plays a bard. He loves music, especially singing, and has a magical kazoo that he toots.

For Tonka, everything is a fun game! And with his friends by his side, he's sure to bring the fun times.

Pickles (she/her)

Pickles plays a fighter. She is fierce and brave, and ready to face off with monsters and evildoers, and especially stand up for her friends.

Her sword, the Eradicator, is her prized possession!

Zoey (she/her)

Zoey plays a cleric. She relies on her brains and her kindness to help her friends through tough times.

With her cleric's Book of Everything, Zoey is always ready for a riddle or sticky situation!

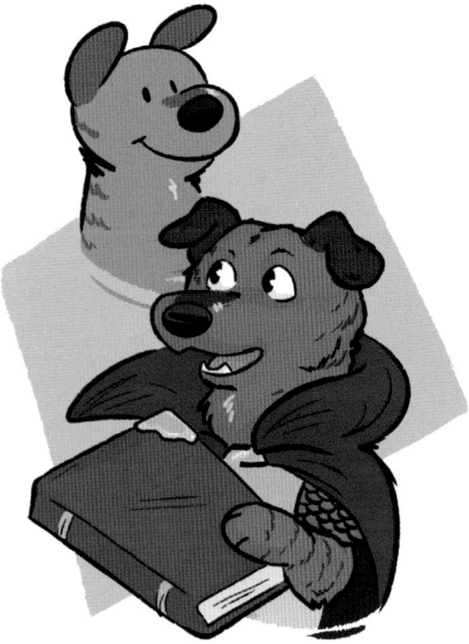

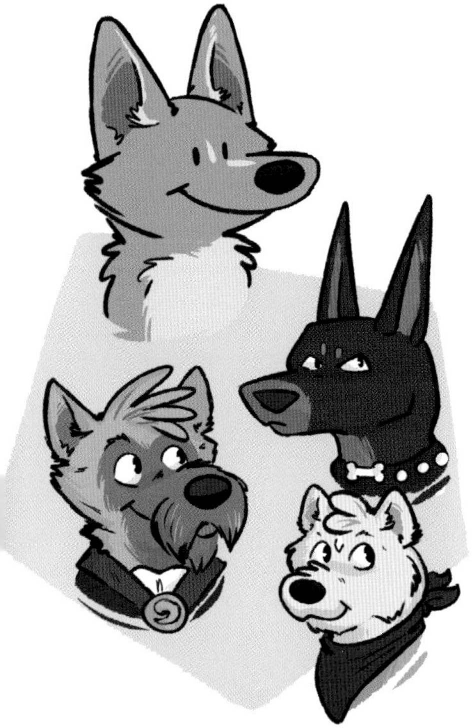

Magnus (he/him)

Magnus plays the Game Master. That means he plans out the epic encounters, all the puzzles, and the extra characters, called NPCs (non-player characters).

That means when you meet Barnabus Barkenstuff and other characters, those are all played by Magnus!

Magnus's narration shows up in boxes like this!

Chapter 1:
A Fetch Quest

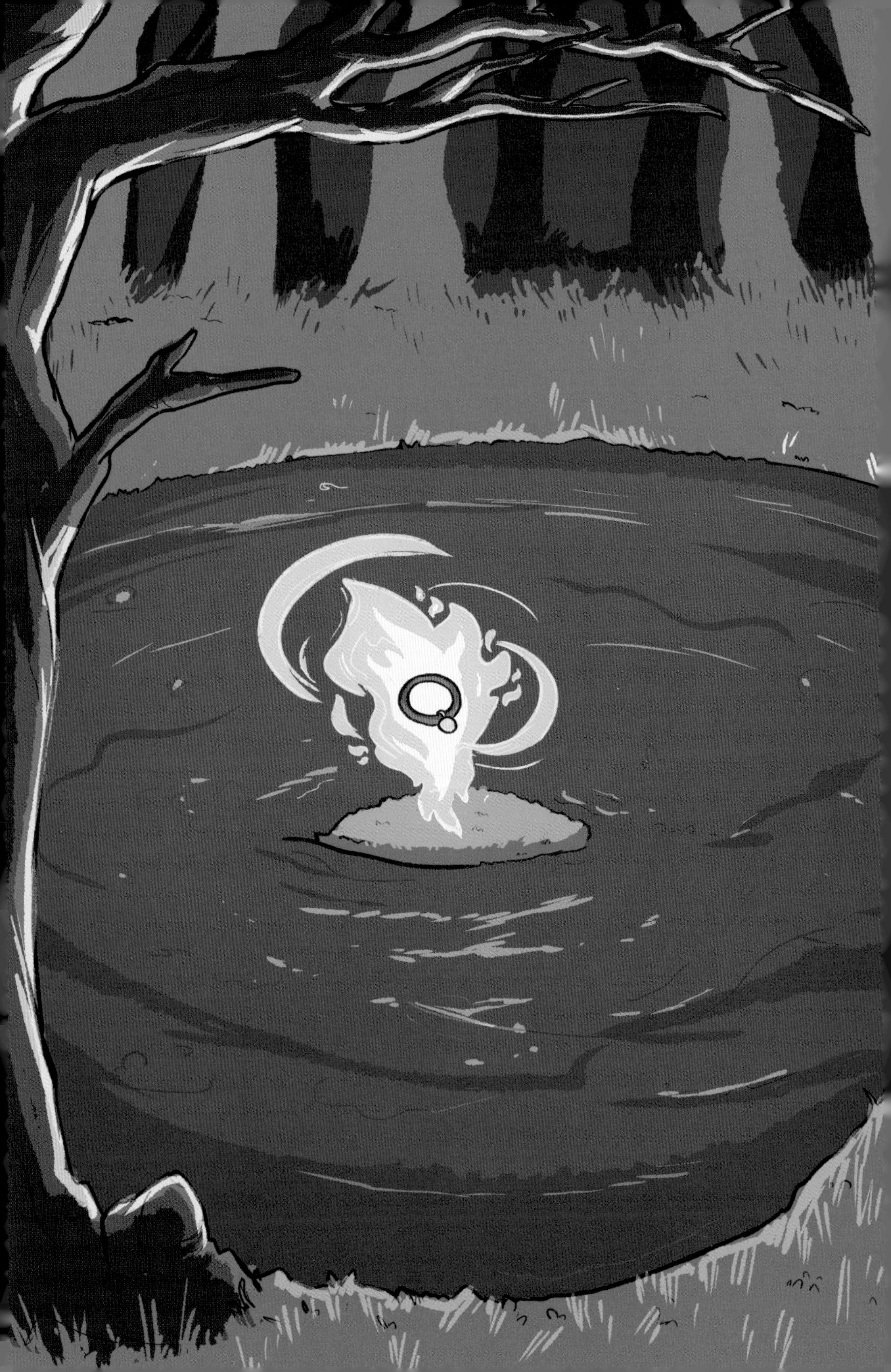

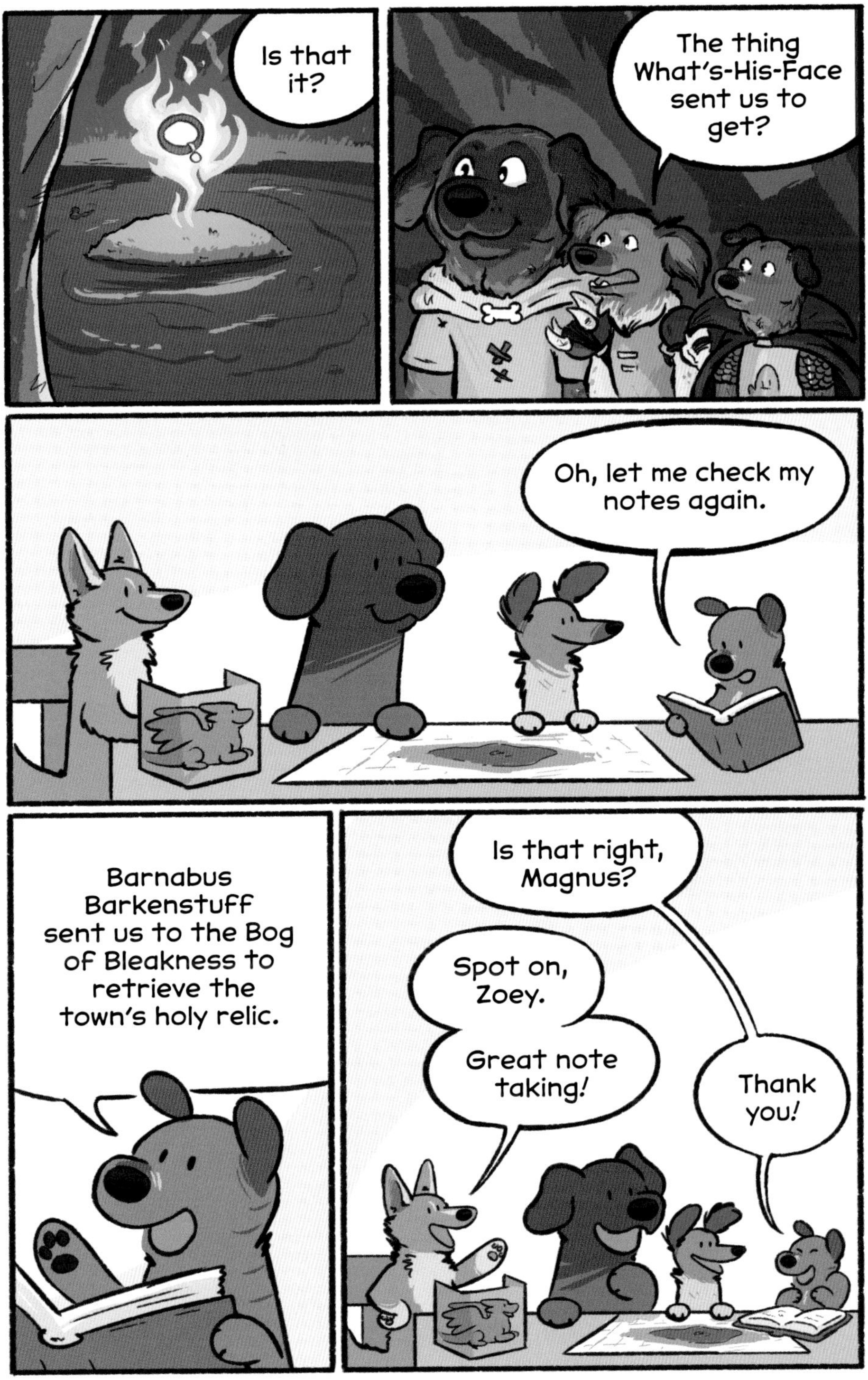
Is that it?
The thing What's-His-Face sent us to get?
Oh, let me check my notes again.
Barnabus Barkenstuff sent us to the Bog of Bleakness to retrieve the town's holy relic.
Is that right, Magnus?
Spot on, Zoey.
Great note taking!
Thank you!

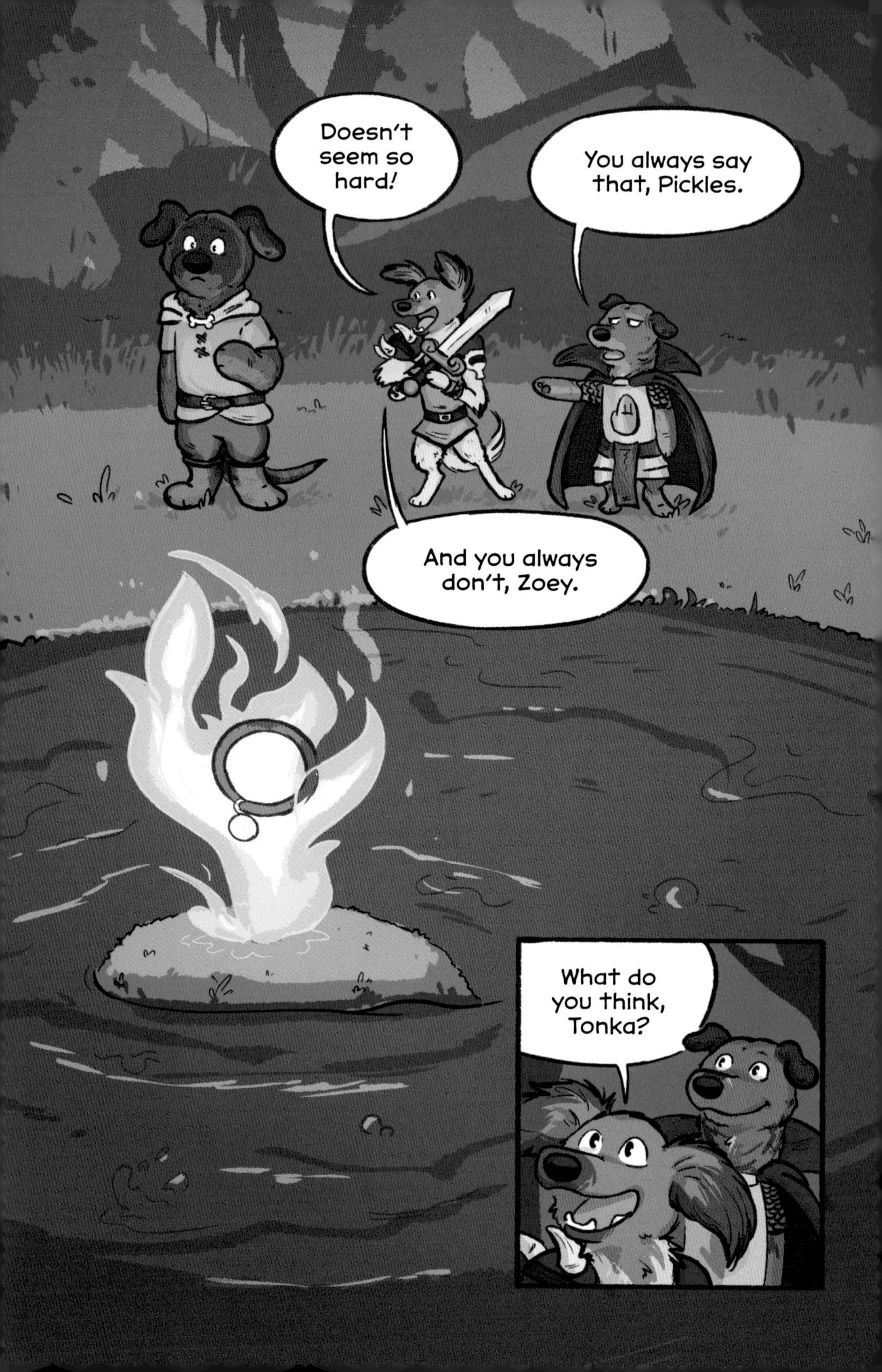
Doesn't seem so hard!
You always say that, Pickles.
And you always don't, Zoey.
What do you think, Tonka?

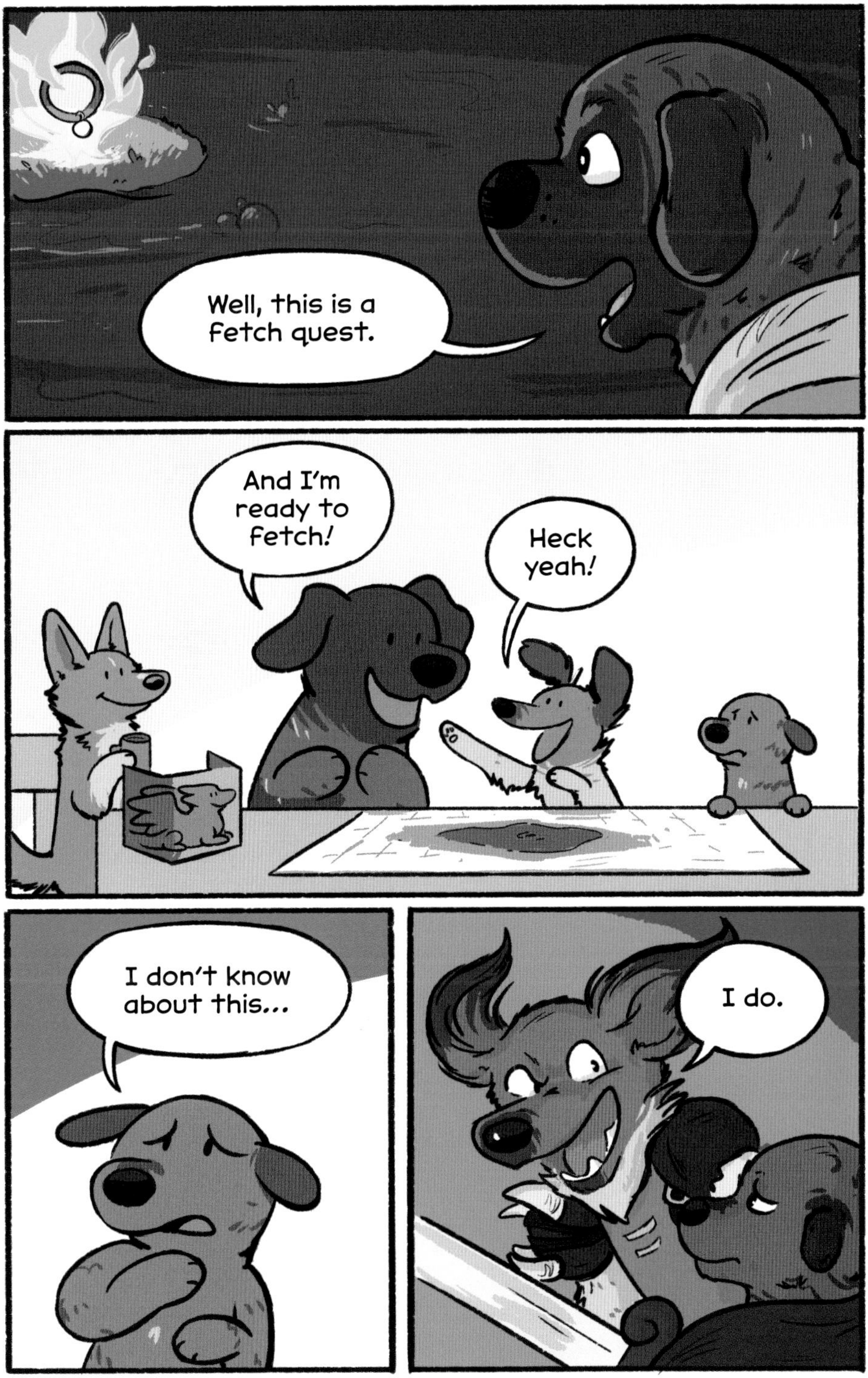
Well, this is a fetch quest.
And I'm ready to fetch!
Heck yeah!
I don't know about this...
I do.

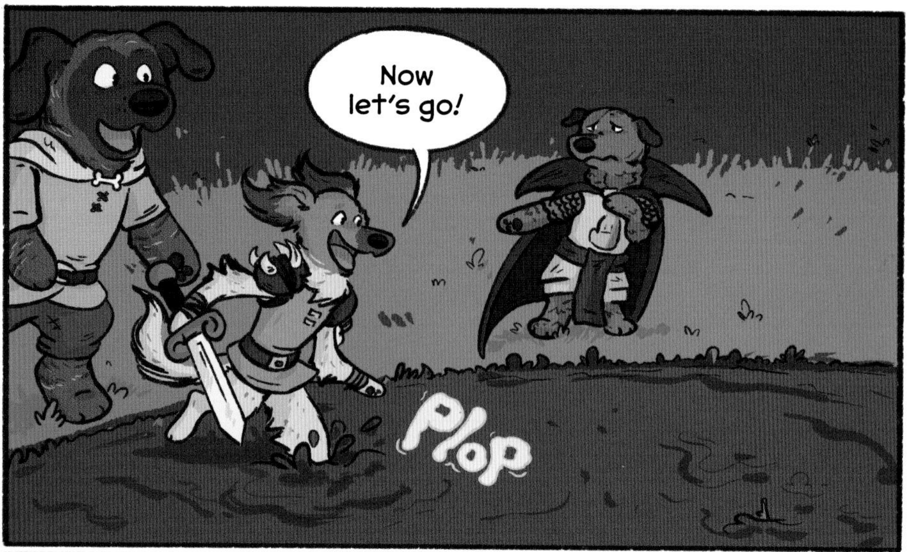
Now let's go!
Plop

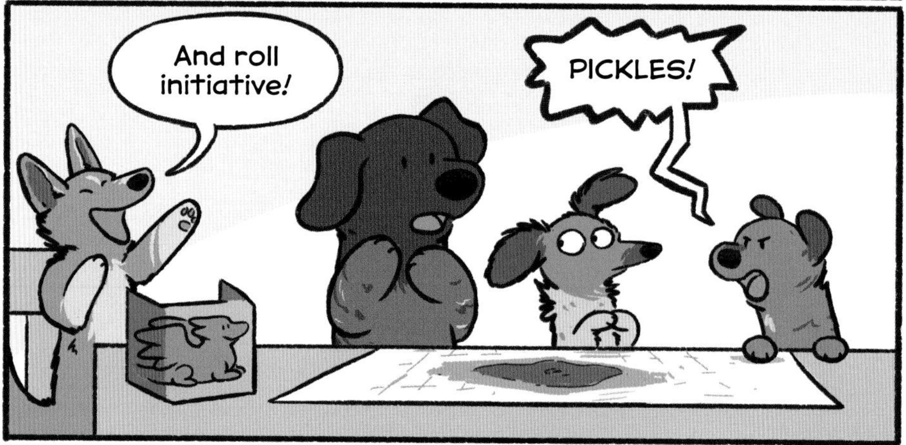
And roll initiative!
PICKLES!

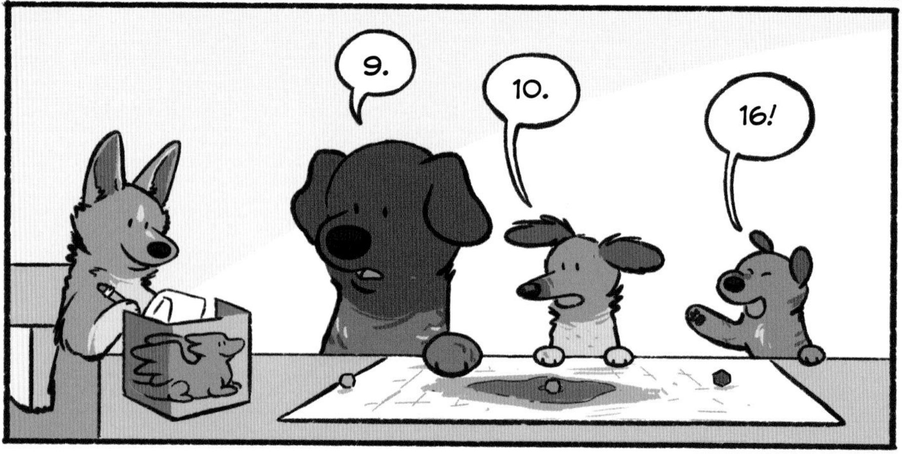
9.
10.
16!

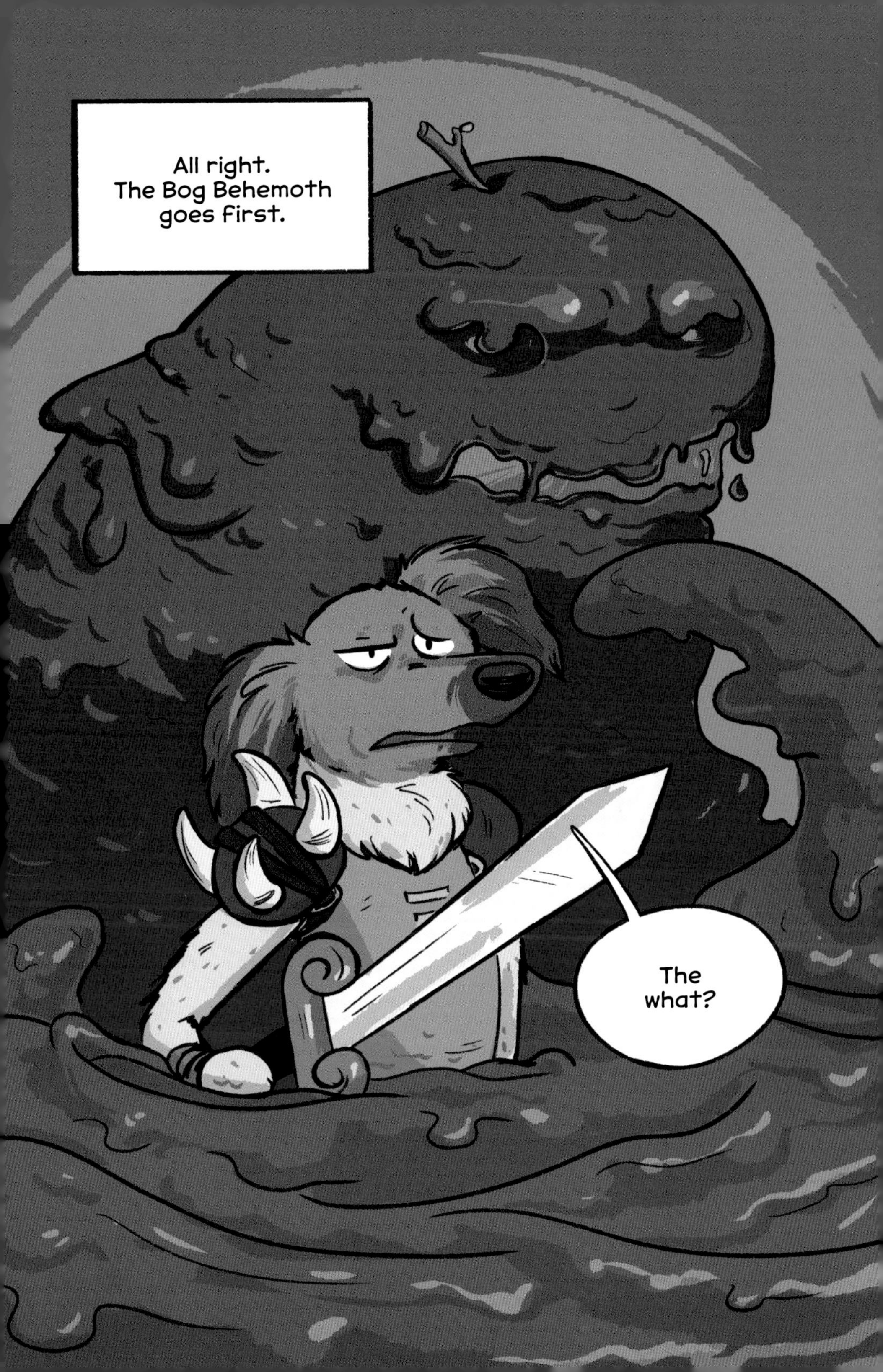
All right.
The Bog Behemoth
goes first.
The
what?

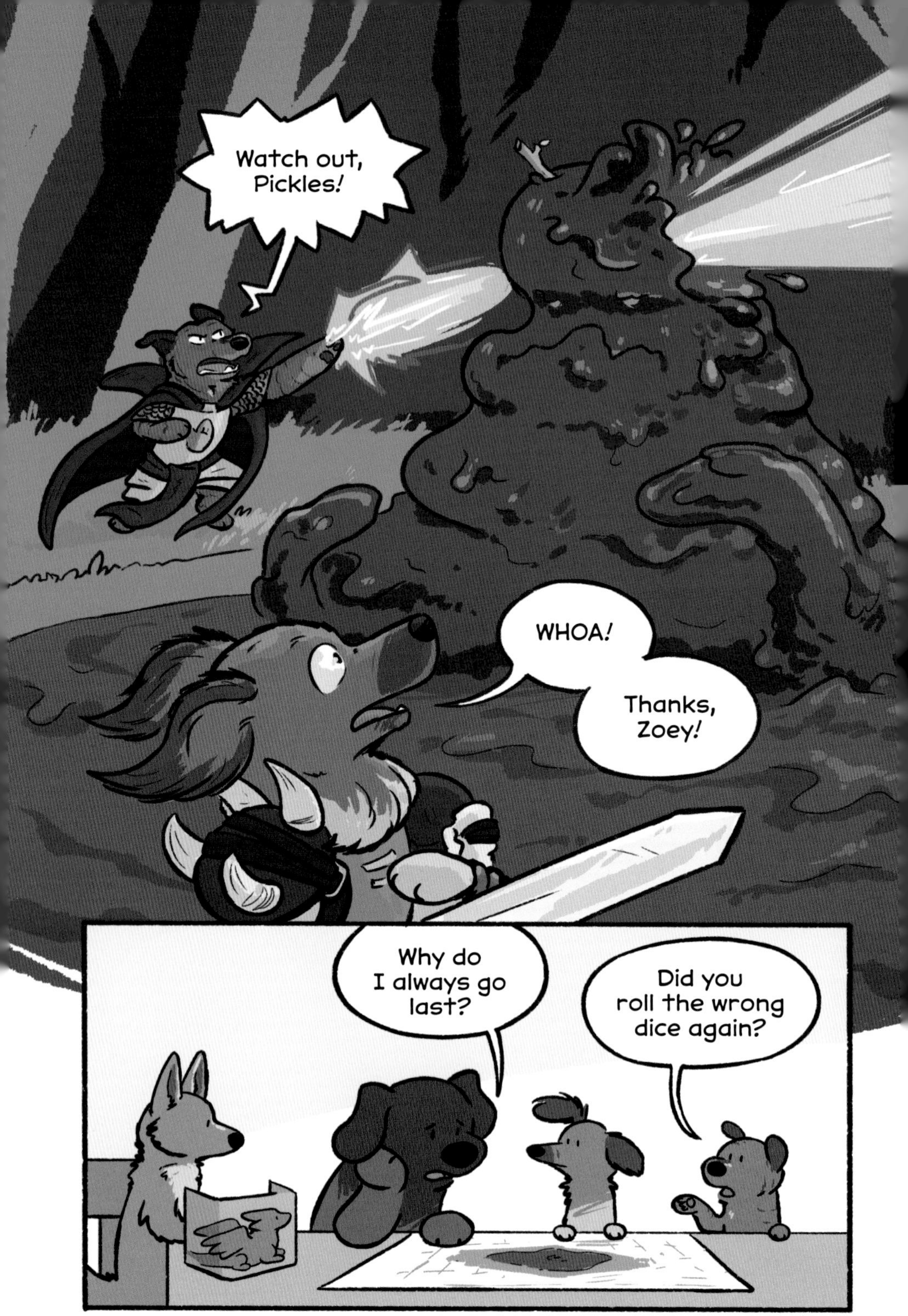
Watch out, Pickles!
WHOA!
Thanks, Zoey!
Why do I always go last?
Did you roll the wrong dice again?

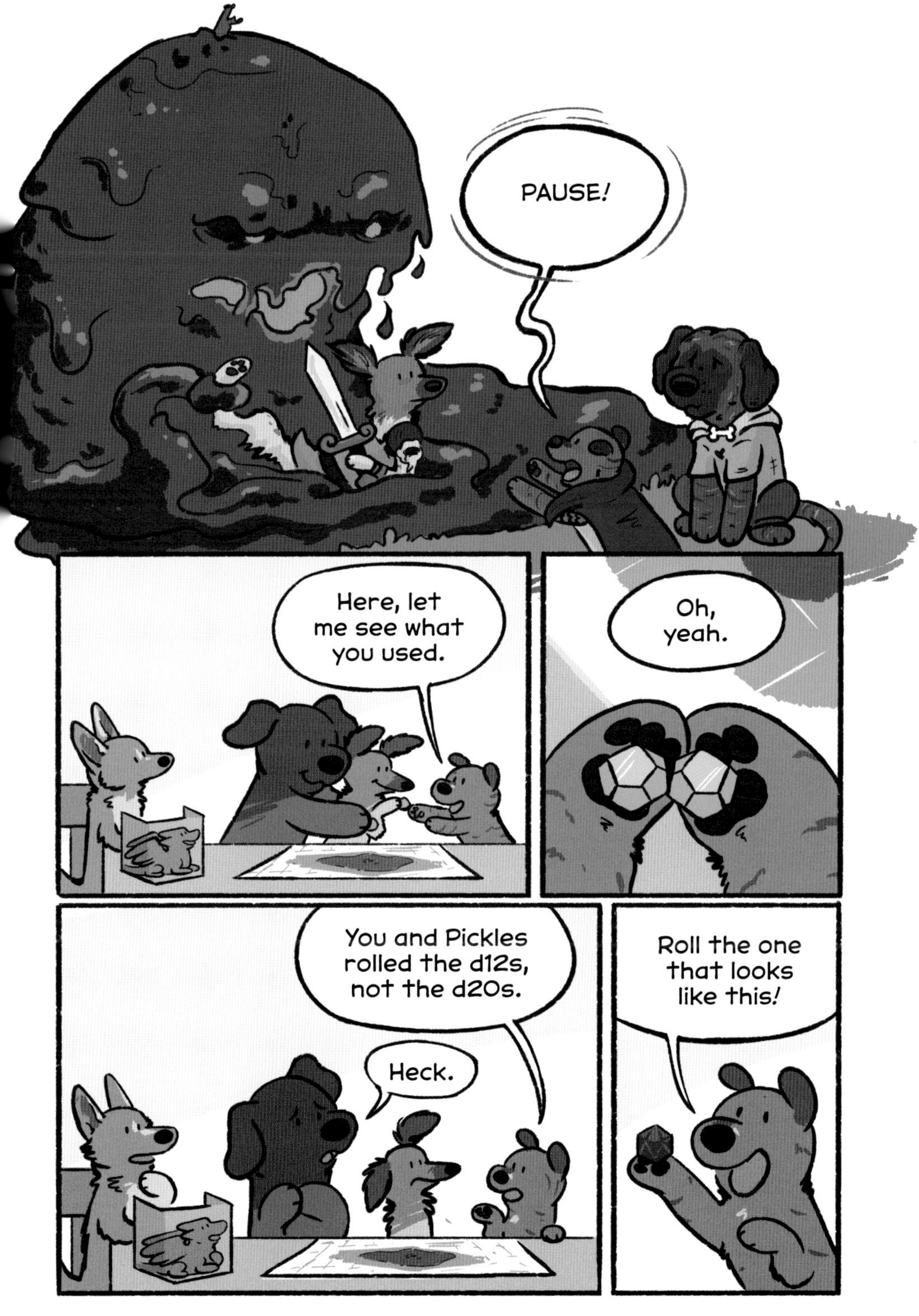
PAUSE!
Here, let me see what you used.
Oh, yeah.
You and Pickles rolled the d12s, not the d20s.
Heck.
Roll the one that looks like this!

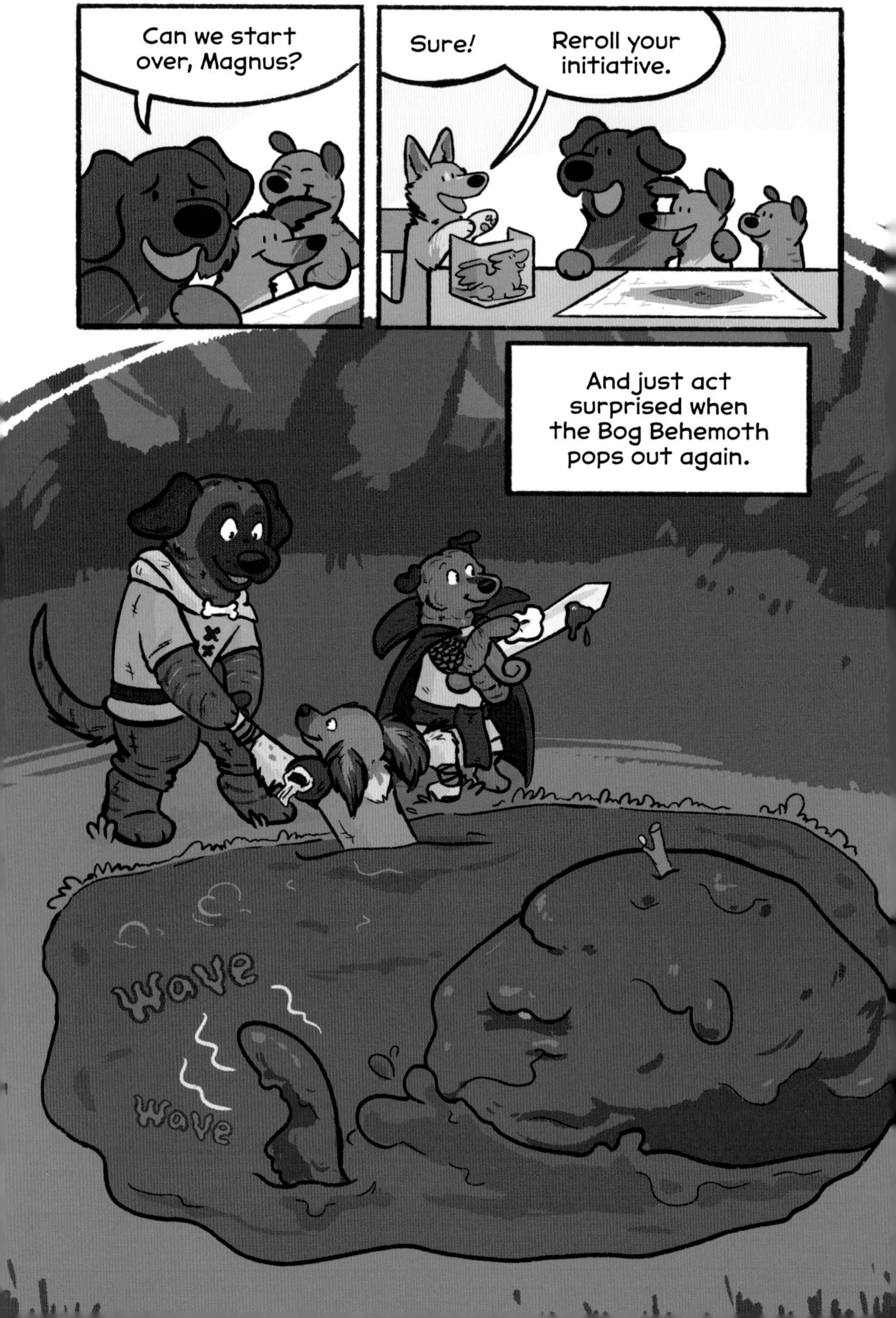

Can we start over, Magnus?
Sure!
Reroll your initiative.
And just act surprised when the Bog Behemoth pops out again.
wave
wave

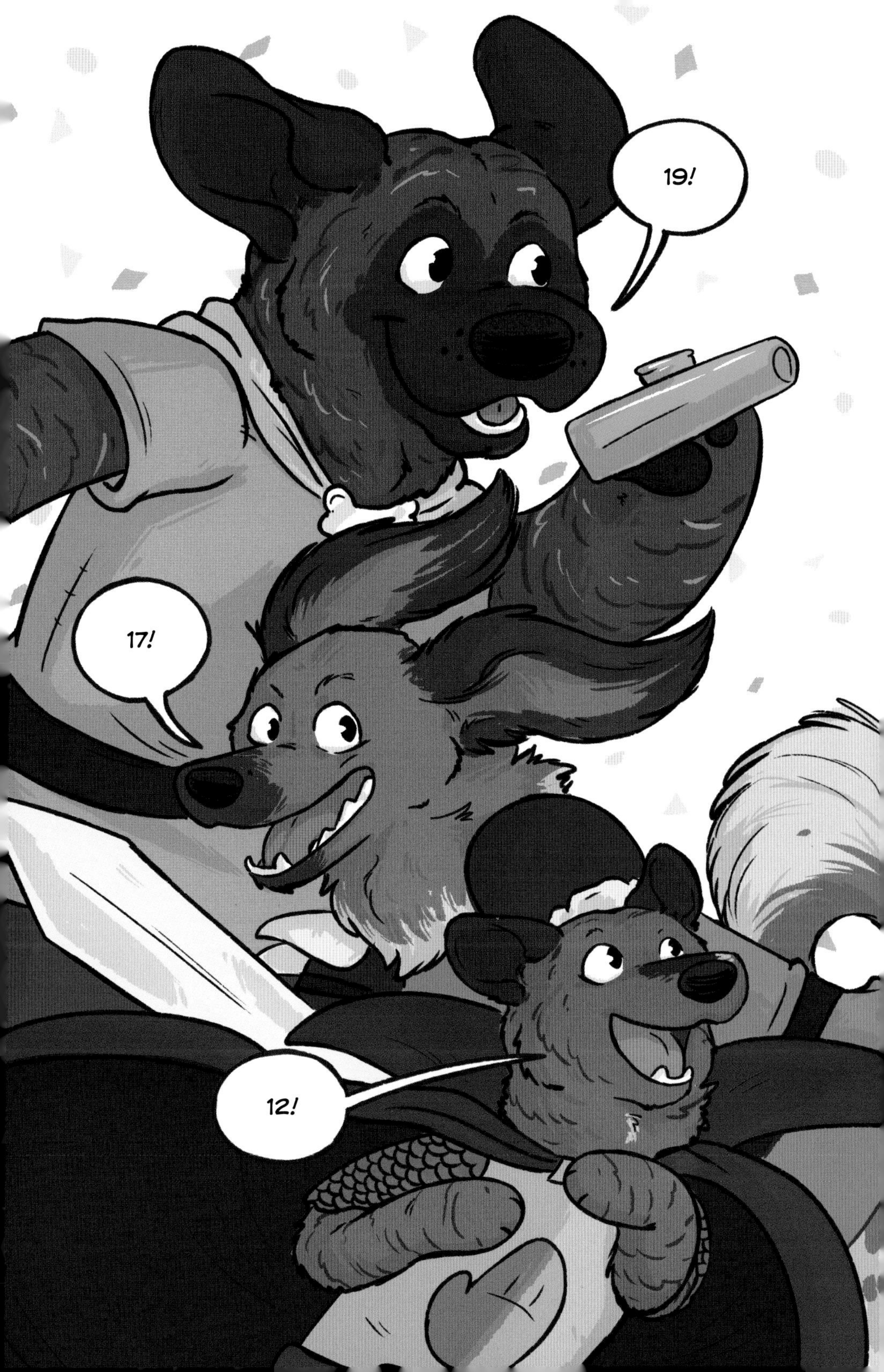
19!
17!
12!

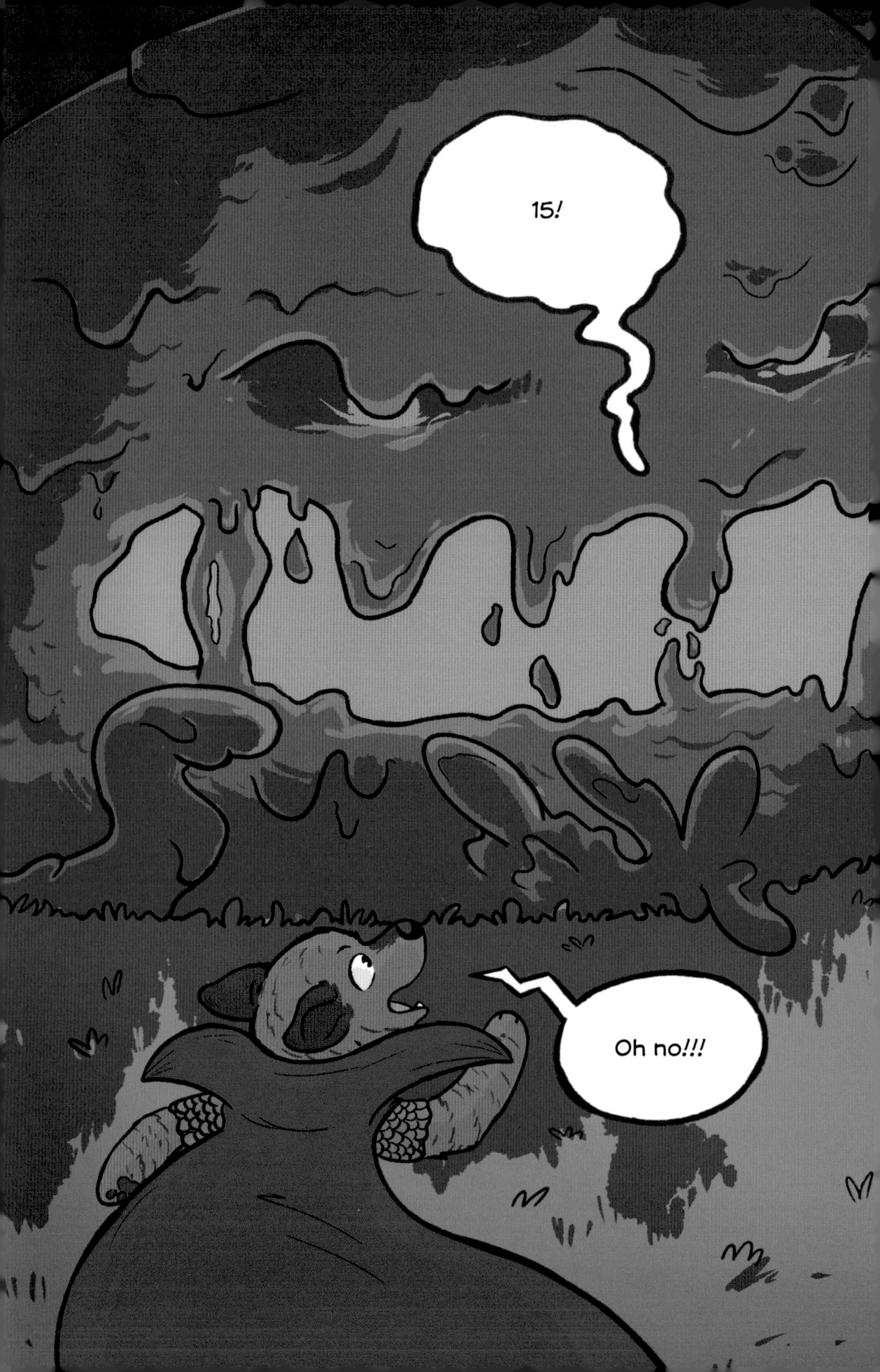
15!
Oh no!!!

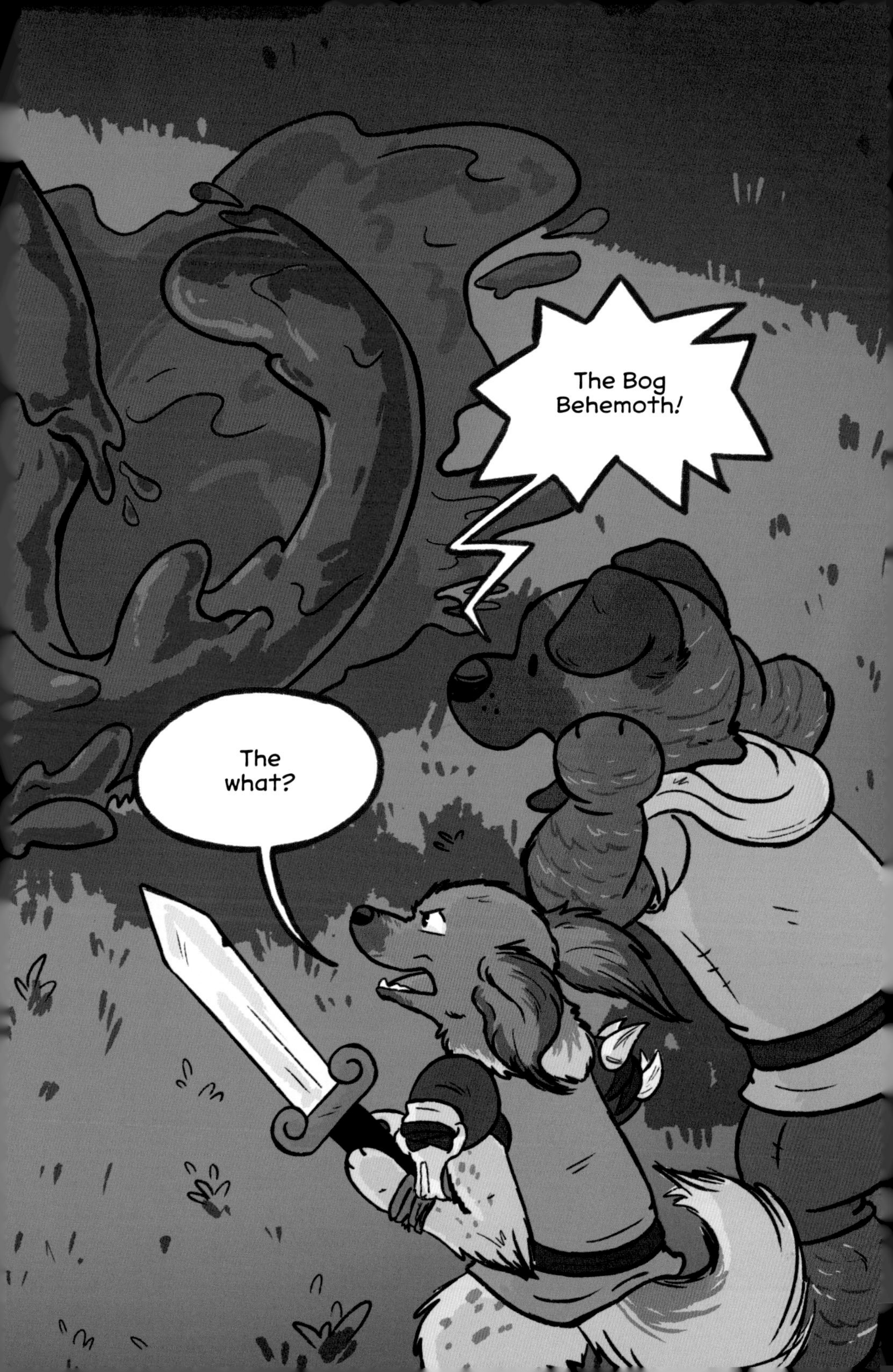
The Bog Behemoth!
The what?

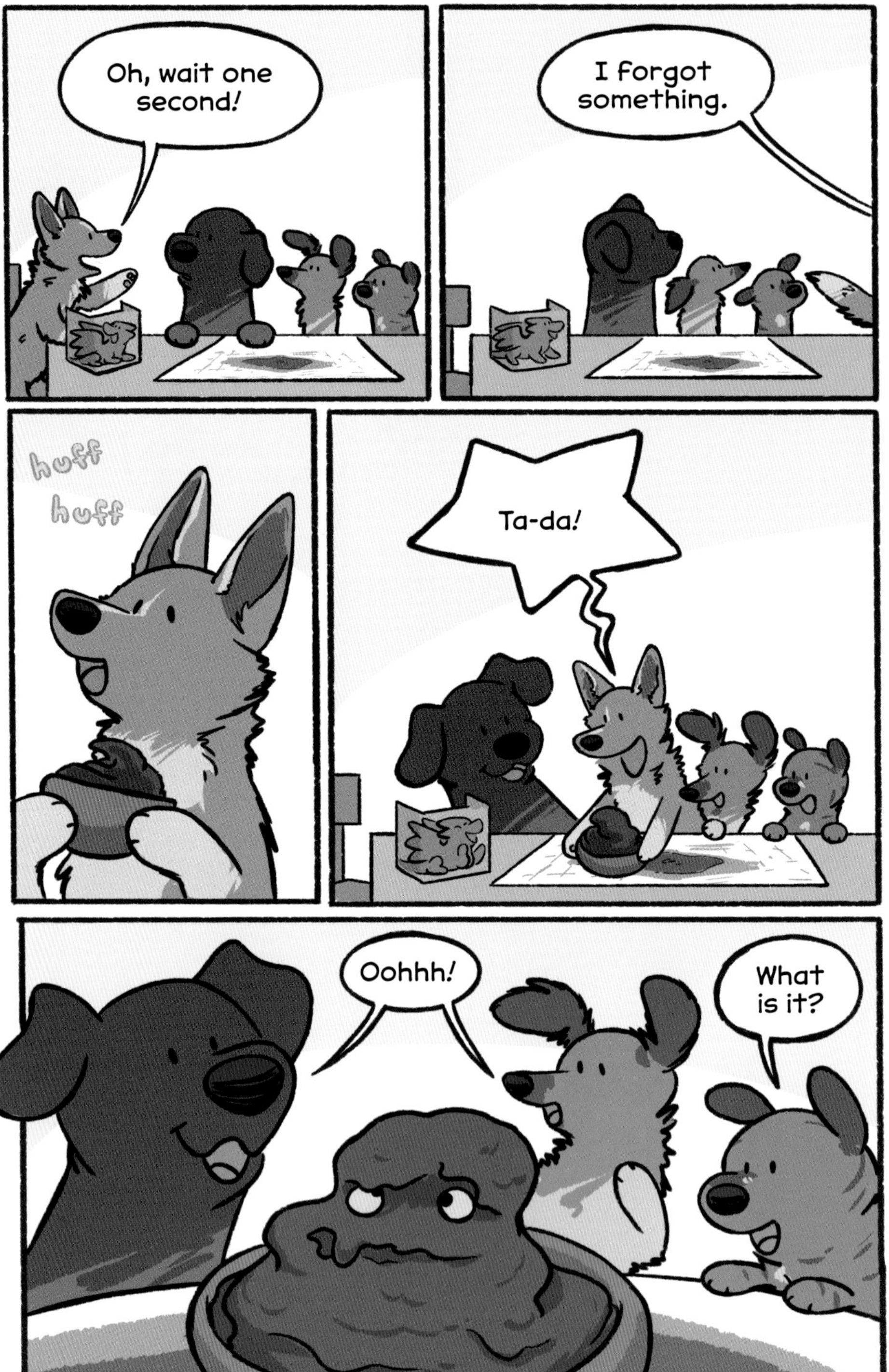
Oh, wait one second!
I forgot something.
huff
huff
Ta-da!
Oohhh!
What is it?

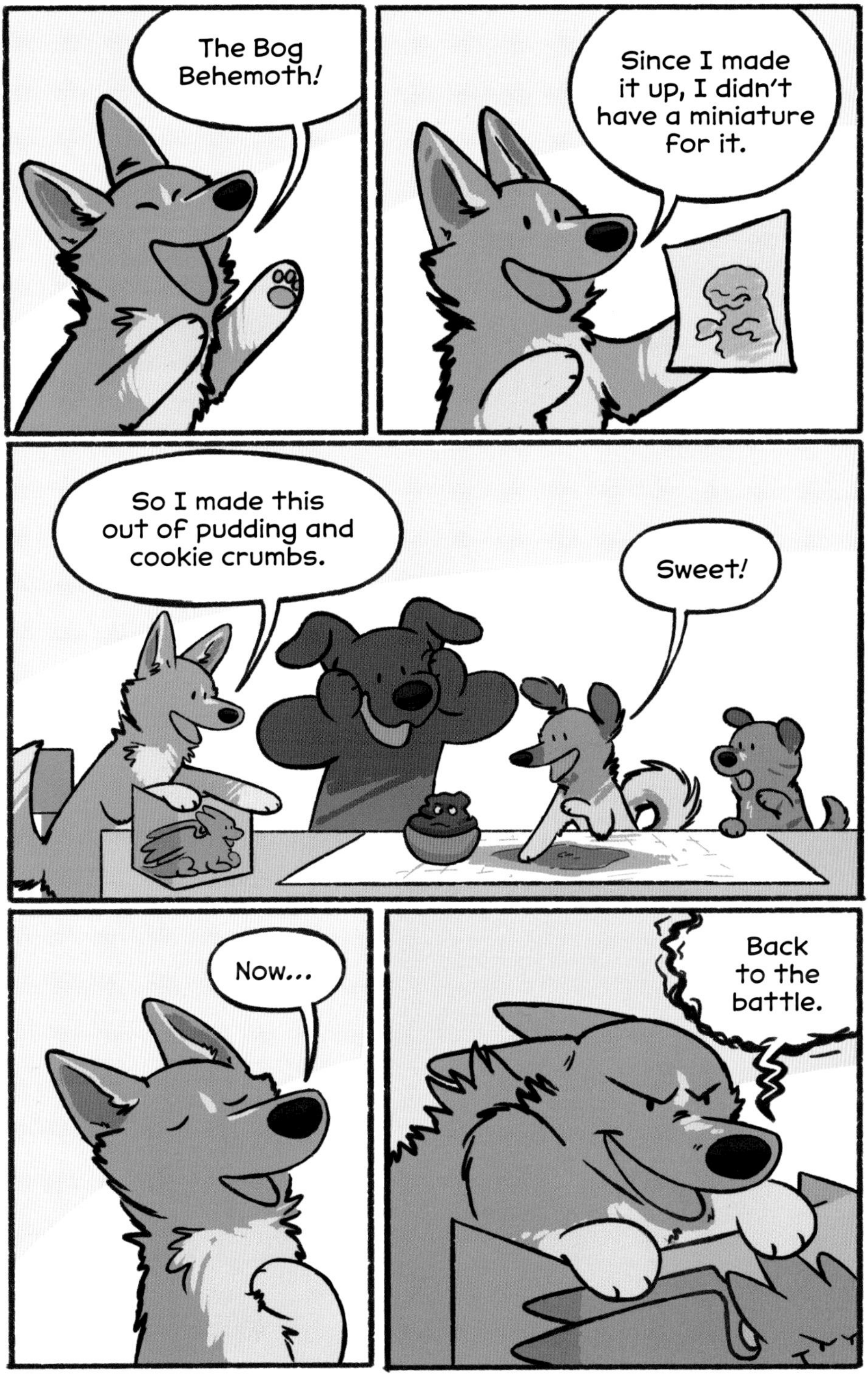
The Bog Behemoth!
Since I made it up, I didn't have a miniature for it.
So I made this out of pudding and cookie crumbs.
Sweet!
Now...
Back to the battle.

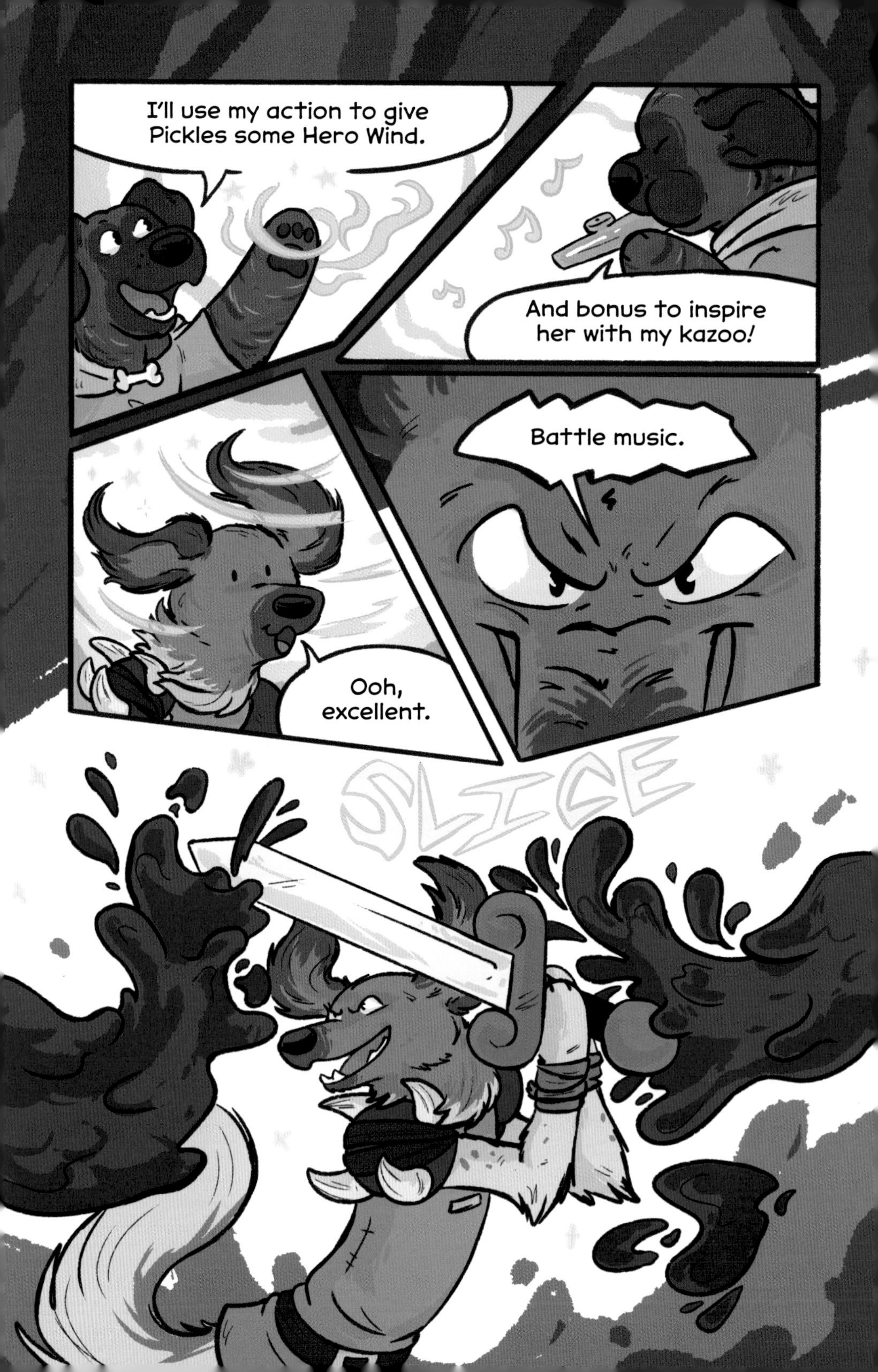
I'll use my action to give Pickles some Hero Wind.
And bonus to inspire her with my kazoo!
Ooh, excellent.
Battle music.
SLICE

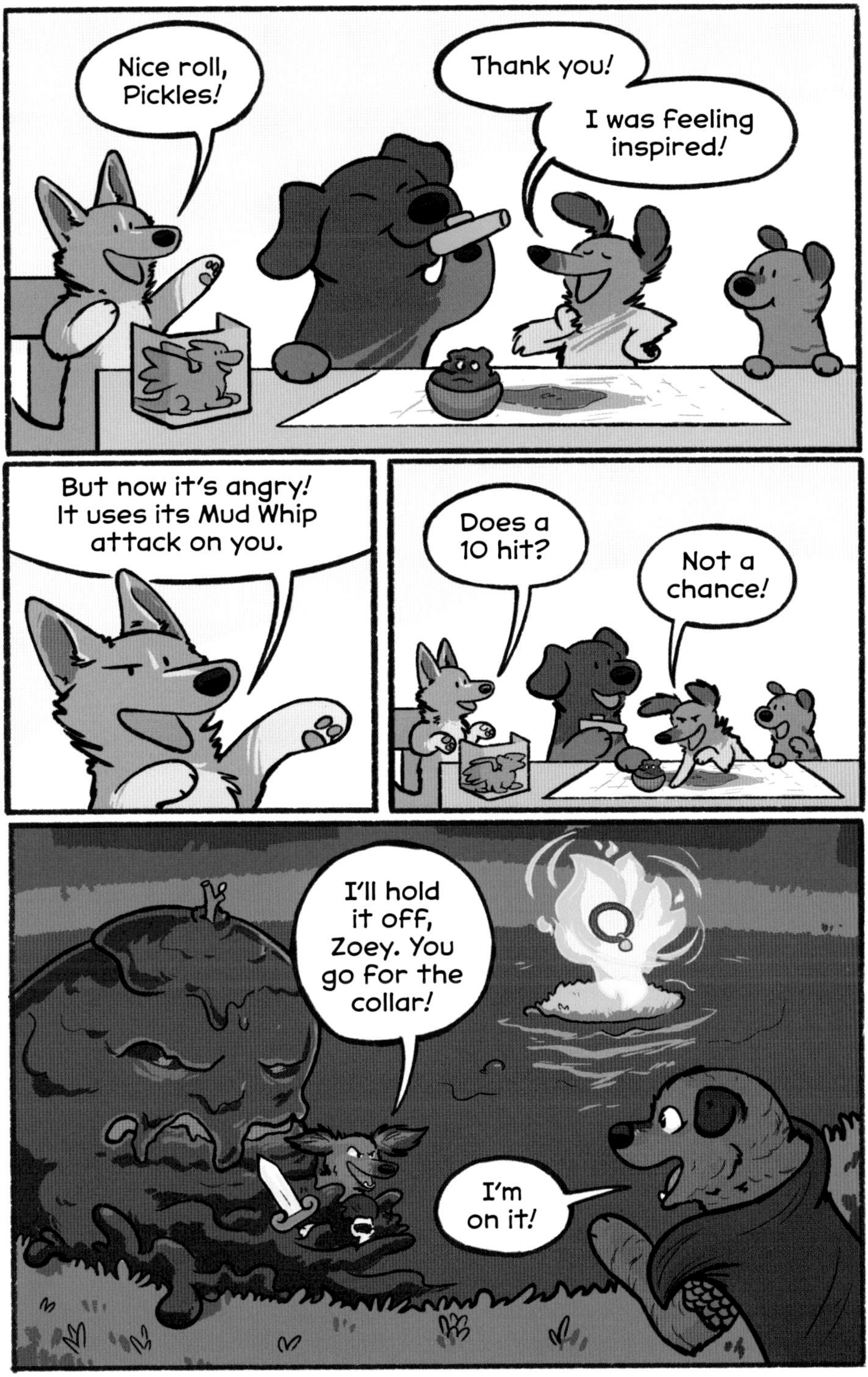
Nice roll, Pickles!
Thank you!
I was feeling inspired!
But now it's angry! It uses its Mud Whip attack on you.
Does a 10 hit?
Not a chance!
I'll hold it off, Zoey. You go for the collar!
I'm on it!

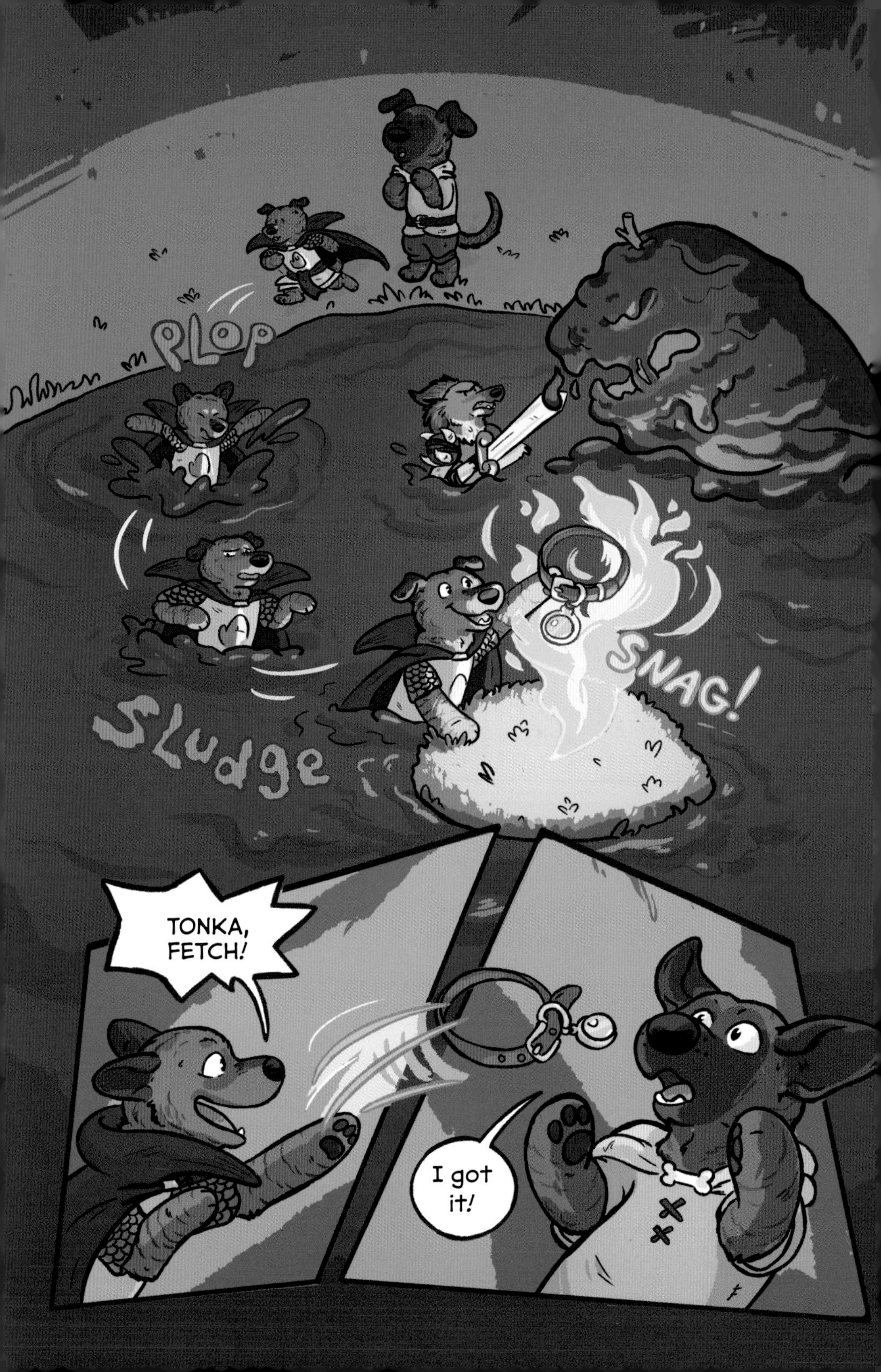
PLOP
SLUDGE
SNAG!
TONKA, FETCH!
I got it!

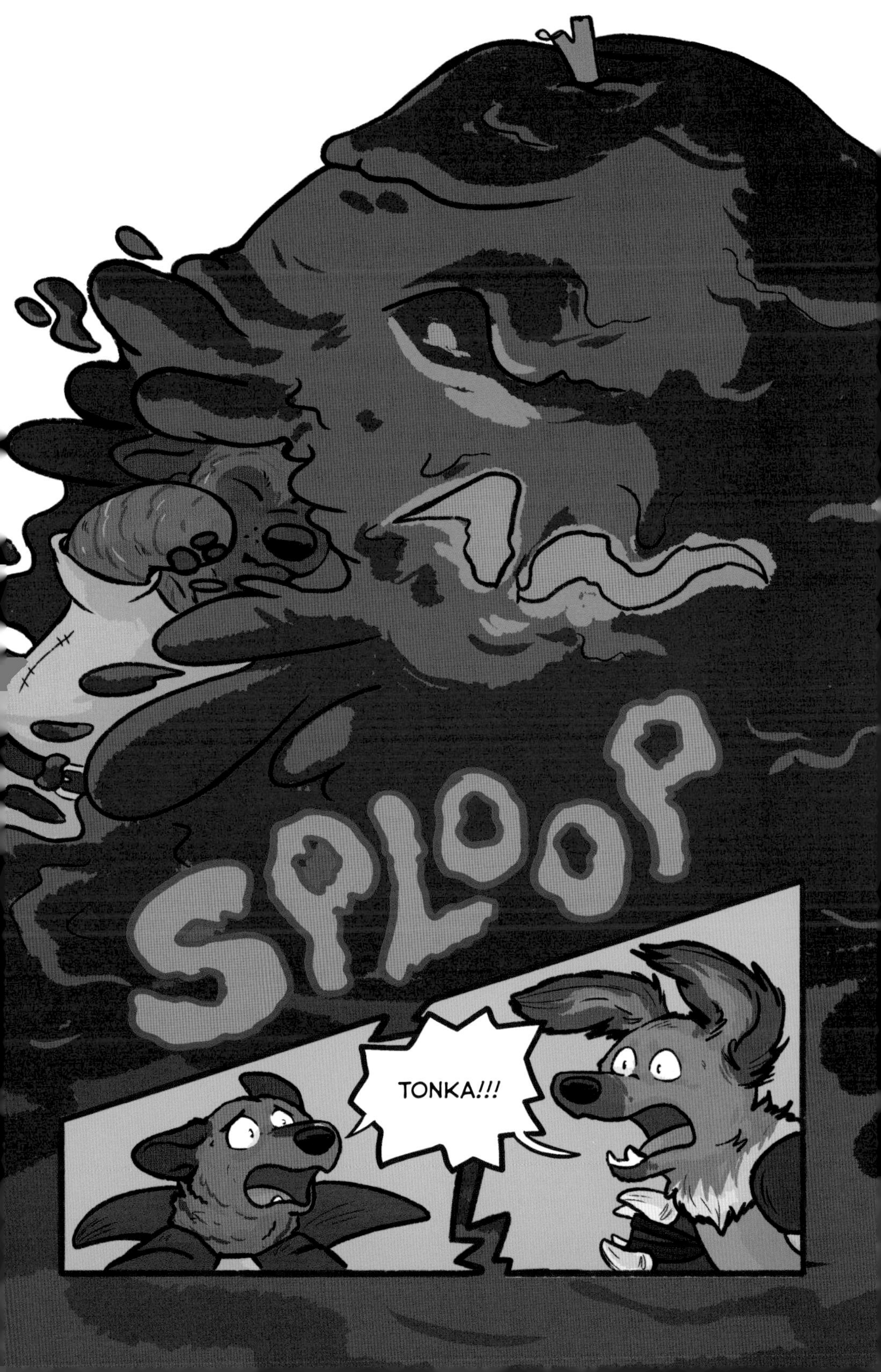
SPLOOP
TONKA!!!

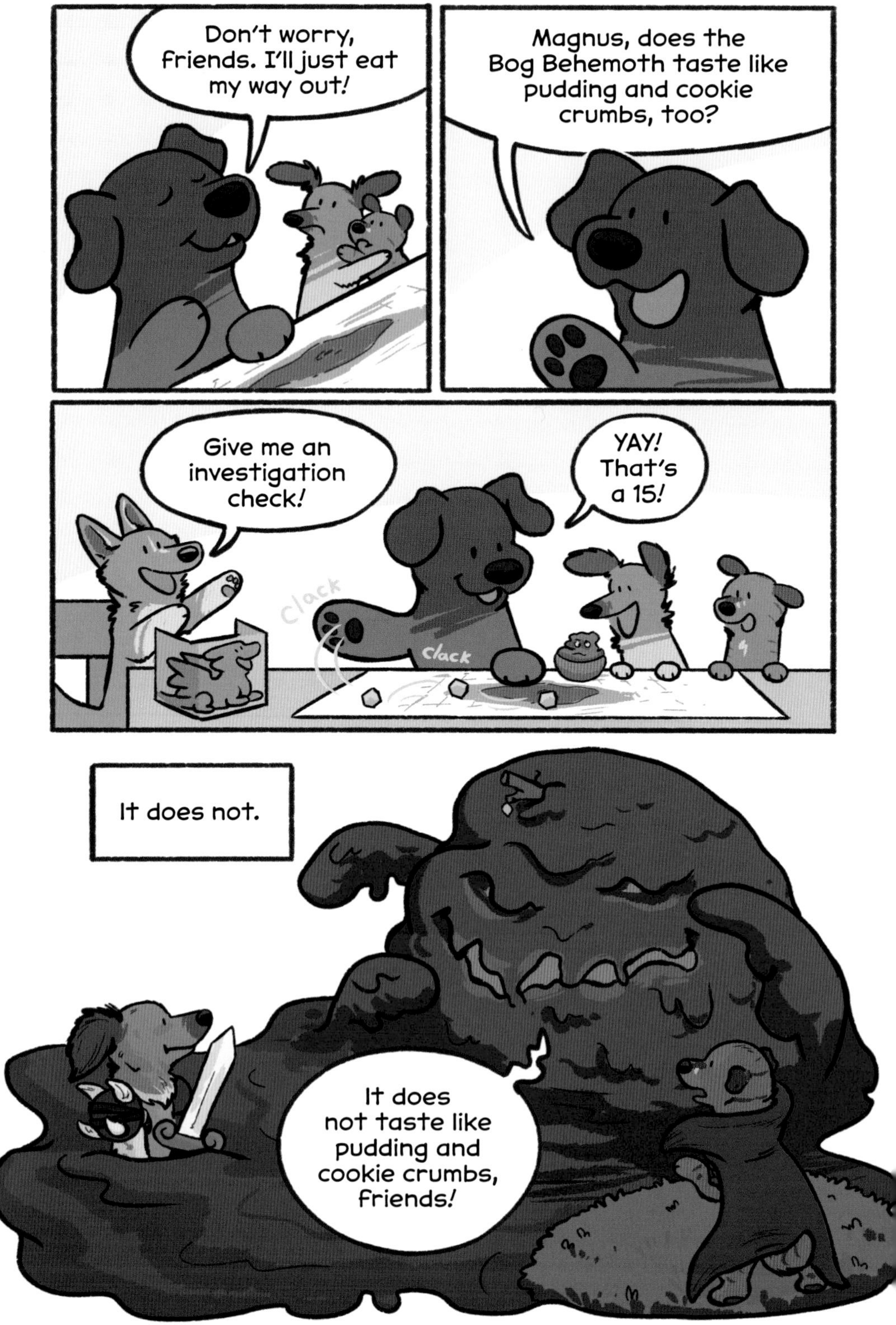
Don't worry, friends. I'll just eat my way out!
Magnus, does the Bog Behemoth taste like pudding and cookie crumbs, too?
Give me an investigation check!
clack
clack
YAY! That's a 15!
It does not.
It does not taste like pudding and cookie crumbs, friends!

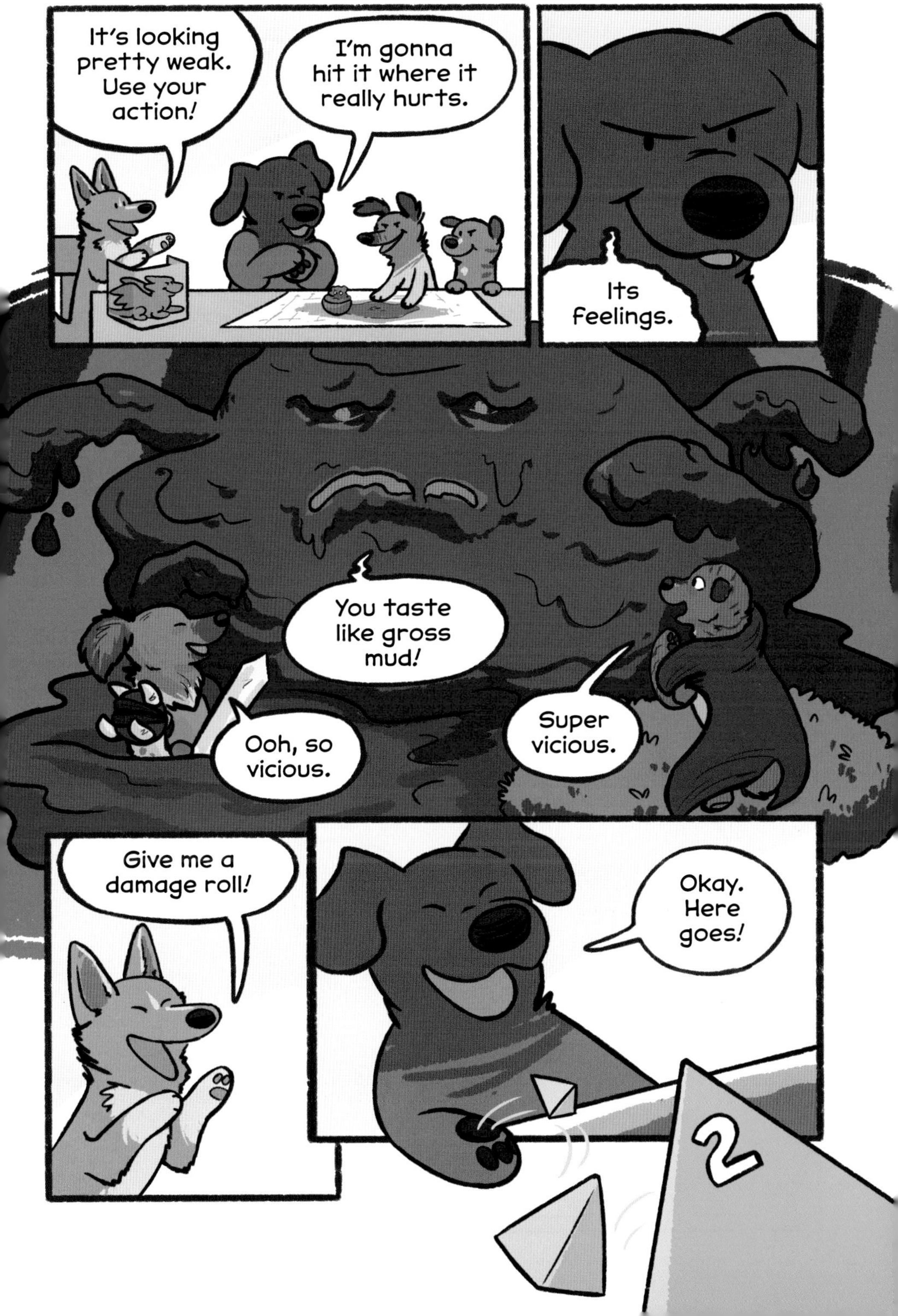
It's looking pretty weak. Use your action!
I'm gonna hit it where it really hurts.
Its feelings.
You taste like gross mud!
Ooh, so vicious.
Super vicious.
Give me a damage roll!
Okay. Here goes!
2

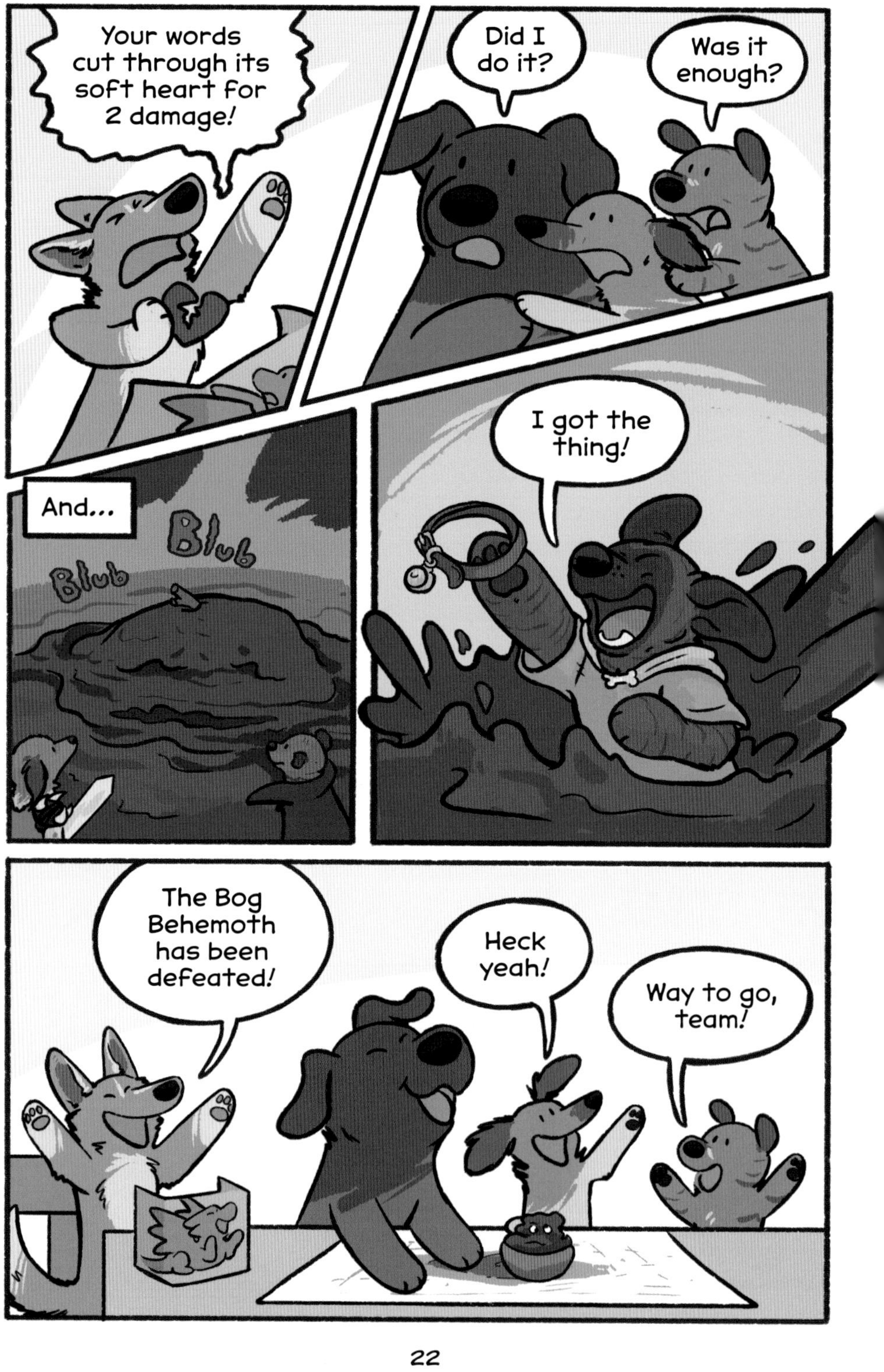
Your words cut through its soft heart for 2 damage!
Did I do it?
Was it enough?
And...
Blub
Blub
I got the thing!
The Bog Behemoth has been defeated!
Heck yeah!
Way to go, team!

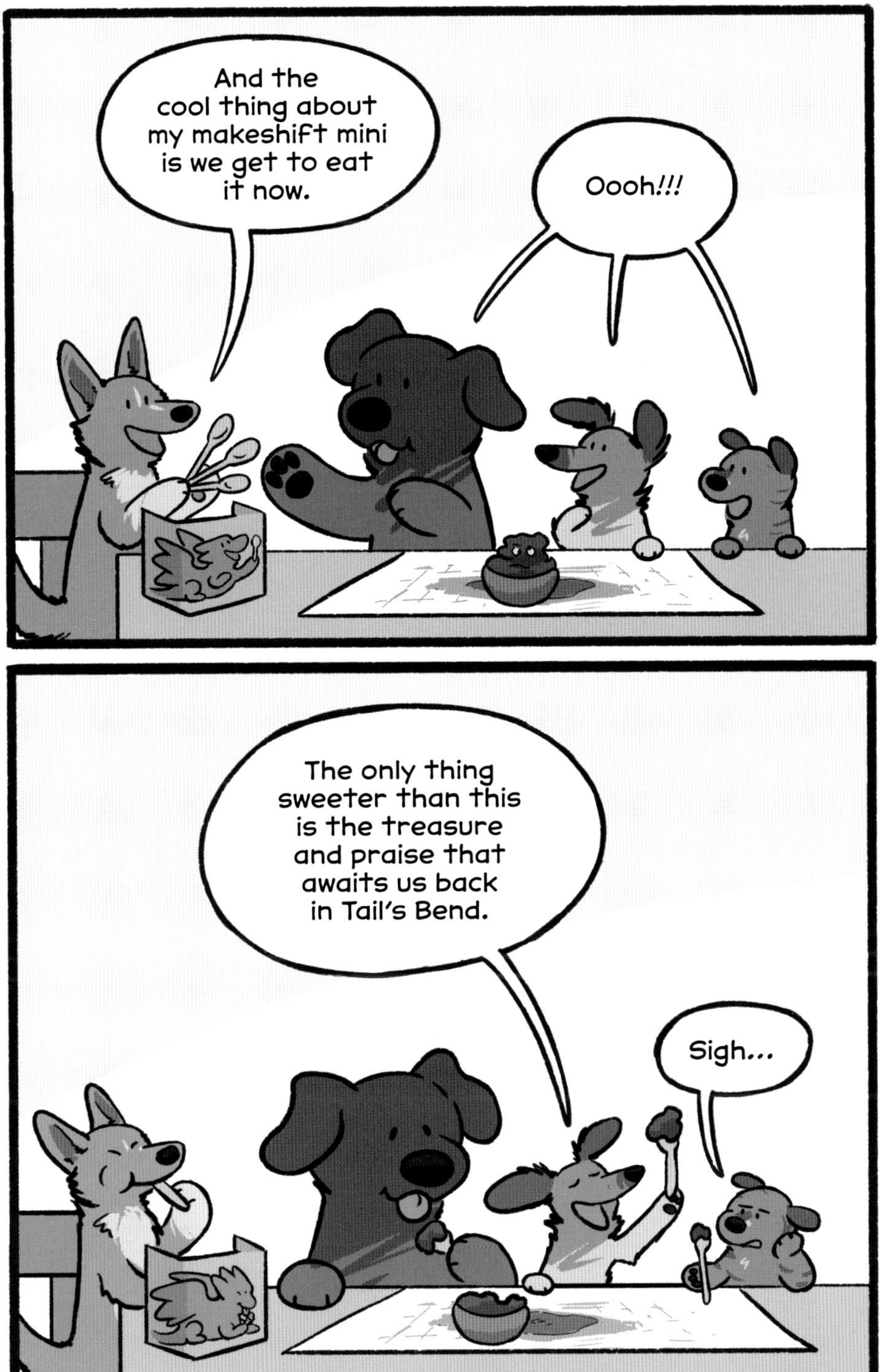
And the cool thing about my makeshift mini is we get to eat it now.
Oooh!!!
The only thing sweeter than this is the treasure and praise that awaits us back in Tail's Bend.
Sigh...

Chapter 2:
Party Time

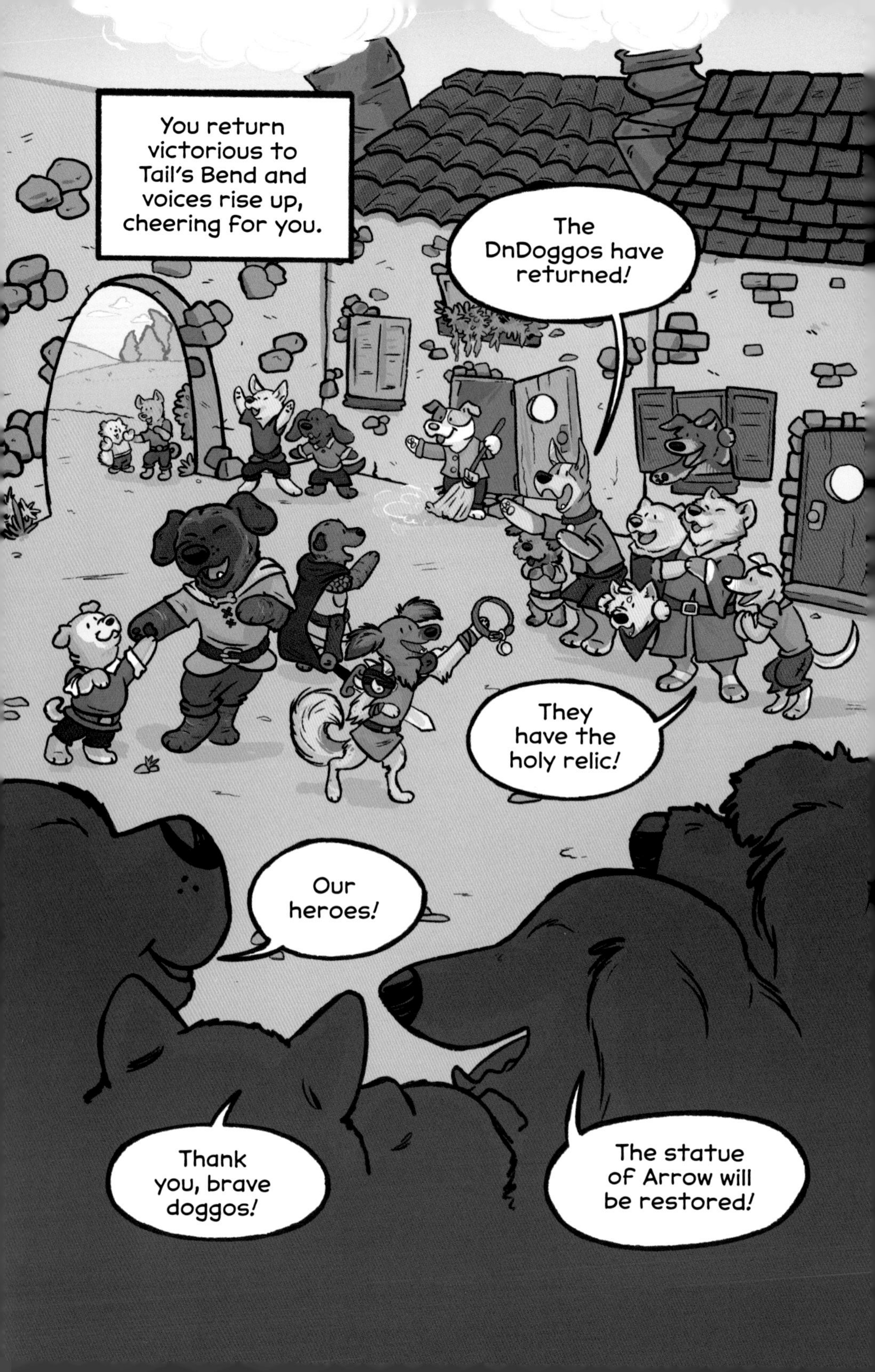
You return victorious to Tail's Bend and voices rise up, cheering for you.
The DnDoggos have returned!
They have the holy relic!
Our heroes!
Thank you, brave doggos!
The statue of Arrow will be restored!

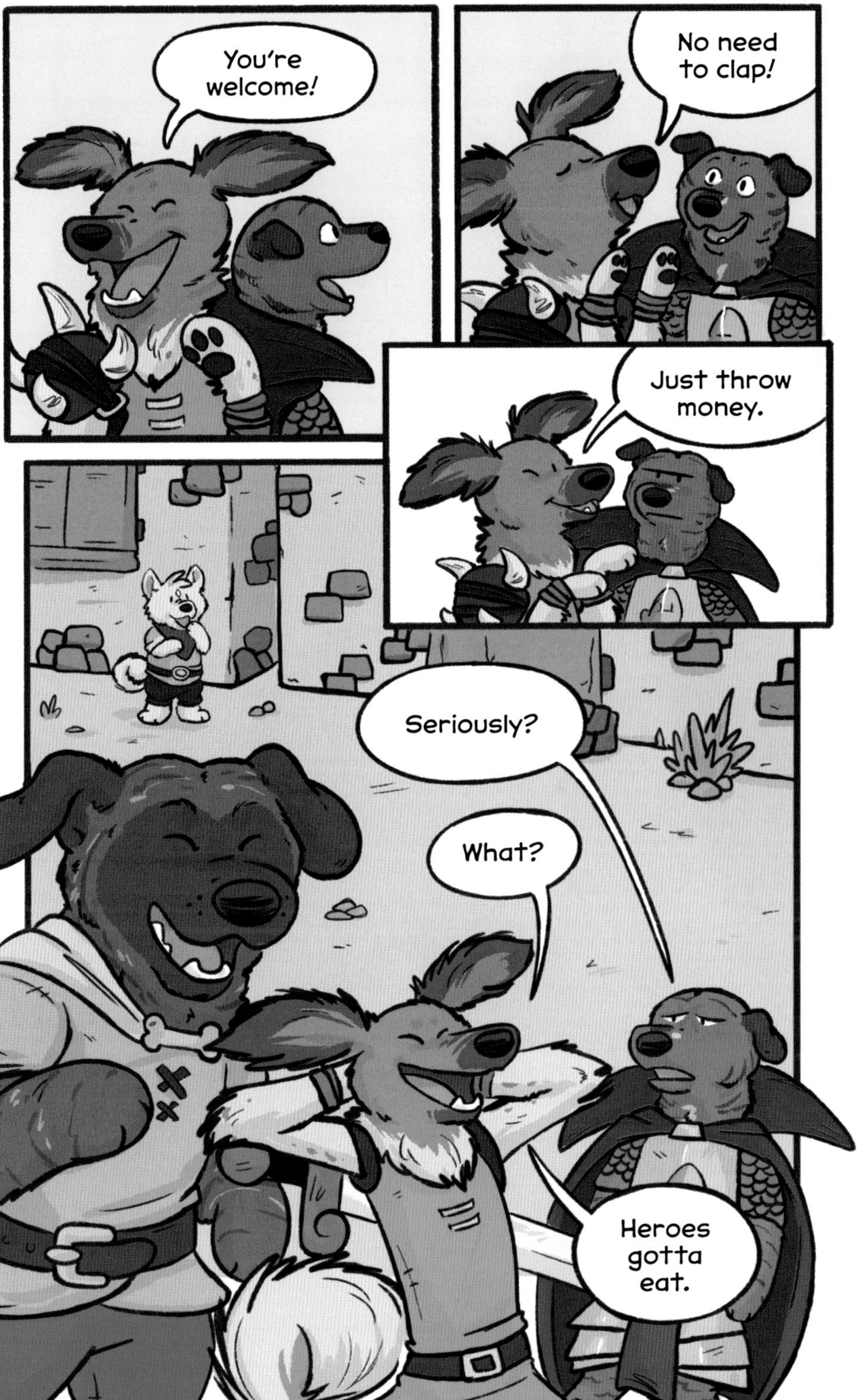
You're welcome!
No need to clap!
Just throw money.
Seriously?
What?
Heroes gotta eat.

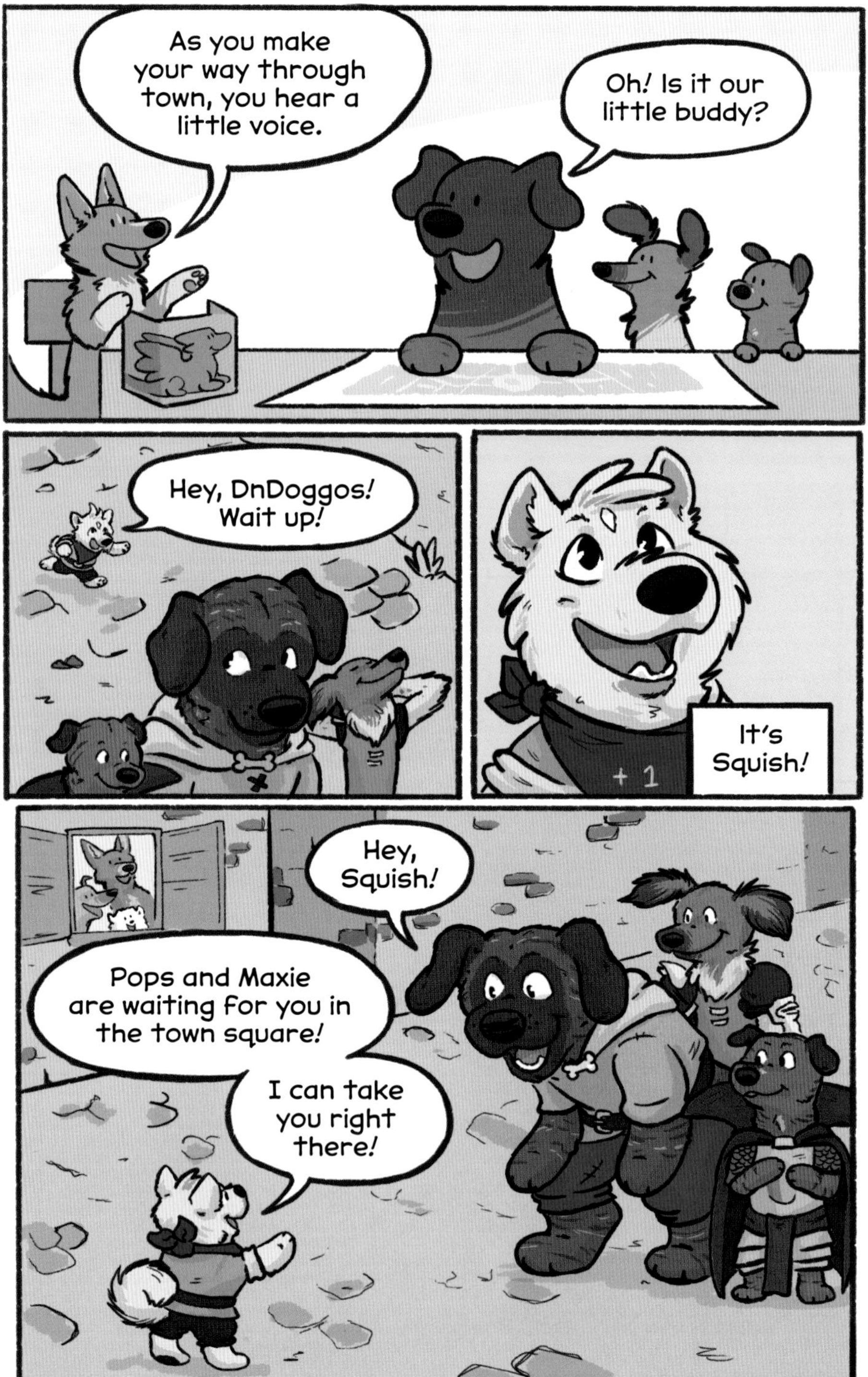
As you make your way through town, you hear a little voice.
Oh! Is it our little buddy?
Hey, DnDoggos! Wait up!
It's Squish!
+1
Hey, Squish!
Pops and Maxie are waiting for you in the town square!
I can take you right there!

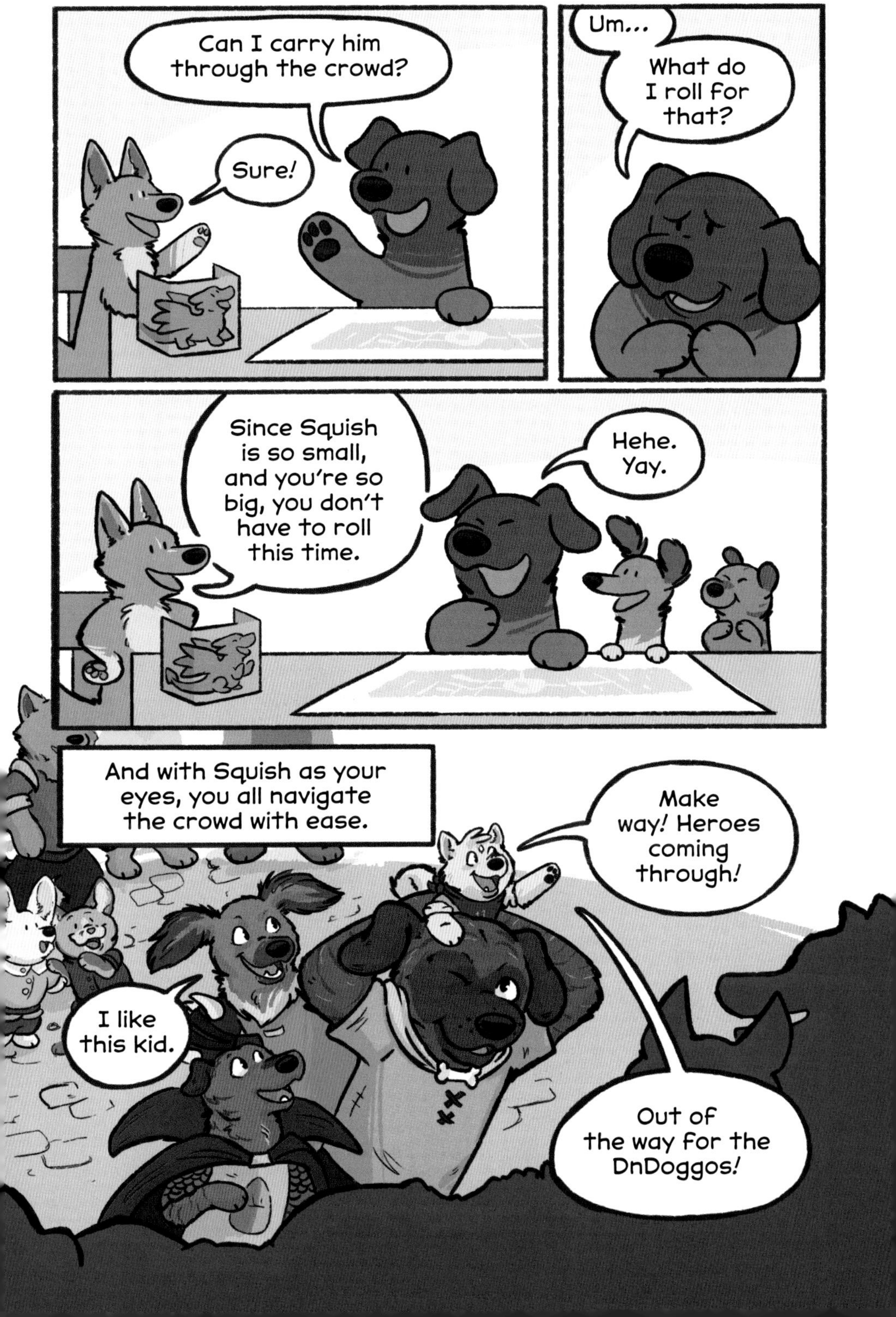
Can I carry him through the crowd?
Sure!
Um...
What do I roll for that?
Since Squish is so small, and you're so big, you don't have to roll this time.
Hehe. Yay.
And with Squish as your eyes, you all navigate the crowd with ease.
Make way! Heroes coming through!
I like this kid.
Out of the way for the DnDoggos!

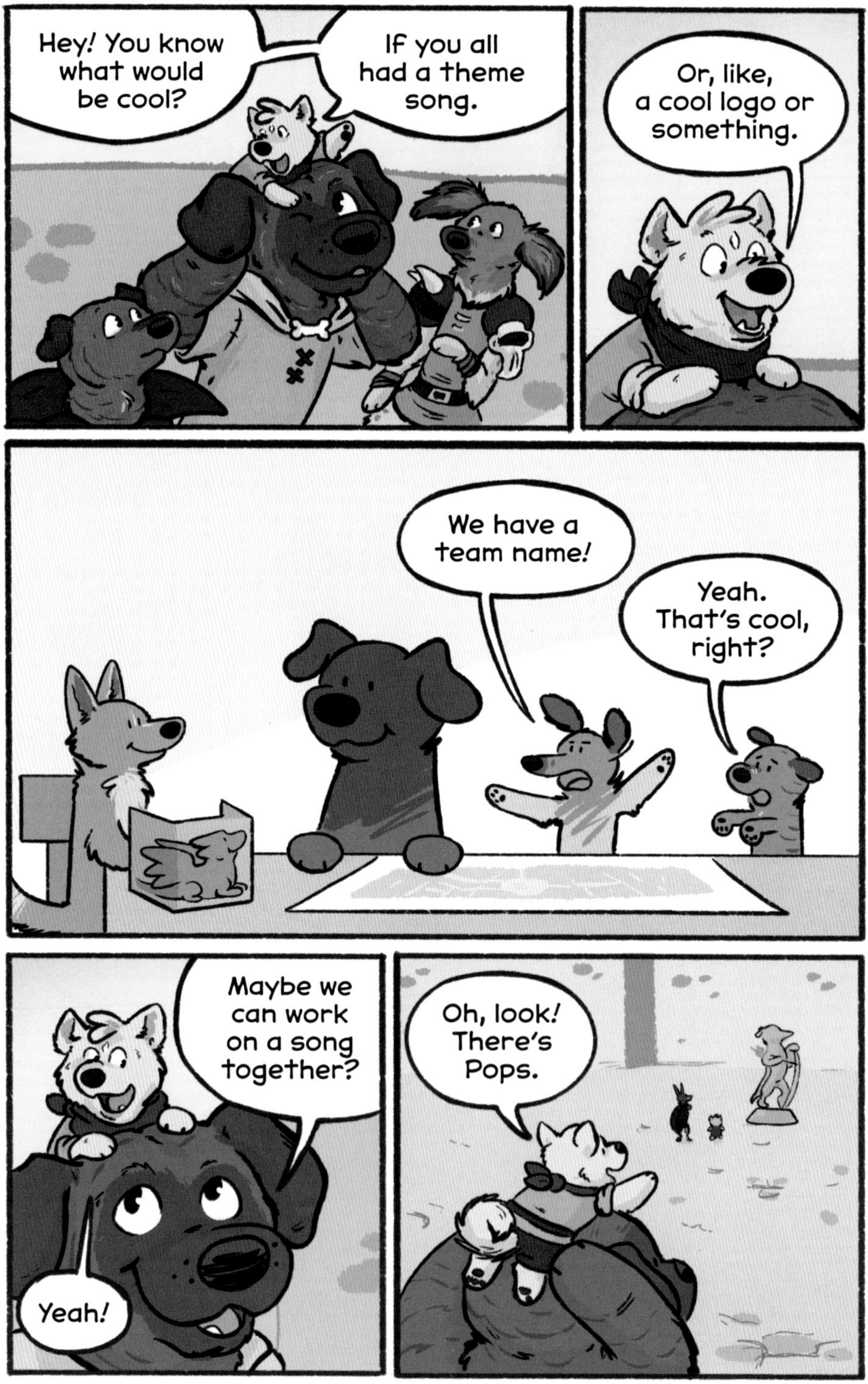
Hey! You know what would be cool?
If you all had a theme song.
Or, like, a cool logo or something.
We have a team name!
Yeah. That's cool, right?
Maybe we can work on a song together?
Yeah!
Oh, look! There's Pops.

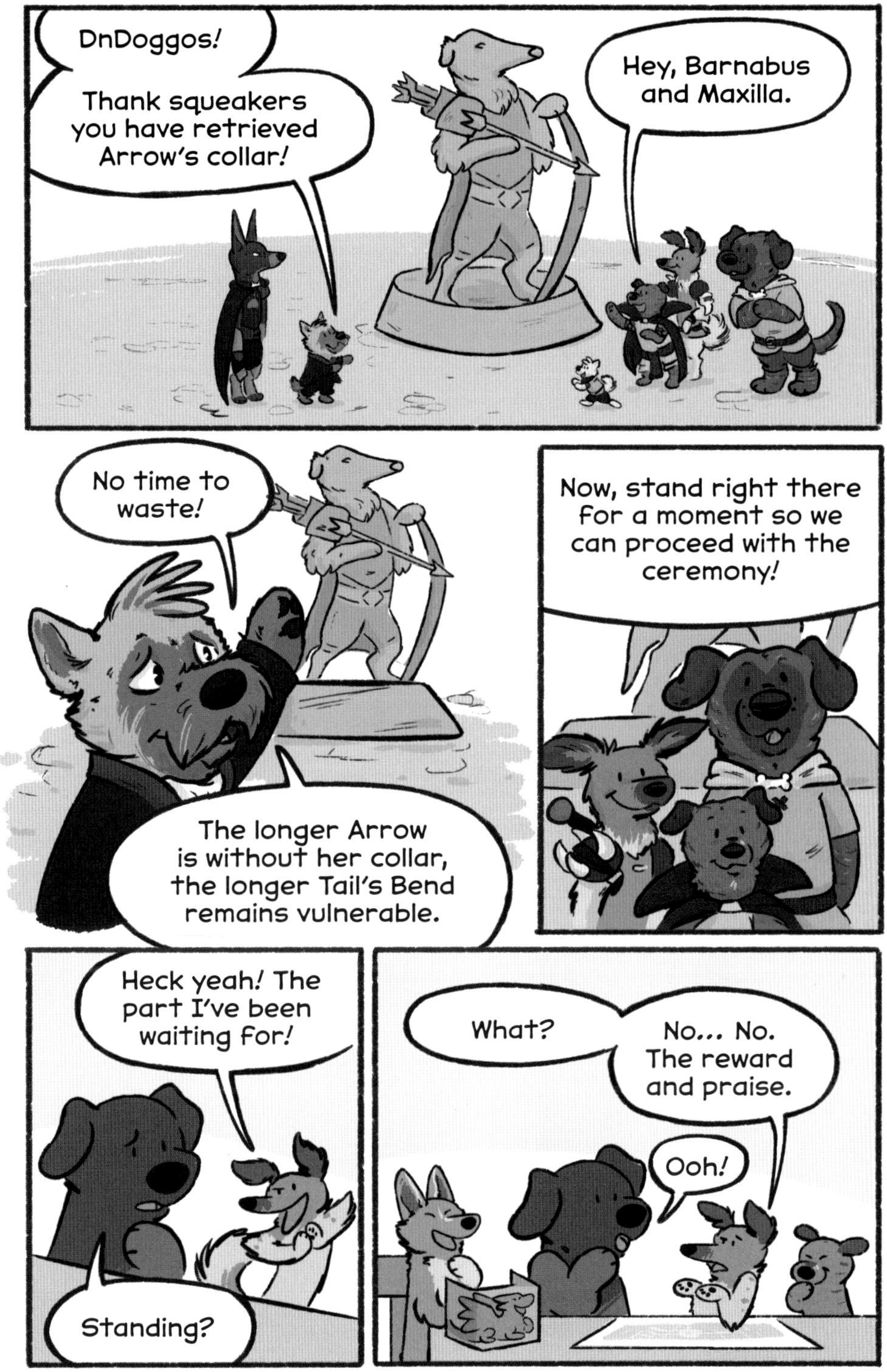
DnDoggos!
Thank squeakers you have retrieved Arrow's collar!
Hey, Barnabus and Maxilla.
No time to waste!
The longer Arrow is without her collar, the longer Tail's Bend remains vulnerable.
Now, stand right there for a moment so we can proceed with the ceremony!
Heck yeah! The part I've been waiting for!
Standing?
What?
No... No. The reward and praise.
Ooh!

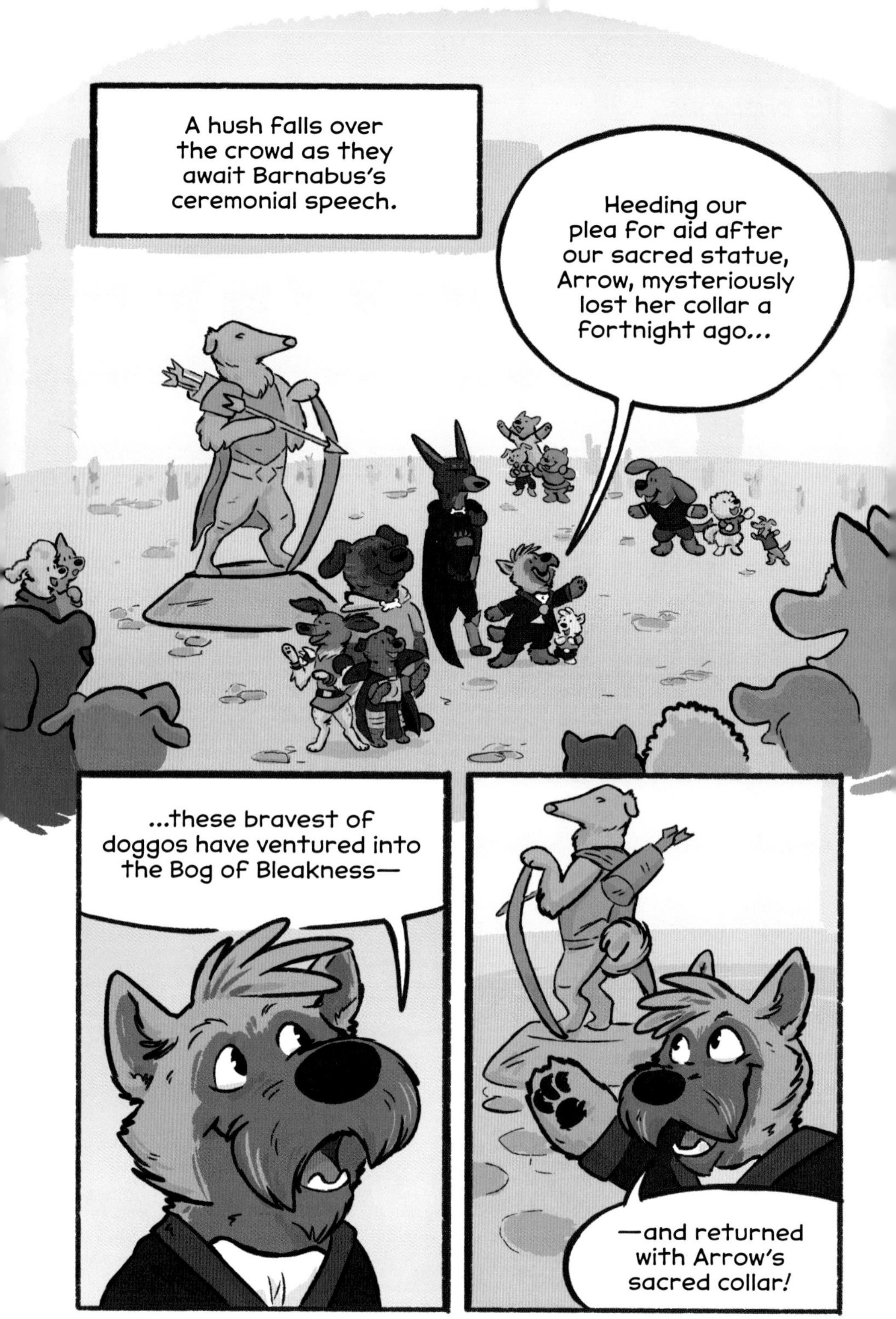
A hush falls over the crowd as they await Barnabus's ceremonial speech.
Heeding our plea for aid after our sacred statue, Arrow, mysteriously lost her collar a fortnight ago...
...these bravest of doggos have ventured into the Bog of Bleakness—
—and returned with Arrow's sacred collar!

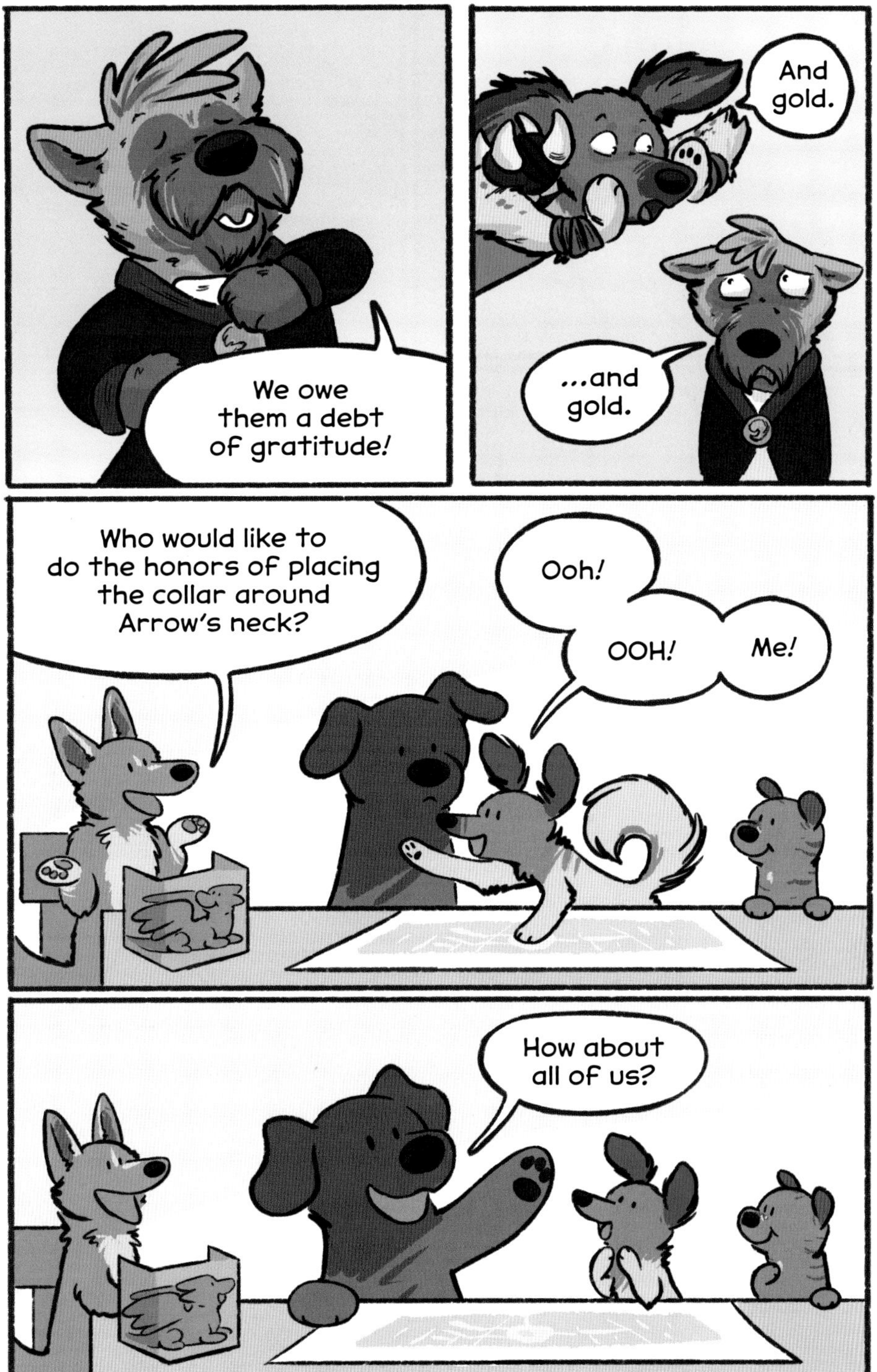
We owe them a debt of gratitude!
And gold.
...and gold.
Who would like to do the honors of placing the collar around Arrow's neck?
Ooh!
OOH!
Me!
How about all of us?

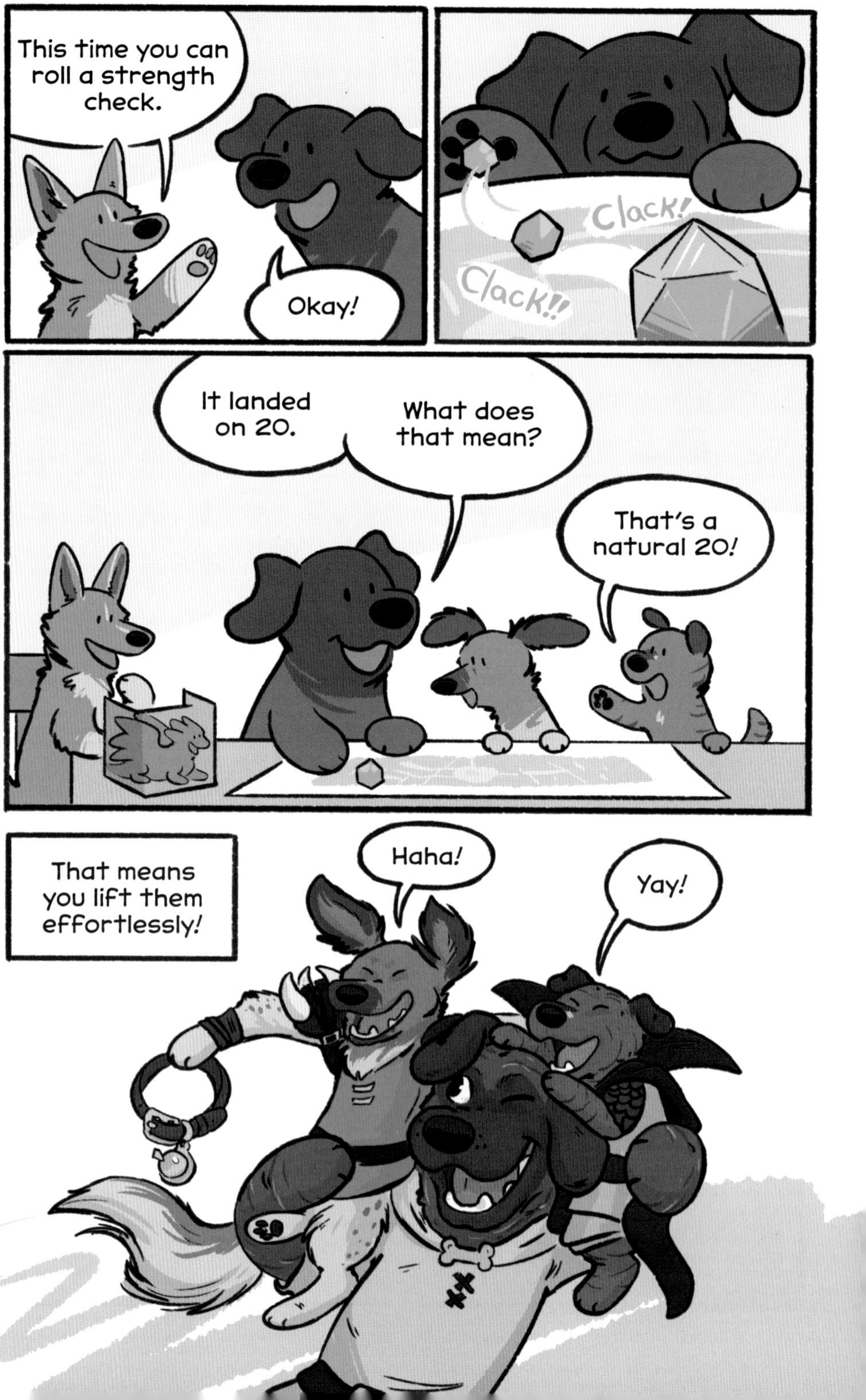
This time you can roll a strength check.
Okay!
Clack!
Clack!!
It landed on 20.
What does that mean?
That's a natural 20!
That means you lift them effortlessly!
Haha!
Yay!

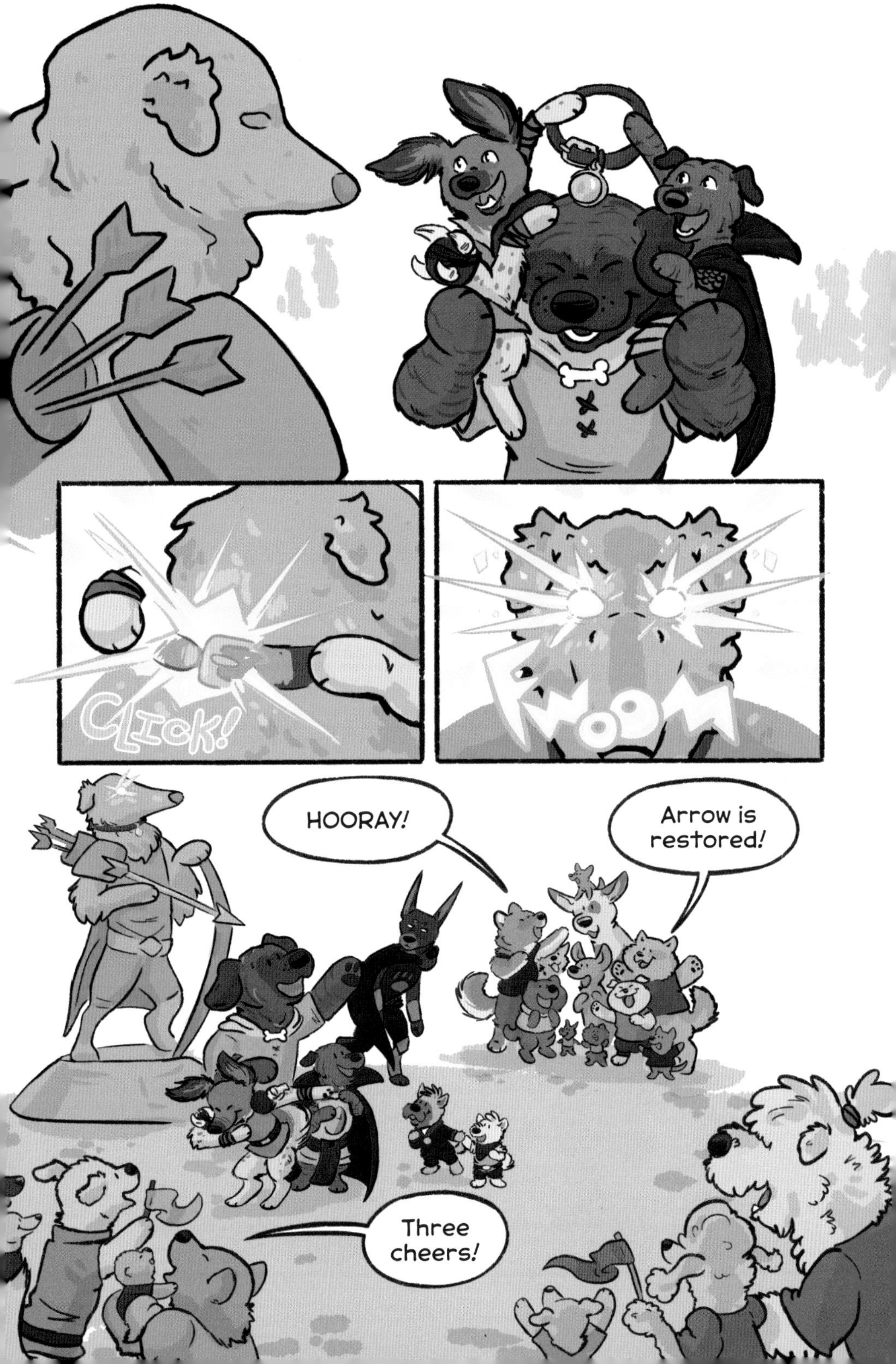
CLICK!
FWOOM
HOORAY!
Arrow is restored!
Three cheers!

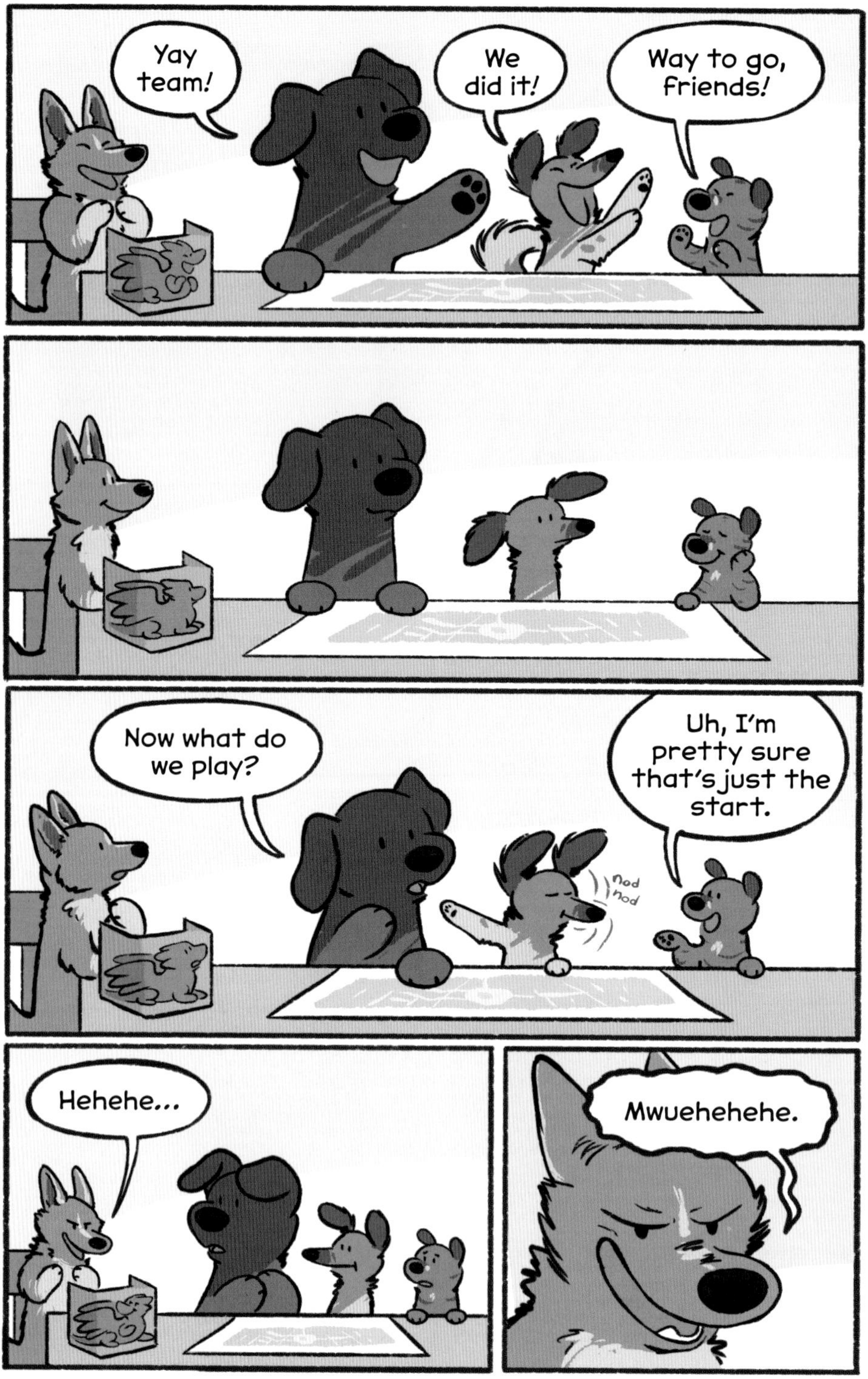
Yay team!
We did it!
Way to go, friends!
Now what do we play?
Uh, I'm pretty sure that's just the start.
nod nod
Hehehe...
Mwuehehehe.

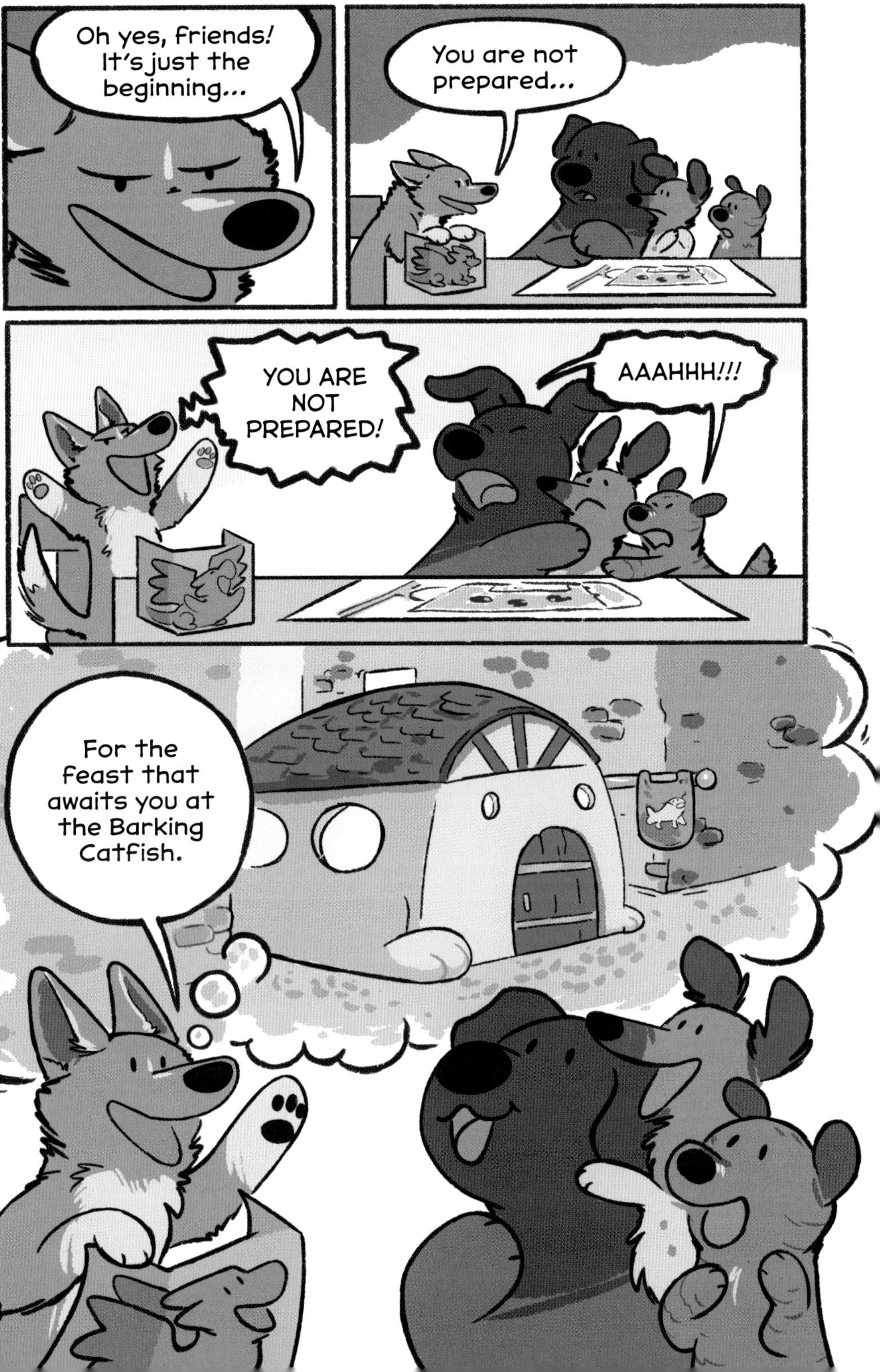
Oh yes, friends! It's just the beginning...
You are not prepared...
YOU ARE NOT PREPARED!
AAAHHH!!!
For the feast that awaits you at the Barking Catfish.

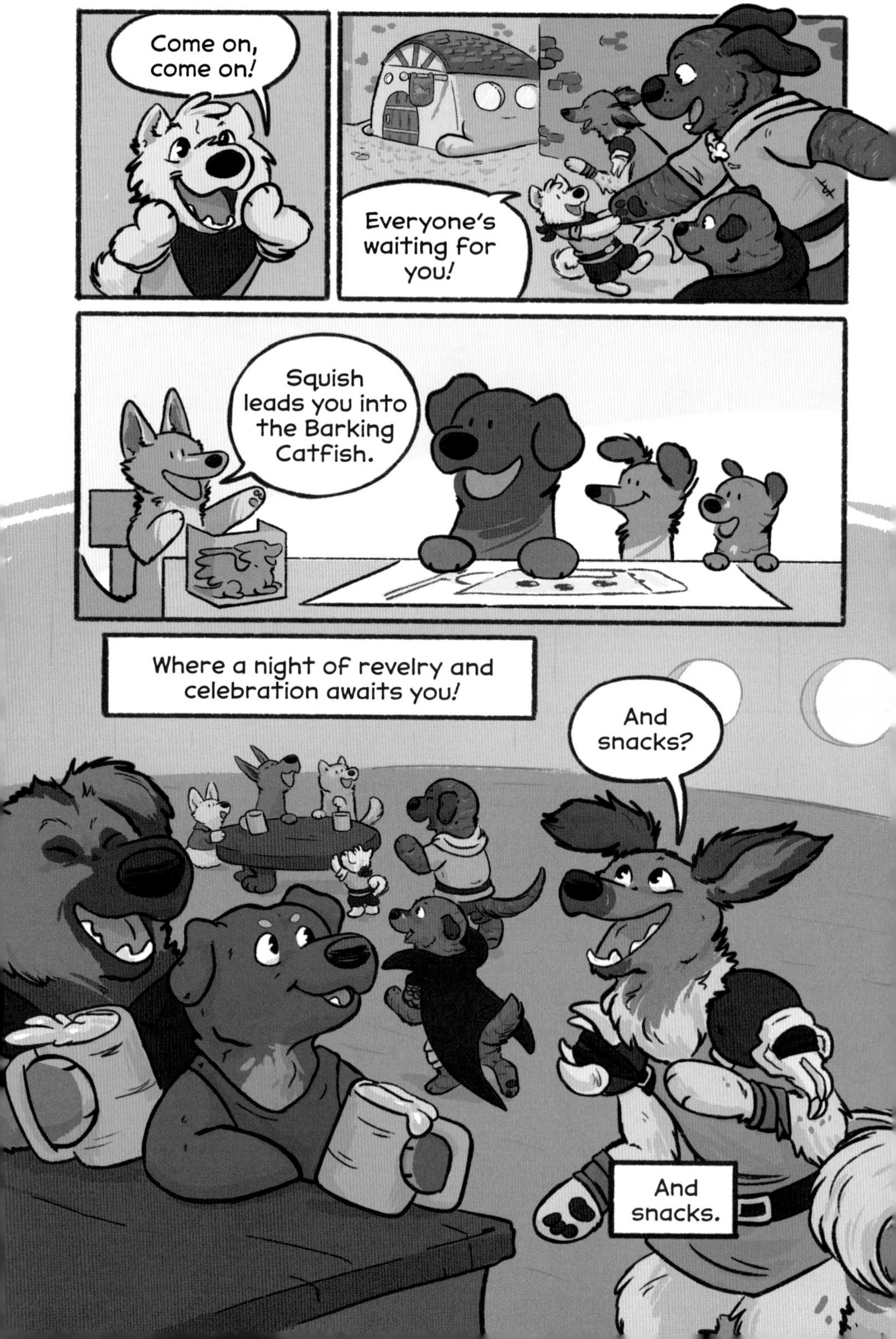
Come on,
come on!
Everyone's
waiting for
you!
Squish
leads you into
the Barking
Catfish.
Where a night of revelry and
celebration awaits you!
And
snacks?
And
snacks.

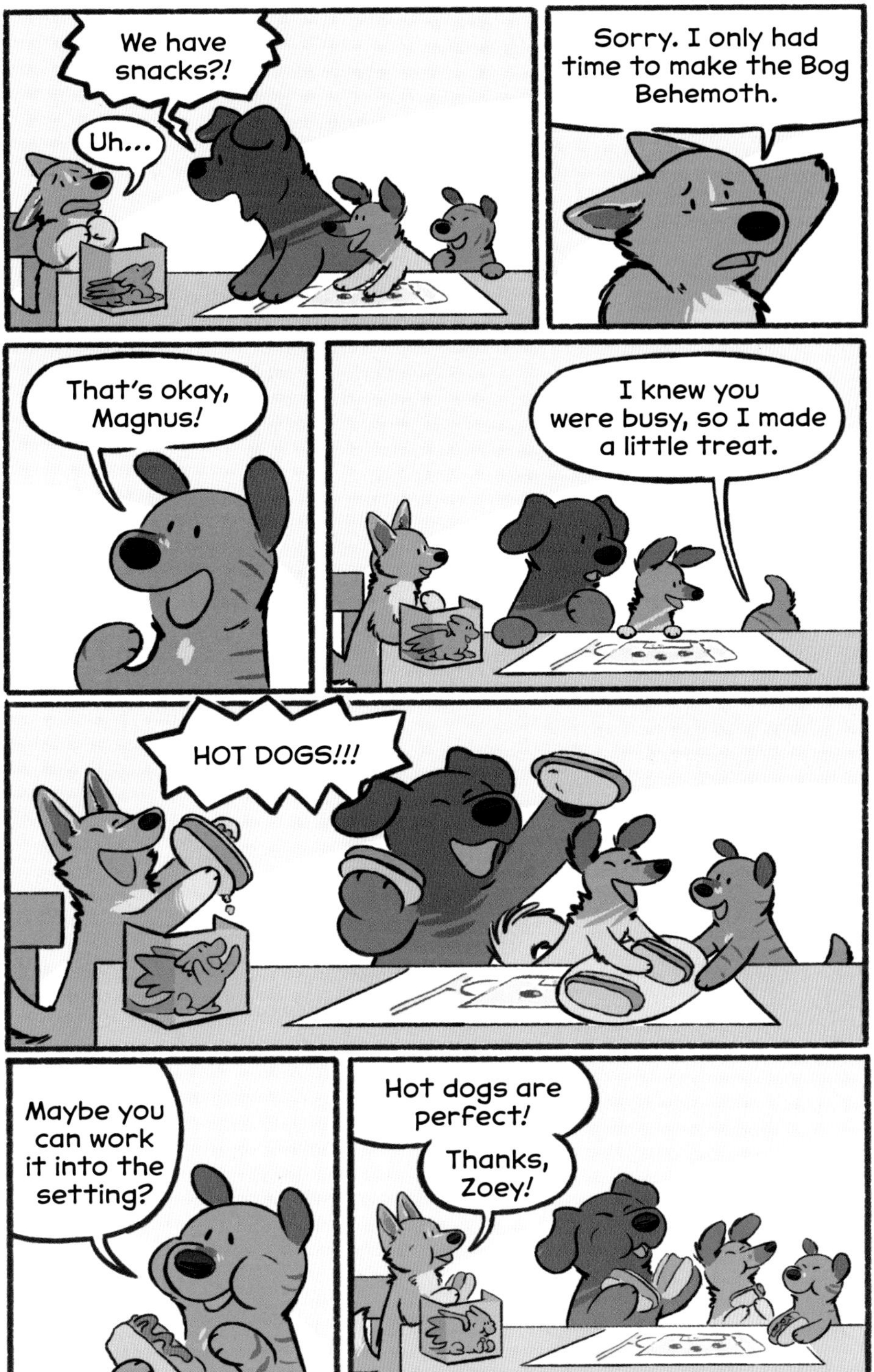
We have snacks?!
Uh...
Sorry. I only had time to make the Bog Behemoth.
That's okay, Magnus!
I knew you were busy, so I made a little treat.
HOT DOGS!!!
Maybe you can work it into the setting?
Hot dogs are perfect!
Thanks, Zoey!

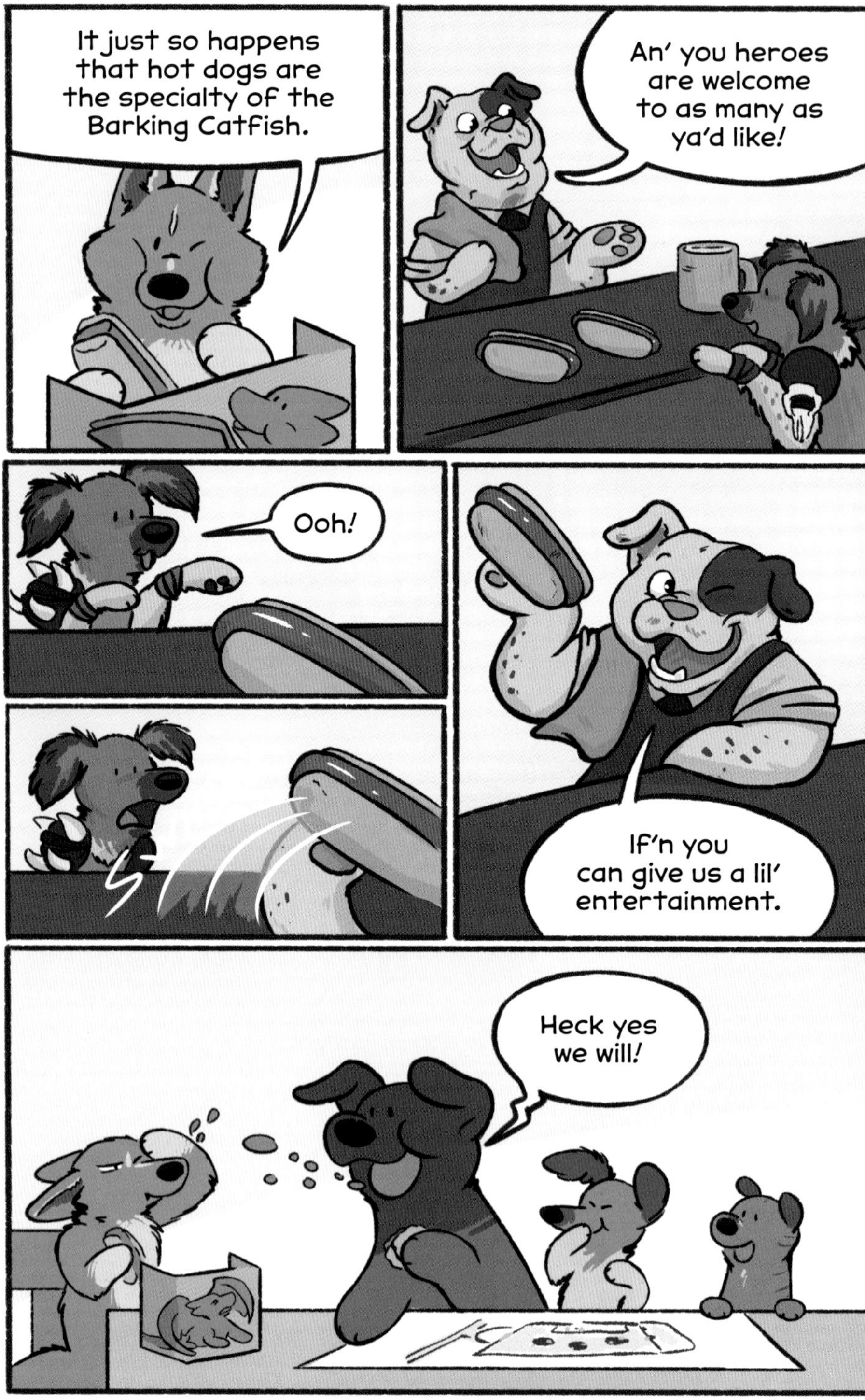
It just so happens that hot dogs are the specialty of the Barking Catfish.
An' you heroes are welcome to as many as ya'd like!
Ooh!
If'n you can give us a lil' entertainment.
Heck yes we will!

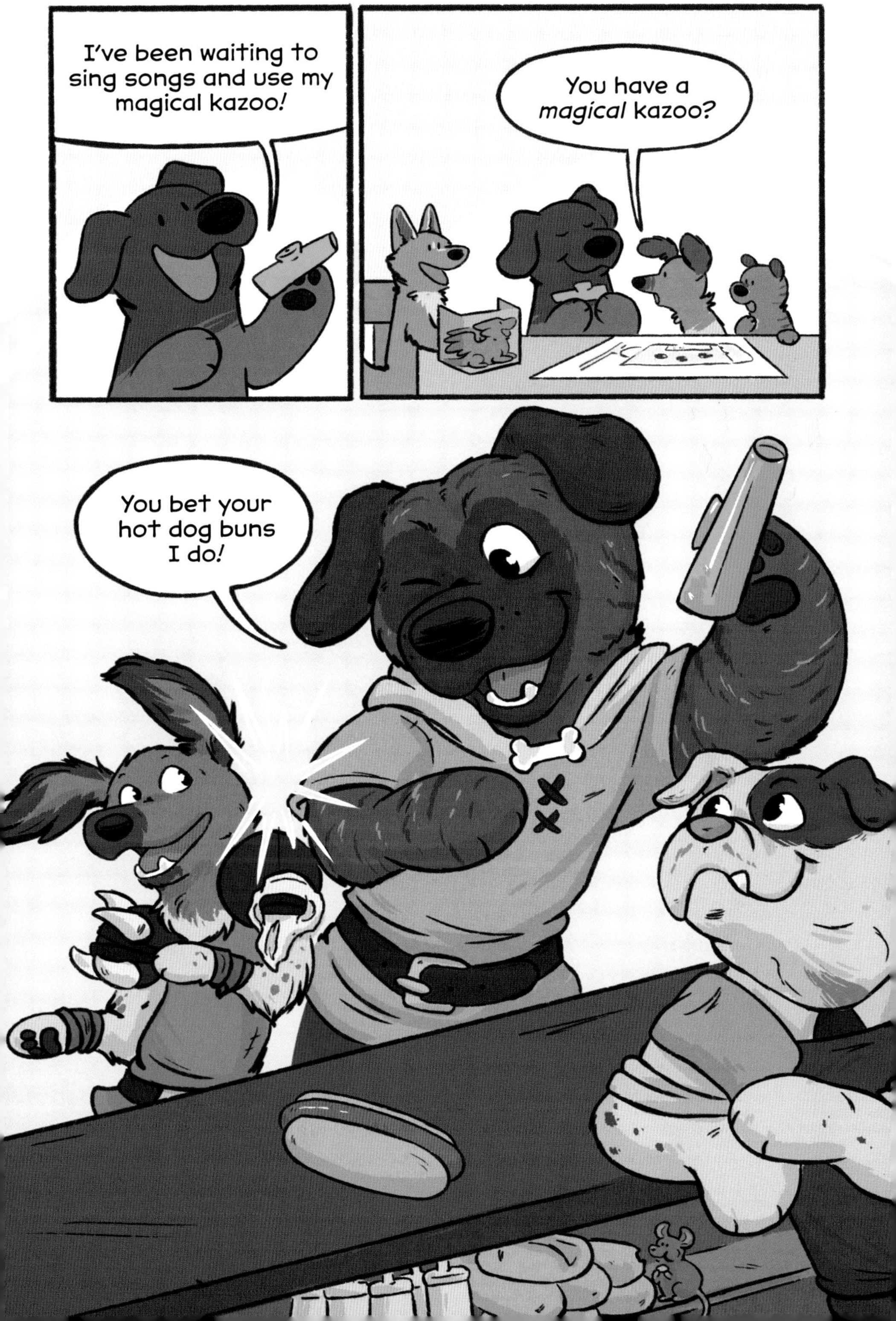
I've been waiting to sing songs and use my *magical kazoo!*
You have a *magical* kazoo?
You bet your hot dog buns I do!

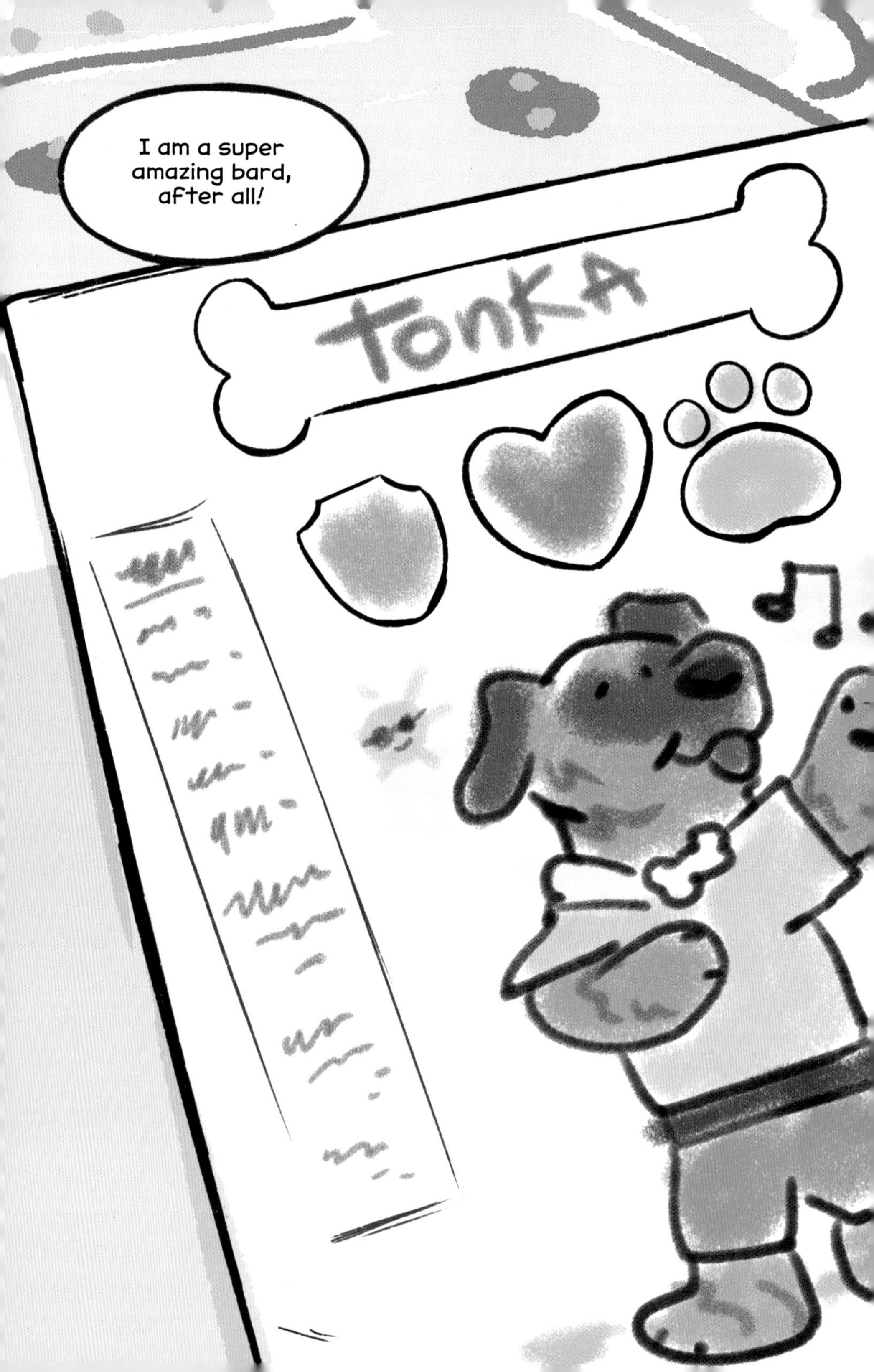
I am a super amazing bard, after all!
TONKA

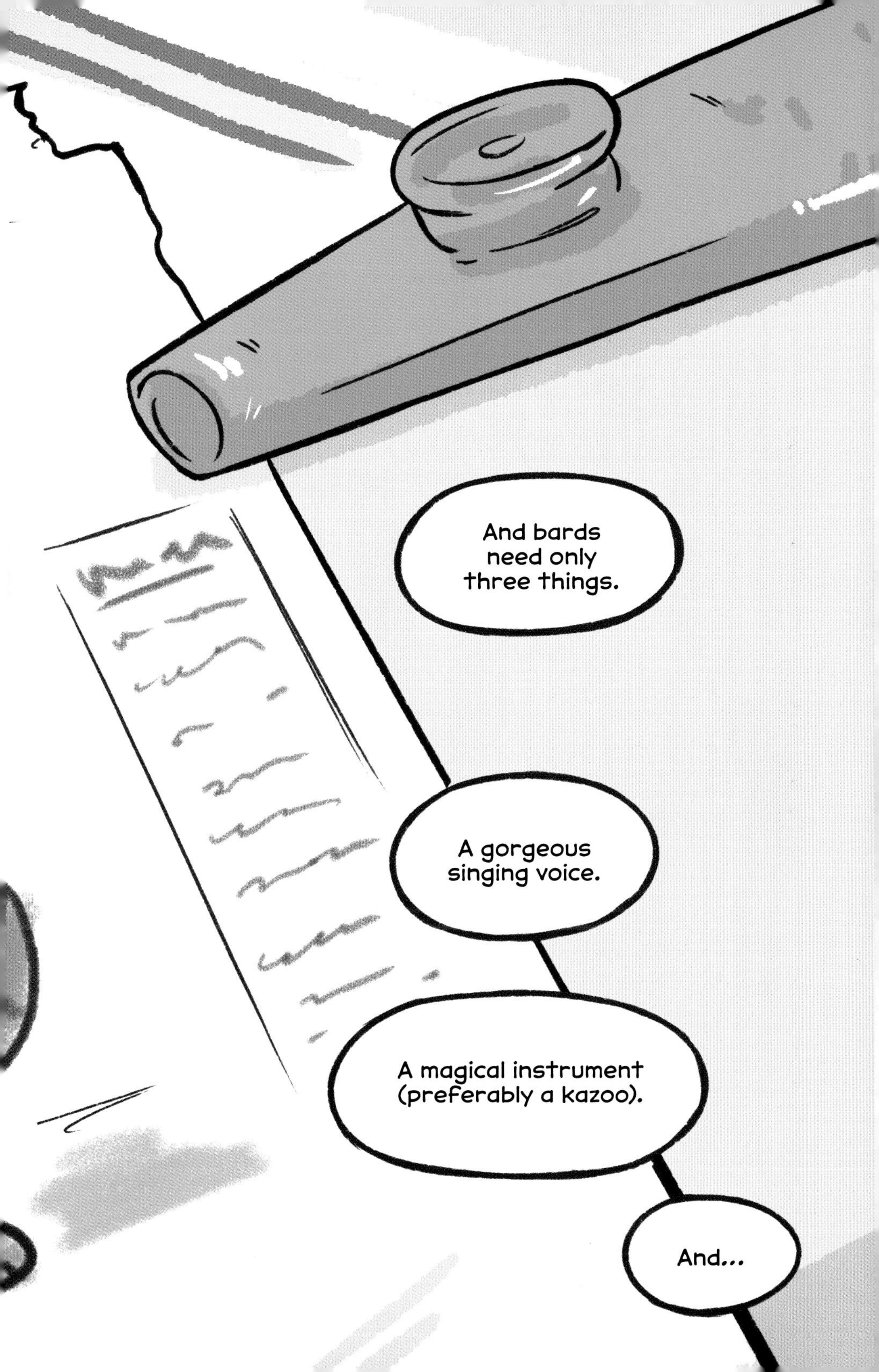
And bards need only three things.
A gorgeous singing voice.
A magical instrument (preferably a kazoo).
And...

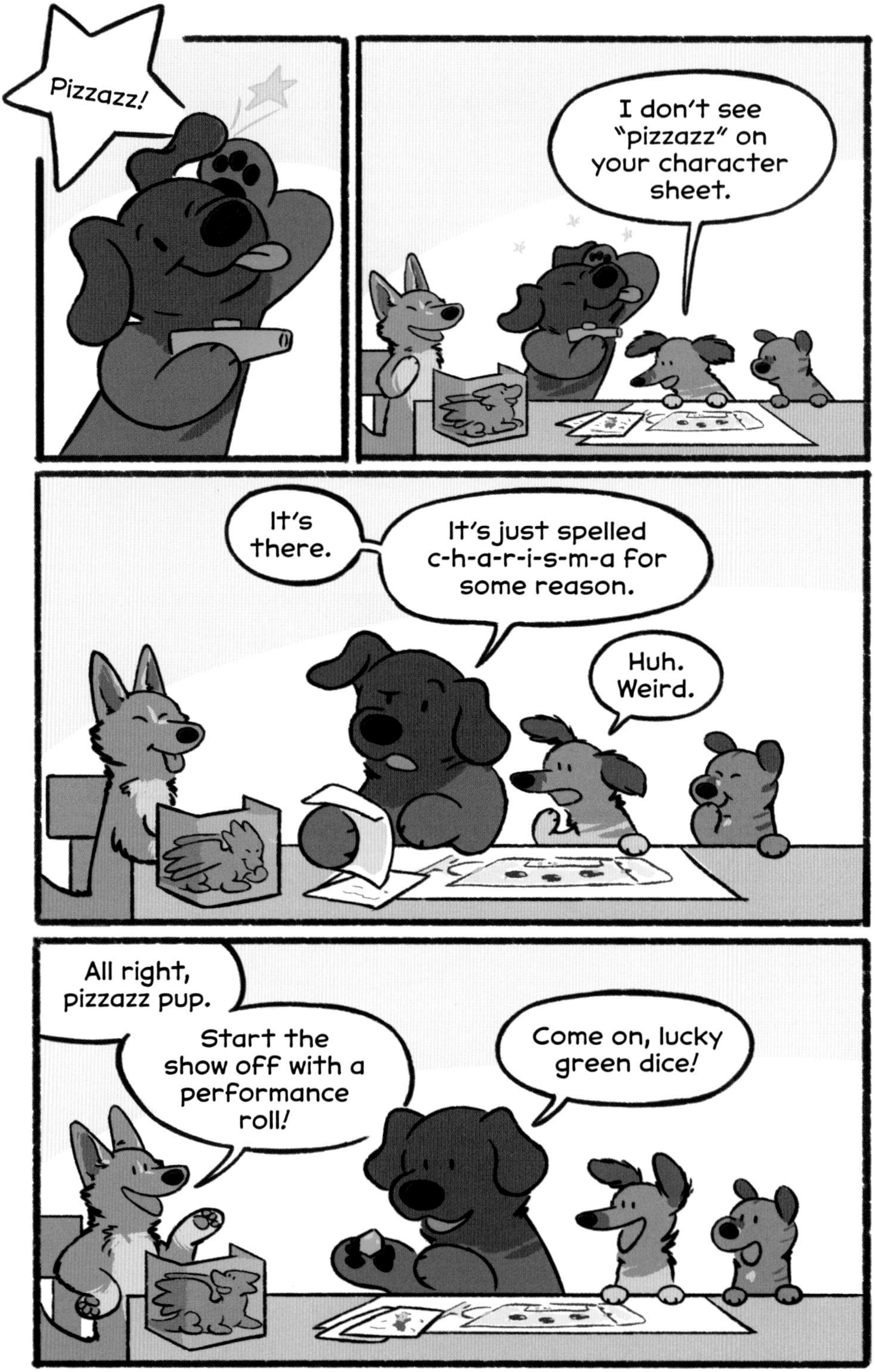
Pizzazz!
I don't see "pizzazz" on your character sheet.
It's there.
It's just spelled c-h-a-r-i-s-m-a for some reason.
Huh. Weird.
All right, pizzazz pup.
Start the show off with a performance roll!
Come on, lucky green dice!

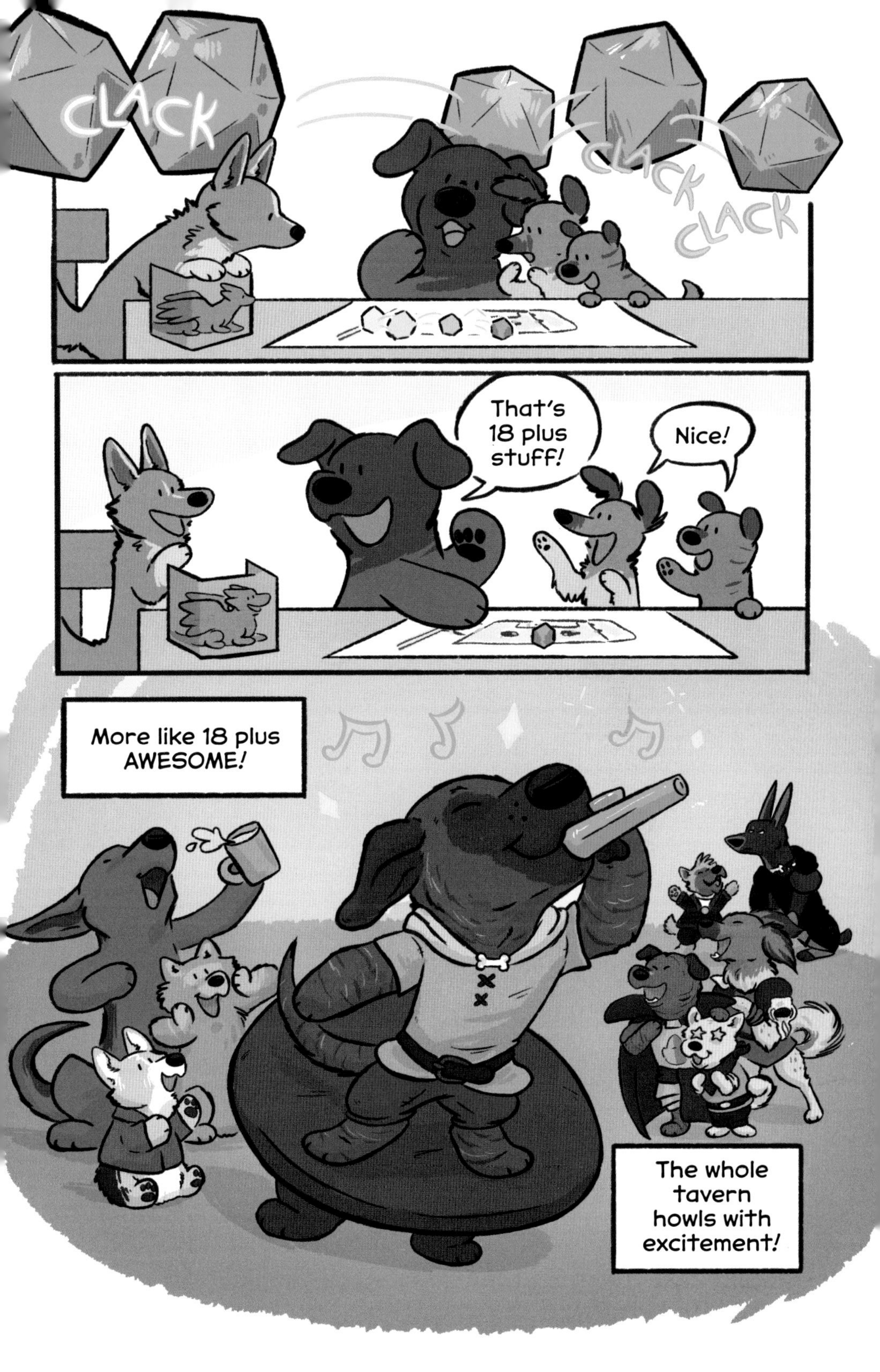
CLACK
CLACK
CLACK
That's 18 plus stuff!
Nice!
More like 18 plus AWESOME!
The whole tavern howls with excitement!

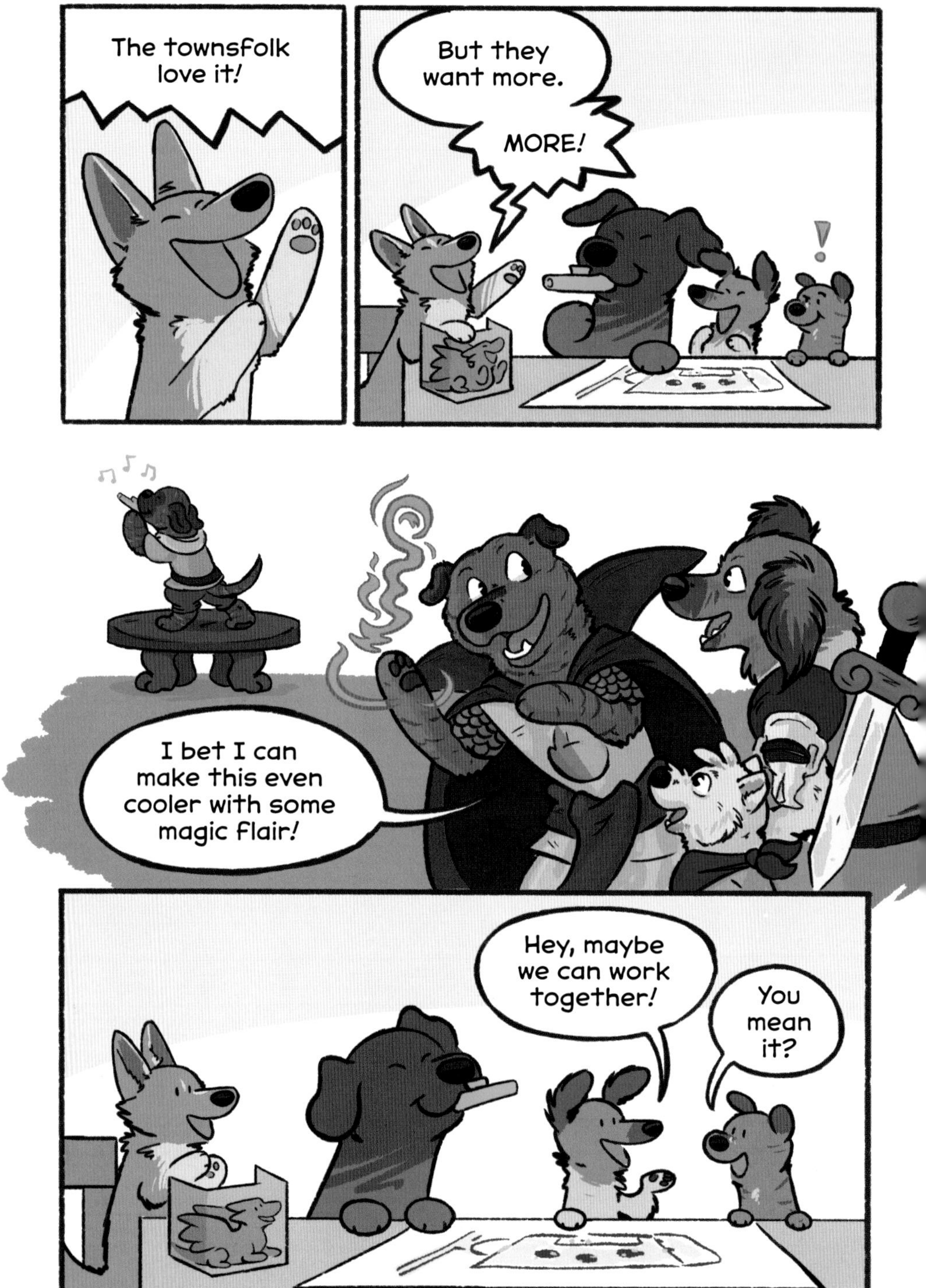

The townsfolk love it!
But they want more.
MORE!
!
I bet I can make this even cooler with some magic flair!
Hey, maybe we can work together!
You mean it?

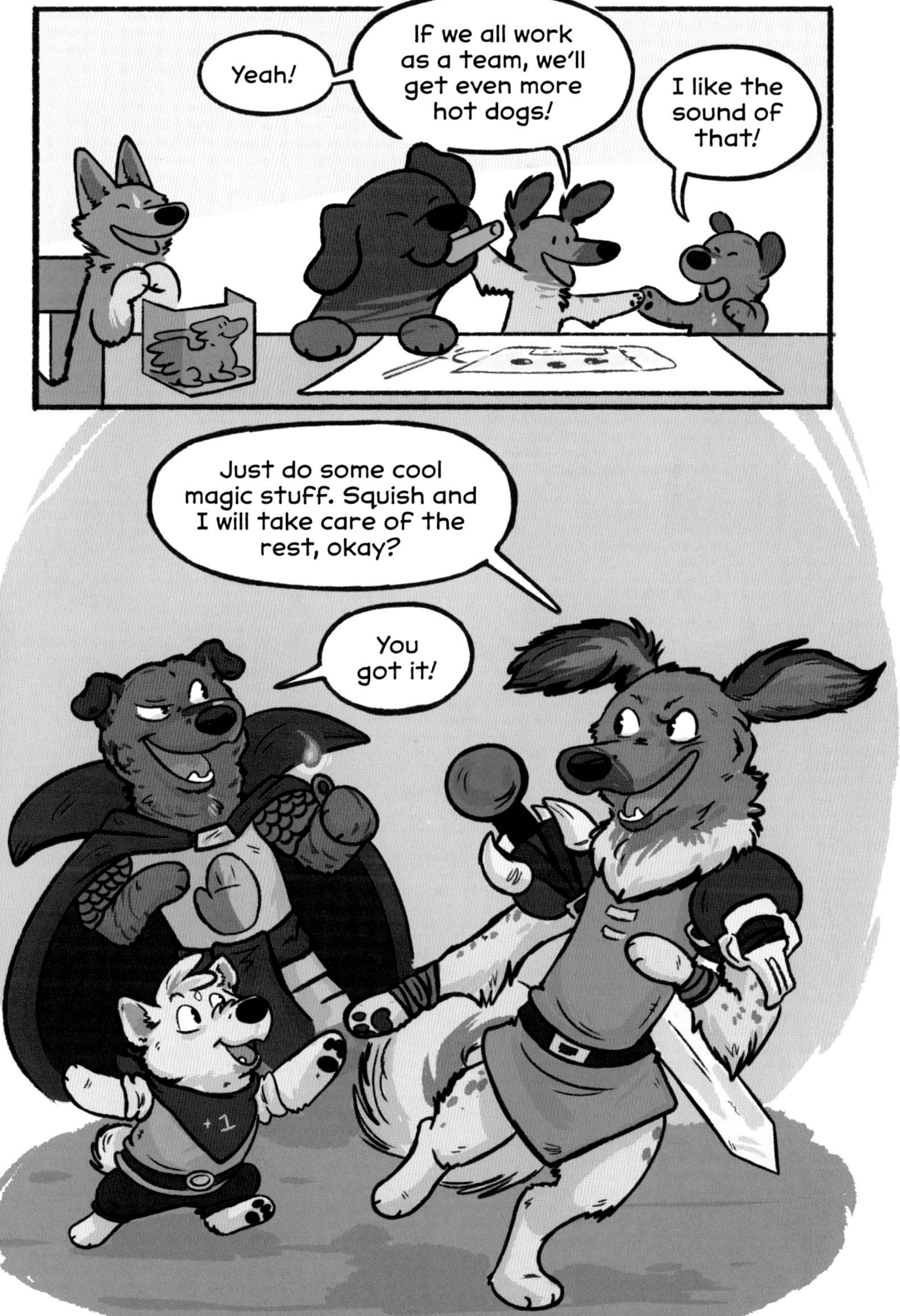
Yeah!
If we all work as a team, we'll get even more hot dogs!
I like the sound of that!
Just do some cool magic stuff. Squish and I will take care of the rest, okay?
You got it!
+1

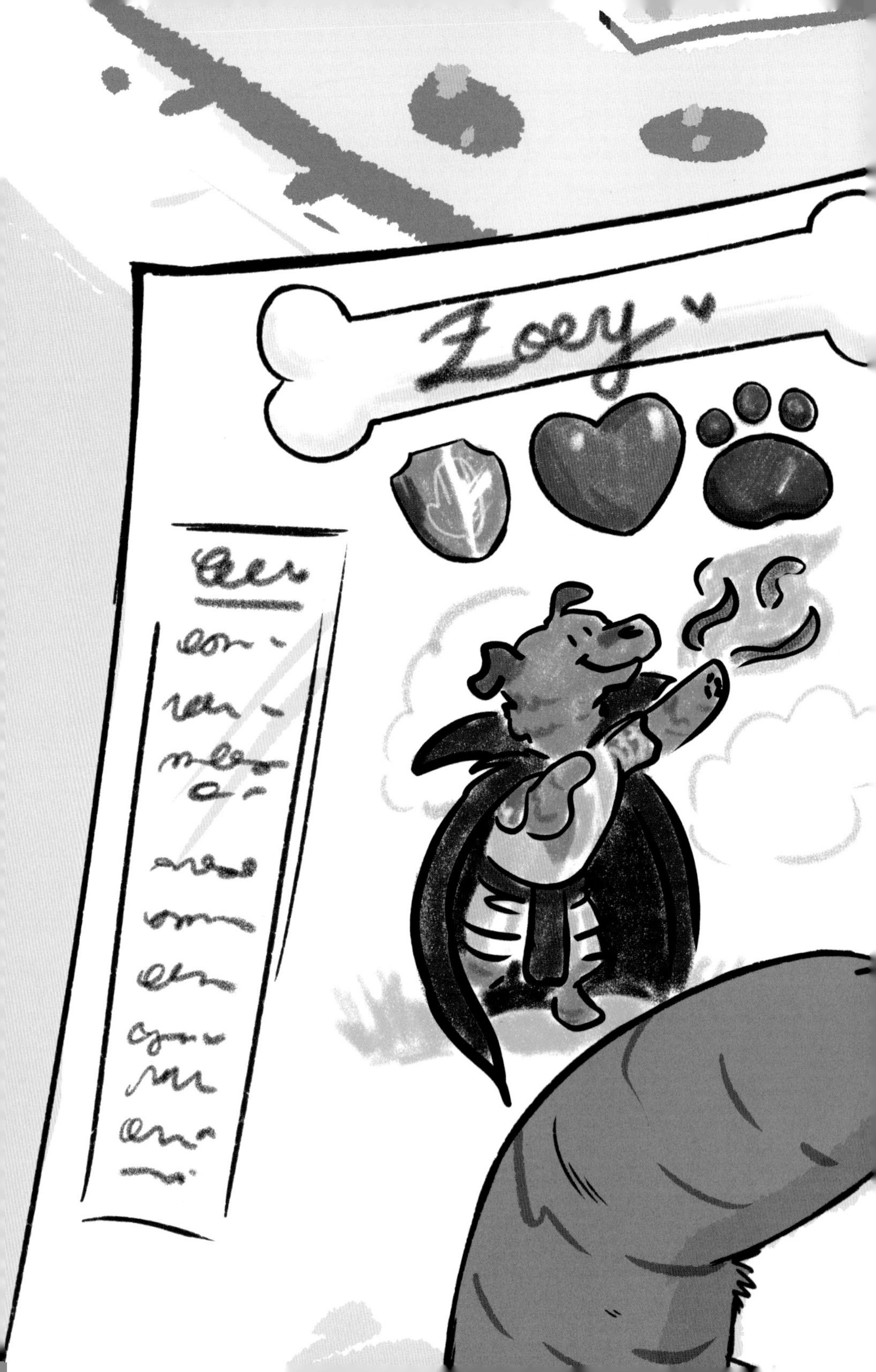
Zoey

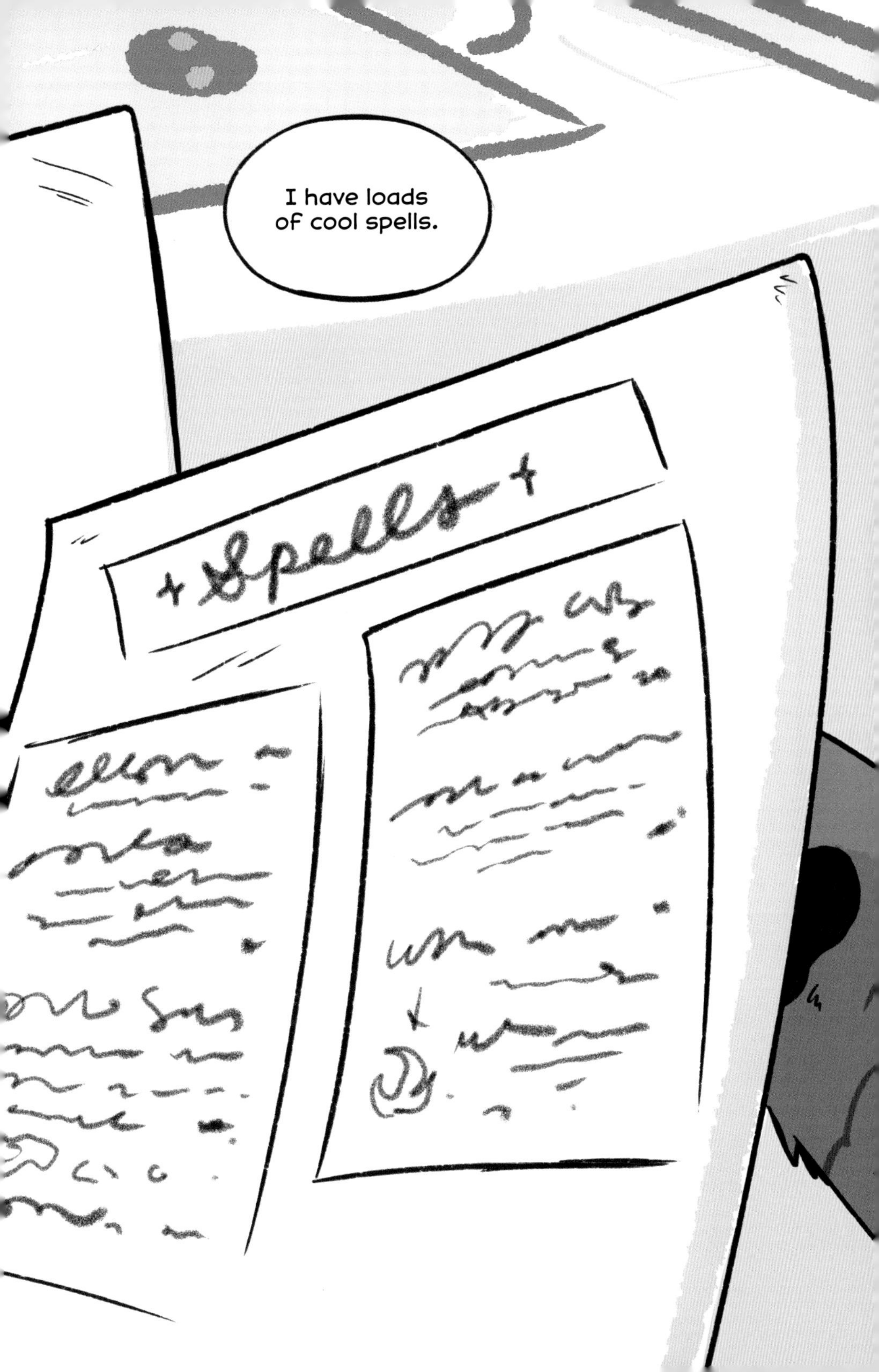
I have loads of cool spells.
Spells

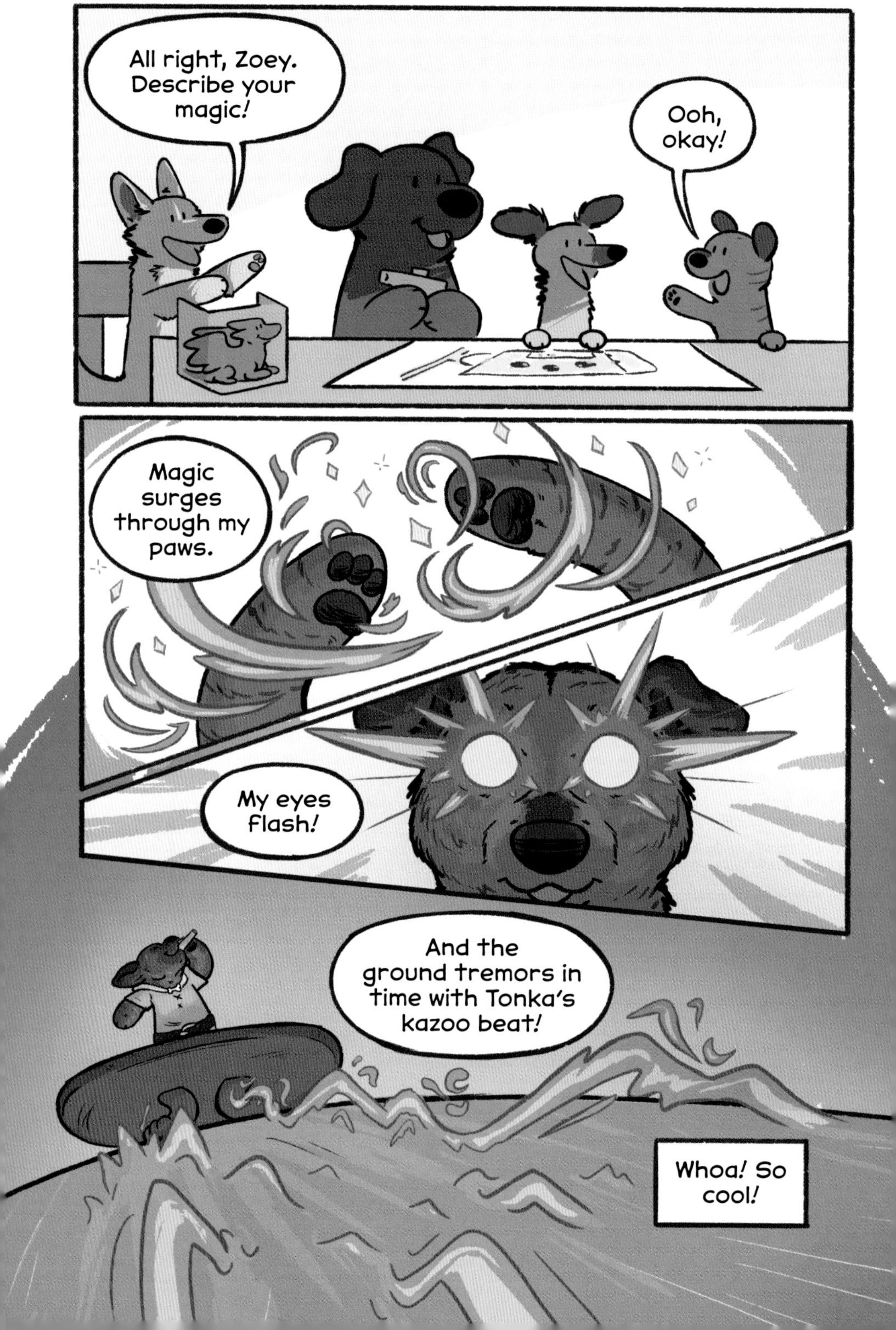

All right, Zoey. Describe your magic!
Ooh, okay!
Magic surges through my paws.
My eyes flash!
And the ground tremors in time with Tonka's kazoo beat!
Whoa! So cool!

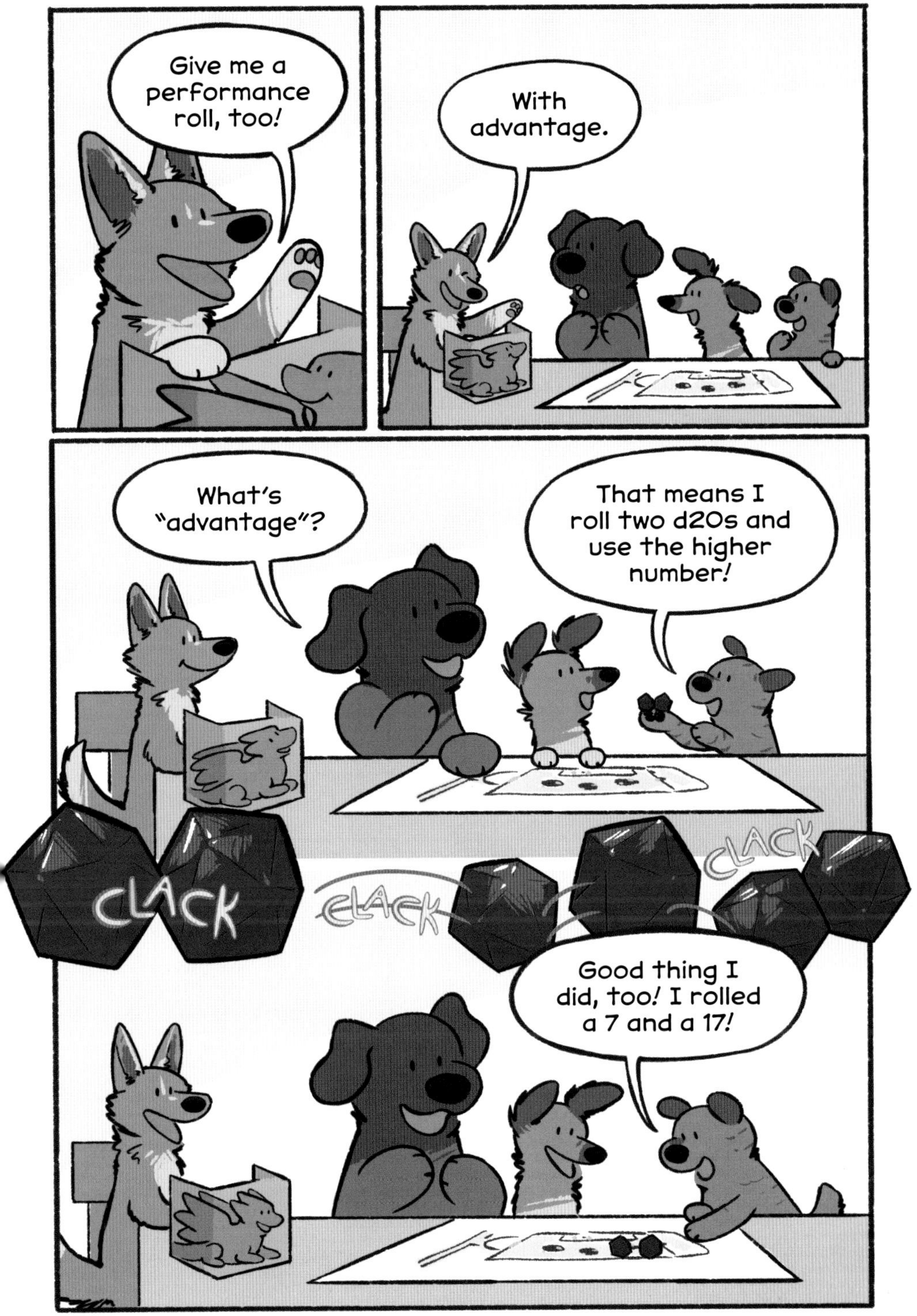
Give me a performance roll, too!
With advantage.
What's "advantage"?
That means I roll two d20s and use the higher number!
CLACK
CLACK
CLACK
Good thing I did, too! I rolled a 7 and a 17!

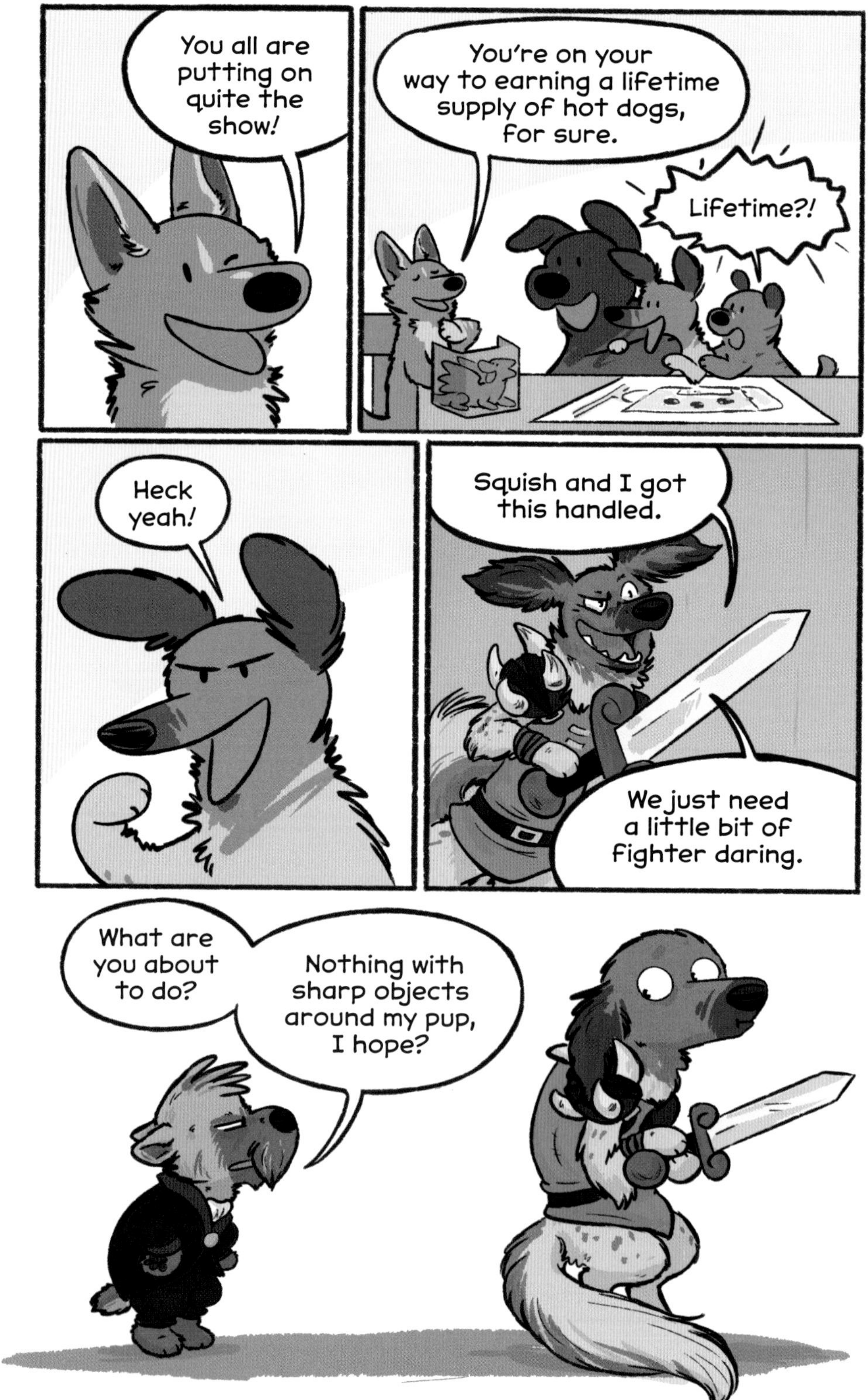
You all are putting on quite the show!
You're on your way to earning a lifetime supply of hot dogs, for sure.
Lifetime?!
Heck yeah!
Squish and I got this handled.
We just need a little bit of fighter daring.
What are you about to do?
Nothing with sharp objects around my pup, I hope?

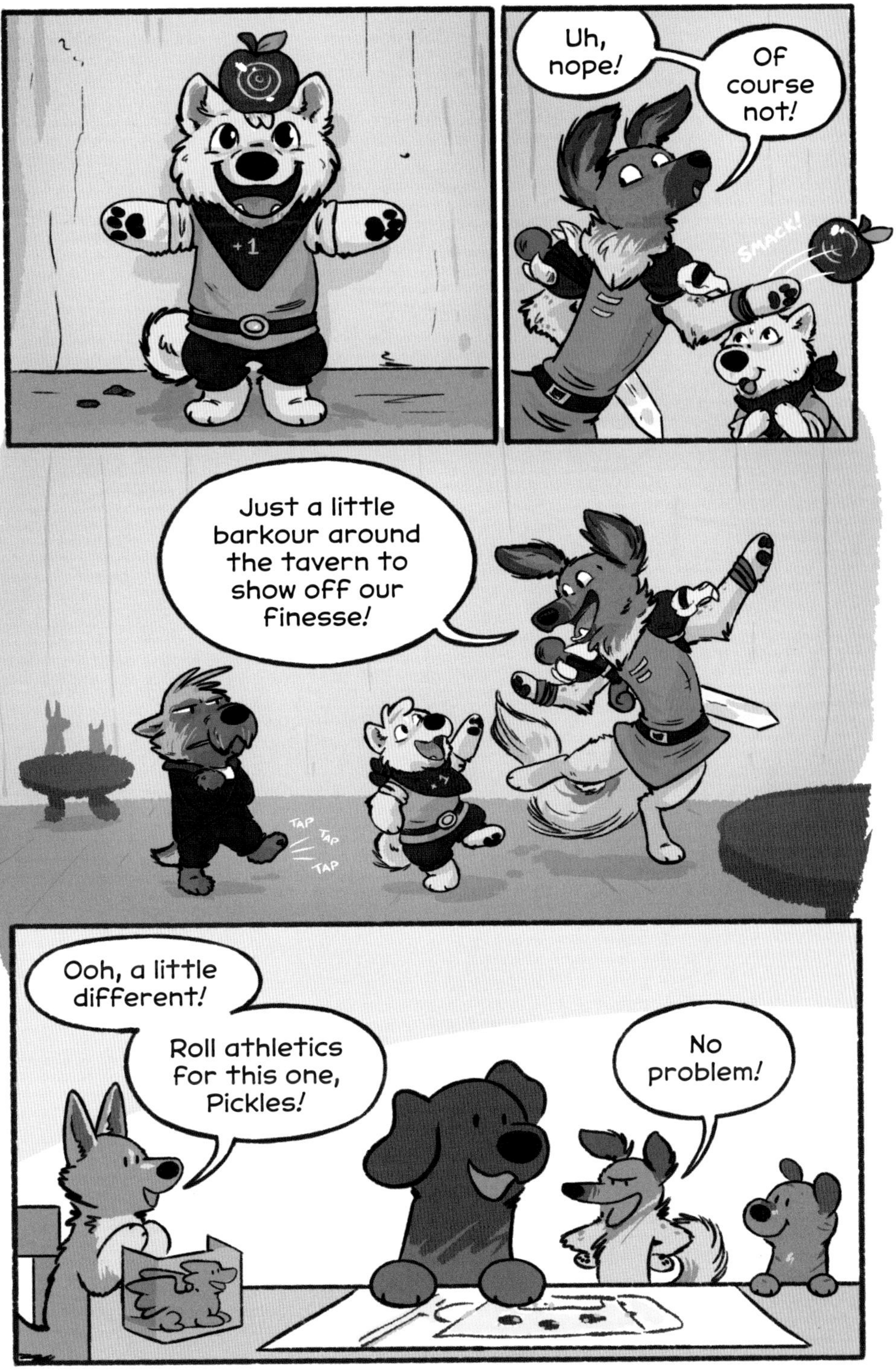
+1
Uh, nope!
Of course not!
SMACK!
Just a little barkour around the tavern to show off our finesse!
TAP
TAP
TAP
Ooh, a little different!
Roll athletics for this one, Pickles!
No problem!

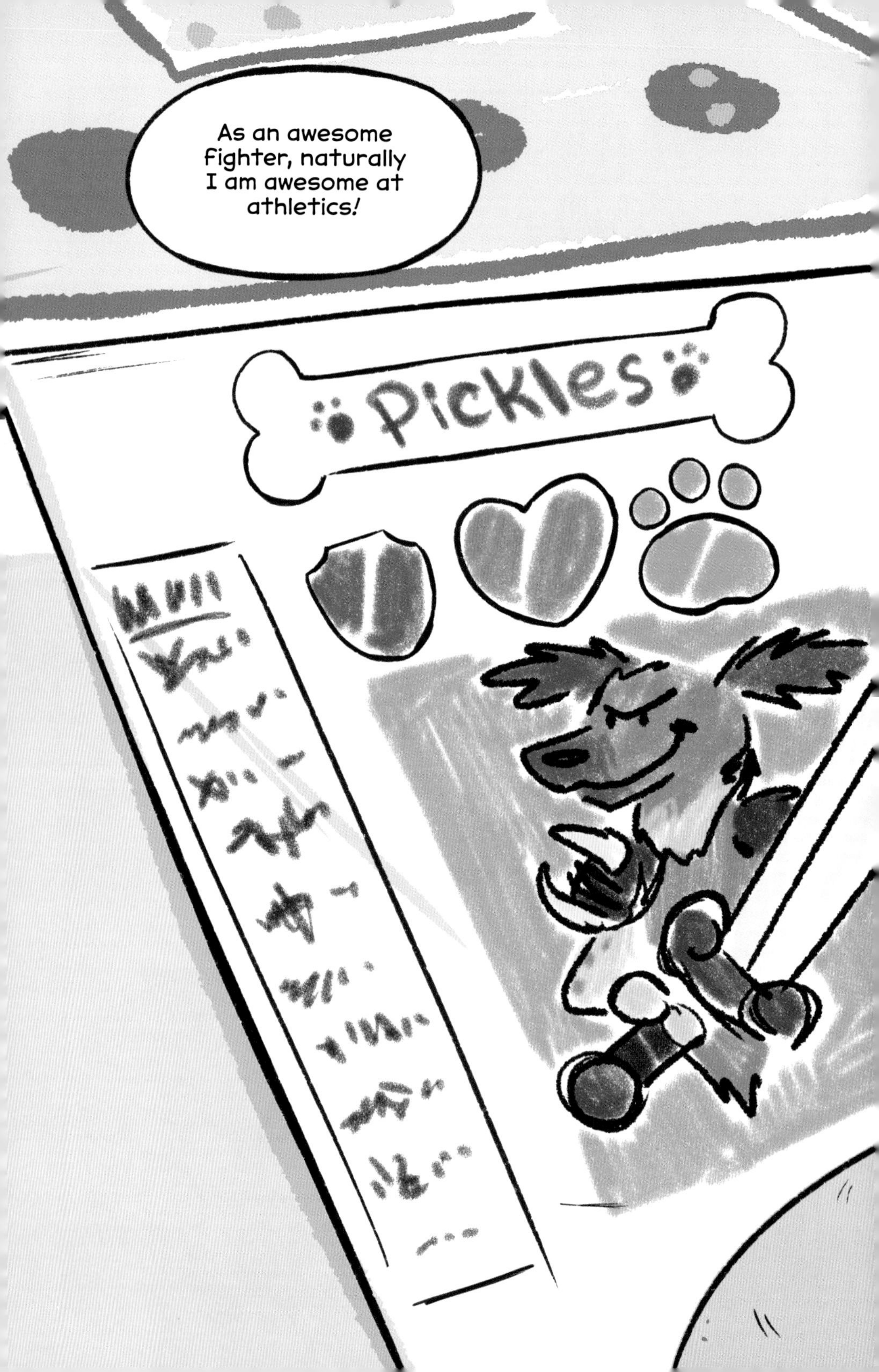
As an awesome fighter, naturally I am awesome at athletics!
Pickles

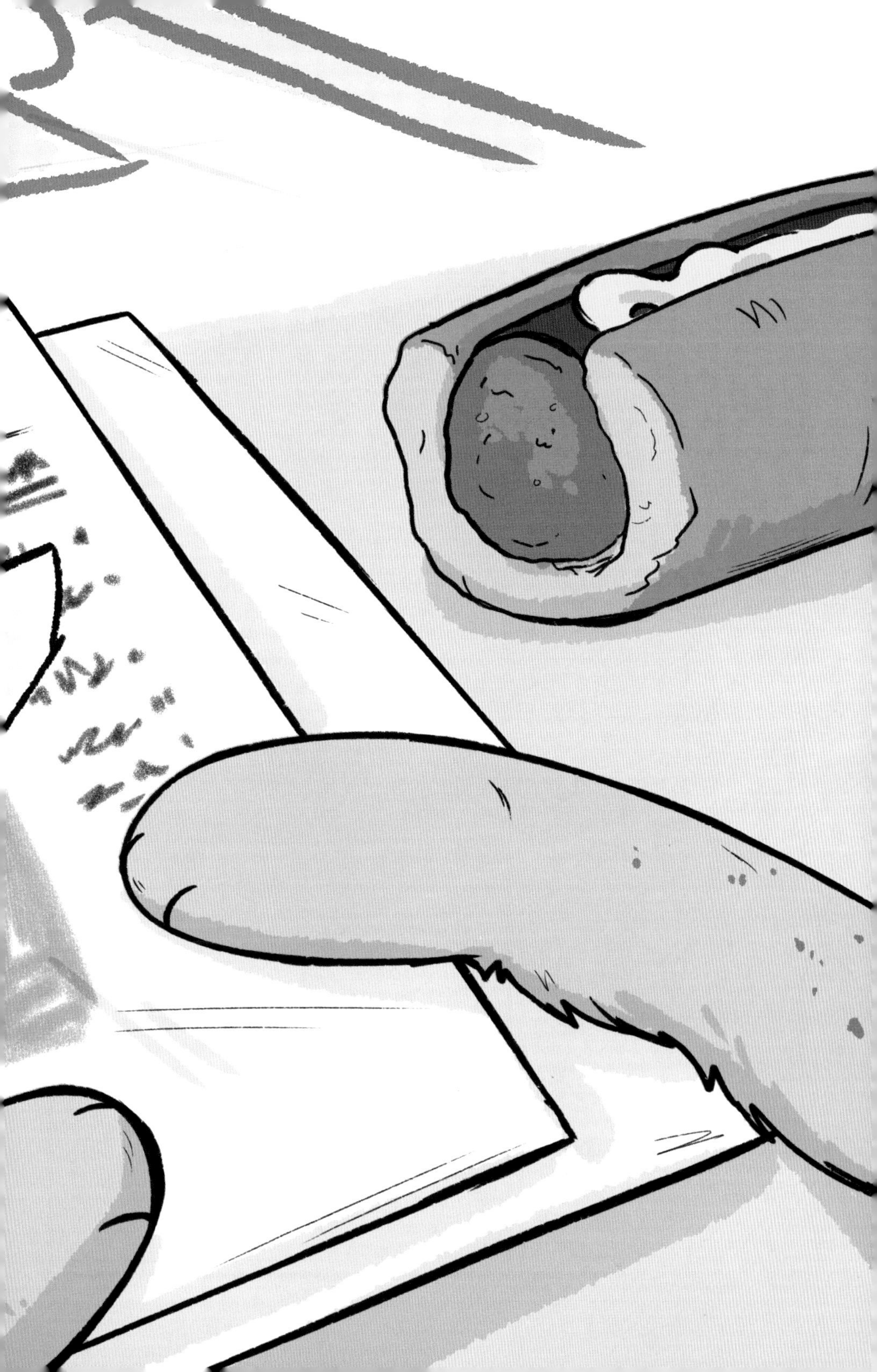

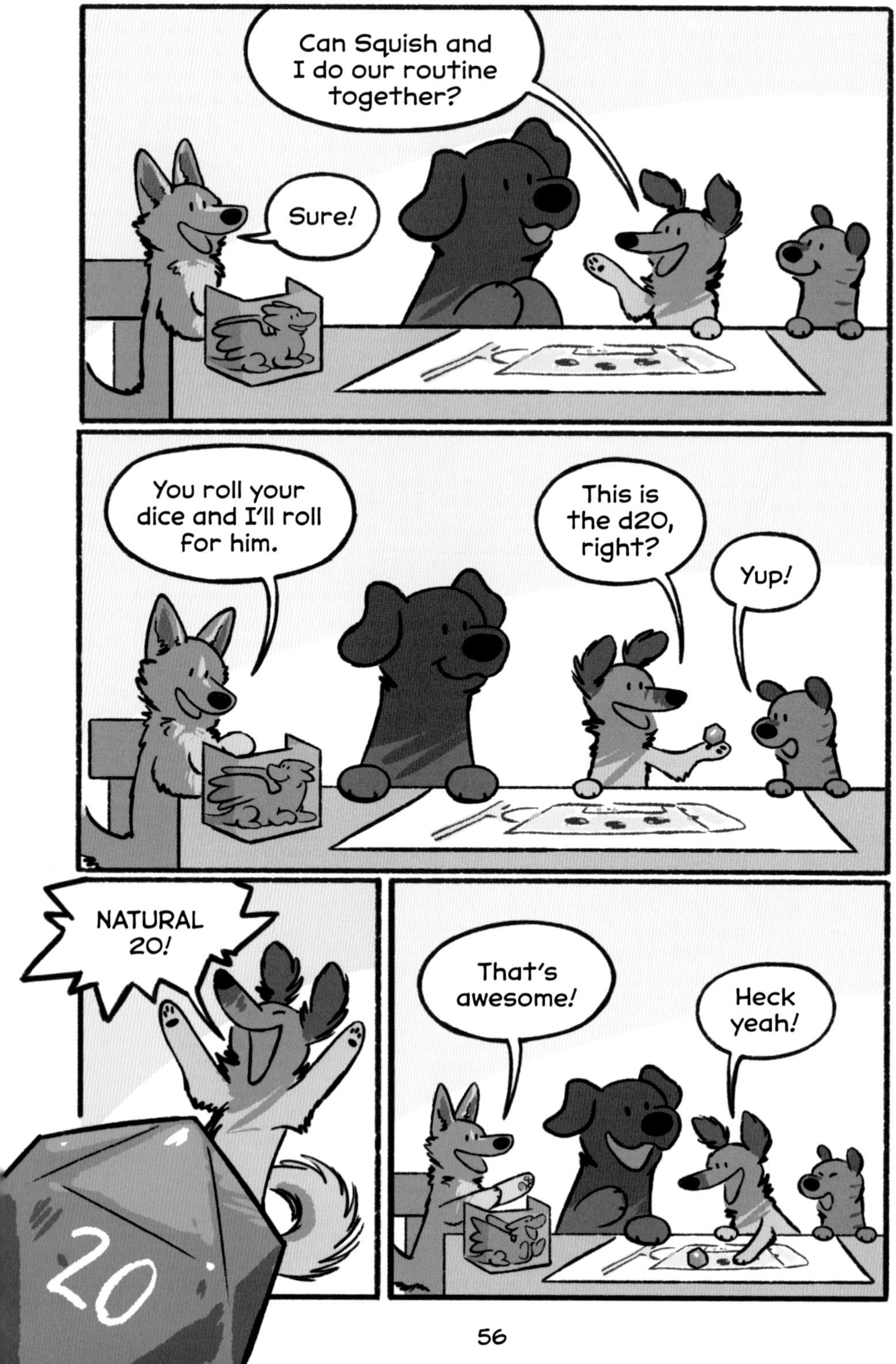
Can Squish and I do our routine together?
Sure!
You roll your dice and I'll roll for him.
This is the d20, right?
Yup!
NATURAL 20!
20
That's awesome!
Heck yeah!

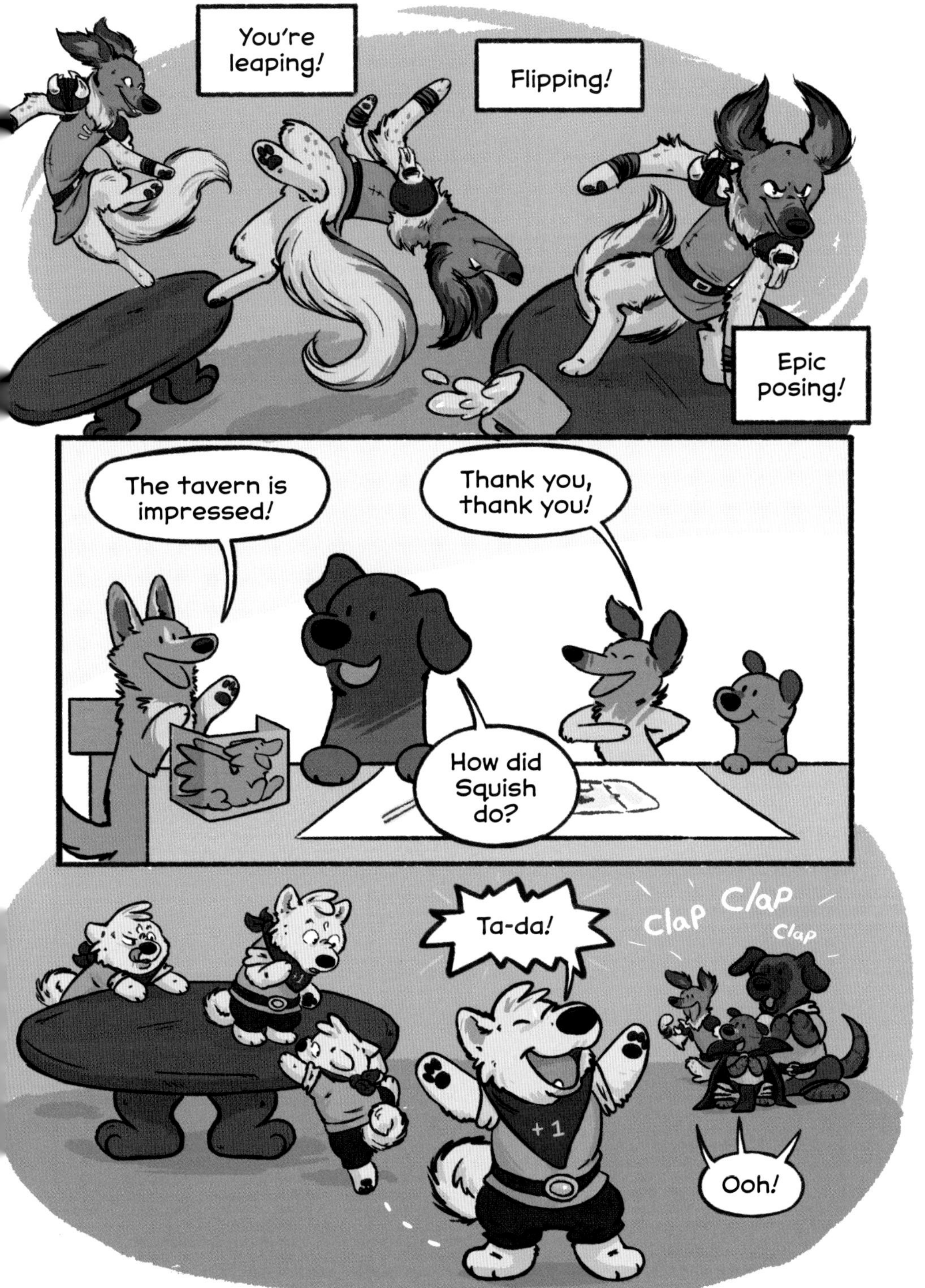
You're leaping!
Flipping!
Epic posing!
The tavern is impressed!
Thank you, thank you!
How did Squish do?
Ta-da!
Clap Clap Clap
Ooh!

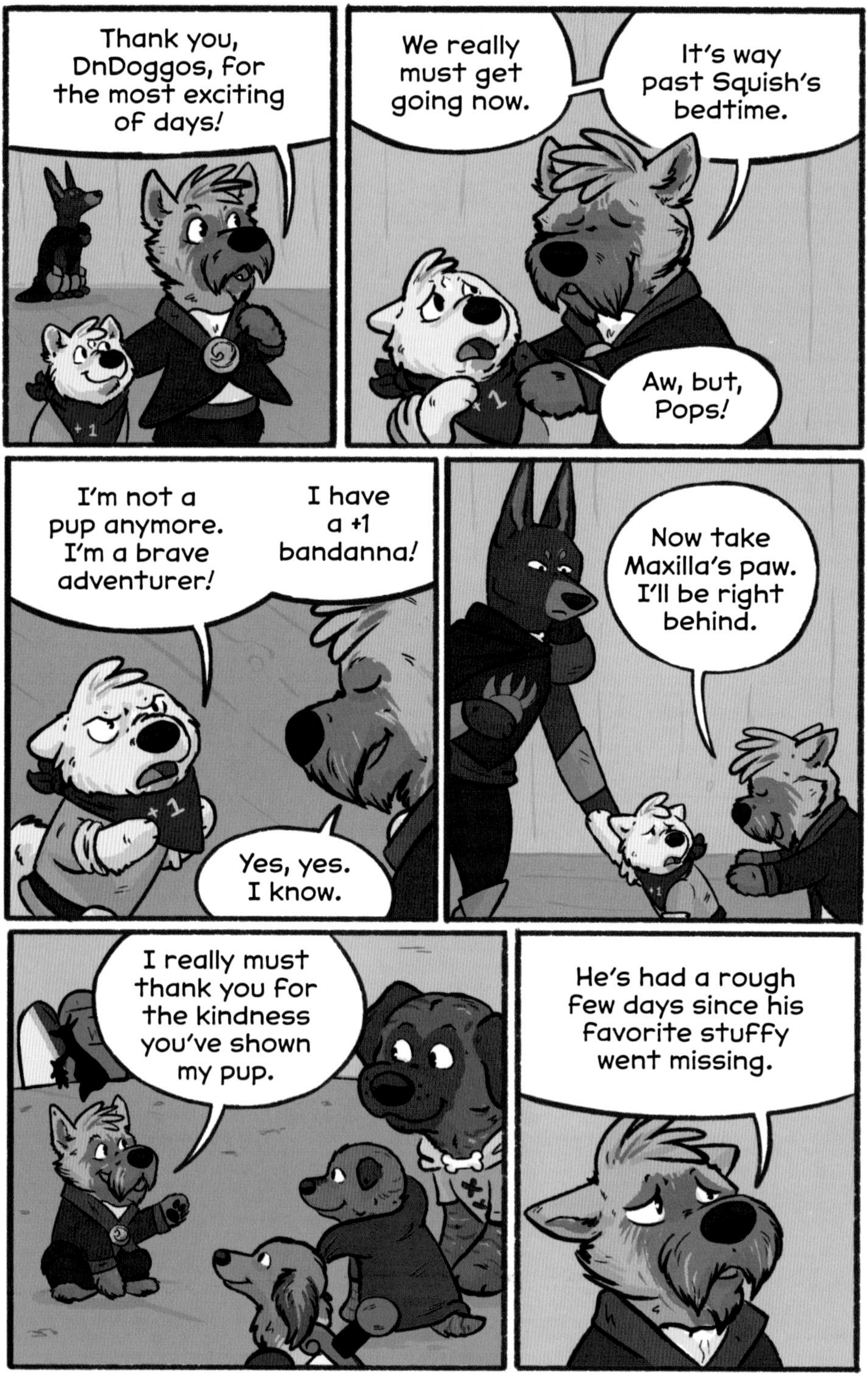
Thank you, DnDoggos, for the most exciting of days!
We really must get going now.
It's way past Squish's bedtime.
Aw, but, Pops!
I'm not a pup anymore. I'm a brave adventurer!
I have a +1 bandanna!
Yes, yes. I know.
Now take Maxilla's paw. I'll be right behind.
I really must thank you for the kindness you've shown my pup.
He's had a rough few days since his favorite stuffy went missing.

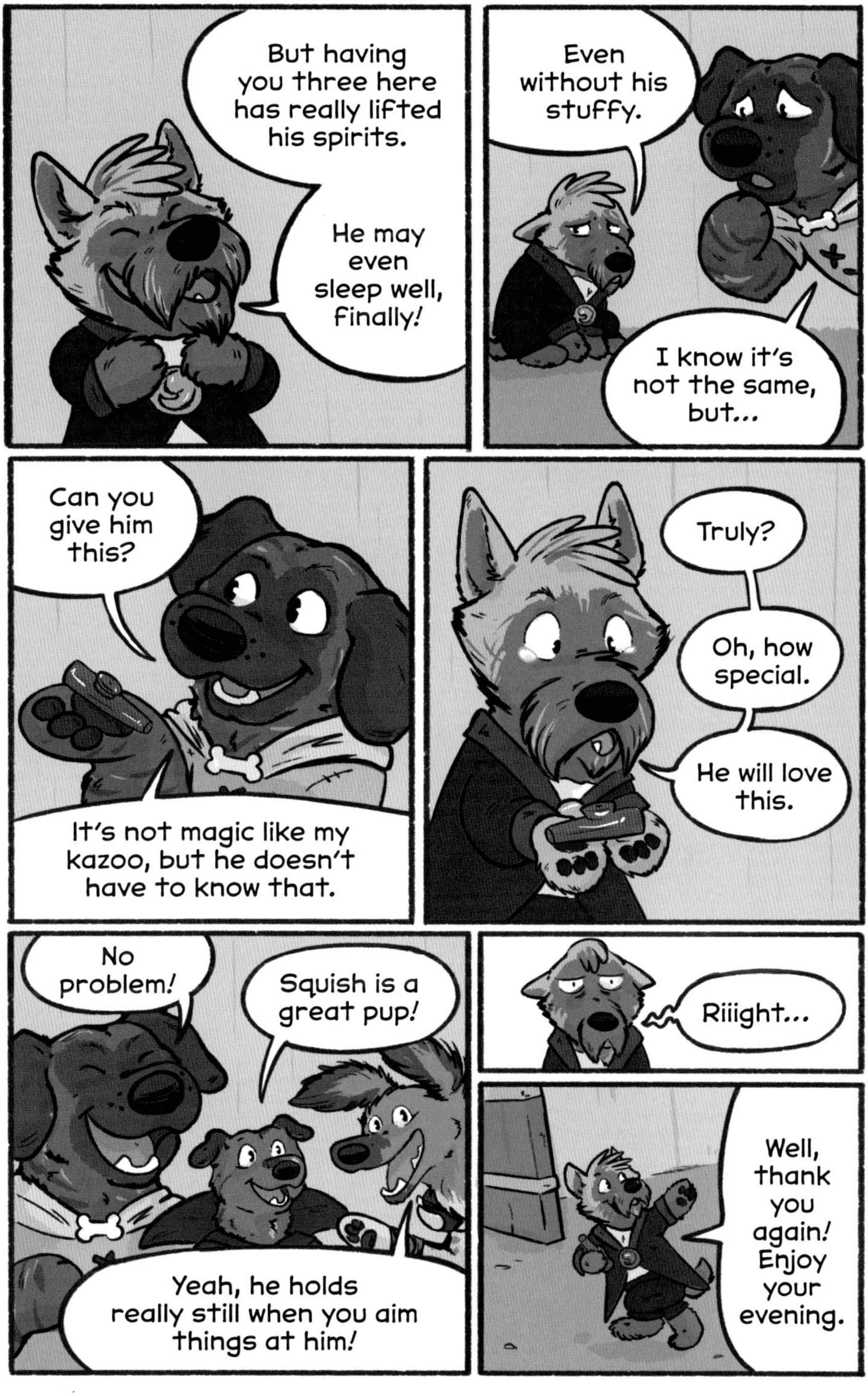
But having you three here has really lifted his spirits.
He may even sleep well, finally!
Even without his stuffy.
I know it's not the same, but...
Can you give him this?
It's not magic like my kazoo, but he doesn't have to know that.
Truly?
Oh, how special.
He will love this.
No problem!
Squish is a great pup!
Yeah, he holds really still when you aim things at him!
Riiight...
Well, thank you again! Enjoy your evening.

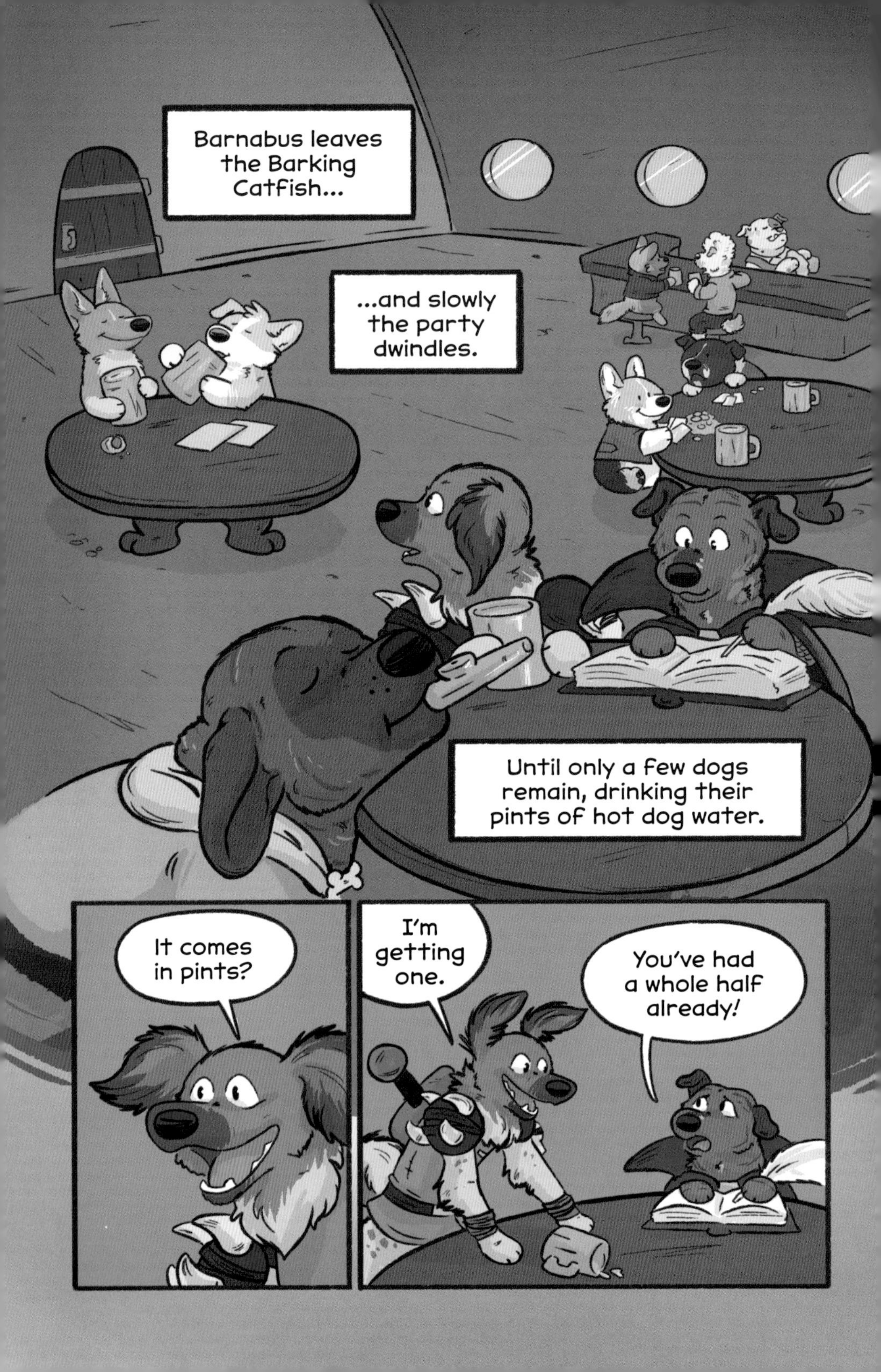

Barnabus leaves the Barking Catfish...
...and slowly the party dwindles.
Until only a few dogs remain, drinking their pints of hot dog water.
It comes in pints?
I'm getting one.
You've had a whole half already!

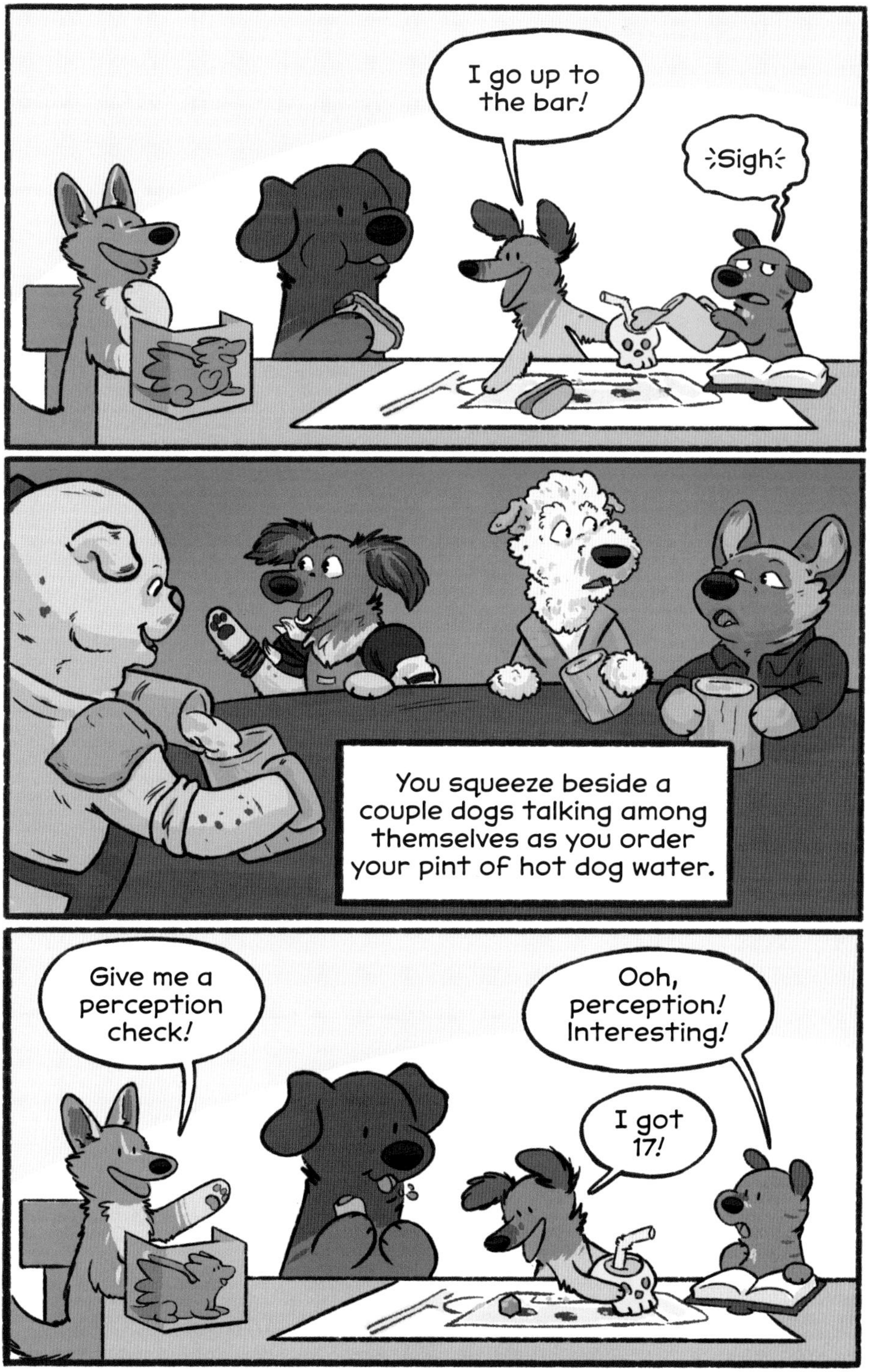
I go up to the bar!
Sigh
You squeeze beside a couple dogs talking among themselves as you order your pint of hot dog water.
Give me a perception check!
Ooh, perception! Interesting!
I got 17!

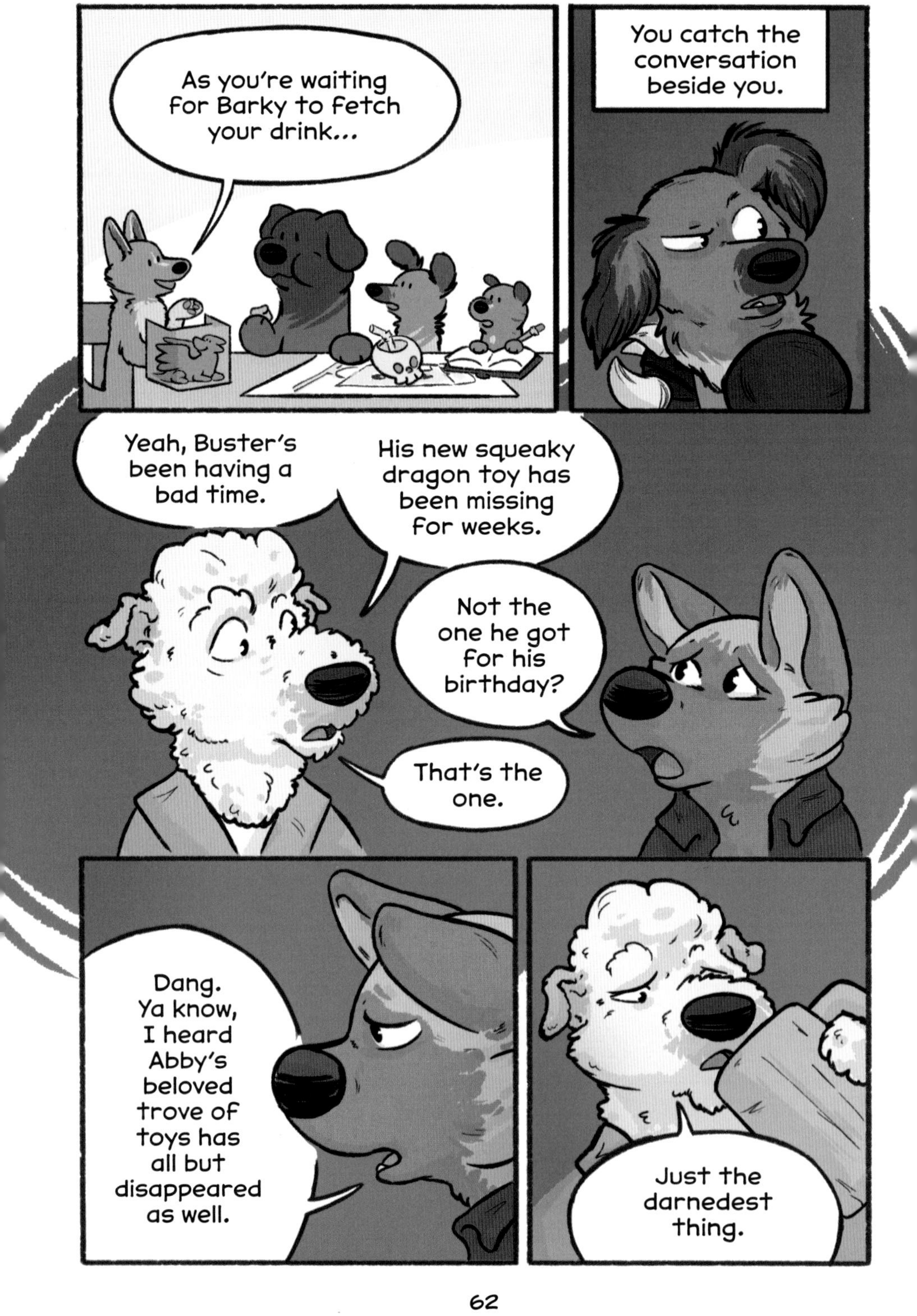
As you're waiting for Barky to fetch your drink...
You catch the conversation beside you.
Yeah, Buster's been having a bad time.
His new squeaky dragon toy has been missing for weeks.
Not the one he got for his birthday?
That's the one.
Dang. Ya know, I heard Abby's beloved trove of toys has all but disappeared as well.
Just the darnedest thing.

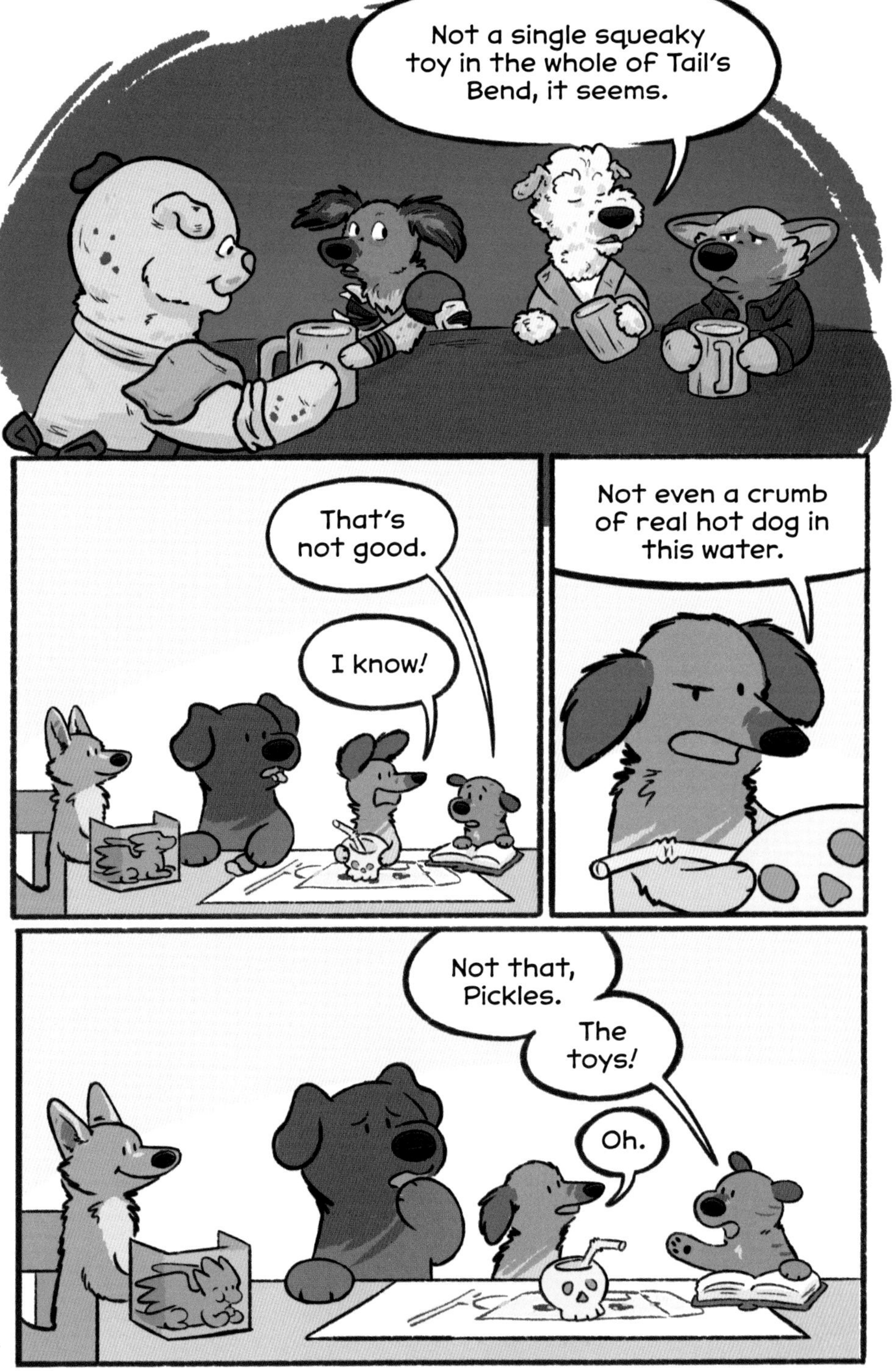
Not a single squeaky toy in the whole of Tail's Bend, it seems.
That's not good.
I know!
Not even a crumb of real hot dog in this water.
Not that, Pickles.
The toys!
Oh.

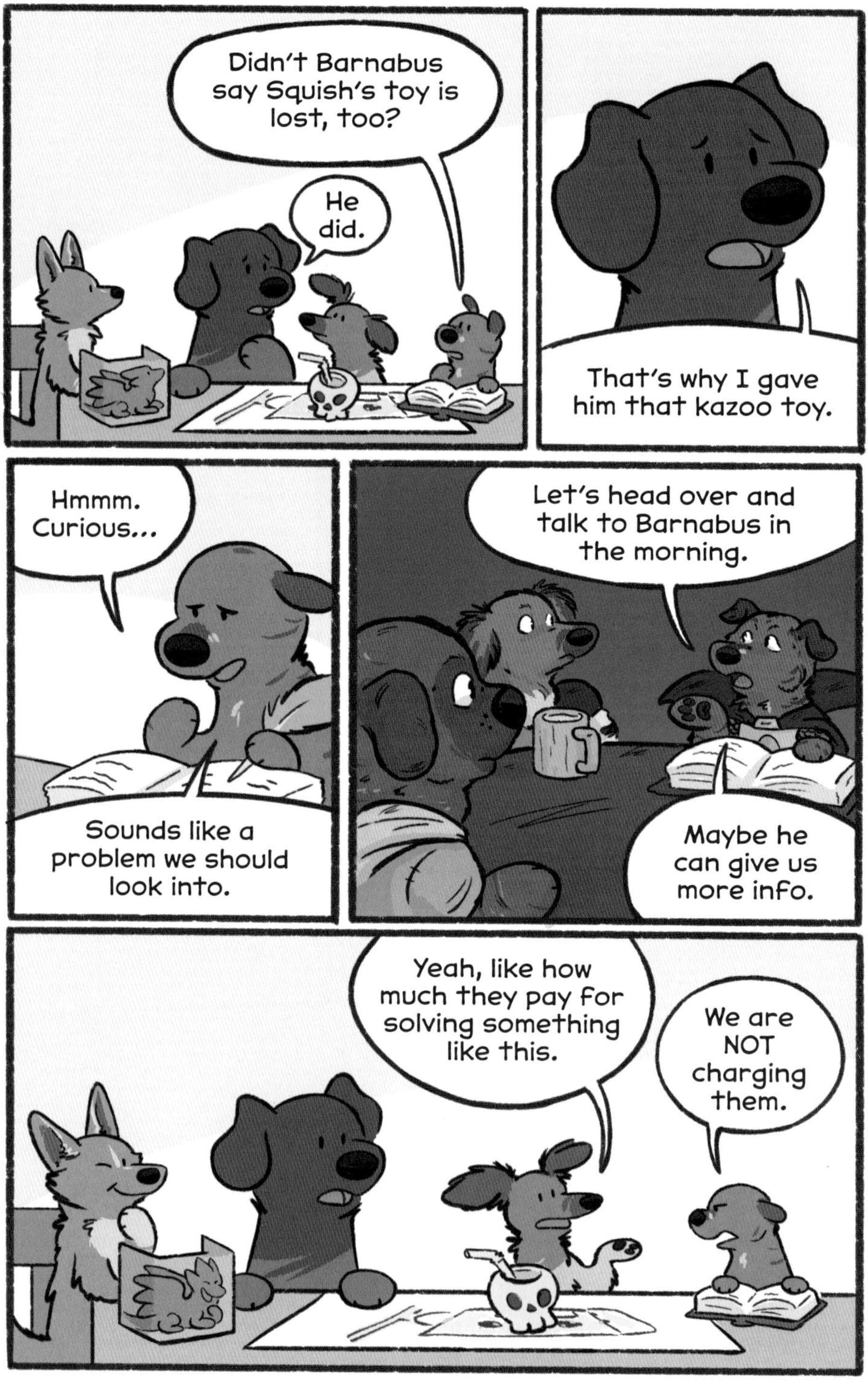

Didn't Barnabus say Squish's toy is lost, too?
He did.
That's why I gave him that kazoo toy.
Hmmm. Curious...
Sounds like a problem we should look into.
Let's head over and talk to Barnabus in the morning.
Maybe he can give us more info.
Yeah, like how much they pay for solving something like this.
We are NOT charging them.

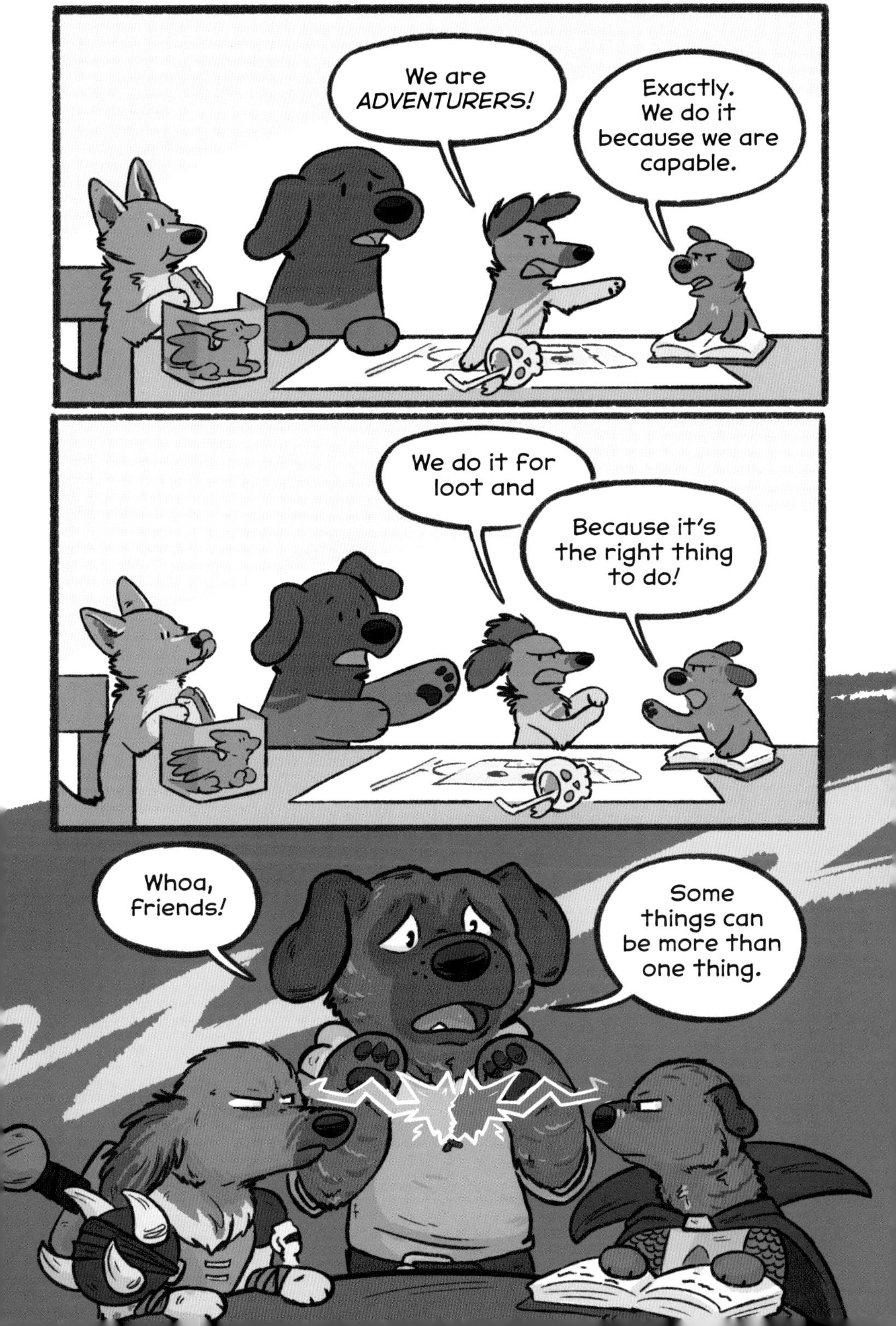
We are ADVENTURERS!
Exactly. We do it because we are capable.
We do it for loot and
Because it's the right thing to do!
Whoa, friends!
Some things can be more than one thing.

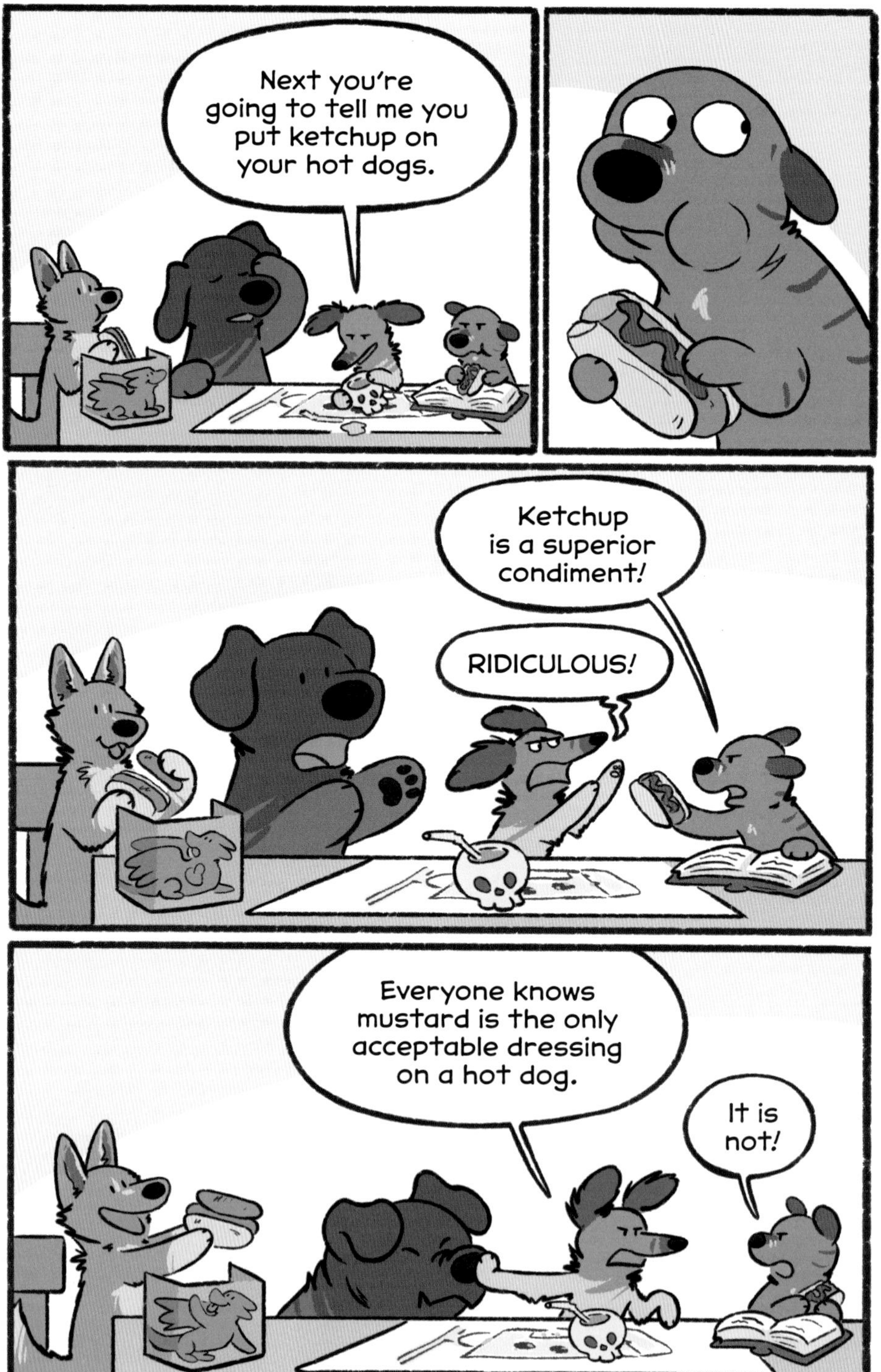
Next you're going to tell me you put ketchup on your hot dogs.
Ketchup is a superior condiment!
RIDICULOUS!
Everyone knows mustard is the only acceptable dressing on a hot dog.
It is not!

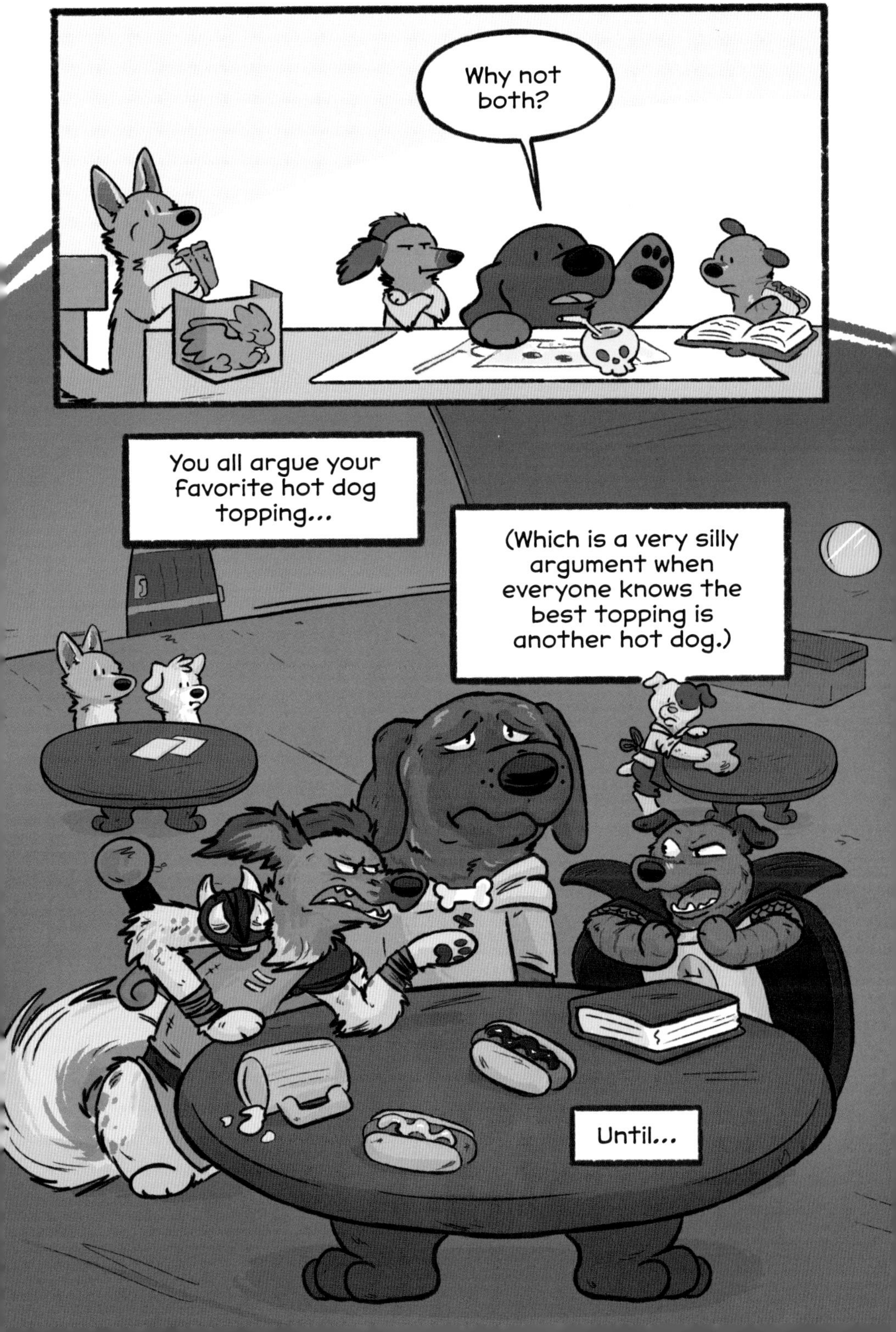
Why not both?
You all argue your favorite hot dog topping...
(Which is a very silly argument when everyone knows the best topping is another hot dog.)
Until...

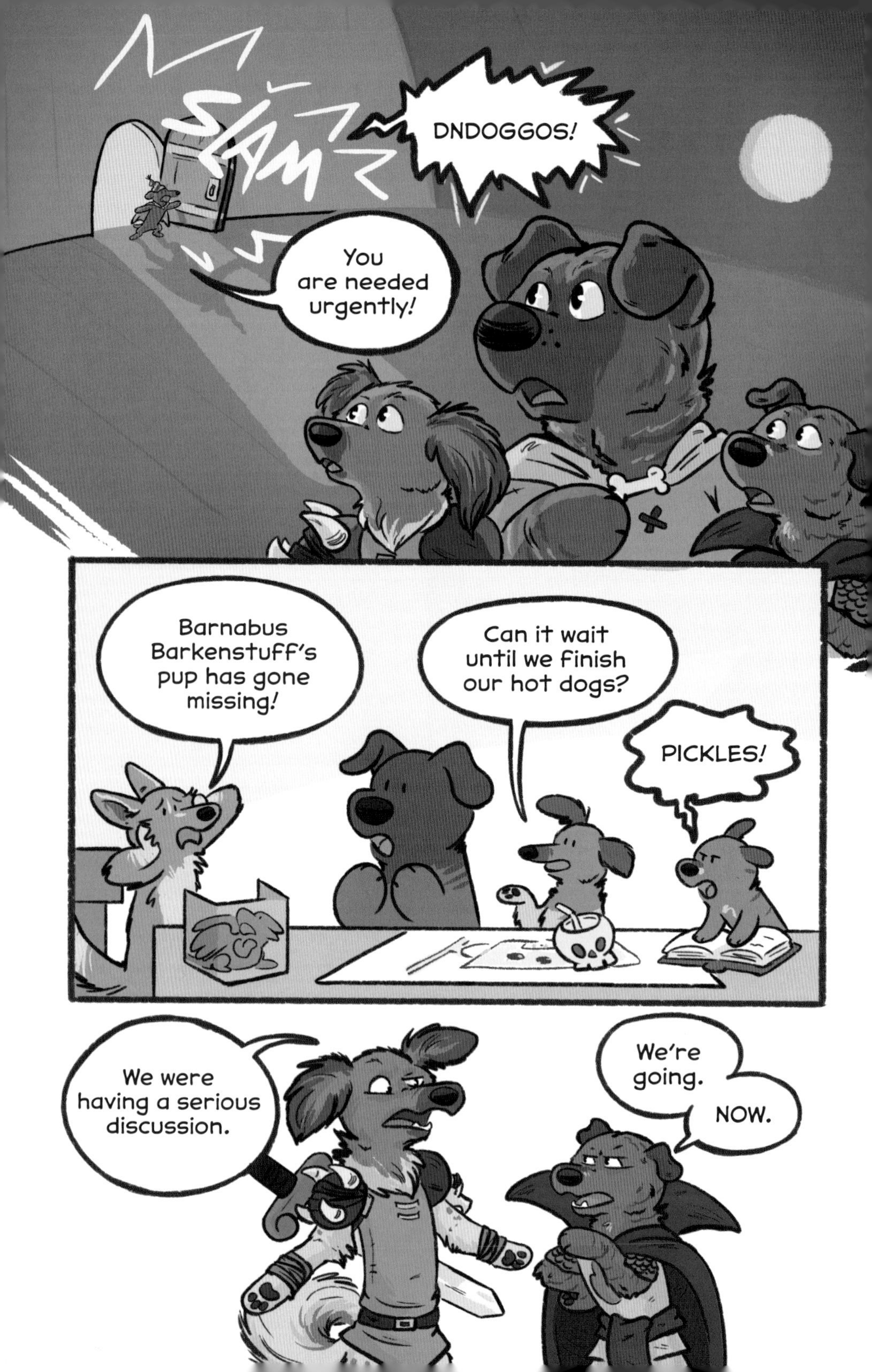
SLAM
DNDOGGOS!
You are needed urgently!
Barnabus Barkenstuff's pup has gone missing!
Can it wait until we finish our hot dogs?
PICKLES!
We were having a serious discussion.
We're going.
NOW.

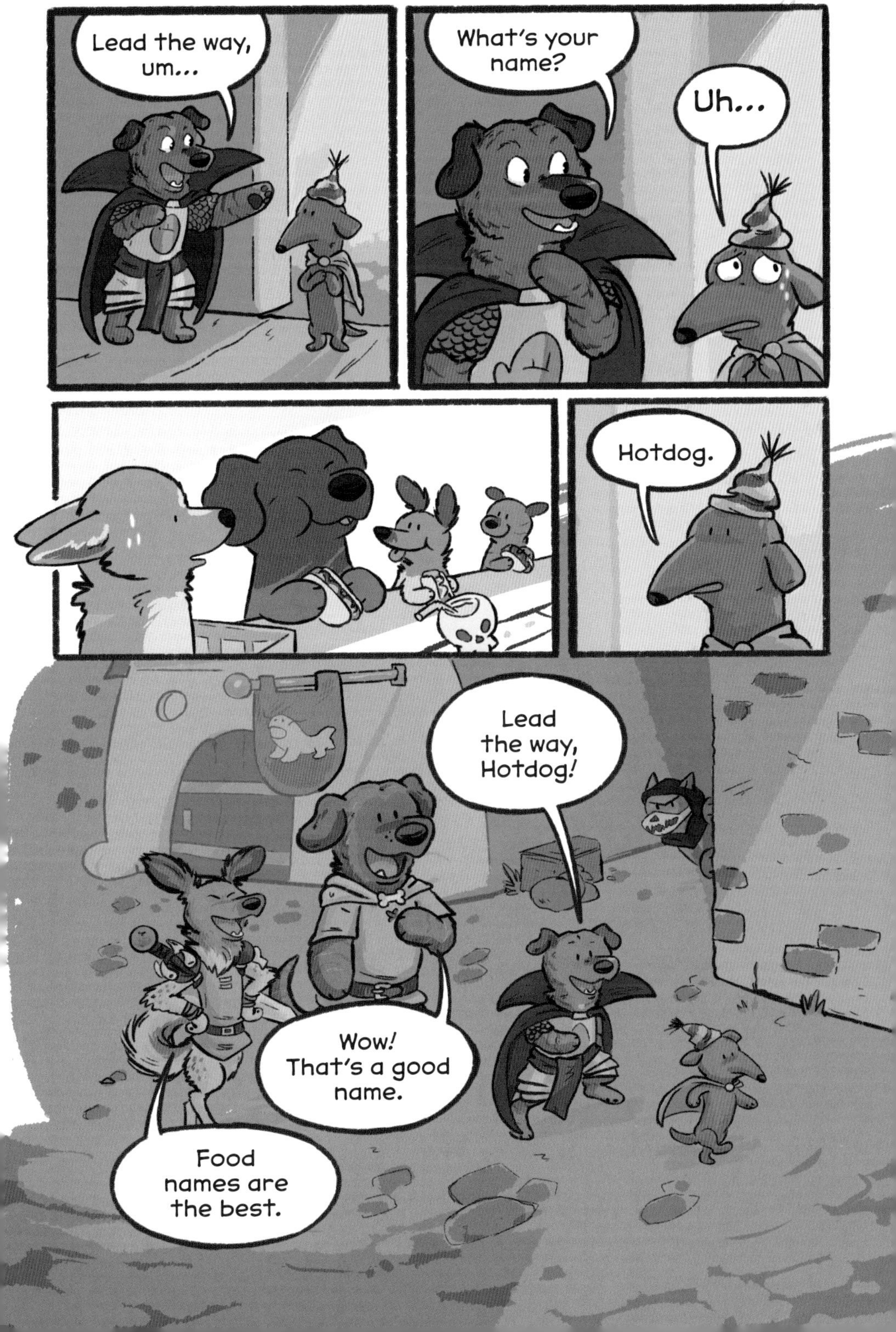
Lead the way, um...
What's your name?
Uh...
Hotdog.
Lead the way, Hotdog!
Wow! That's a good name.
Food names are the best.

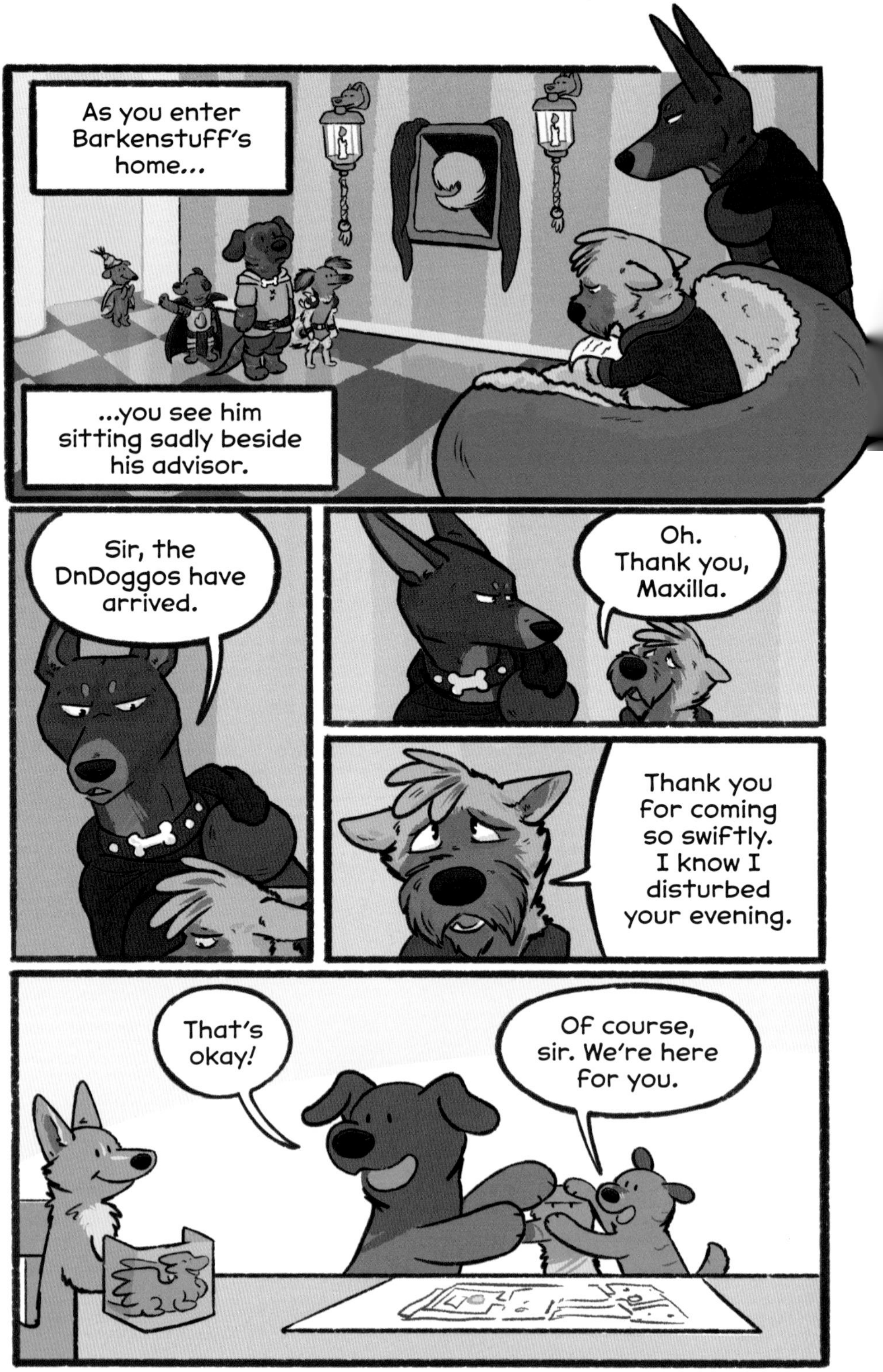
As you enter Barkenstuff's home...
...you see him sitting sadly beside his advisor.
Sir, the DnDoggos have arrived.
Oh. Thank you, Maxilla.
Thank you for coming so swiftly. I know I disturbed your evening.
That's okay!
Of course, sir. We're here for you.

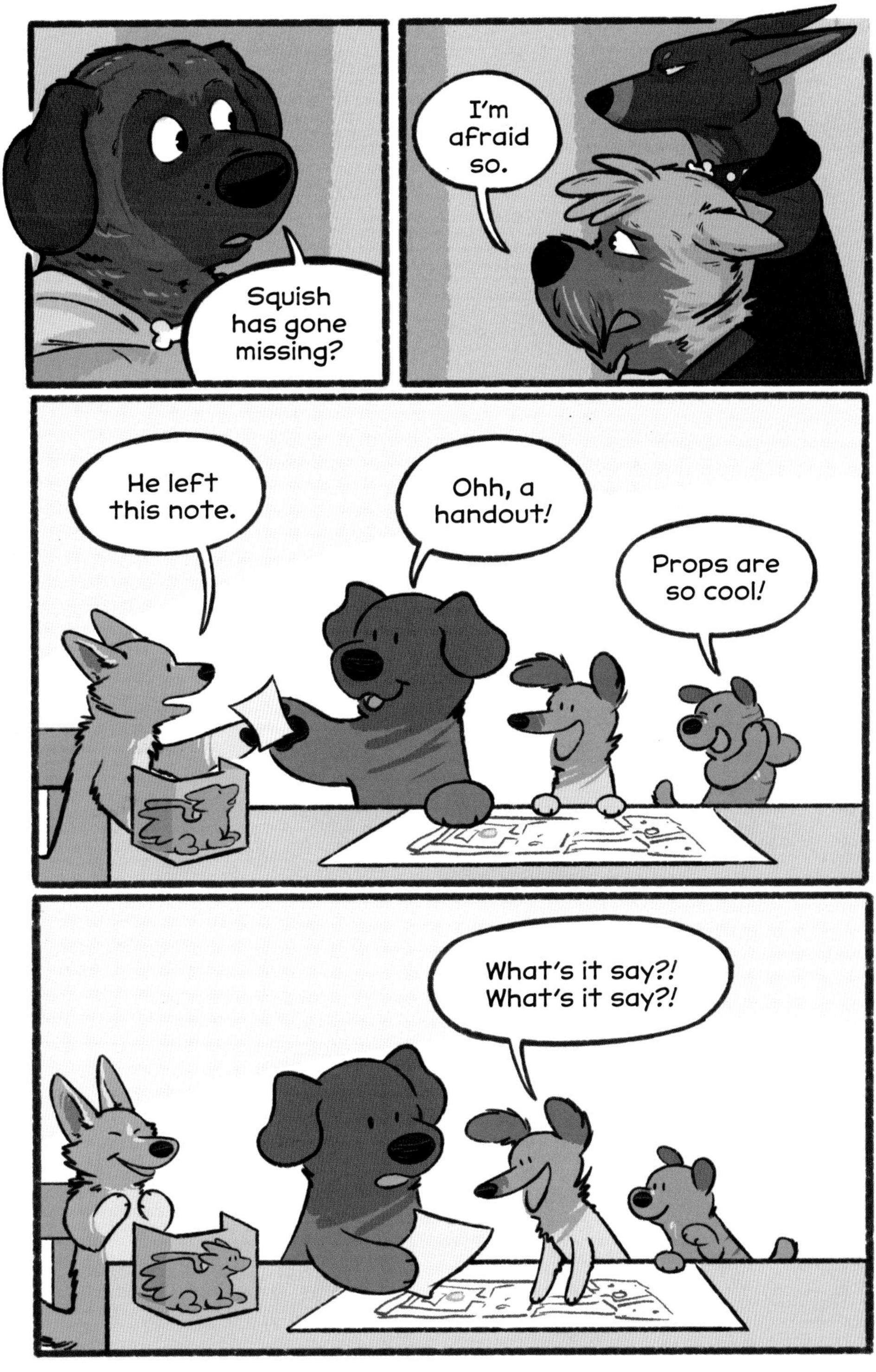
Squish has gone missing?
I'm afraid so.
He left this note.
Ohh, a handout!
Props are so cool!
What's it say?! What's it say?!

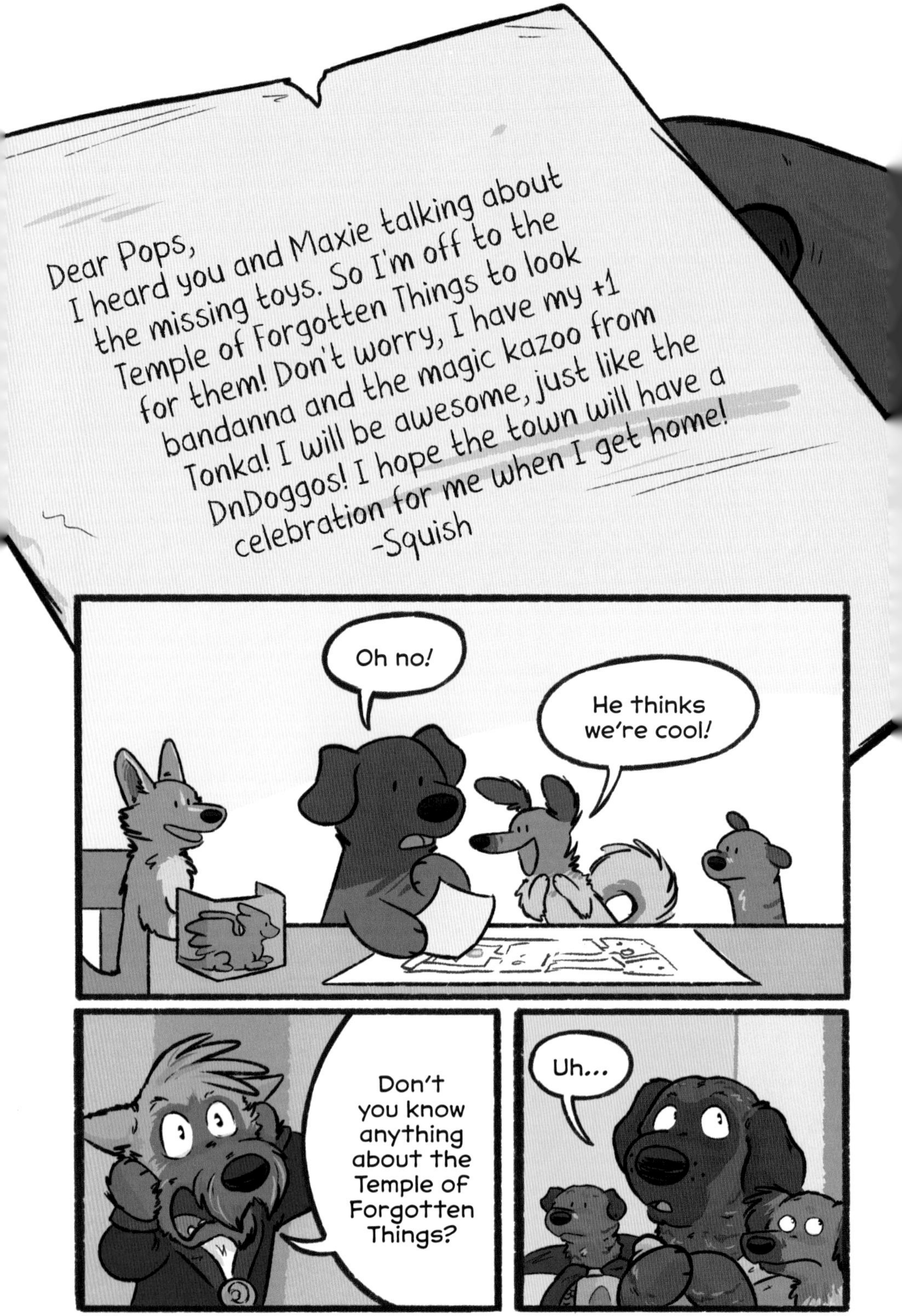

Dear Pops,
I heard you and Maxie talking about the missing toys. So I'm off to the Temple of Forgotten Things to look for them! Don't worry, I have my +1 bandanna and the magic kazoo from Tonka! I will be awesome, just like the DnDoggos! I hope the town will have a celebration for me when I get home!
-Squish
Oh no!
He thinks we're cool!
Don't you know anything about the Temple of Forgotten Things?
Uh...

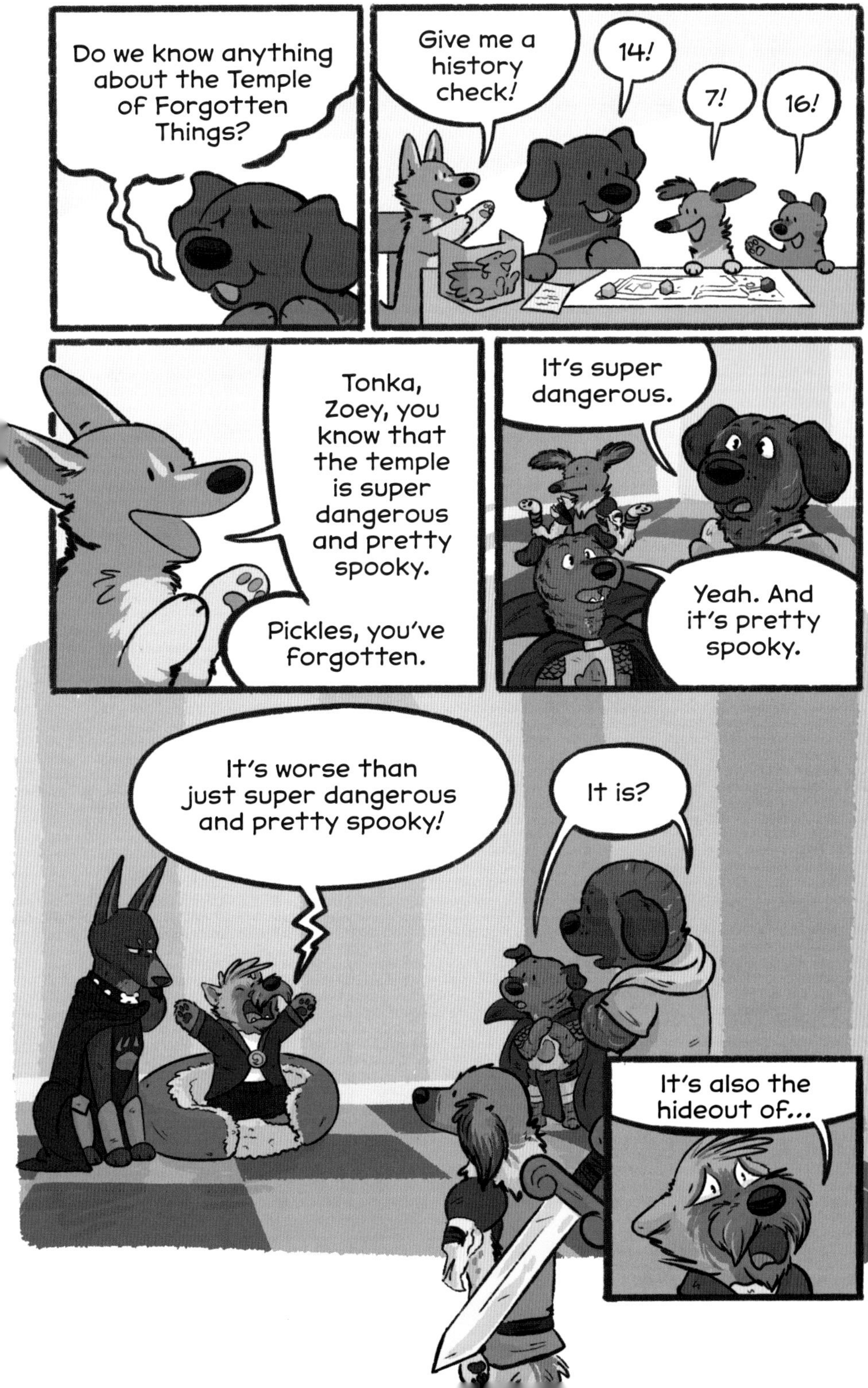
Do we know anything about the Temple of Forgotten Things?
Give me a history check!
14!
7!
16!
Tonka, Zoey, you know that the temple is super dangerous and pretty spooky.
Pickles, you've forgotten.
It's super dangerous.
Yeah. And it's pretty spooky.
It's worse than just super dangerous and pretty spooky!
It is?
It's also the hideout of...

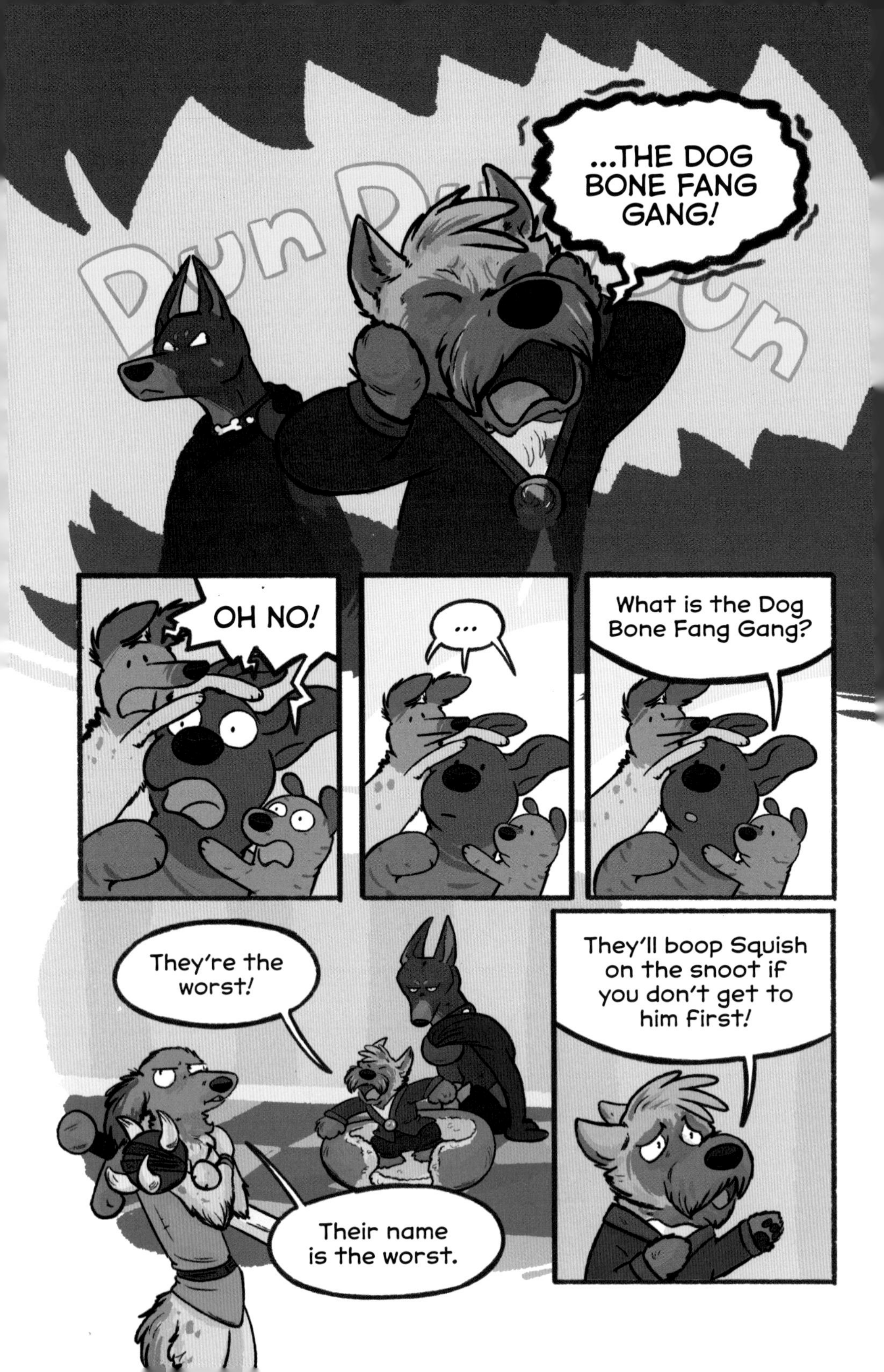

...THE DOG BONE FANG GANG!
OH NO!
...
What is the Dog Bone Fang Gang?
They're the worst!
Their name is the worst.
They'll boop Squish on the snoot if you don't get to him first!

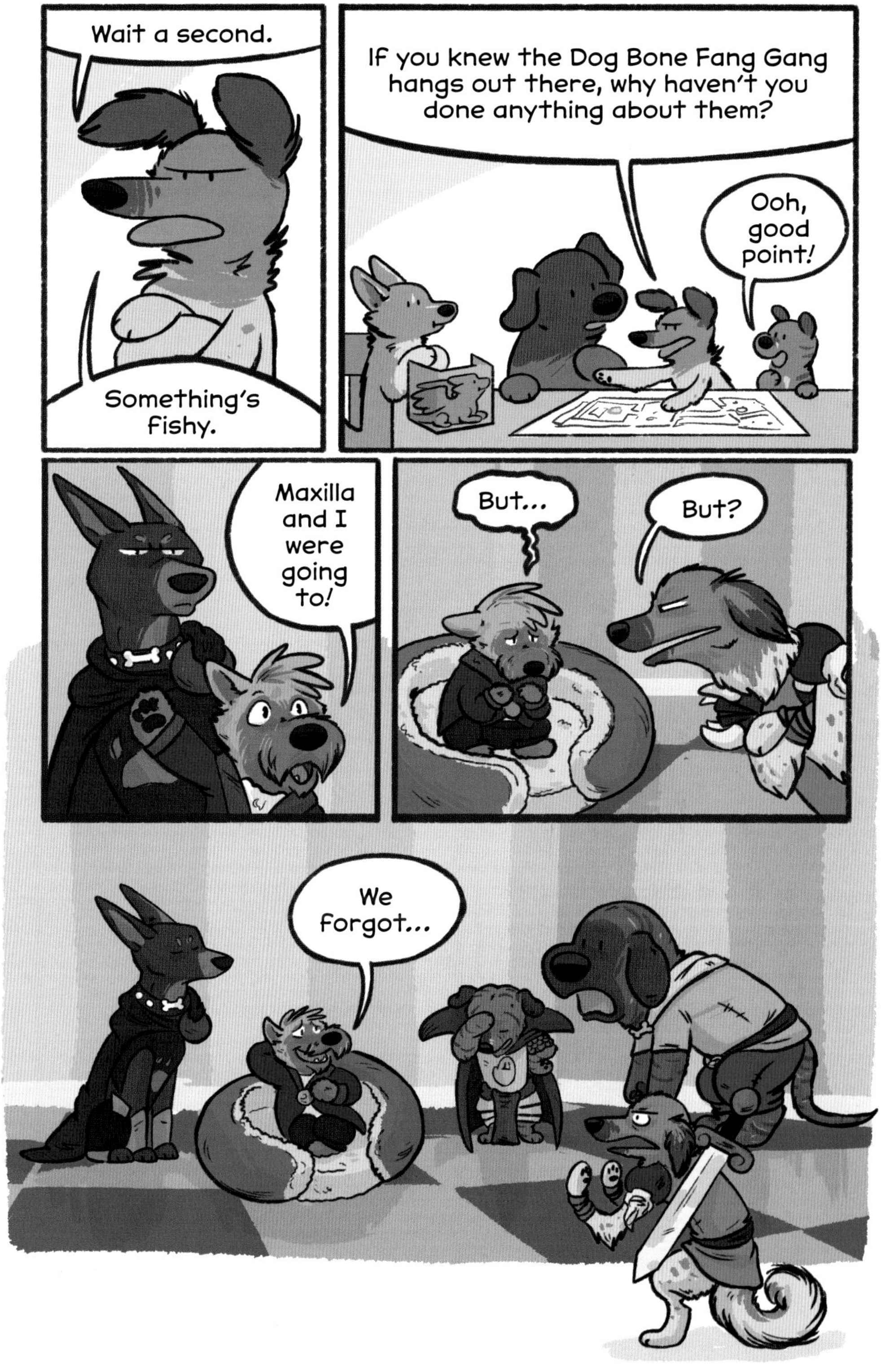
Wait a second.
Something's fishy.
If you knew the Dog Bone Fang Gang hangs out there, why haven't you done anything about them?
Ooh, good point!
Maxilla and I were going to!
But...
But?
We forgot...

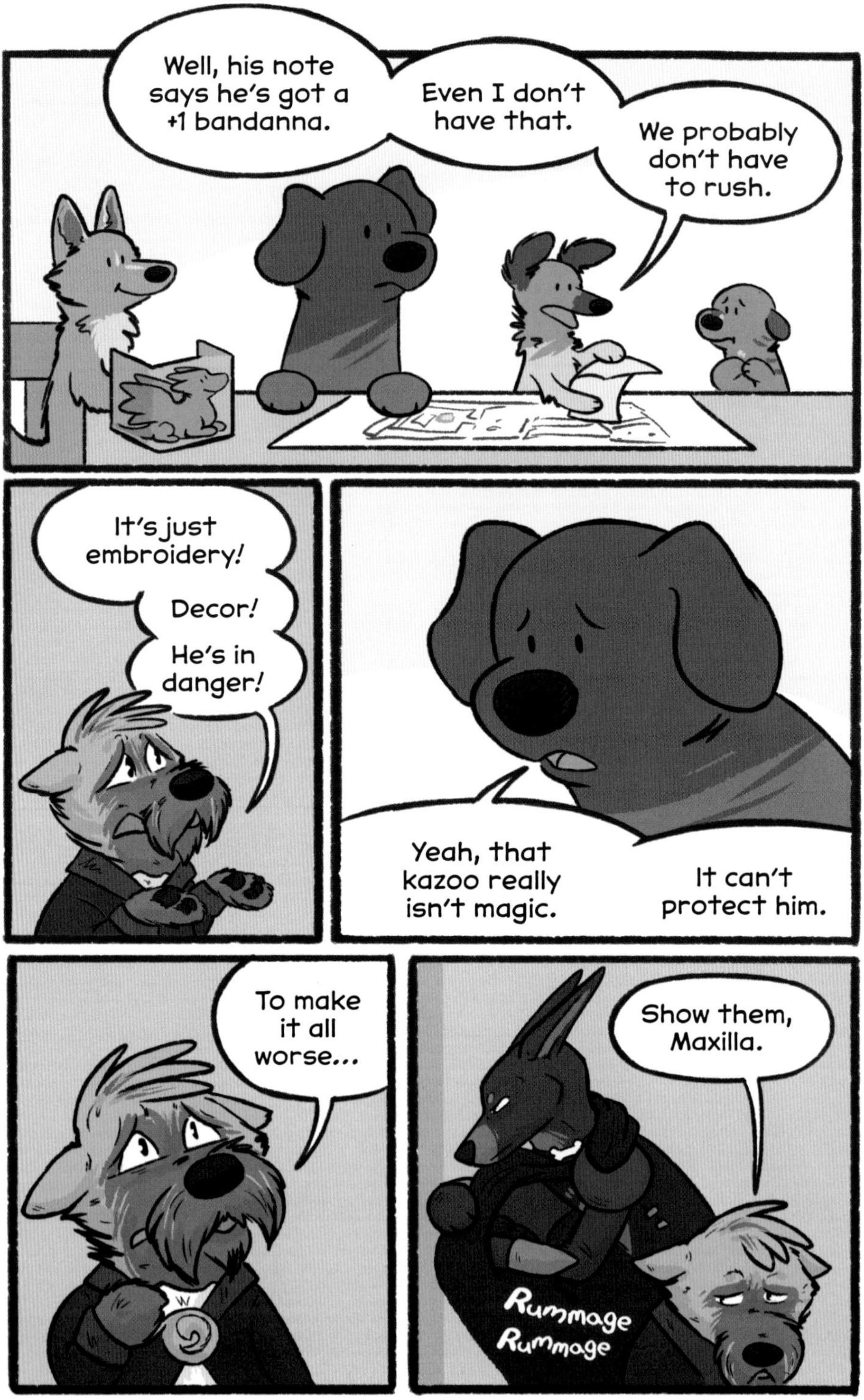
Well, his note says he's got a +1 bandanna.
Even I don't have that.
We probably don't have to rush.
It's just embroidery!
Decor!
He's in danger!
Yeah, that kazoo really isn't magic.
It can't protect him.
To make it all worse...
Show them, Maxilla.
Rummage Rummage

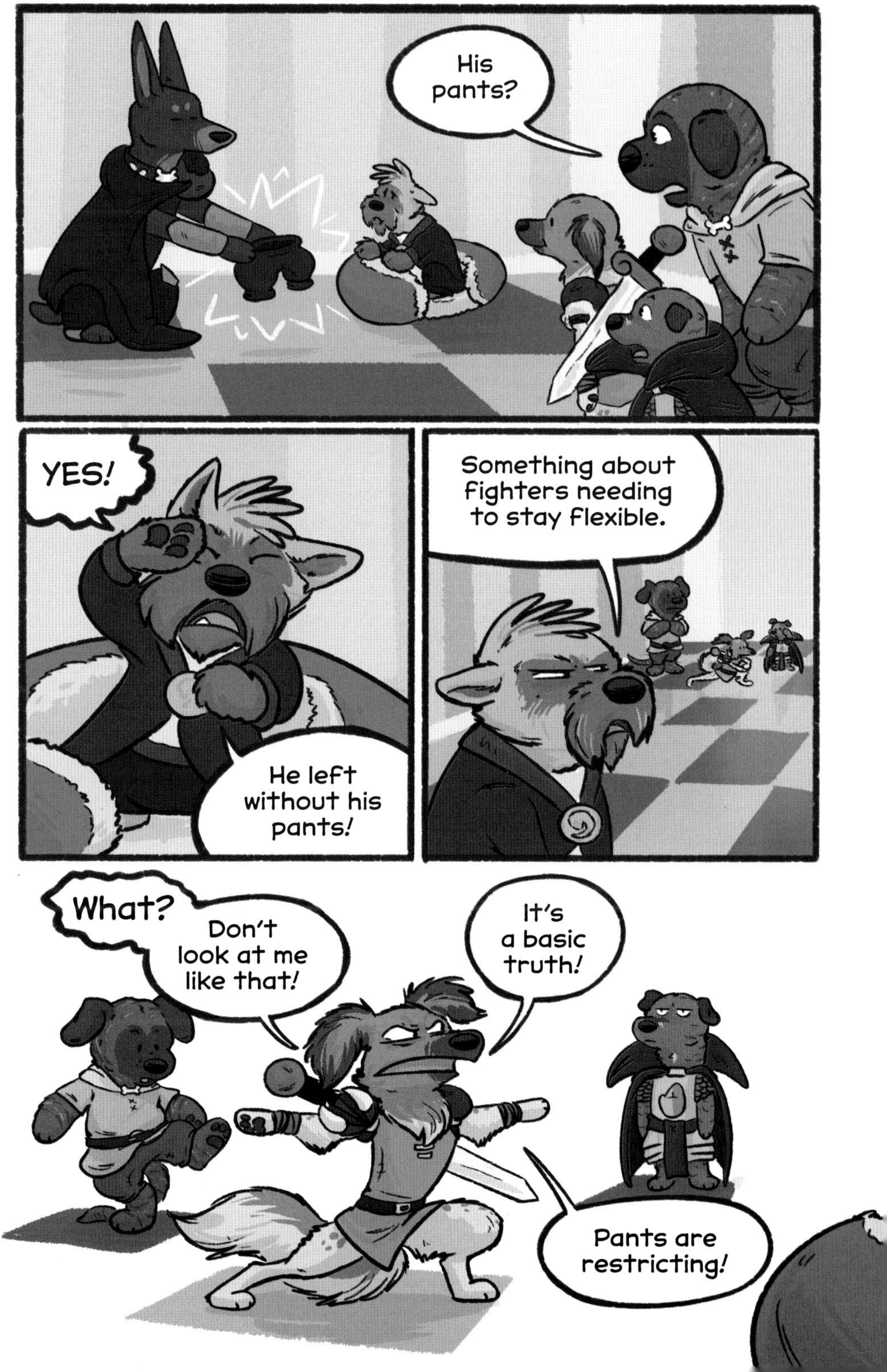
His pants?
YES!
He left without his pants!
Something about fighters needing to stay flexible.
What?
Don't look at me like that!
It's a basic truth!
Pants are restricting!

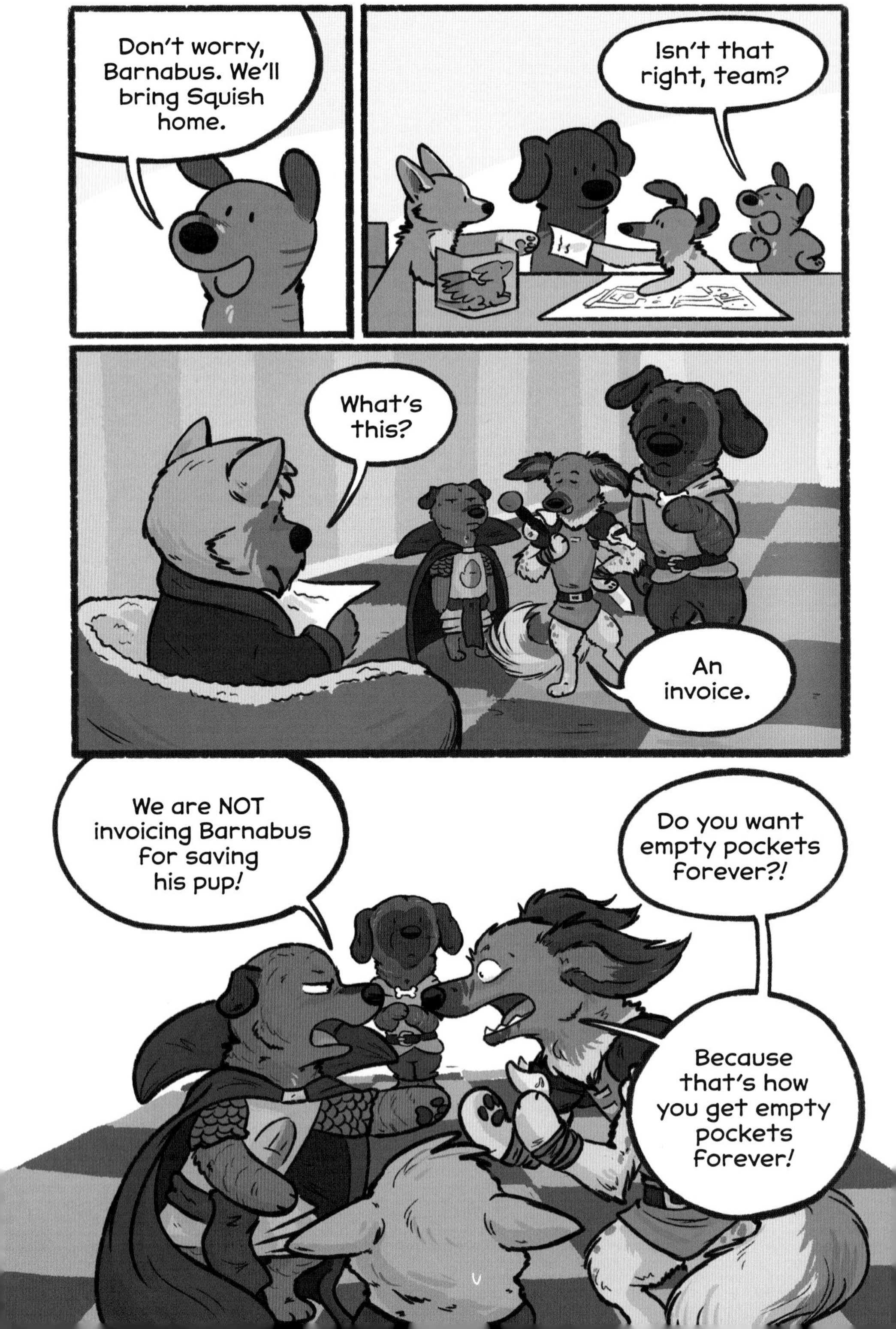
Don't worry, Barnabus. We'll bring Squish home.
Isn't that right, team?
What's this?
An invoice.
We are NOT invoicing Barnabus for saving his pup!
Do you want empty pockets forever?!
Because that's how you get empty pockets forever!

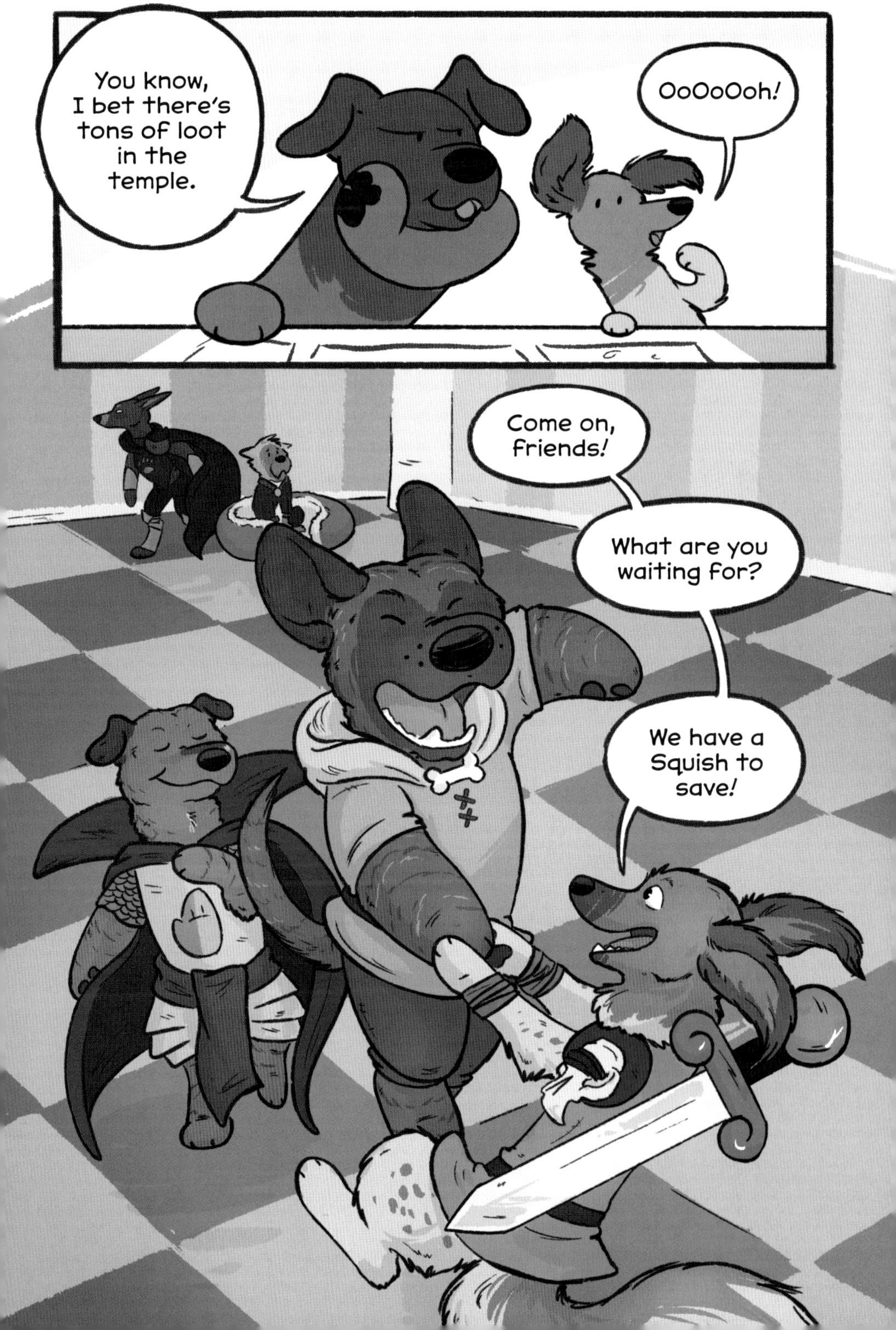

You know, I bet there's tons of loot in the temple.
OoOoOoh!
Come on, friends!
What are you waiting for?
We have a Squish to save!

Chapter 3:
No Sense of Humor

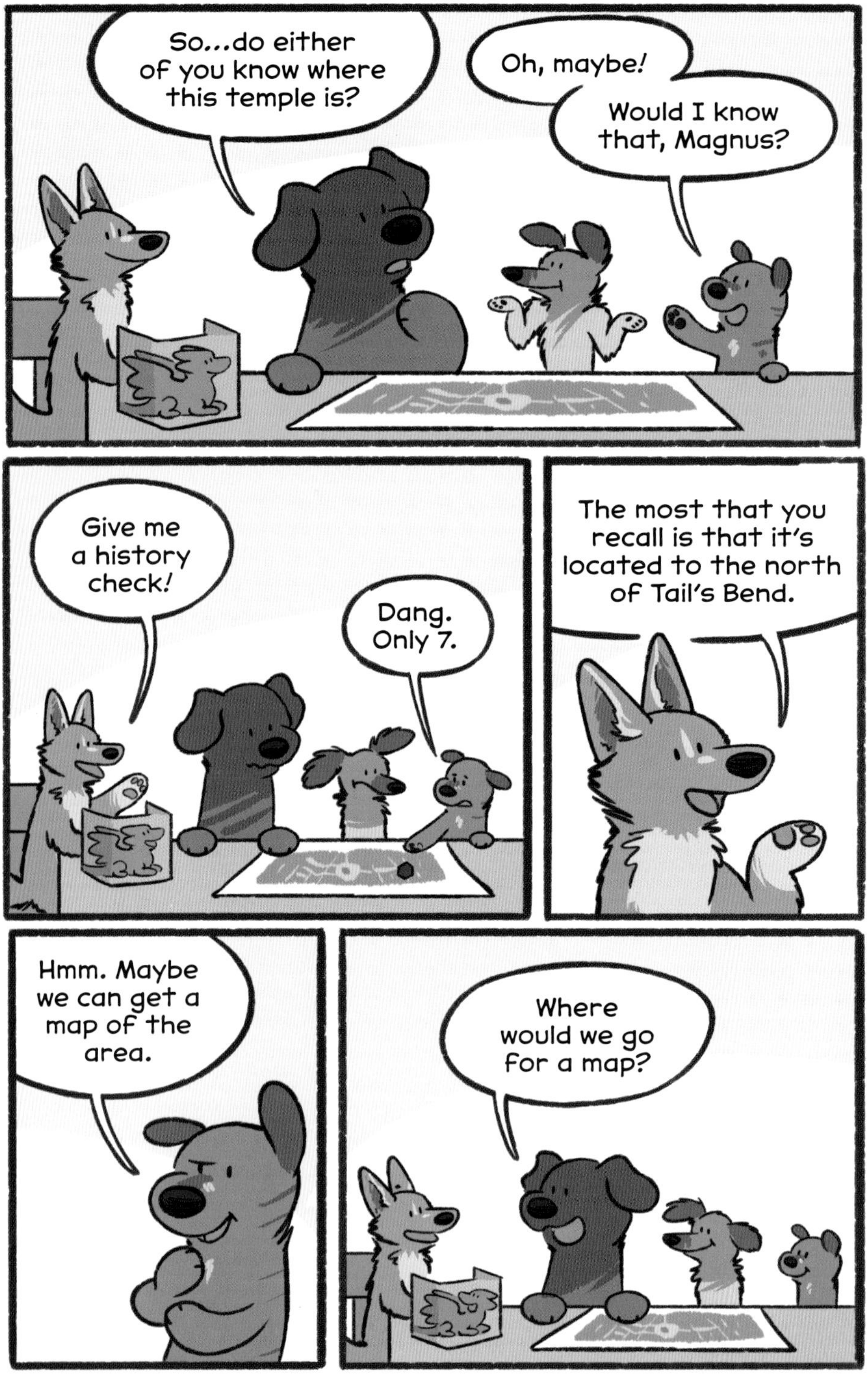
So...do either of you know where this temple is?
Oh, maybe!
Would I know that, Magnus?
Give me a history check!
Dang. Only 7.
The most that you recall is that it's located to the north of Tail's Bend.
Hmm. Maybe we can get a map of the area.
Where would we go for a map?

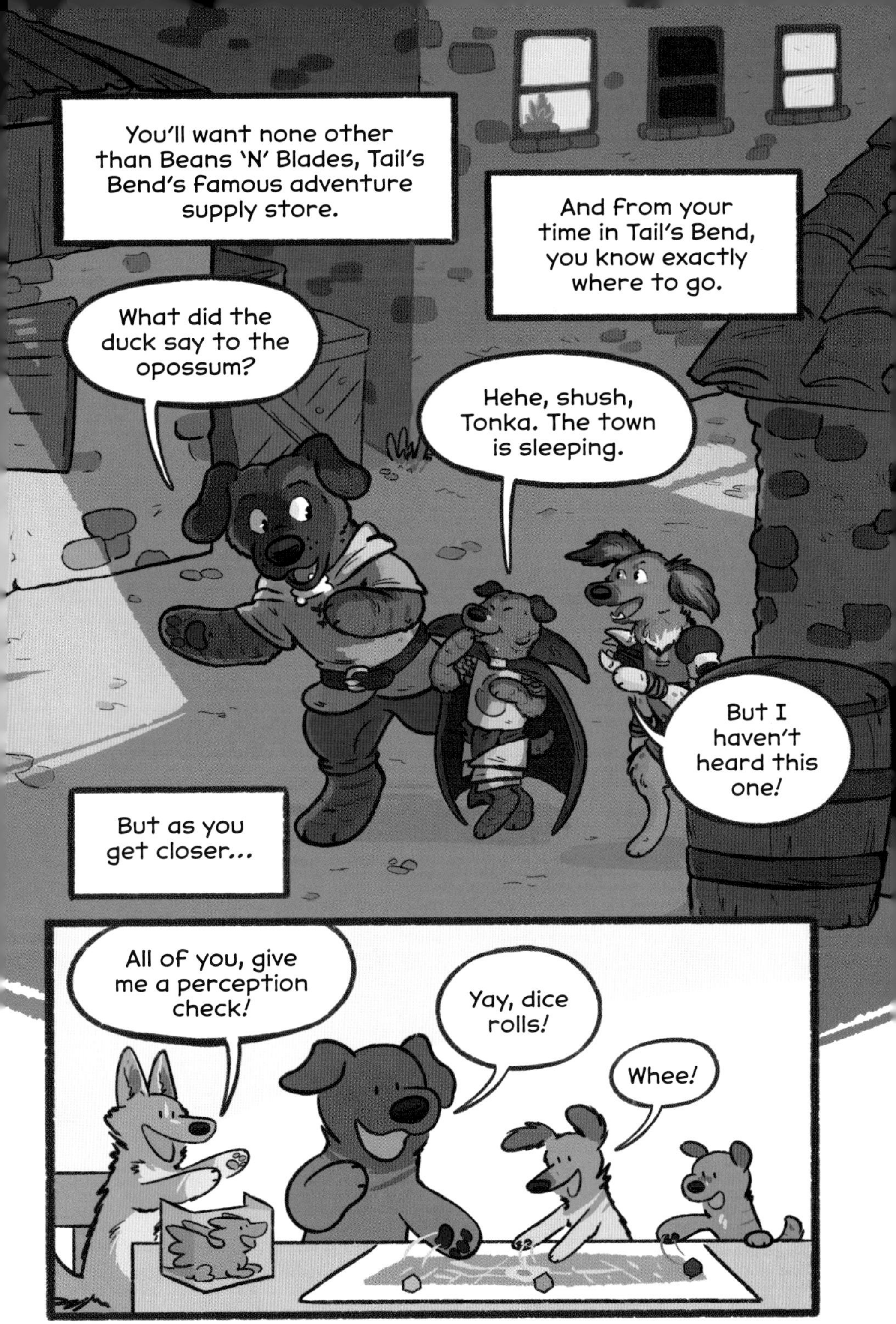
You'll want none other than Beans 'N' Blades, Tail's Bend's famous adventure supply store.
And from your time in Tail's Bend, you know exactly where to go.
What did the duck say to the opossum?
Hehe, shush, Tonka. The town is sleeping.
But I haven't heard this one!
But as you get closer...
All of you, give me a perception check!
Yay, dice rolls!
Whee!

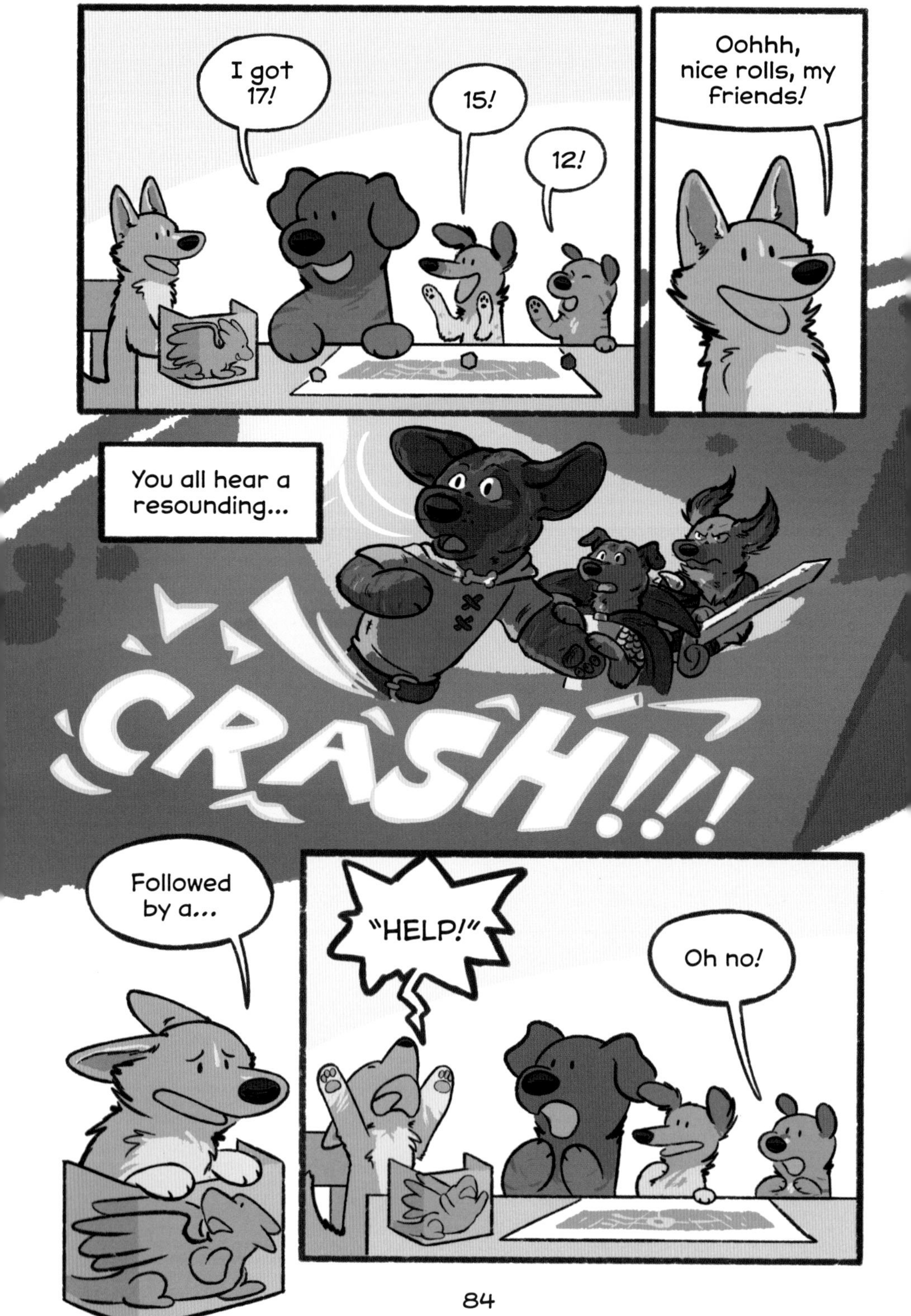
I got 17!
15!
12!
Oohhh, nice rolls, my friends!
You all hear a resounding...
CRASH!!!
Followed by a...
"HELP!"
Oh no!

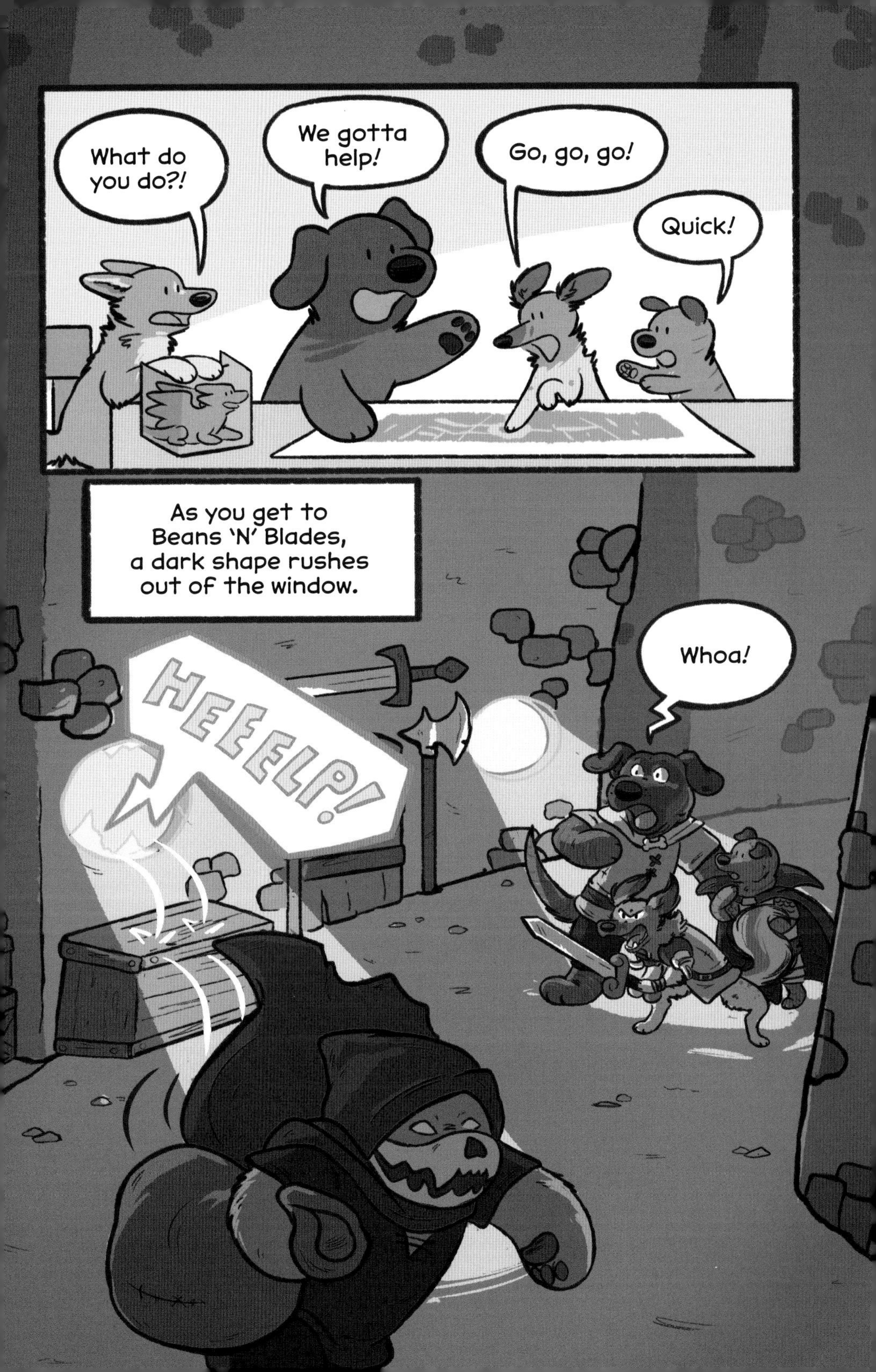
What do you do?!
We gotta help!
Go, go, go!
Quick!
As you get to Beans 'N' Blades, a dark shape rushes out of the window.
HEEELP!
Whoa!

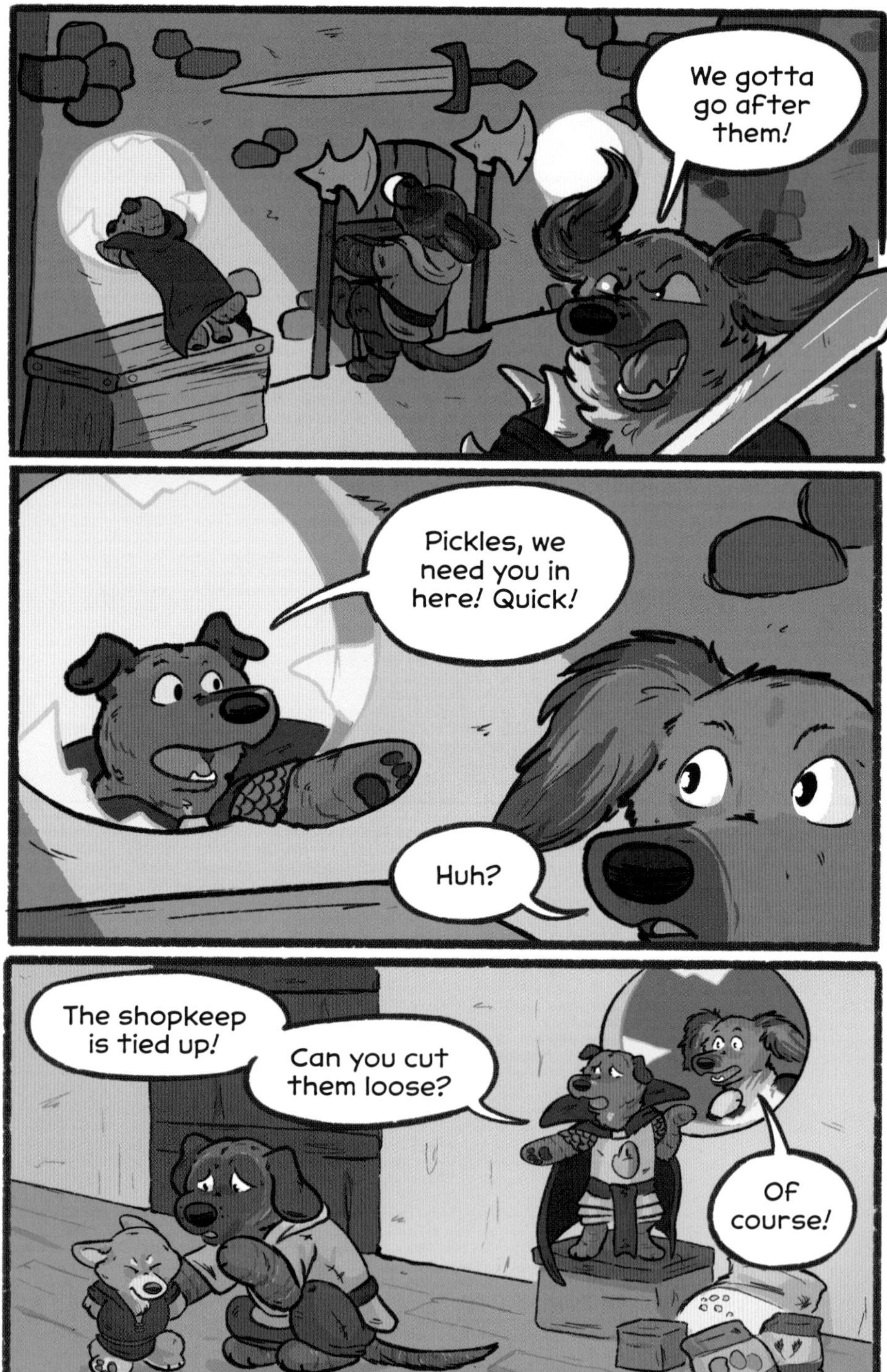
We gotta go after them!
Pickles, we need you in here! Quick!
Huh?
The shopkeep is tied up!
Can you cut them loose?
Of course!

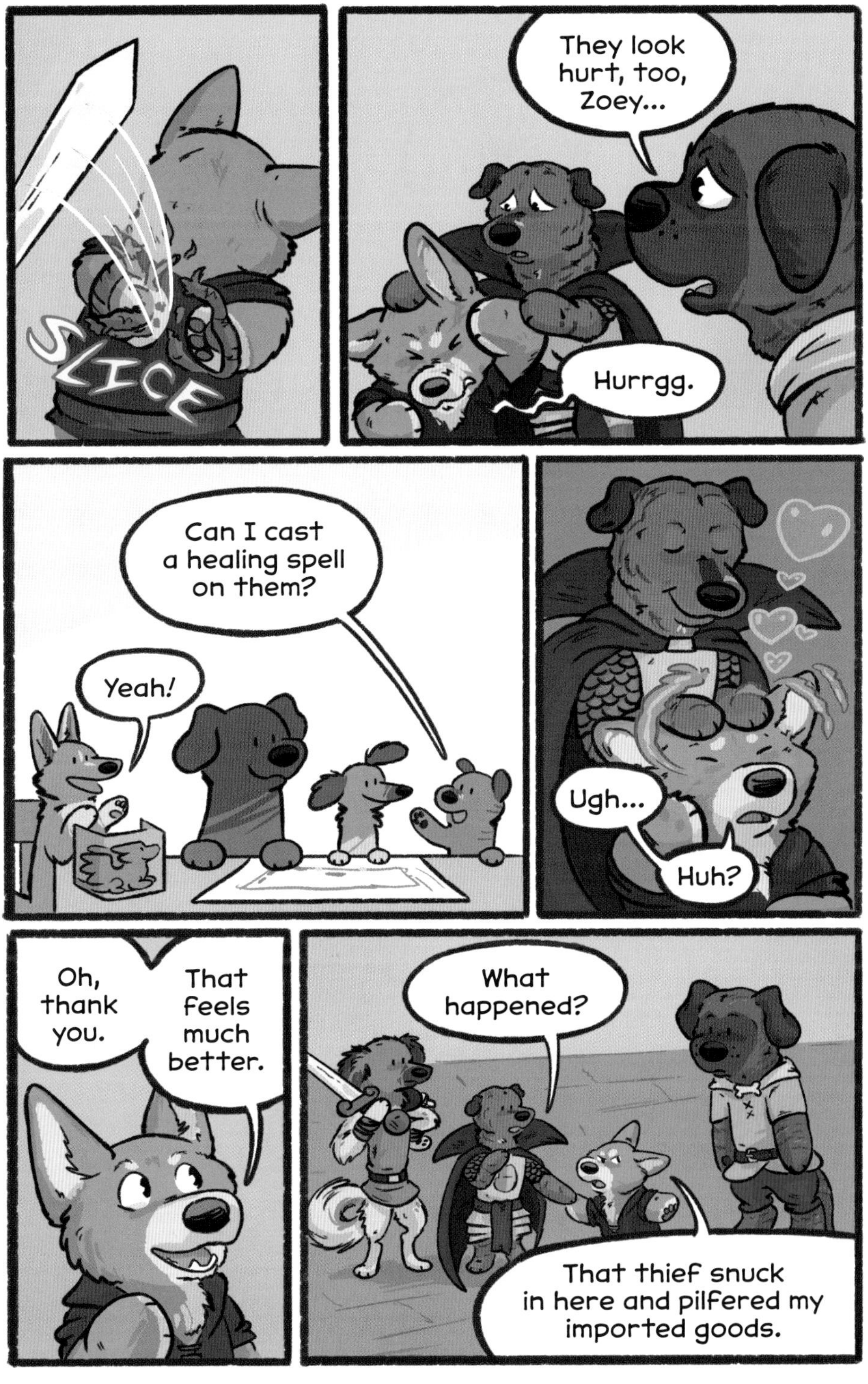
SLICE
They look hurt, too, Zoey...
Hurrgg.
Can I cast a healing spell on them?
Yeah!
Ugh...
Huh?
Oh, thank you.
That feels much better.
What happened?
That thief snuck in here and pilfered my imported goods.

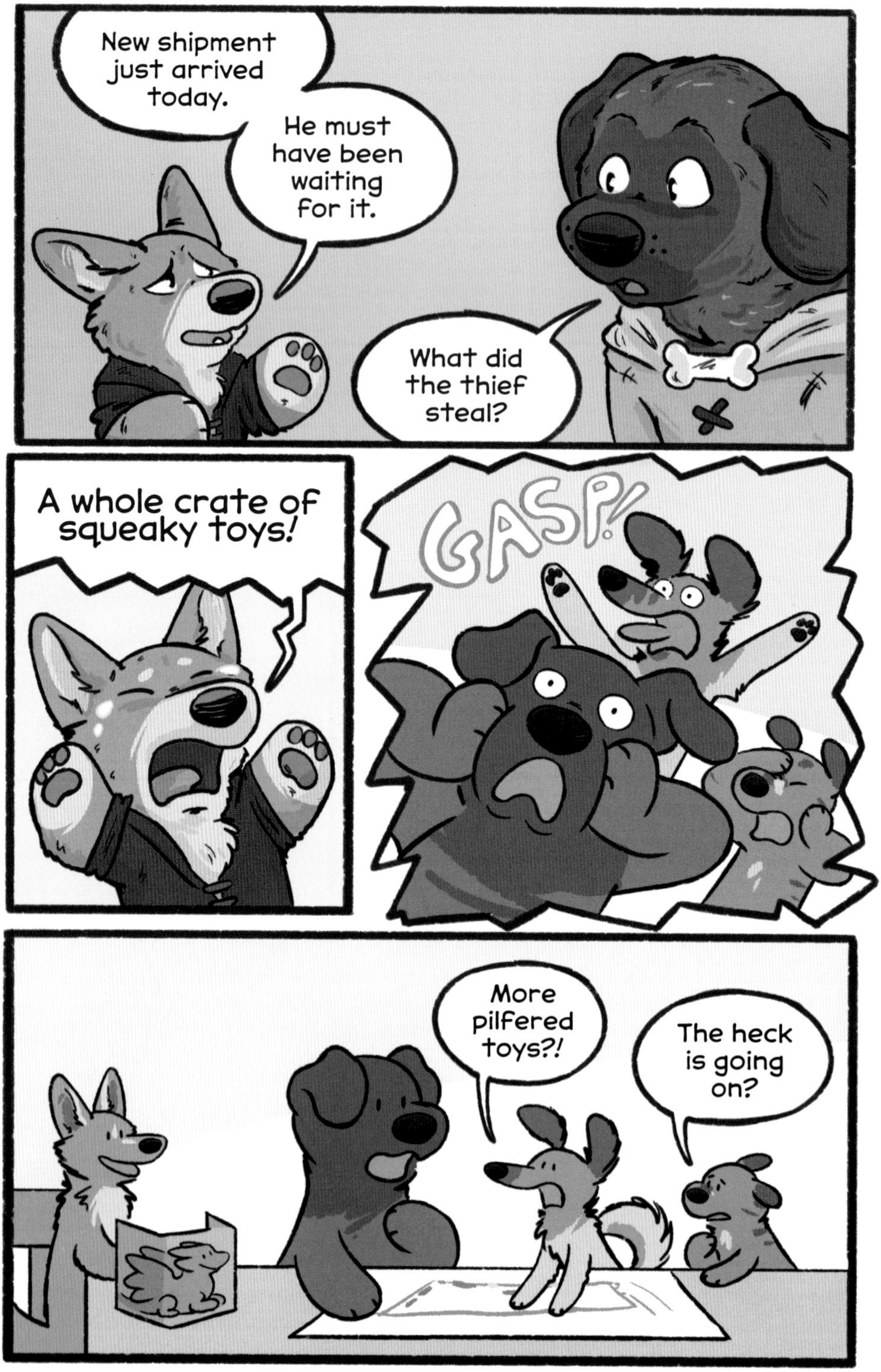
New shipment just arrived today.
He must have been waiting for it.
What did the thief steal?
A whole crate of squeaky toys!
GASP!
More pilfered toys?!
The heck is going on?

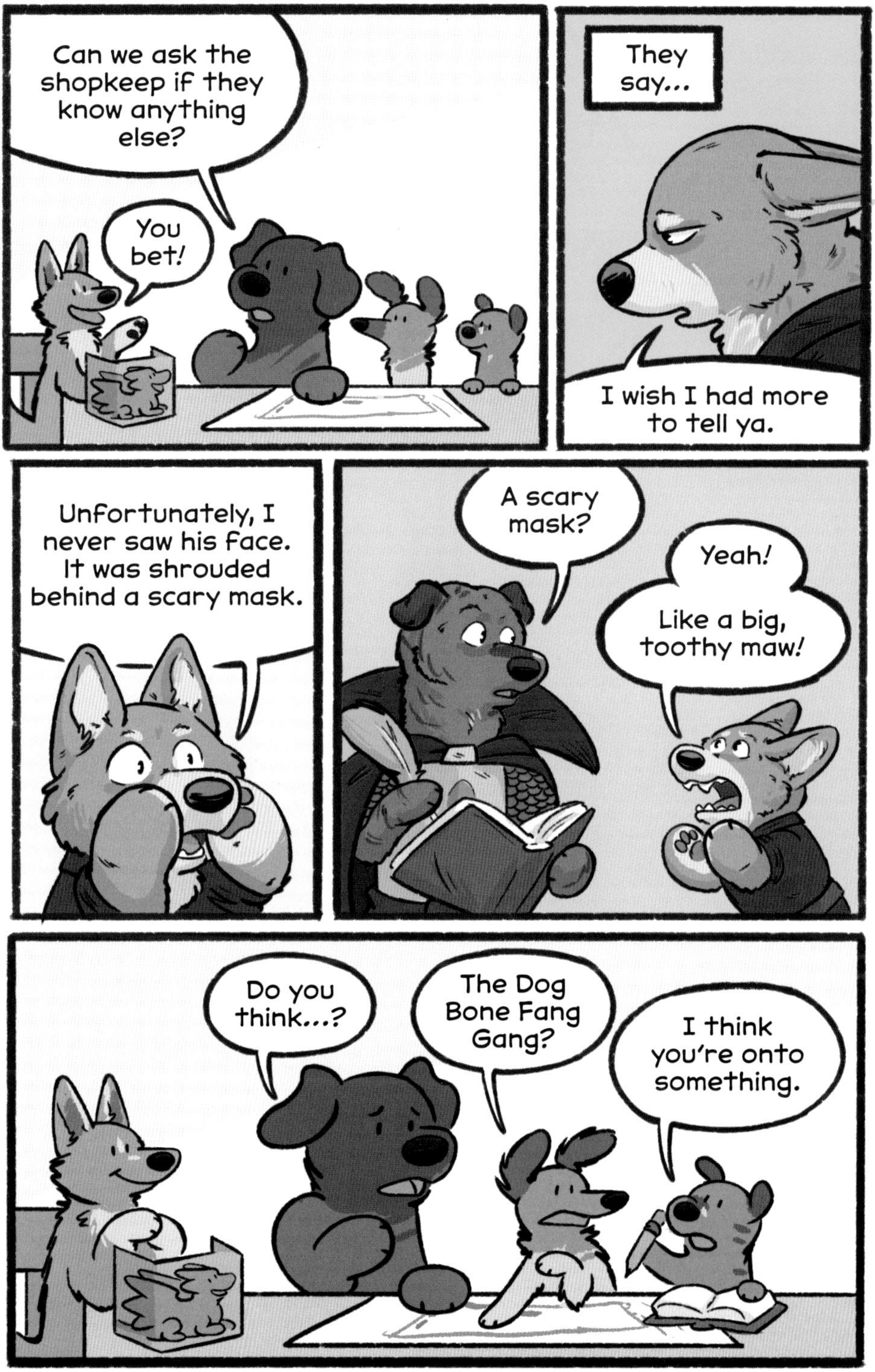

Can we ask the shopkeep if they know anything else?
You bet!
They say...
I wish I had more to tell ya.
Unfortunately, I never saw his face. It was shrouded behind a scary mask.
A scary mask?
Yeah!
Like a big, toothy maw!
Do you think...?
The Dog Bone Fang Gang?
I think you're onto something.

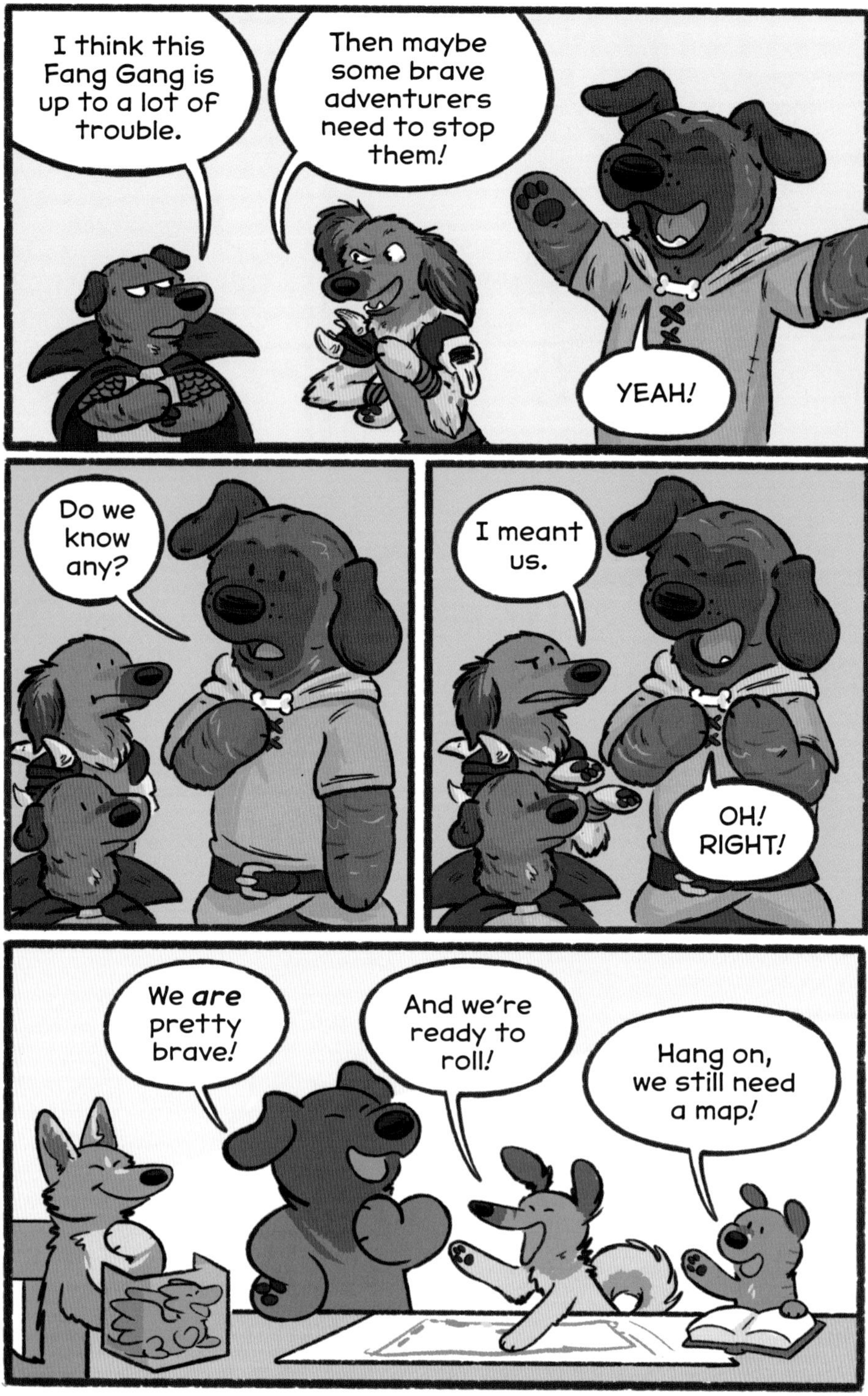
I think this Fang Gang is up to a lot of trouble.
Then maybe some brave adventurers need to stop them!
YEAH!
Do we know any?
I meant us.
OH! RIGHT!
We *are* pretty brave!
And we're ready to roll!
Hang on, we still need a map!

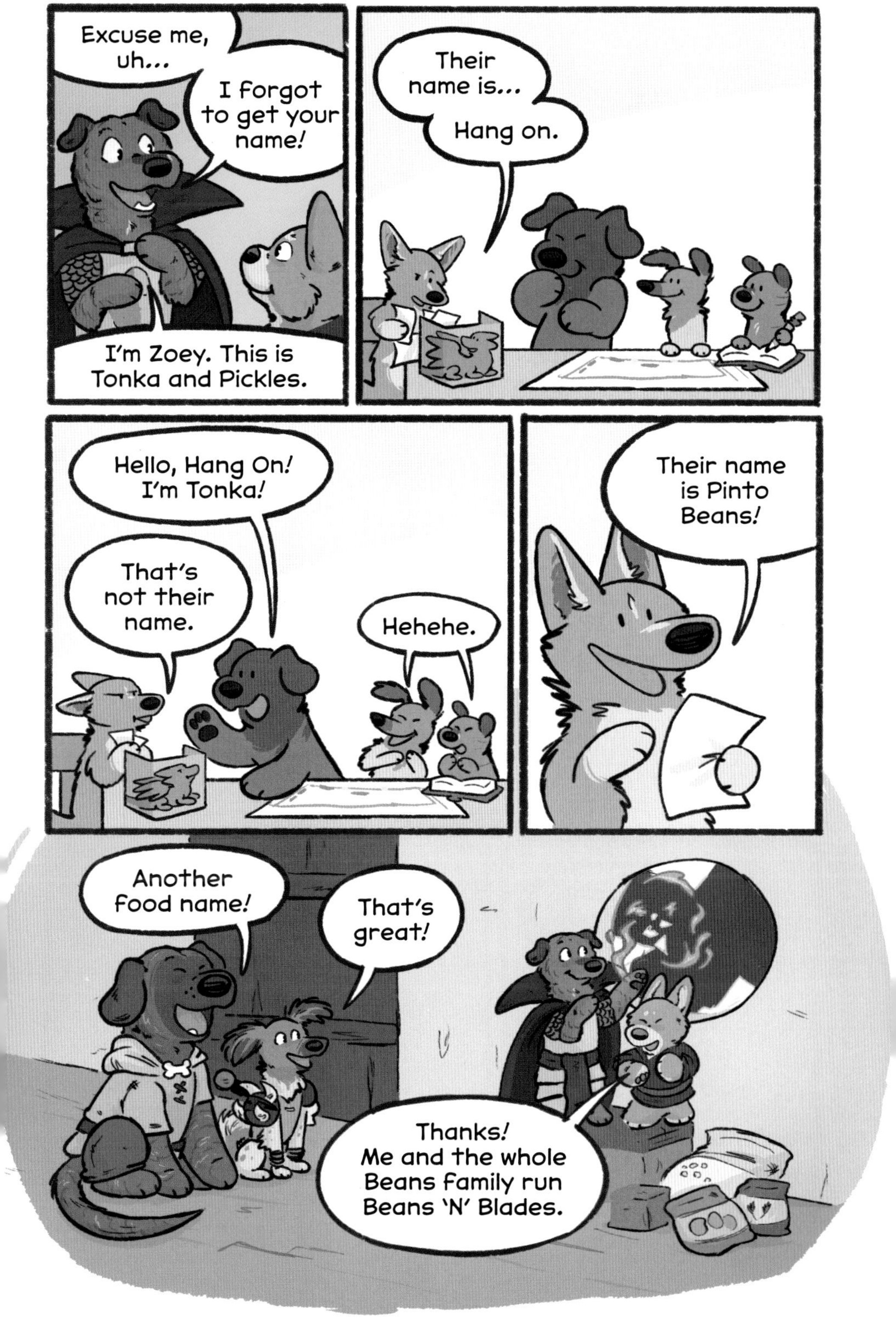
Excuse me, uh...
I forgot to get your name!
I'm Zoey. This is Tonka and Pickles.
Their name is...
Hang on.
Hello, Hang On! I'm Tonka!
That's not their name.
Hehehe.
Their name is Pinto Beans!
Another food name!
That's great!
Thanks! Me and the whole Beans family run Beans 'N' Blades.

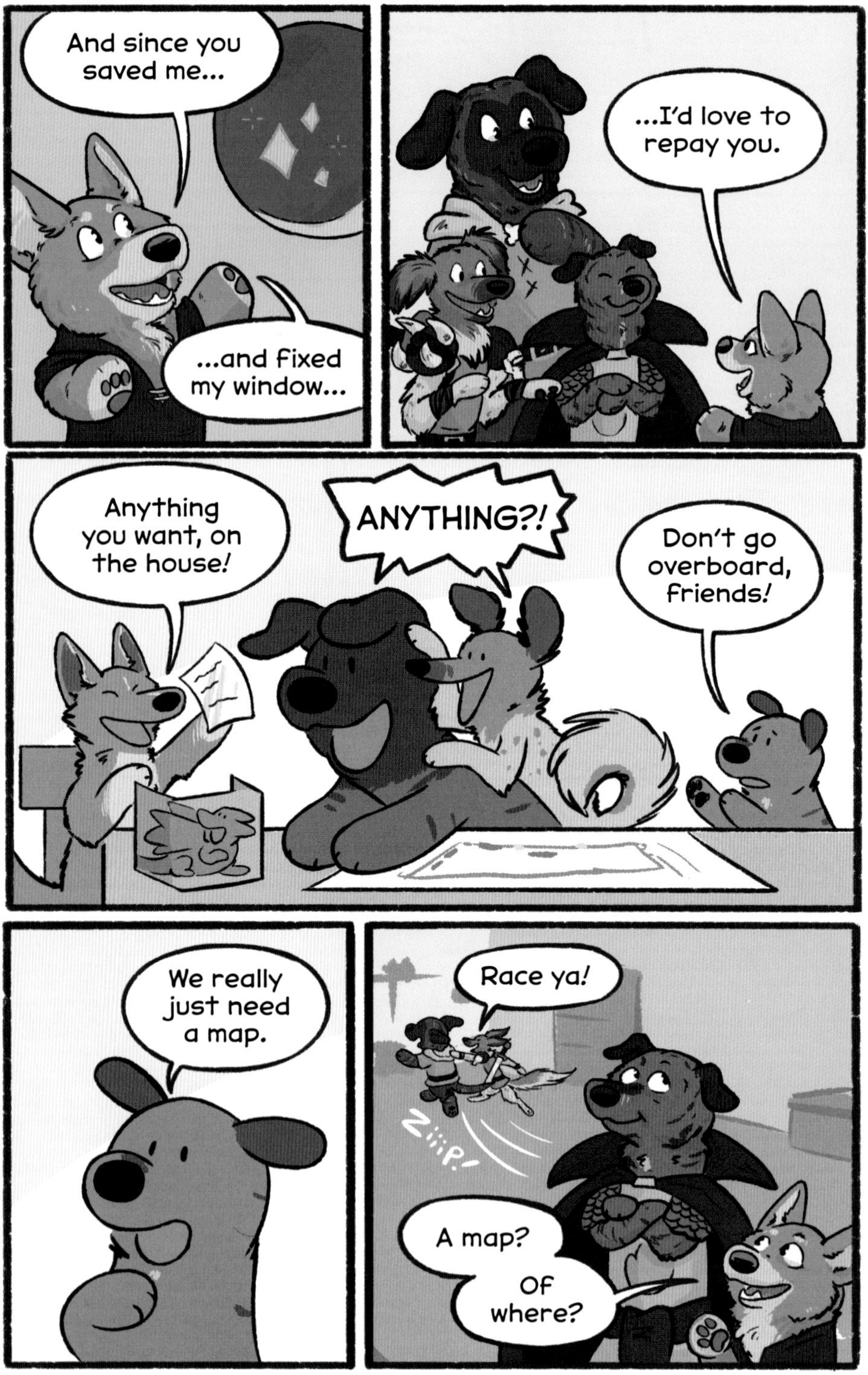
And since you saved me...
...and fixed my window...
...I'd love to repay you.
Anything you want, on the house!
ANYTHING?!
Don't go overboard, friends!
We really just need a map.
Race ya!
ZIIIP!
A map?
Of where?

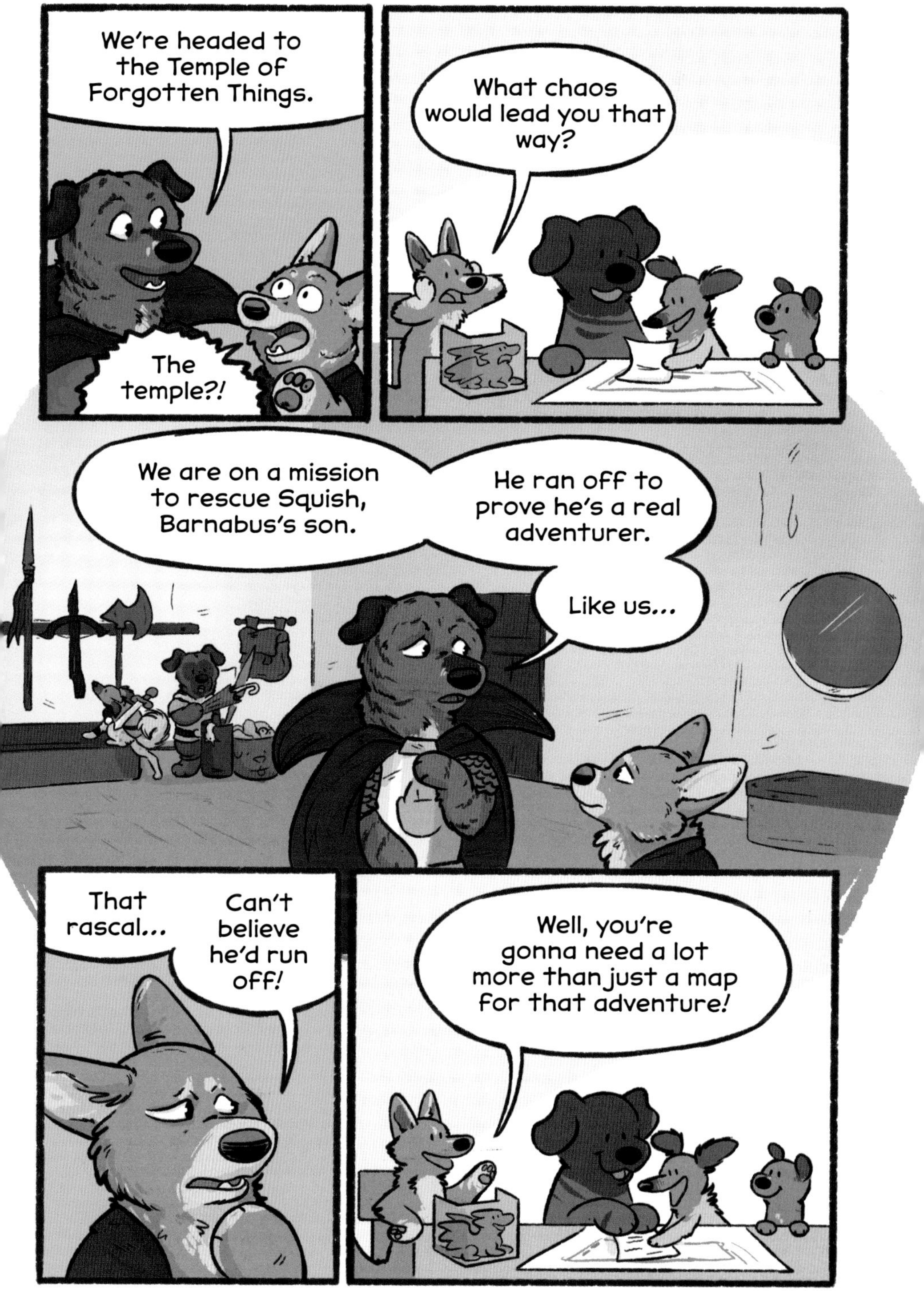
We're headed to the Temple of Forgotten Things.
The temple?!
What chaos would lead you that way?
We are on a mission to rescue Squish, Barnabus's son.
He ran off to prove he's a real adventurer.
Like us...
That rascal...
Can't believe he'd run off!
Well, you're gonna need a lot more than just a map for that adventure!

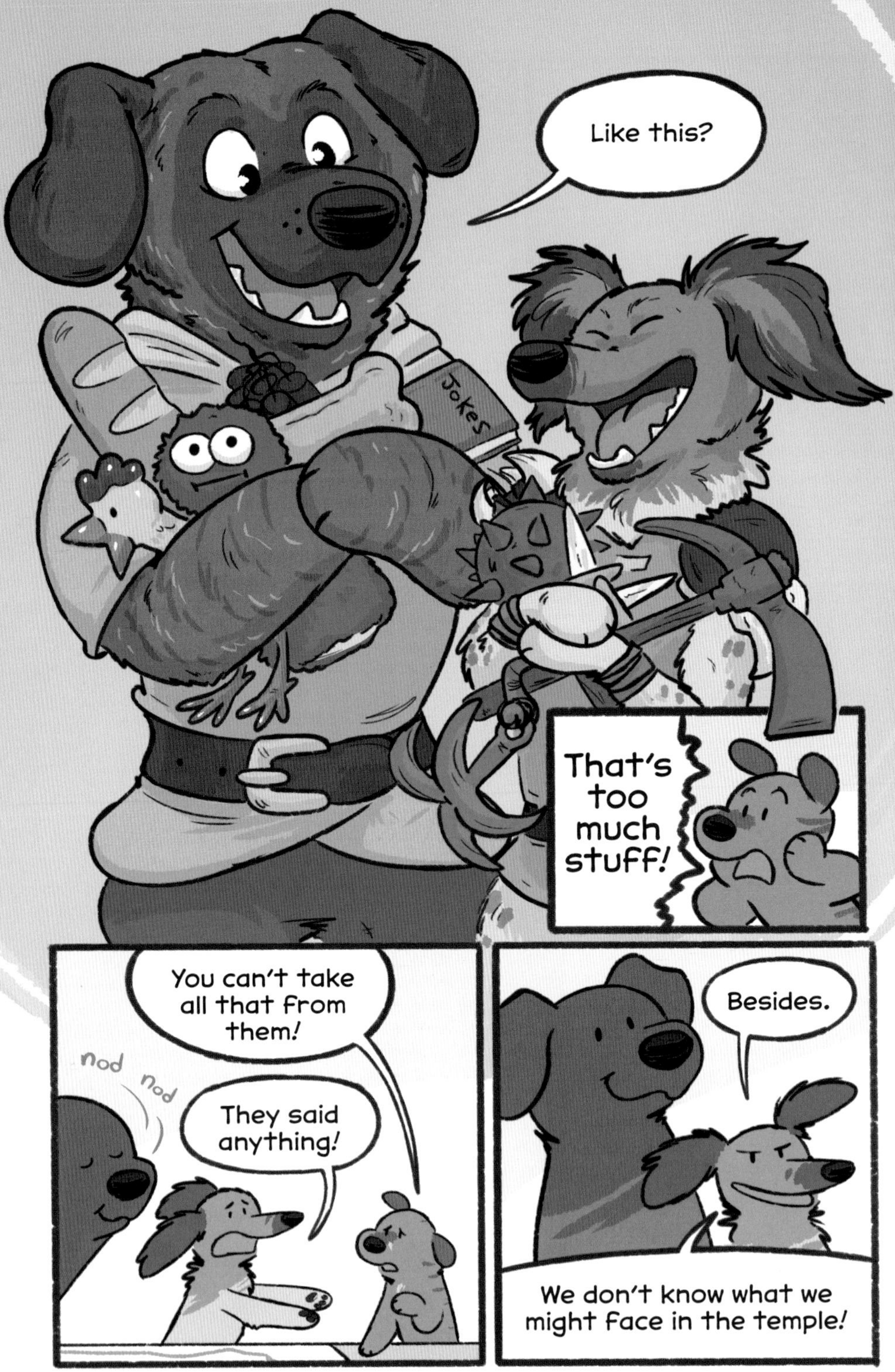
Like this?
Jokes
That's too much stuff!
You can't take all that from them!
nod nod
They said anything!
Besides.
We don't know what we might face in the temple!

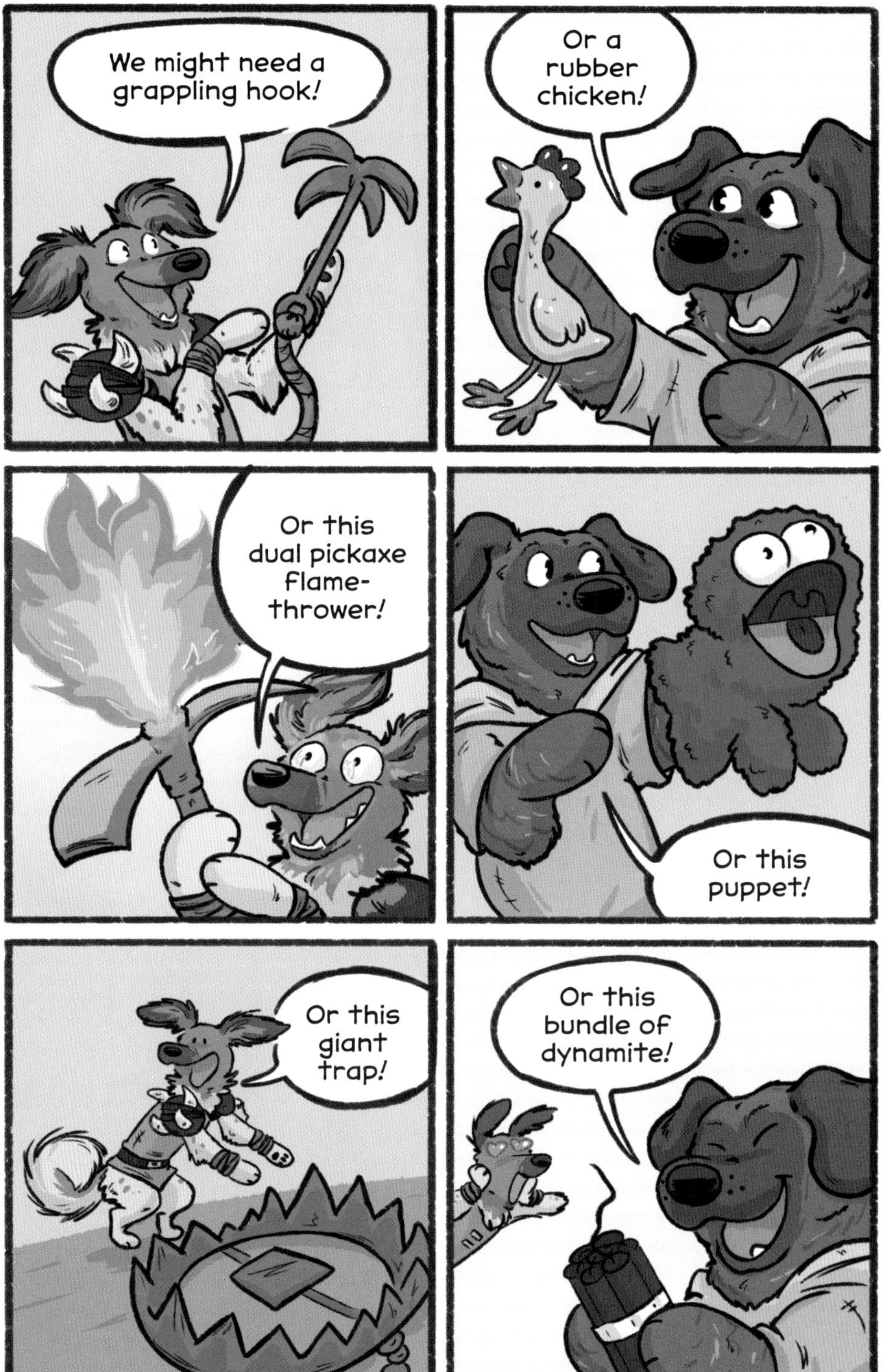
We might need a grappling hook!
Or a rubber chicken!
Or this dual pickaxe flame-thrower!
Or this puppet!
Or this giant trap!
Or this bundle of dynamite!

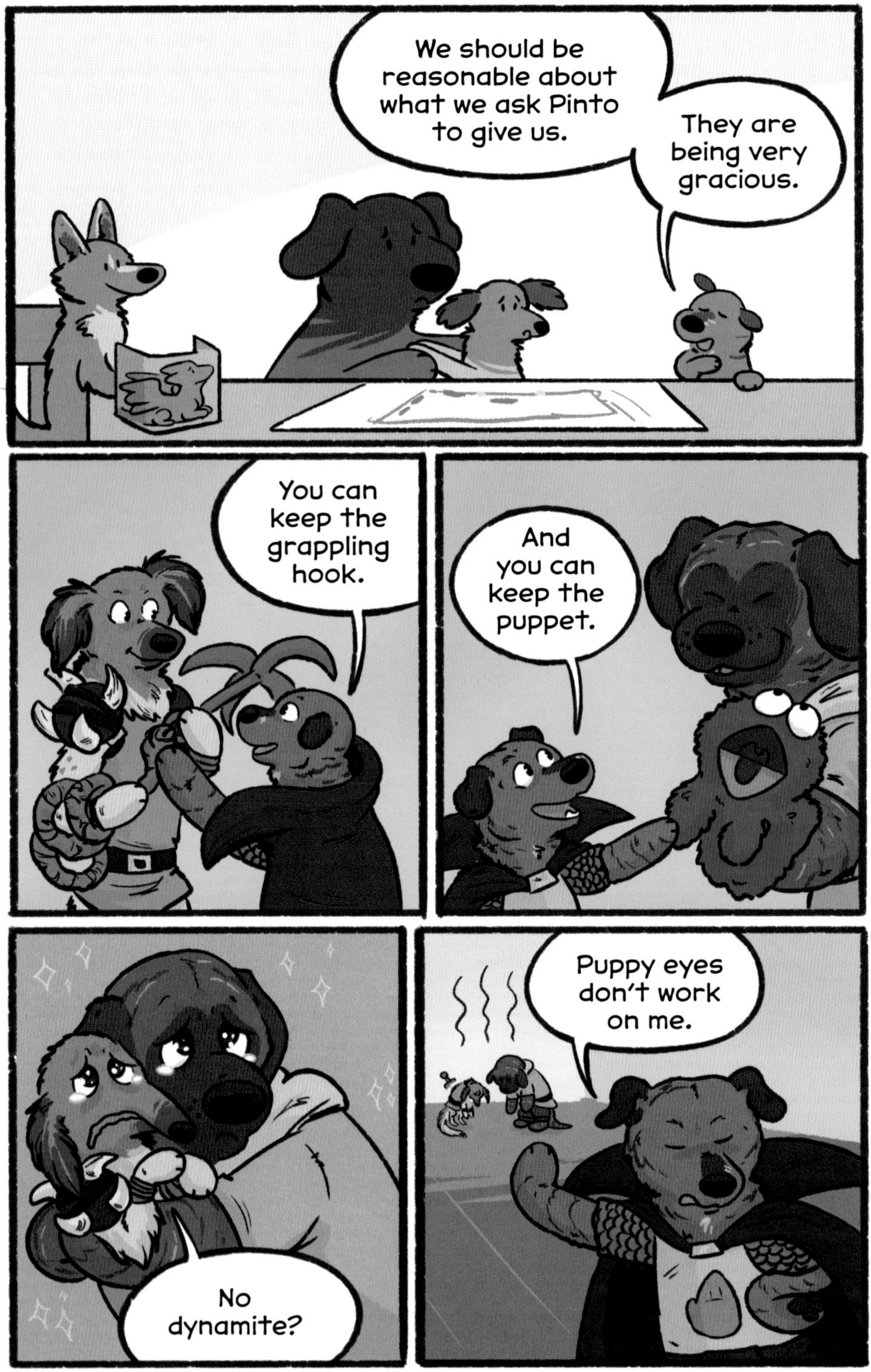
We should be reasonable about what we ask Pinto to give us.
They are being very gracious.
You can keep the grappling hook.
And you can keep the puppet.
No dynamite?
Puppy eyes don't work on me.

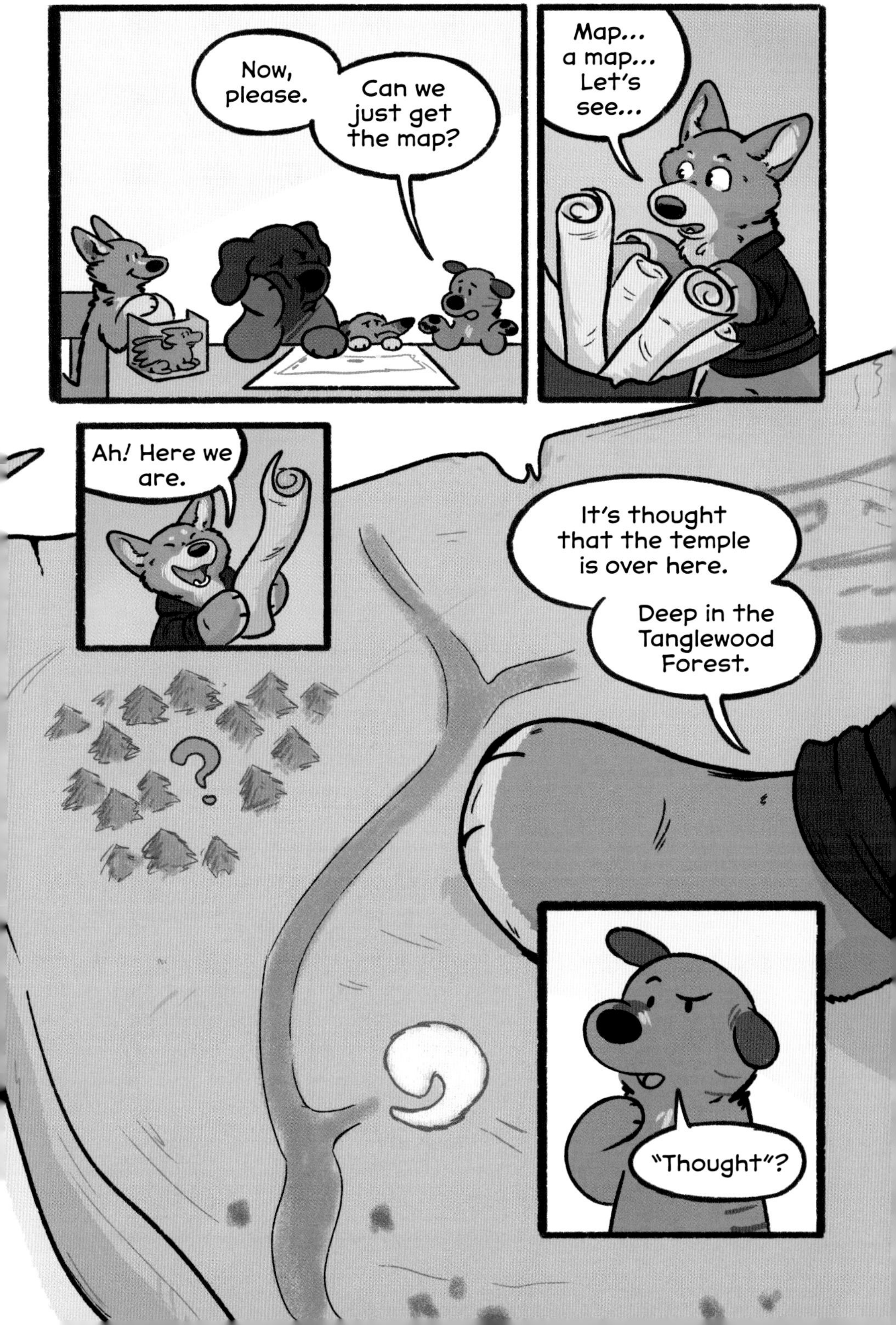
Now, please.
Can we just get the map?
Map... a map... Let's see...
Ah! Here we are.
It's thought that the temple is over here.
Deep in the Tanglewood Forest.
"Thought"?

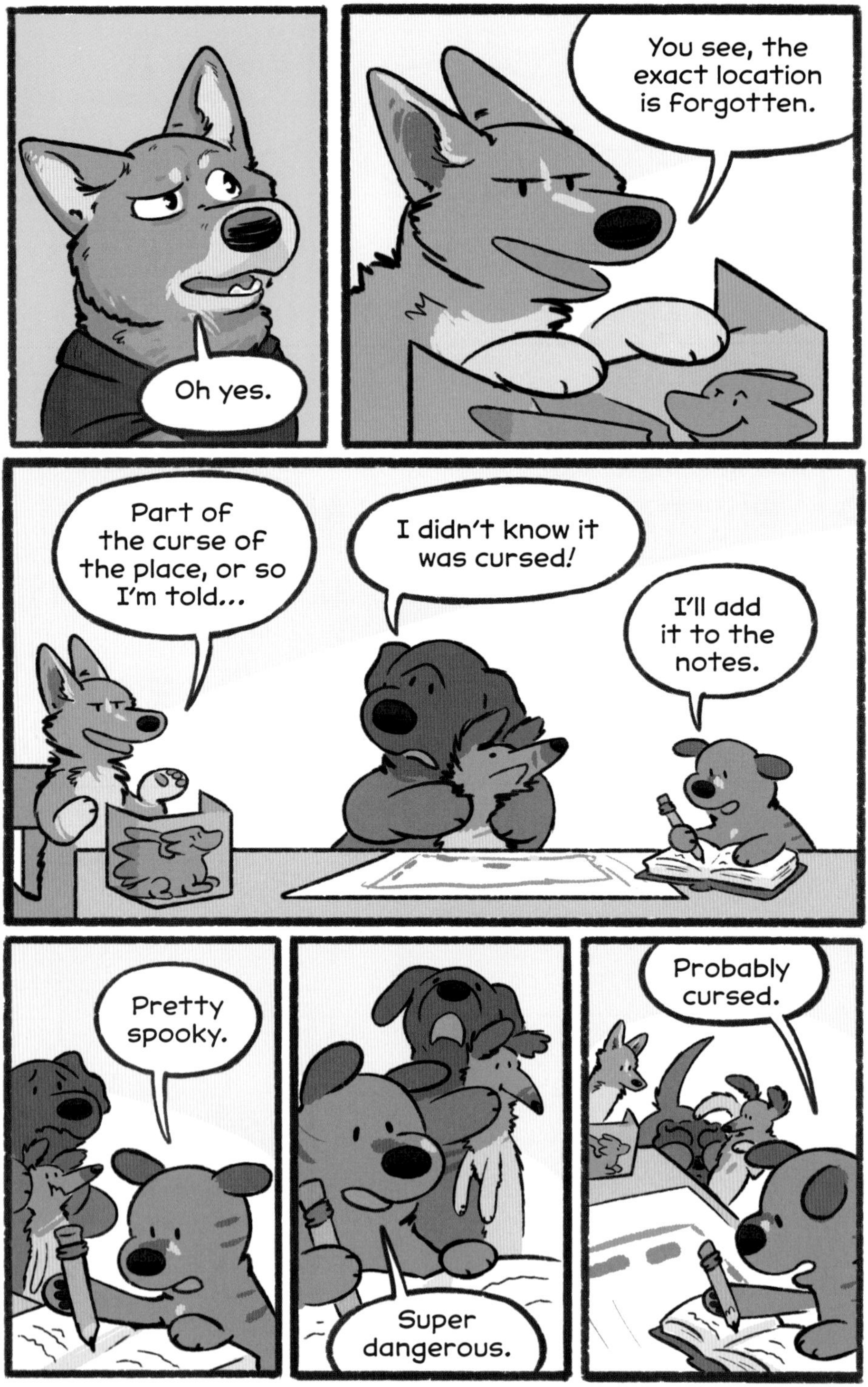
Oh yes.
You see, the exact location is forgotten.
Part of the curse of the place, or so I'm told...
I didn't know it was cursed!
I'll add it to the notes.
Pretty spooky.
Super dangerous.
Probably cursed.

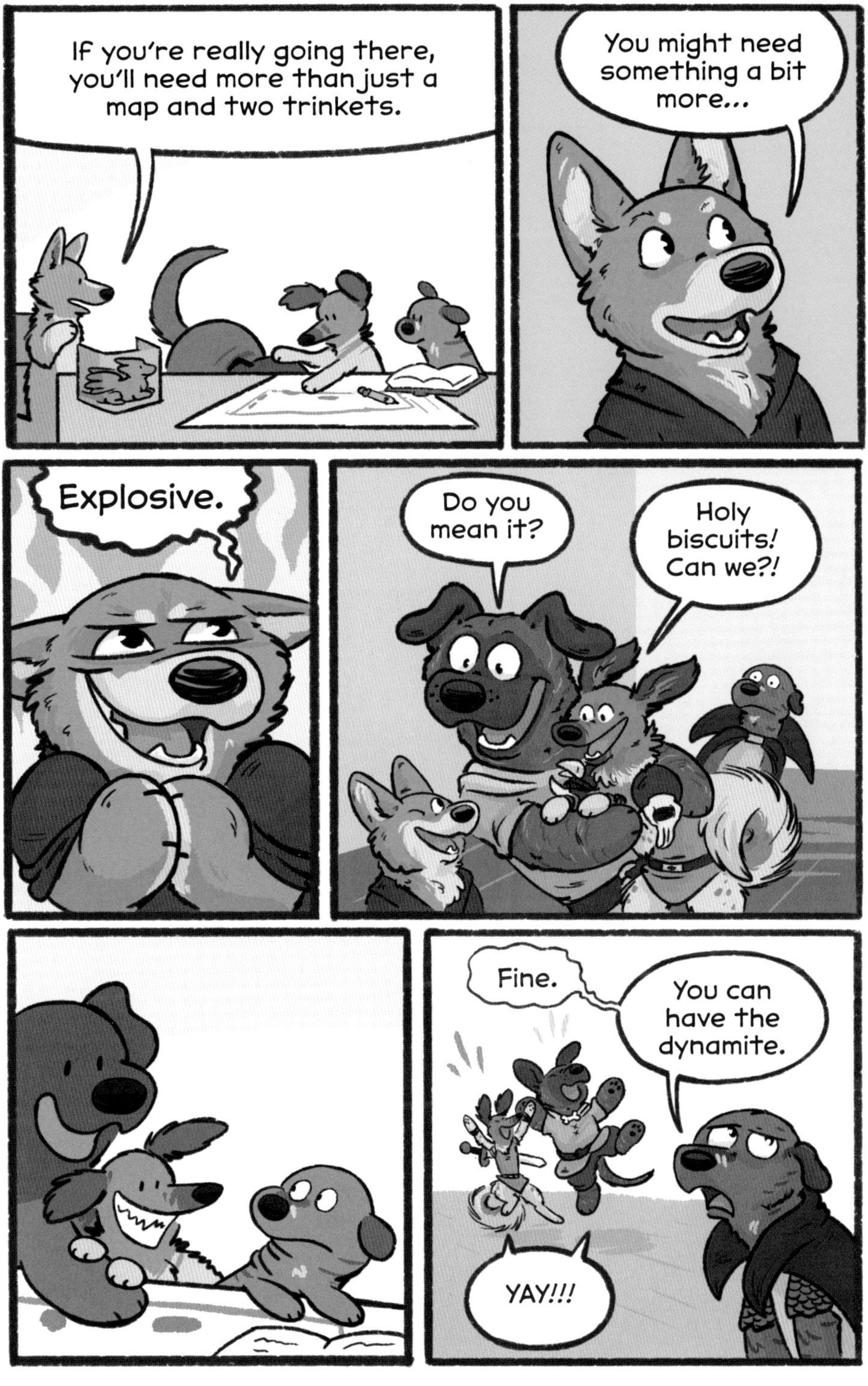
If you're really going there, you'll need more than just a map and two trinkets.
You might need something a bit more...
Explosive.
Do you mean it?
Holy biscuits! Can we?!
Fine.
You can have the dynamite.
YAY!!!

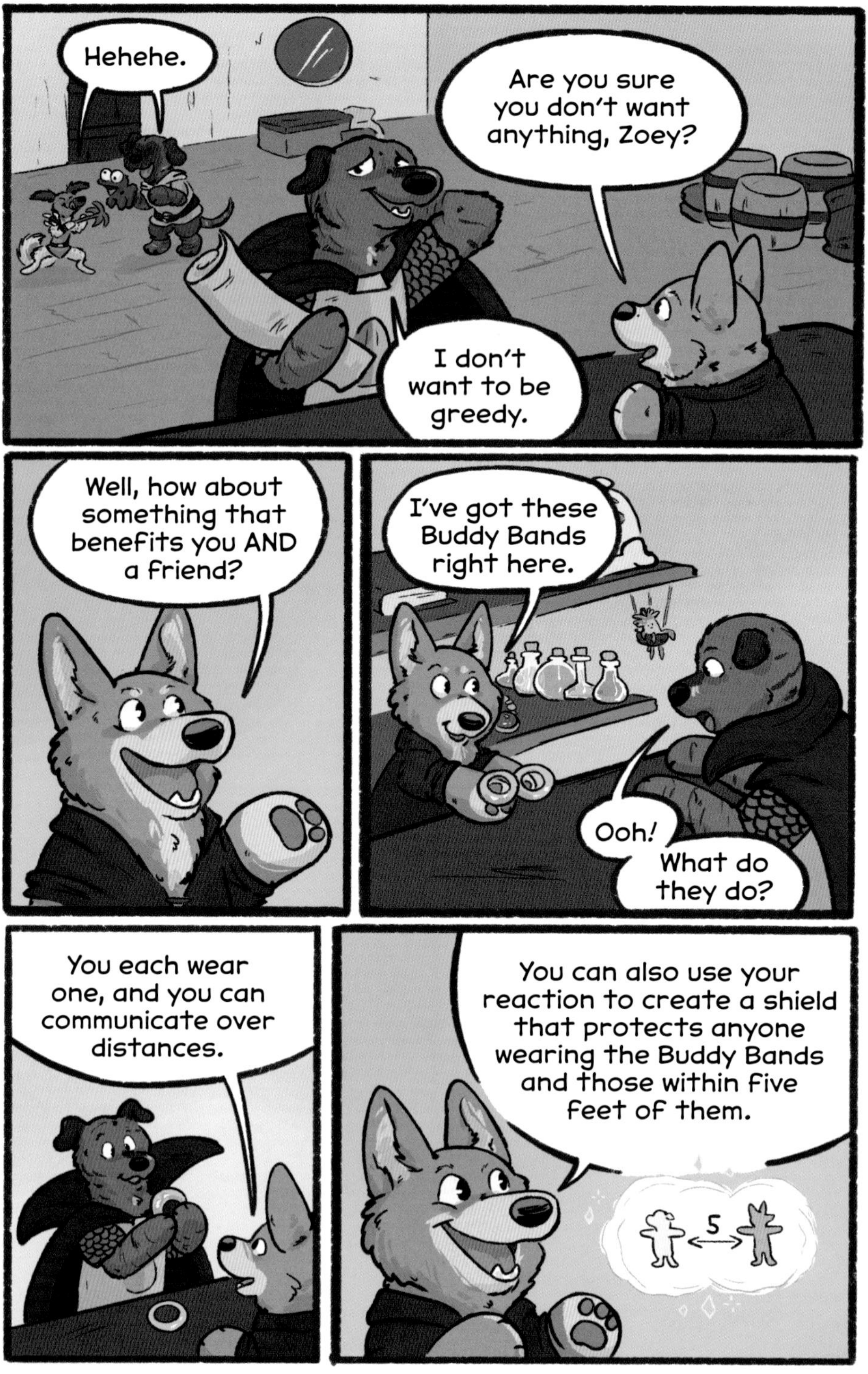
Hehehe.
Are you sure you don't want anything, Zoey?
I don't want to be greedy.
Well, how about something that benefits you AND a friend?
I've got these Buddy Bands right here.
Ooh!
What do they do?
You each wear one, and you can communicate over distances.
You can also use your reaction to create a shield that protects anyone wearing the Buddy Bands and those within five feet of them.
5

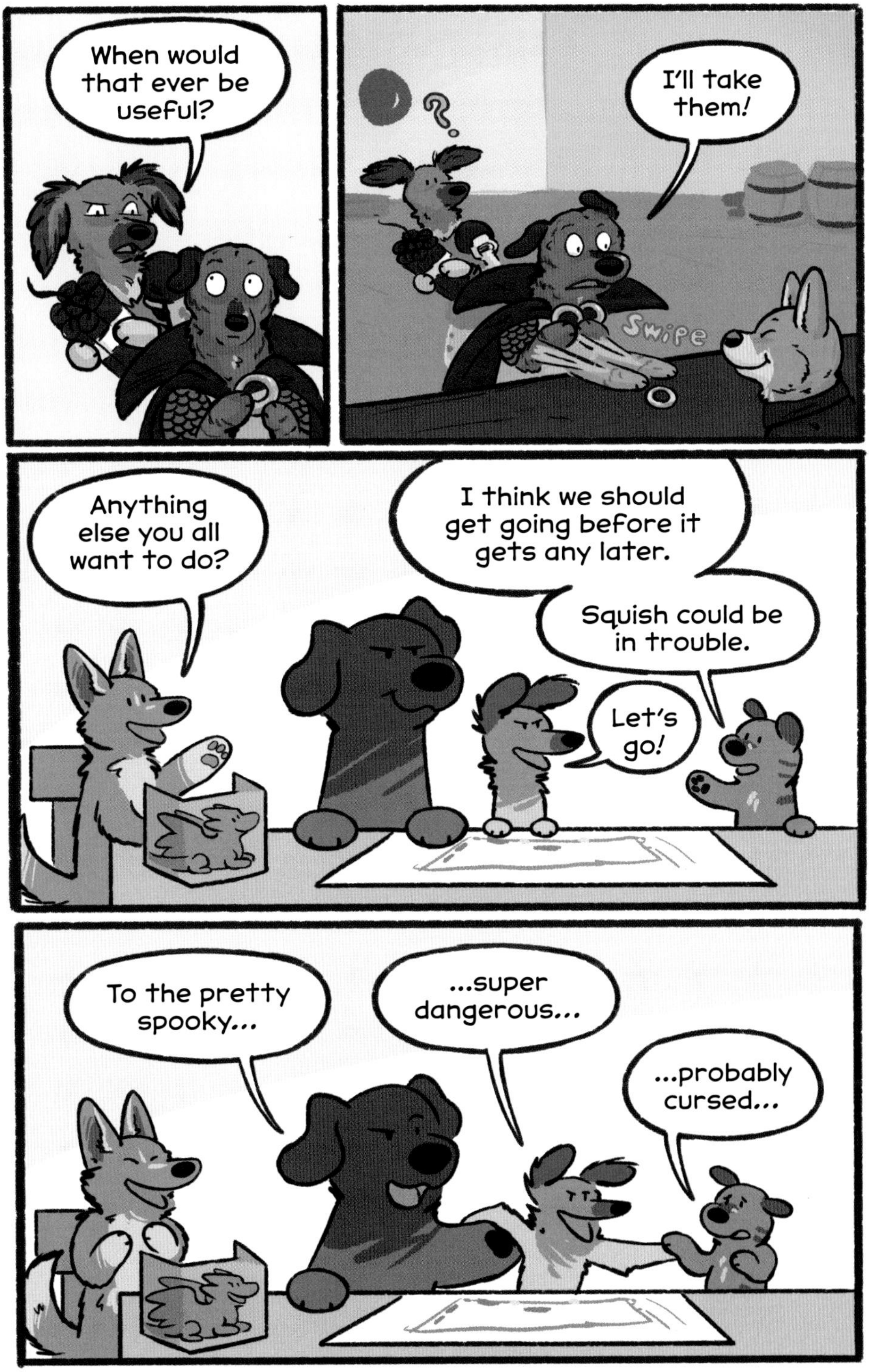
When would that ever be useful?
I'll take them!
Swipe
Anything else you all want to do?
I think we should get going before it gets any later.
Squish could be in trouble.
Let's go!
To the pretty spooky...
...super dangerous...
...probably cursed...

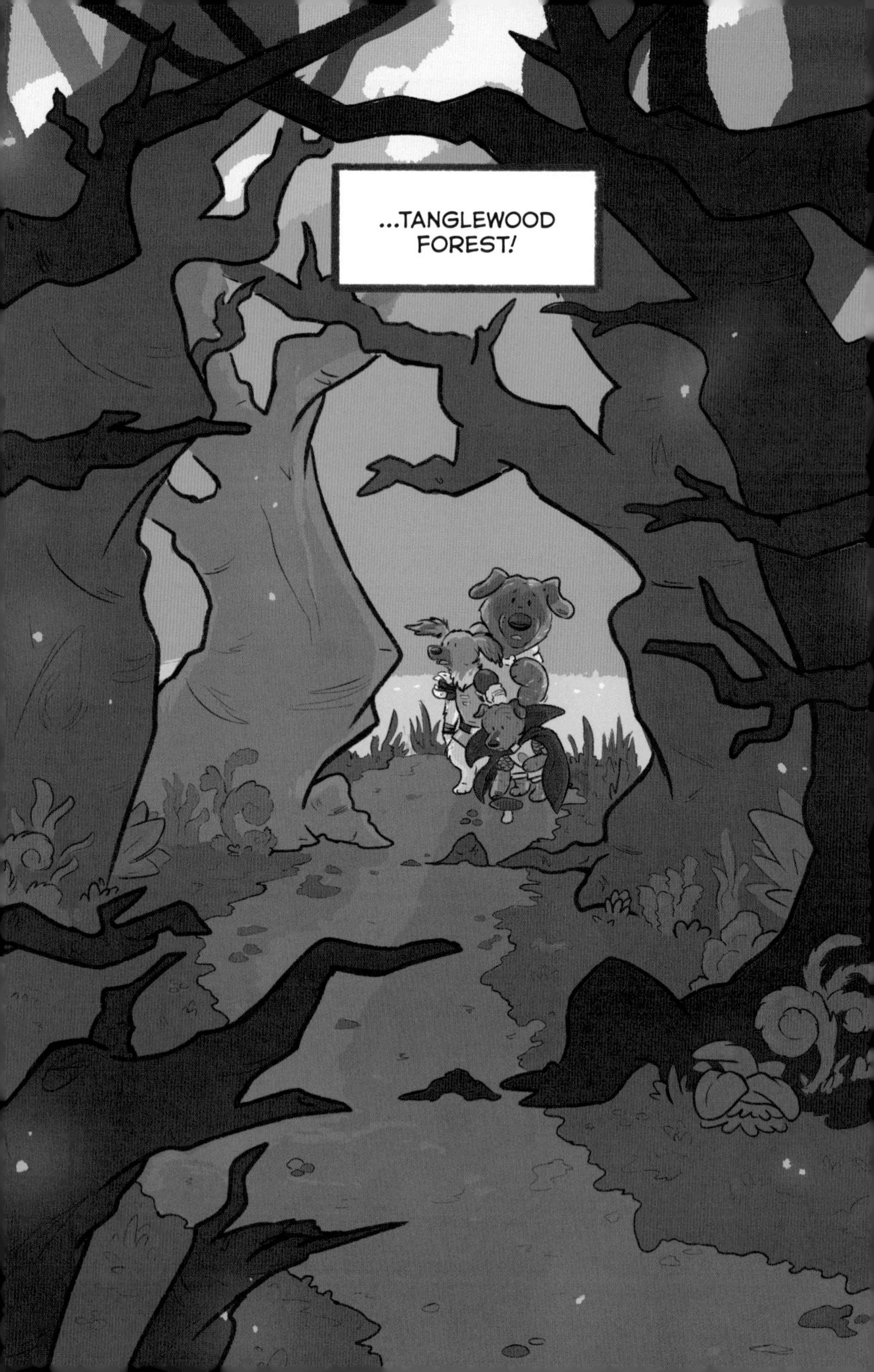
...TANGLEWOOD FOREST!

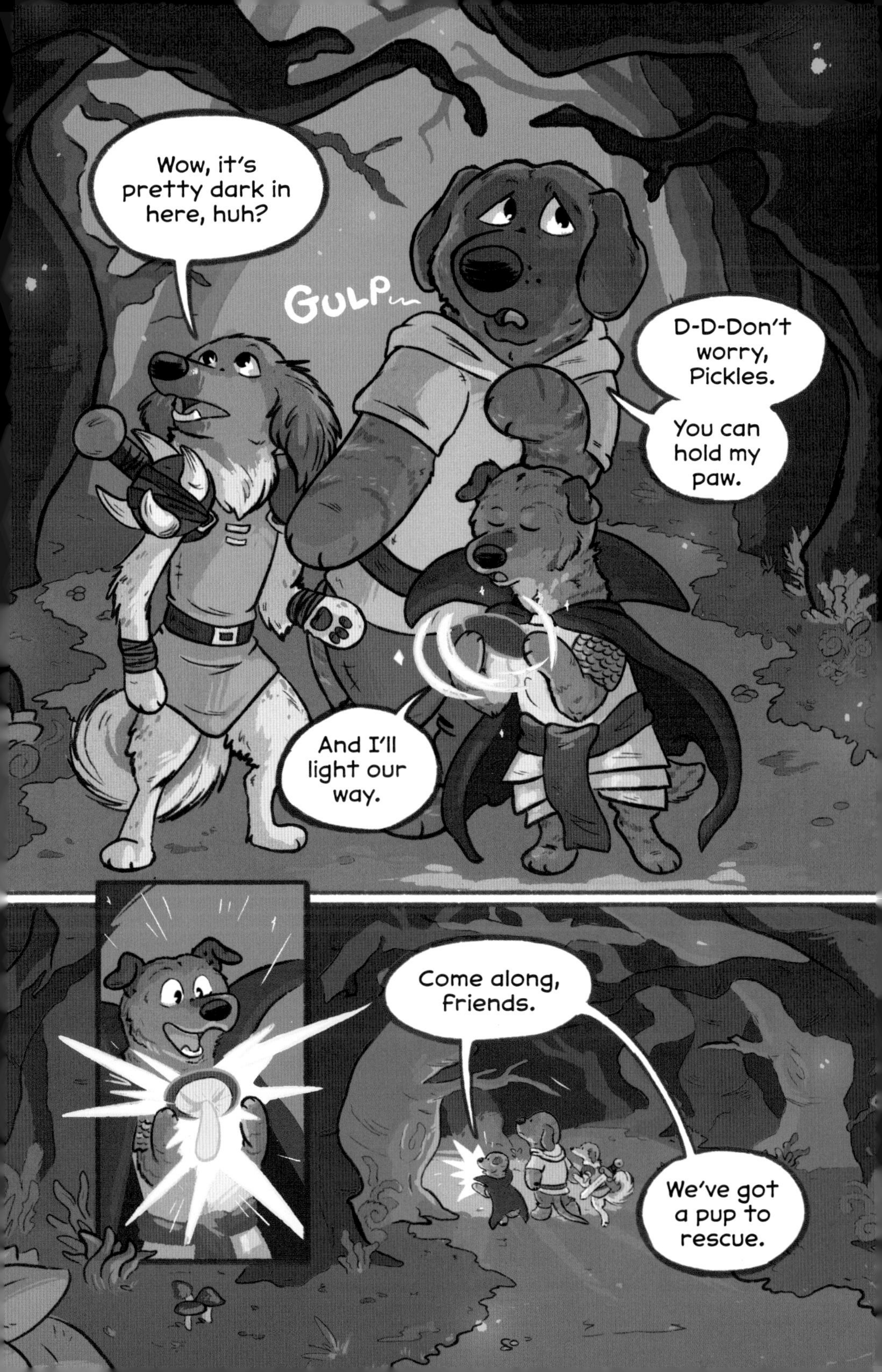
Wow, it's pretty dark in here, huh?
GULP
D-D-Don't worry, Pickles.
You can hold my paw.
And I'll light our way.
Come along, friends.
We've got a pup to rescue.

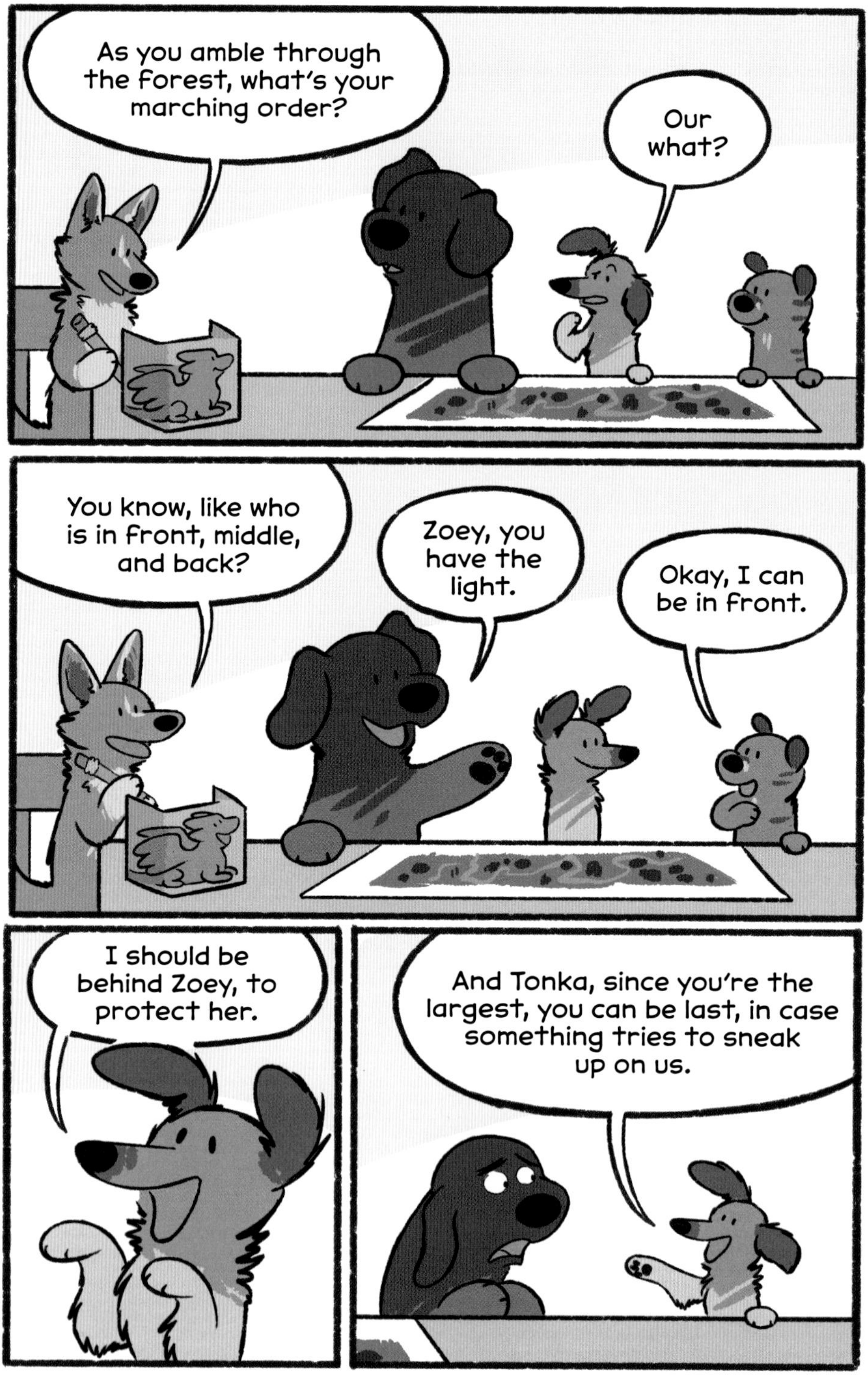
As you amble through the forest, what's your marching order?
Our what?
You know, like who is in front, middle, and back?
Zoey, you have the light.
Okay, I can be in front.
I should be behind Zoey, to protect her.
And Tonka, since you're the largest, you can be last, in case something tries to sneak up on us.

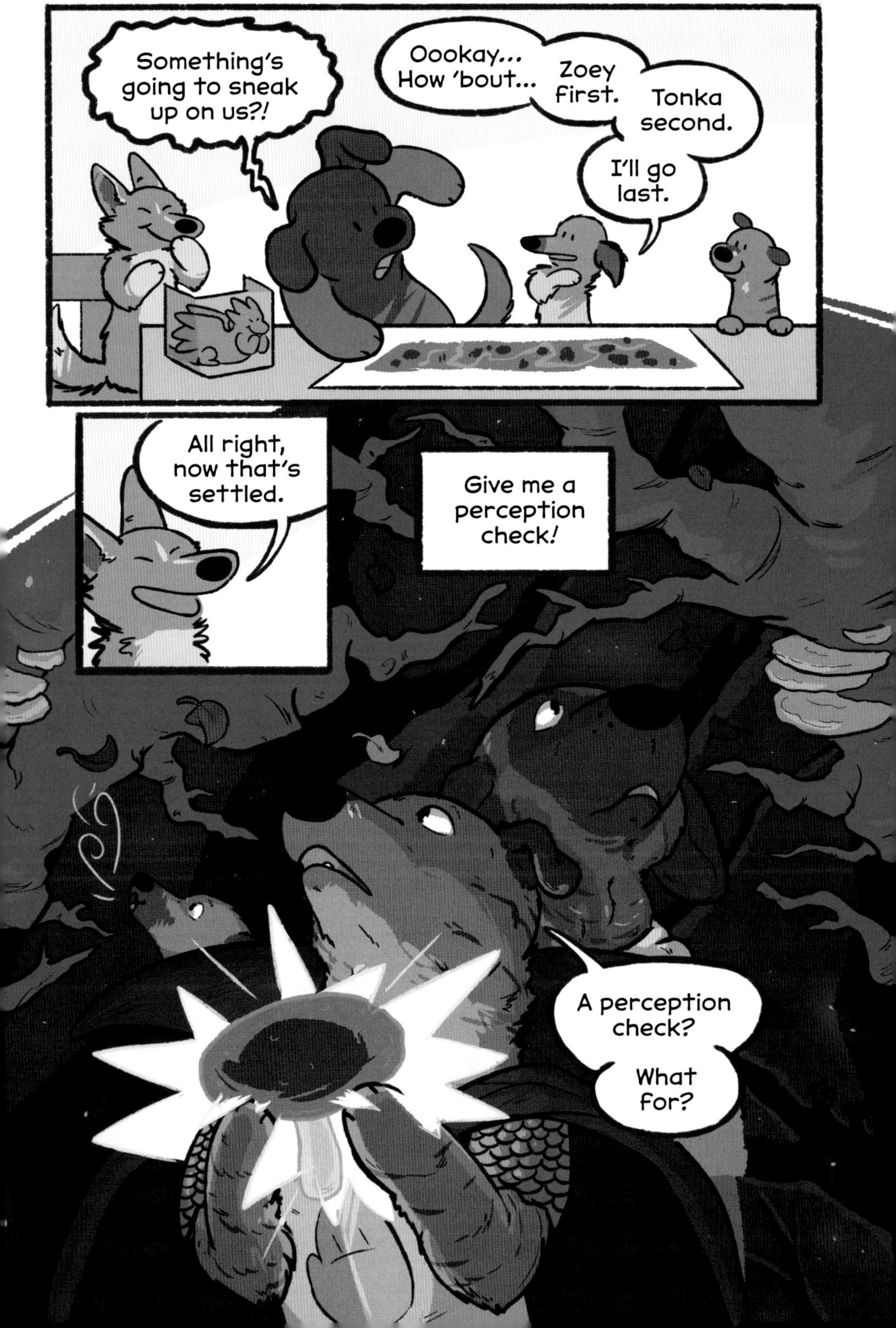
Something's going to sneak up on us?!
Oookay... How 'bout...
Zoey first.
Tonka second.
I'll go last.
All right, now that's settled.
Give me a perception check!
A perception check?
What for?

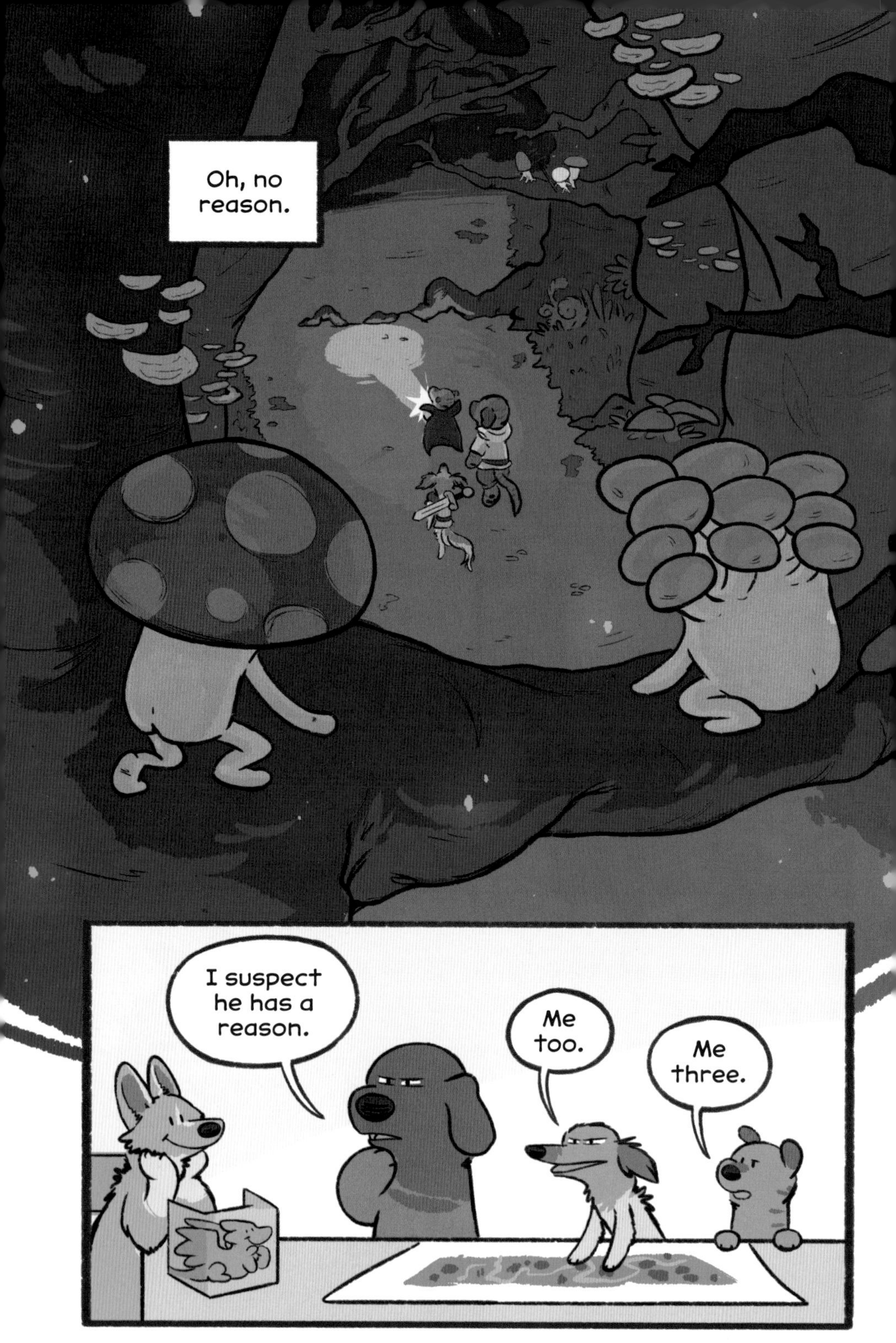
Oh, no reason.
I suspect he has a reason.
Me too.
Me three.

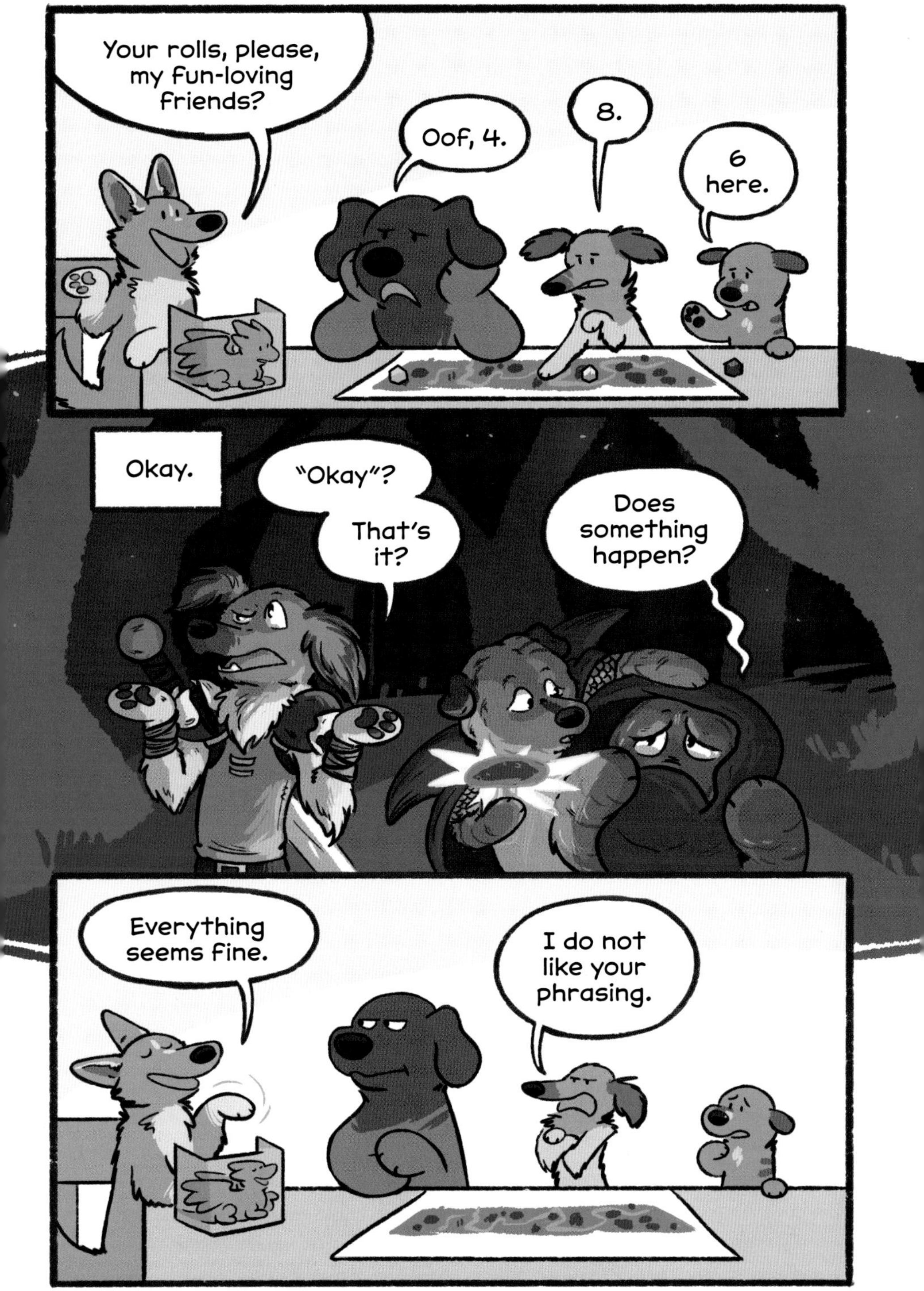
Your rolls, please, my fun-loving friends?
Oof, 4.
8.
6 here.
Okay.
"Okay"?
That's it?
Does something happen?
Everything seems fine.
I do not like your phrasing.

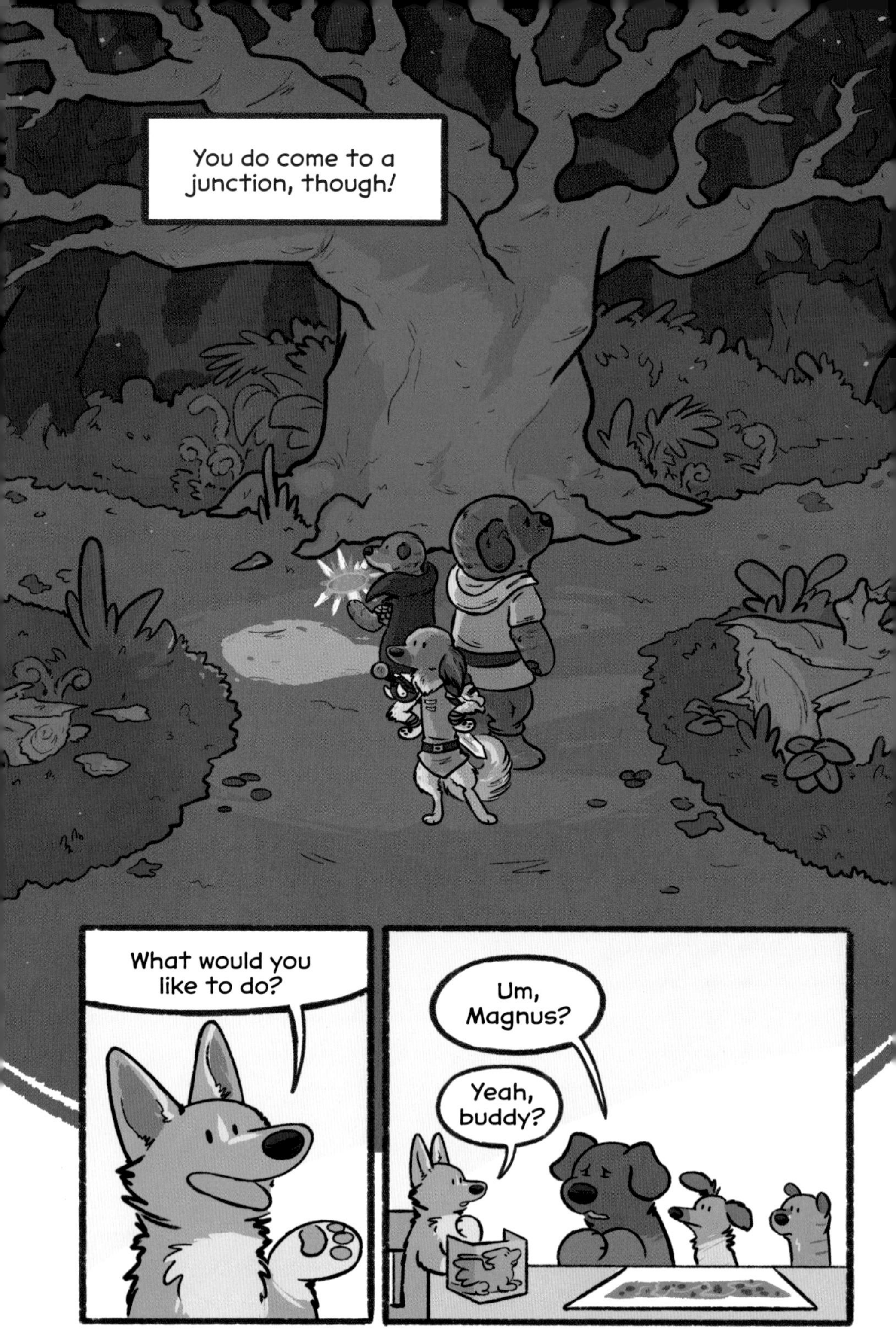
You do come to a junction, though!
What would you like to do?
Um, Magnus?
Yeah, buddy?

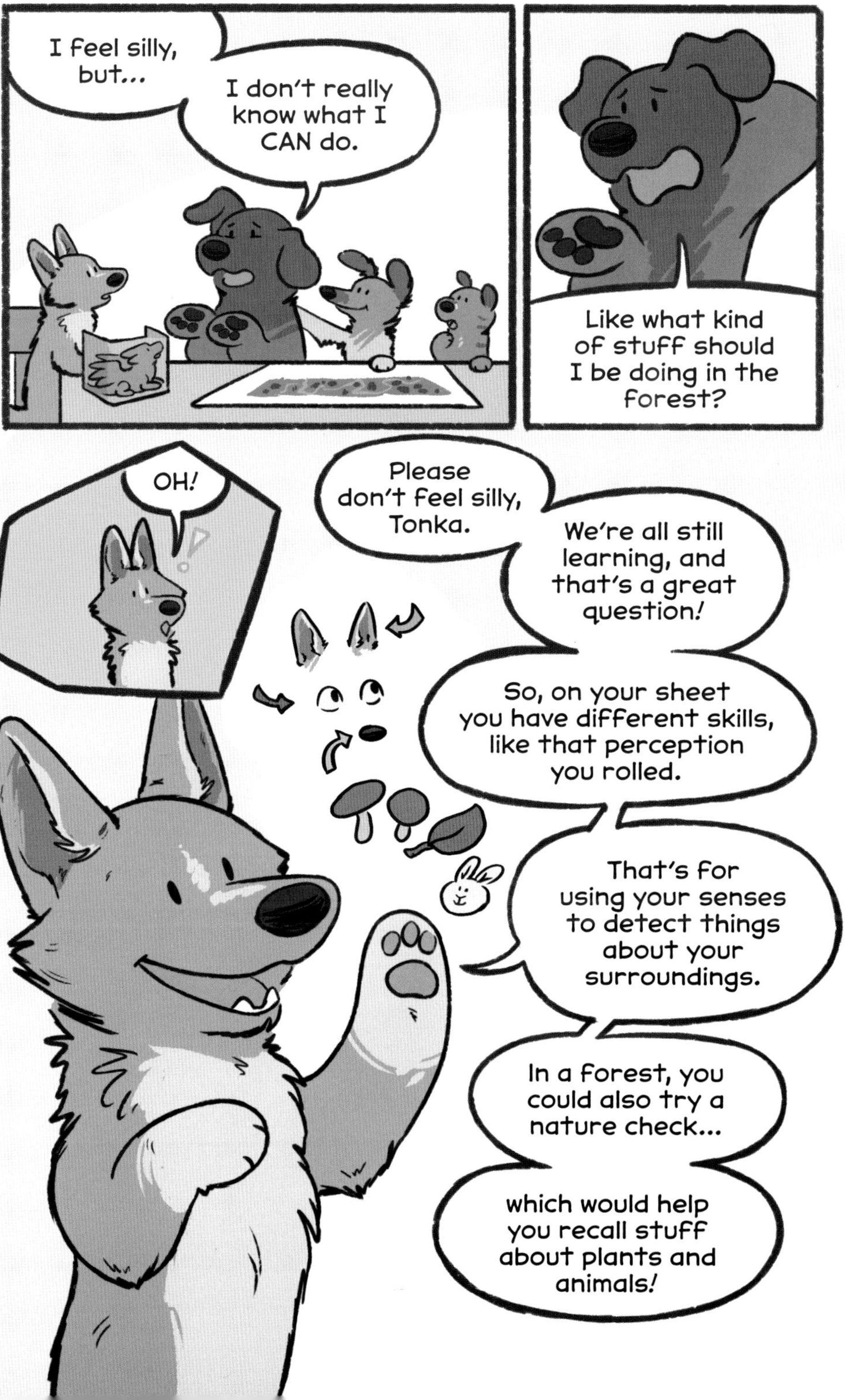
I feel silly, but...
I don't really know what I CAN do.
Like what kind of stuff should I be doing in the forest?
OH!
Please don't feel silly, Tonka.
We're all still learning, and that's a great question!
So, on your sheet you have different skills, like that perception you rolled.
That's for using your senses to detect things about your surroundings.
In a forest, you could also try a nature check...
which would help you recall stuff about plants and animals!

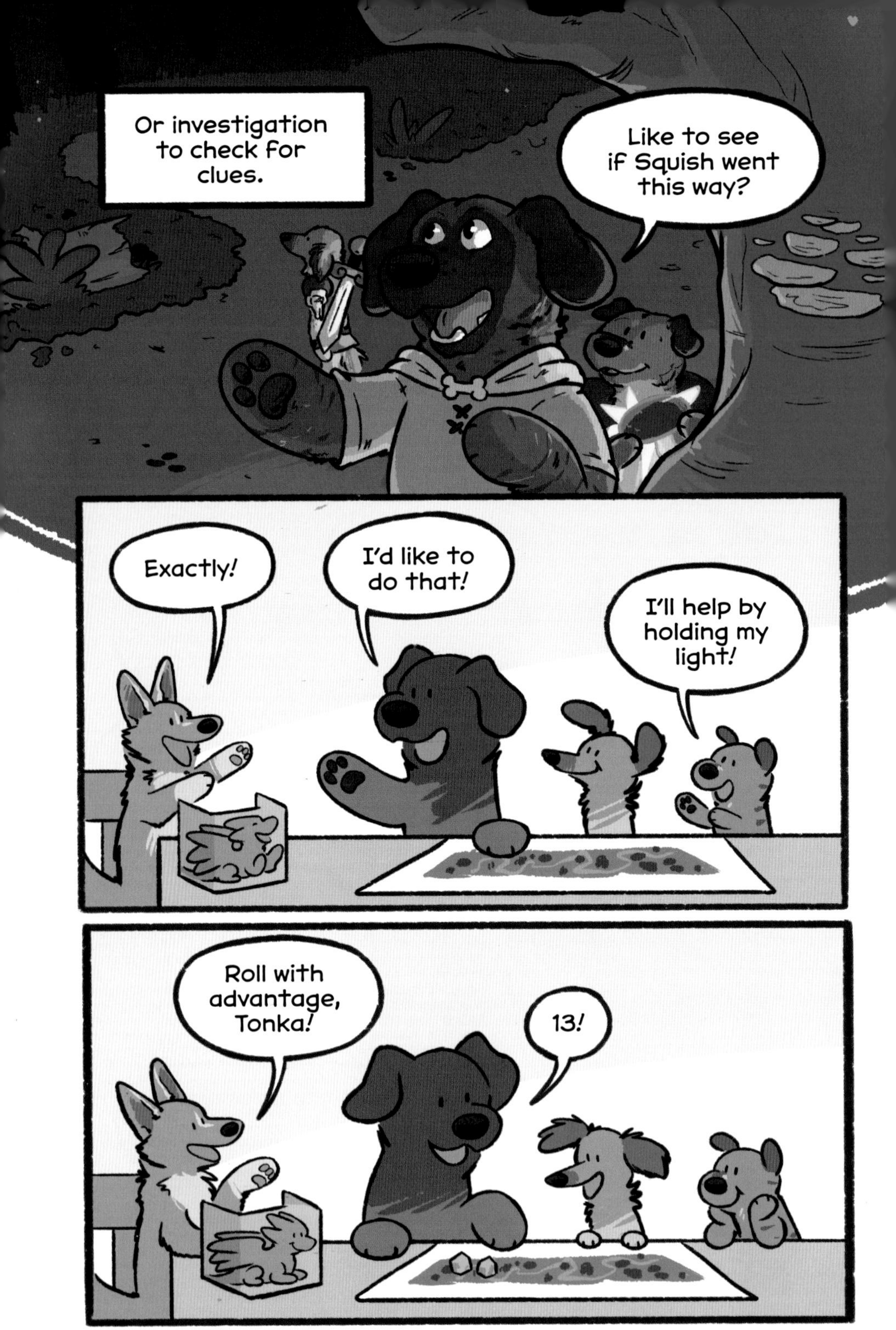
Or investigation to check for clues.
Like to see if Squish went this way?
Exactly!
I'd like to do that!
I'll help by holding my light!
Roll with advantage, Tonka!
13!

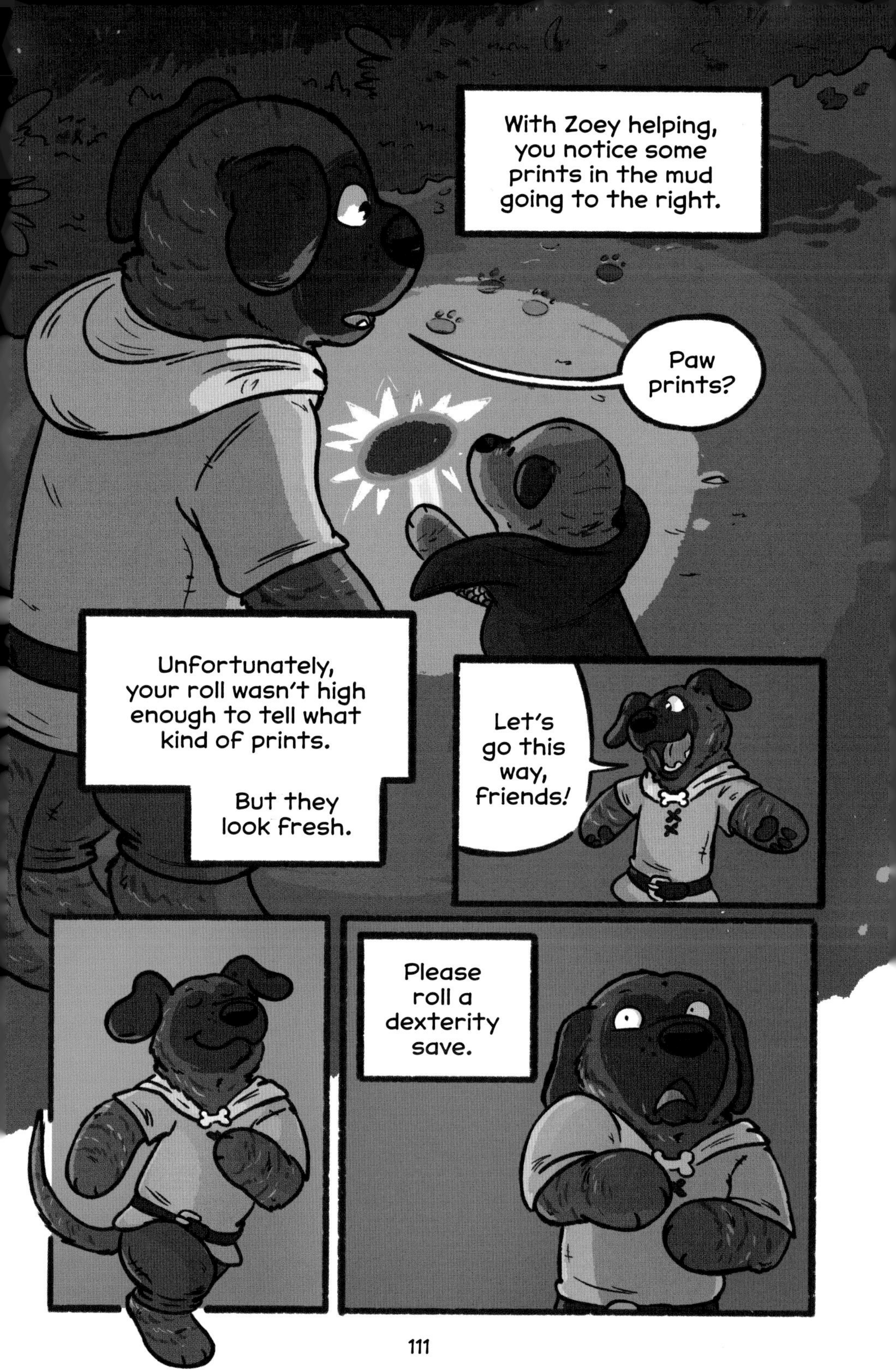
With Zoey helping, you notice some prints in the mud going to the right.
Paw prints?
Unfortunately, your roll wasn't high enough to tell what kind of prints.
But they look fresh.
Let's go this way, friends!
Please roll a dexterity save.

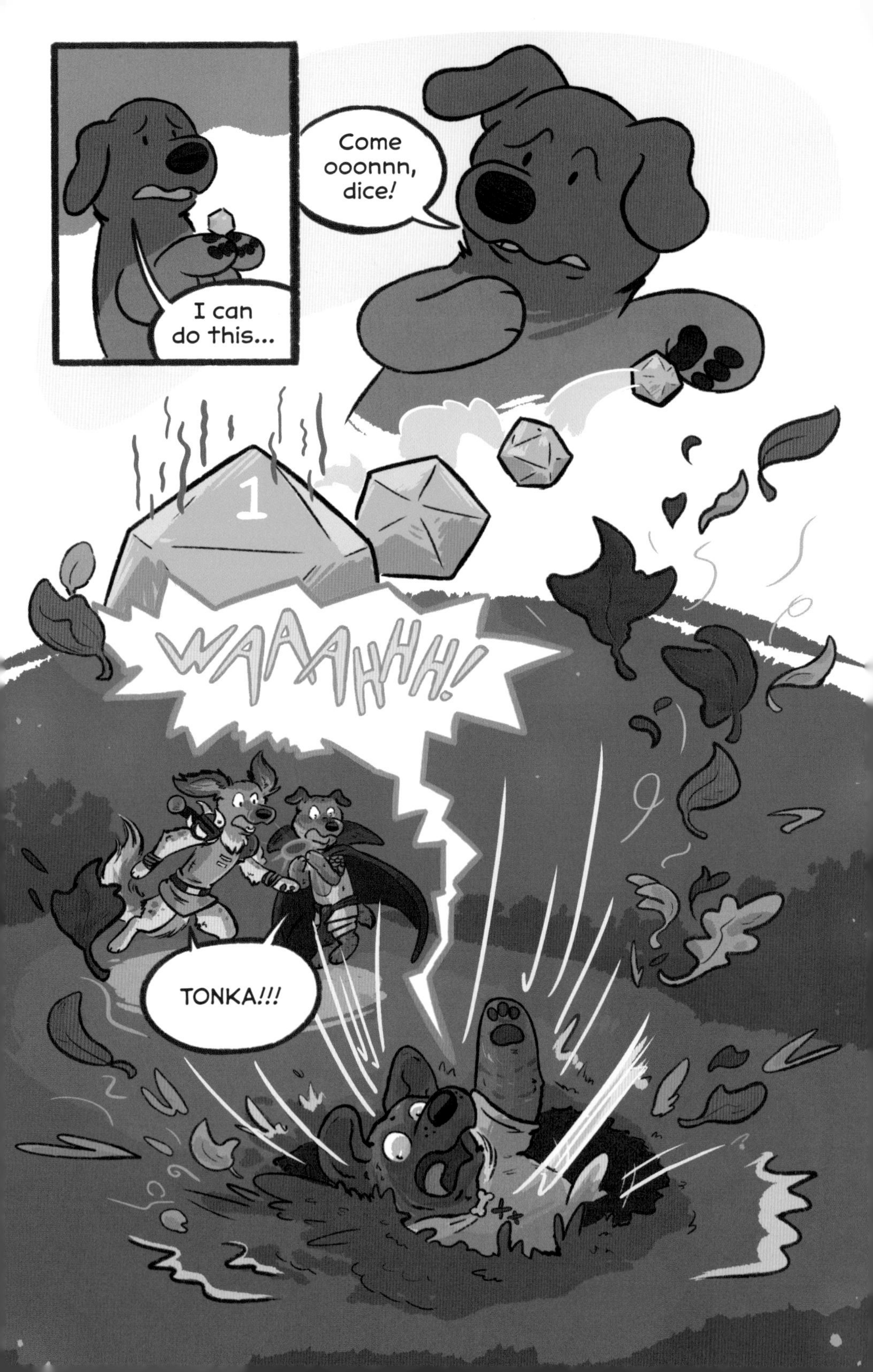
I can do this...
Come ooonnn, dice!
1
WAAAHHH!
TONKA!!!

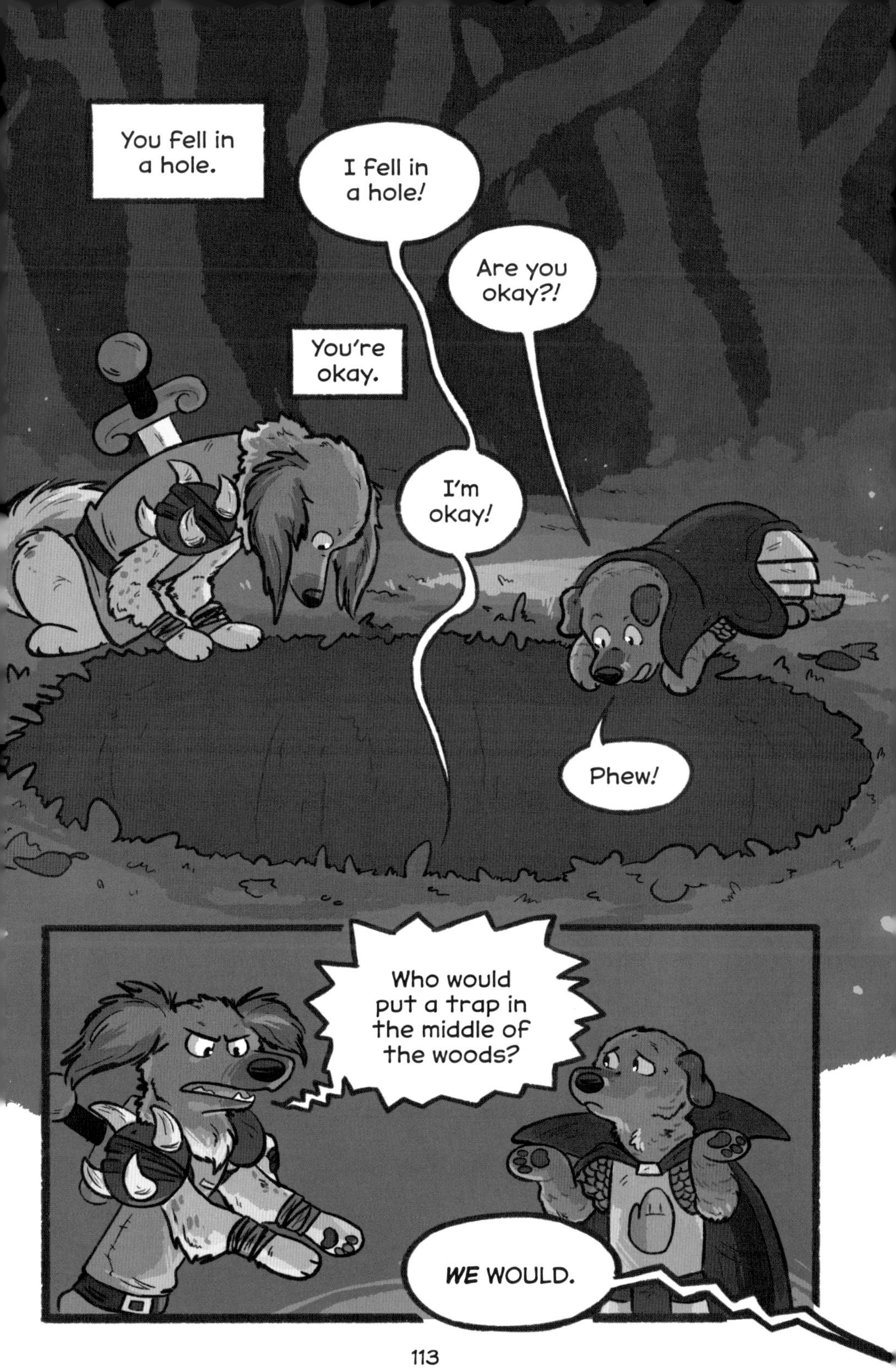
You fell in a hole.
I fell in a hole!
Are you okay?!
You're okay.
I'm okay!
Phew!
Who would put a trap in the middle of the woods?
WE WOULD.

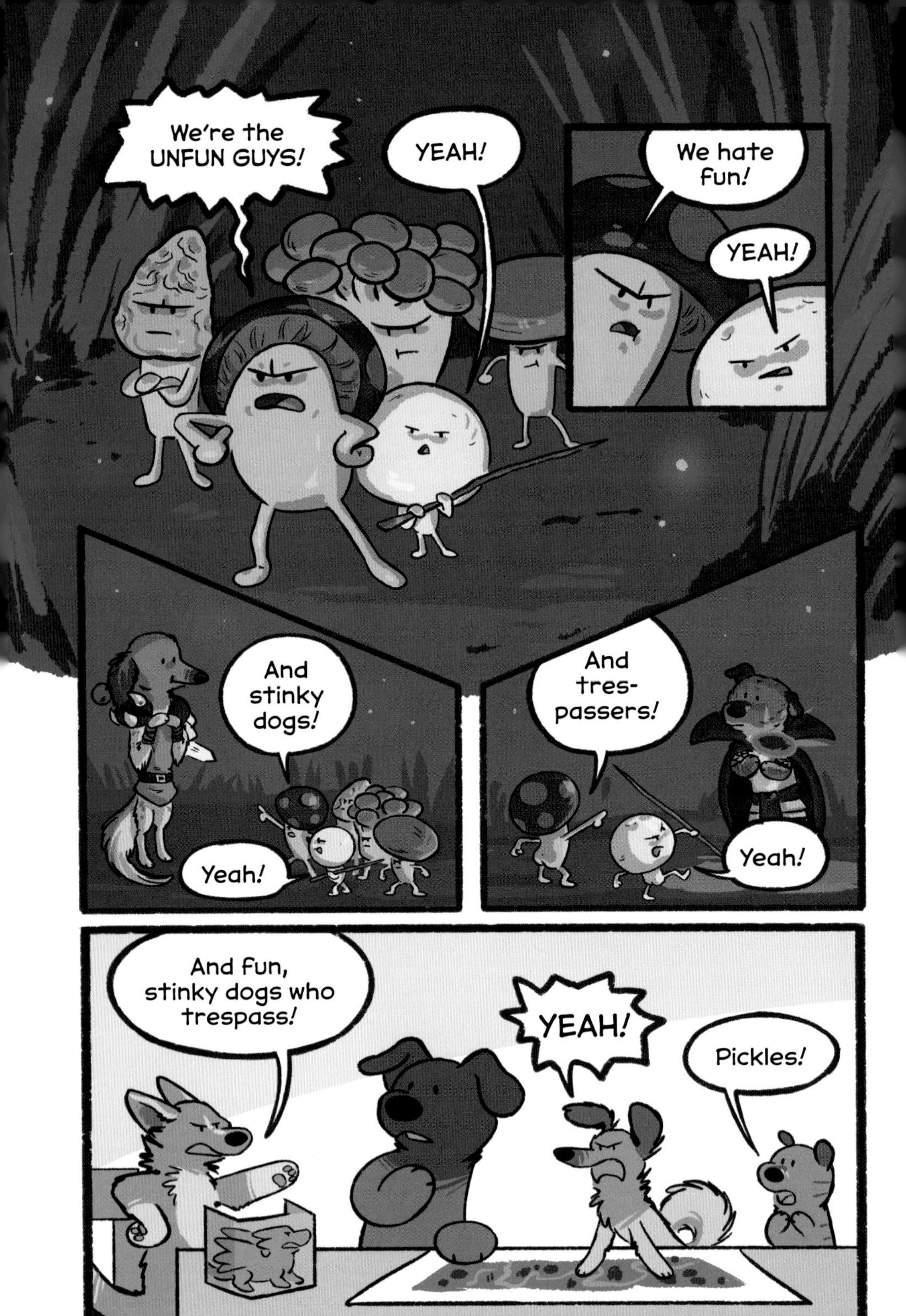
We're the UNFUN GUYS!
YEAH!
We hate fun!
YEAH!
And stinky dogs!
Yeah!
And tres-passers!
Yeah!
And fun, stinky dogs who trespass!
YEAH!
Pickles!

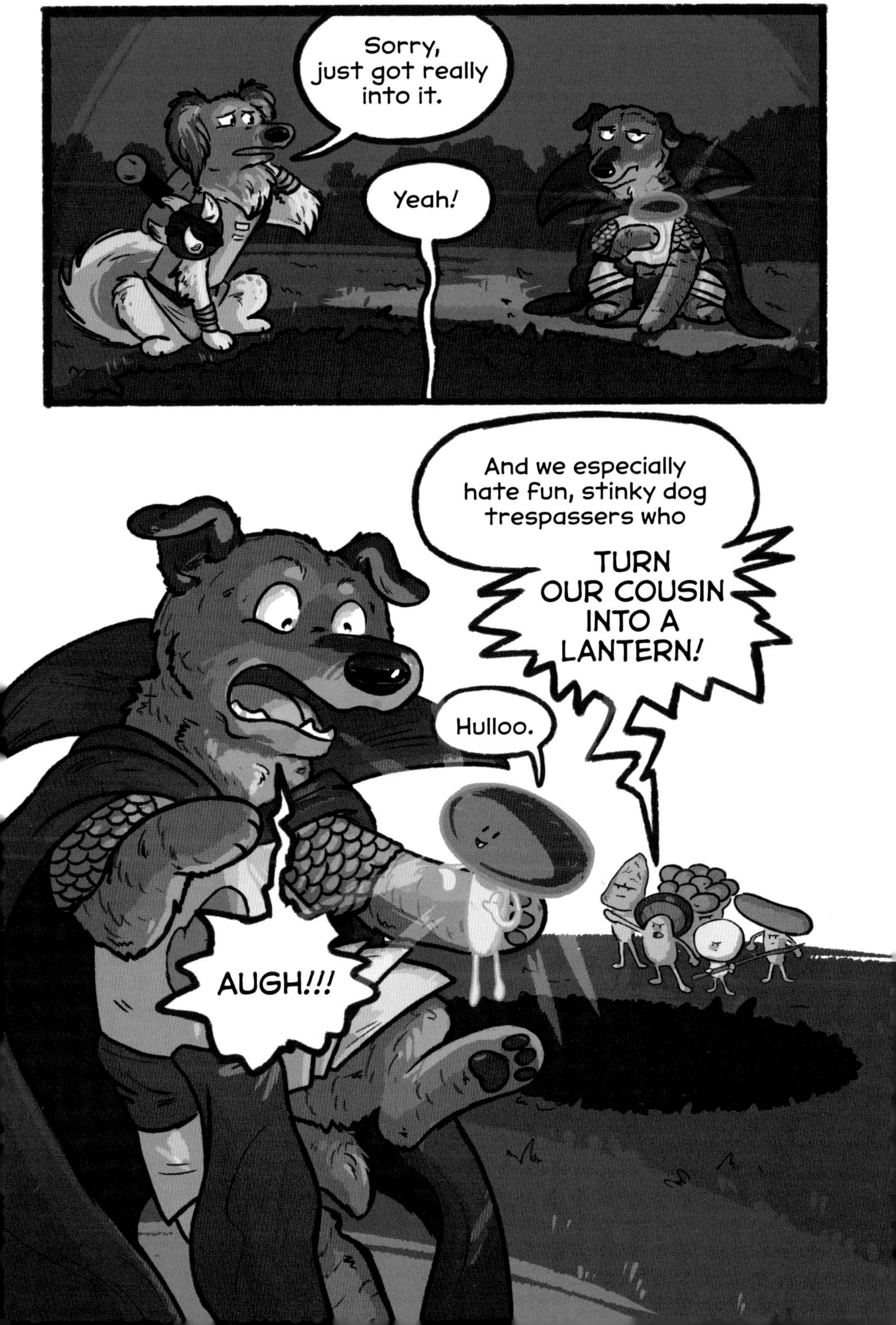
Sorry, just got really into it.
Yeah!
And we especially hate fun, stinky dog trespassers who
TURN OUR COUSIN INTO A LANTERN!
Hulloo.
AUGH!!!

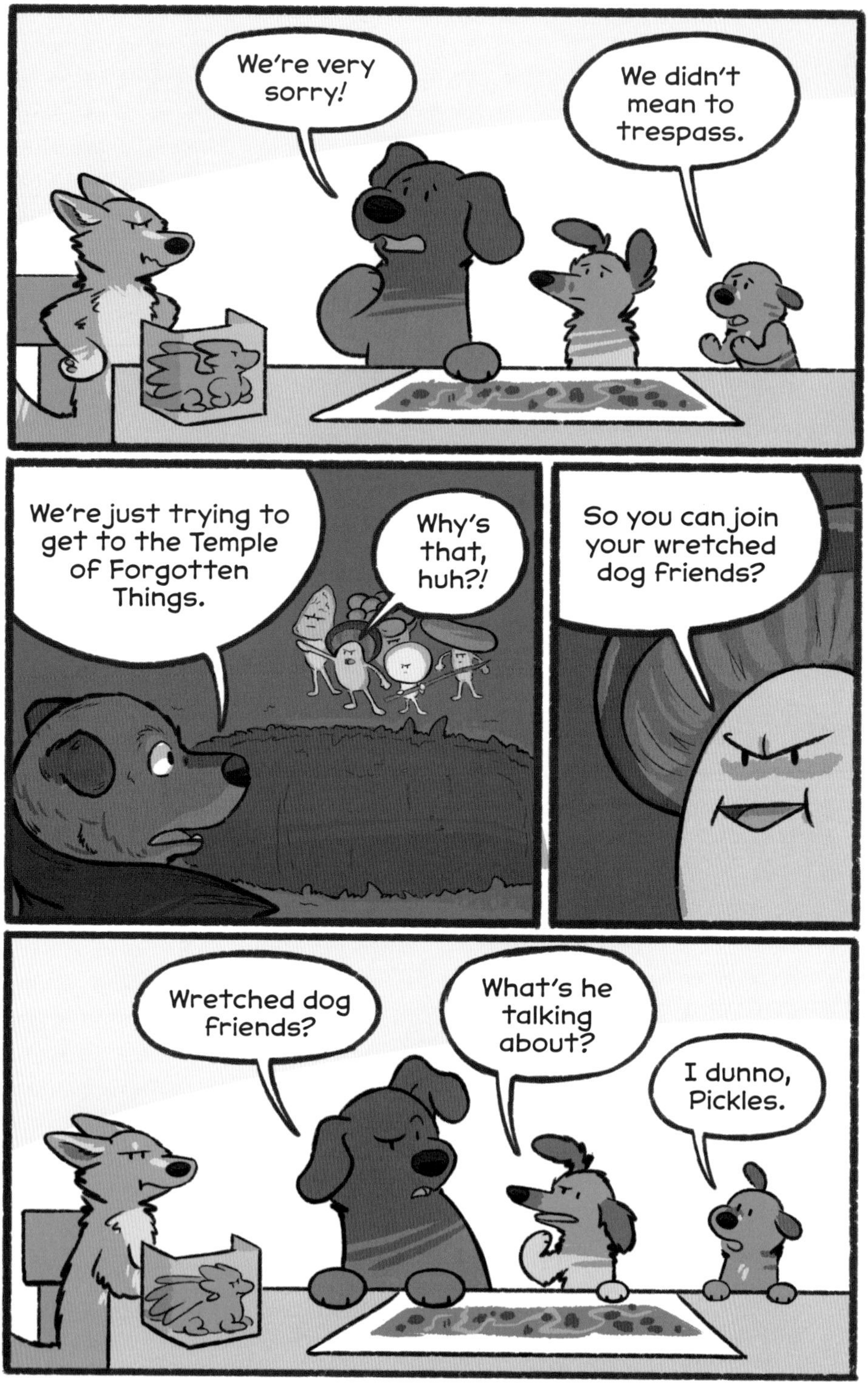
We're very sorry!
We didn't mean to trespass.
We're just trying to get to the Temple of Forgotten Things.
Why's that, huh?!
So you can join your wretched dog friends?
Wretched dog friends?
What's he talking about?
I dunno, Pickles.

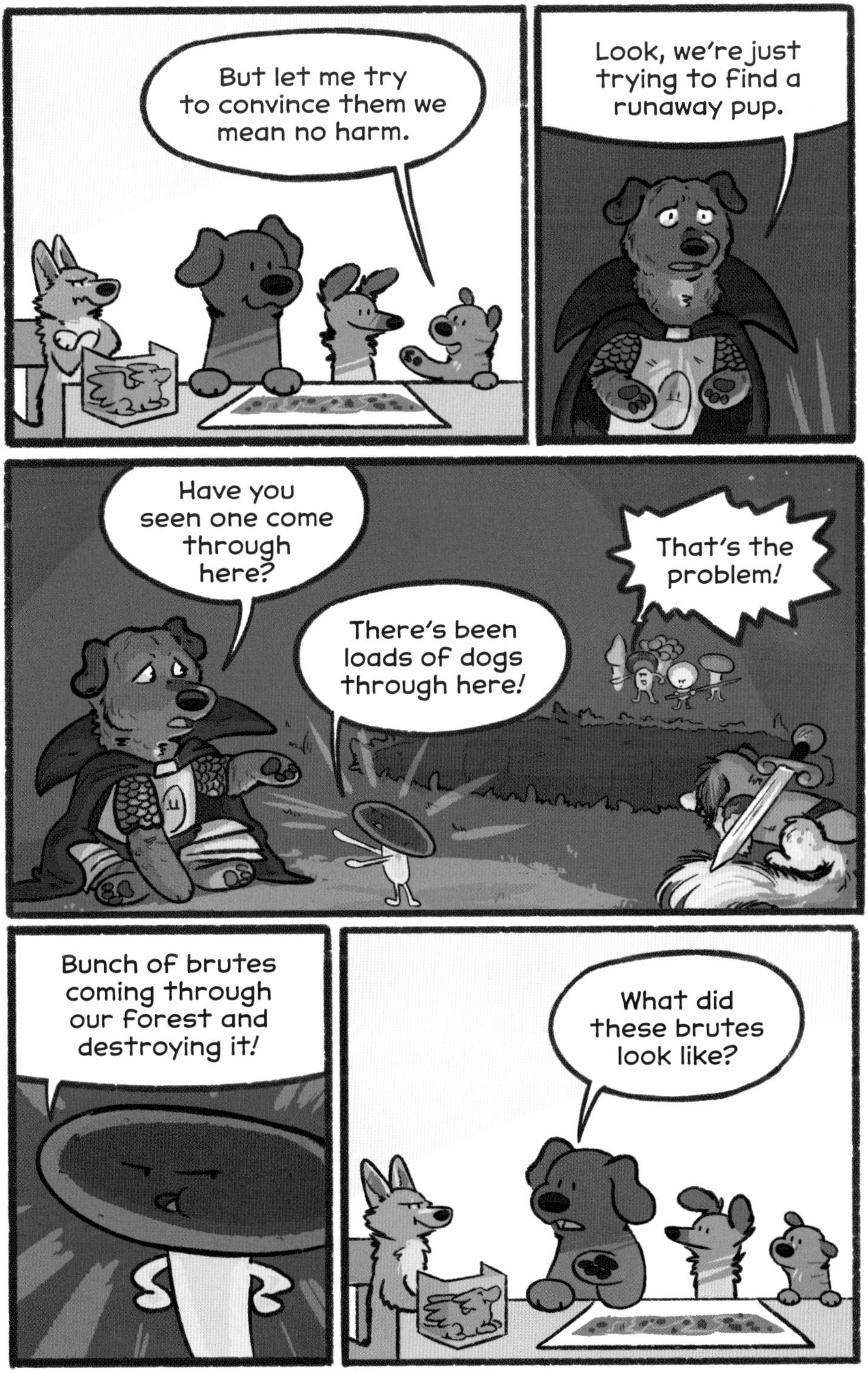
But let me try
to convince them we
mean no harm.
Look, we're just
trying to find a
runaway pup.
Have you
seen one come
through
here?
That's the
problem!
There's been
loads of dogs
through here!
Bunch of brutes
coming through
our forest and
destroying it!
What did
these brutes
look like?

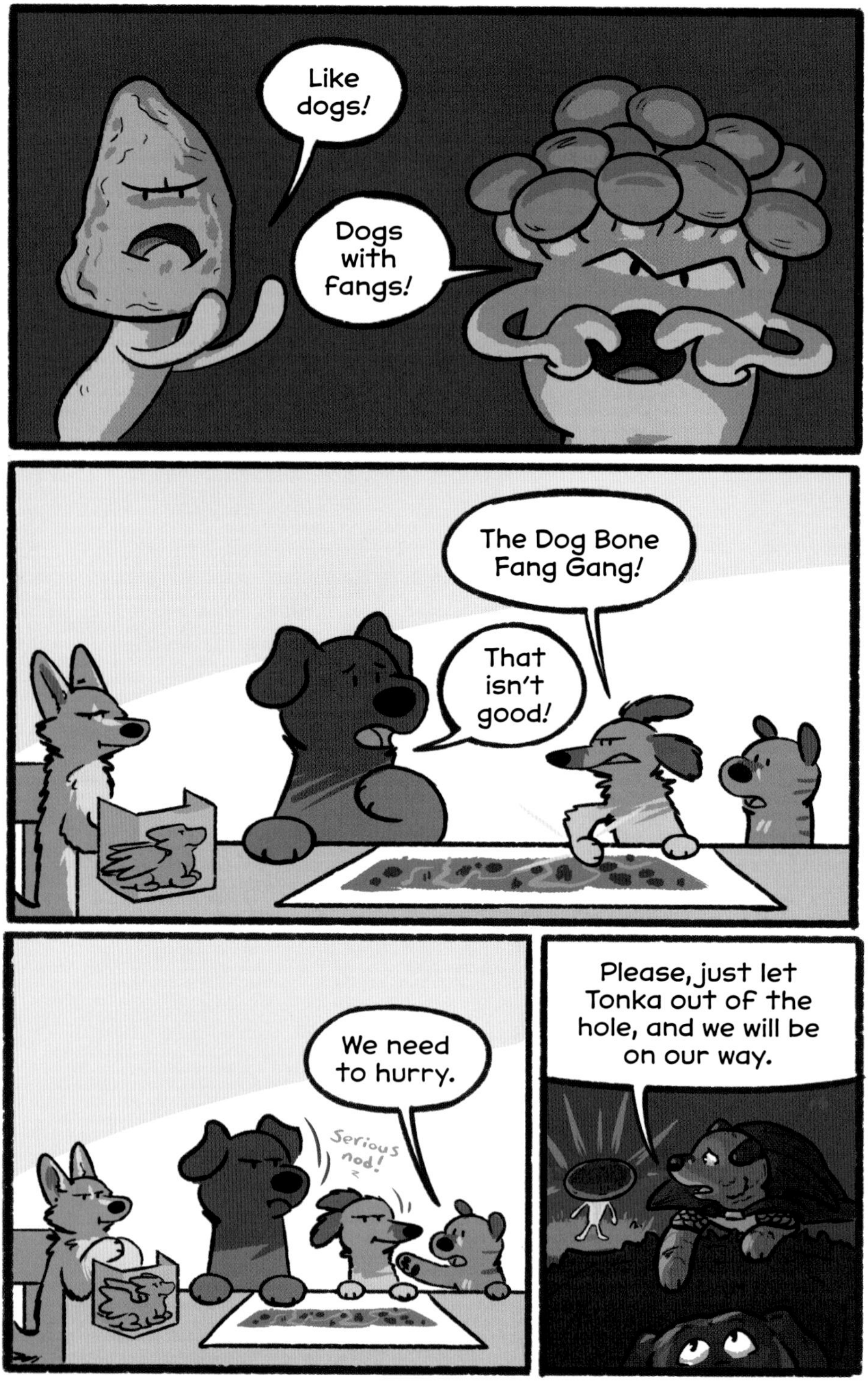
Like dogs!
Dogs with fangs!
The Dog Bone Fang Gang!
That isn't good!
We need to hurry.
Serious nod!
Please, just let Tonka out of the hole, and we will be on our way.

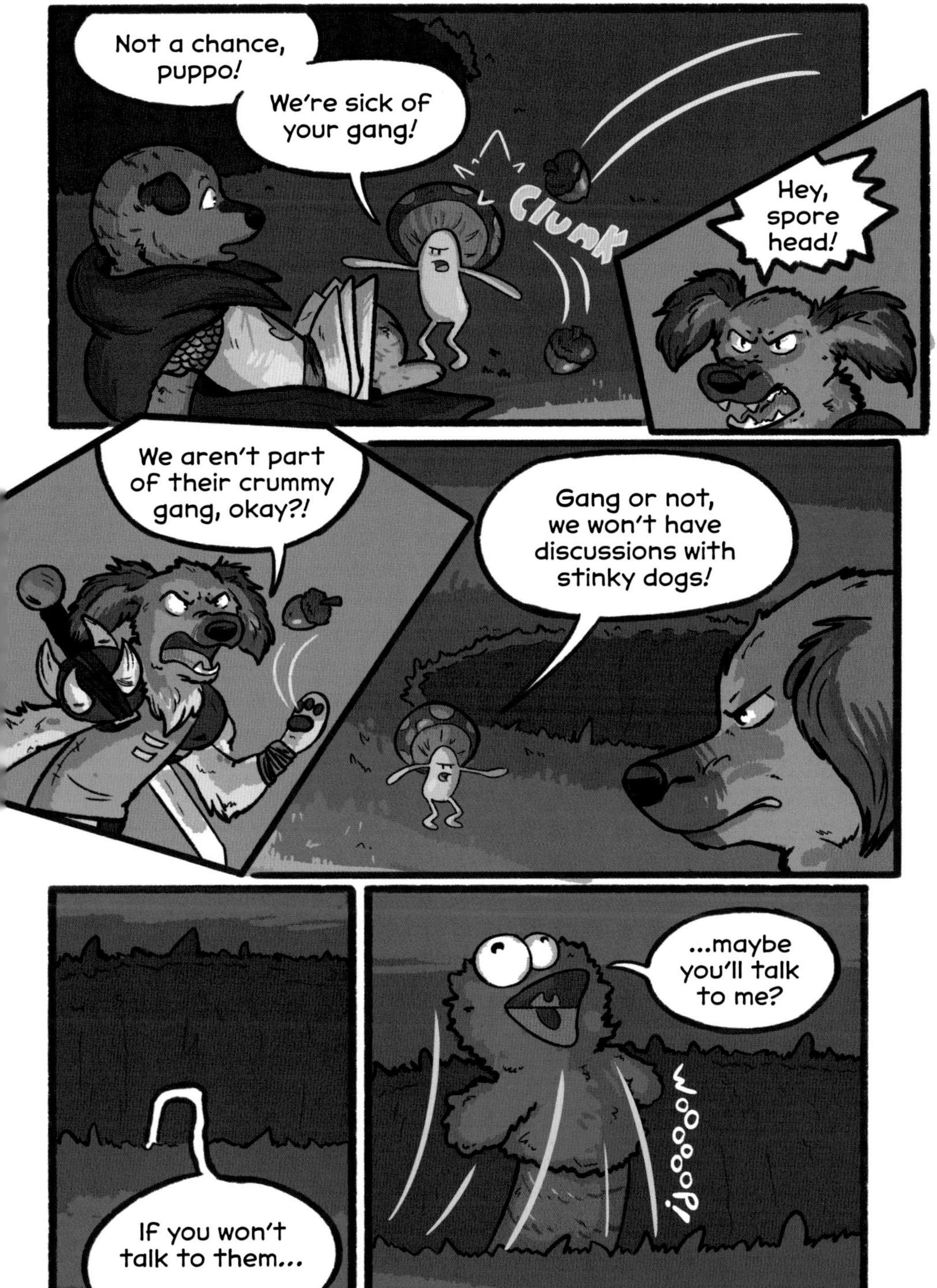
Not a chance, puppo!
We're sick of your gang!
CLUNK
Hey, spore head!
We aren't part of their crummy gang, okay?!
Gang or not, we won't have discussions with stinky dogs!
If you won't talk to them...
...maybe you'll talk to me?
WOOOOOP!

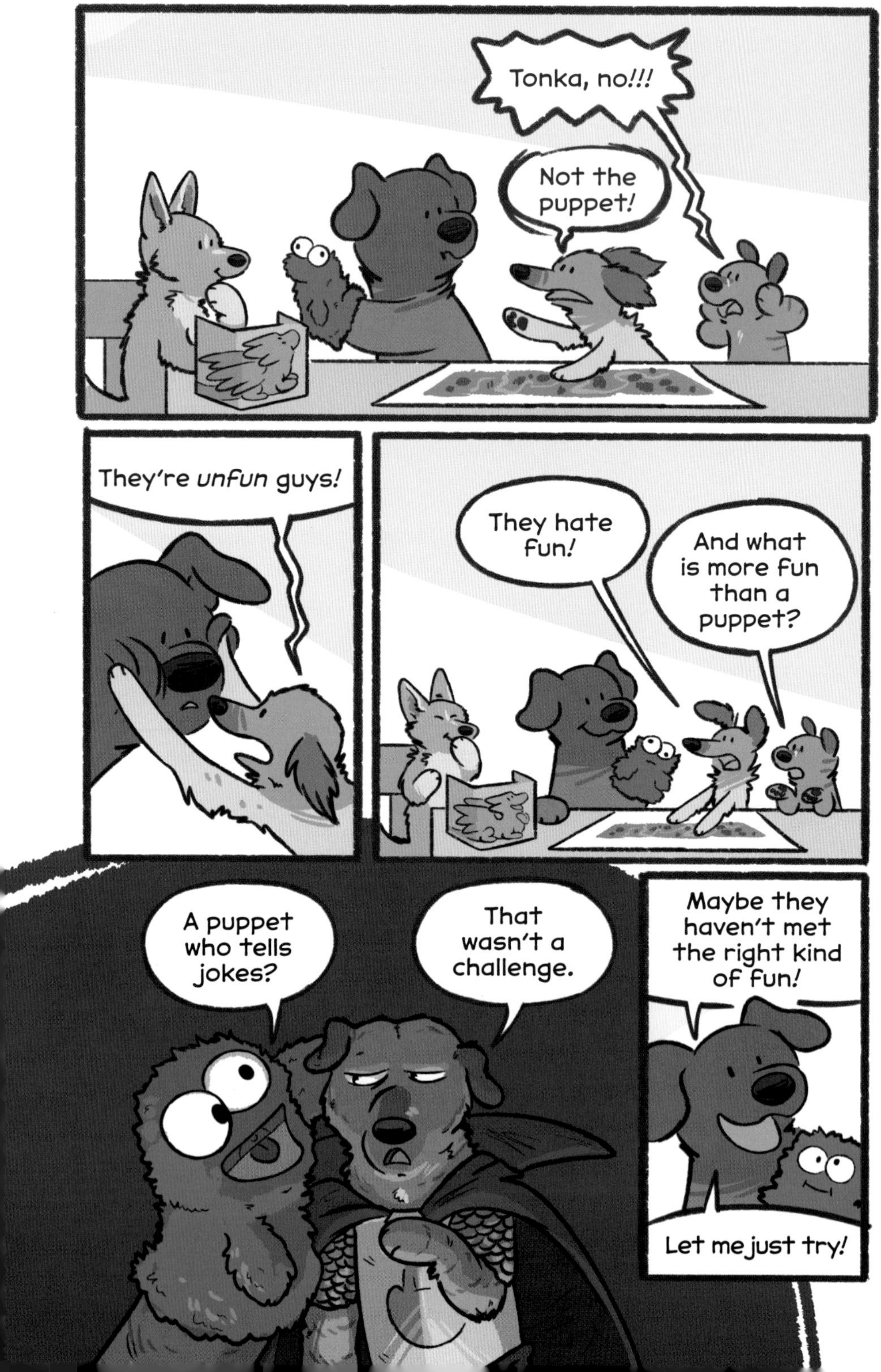
Tonka, no!!!
Not the puppet!
They're *unfun* guys!
They hate fun!
And what is more fun than a puppet?
A puppet who tells jokes?
That wasn't a challenge.
Maybe they haven't met the right kind of fun!
Let me just try!

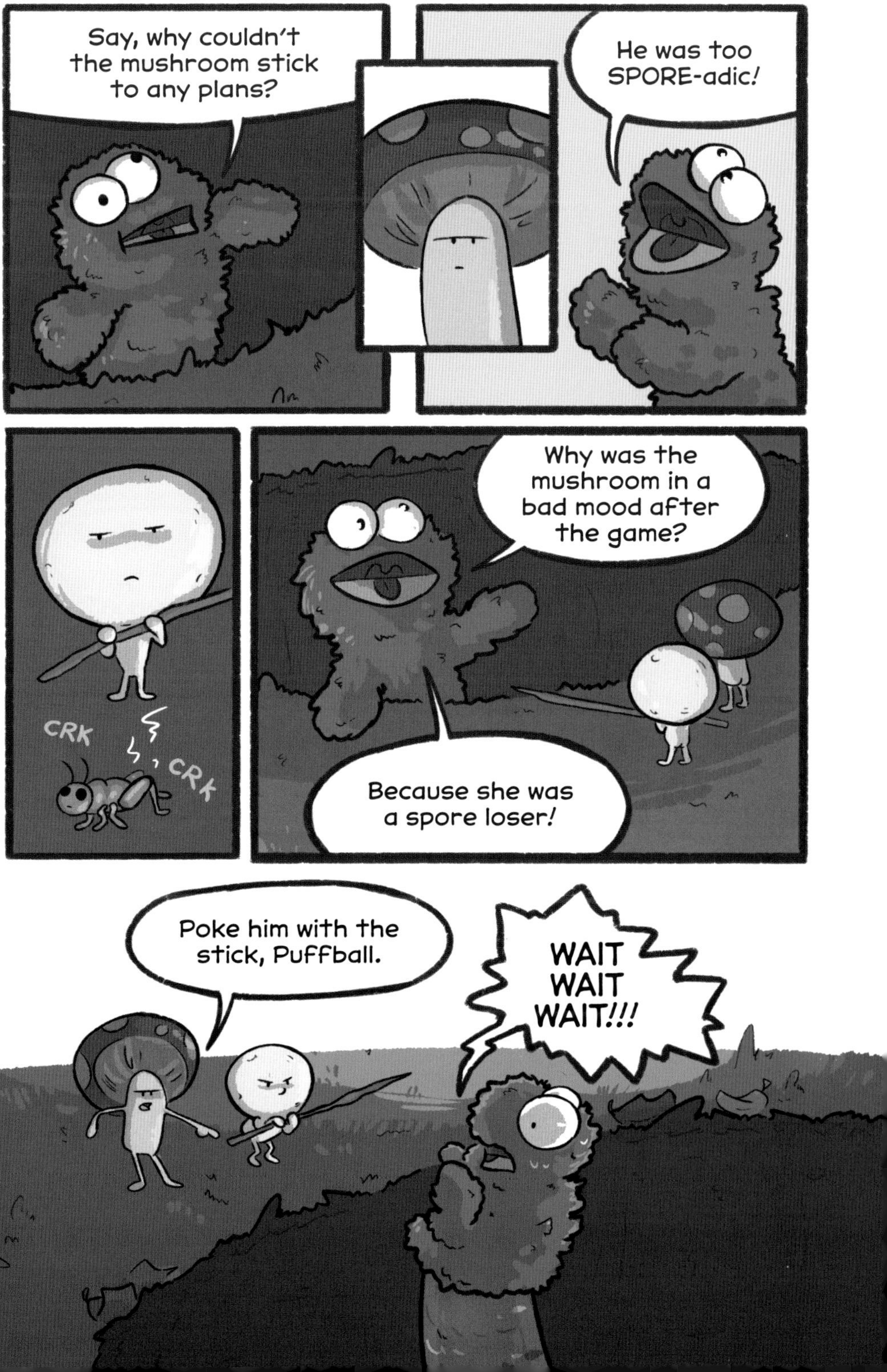
Say, why couldn't the mushroom stick to any plans?
He was too SPORE-adic!
CRK
CRK
Why was the mushroom in a bad mood after the game?
Because she was a spore loser!
Poke him with the stick, Puffball.
WAIT WAIT WAIT!!!

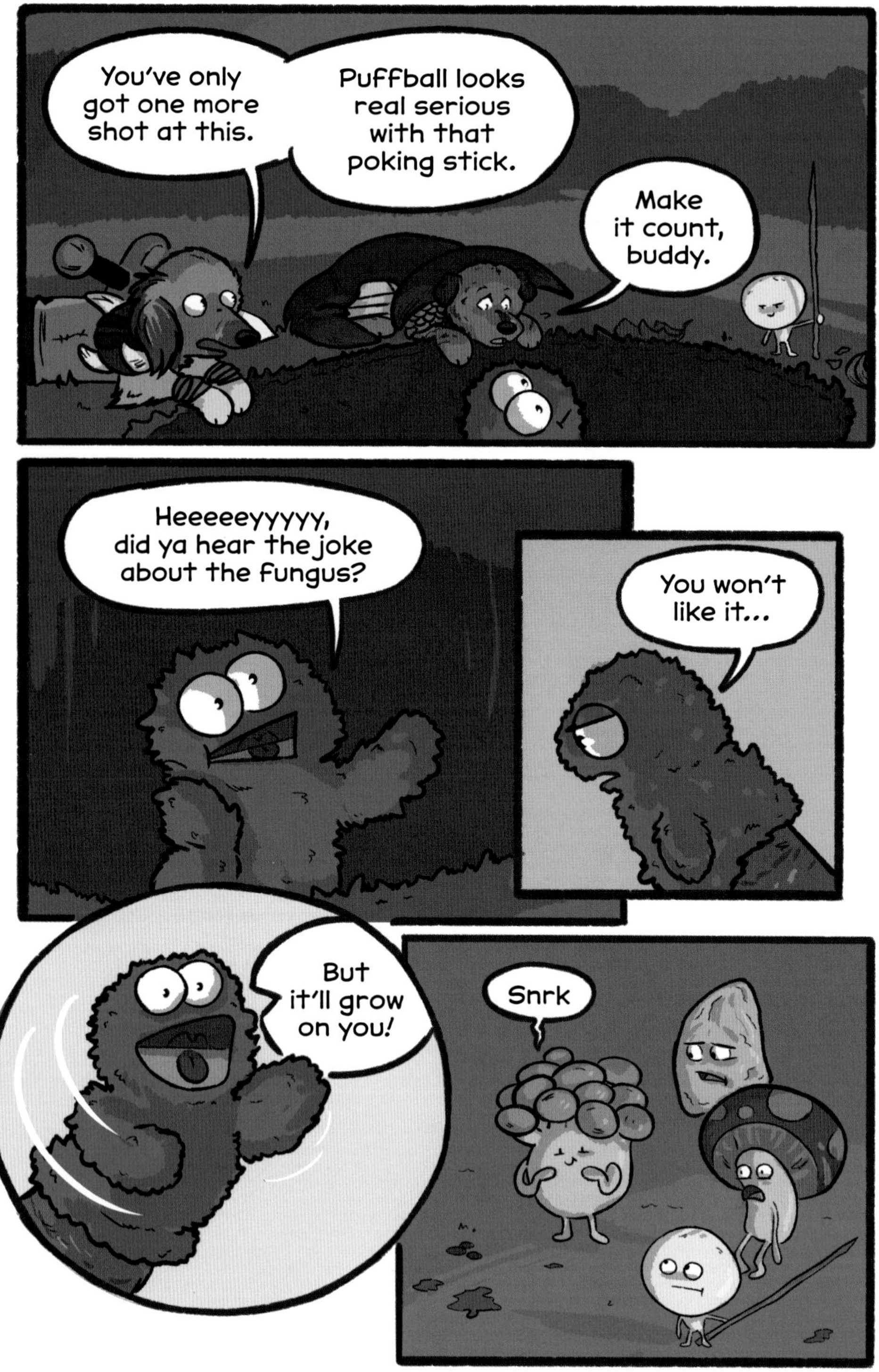
You've only got one more shot at this.
Puffball looks real serious with that poking stick.
Make it count, buddy.
Heeeeeyyyyy, did ya hear the joke about the fungus?
You won't like it...
But it'll grow on you!
Snrk

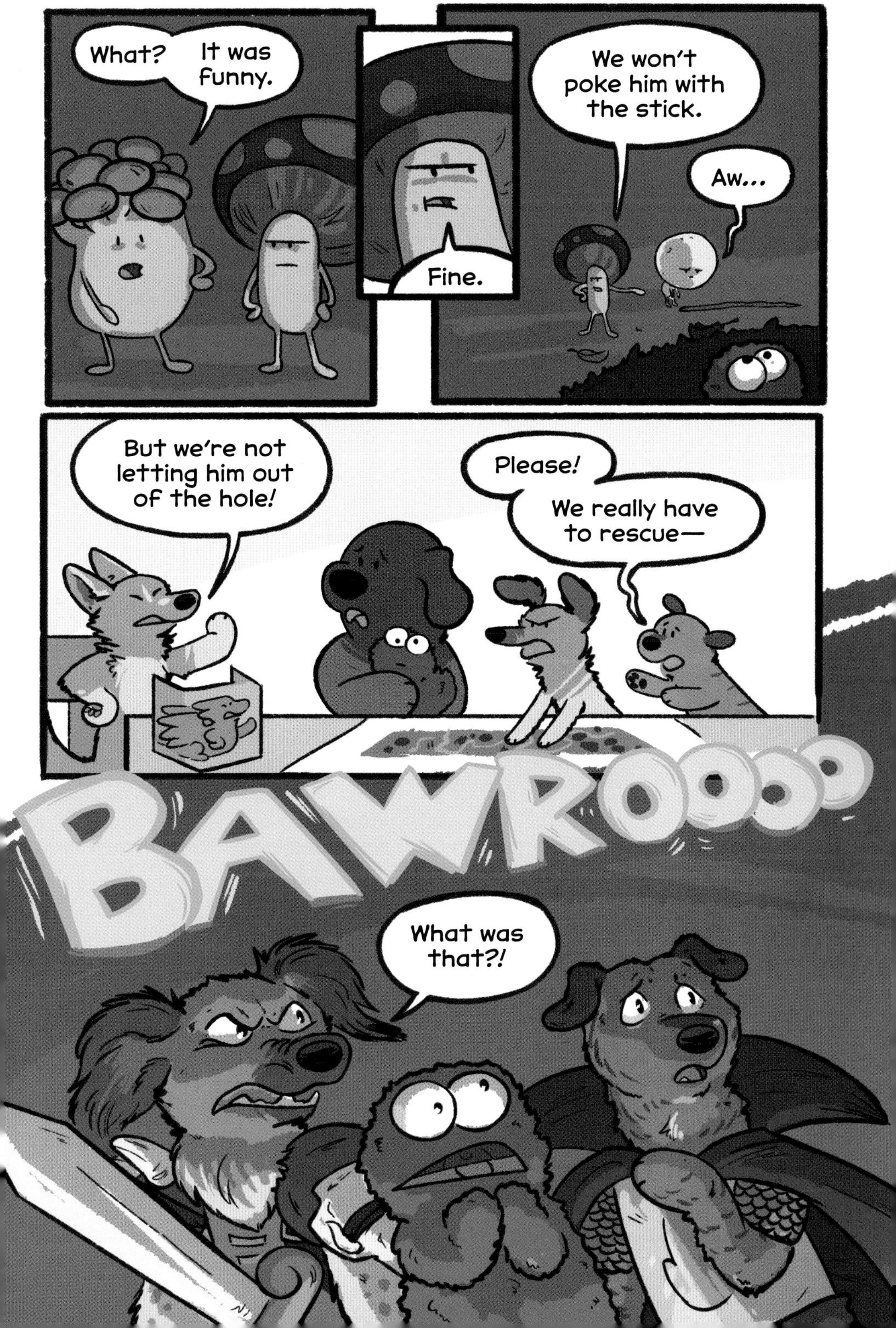
What?
It was funny.
Fine.
We won't poke him with the stick.
Aw...
But we're not letting him out of the hole!
Please!
We really have to rescue—
BAWROOOO
What was that?!

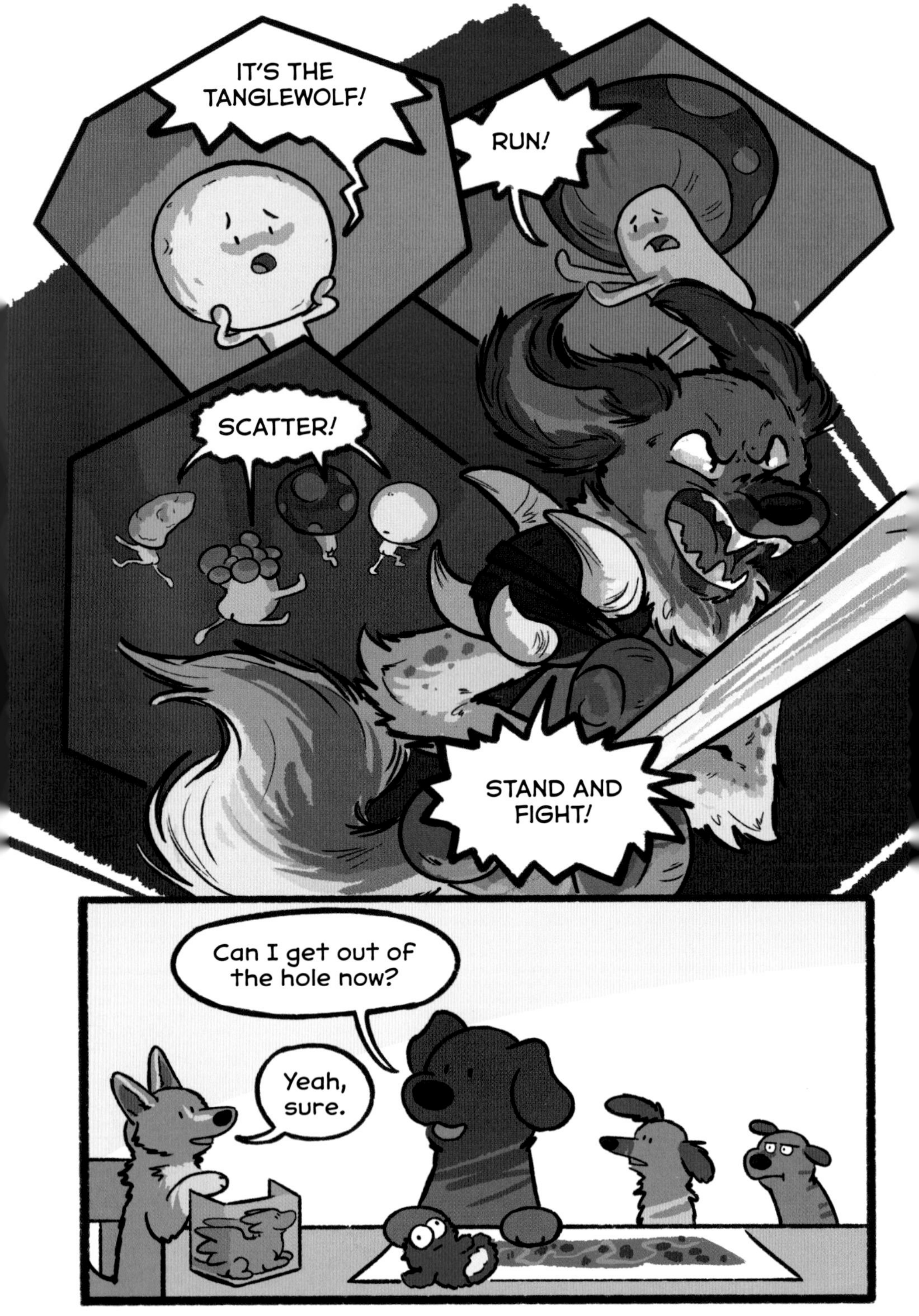
IT'S THE TANGLEWOLF!
RUN!
SCATTER!
STAND AND FIGHT!
Can I get out of the hole now?
Yeah, sure.

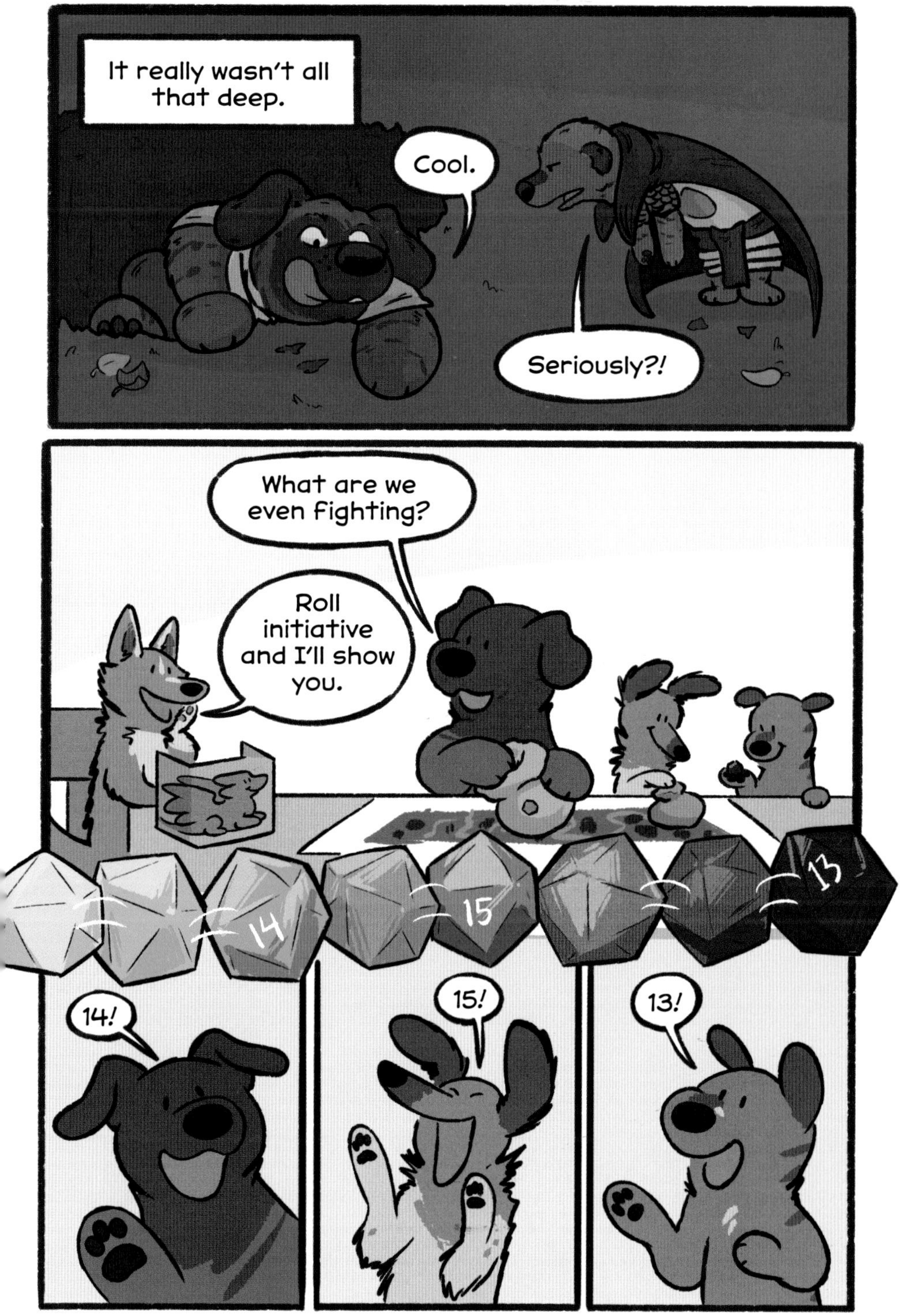

It really wasn't all that deep.
Cool.
Seriously?!
What are we even fighting?
Roll initiative and I'll show you.
14
15
13
14!
15!
13!

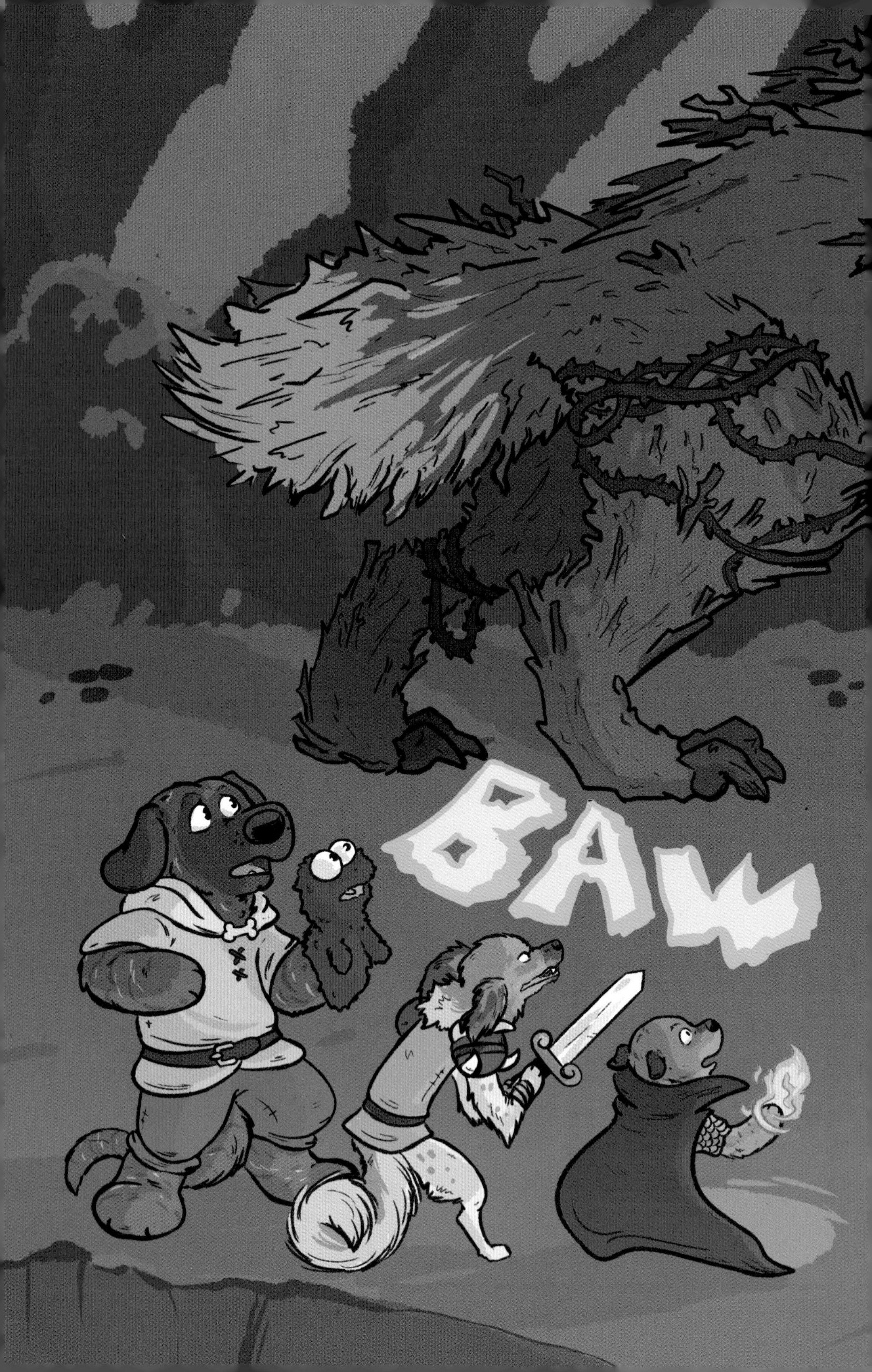
BAW

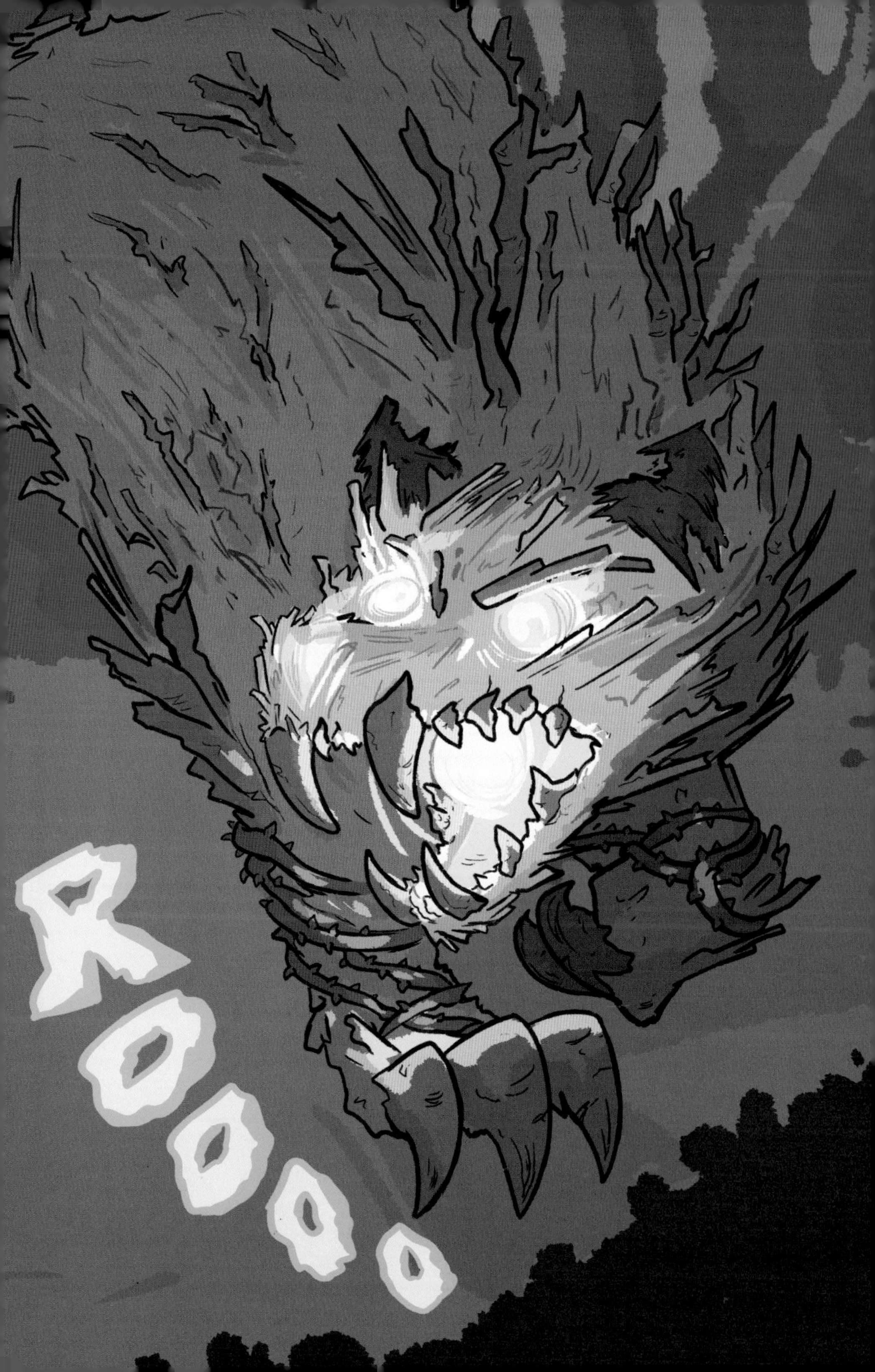
ROOOO

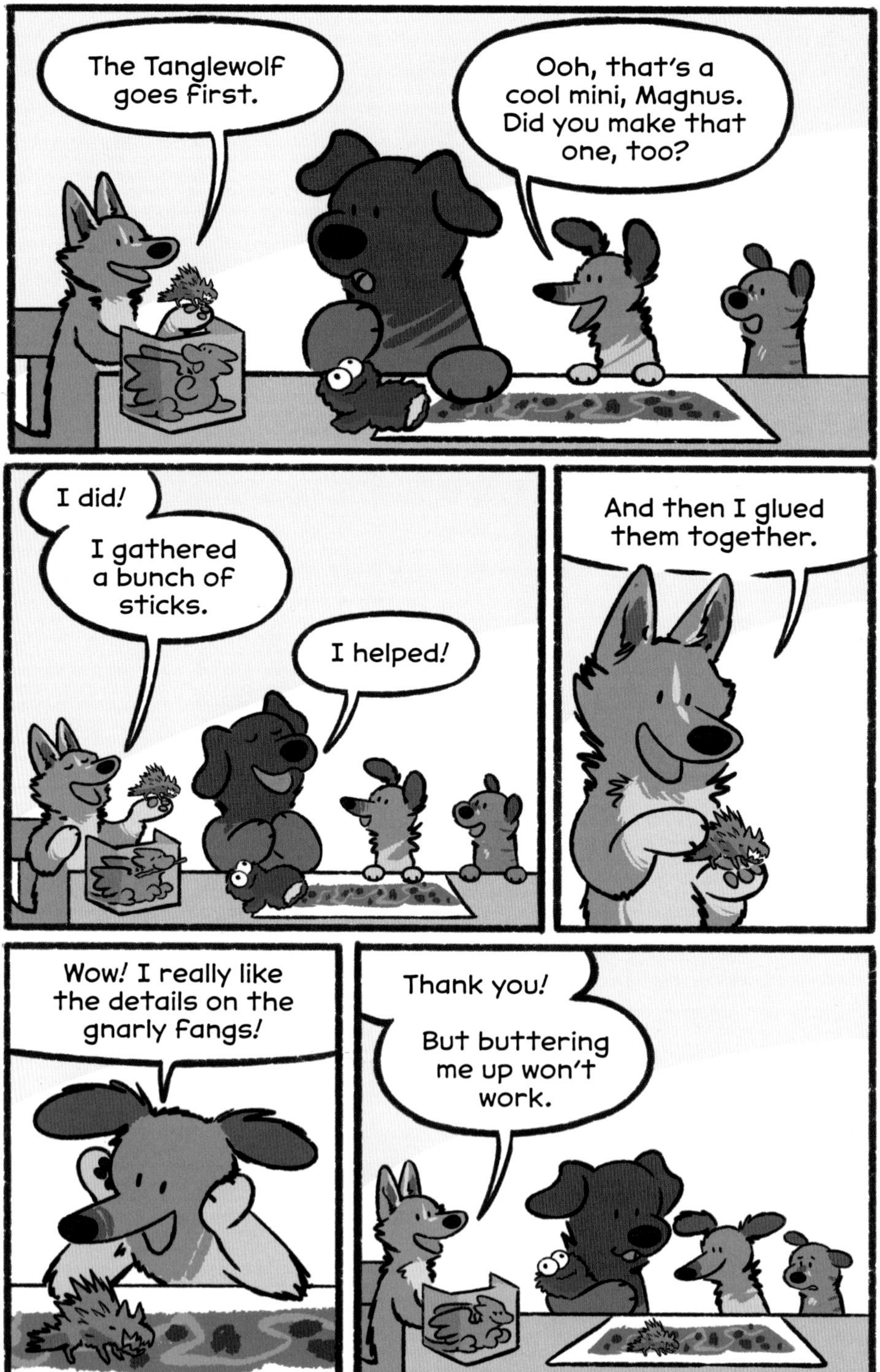
The Tanglewolf goes first.
Ooh, that's a cool mini, Magnus. Did you make that one, too?
I did!
I gathered a bunch of sticks.
I helped!
And then I glued them together.
Wow! I really like the details on the gnarly fangs!
Thank you!
But buttering me up won't work.

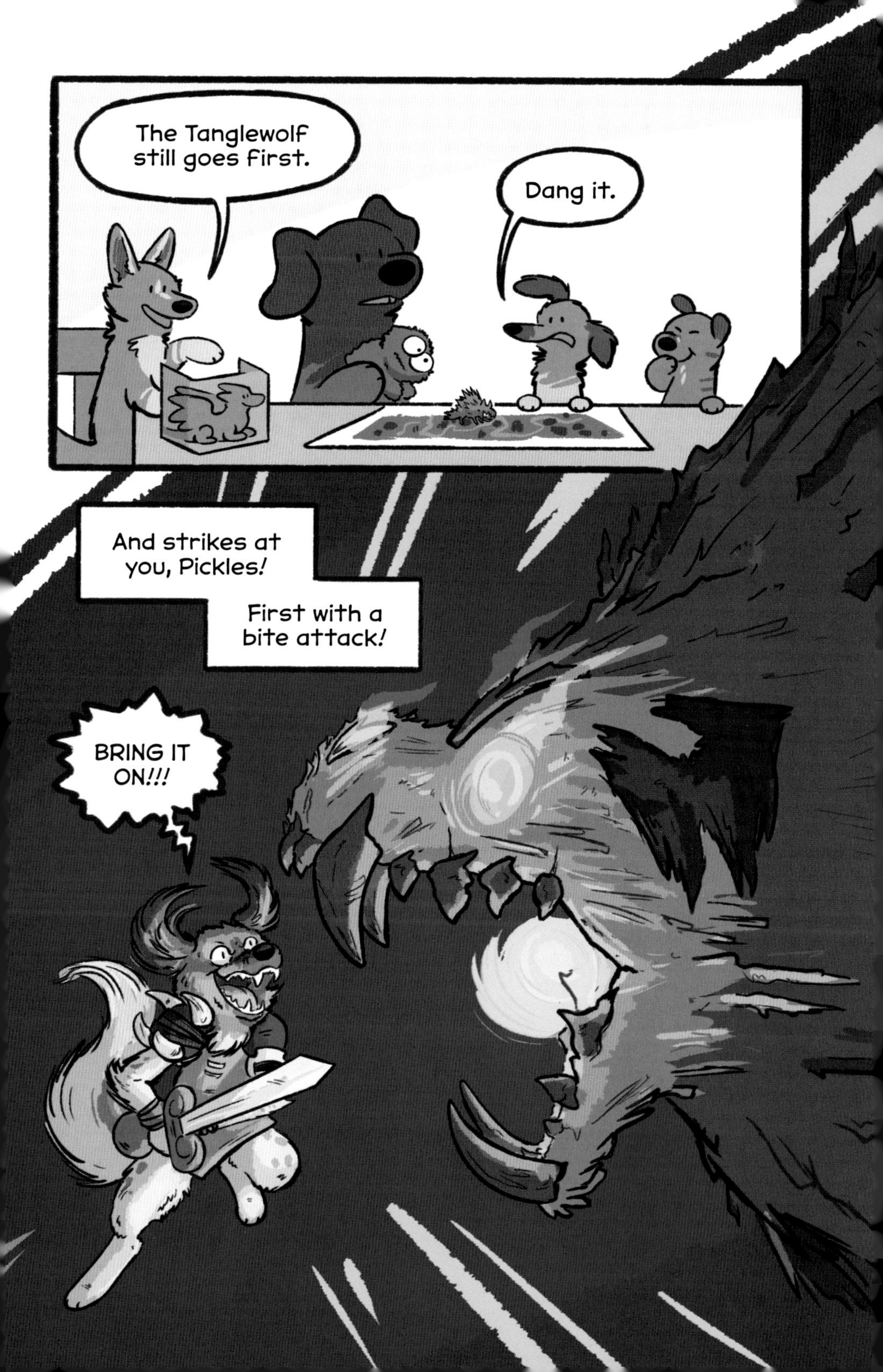
The Tanglewolf still goes first.
Dang it.
And strikes at you, Pickles!
First with a bite attack!
BRING IT ON!!!

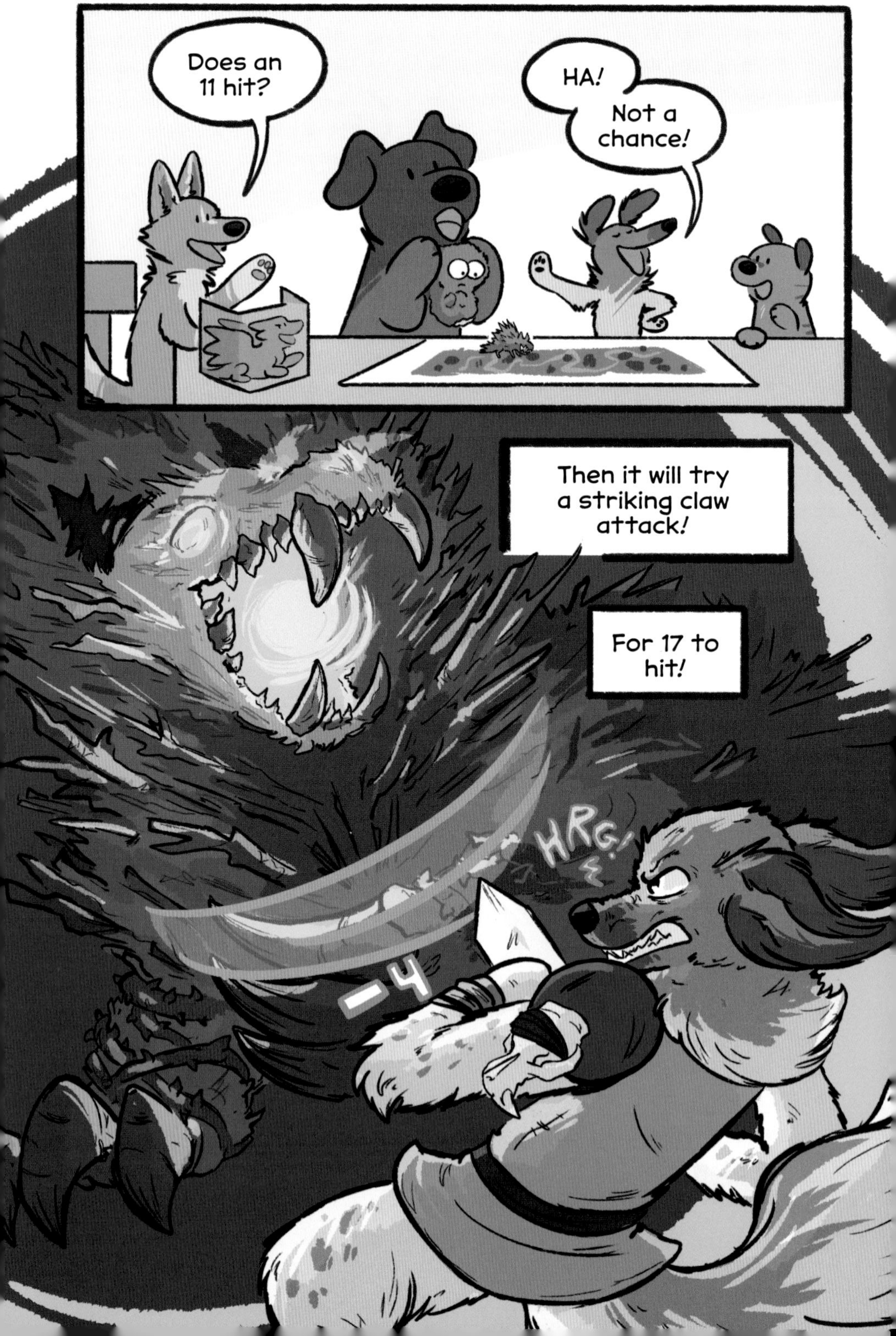

Does an 11 hit?
HA!
Not a chance!
Then it will try a striking claw attack!
For 17 to hit!
HRG!
-4

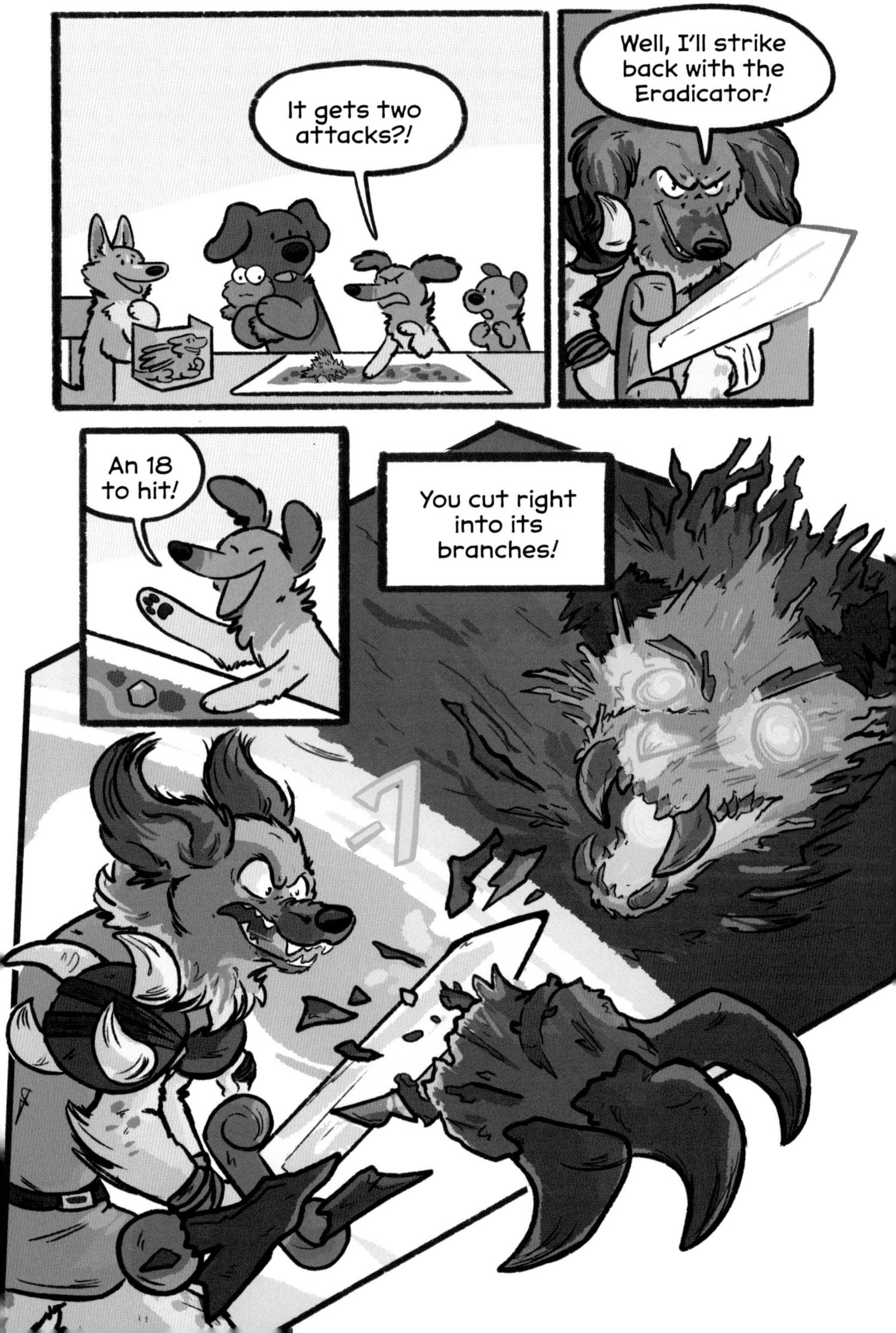
It gets two attacks?!
Well, I'll strike back with the Eradicator!
An 18 to hit!
You cut right into its branches!

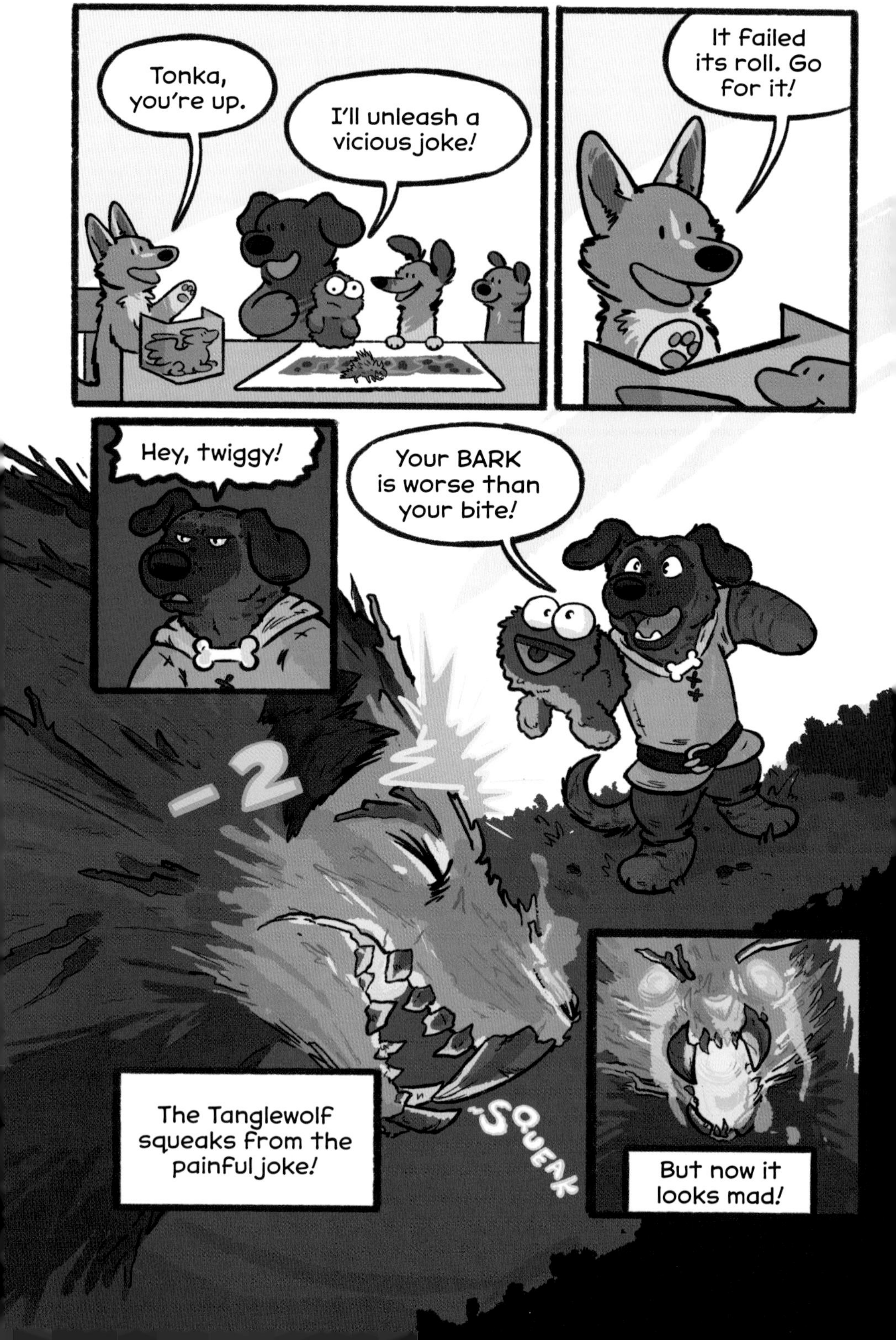
Tonka, you're up.
I'll unleash a vicious joke!
It failed its roll. Go for it!
Hey, twiggy!
Your BARK is worse than your bite!
-2
The Tanglewolf squeaks from the painful joke!
SQUEAK
But now it looks mad!

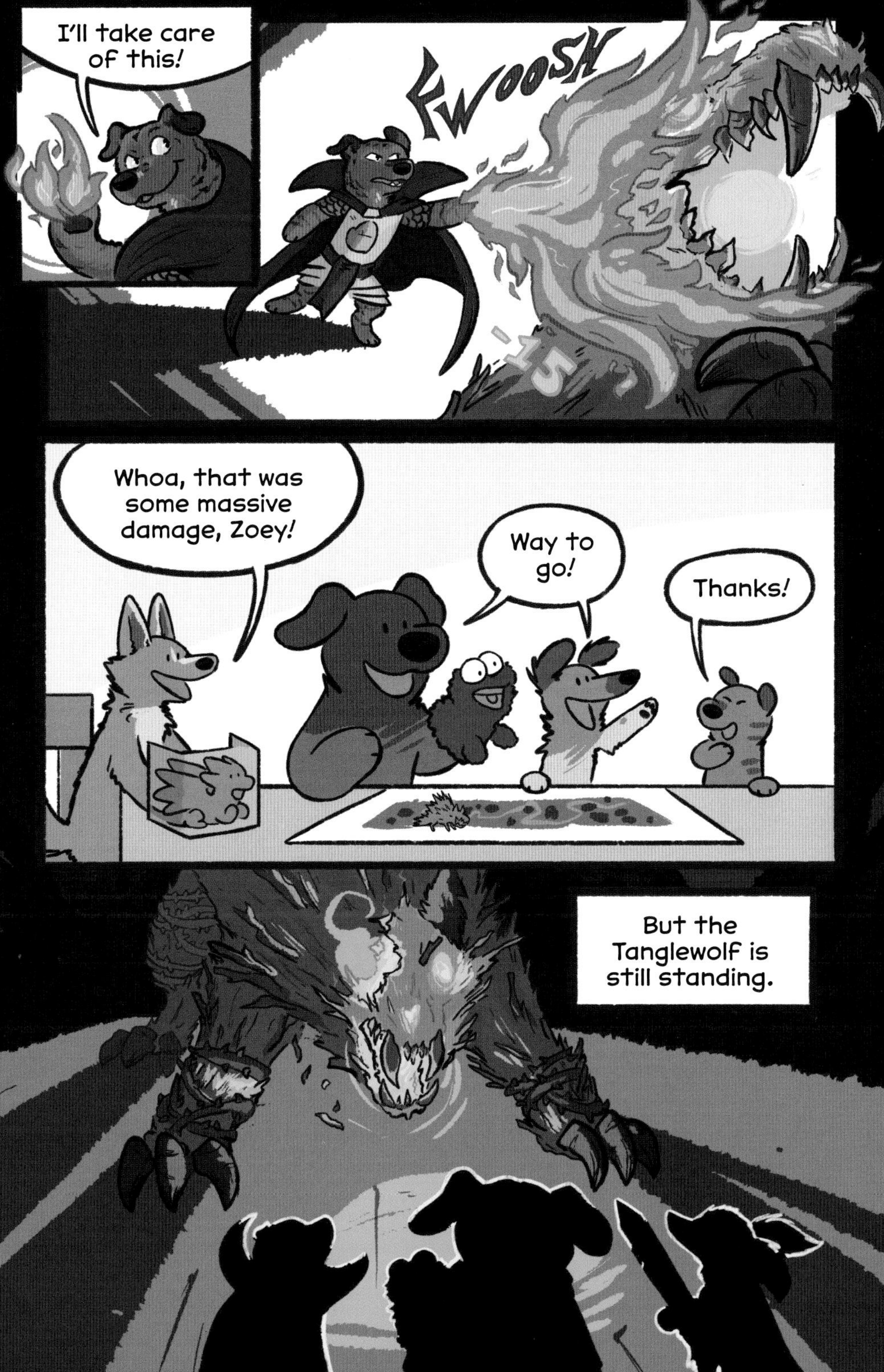

I'll take care of this!
FWOOSH
-15
Whoa, that was some massive damage, Zoey!
Way to go!
Thanks!
But the Tanglewolf is still standing.

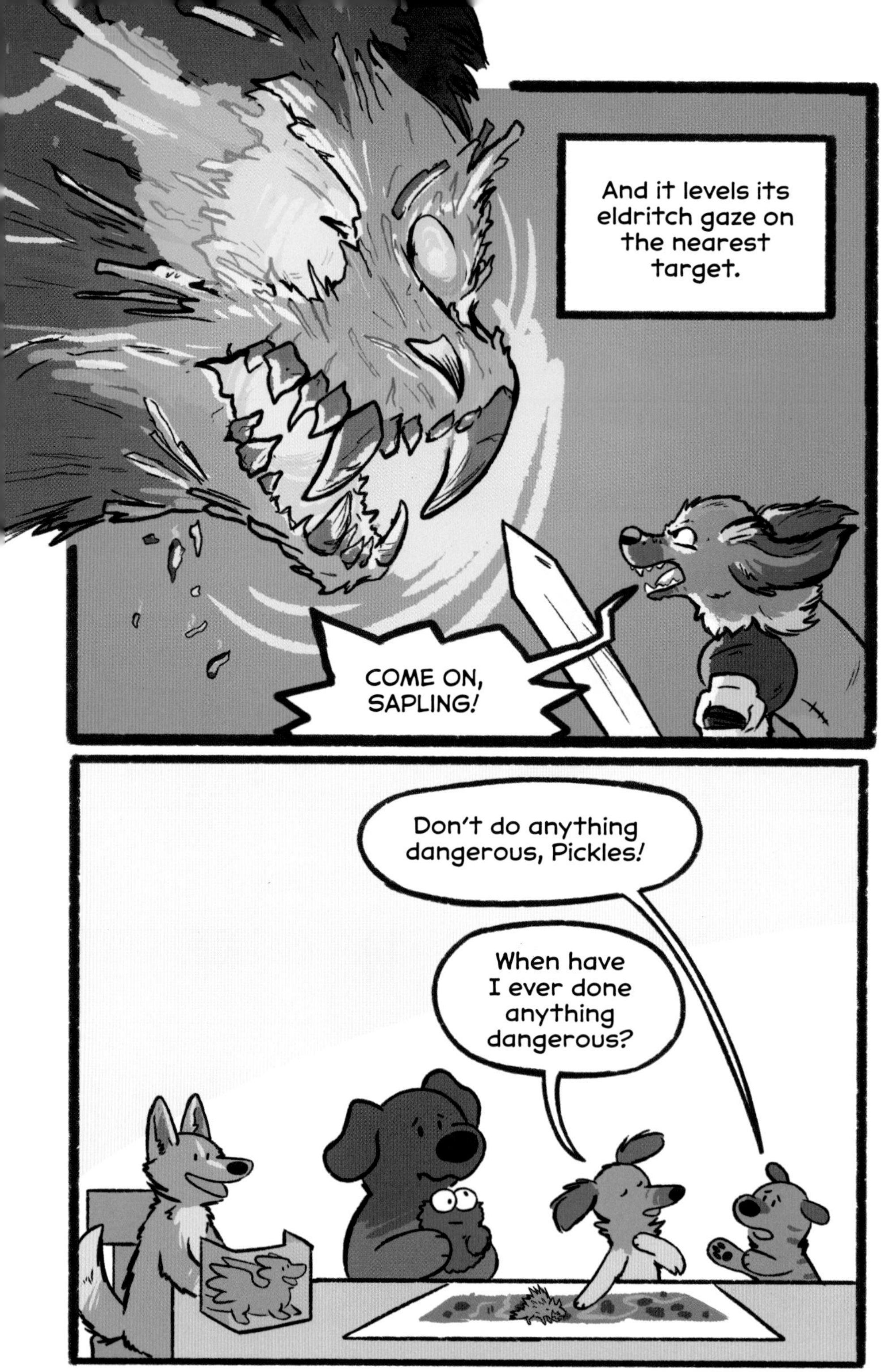
And it levels its eldritch gaze on the nearest target.
COME ON, SAPLING!
Don't do anything dangerous, Pickles!
When have I ever done anything dangerous?

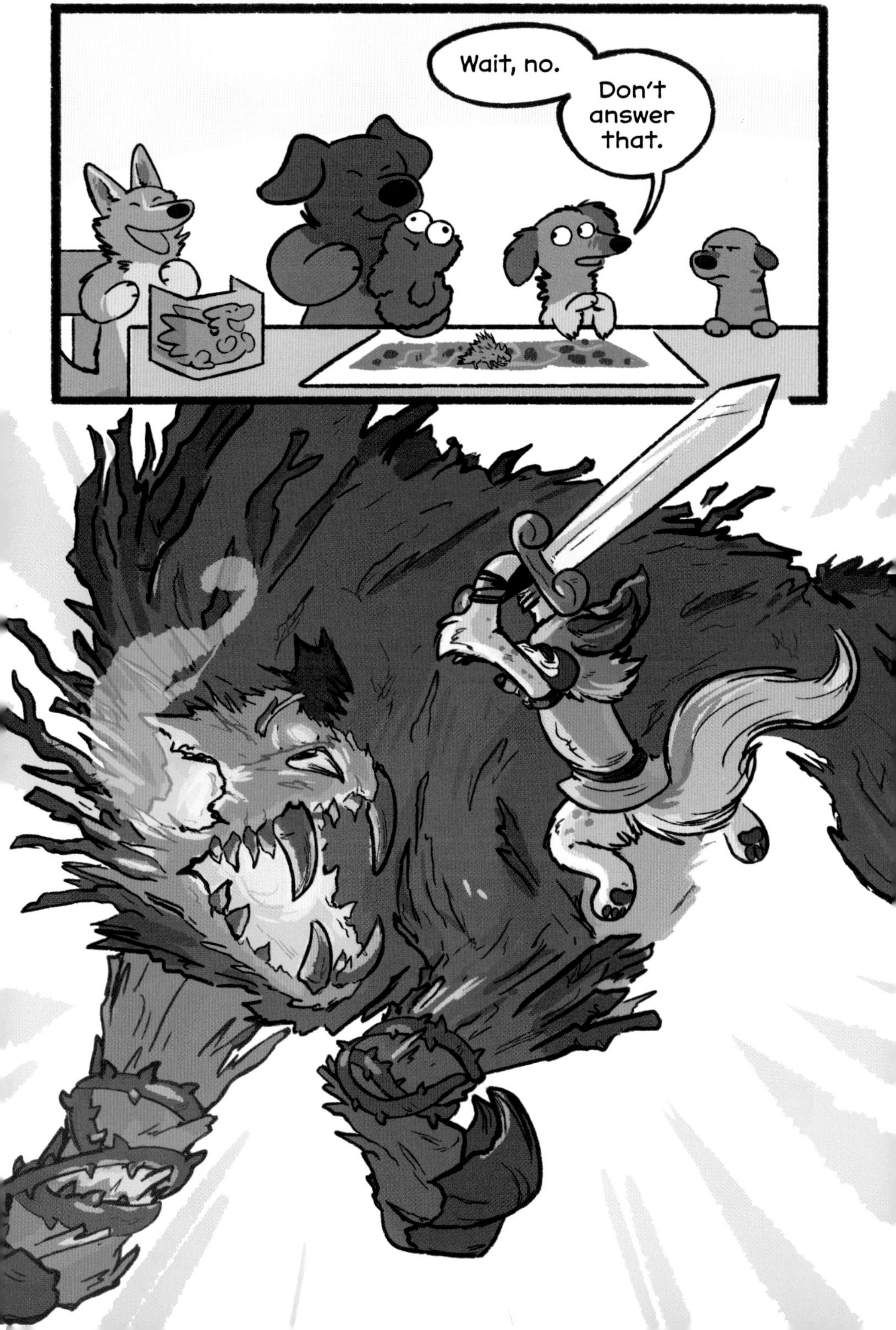
Wait, no.
Don't answer that.

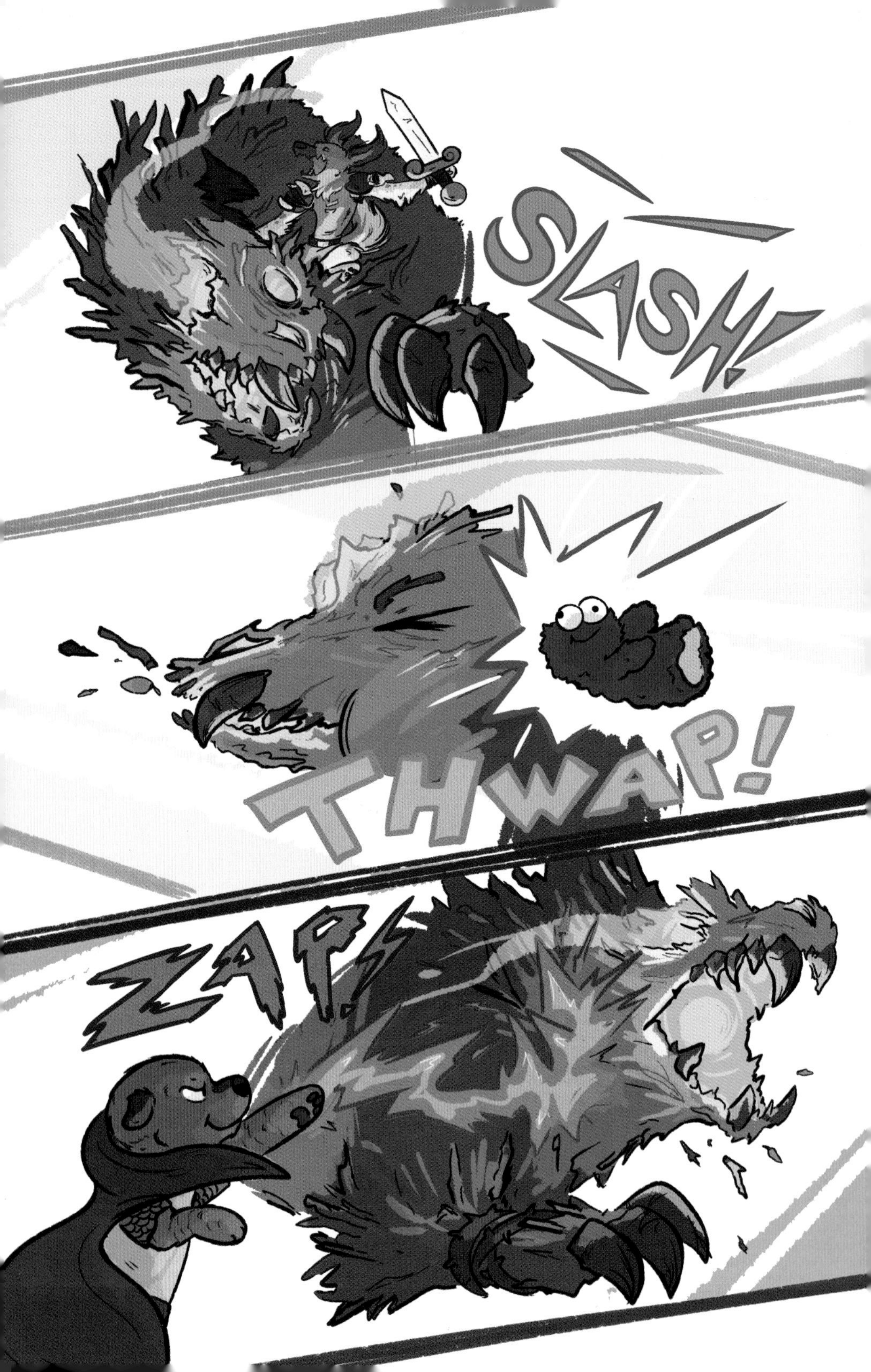
SLASH!
THWAP!
ZAP!

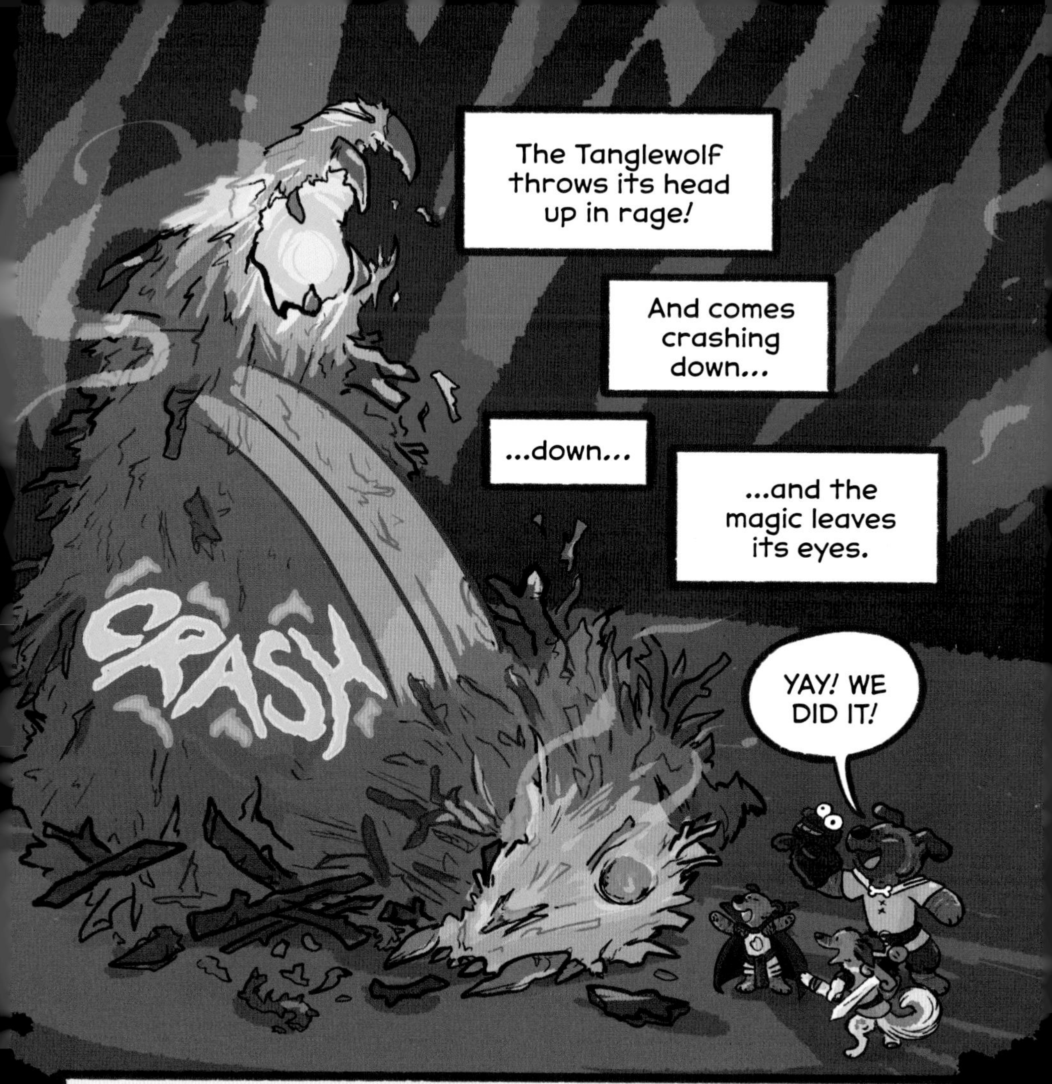
The Tanglewolf throws its head up in rage!
And comes crashing down...
...down...
...and the magic leaves its eyes.
CRASH
YAY! WE DID IT!

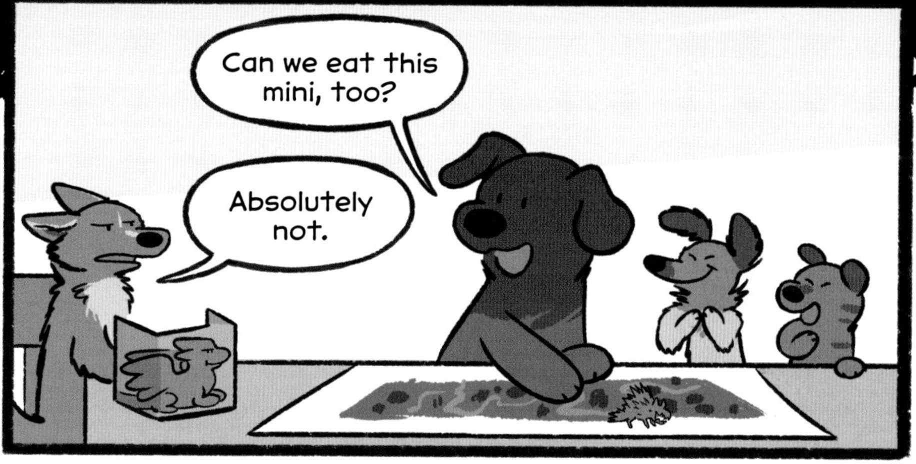
Can we eat this mini, too?
Absolutely not.

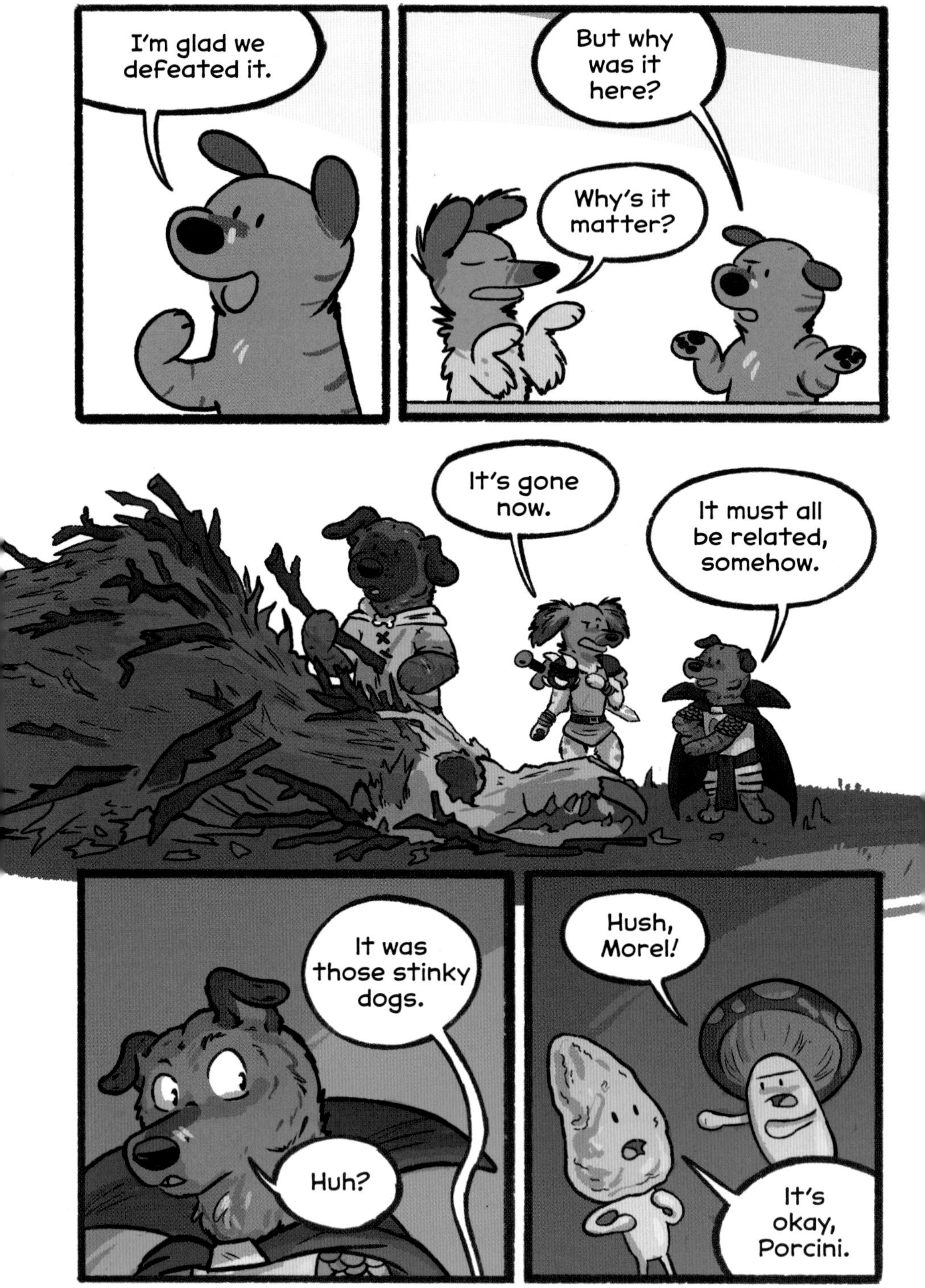

I'm glad we defeated it.
But why was it here?
Why's it matter?
It's gone now.
It must all be related, somehow.
It was those stinky dogs.
Huh?
Hush, Morel!
It's okay, Porcini.

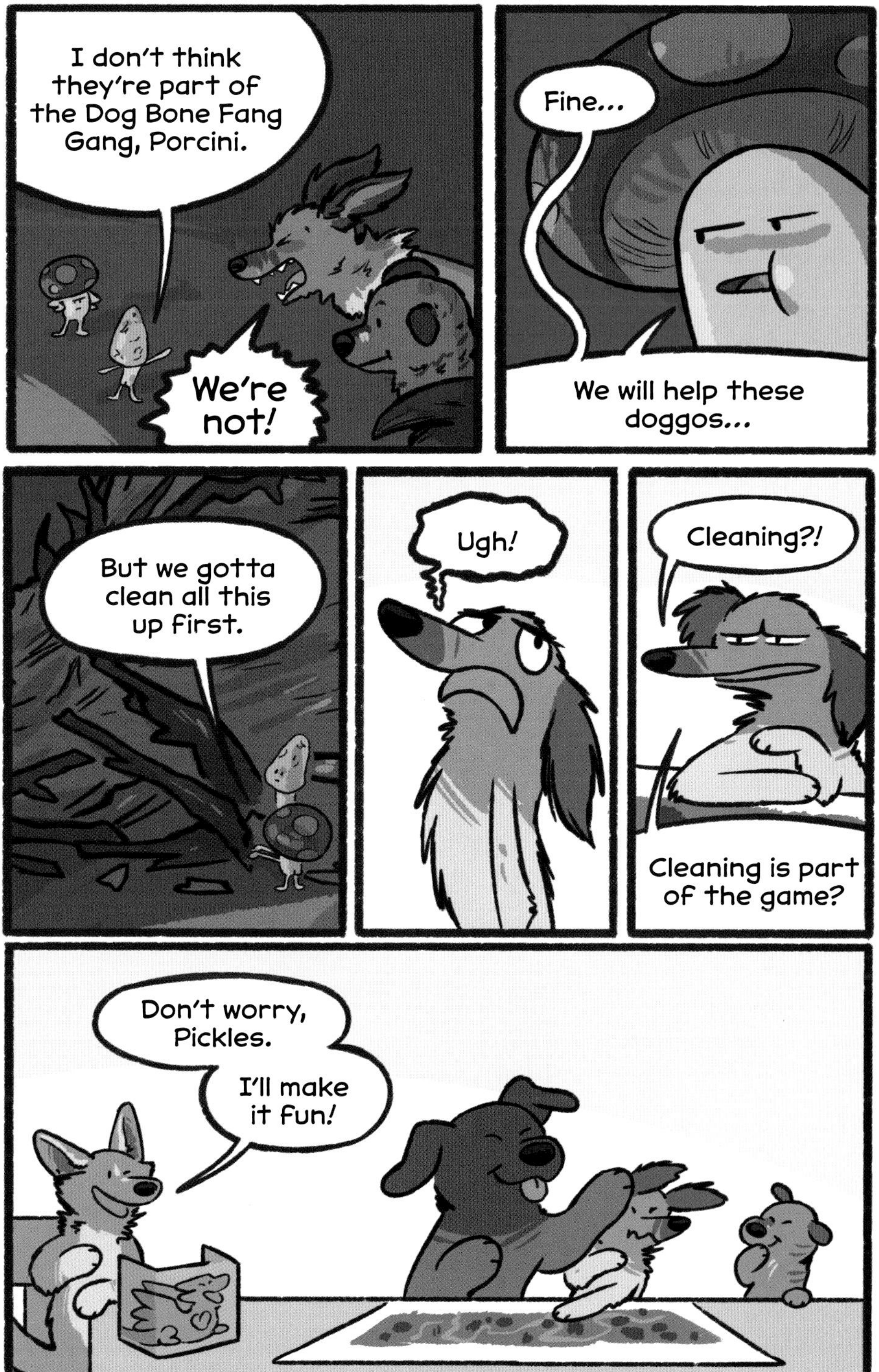
I don't think they're part of the Dog Bone Fang Gang, Porcini.
We're not!
Fine...
We will help these doggos...
But we gotta clean all this up first.
Ugh!
Cleaning?!
Cleaning is part of the game?
Don't worry, Pickles.
I'll make it fun!

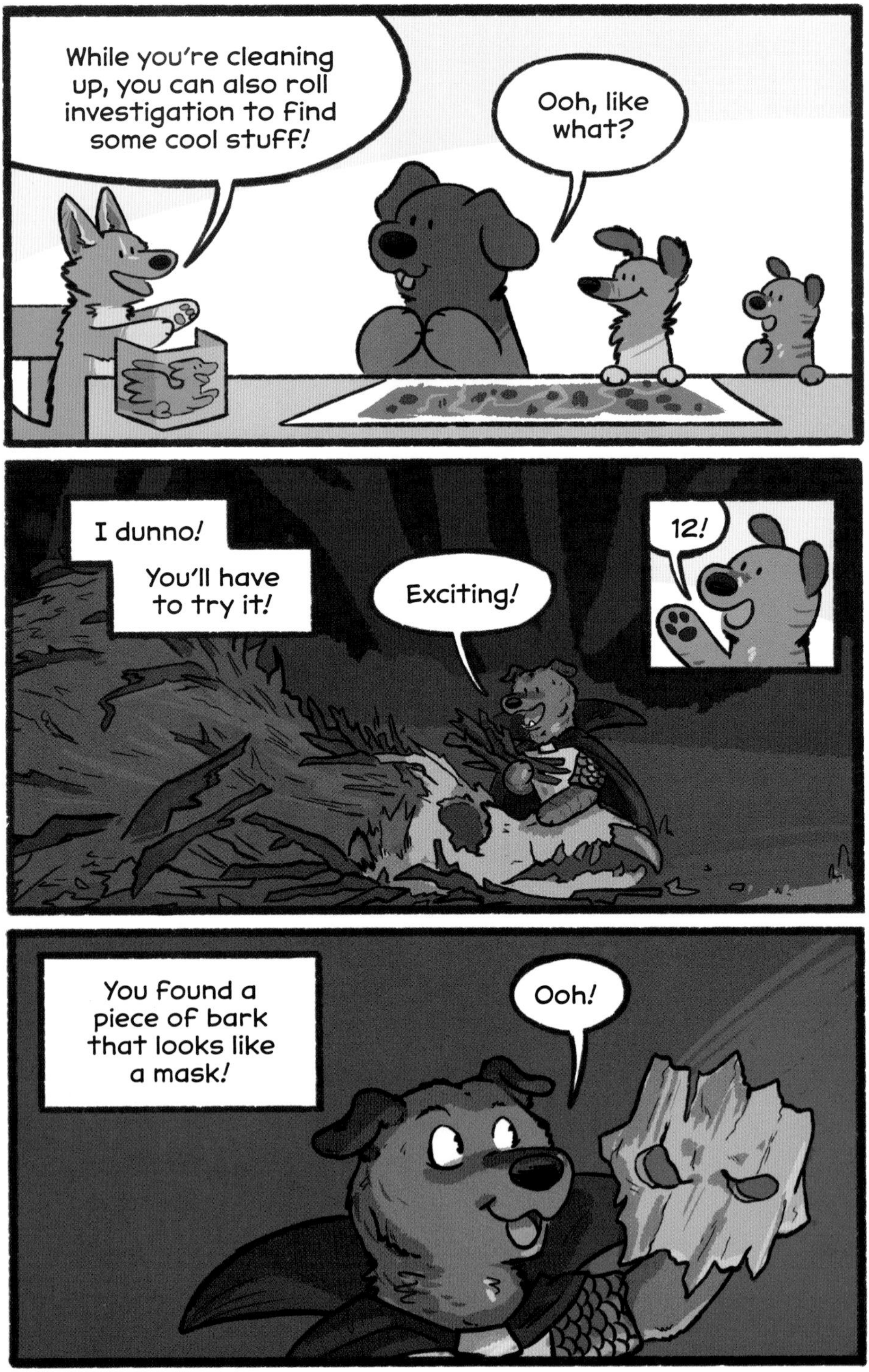
While you're cleaning up, you can also roll investigation to find some cool stuff!
Ooh, like what?
I dunno!
You'll have to try it!
Exciting!
12!
You found a piece of bark that looks like a mask!
Ooh!

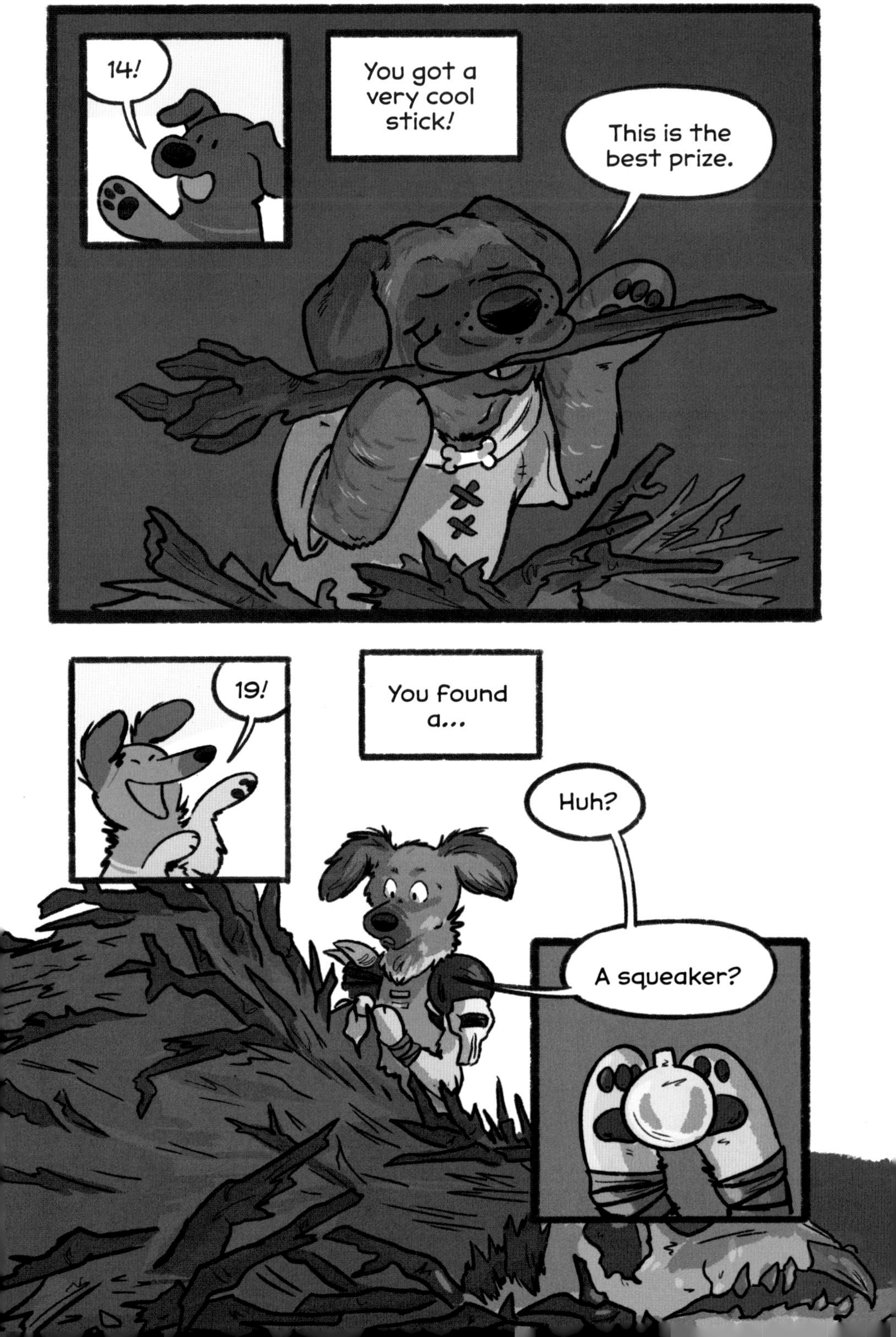
14!
You got a very cool stick!
This is the best prize.
19!
You found a...
Huh?
A squeaker?

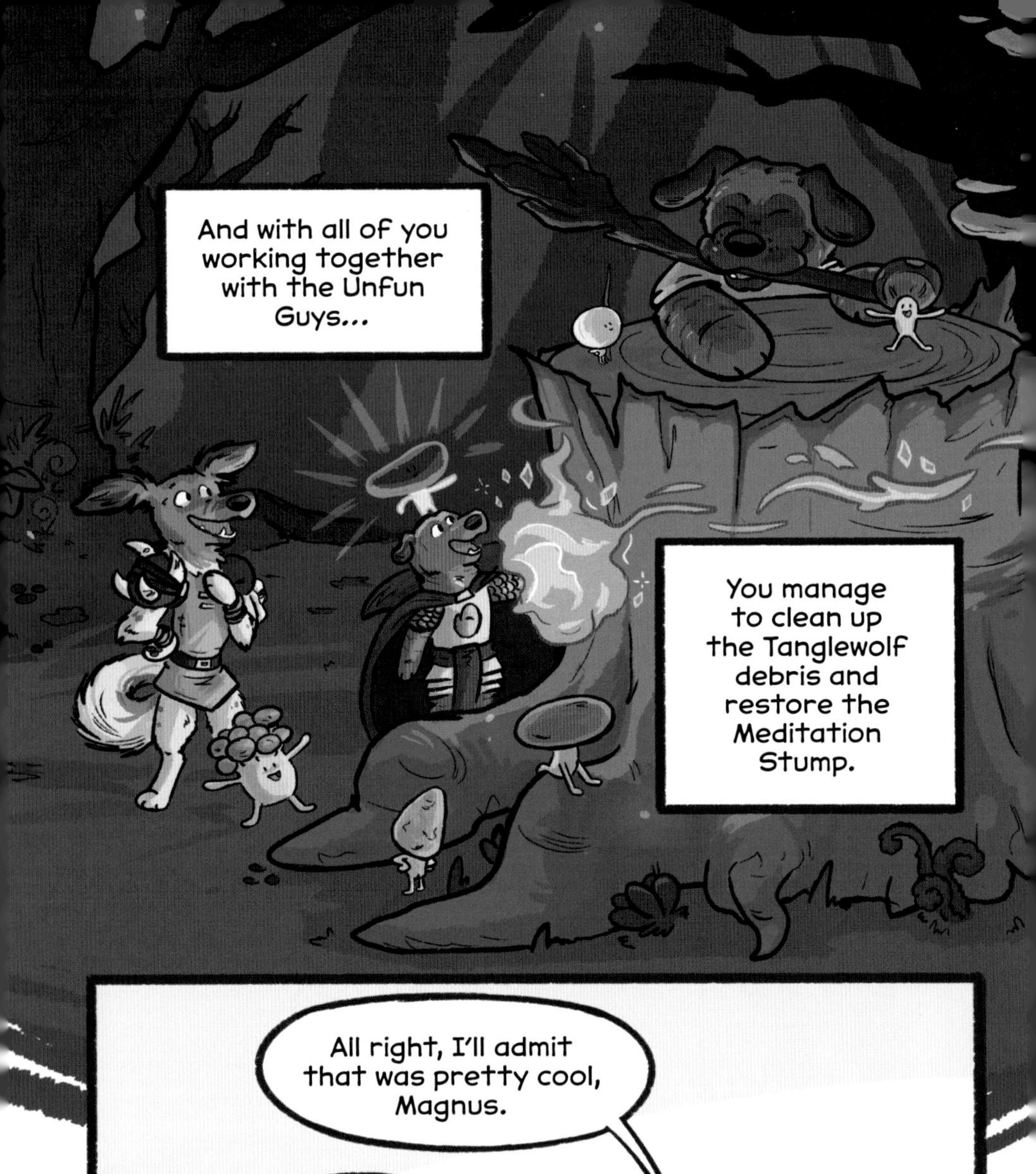
And with all of you working together with the Unfun Guys...
You manage to clean up the Tanglewolf debris and restore the Meditation Stump.

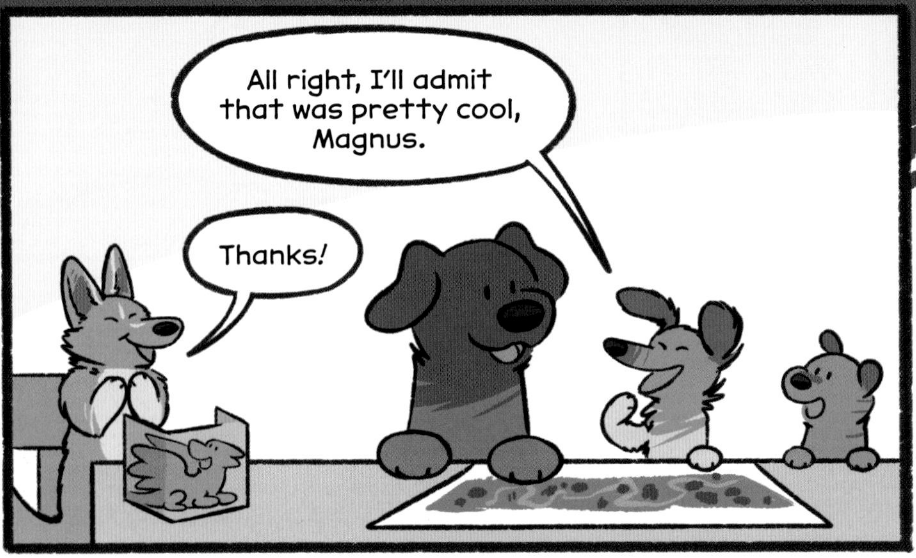
All right, I'll admit that was pretty cool, Magnus.
Thanks!

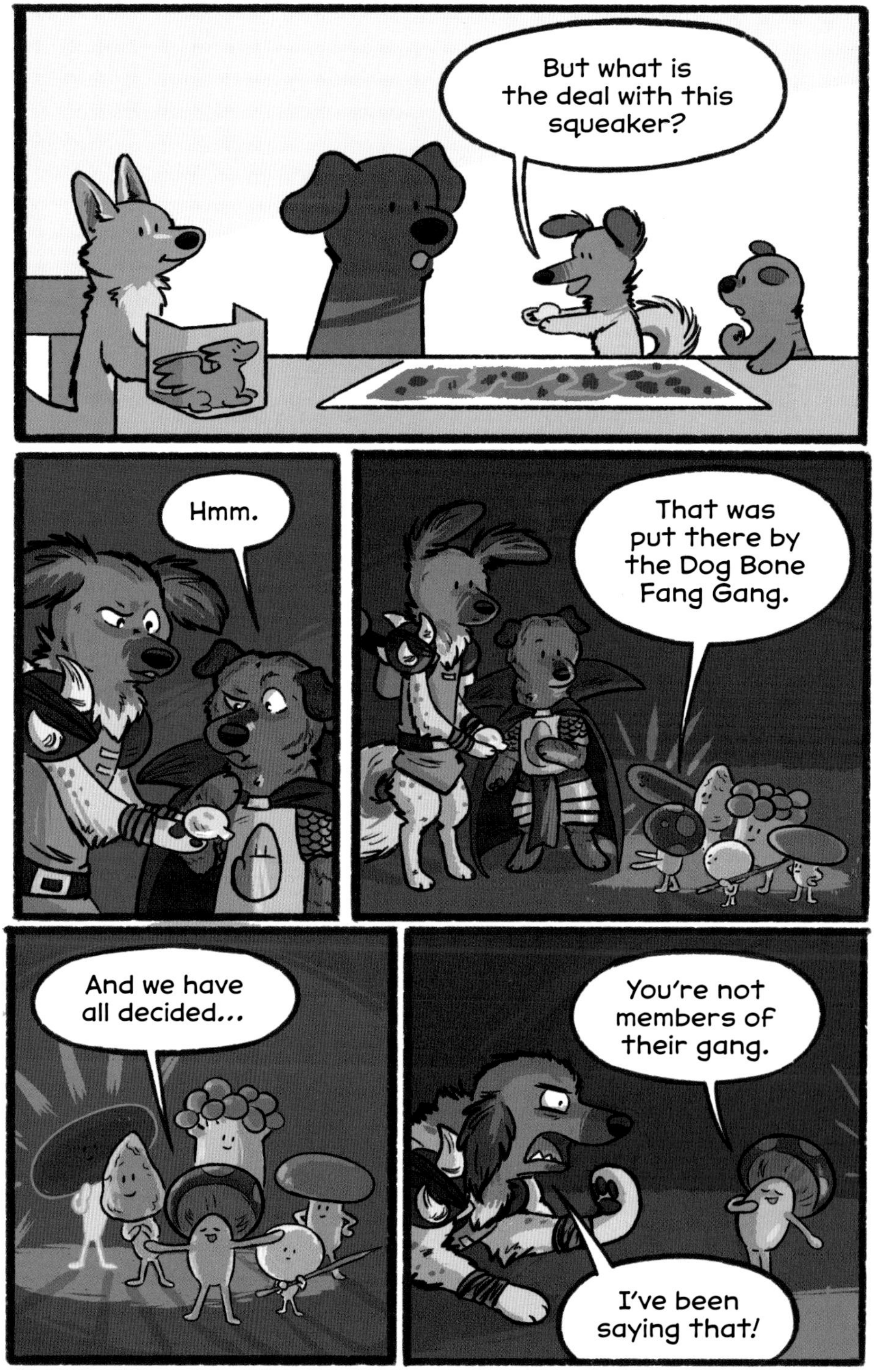
But what is the deal with this squeaker?
Hmm.
That was put there by the Dog Bone Fang Gang.
And we have all decided...
You're not members of their gang.
I've been saying that!

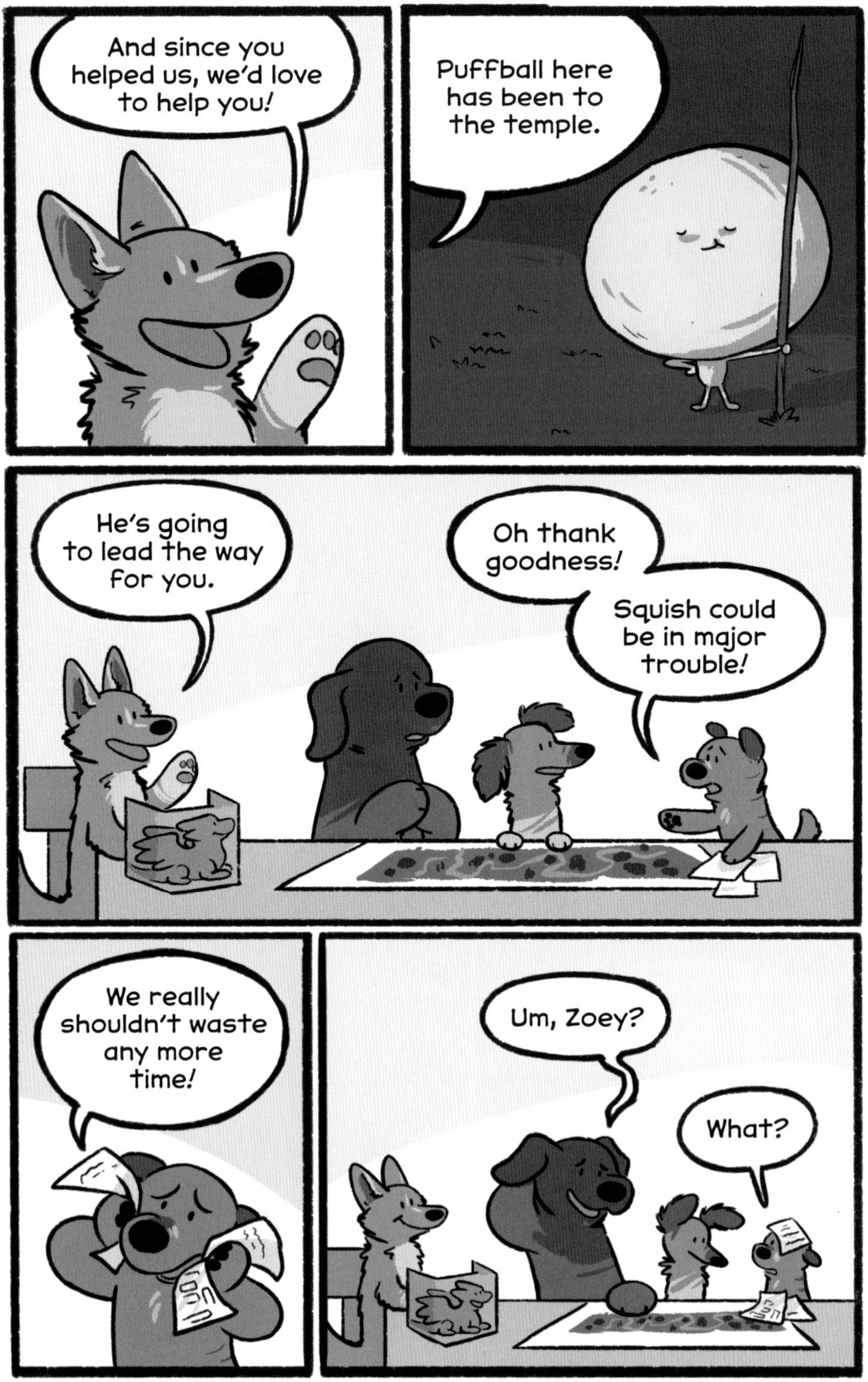
And since you helped us, we'd love to help you!
Puffball here has been to the temple.
He's going to lead the way for you.
Oh thank goodness!
Squish could be in major trouble!
We really shouldn't waste any more time!
Um, Zoey?
What?

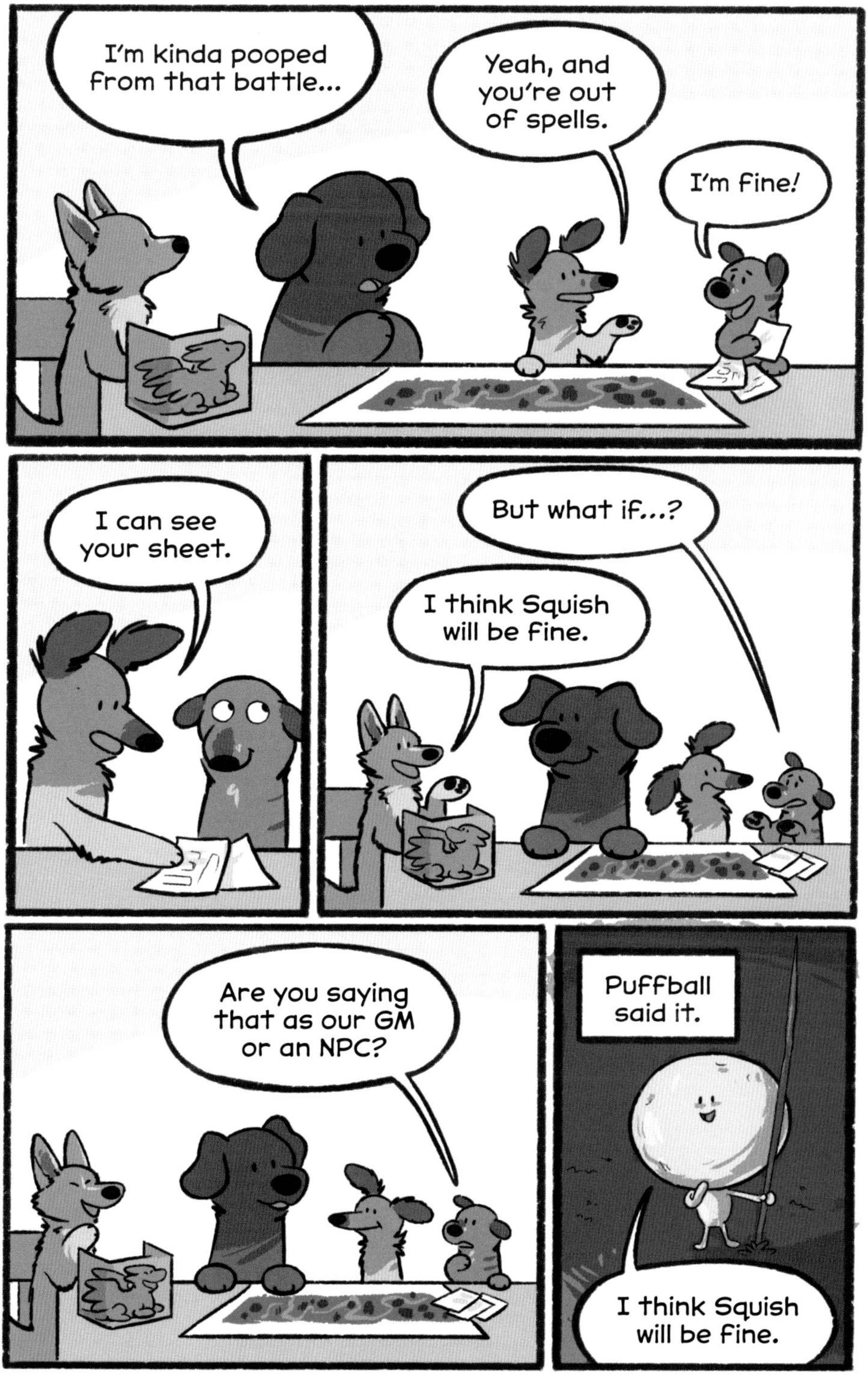
I'm kinda pooped from that battle...
Yeah, and you're out of spells.
I'm fine!
I can see your sheet.
But what if...?
I think Squish will be fine.
Are you saying that as our GM or an NPC?
Puffball said it.
I think Squish will be fine.

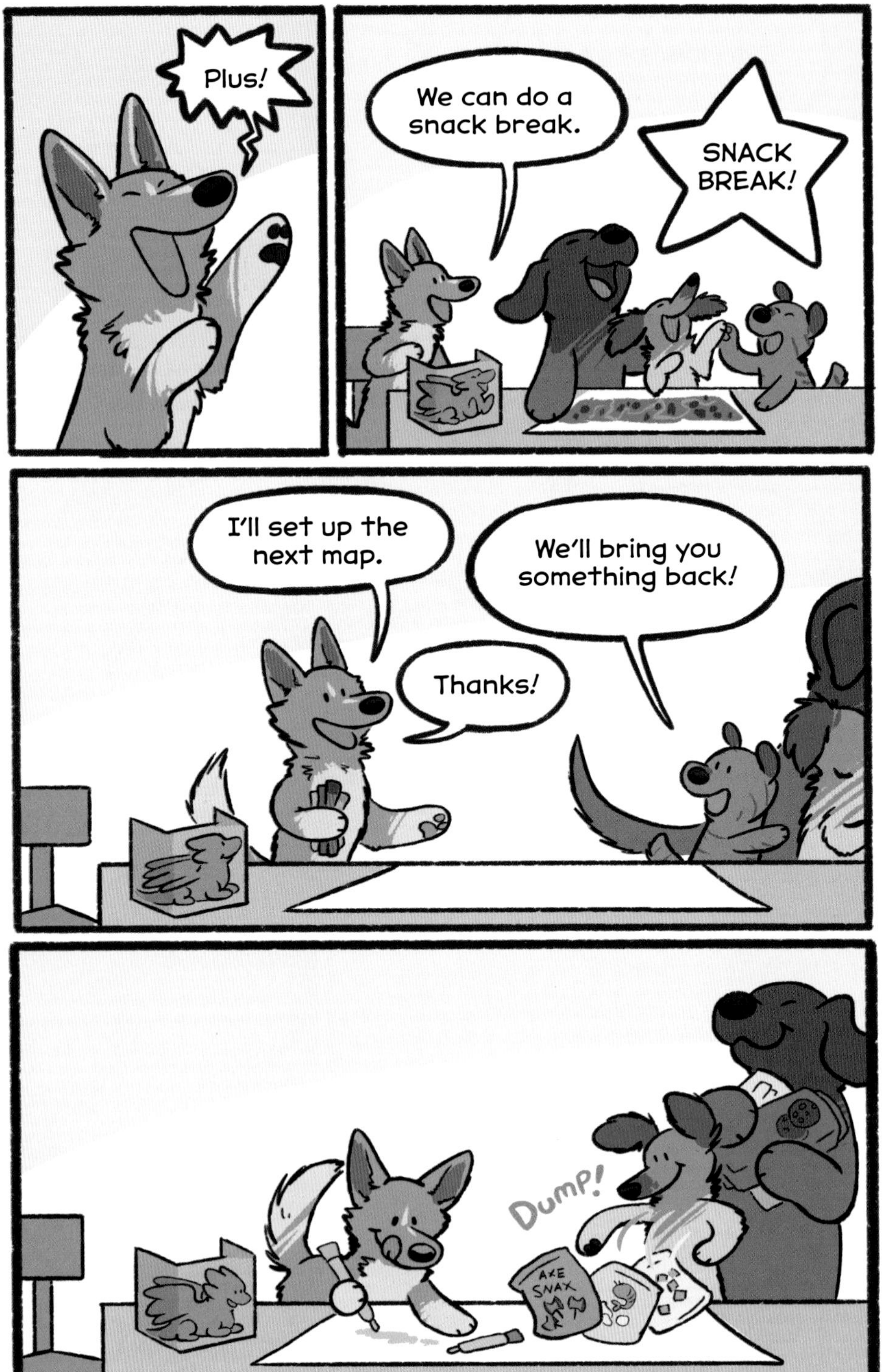
Plus!
We can do a snack break.
SNACK BREAK!
I'll set up the next map.
We'll bring you something back!
Thanks!
Dump!
AXE SNAX

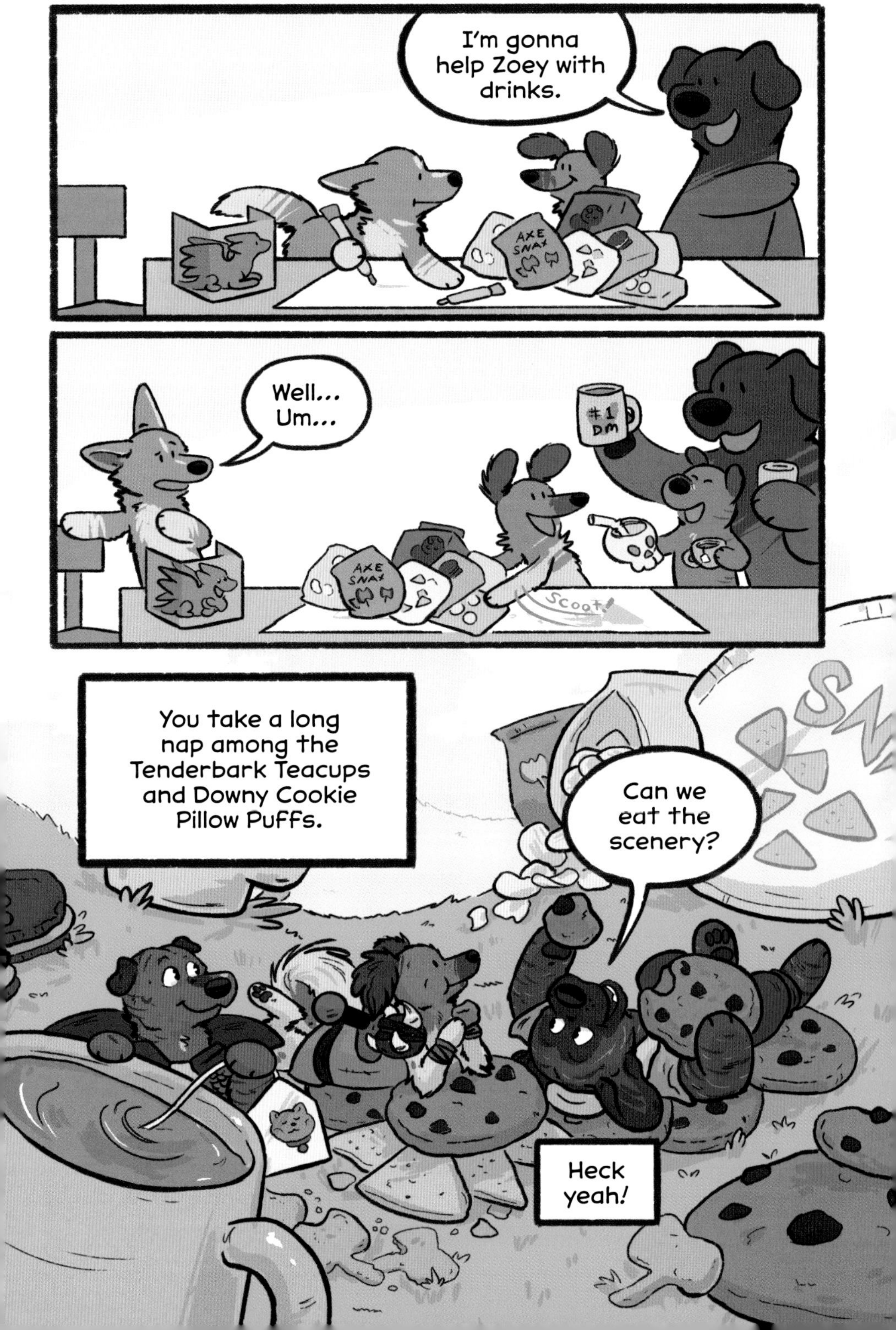
I'm gonna help Zoey with drinks.
AXE SNAX
Well... Um...
#1 DM
AXE SNAX
Scoot!
You take a long nap among the Tenderbark Teacups and Downy Cookie Pillow Puffs.
Can we eat the scenery?
Heck yeah!

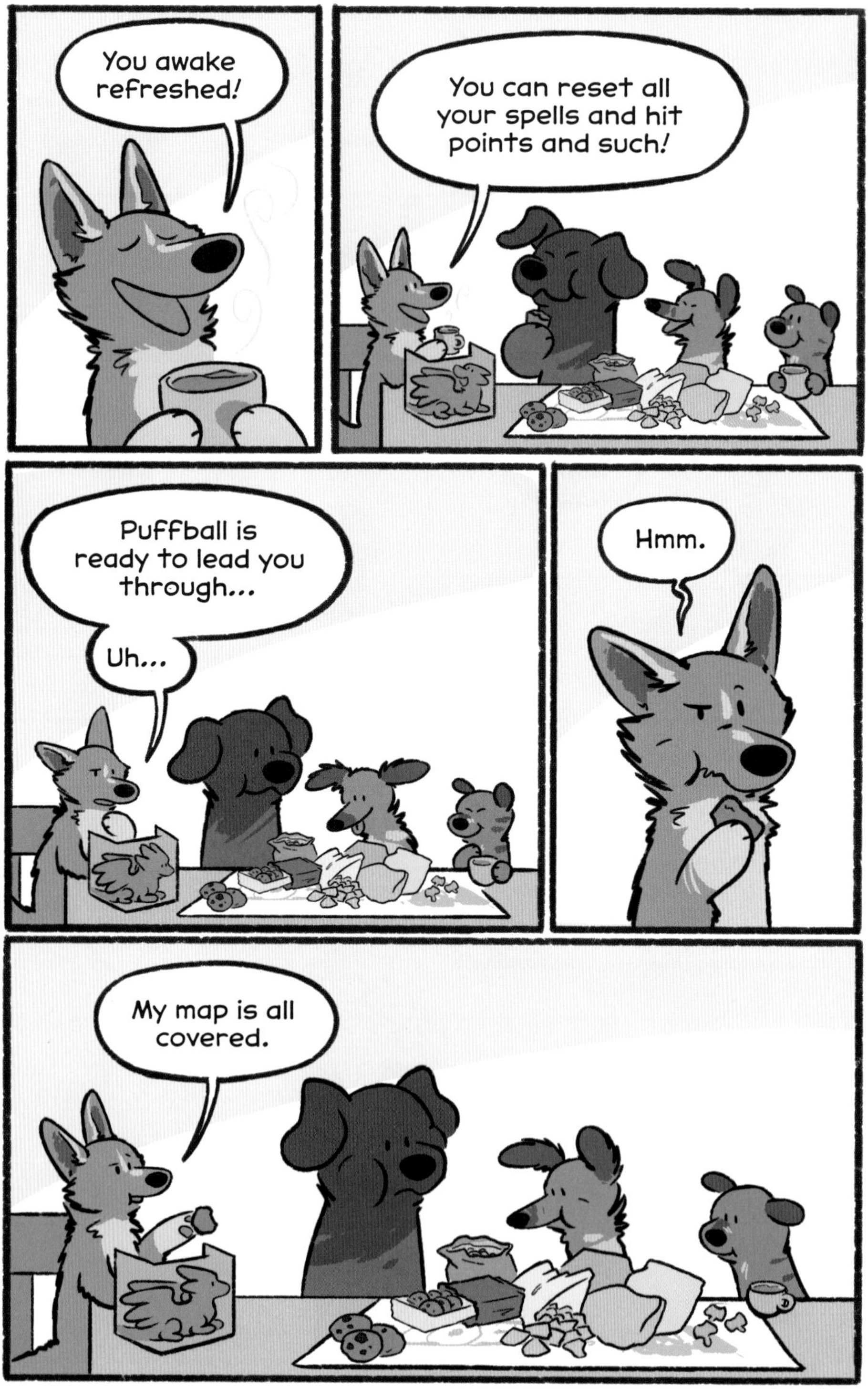
You awake refreshed!
You can reset all your spells and hit points and such!
Puffball is ready to lead you through...
Uh...
Hmm.
My map is all covered.

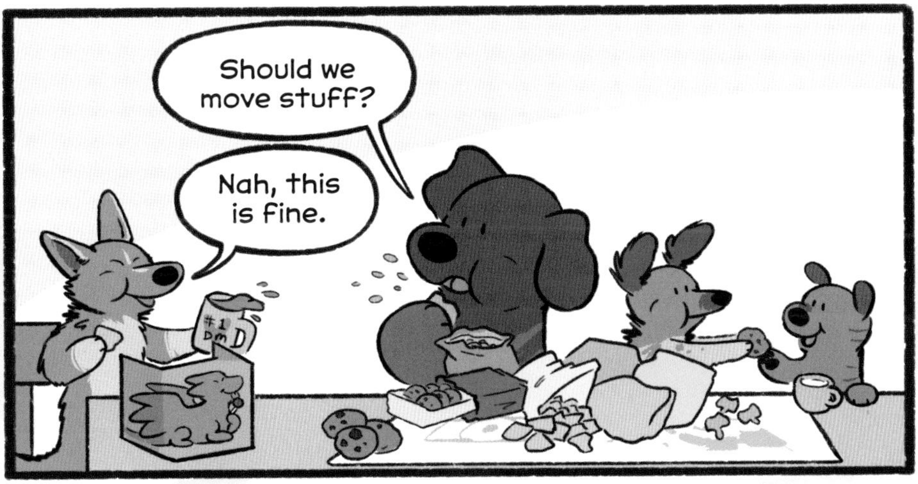
Should we move stuff?
Nah, this is fine.
#1 DM

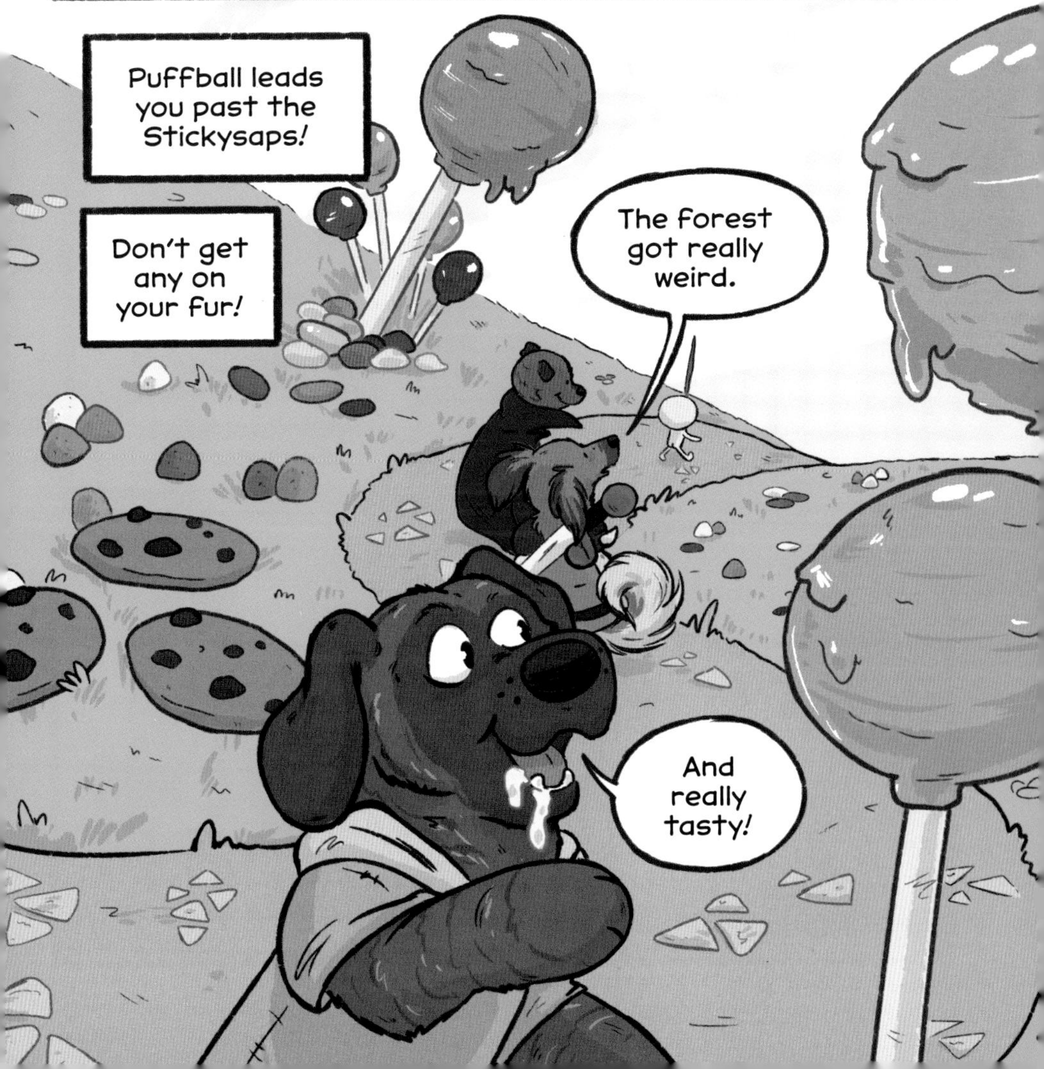
Puffball leads you past the Stickysaps!
Don't get any on your fur!
The forest got really weird.
And really tasty!

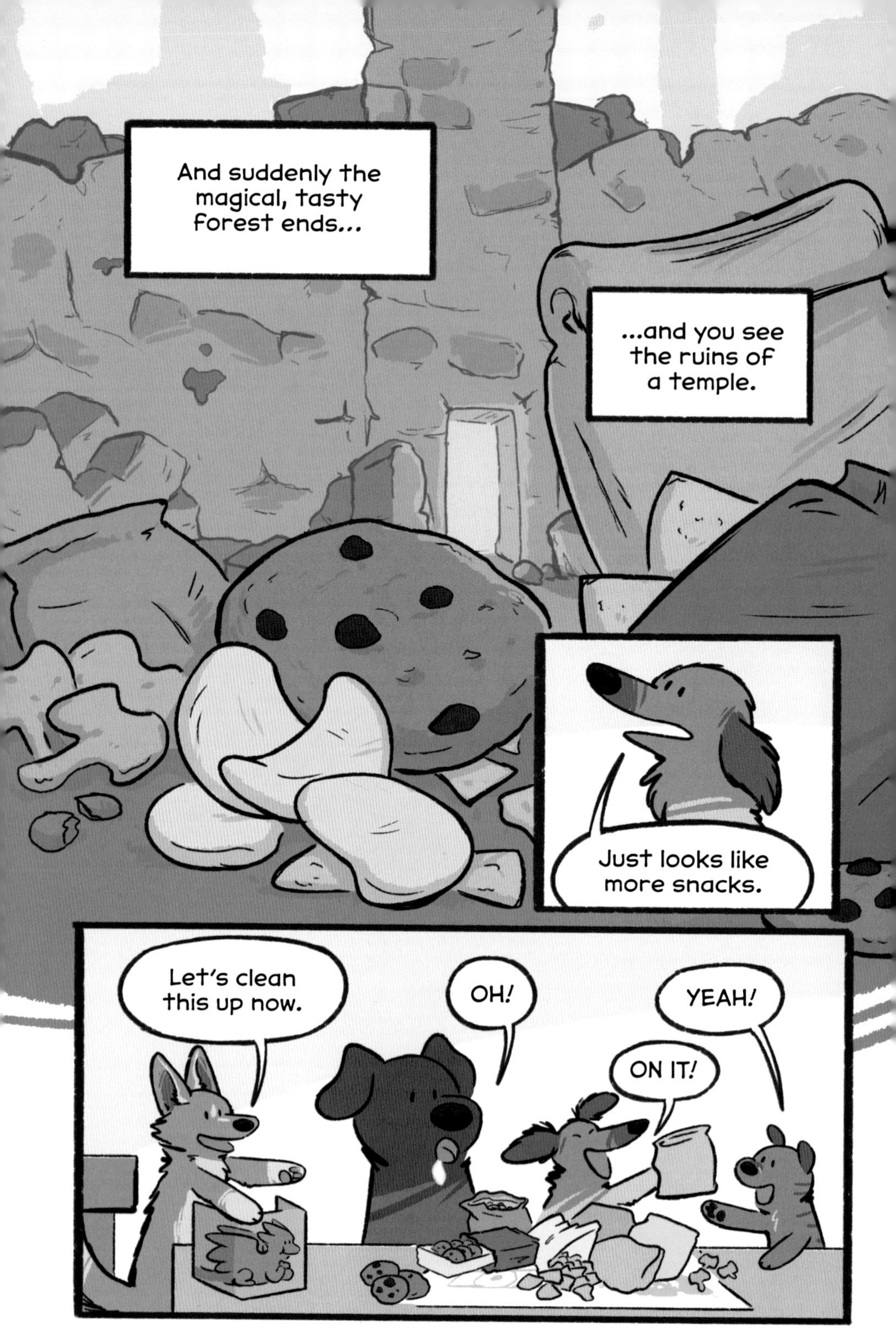

And suddenly the magical, tasty forest ends...
...and you see the ruins of a temple.
Just looks like more snacks.
Let's clean this up now.
OH!
YEAH!
ON IT!

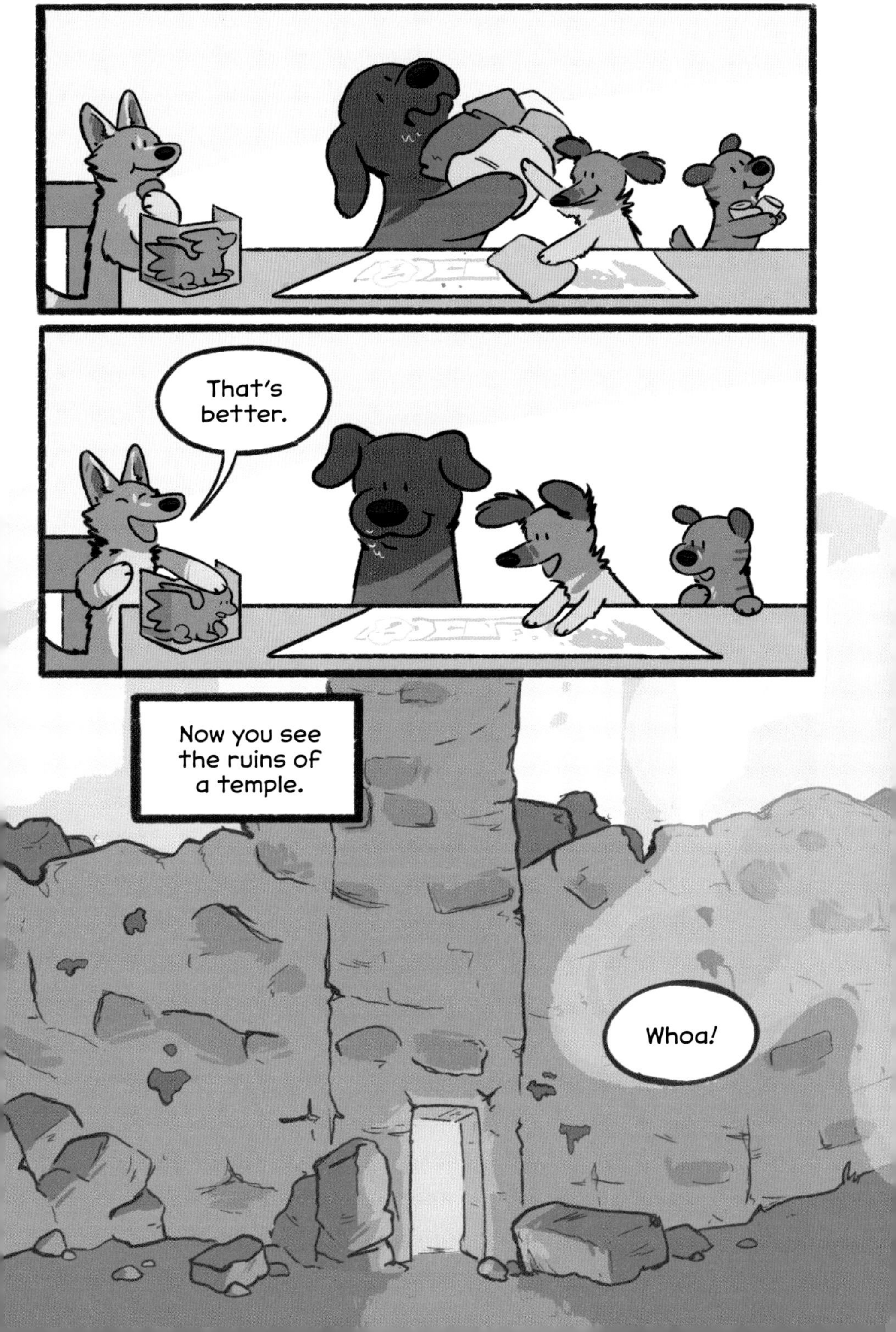
That's better.
Now you see the ruins of a temple.
Whoa!

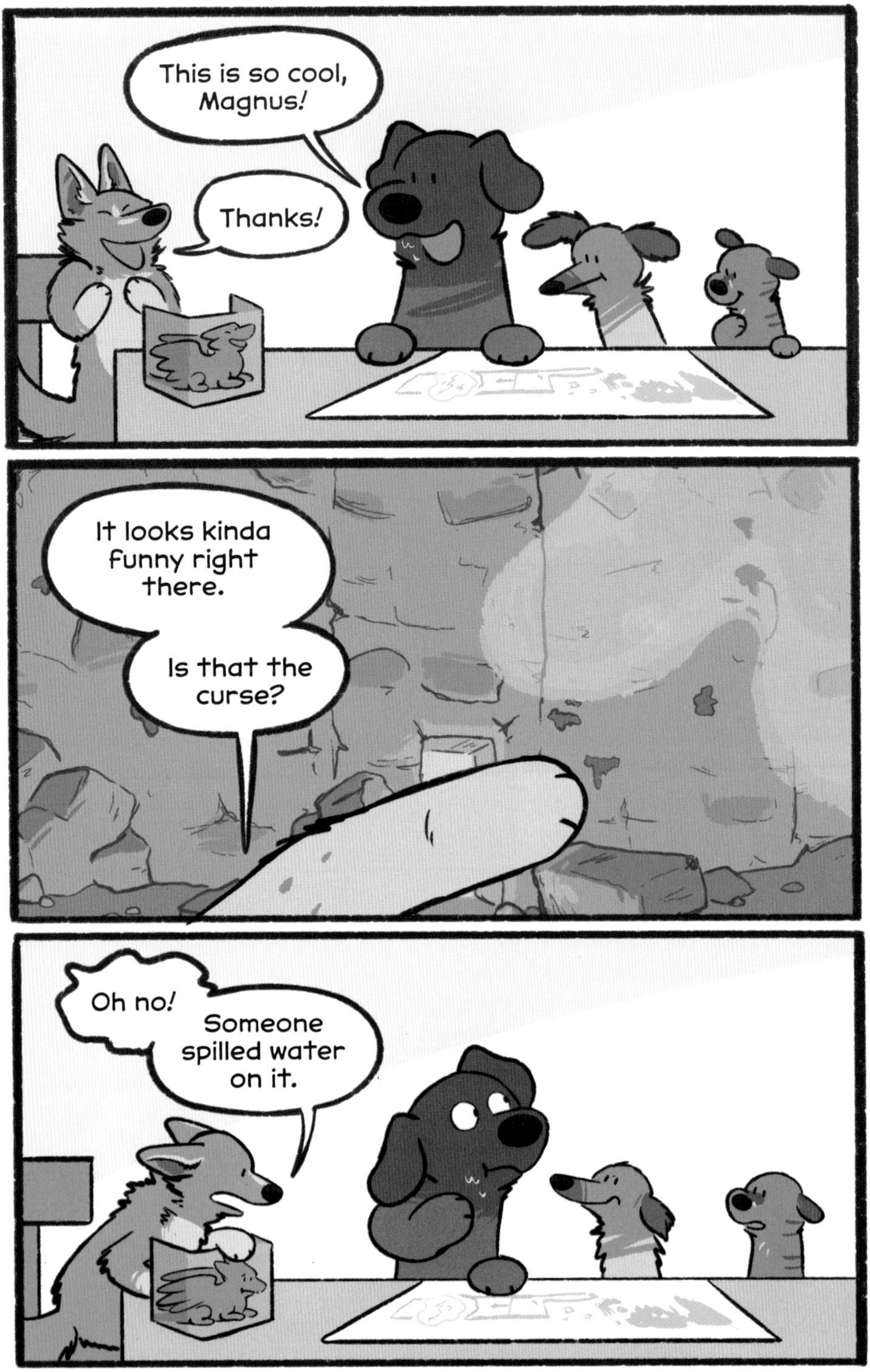
This is so cool, Magnus!
Thanks!
It looks kinda funny right there.
Is that the curse?
Oh no!
Someone spilled water on it.

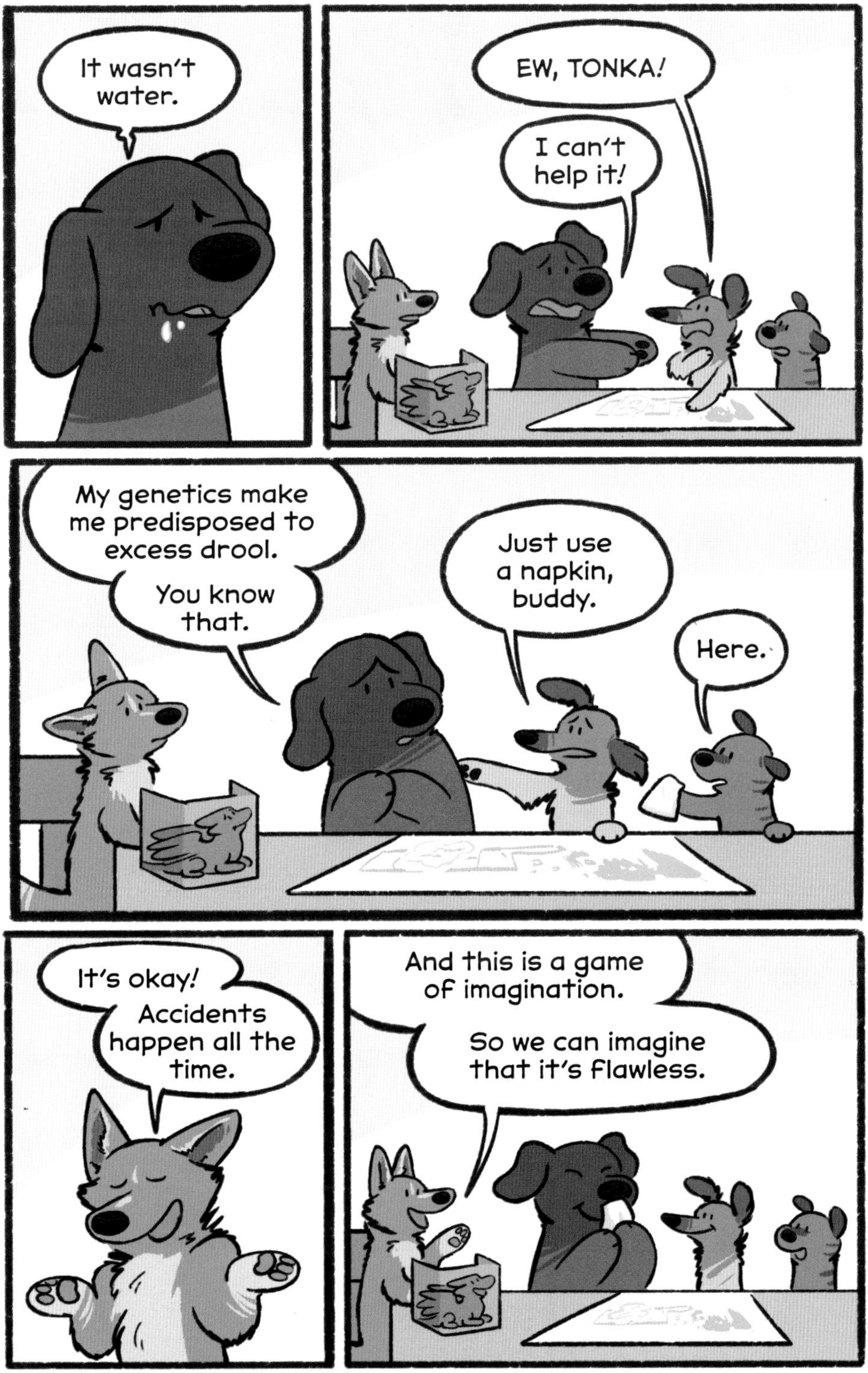

It wasn't water.
EW, TONKA!
I can't help it!
My genetics make me predisposed to excess drool.
You know that.
Just use a napkin, buddy.
Here.
It's okay!
Accidents happen all the time.
And this is a game of imagination.
So we can imagine that it's flawless.

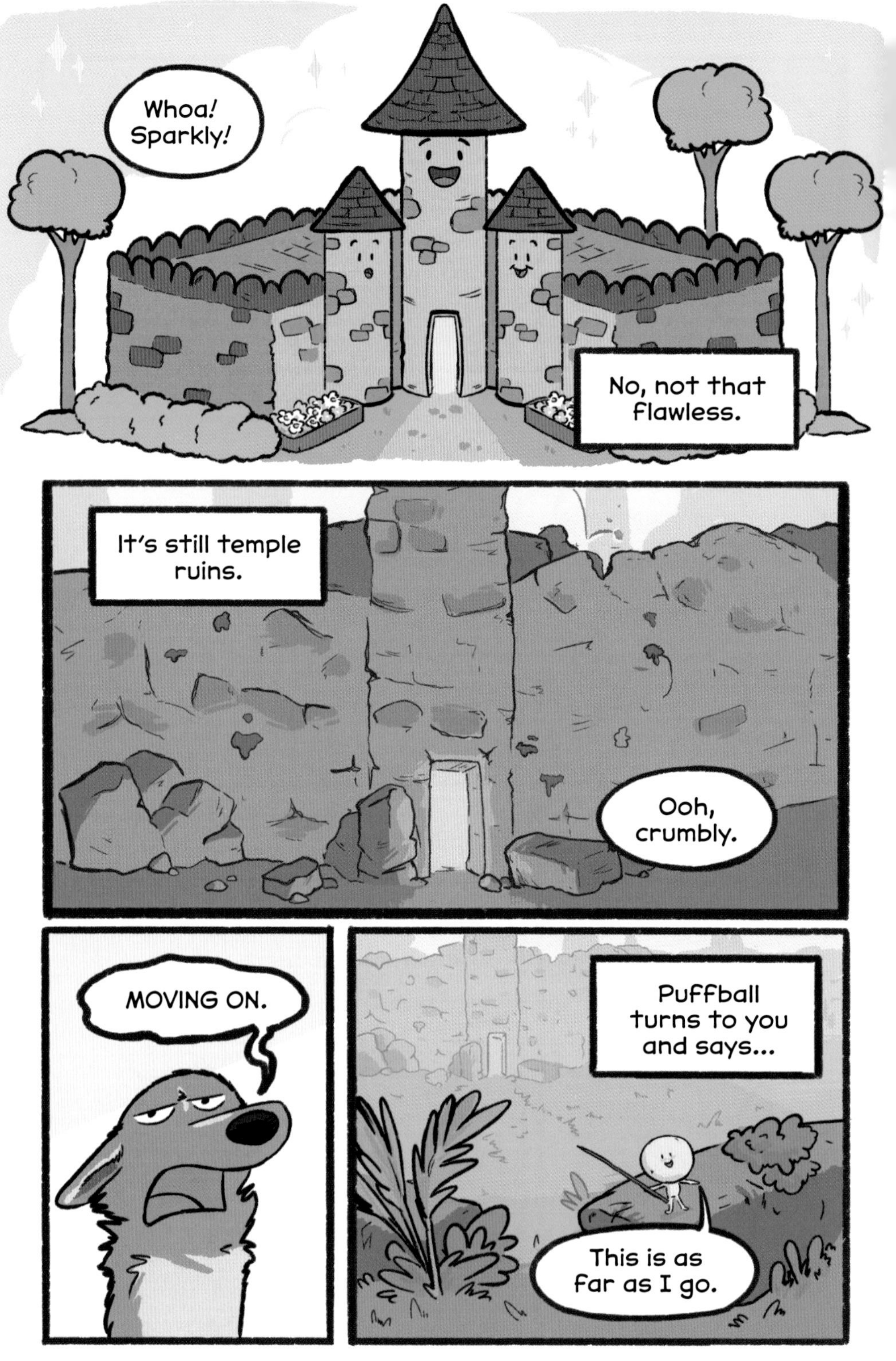
Whoa! Sparkly!
No, not that flawless.
It's still temple ruins.
Ooh, crumbly.
MOVING ON.
Puffball turns to you and says...
This is as far as I go.

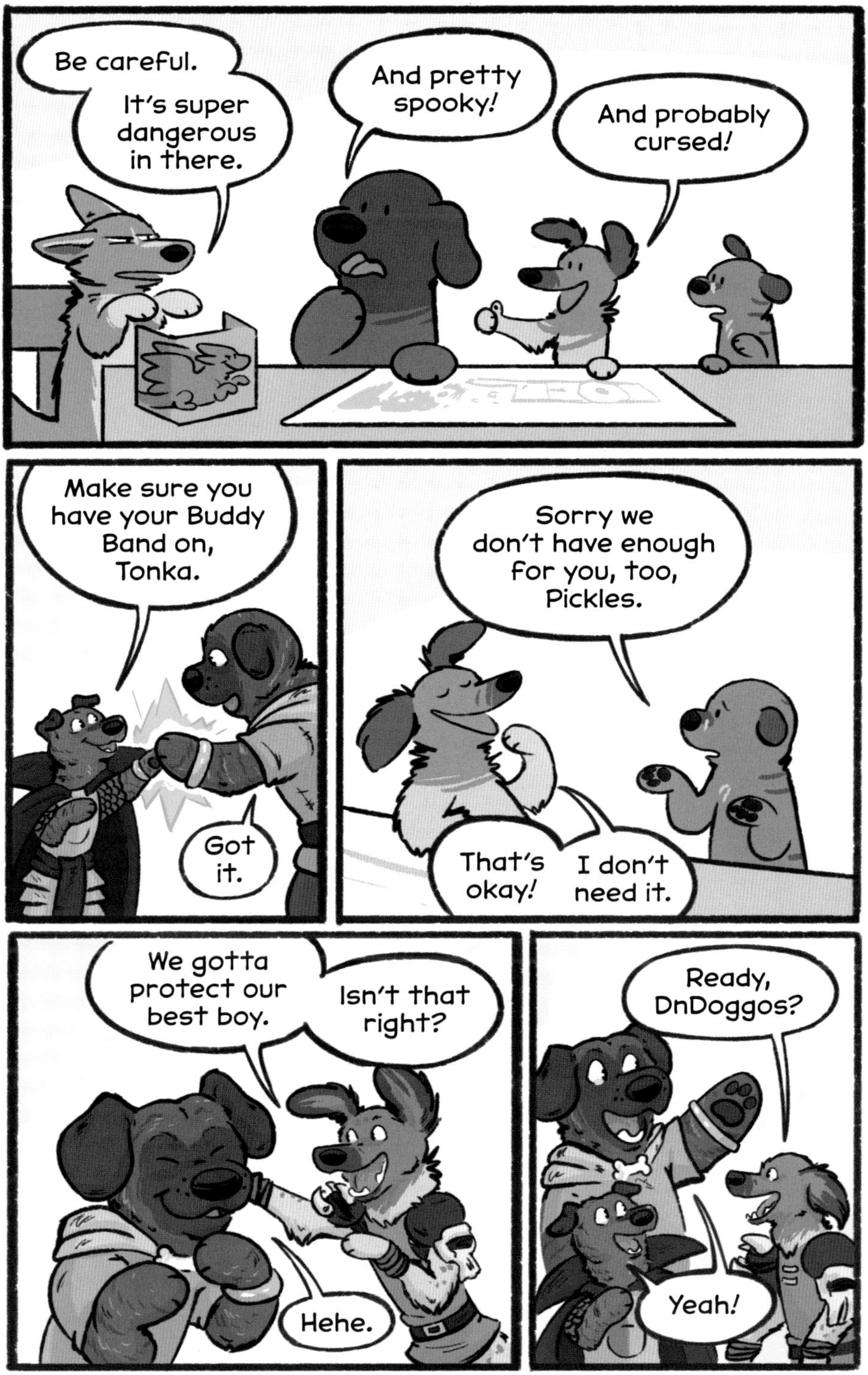
Be careful.
It's super dangerous in there.
And pretty spooky!
And probably cursed!
Make sure you have your Buddy Band on, Tonka.
Got it.
Sorry we don't have enough for you, too, Pickles.
That's okay!
I don't need it.
We gotta protect our best boy.
Isn't that right?
Hehe.
Ready, DnDoggos?
Yeah!

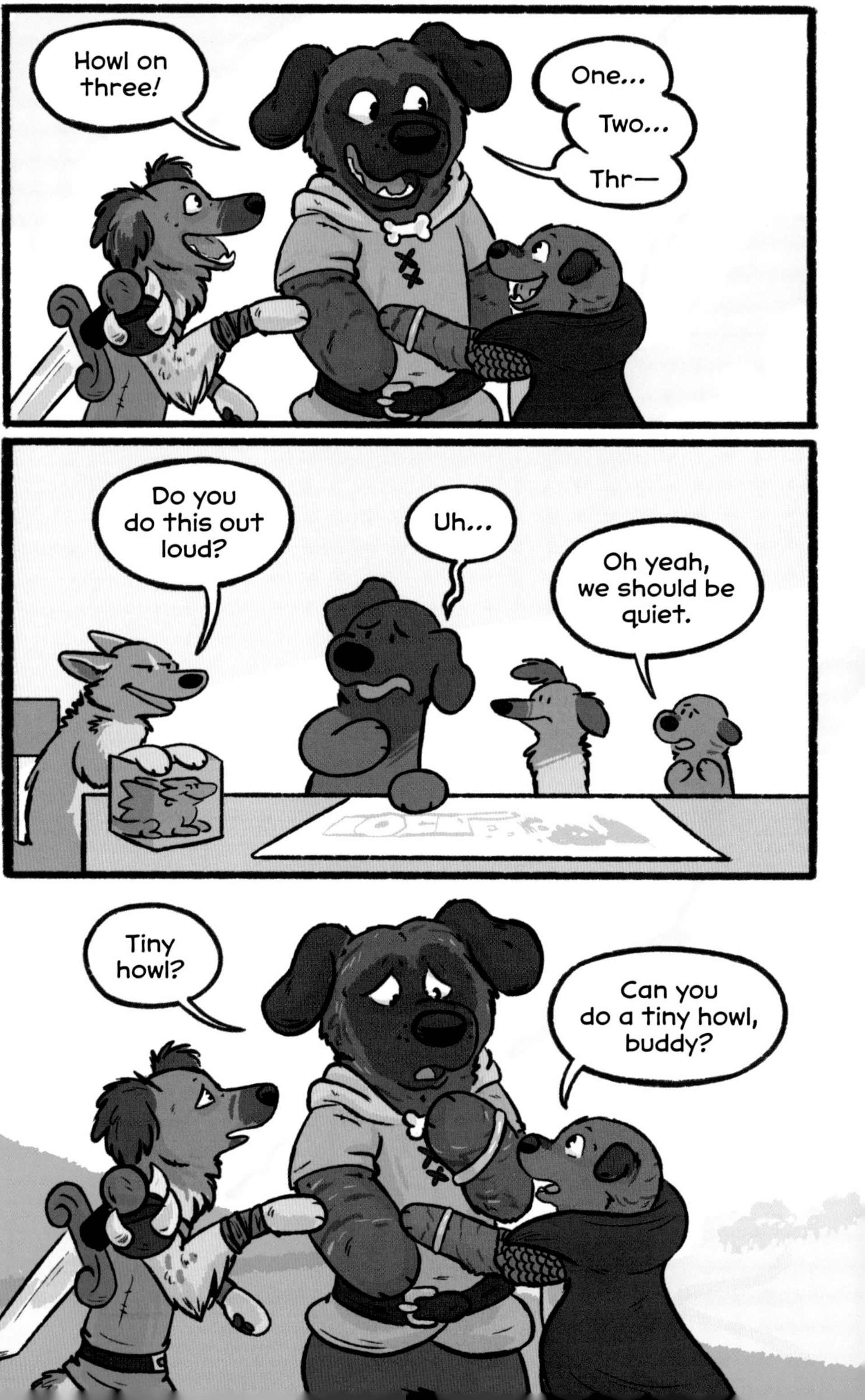

Howl on three!
One...
Two...
Thr—
Do you do this out loud?
Uh...
Oh yeah, we should be quiet.
Tiny howl?
Can you do a tiny howl, buddy?

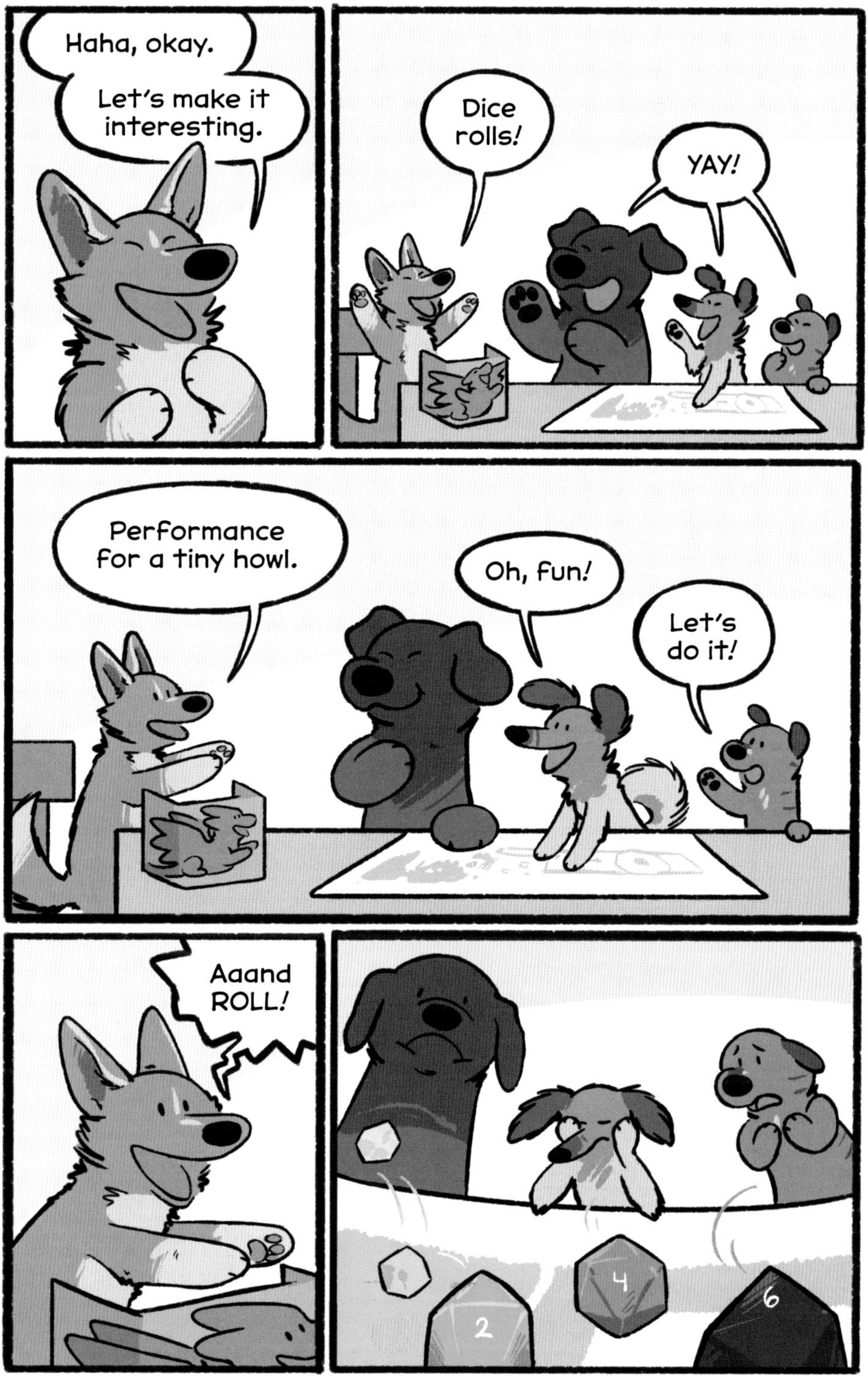
Haha, okay.
Let's make it interesting.
Dice rolls!
YAY!
Performance for a tiny howl.
Oh, fun!
Let's do it!
Aaand ROLL!
4
2
6

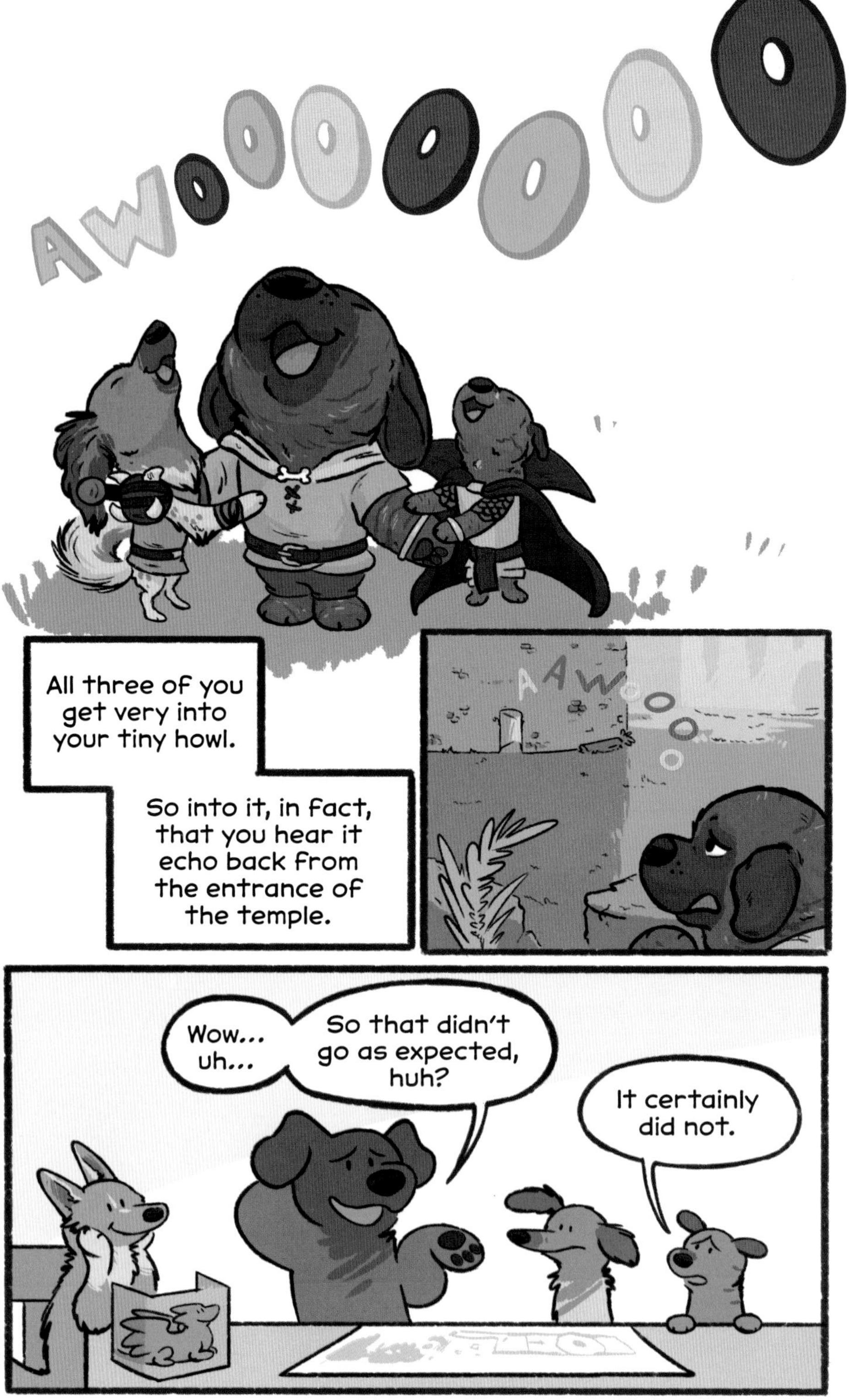
AWOOOOOOOO
All three of you get very into your tiny howl.
So into it, in fact, that you hear it echo back from the entrance of the temple.
AAWOOOO
Wow... uh...
So that didn't go as expected, huh?
It certainly did not.

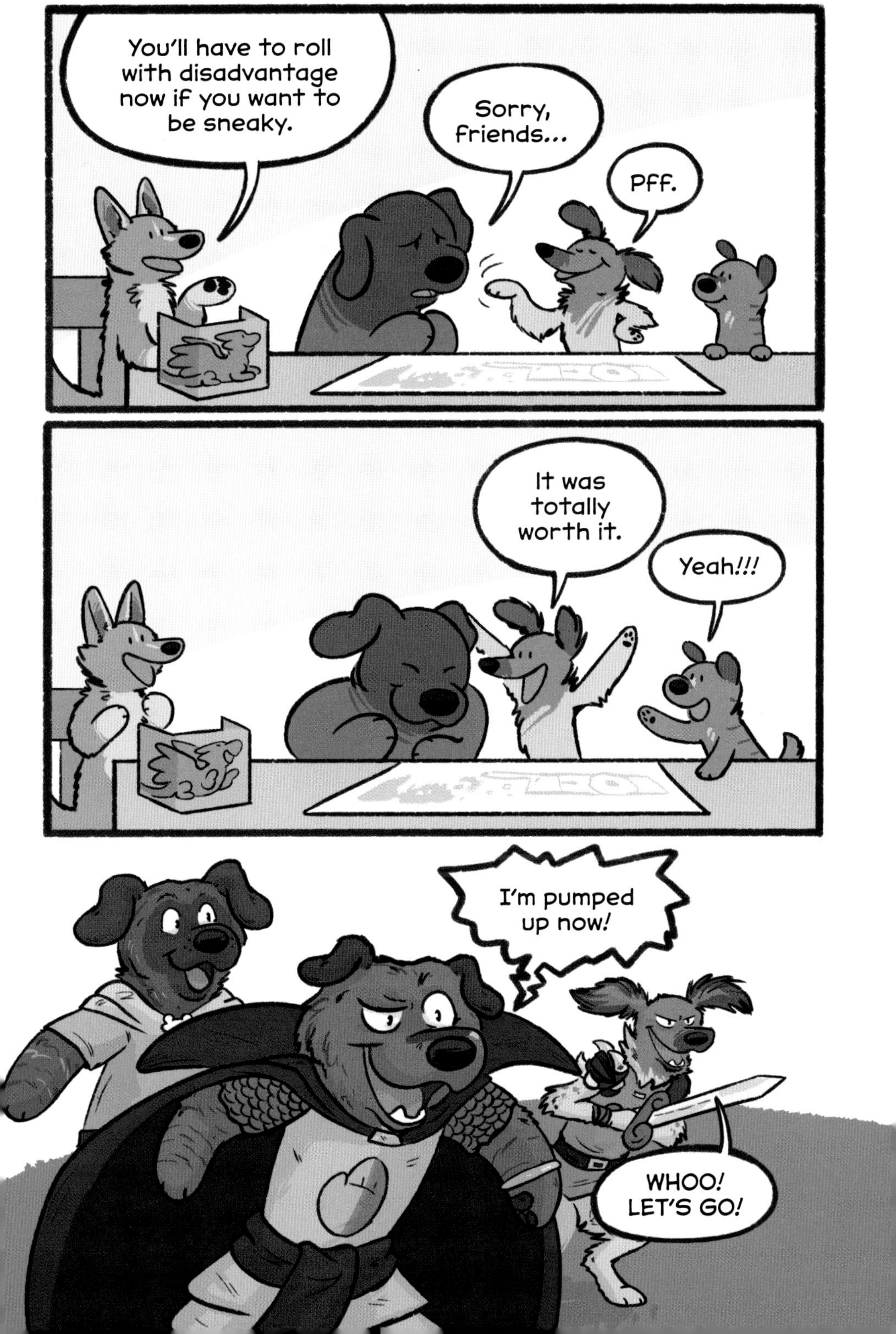
You'll have to roll with disadvantage now if you want to be sneaky.
Sorry, friends...
Pff.
It was totally worth it.
Yeah!!!
I'm pumped up now!
WHOO! LET'S GO!

Chapter 4:
Forgotten Things

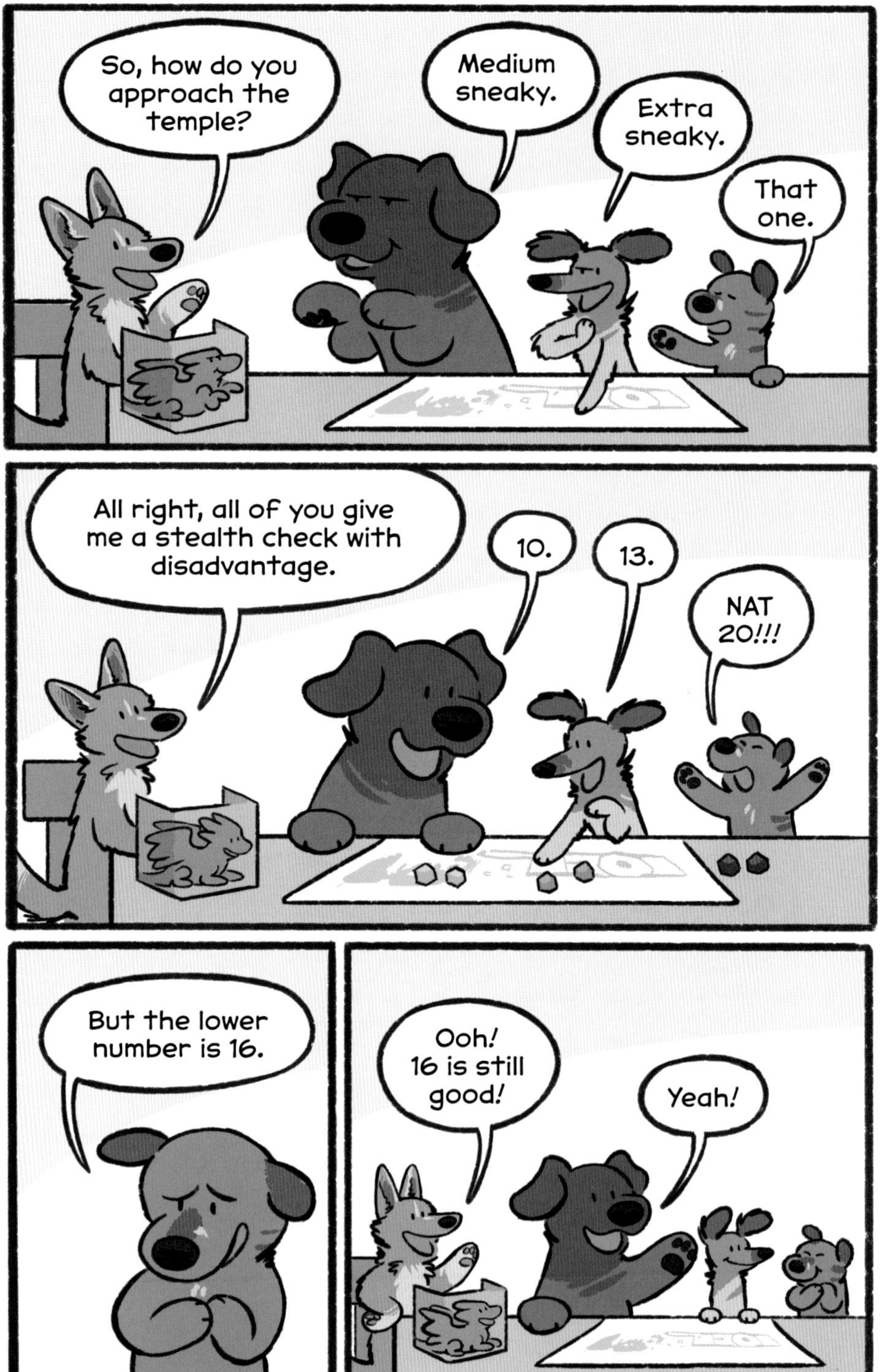
So, how do you approach the temple?
Medium sneaky.
Extra sneaky.
That one.
All right, all of you give me a stealth check with disadvantage.
10.
13.
NAT 20!!!
But the lower number is 16.
Ooh! 16 is still good!
Yeah!

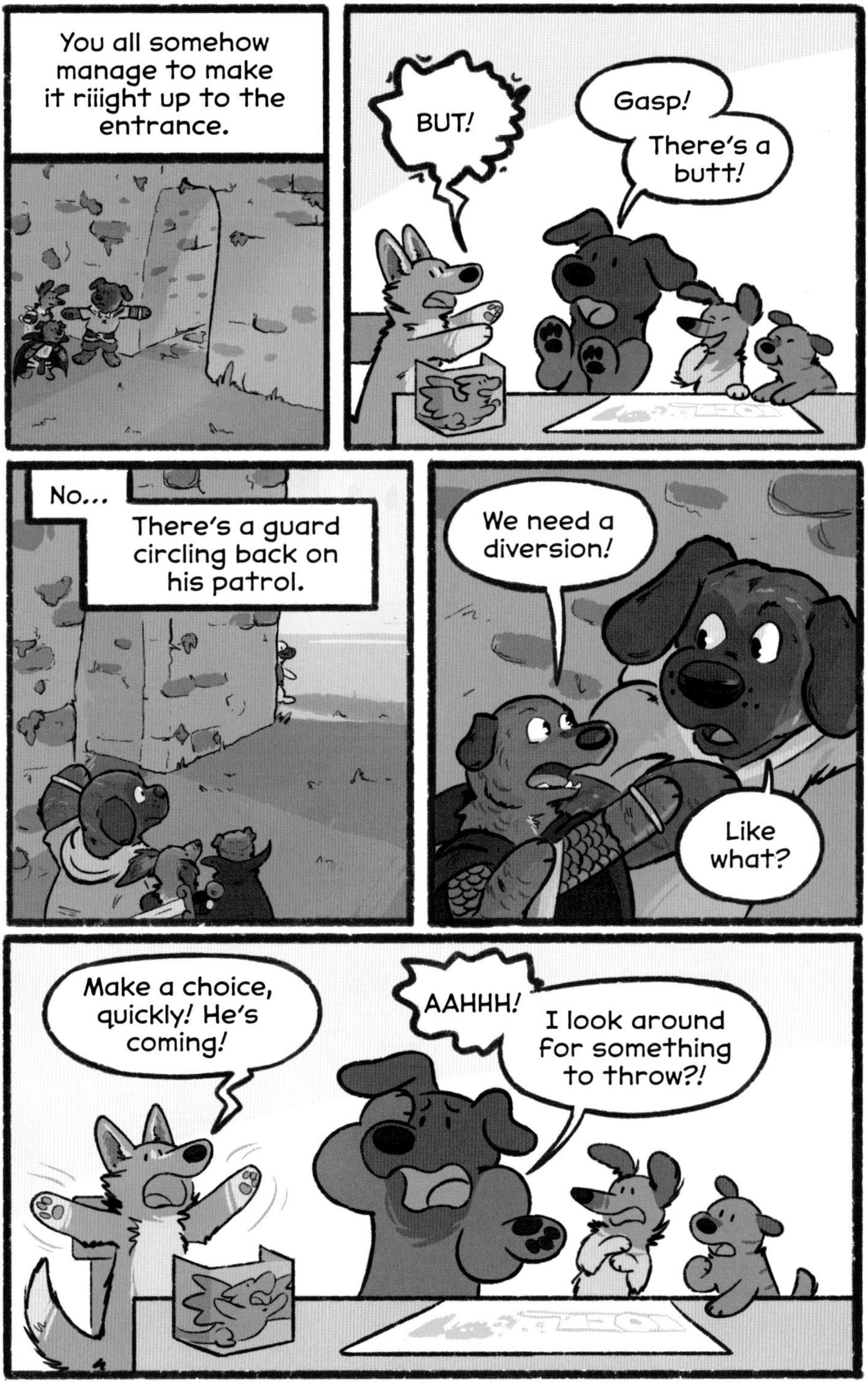
You all somehow manage to make it riiight up to the entrance.
BUT!
Gasp!
There's a butt!
No...
There's a guard circling back on his patrol.
We need a diversion!
Like what?
Make a choice, quickly! He's coming!
AAHHH!
I look around for something to throw?!

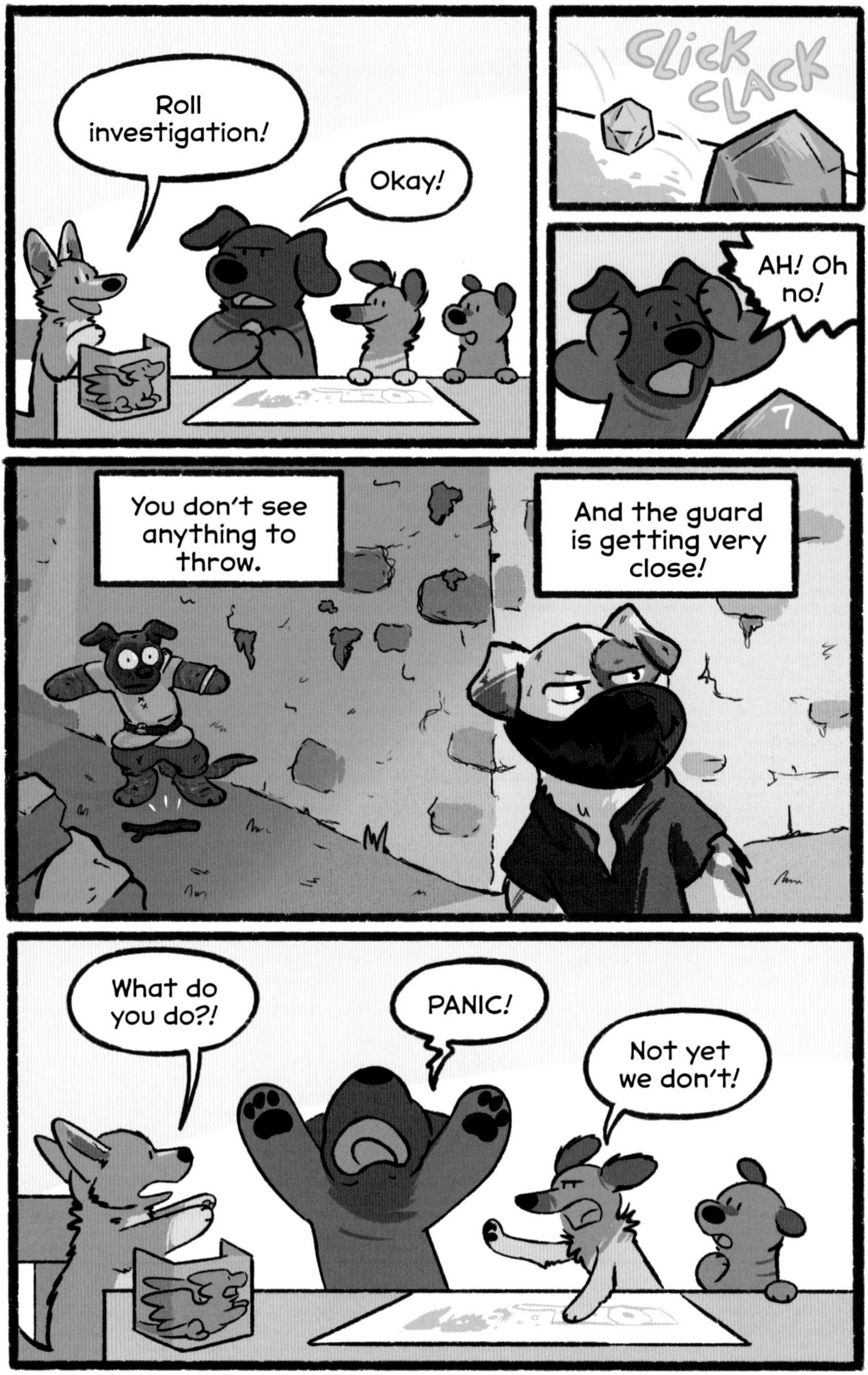

Roll investigation!
Okay!
CLICK CLACK
AH! Oh no!
7
You don't see anything to throw.
And the guard is getting very close!
What do you do?!
PANIC!
Not yet we don't!

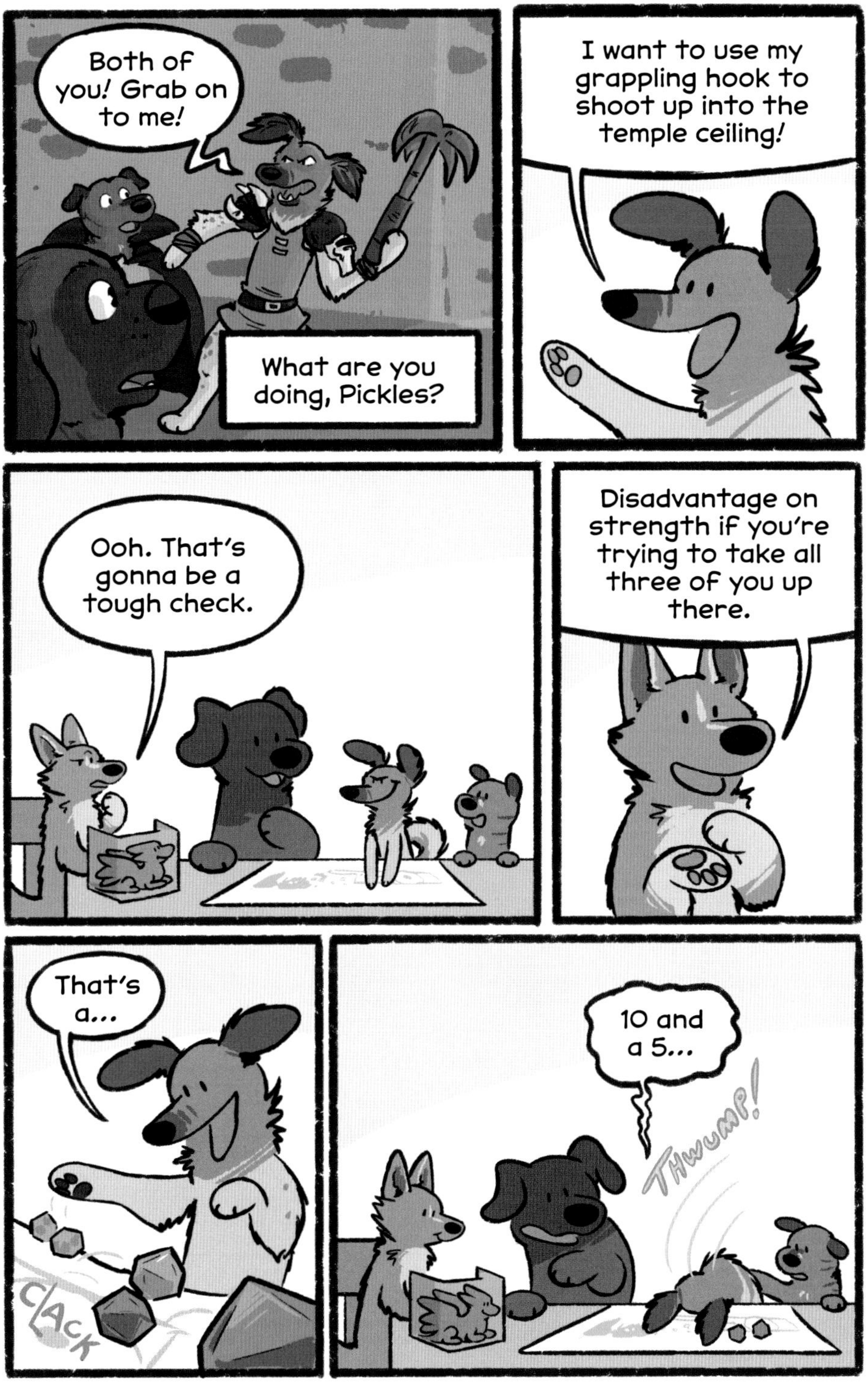
Both of you! Grab on to me!
What are you doing, Pickles?
I want to use my grappling hook to shoot up into the temple ceiling!
Ooh. That's gonna be a tough check.
Disadvantage on strength if you're trying to take all three of you up there.
That's a...
CLACK
10 and a 5...
THWUMP!

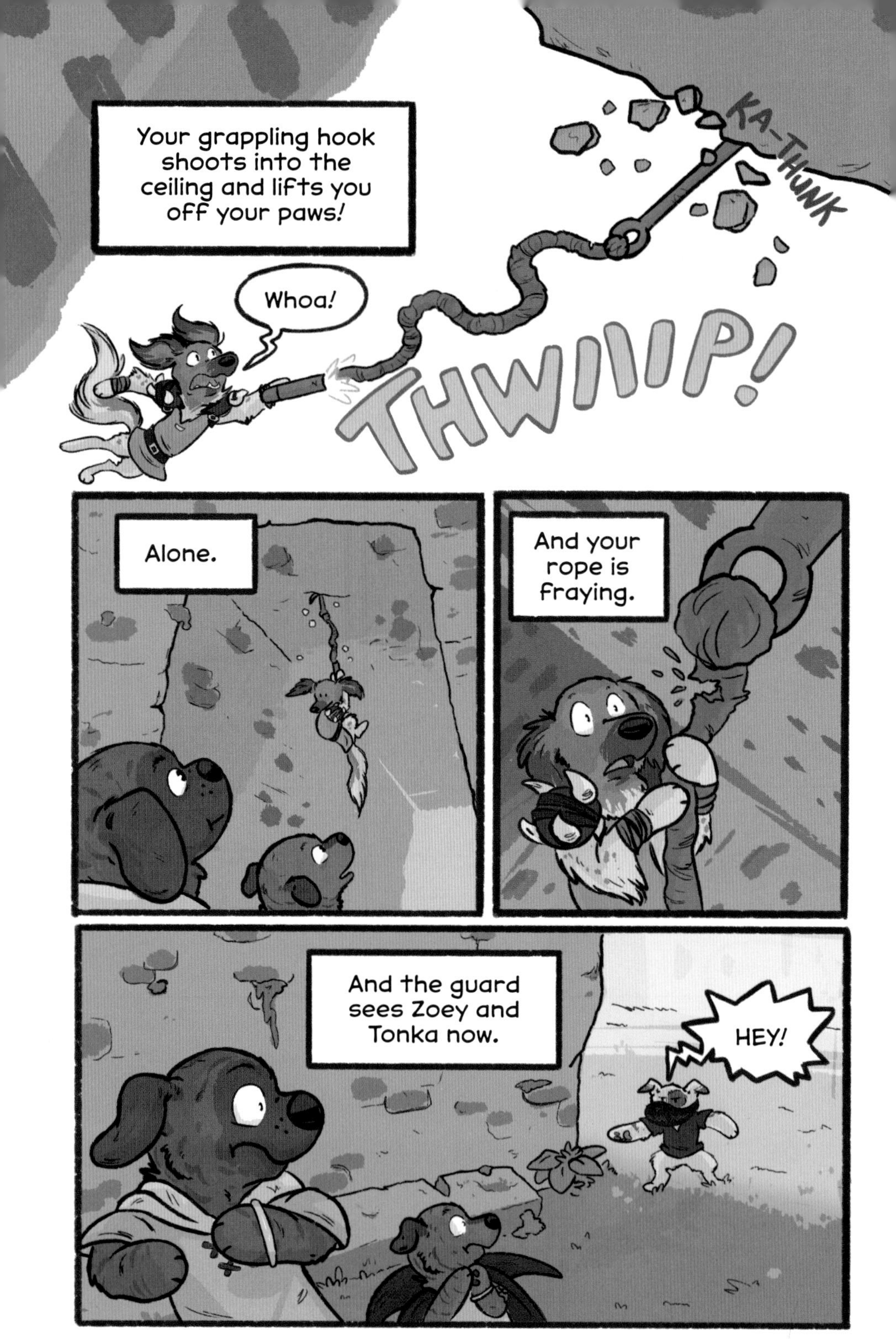
Your grappling hook shoots into the ceiling and lifts you off your paws!
KA-THUNK
Whoa!
THWIIIP!
Alone.
And your rope is fraying.
And the guard sees Zoey and Tonka now.
HEY!

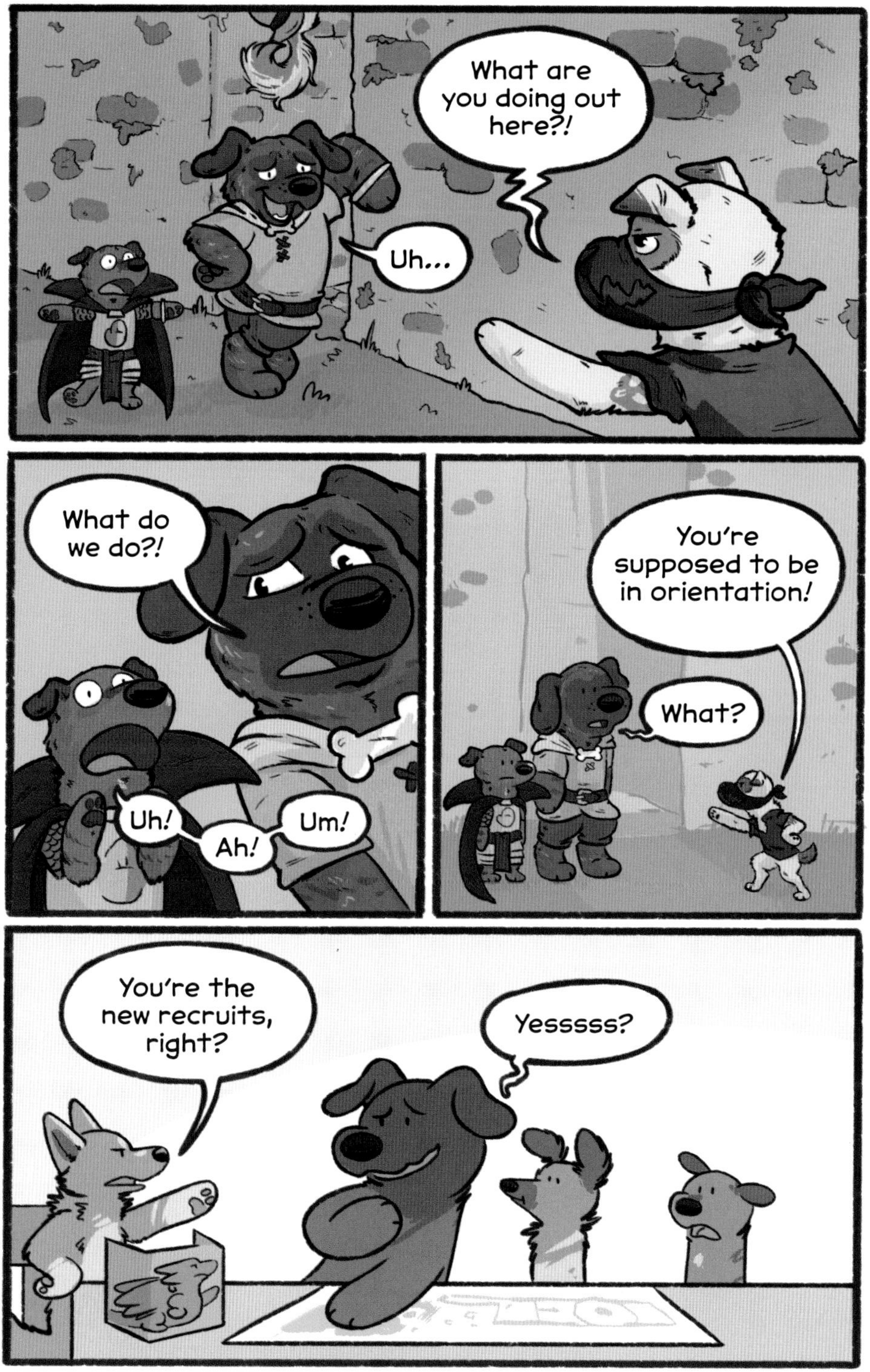
What are you doing out here?!
Uh...
What do we do?!
Uh!
Ah!
Um!
You're supposed to be in orientation!
What?
You're the new recruits, right?
Yesssss?

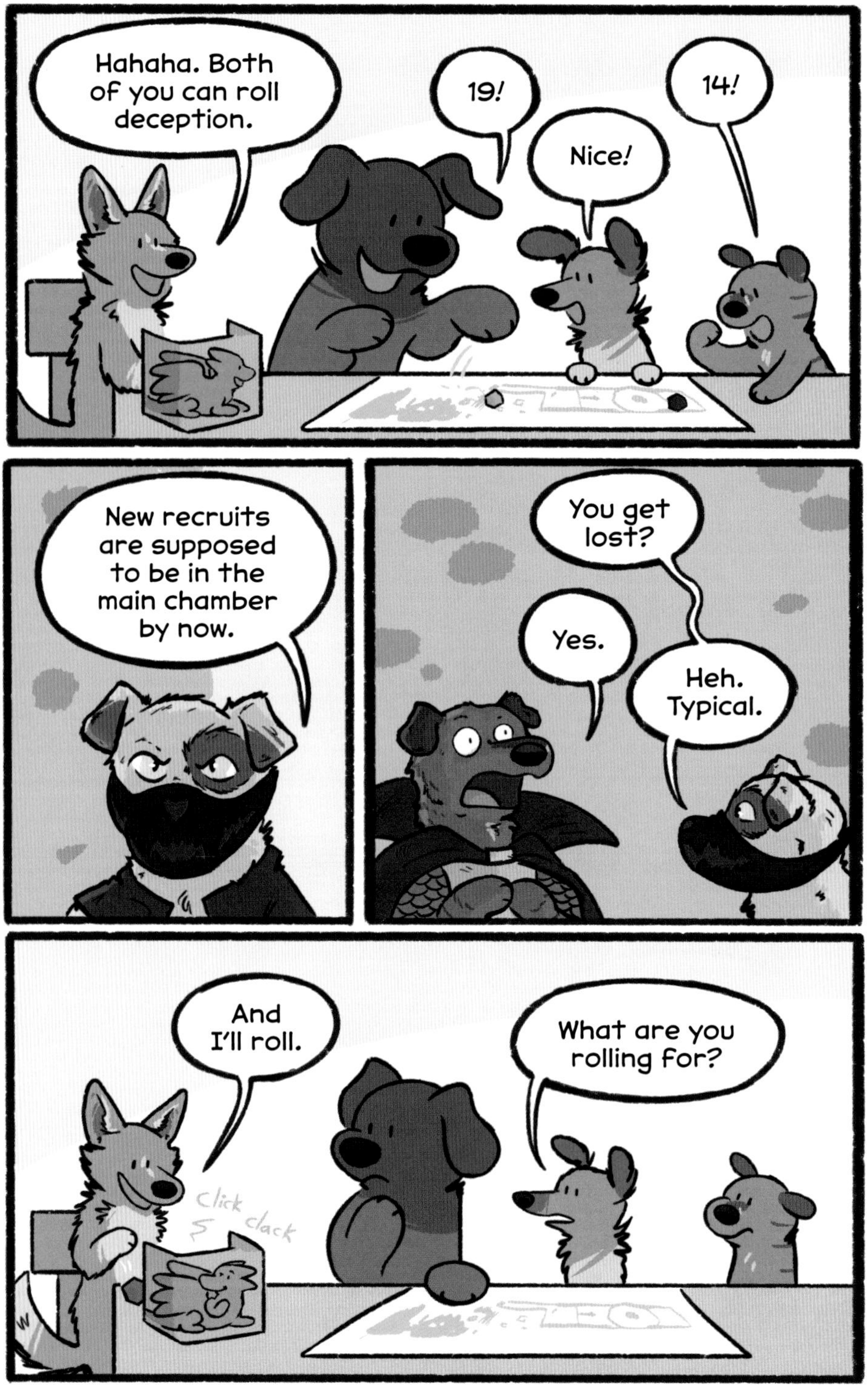
Hahaha. Both of you can roll deception.
19!
Nice!
14!
New recruits are supposed to be in the main chamber by now.
You get lost?
Yes.
Heh. Typical.
And I'll roll.
Click clack
What are you rolling for?

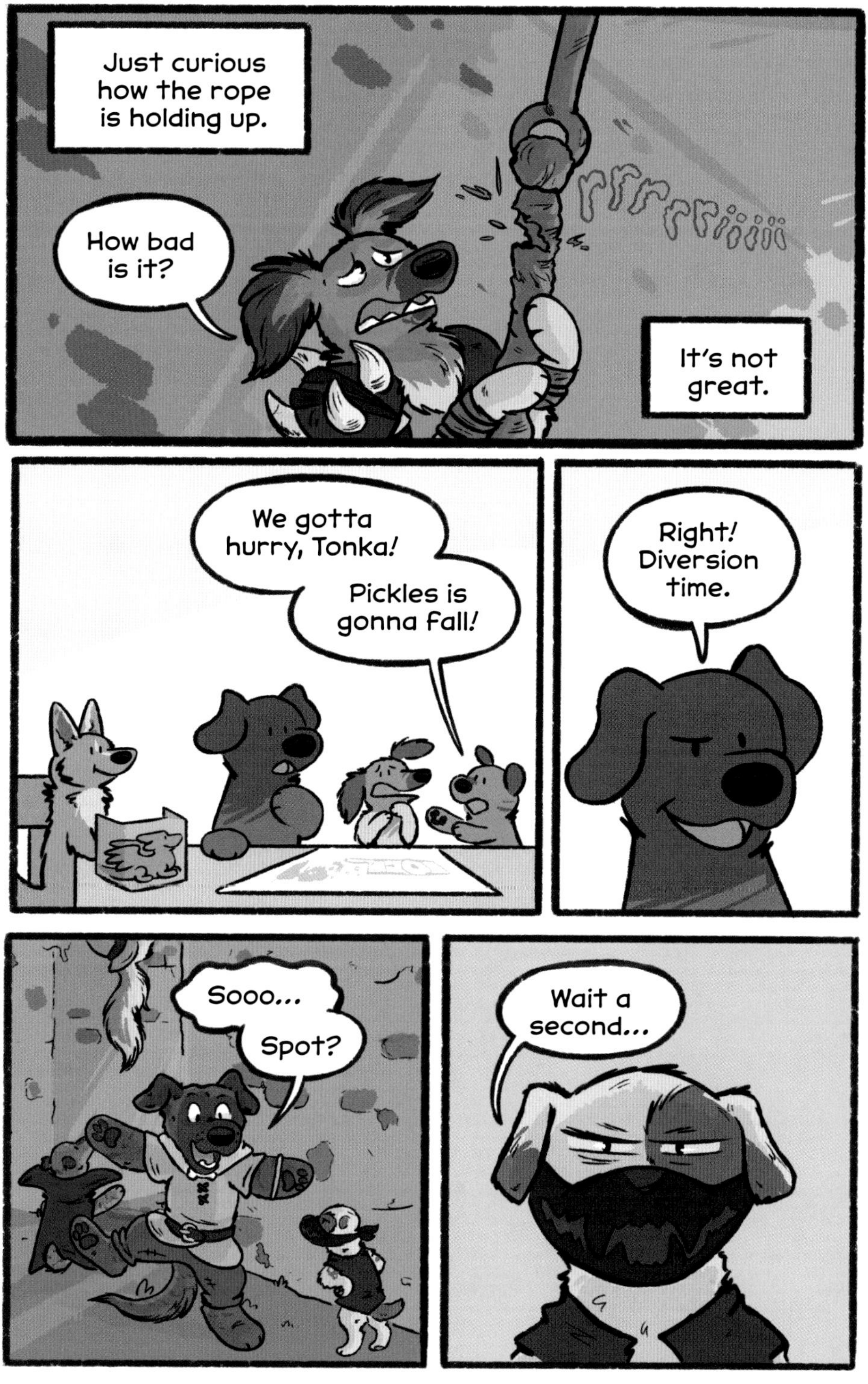
Just curious how the rope is holding up.
How bad is it?
rrrrriiiii
It's not great.
We gotta hurry, Tonka!
Pickles is gonna fall!
Right! Diversion time.
Sooo...
Spot?
Wait a second...

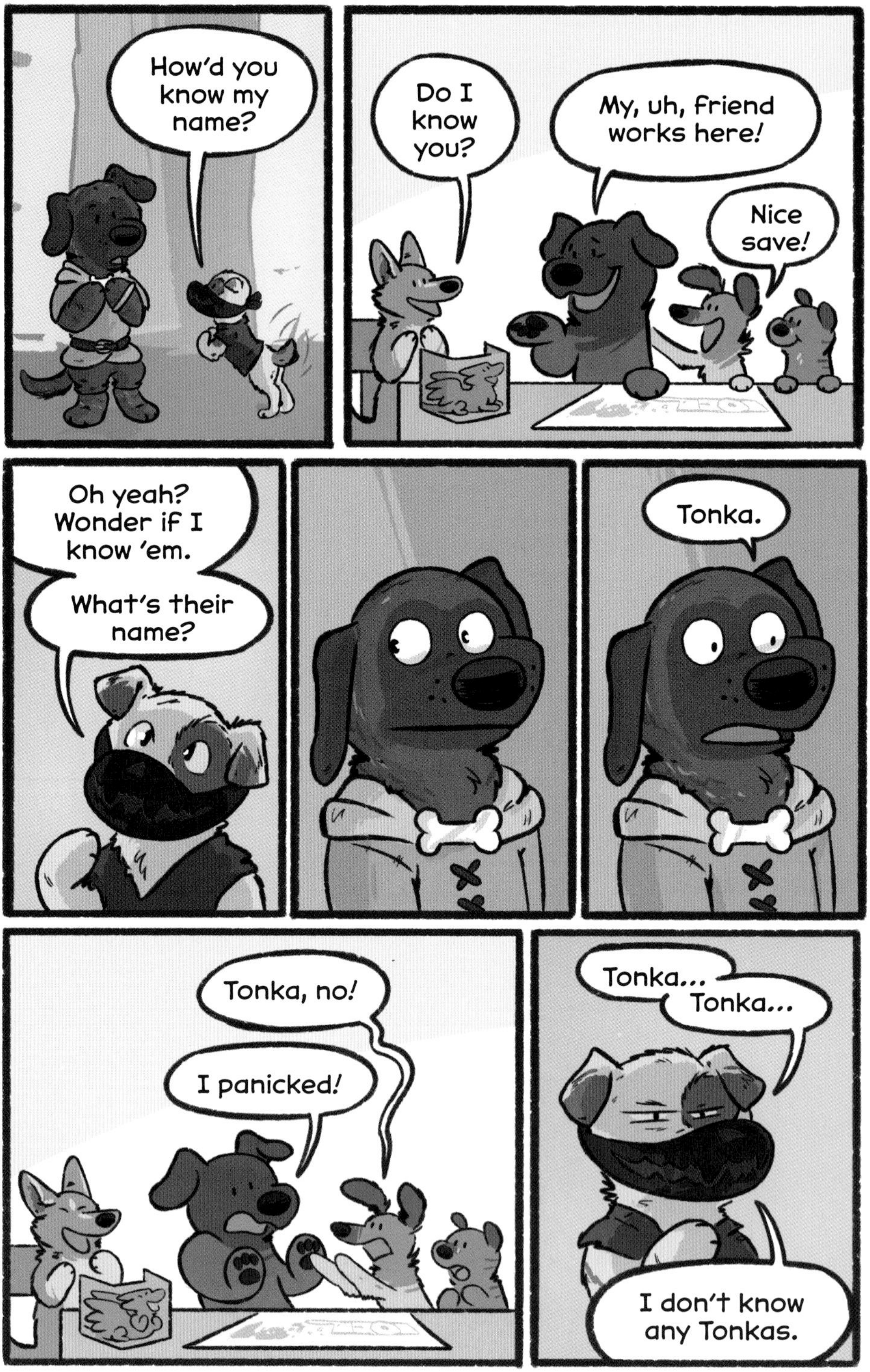
How'd you know my name?
Do I know you?
My, uh, friend works here!
Nice save!
Oh yeah? Wonder if I know 'em.
What's their name?
Tonka.
Tonka, no!
I panicked!
Tonka... Tonka...
I don't know any Tonkas.

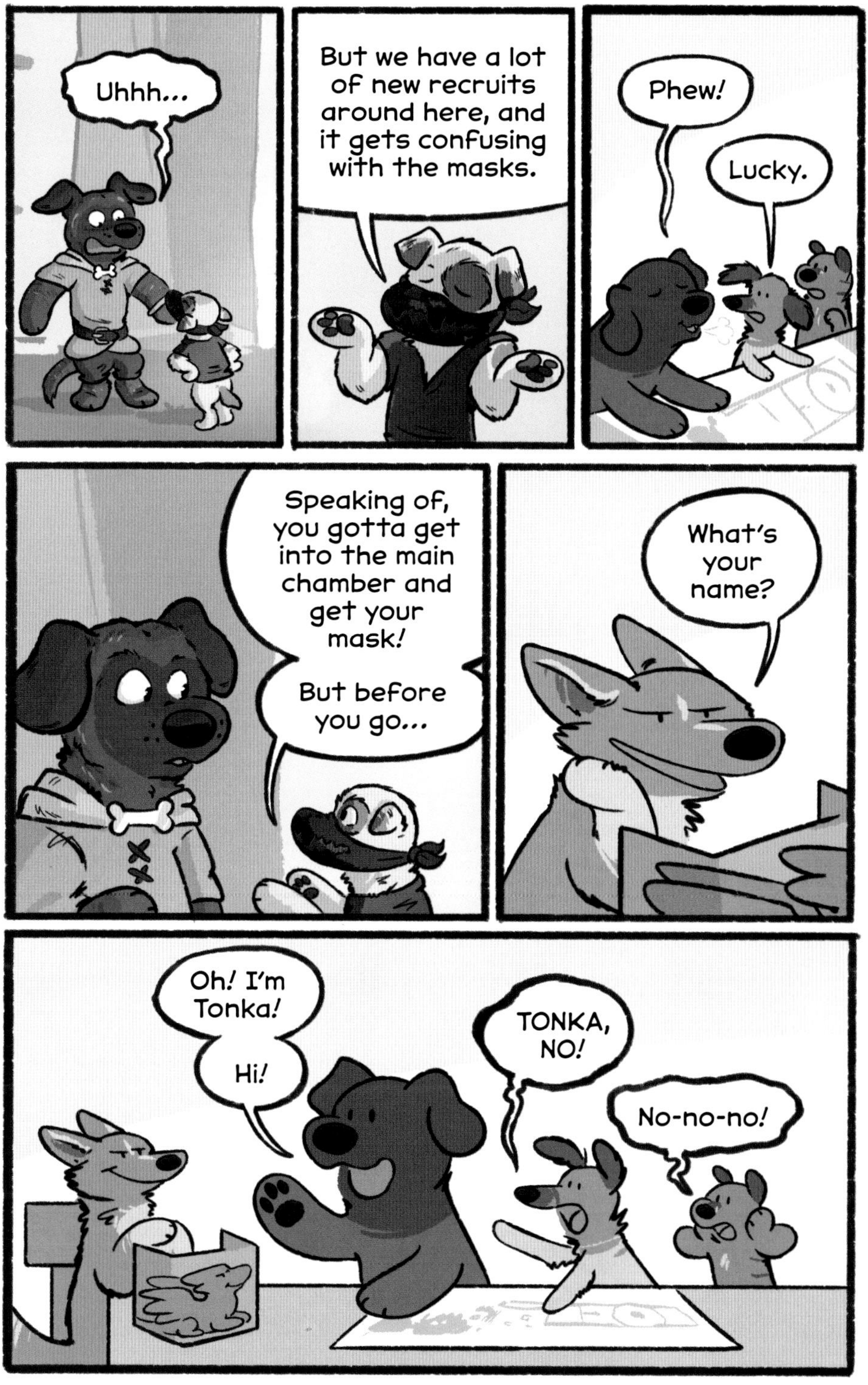
Uhhh...
But we have a lot of new recruits around here, and it gets confusing with the masks.
Phew!
Lucky.
Speaking of, you gotta get into the main chamber and get your mask!
But before you go...
What's your name?
Oh! I'm Tonka!
Hi!
TONKA, NO!
No-no-no!

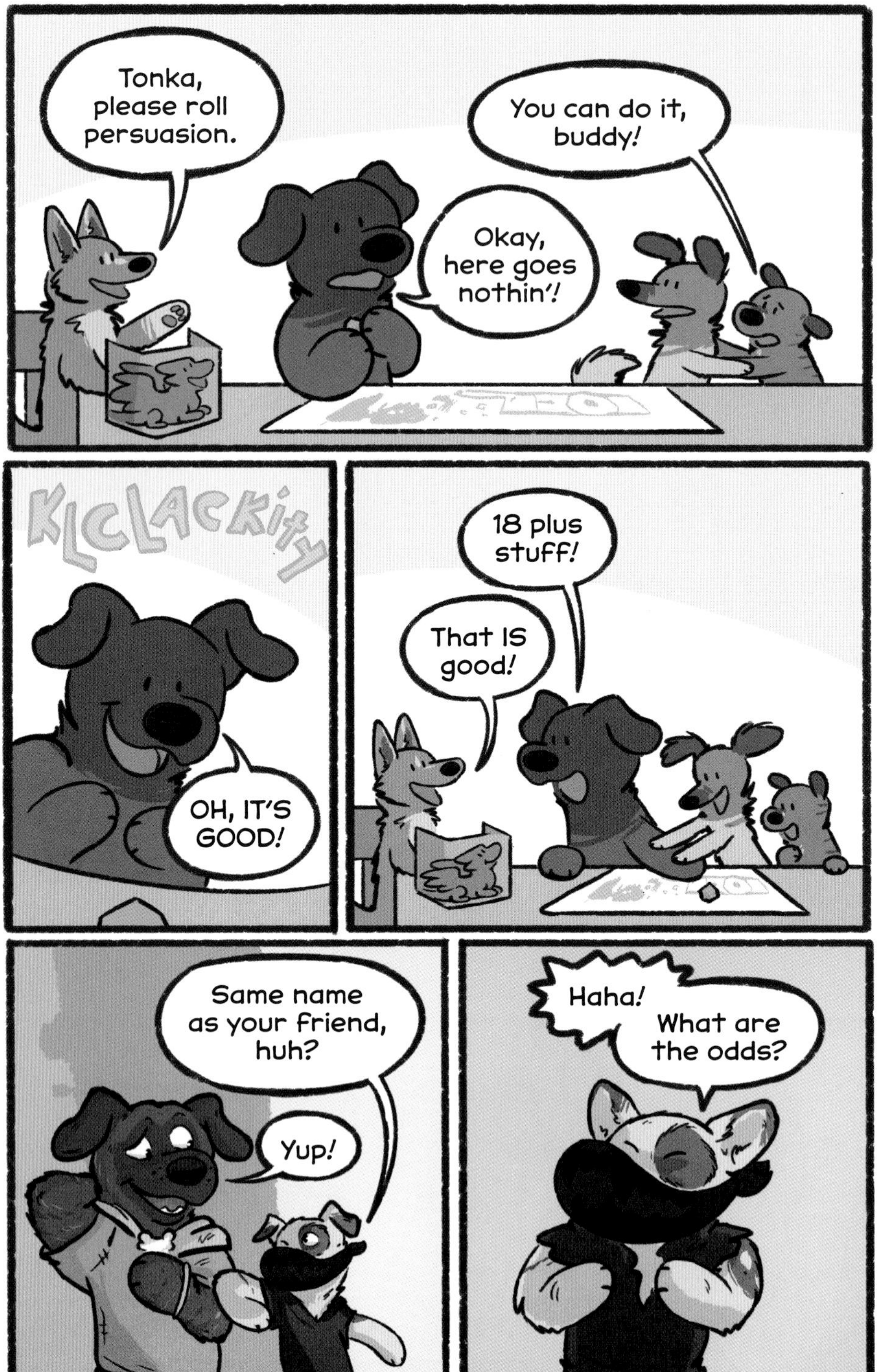
Tonka, please roll persuasion.
You can do it, buddy!
Okay, here goes nothin'!
KLCLACKity
OH, IT'S GOOD!
18 plus stuff!
That IS good!
Same name as your friend, huh?
Yup!
Haha!
What are the odds?

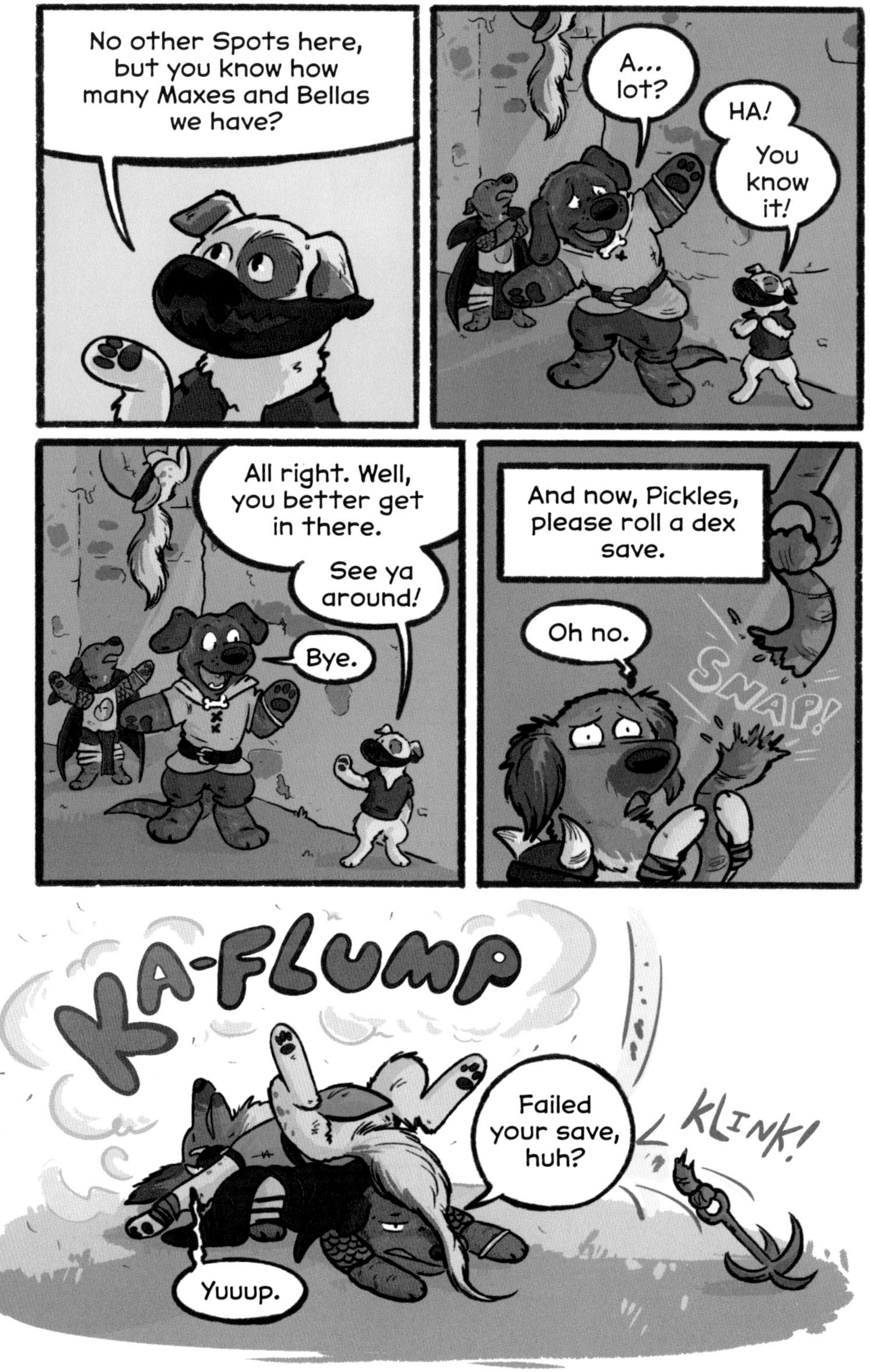
No other Spots here, but you know how many Maxes and Bellas we have?
A... lot?
HA!
You know it!
All right. Well, you better get in there.
See ya around!
Bye.
And now, Pickles, please roll a dex save.
Oh no.
SNAP!
KA-FLUMP
Failed your save, huh?
KLINK!
Yuuup.

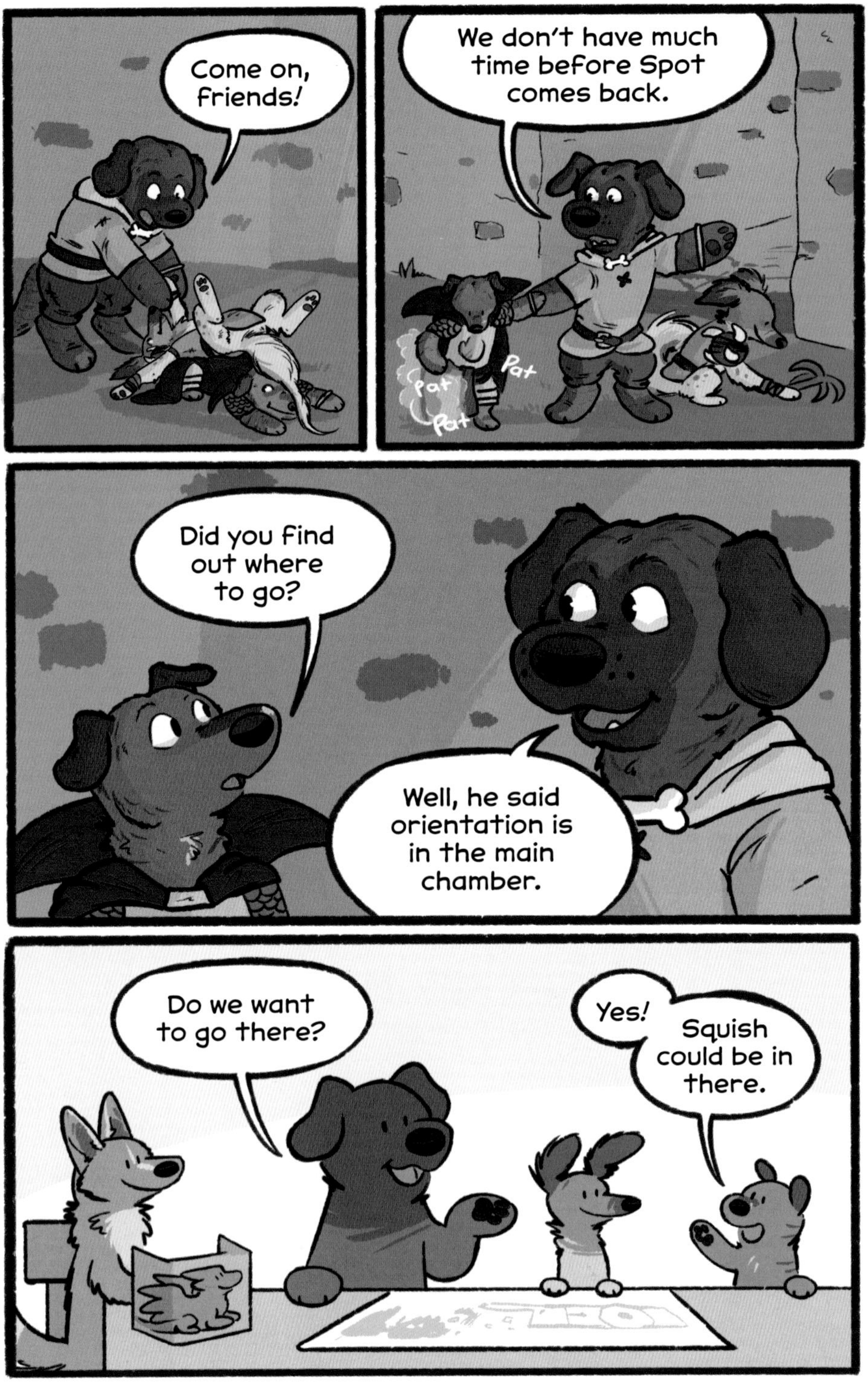
Come on, friends!
We don't have much time before Spot comes back.
Pat
Pat
Pat
Did you find out where to go?
Well, he said orientation is in the main chamber.
Do we want to go there?
Yes!
Squish could be in there.

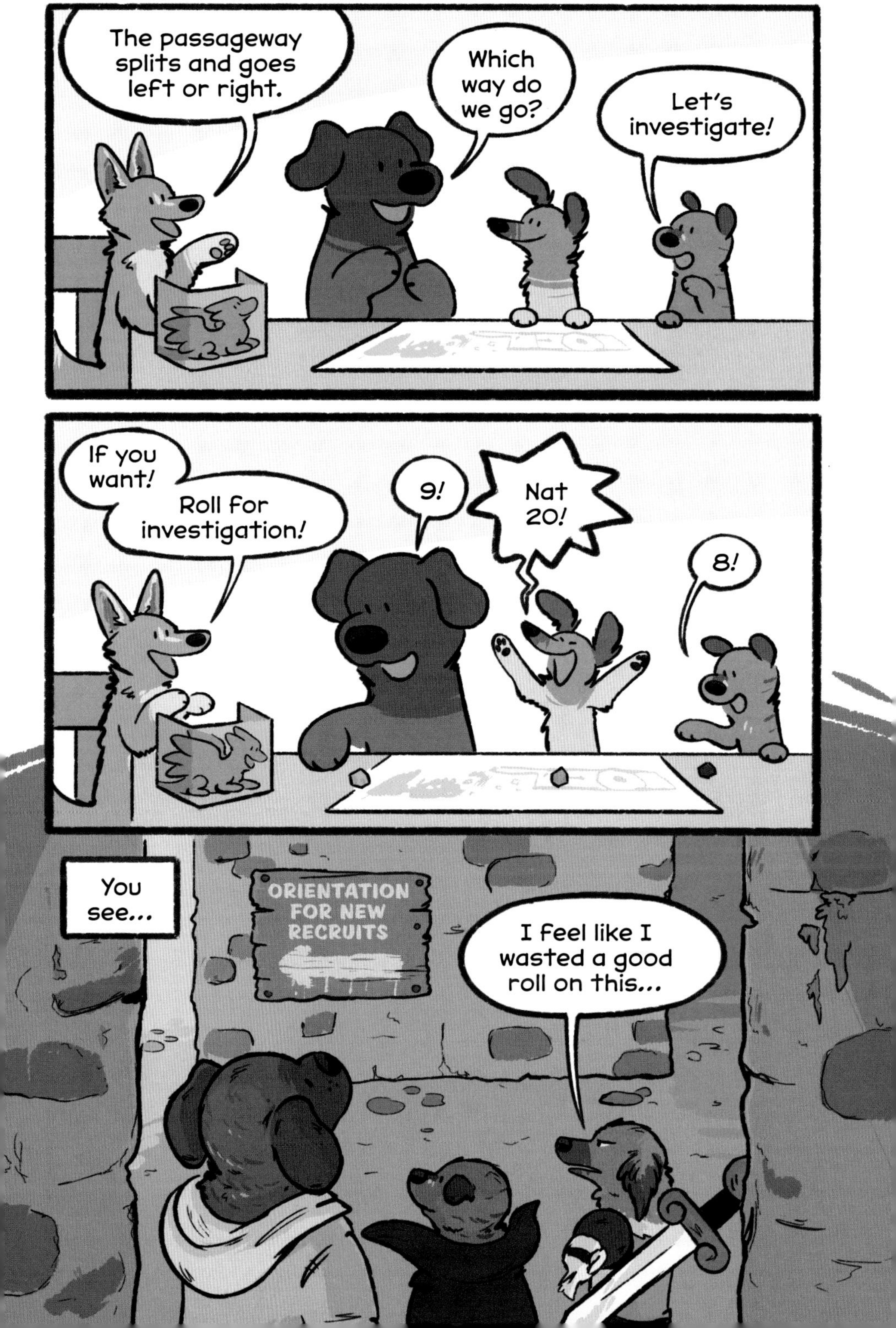
The passageway splits and goes left or right.
Which way do we go?
Let's investigate!
If you want!
Roll for investigation!
9!
Nat 20!
8!
You see...
ORIENTATION FOR NEW RECRUITS
I feel like I wasted a good roll on this...

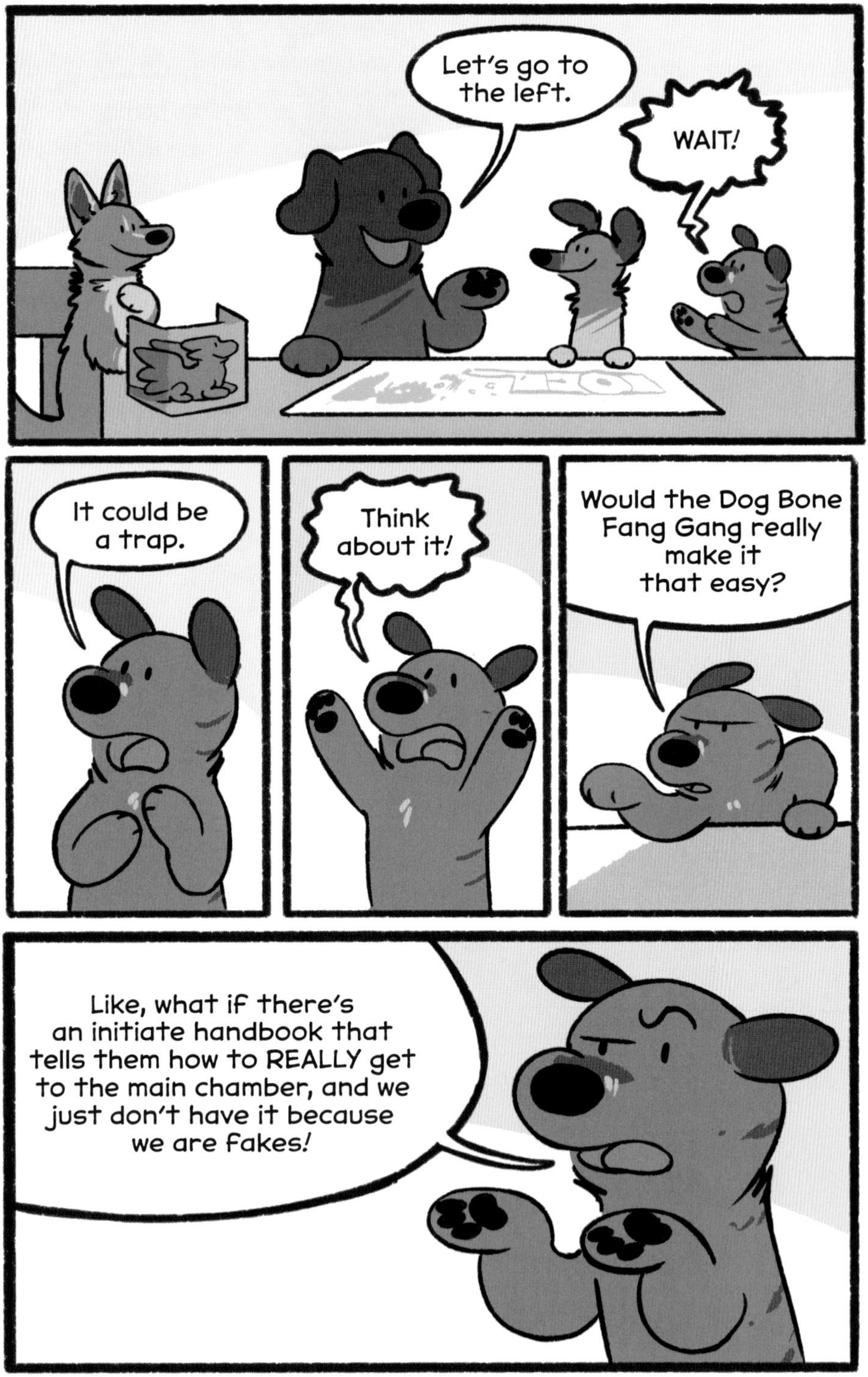
Let's go to the left.
WAIT!
It could be a trap.
Think about it!
Would the Dog Bone Fang Gang really make it that easy?
Like, what if there's an initiate handbook that tells them how to REALLY get to the main chamber, and we just don't have it because we are fakes!

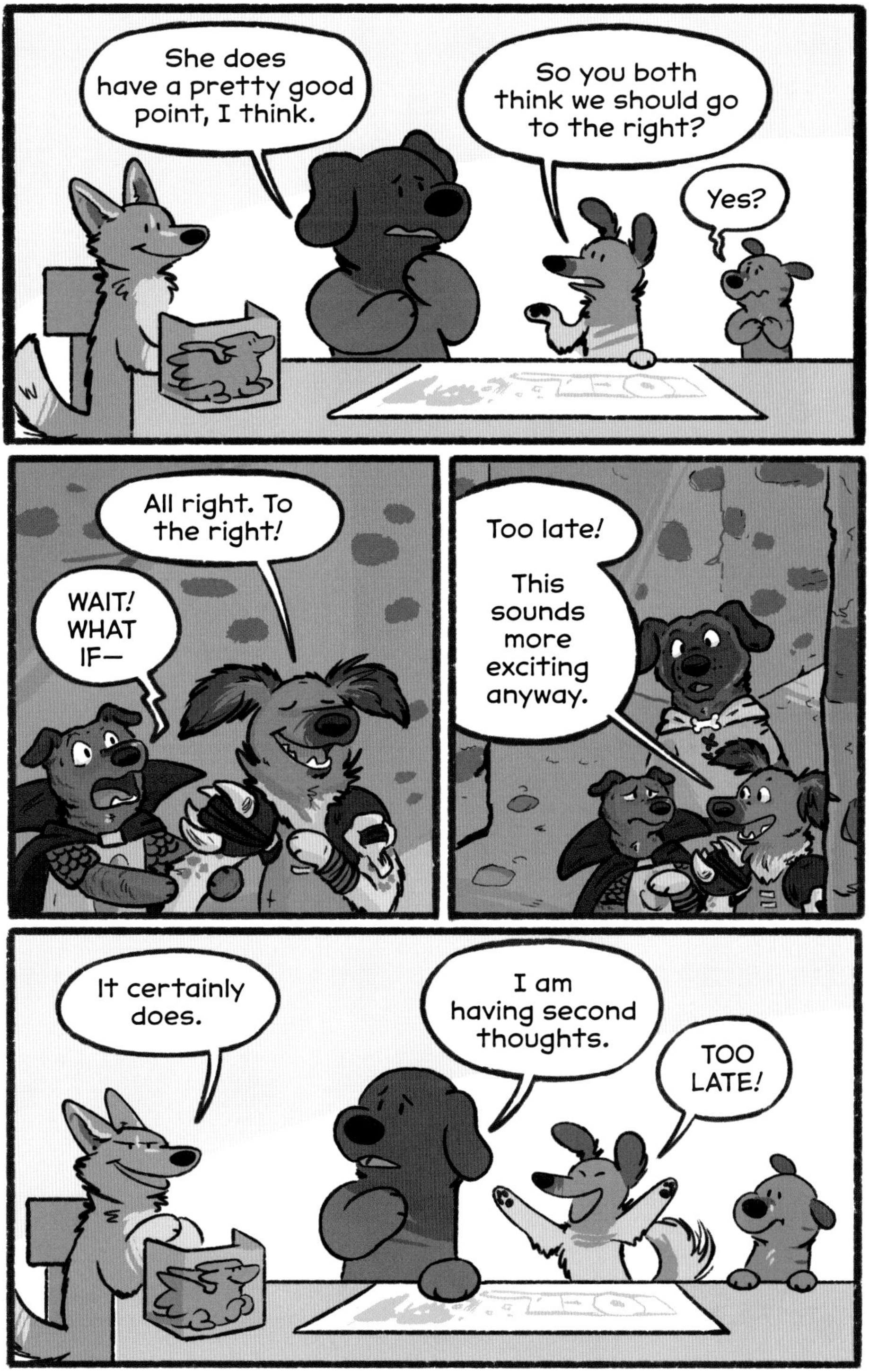
She does have a pretty good point, I think.
So you both think we should go to the right?
Yes?
All right. To the right!
WAIT! WHAT IF—
Too late!
This sounds more exciting anyway.
It certainly does.
I am having second thoughts.
TOO LATE!

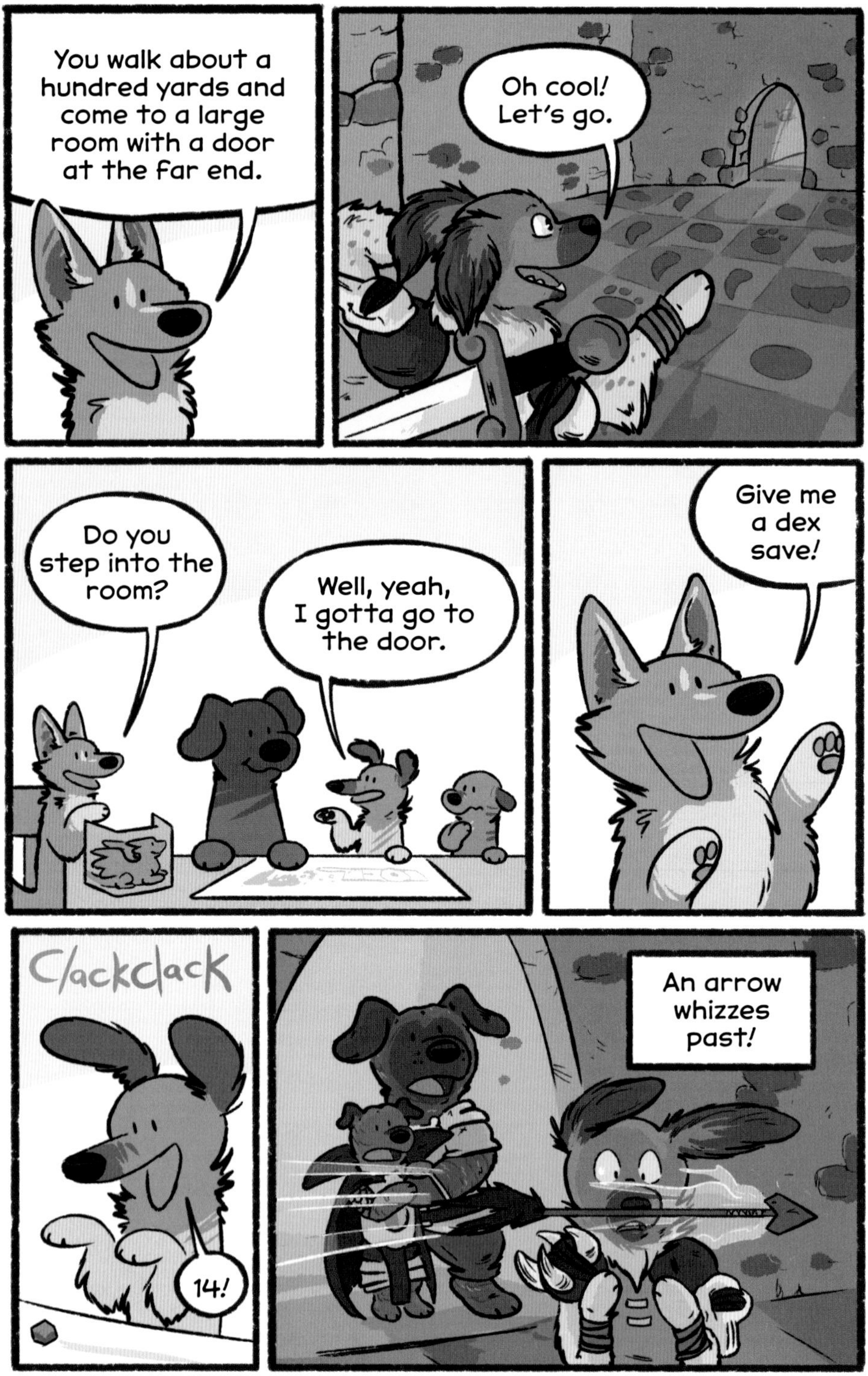
You walk about a hundred yards and come to a large room with a door at the far end.
Oh cool! Let's go.
Do you step into the room?
Well, yeah, I gotta go to the door.
Give me a dex save!
Clackclack
14!
An arrow whizzes past!

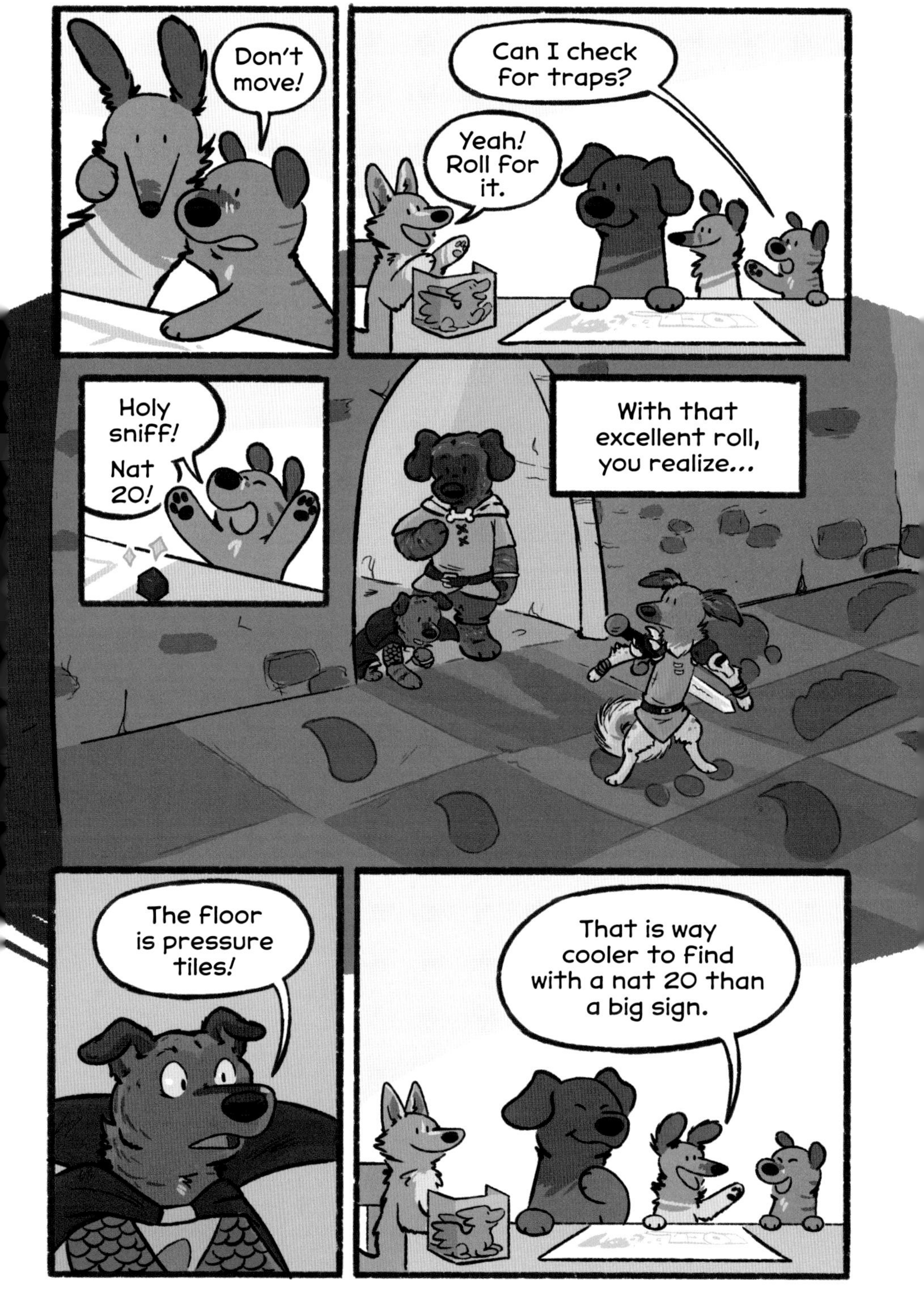
Don't move!
Can I check for traps?
Yeah! Roll for it.
Holy sniff!
Nat 20!
With that excellent roll, you realize...
The floor is pressure tiles!
That is way cooler to find with a nat 20 than a big sign.

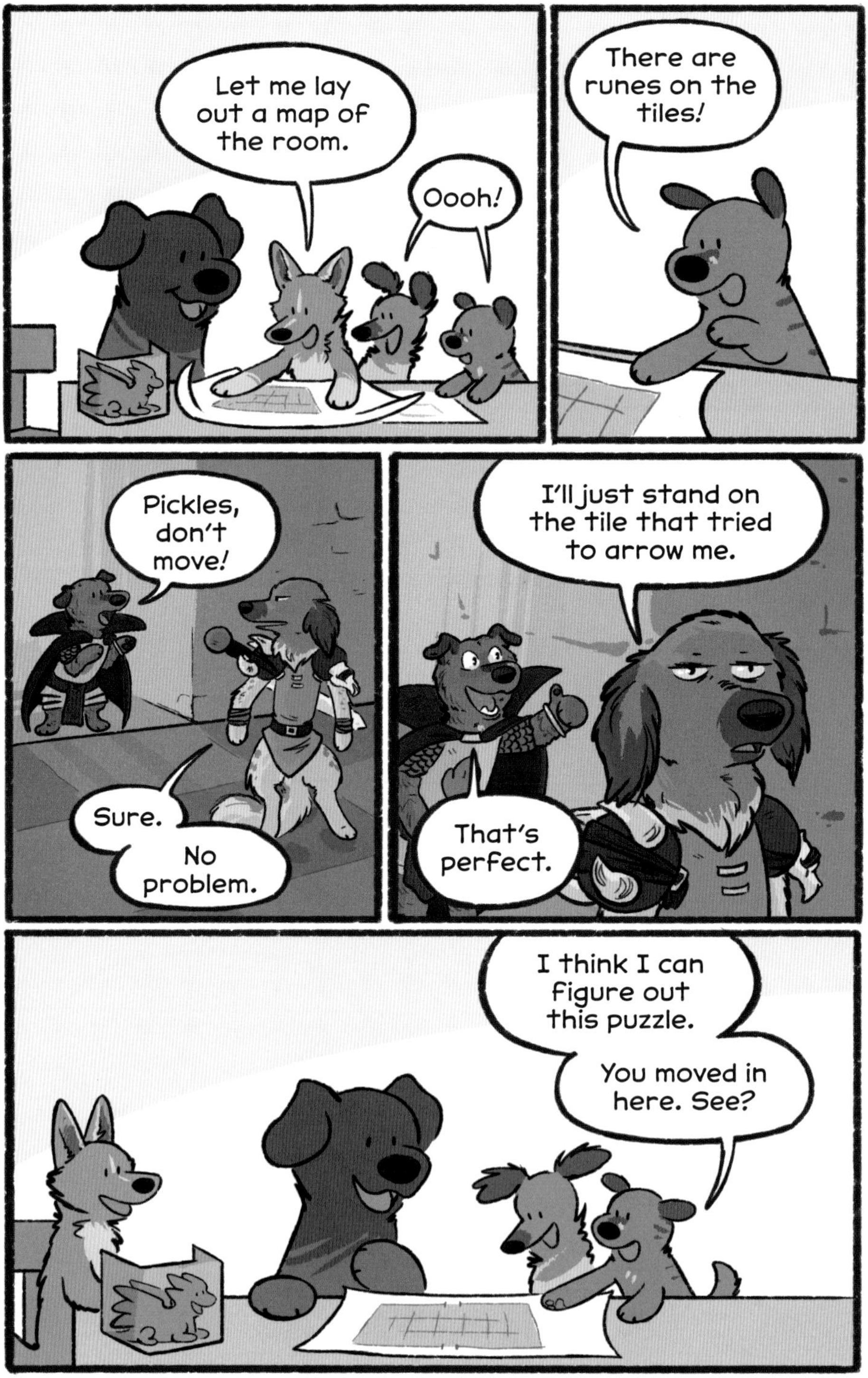
Let me lay out a map of the room.
Oooh!
There are runes on the tiles!
Pickles, don't move!
Sure.
No problem.
I'll just stand on the tile that tried to arrow me.
That's perfect.
I think I can figure out this puzzle.
You moved in here. See?

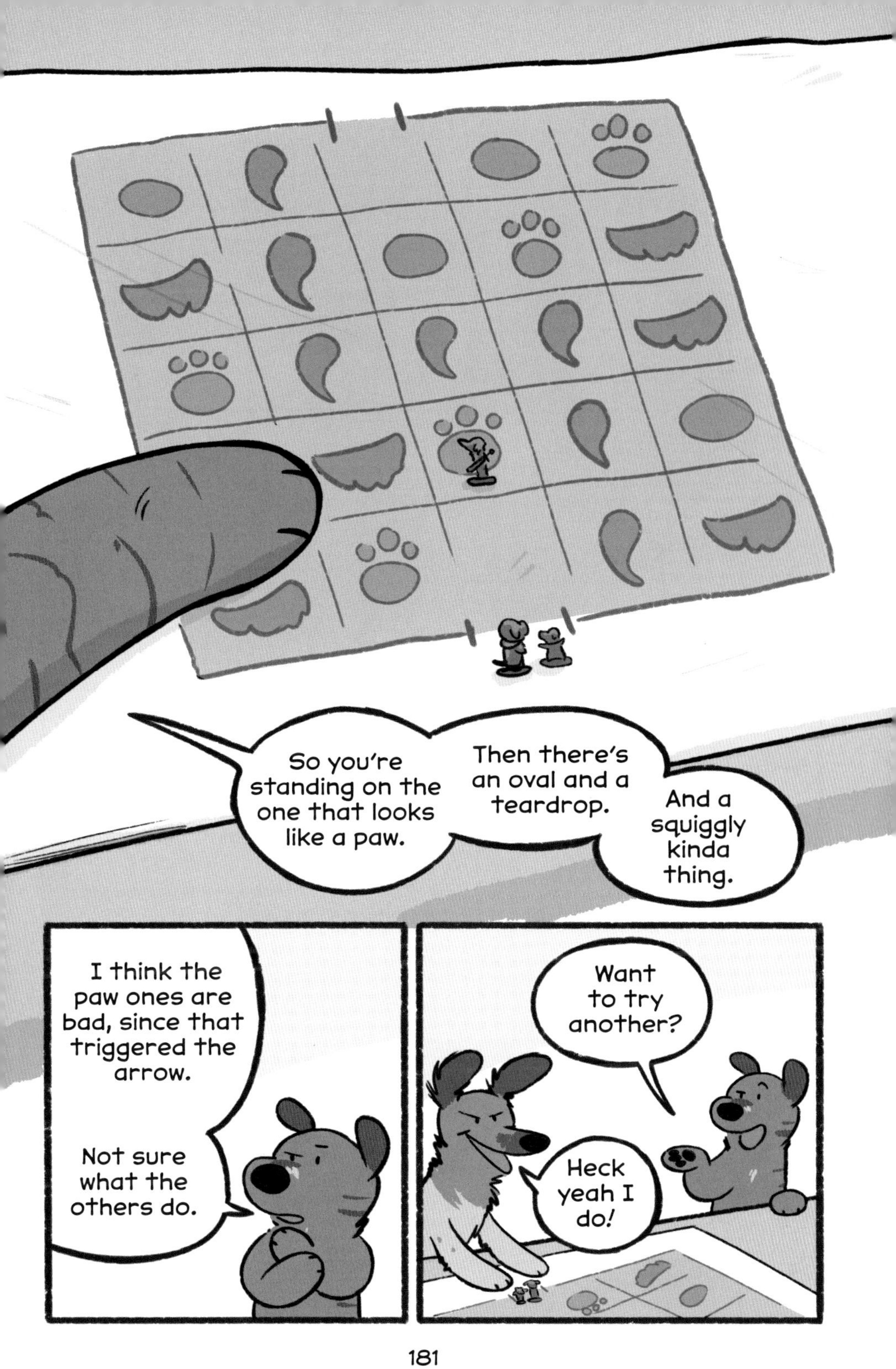
So you're standing on the one that looks like a paw.
Then there's an oval and a teardrop.
And a squiggly kinda thing.
I think the paw ones are bad, since that triggered the arrow.
Not sure what the others do.
Want to try another?
Heck yeah I do!

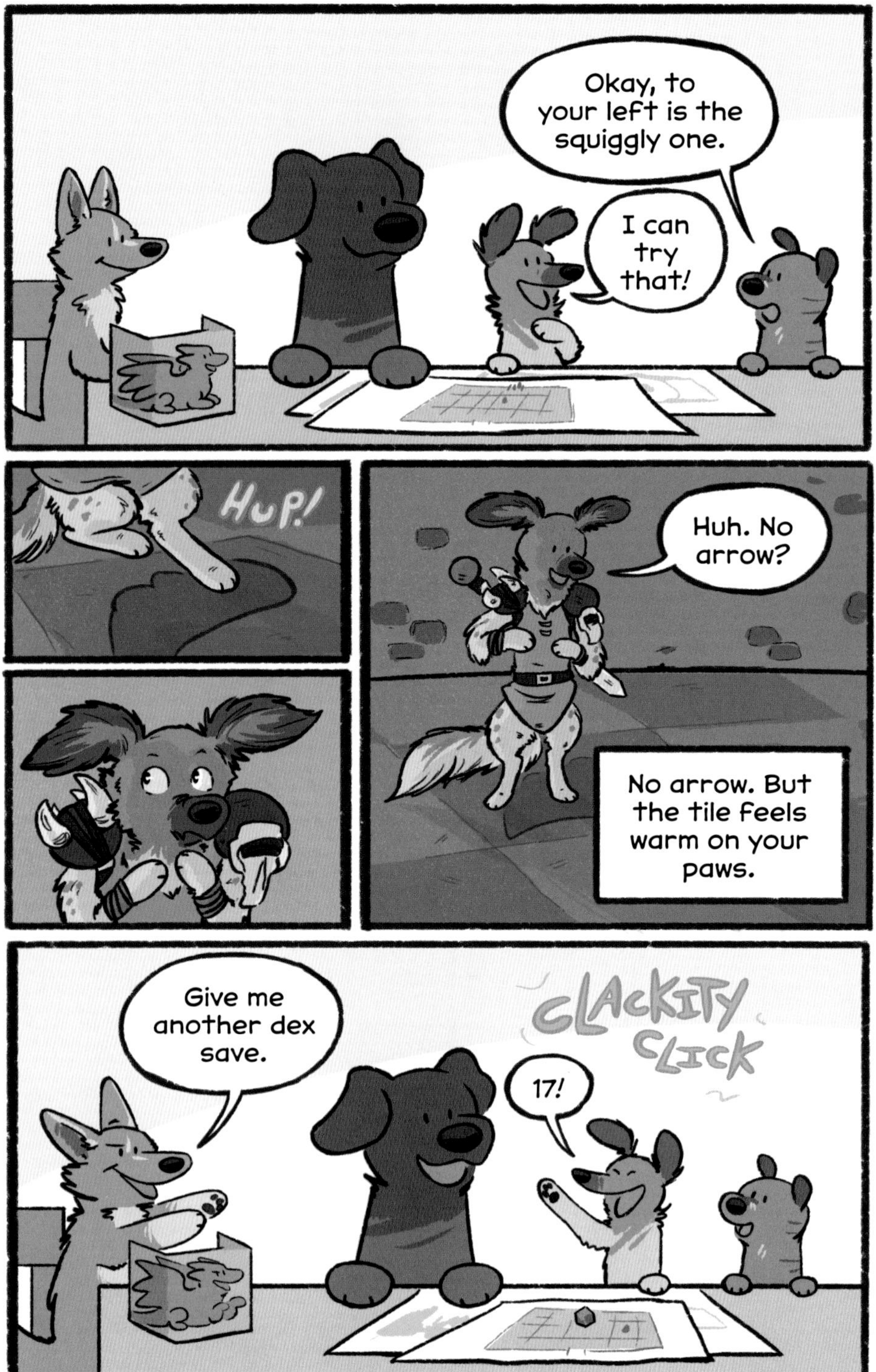
Okay, to your left is the squiggly one.
I can try that!
HUP!
Huh. No arrow?
No arrow. But the tile feels warm on your paws.
Give me another dex save.
CLACKITY CLICK
17!

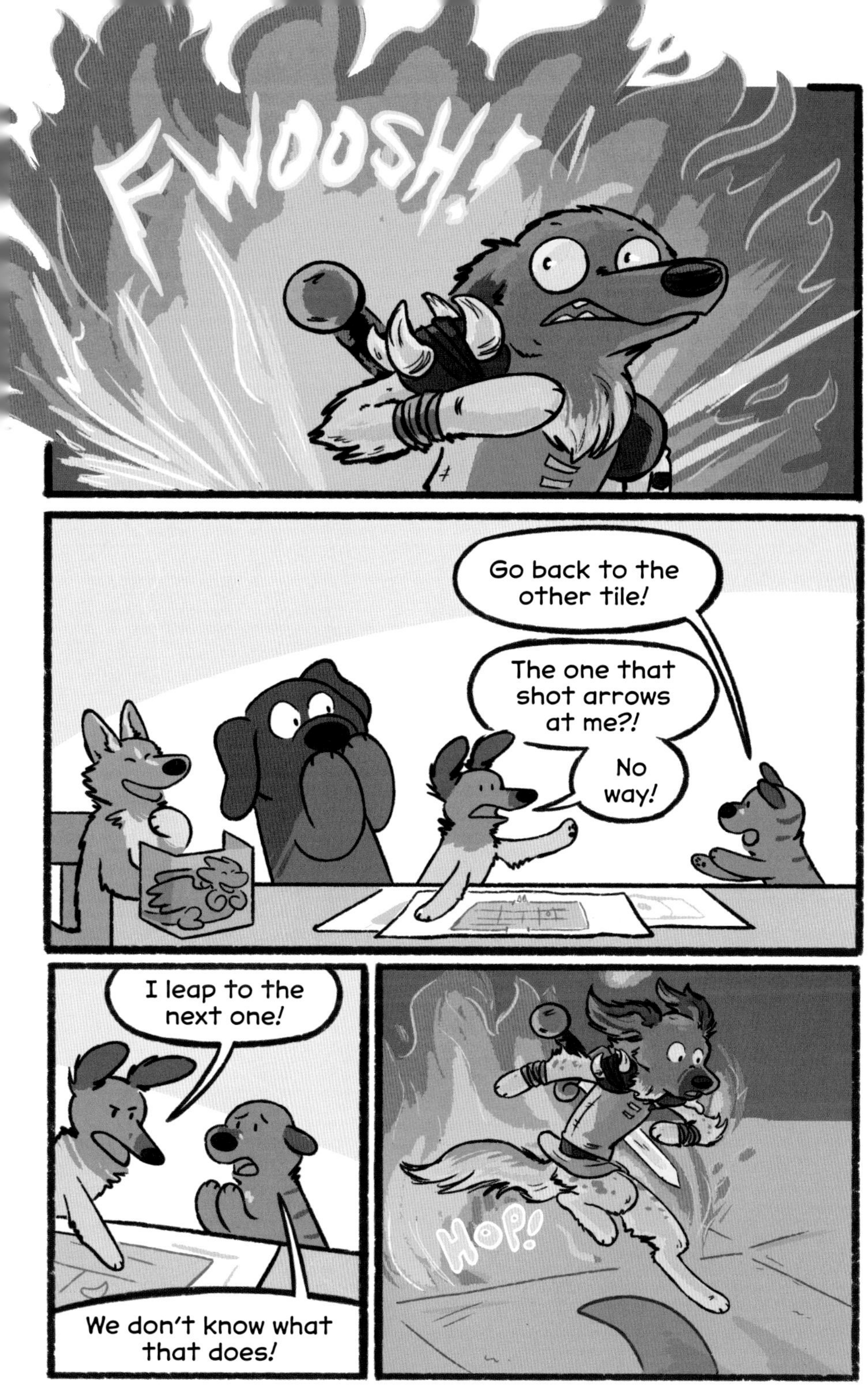
FWOOSH!
Go back to the other tile!
The one that shot arrows at me?!
No way!
I leap to the next one!
We don't know what that does!
HOP!

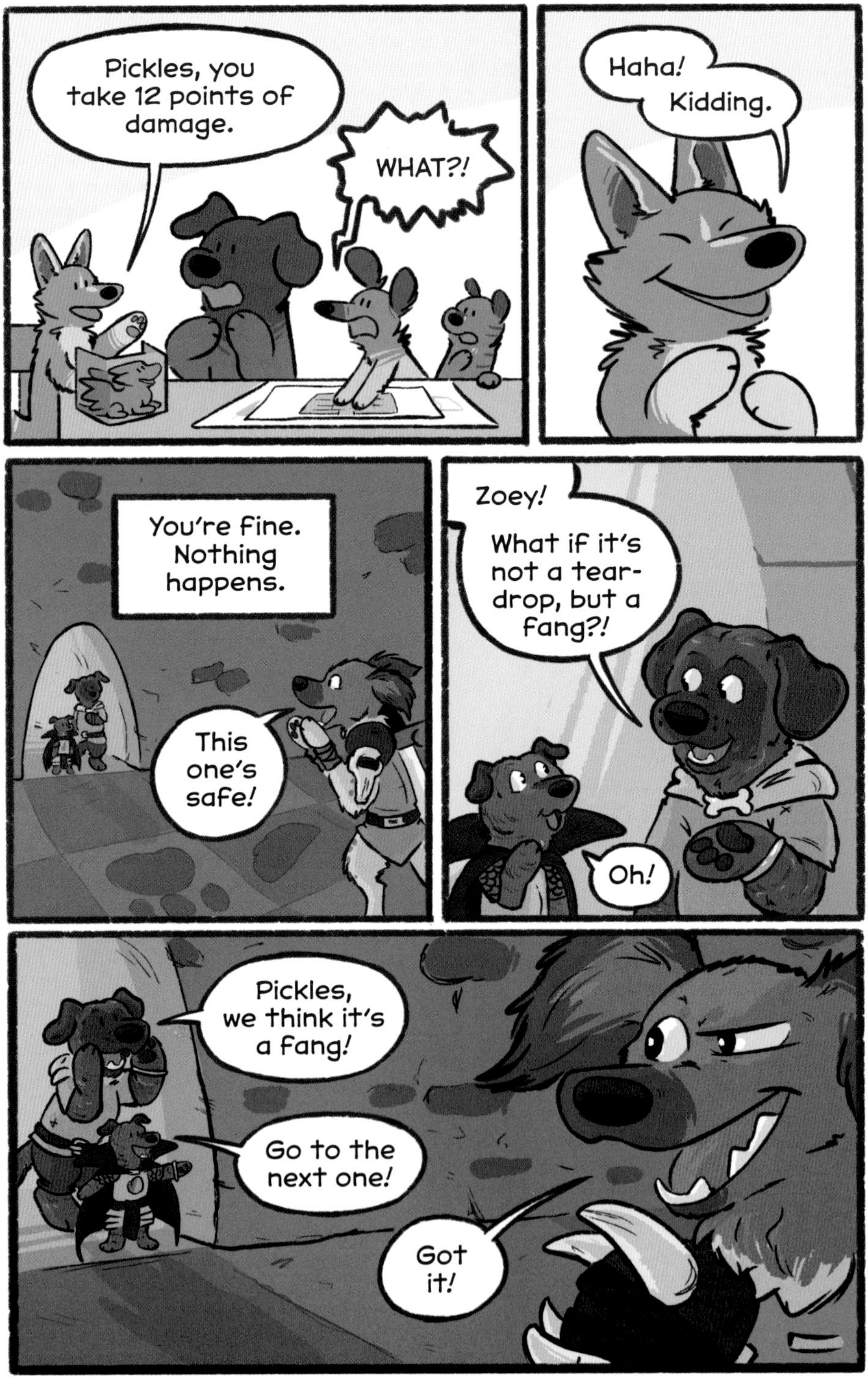
Pickles, you take 12 points of damage.
WHAT?!
Haha!
Kidding.
You're fine. Nothing happens.
This one's safe!
Zoey!
What if it's not a tear-drop, but a fang?!
Oh!
Pickles, we think it's a fang!
Go to the next one!
Got it!

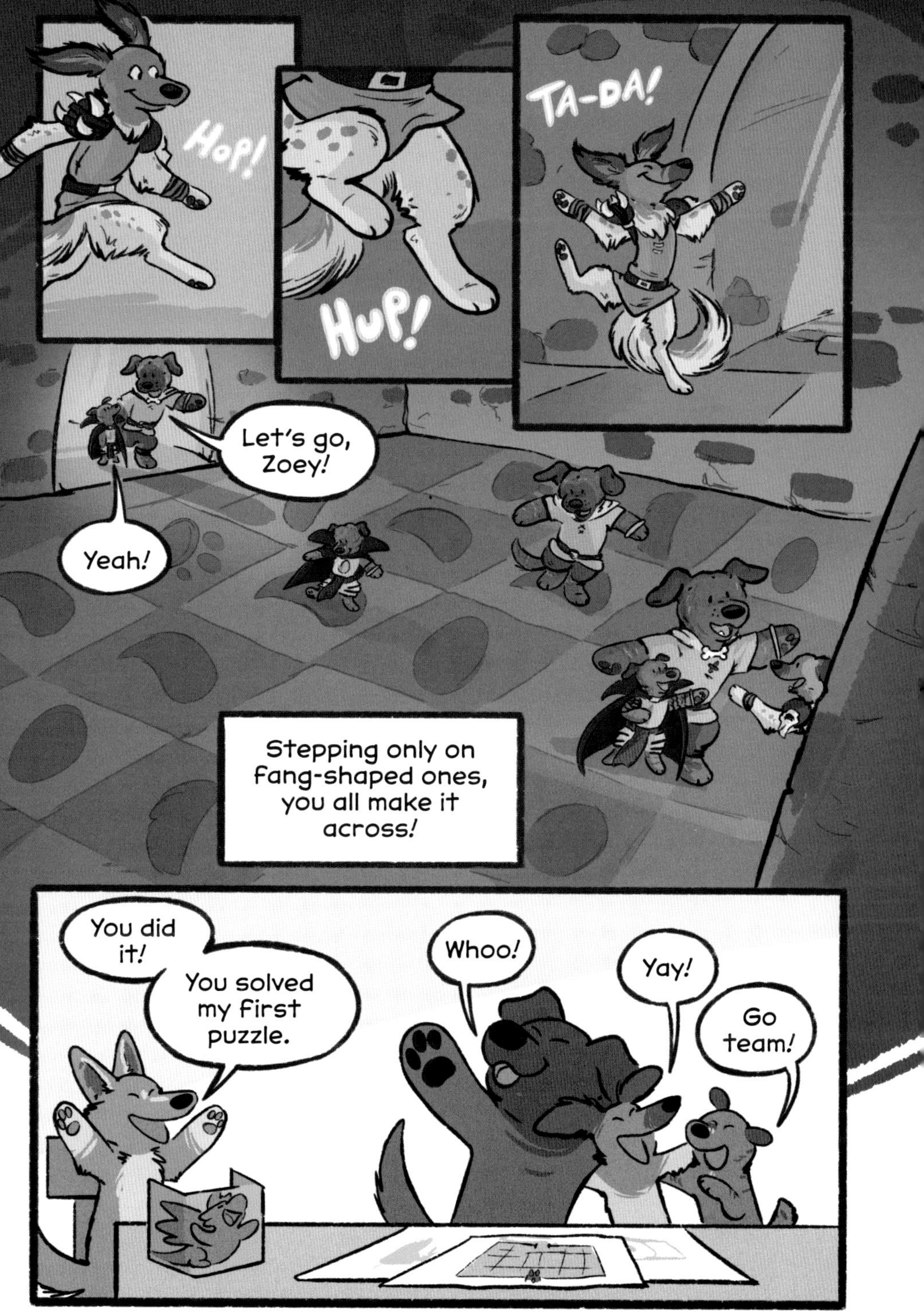
HOP!
HUP!
TA-DA!
Let's go, Zoey!
Yeah!
Stepping only on fang-shaped ones, you all make it across!
You did it!
You solved my first puzzle.
Whoo!
Yay!
Go team!

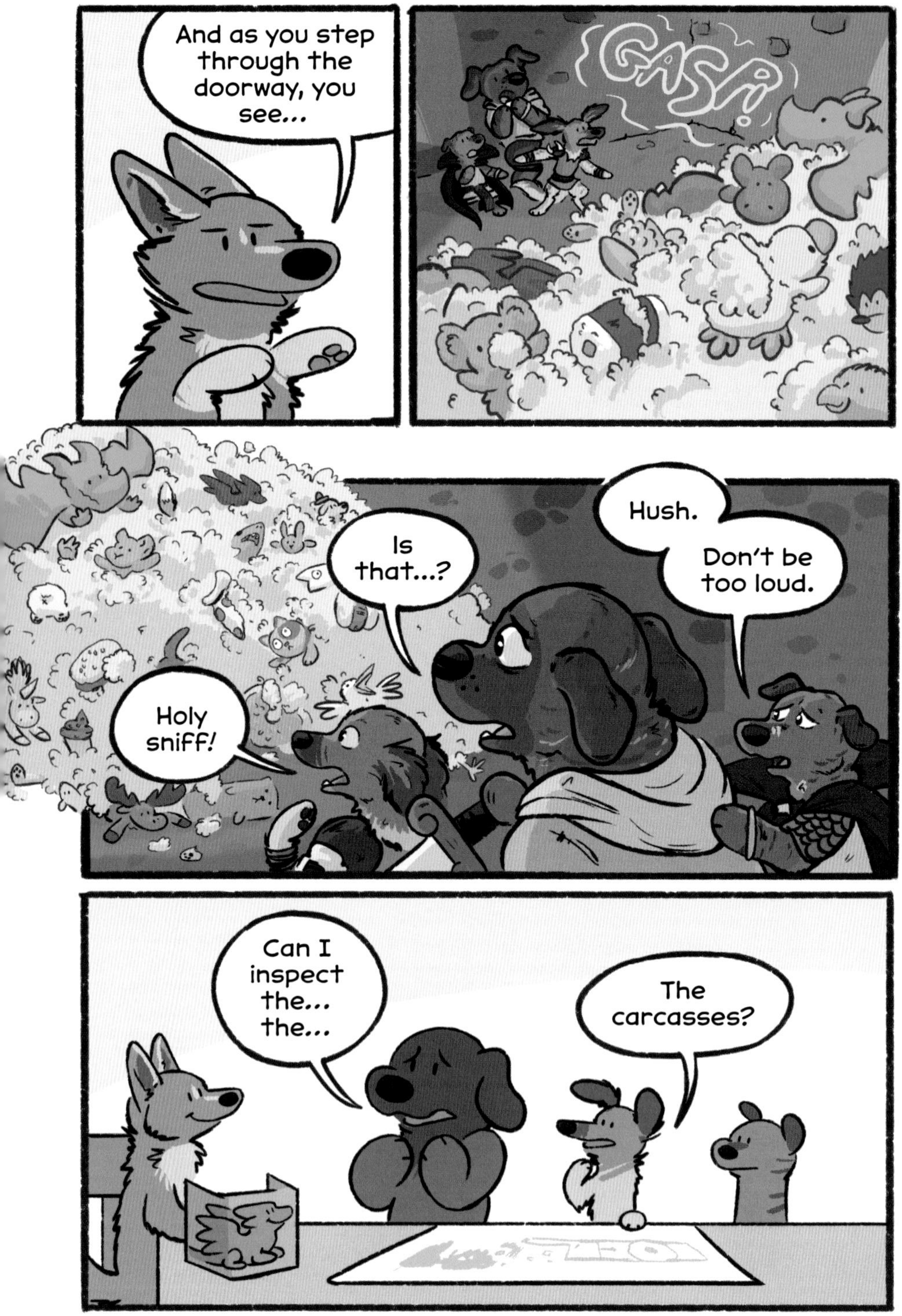
And as you step through the doorway, you see...
GASP!
Is that...?
Hush.
Don't be too loud.
Holy sniff!
Can I inspect the... the...
The carcasses?

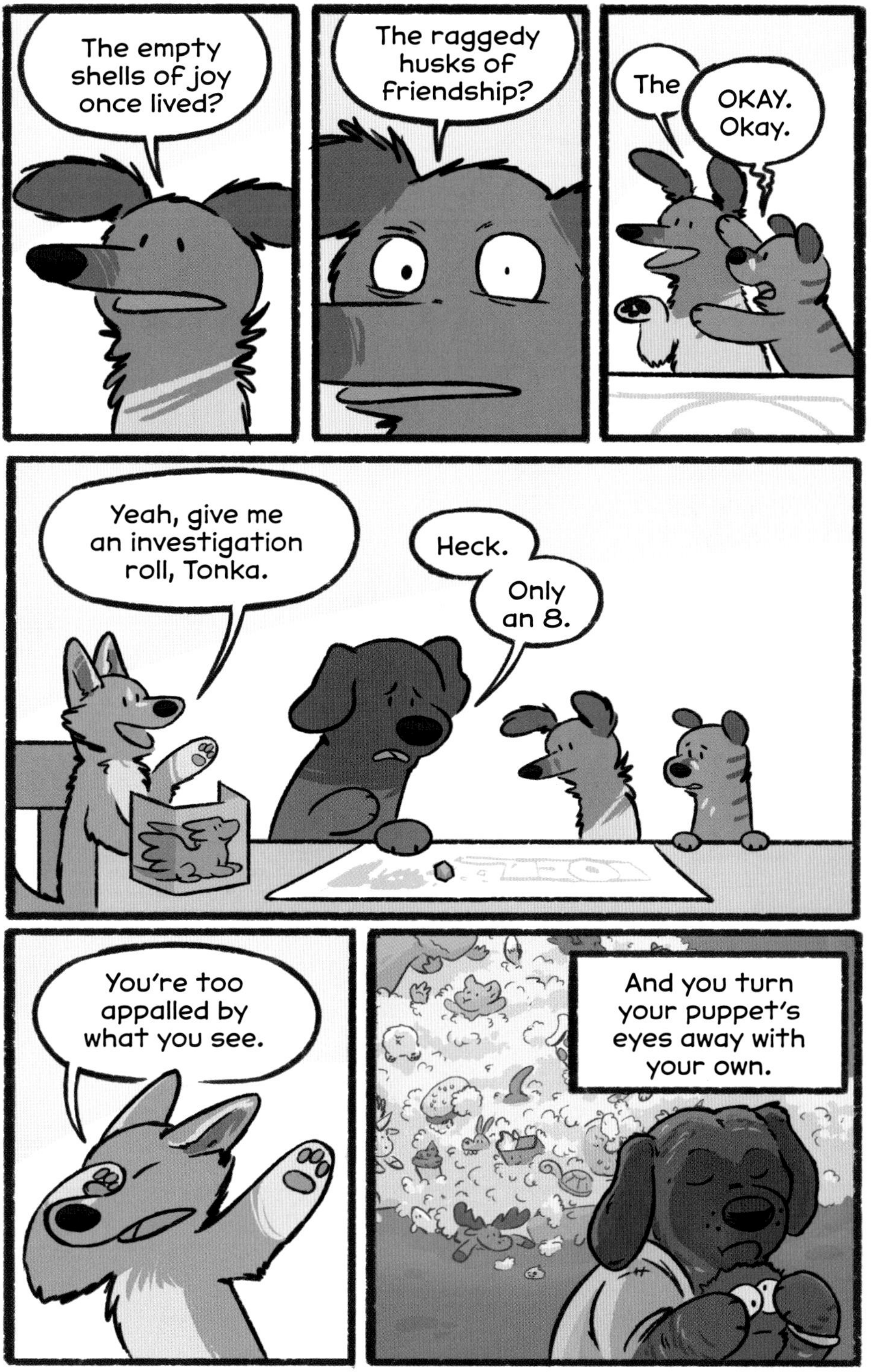
The empty shells of joy once lived?
The raggedy husks of friendship?
The
OKAY. Okay.
Yeah, give me an investigation roll, Tonka.
Heck.
Only an 8.
You're too appalled by what you see.
And you turn your puppet's eyes away with your own.

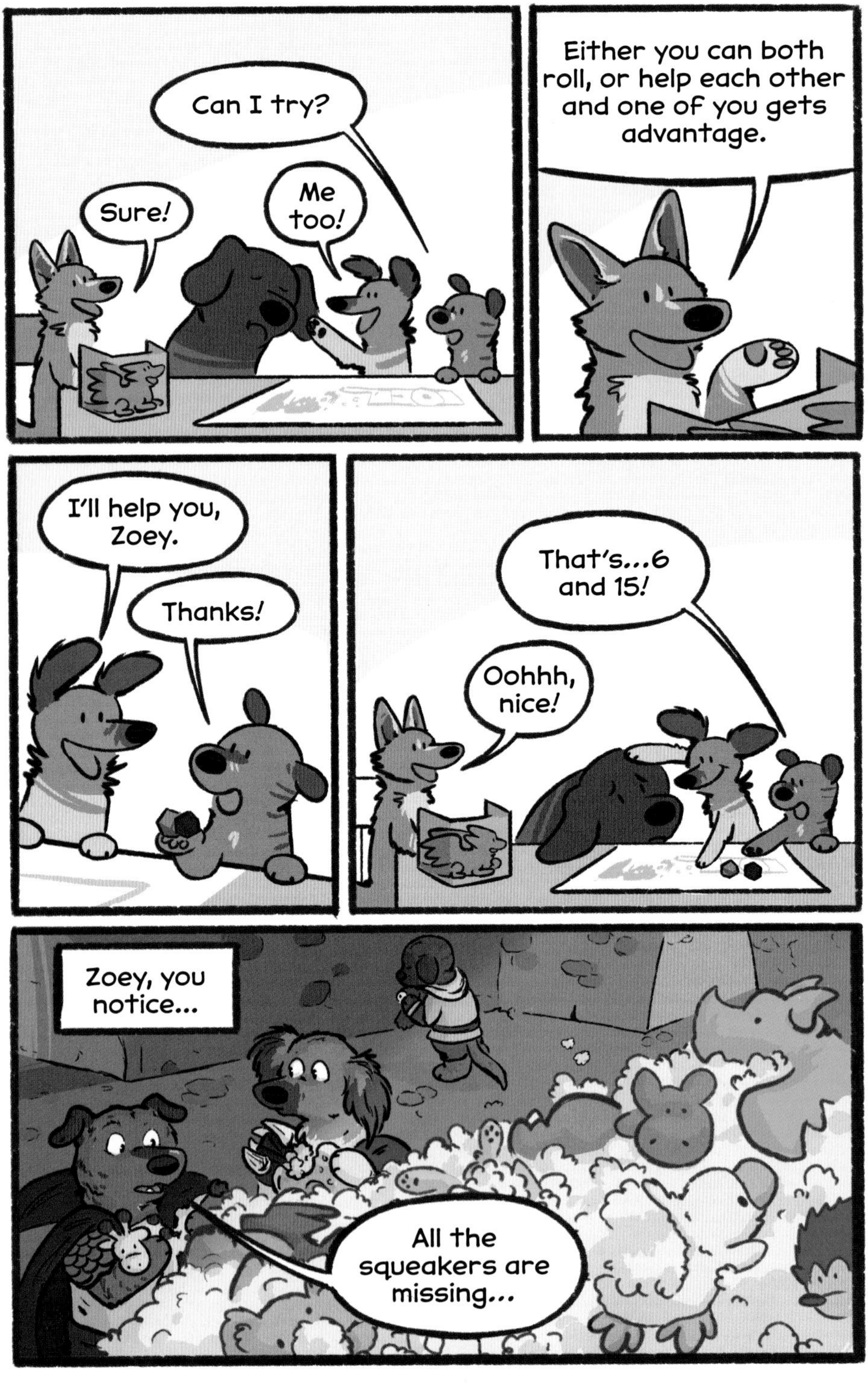
Can I try?
Sure!
Me too!
Either you can both roll, or help each other and one of you gets advantage.
I'll help you, Zoey.
Thanks!
That's...6 and 15!
Oohhh, nice!
Zoey, you notice...
All the squeakers are missing...

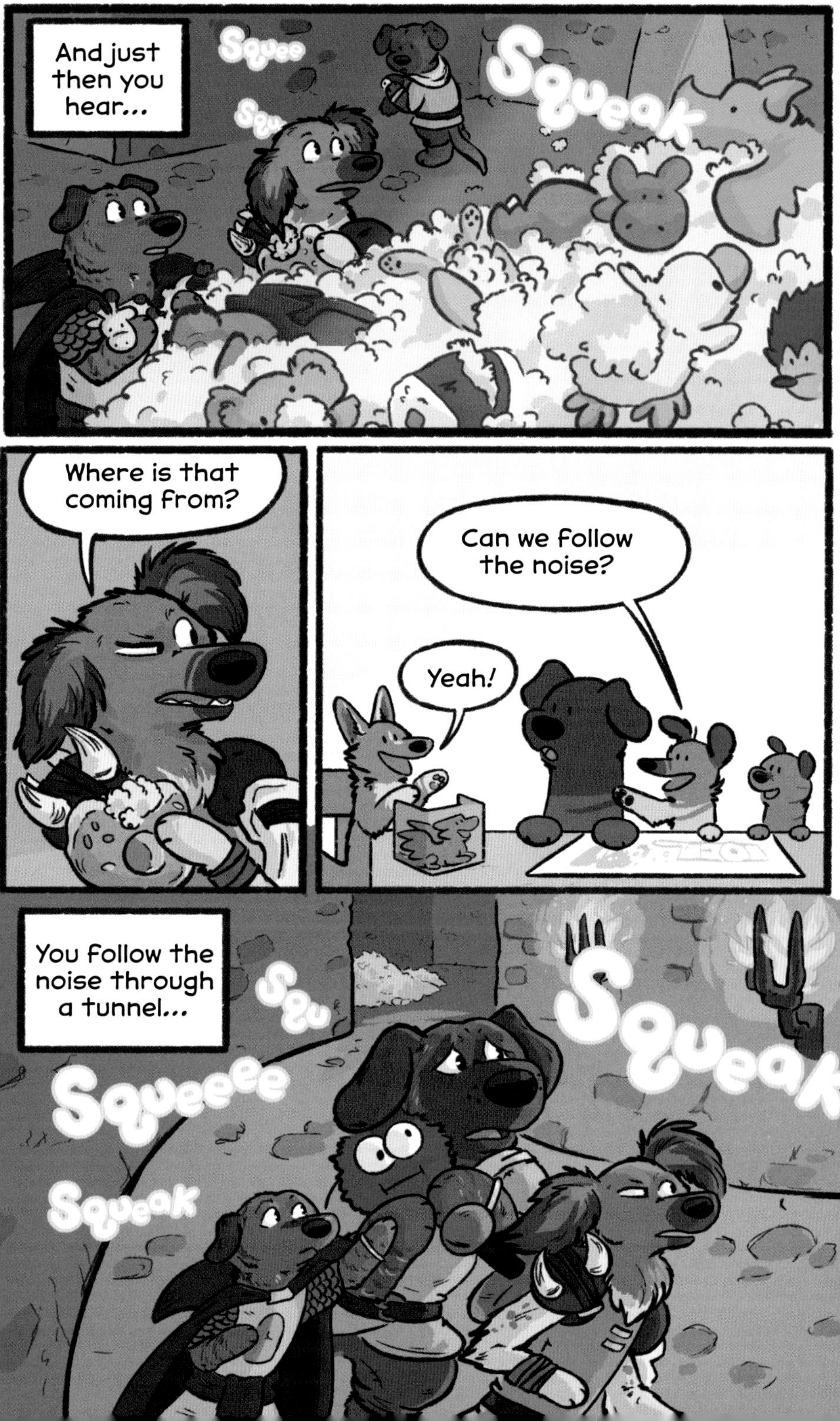
And just then you hear...
Squee
Squ
Squeak
Where is that coming from?
Can we follow the noise?
Yeah!
You follow the noise through a tunnel...
Squ
Squeak
Squeeee
Squeak

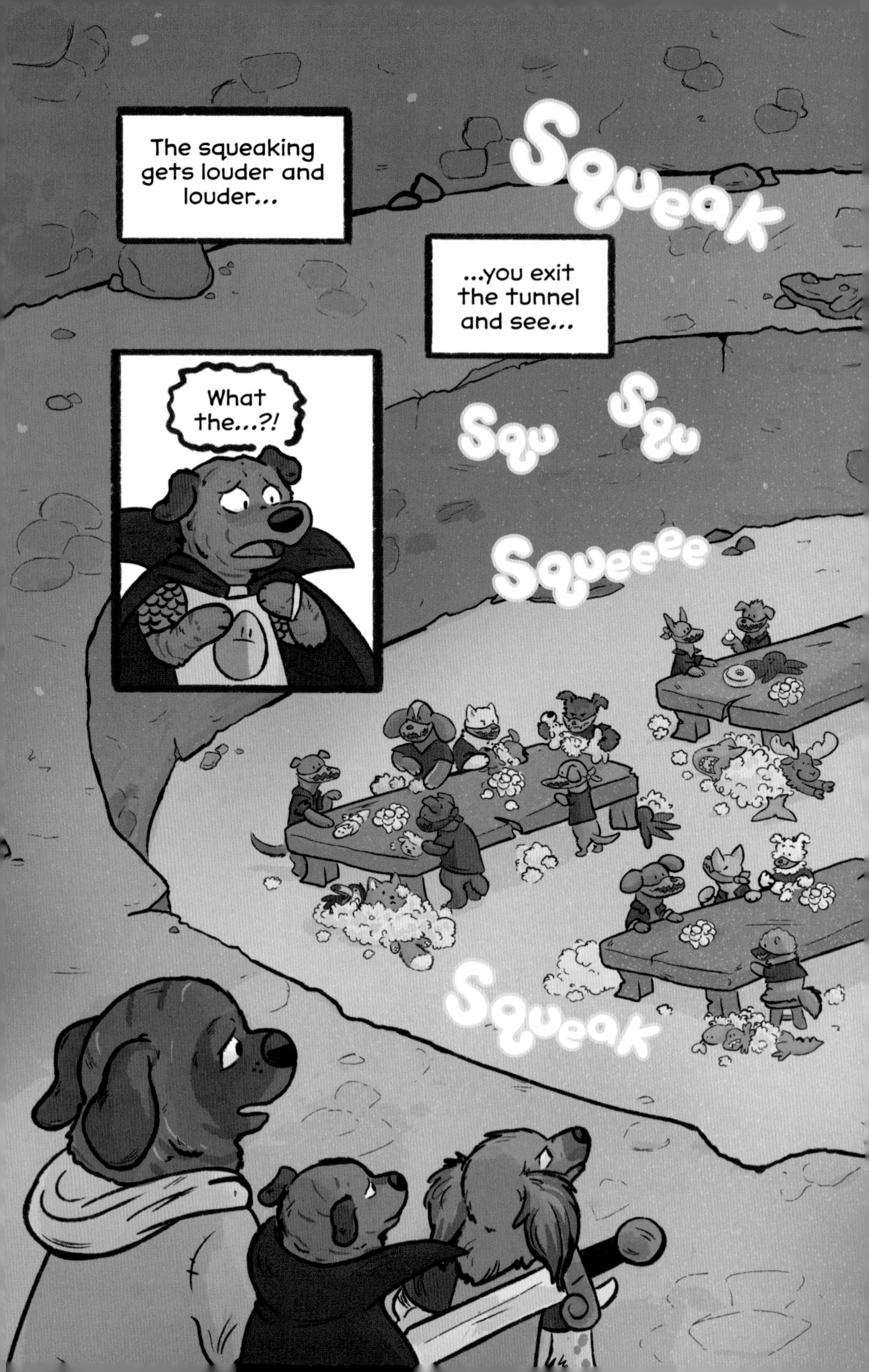

The squeaking gets louder and louder...
Squeak
...you exit the tunnel and see...
What the...?!
Squ
Squ
Squeeee
Squeak

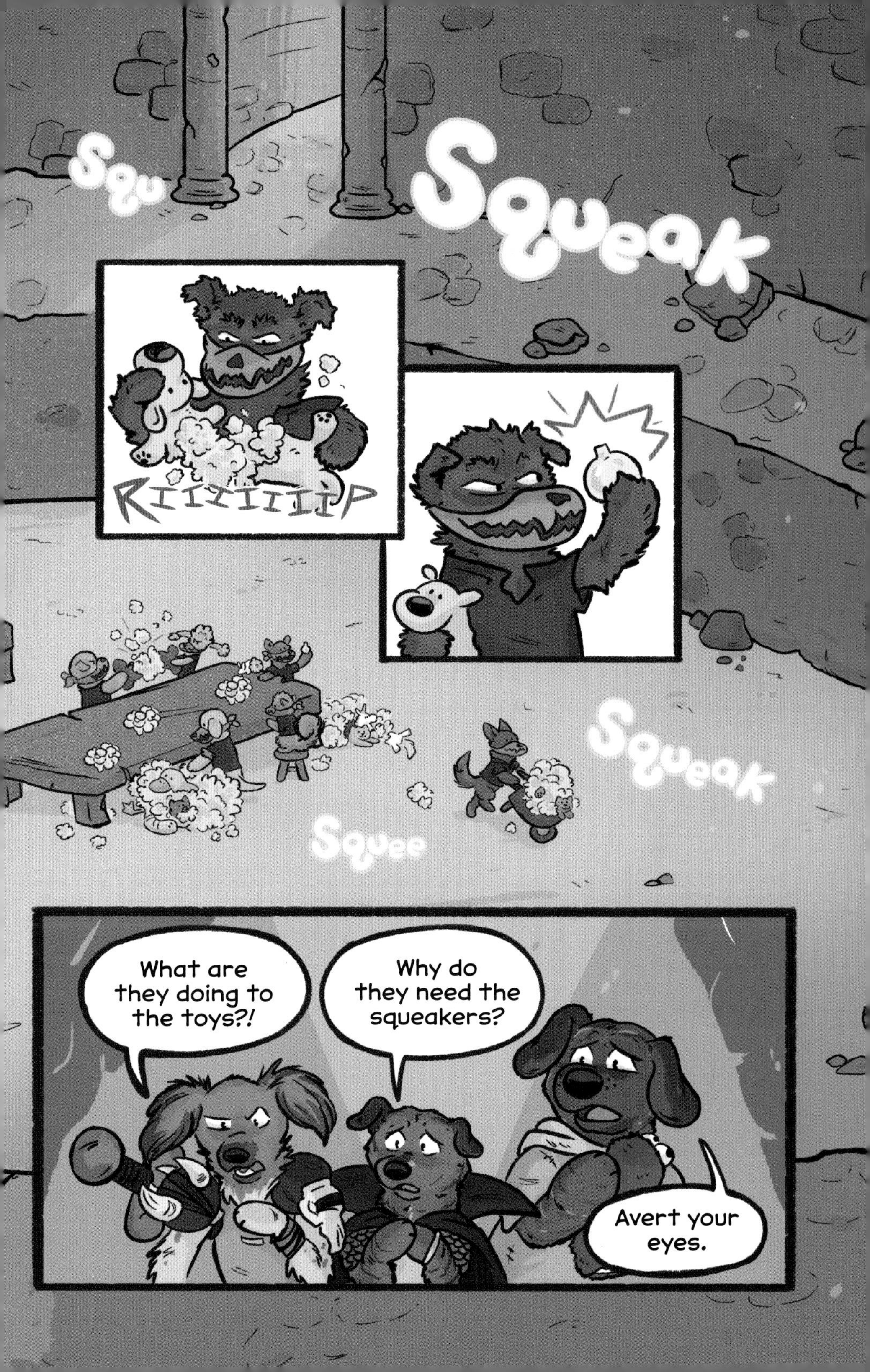
Squ
Squeak
RIIIIIIIP
Squeak
Squee
What are they doing to the toys?!
Why do they need the squeakers?
Avert your eyes.

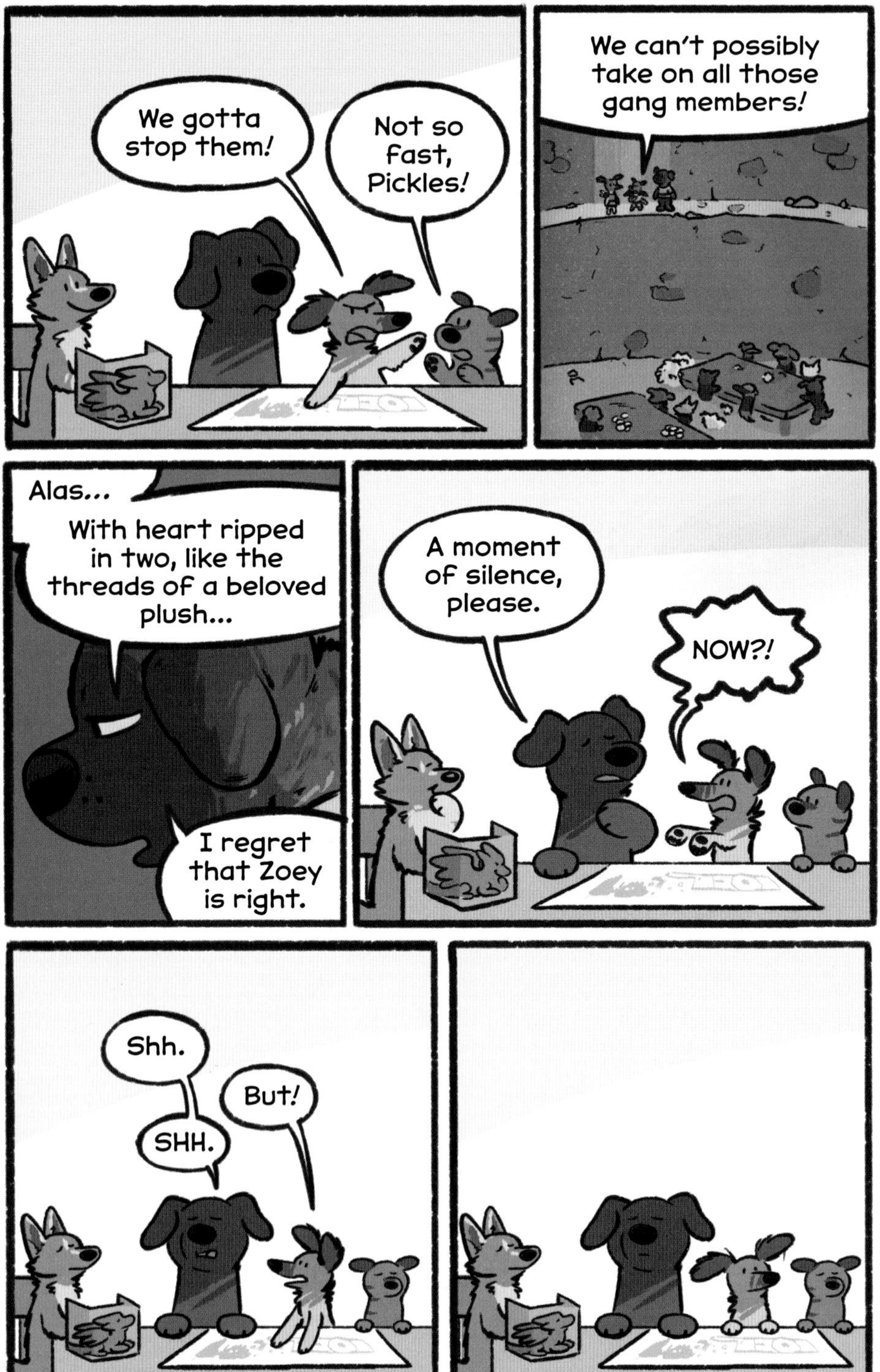
We gotta stop them!
Not so fast, Pickles!
We can't possibly take on all those gang members!
Alas...
With heart ripped in two, like the threads of a beloved plush...
I regret that Zoey is right.
A moment of silence, please.
NOW?!
Shh.
SHH.
But!

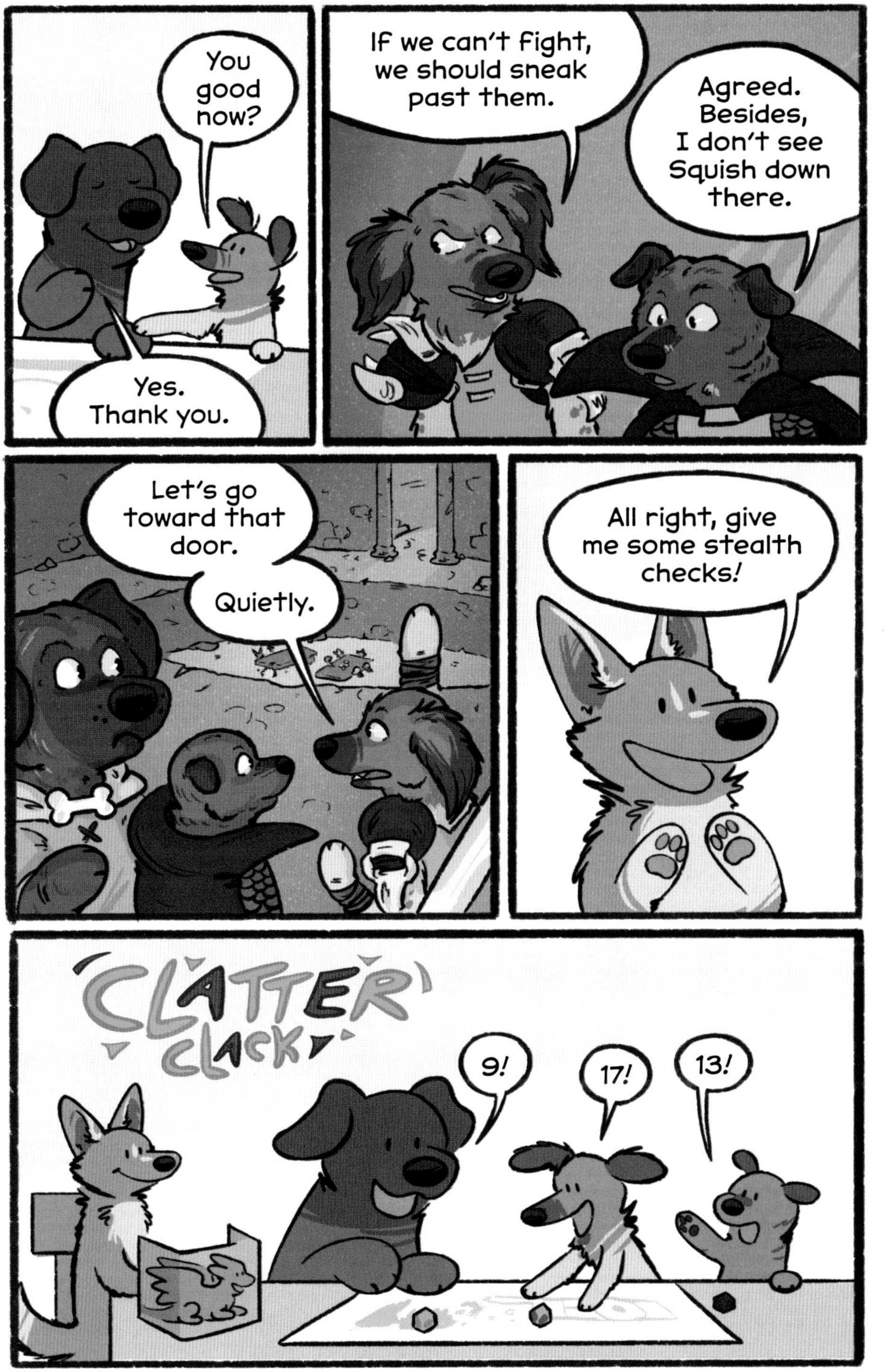
You good now?
Yes. Thank you.
If we can't fight, we should sneak past them.
Agreed. Besides, I don't see Squish down there.
Let's go toward that door.
Quietly.
All right, give me some stealth checks!
CLATTER
CLACK
9!
17!
13!

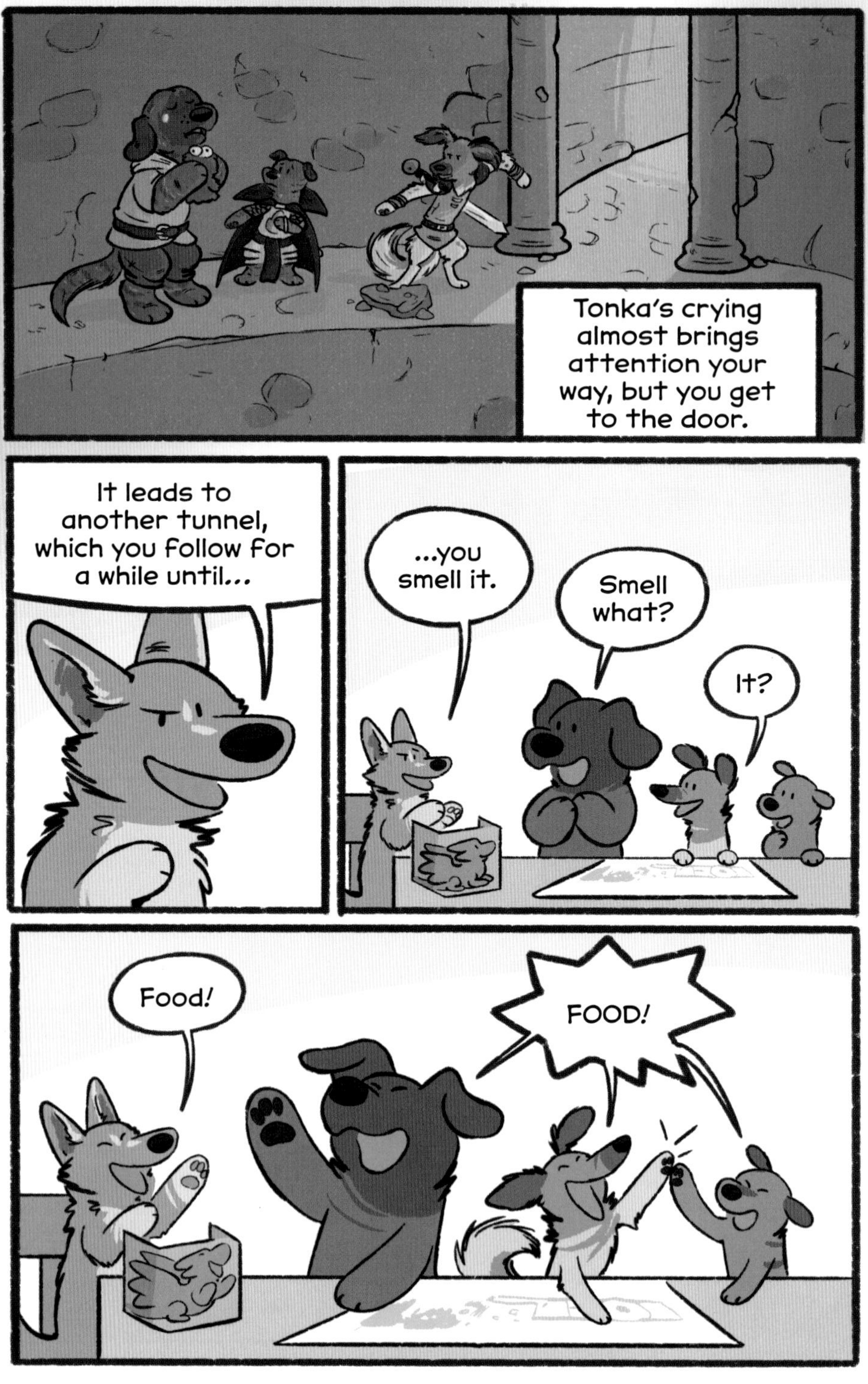

Tonka's crying almost brings attention your way, but you get to the door.
It leads to another tunnel, which you follow for a while until...
...you smell it.
Smell what?
It?
Food!
FOOD!

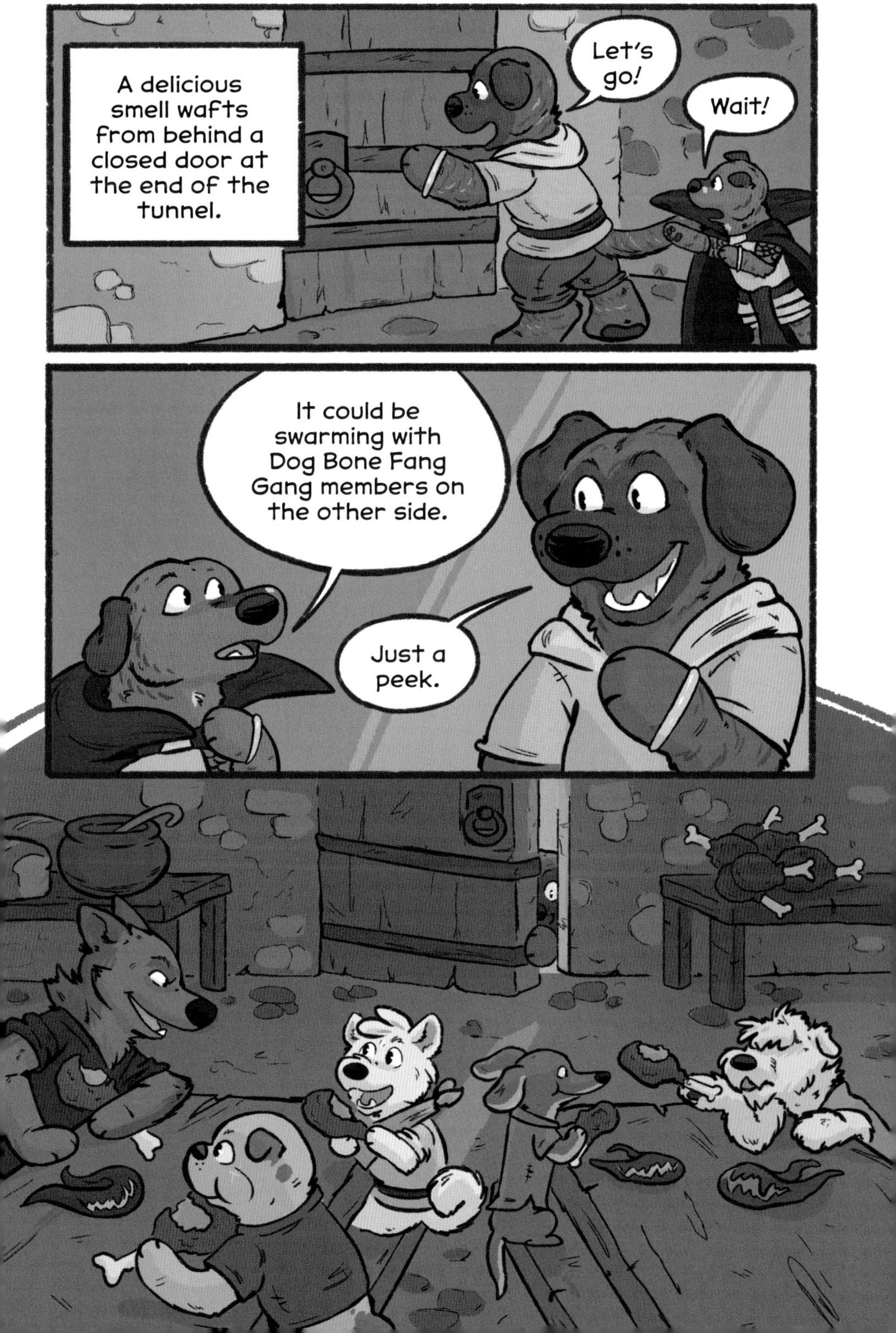
A delicious smell wafts from behind a closed door at the end of the tunnel.
Let's go!
Wait!
It could be swarming with Dog Bone Fang Gang members on the other side.
Just a peek.

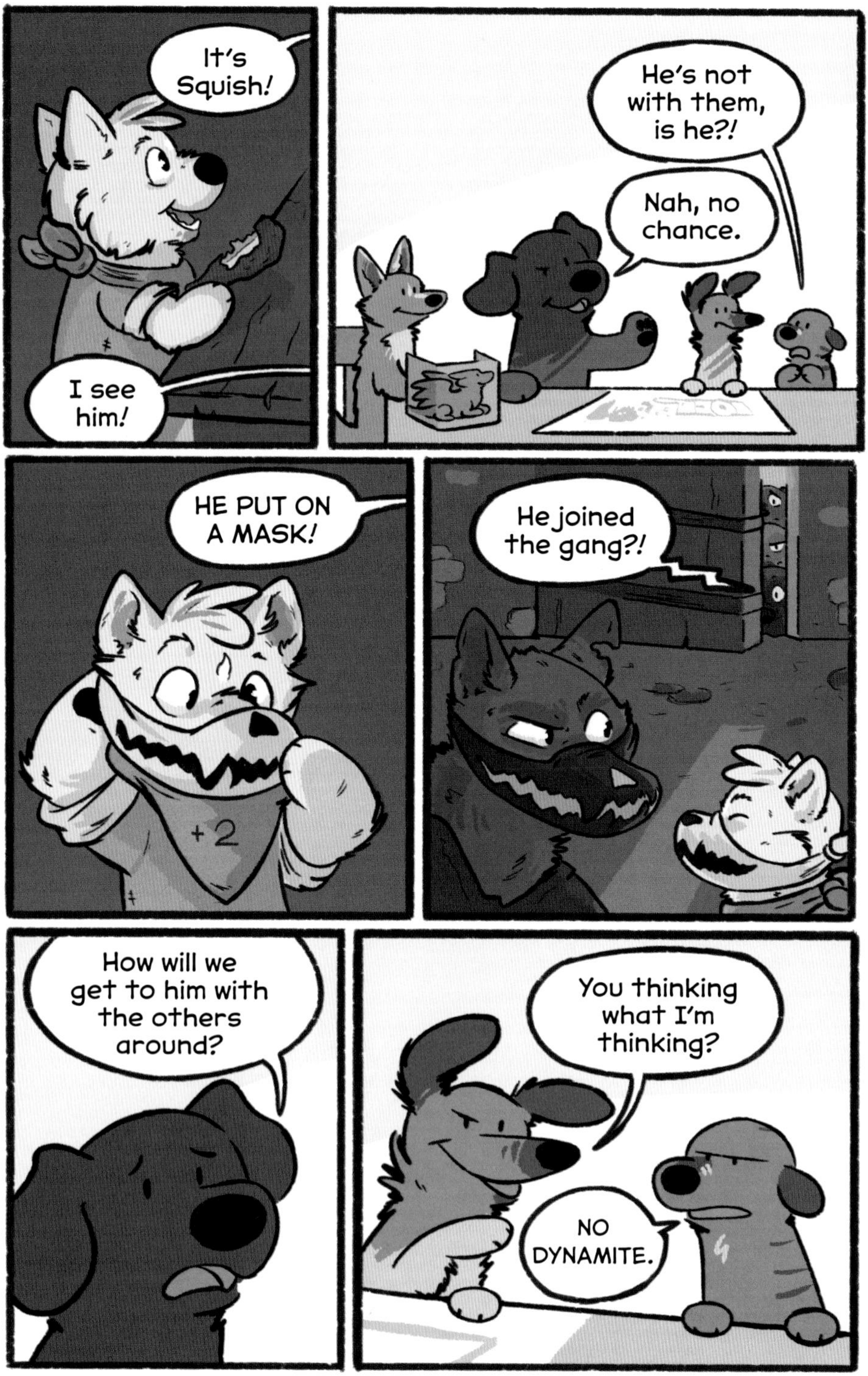
It's Squish!
I see him!
He's not with them, is he?!
Nah, no chance.
HE PUT ON A MASK!
He joined the gang?!
How will we get to him with the others around?
You thinking what I'm thinking?
NO DYNAMITE.

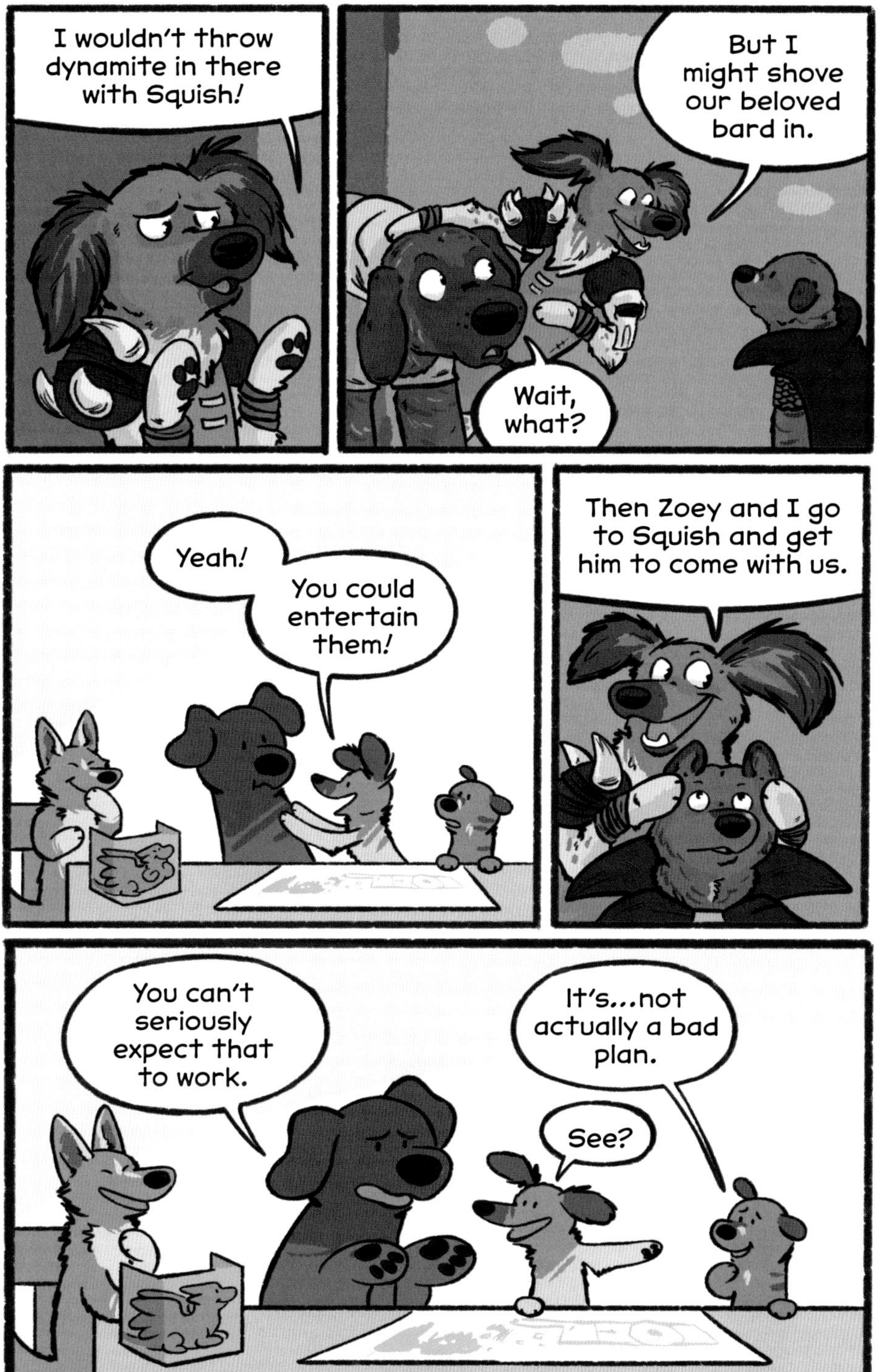

I wouldn't throw dynamite in there with Squish!
But I might shove our beloved bard in.
Wait, what?
Yeah!
You could entertain them!
Then Zoey and I go to Squish and get him to come with us.
You can't seriously expect that to work.
It's...not actually a bad plan.
See?

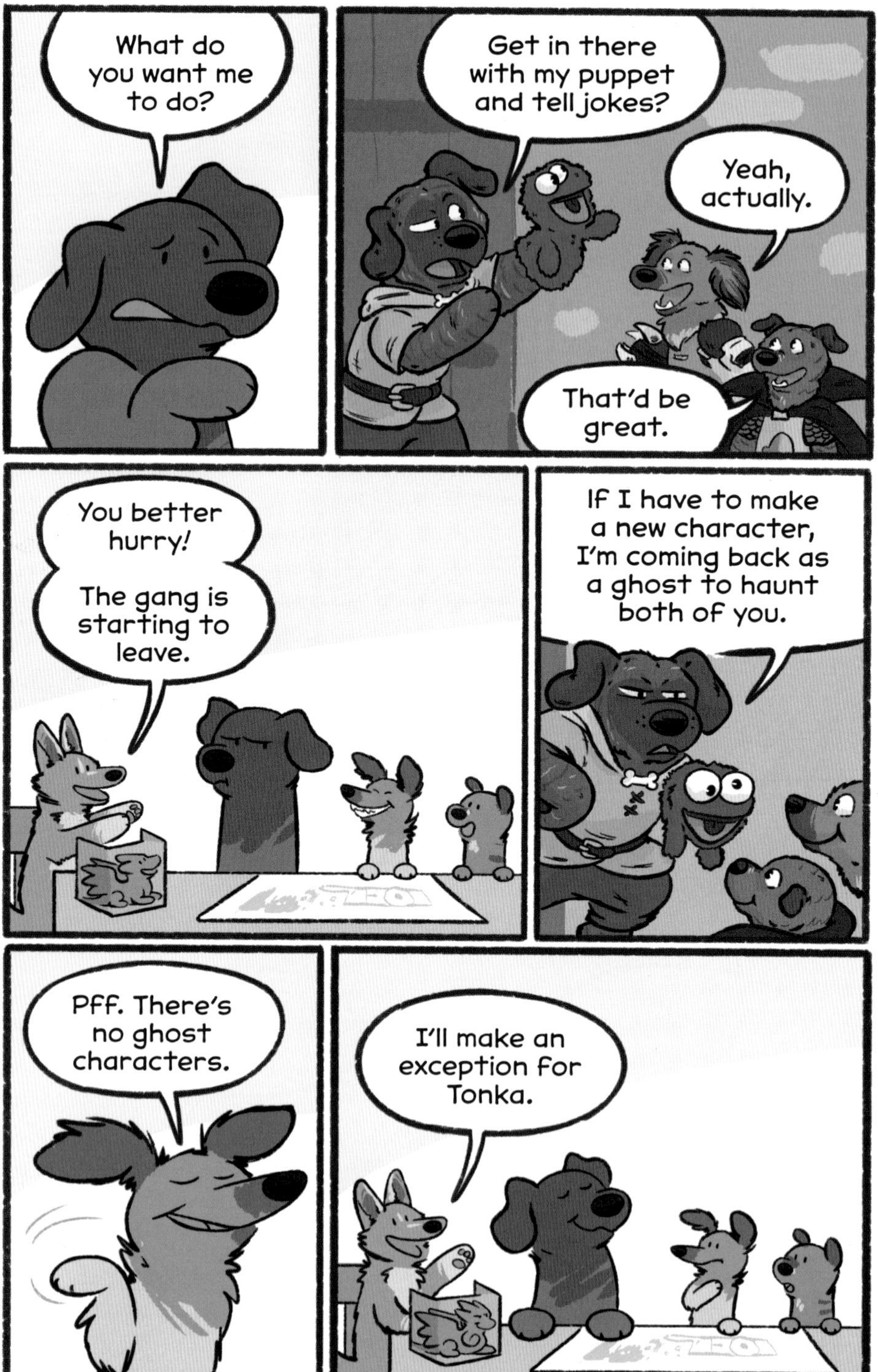
What do you want me to do?
Get in there with my puppet and tell jokes?
Yeah, actually.
That'd be great.
You better hurry!
The gang is starting to leave.
If I have to make a new character, I'm coming back as a ghost to haunt both of you.
Pff. There's no ghost characters.
I'll make an exception for Tonka.

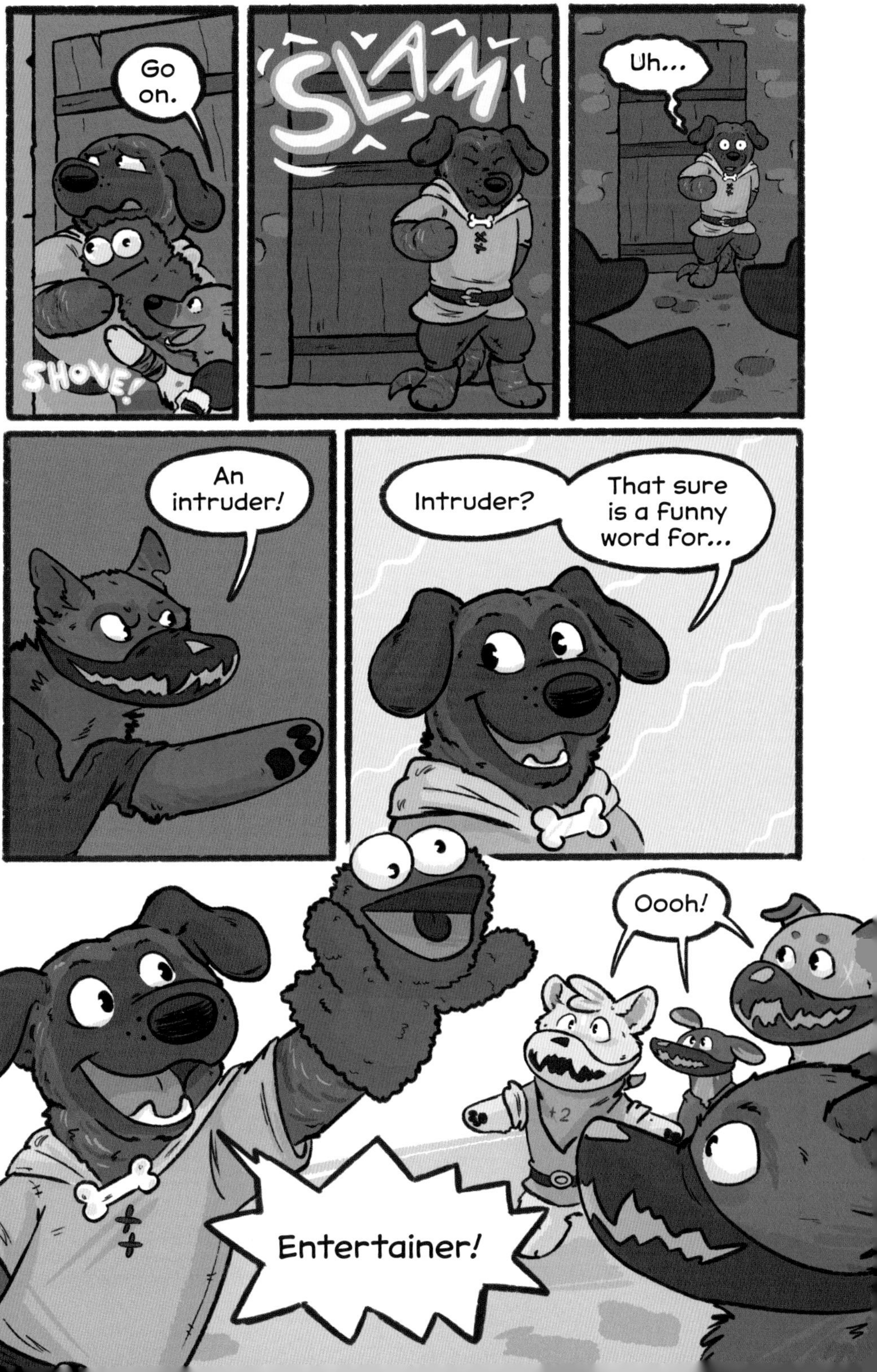
Go on.
SHOVE!
SLAM
Uh...
An intruder!
Intruder?
That sure is a funny word for...
Entertainer!
Oooh!

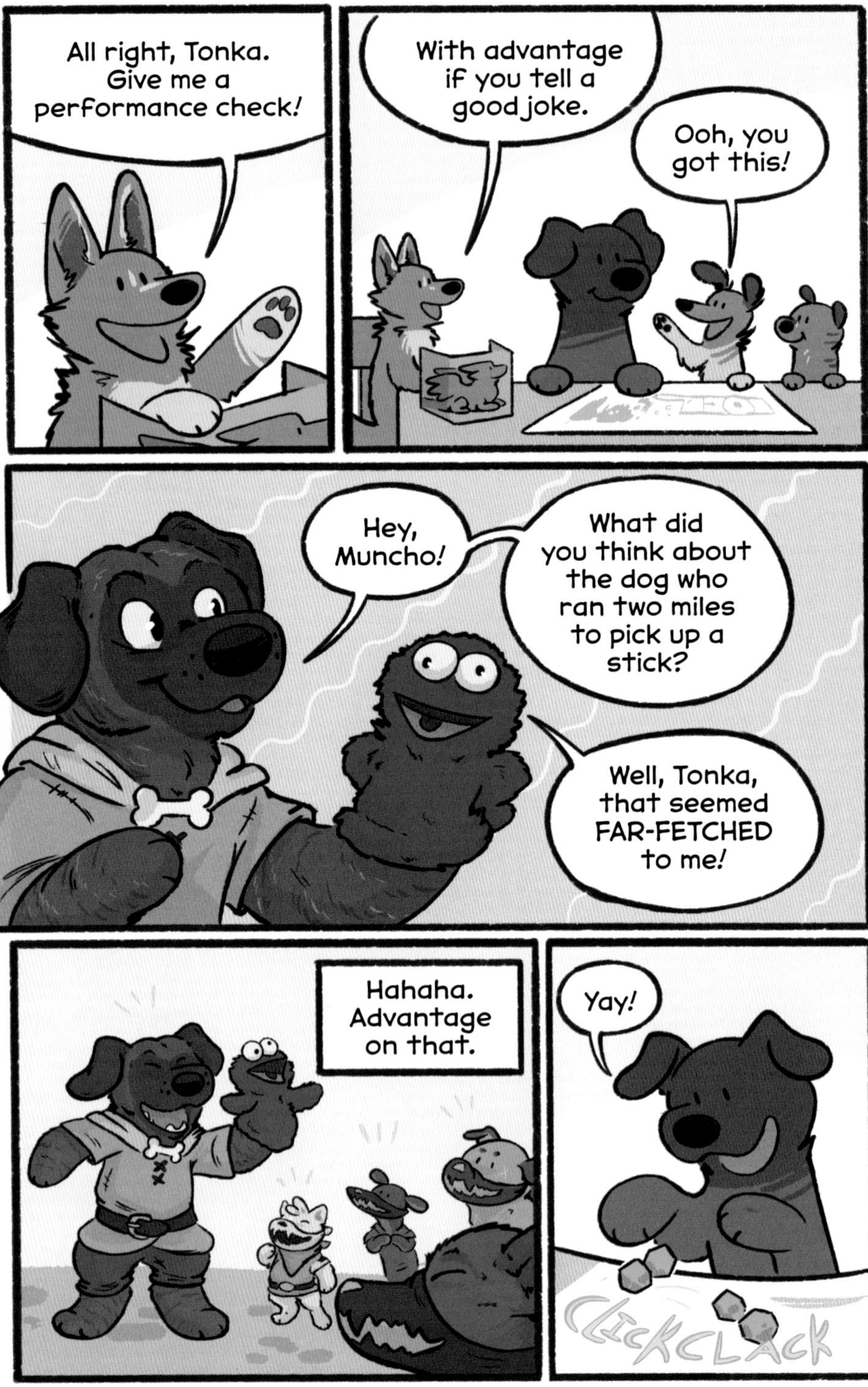
All right, Tonka. Give me a performance check!
With advantage if you tell a good joke.
Ooh, you got this!
Hey, Muncho!
What did you think about the dog who ran two miles to pick up a stick?
Well, Tonka, that seemed FAR-FETCHED to me!
Hahaha. Advantage on that.
Yay!
CLICKCLACK

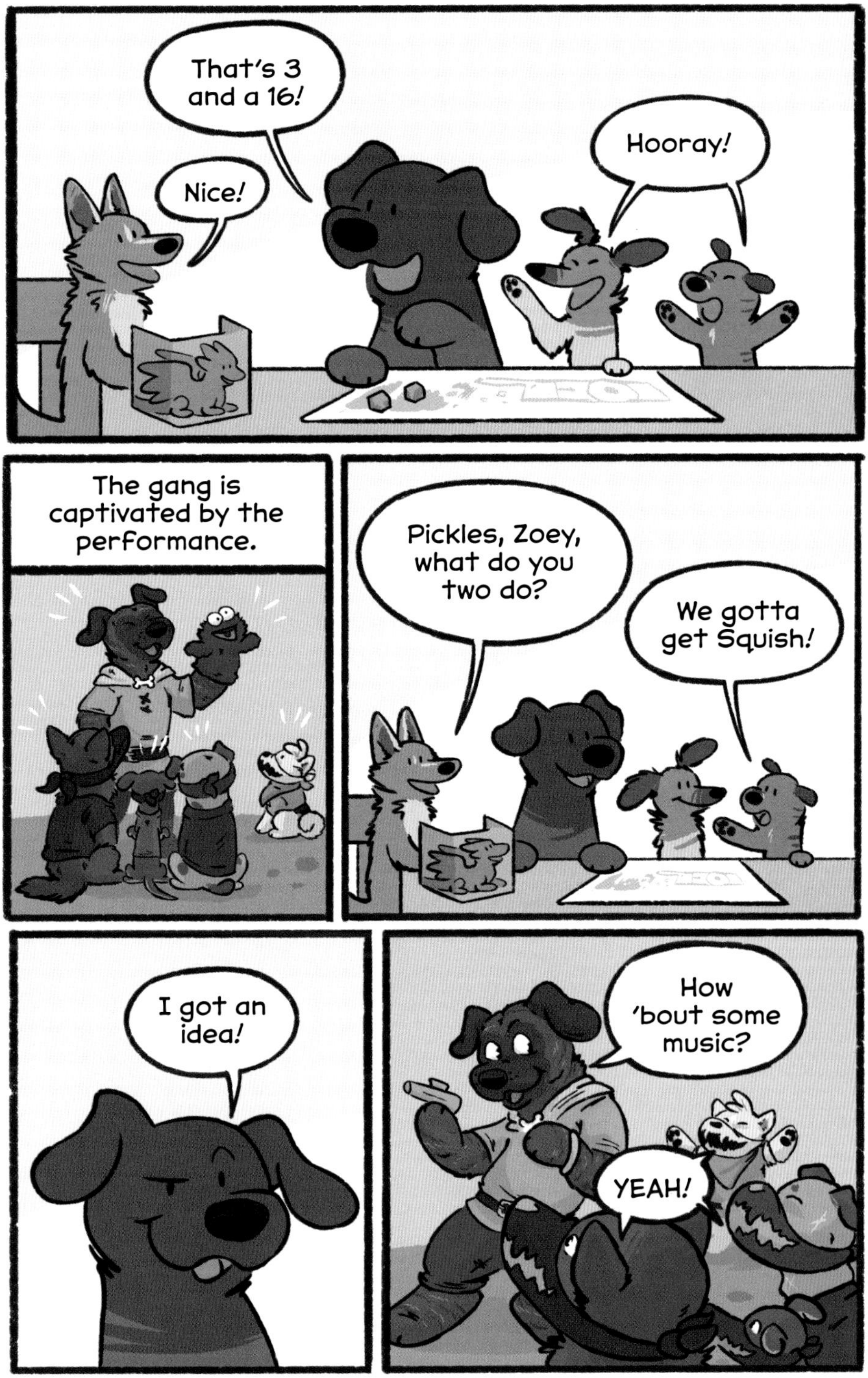

That's 3 and a 16!
Nice!
Hooray!
The gang is captivated by the performance.
Pickles, Zoey, what do you two do?
We gotta get Squish!
I got an idea!
How 'bout some music?
YEAH!

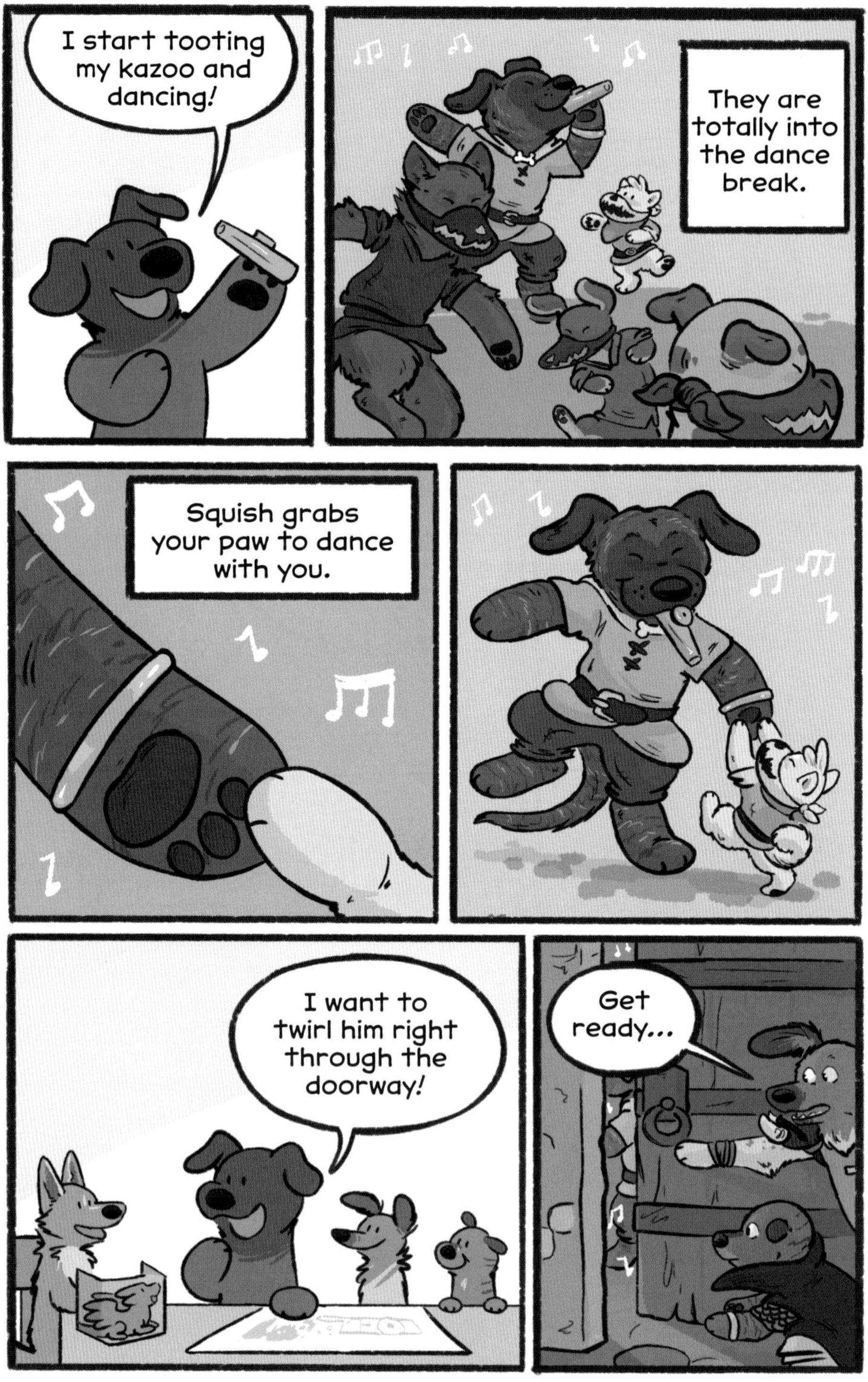
I start tooting my kazoo and dancing!
They are totally into the dance break.
Squish grabs your paw to dance with you.
I want to twirl him right through the doorway!
Get ready...

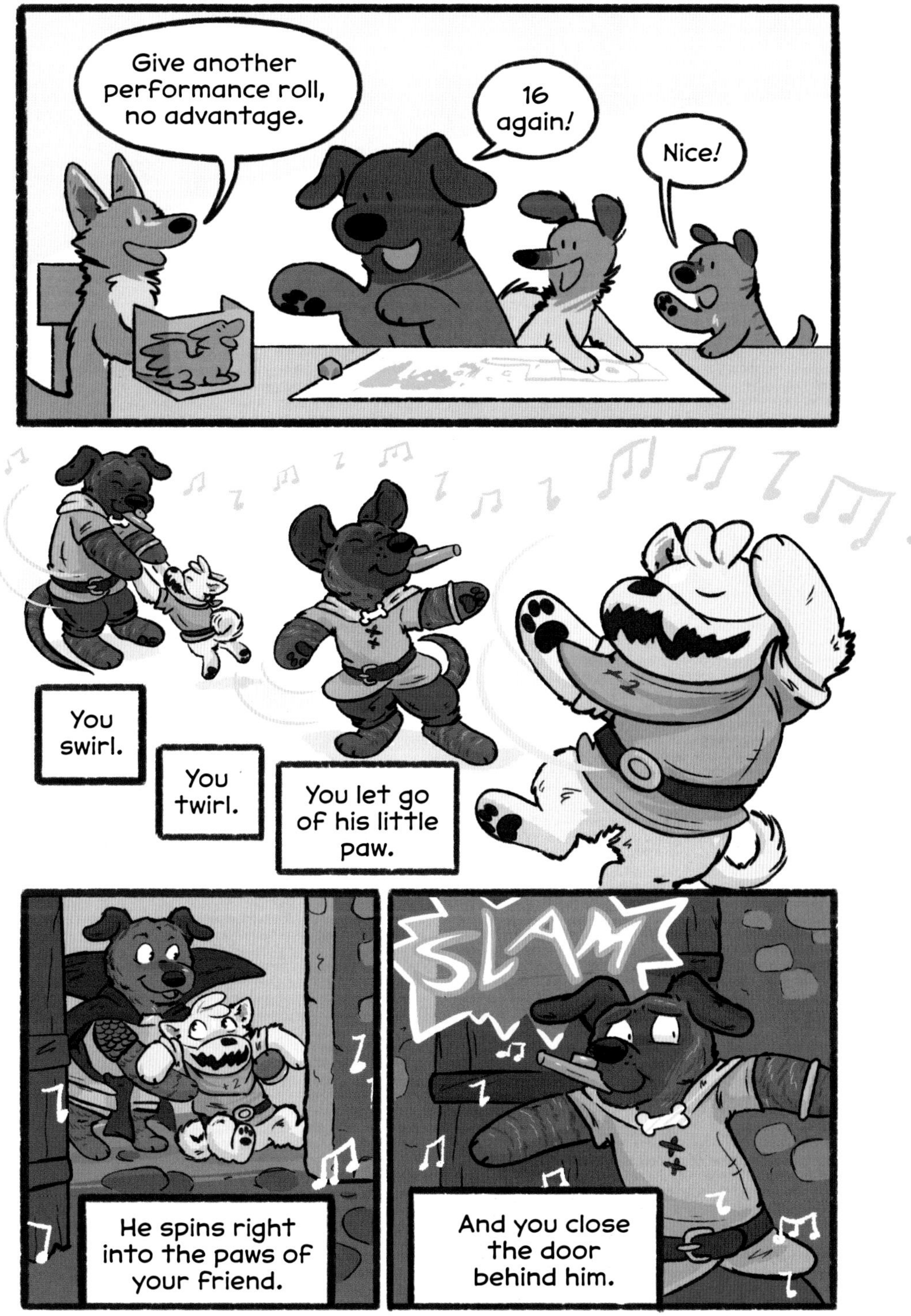
Give another performance roll, no advantage.
16 again!
Nice!
You swirl.
You twirl.
You let go of his little paw.
SLAM
He spins right into the paws of your friend.
And you close the door behind him.

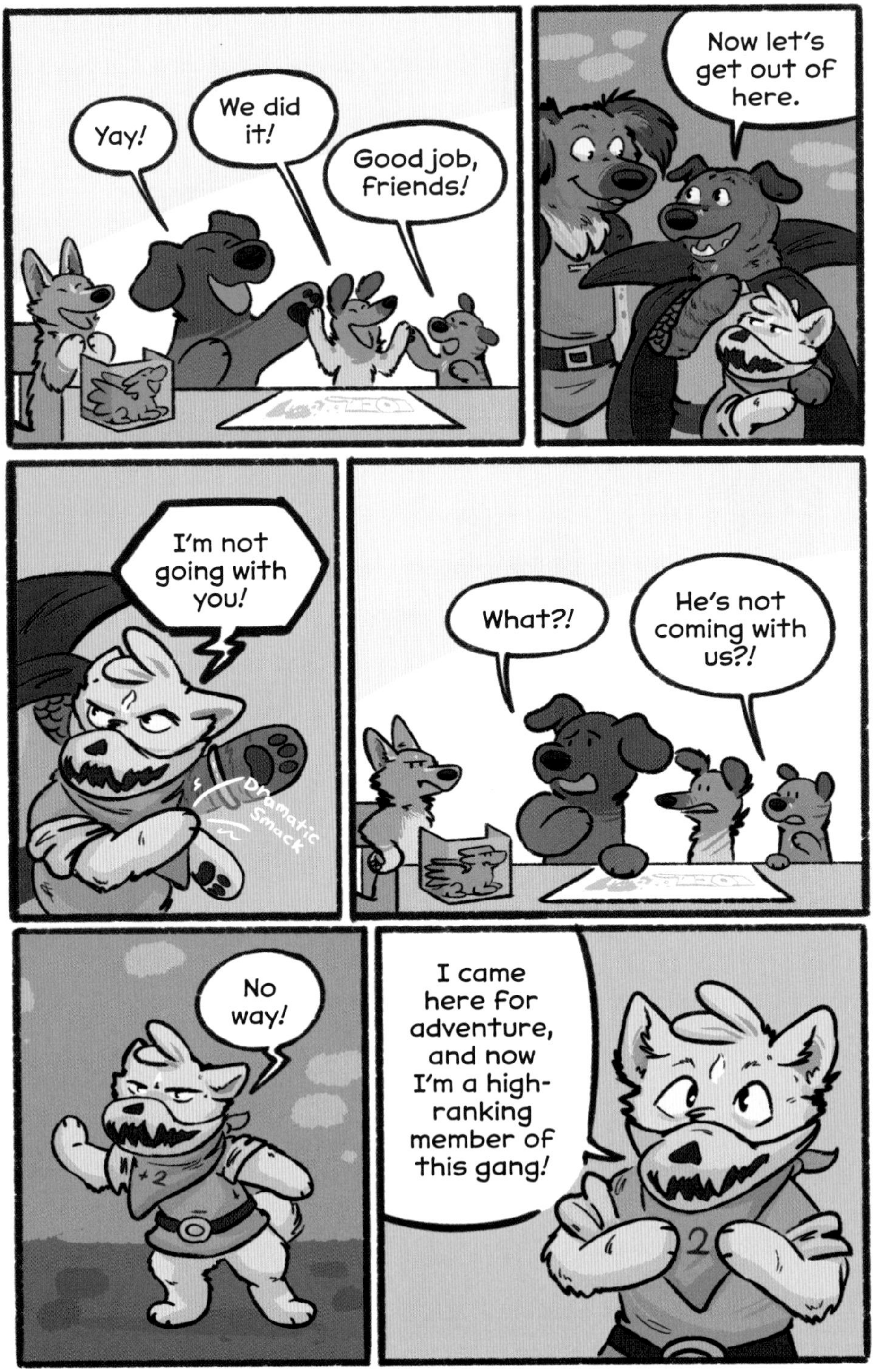
Yay!
We did it!
Good job, friends!
Now let's get out of here.
I'm not going with you!
Dramatic Smack
What?!
He's not coming with us?!
No way!
I came here for adventure, and now I'm a high-ranking member of this gang!

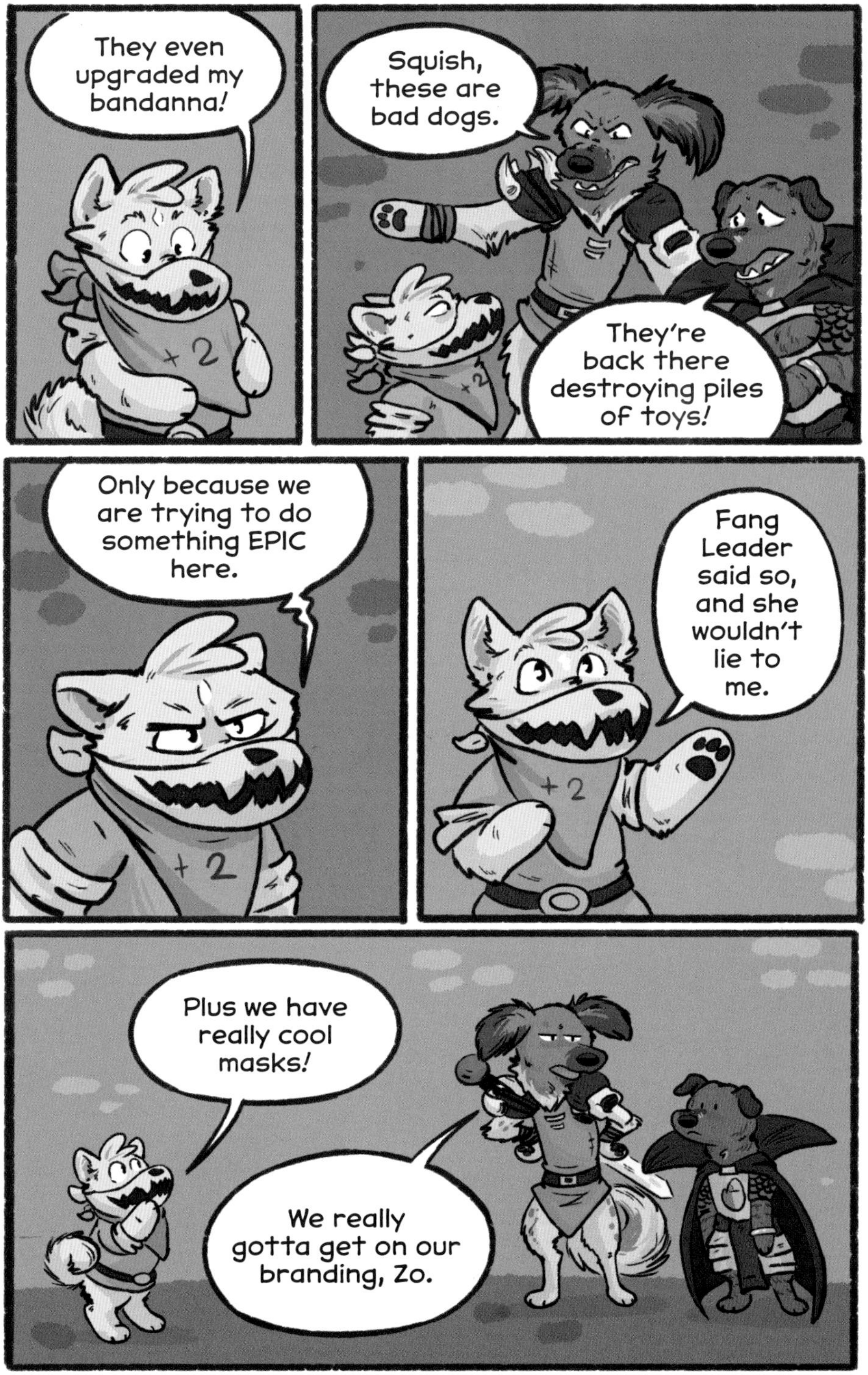
They even upgraded my bandanna!
Squish, these are bad dogs.
They're back there destroying piles of toys!
+2
Only because we are trying to do something EPIC here.
+2
Fang Leader said so, and she wouldn't lie to me.
+2
Plus we have really cool masks!
We really gotta get on our branding, Zo.

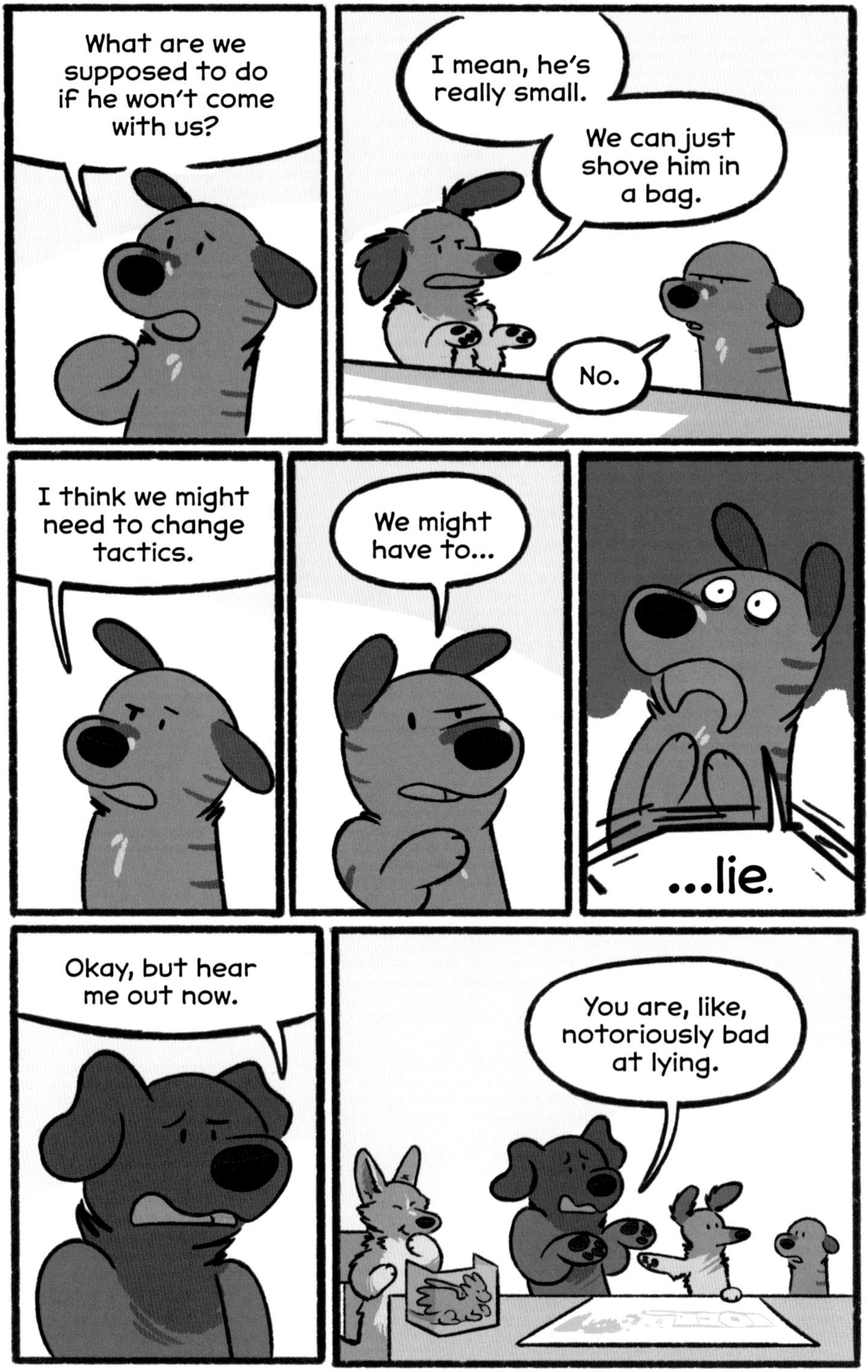
What are we supposed to do if he won't come with us?
I mean, he's really small.
We can just shove him in a bag.
No.
I think we might need to change tactics.
We might have to...
...lie.
Okay, but hear me out now.
You are, like, notoriously bad at lying.

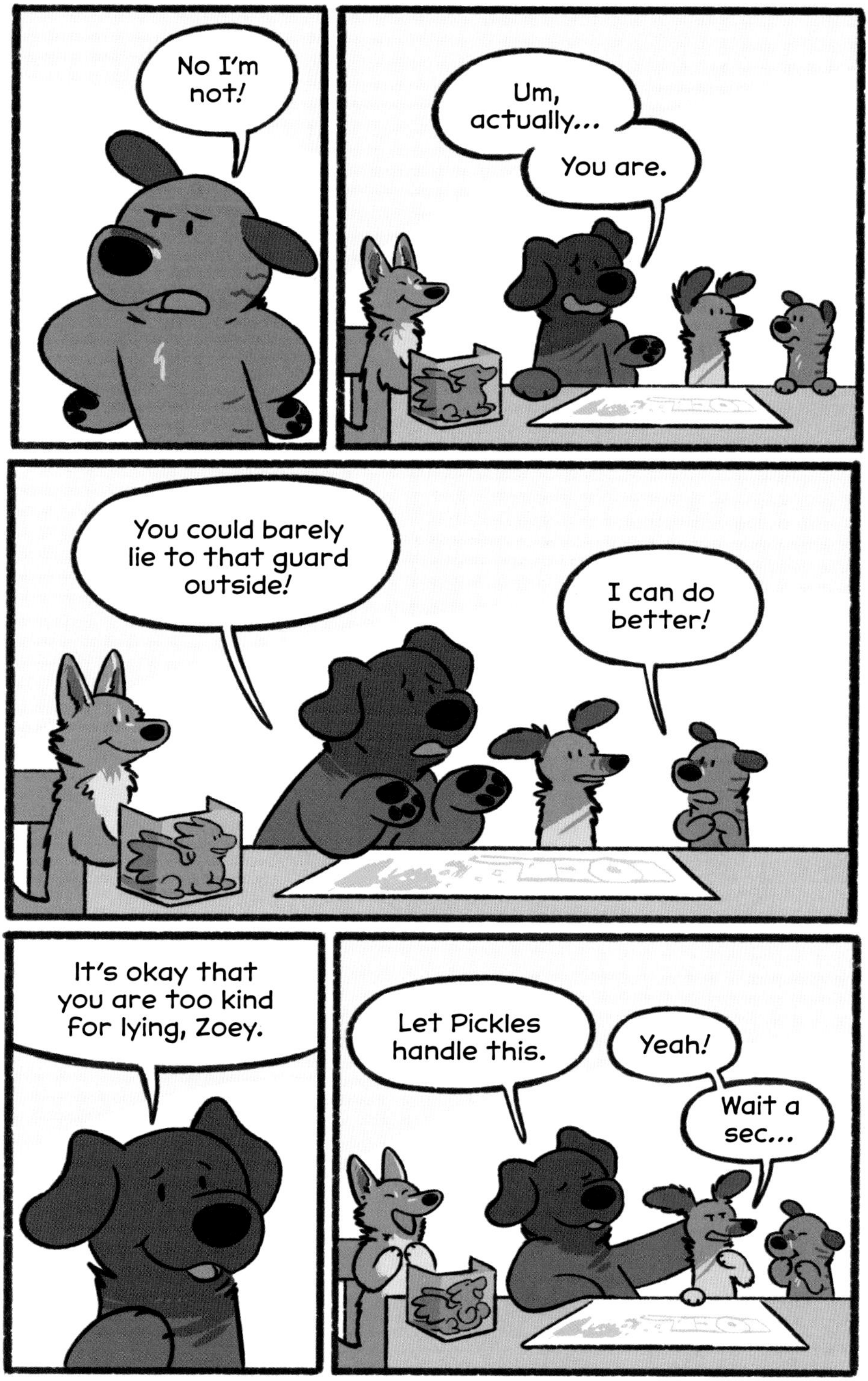
No I'm not!
Um, actually...
You are.
You could barely lie to that guard outside!
I can do better!
It's okay that you are too kind for lying, Zoey.
Let Pickles handle this.
Yeah!
Wait a sec...

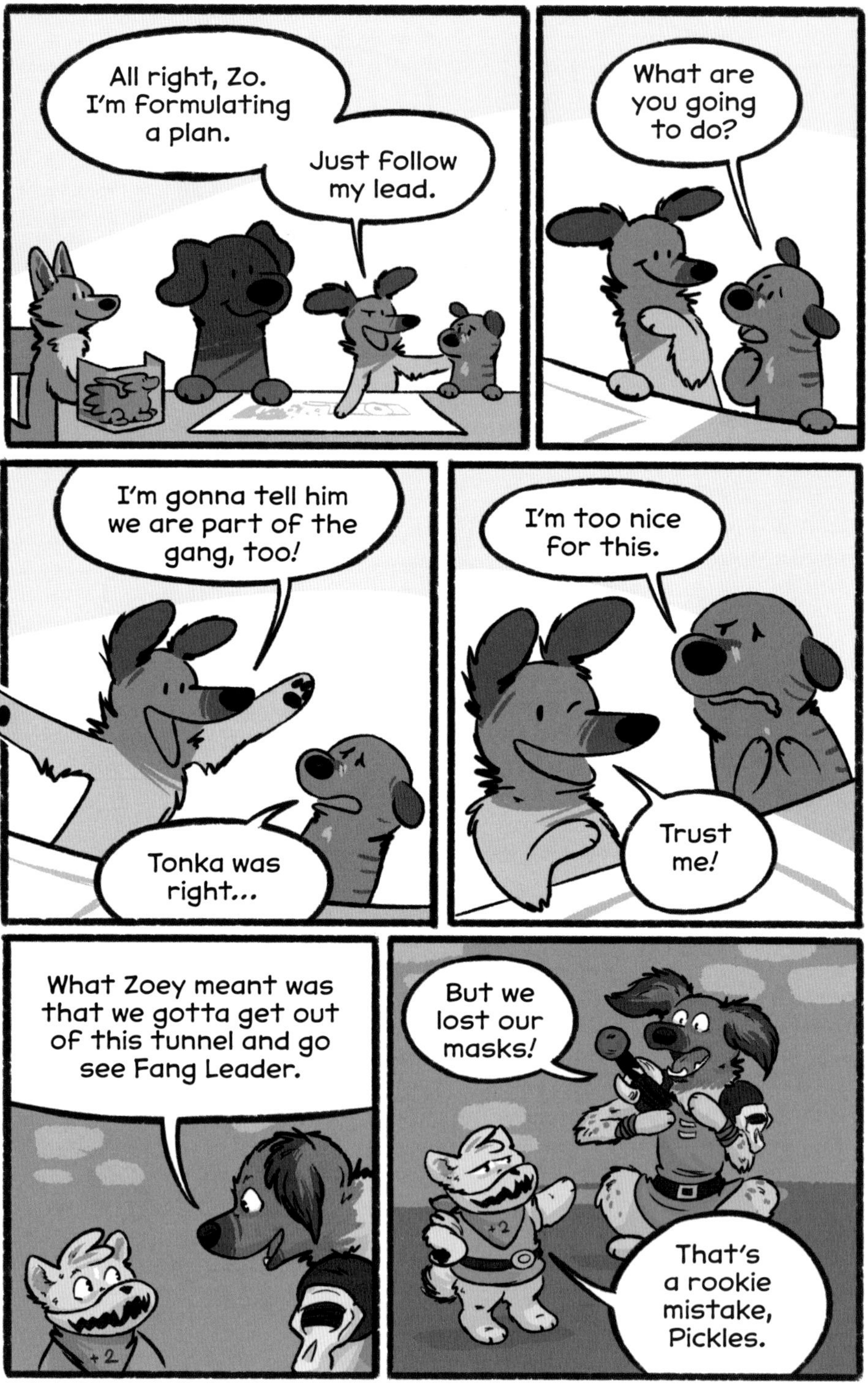
All right, Zo. I'm formulating a plan.
Just follow my lead.
What are you going to do?
I'm gonna tell him we are part of the gang, too!
Tonka was right...
I'm too nice for this.
Trust me!
What Zoey meant was that we gotta get out of this tunnel and go see Fang Leader.
But we lost our masks!
That's a rookie mistake, Pickles.

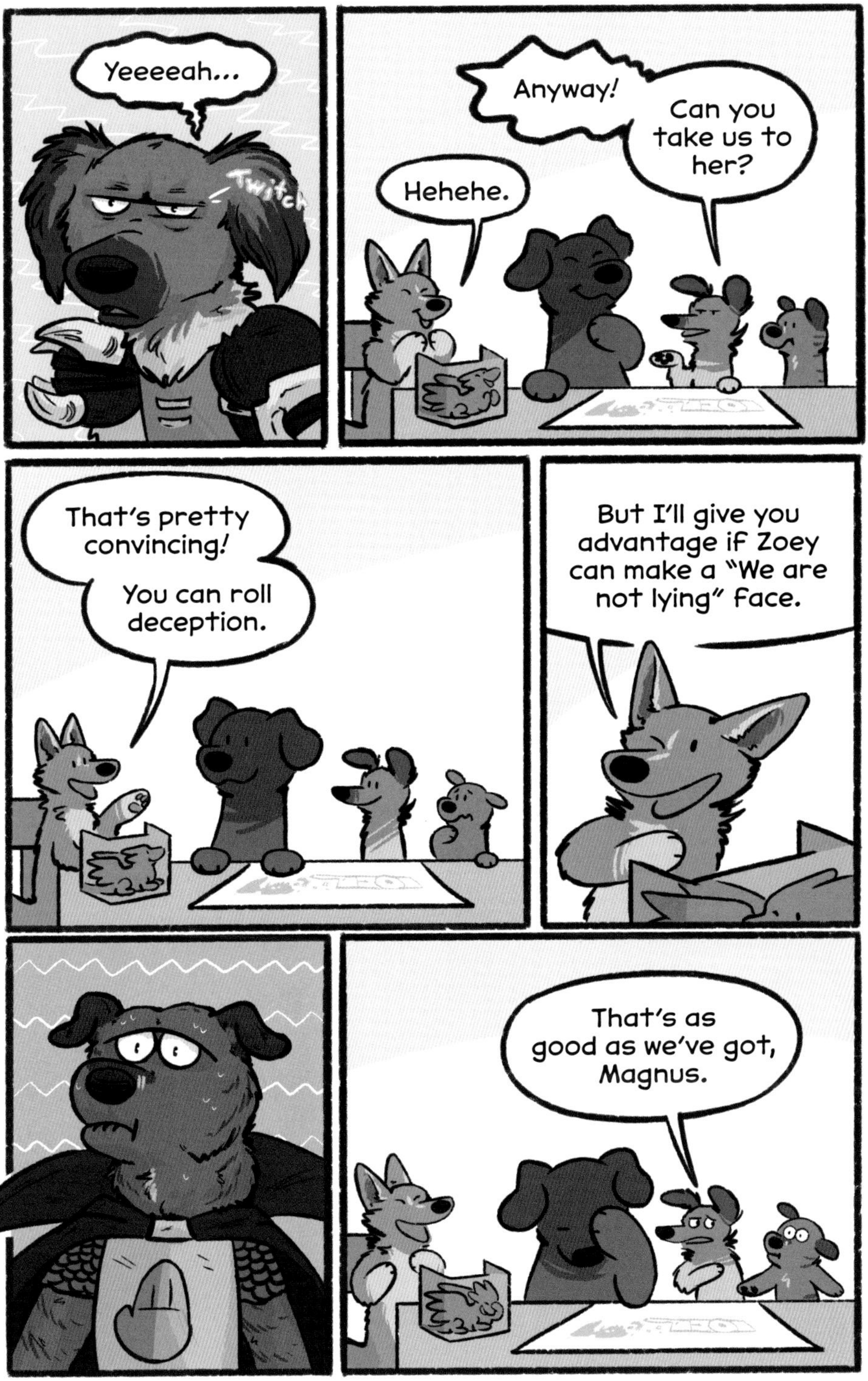
Yeeeeah...
Twitch
Hehehe.
Anyway!
Can you take us to her?
That's pretty convincing!
You can roll deception.
But I'll give you advantage if Zoey can make a "We are not lying" face.
That's as good as we've got, Magnus.

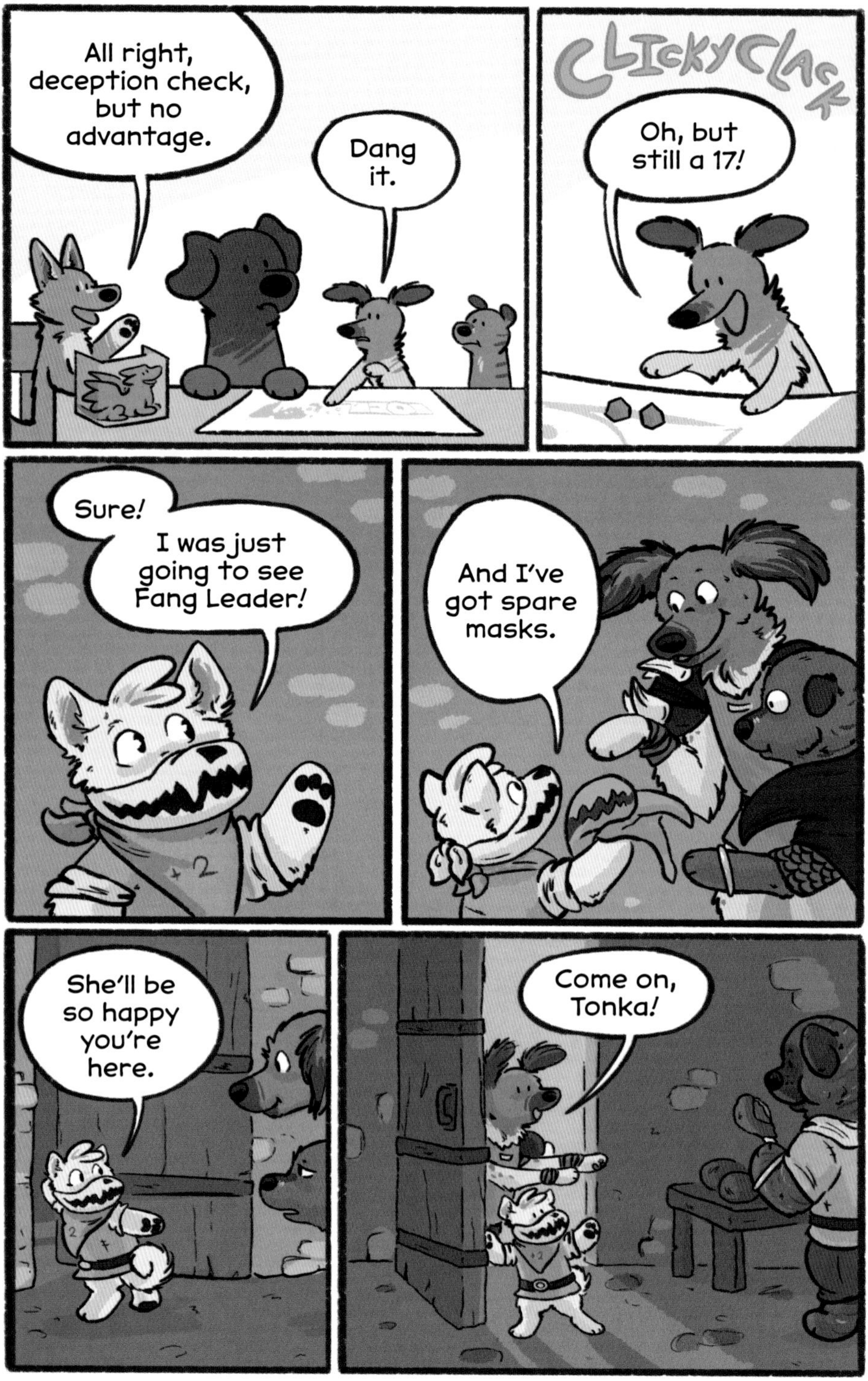
All right, deception check, but no advantage.
Dang it.
CLICKYCLACK
Oh, but still a 17!
Sure!
I was just going to see Fang Leader!
And I've got spare masks.
She'll be so happy you're here.
Come on, Tonka!

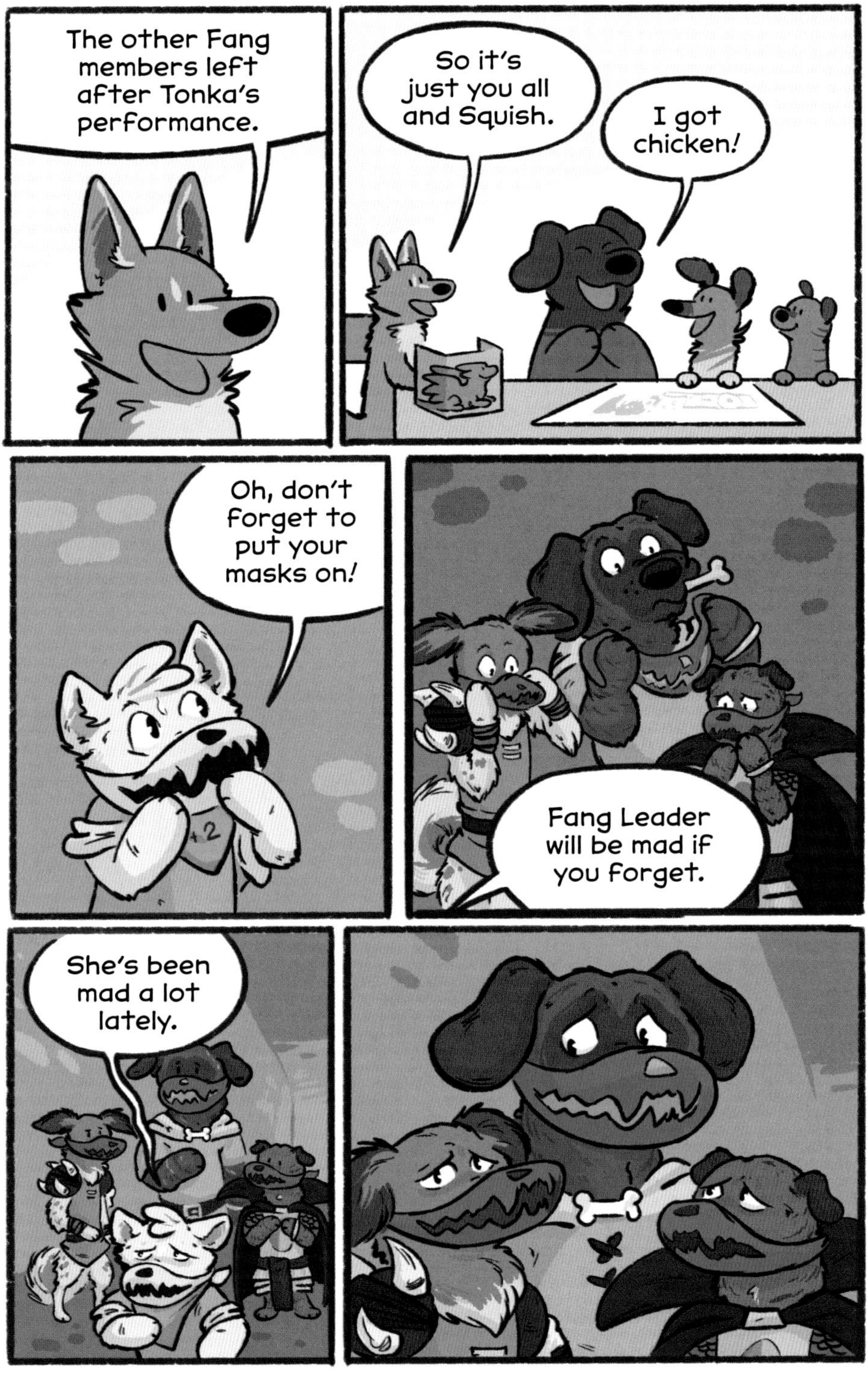
The other Fang members left after Tonka's performance.
So it's just you all and Squish.
I got chicken!
Oh, don't forget to put your masks on!
Fang Leader will be mad if you forget.
She's been mad a lot lately.

Chapter 5:
Boss Fight

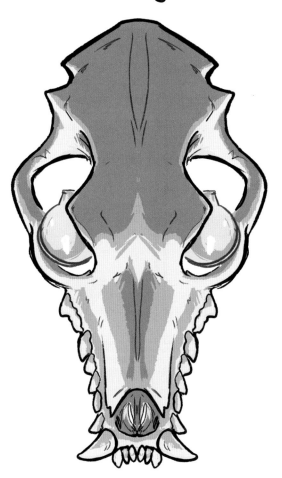

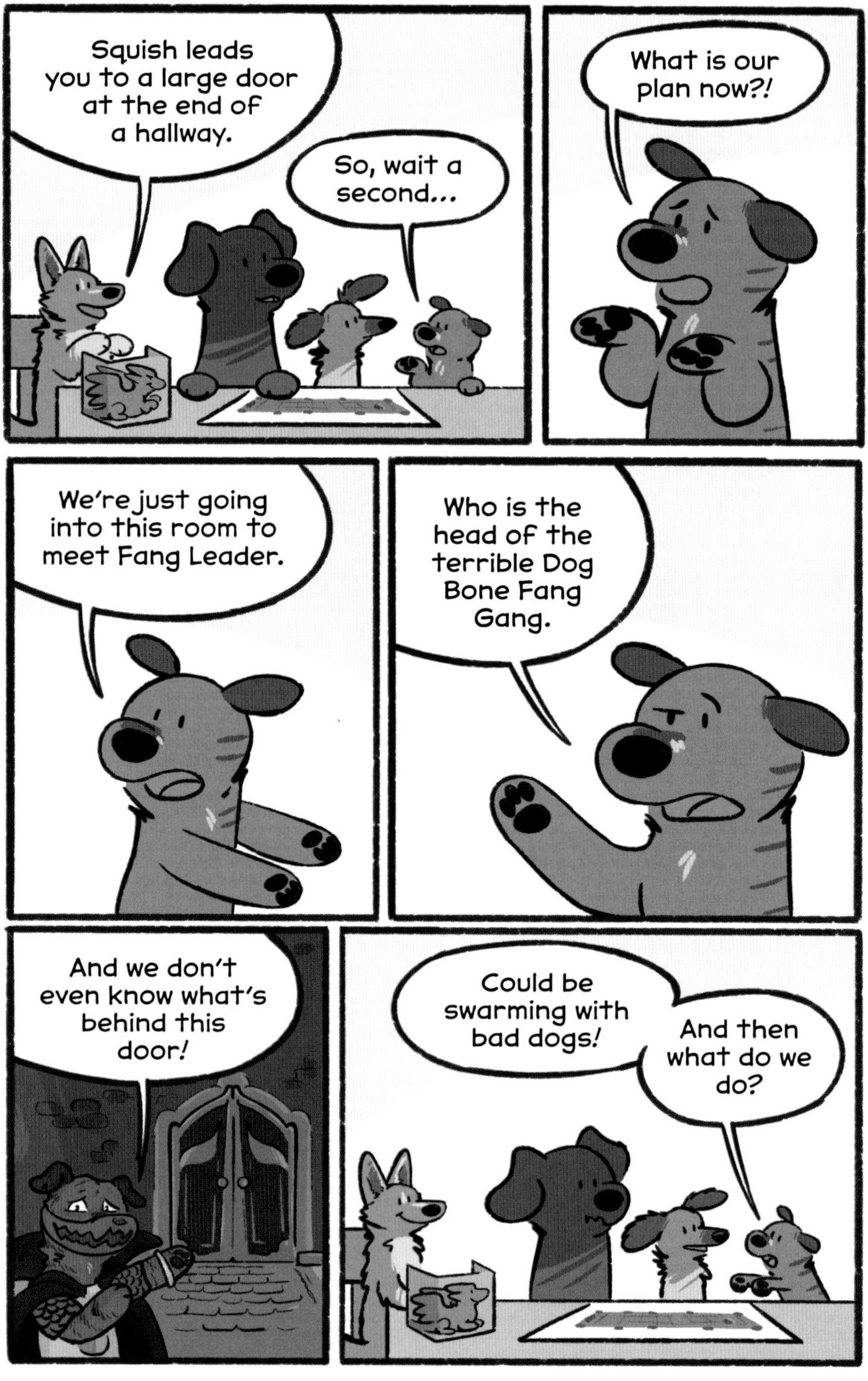
Squish leads you to a large door at the end of a hallway.
So, wait a second...
What is our plan now?!
We're just going into this room to meet Fang Leader.
Who is the head of the terrible Dog Bone Fang Gang.
And we don't even know what's behind this door!
Could be swarming with bad dogs!
And then what do we do?

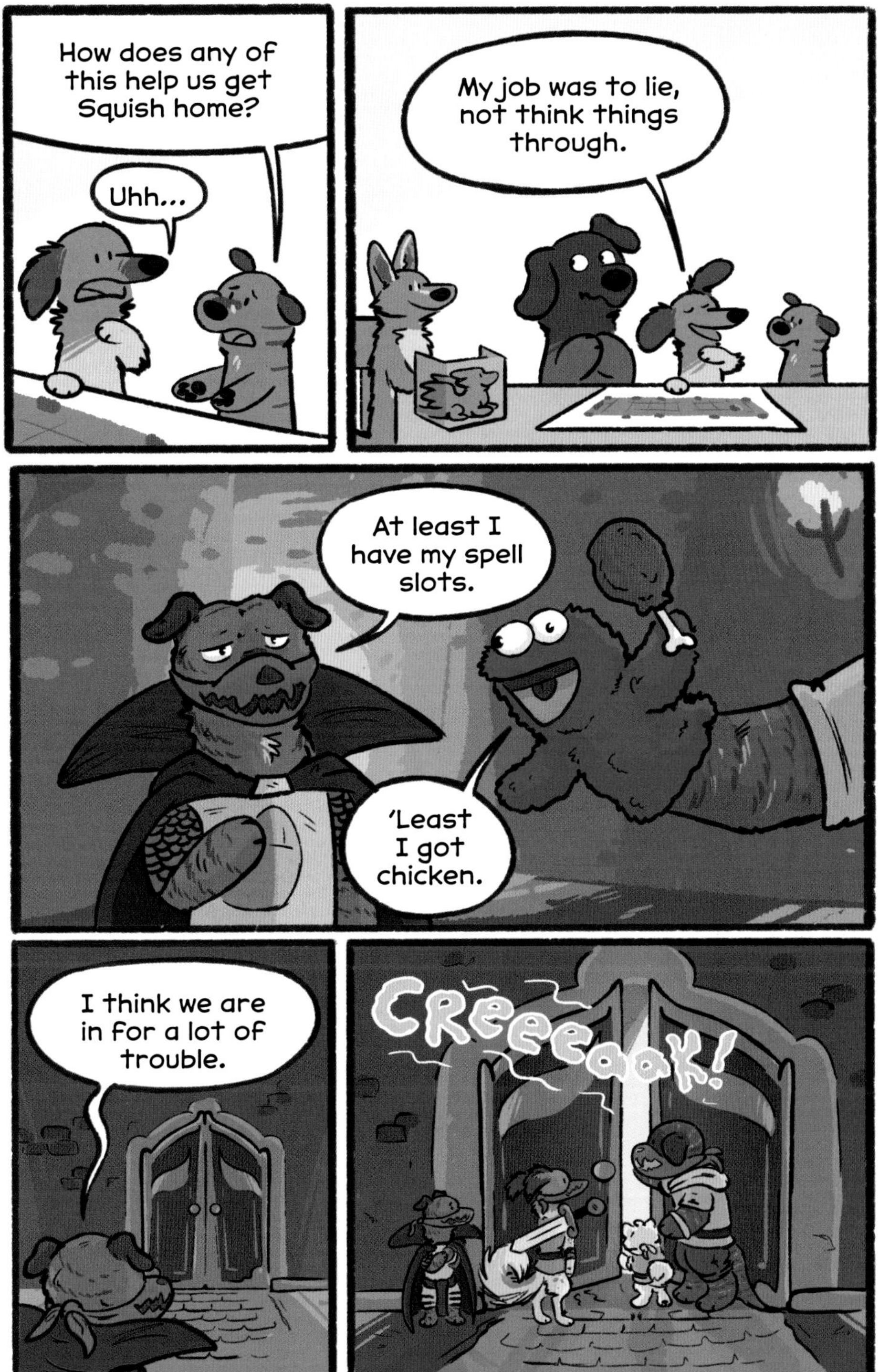
How does any of this help us get Squish home?
Uhh...
My job was to lie, not think things through.
At least I have my spell slots.
'Least I got chicken.
I think we are in for a lot of trouble.
CReeeaak!

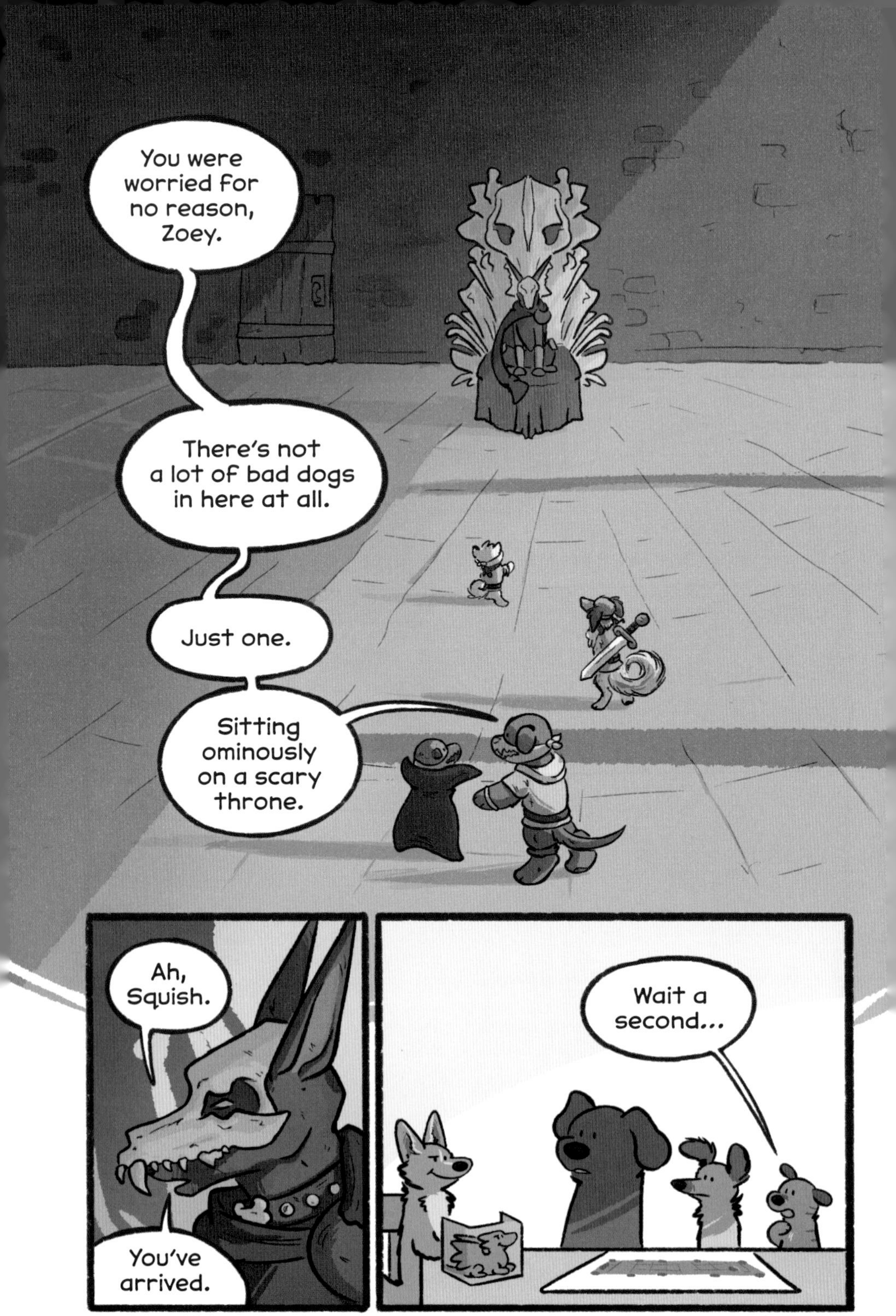
You were worried for no reason, Zoey.
There's not a lot of bad dogs in here at all.
Just one.
Sitting ominously on a scary throne.
Ah, Squish.
You've arrived.
Wait a second...

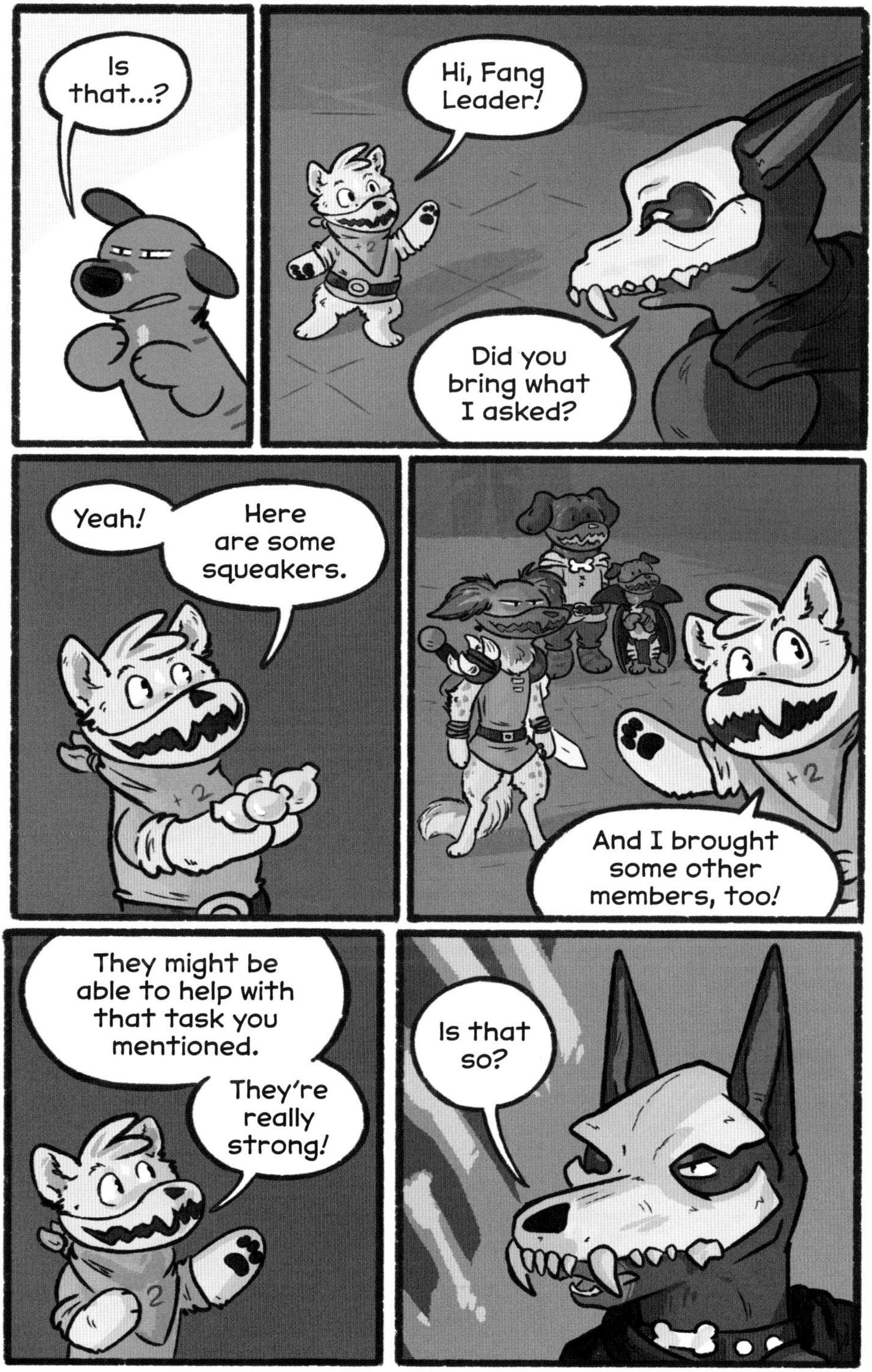
Is that...?
Hi, Fang Leader!
Did you bring what I asked?
Yeah!
Here are some squeakers.
And I brought some other members, too!
They might be able to help with that task you mentioned.
They're really strong!
Is that so?

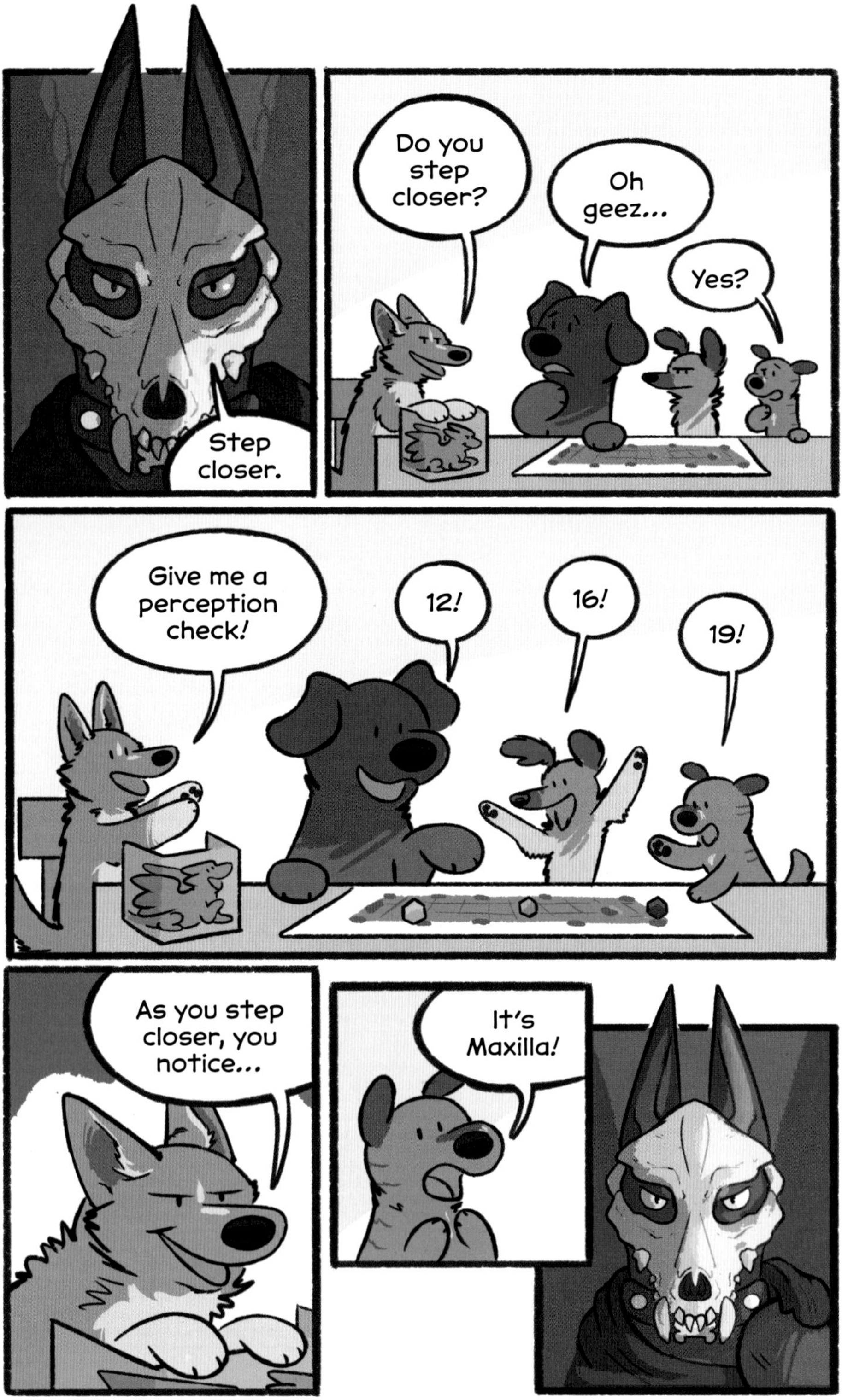
Step closer.
Do you step closer?
Oh geez...
Yes?
Give me a perception check!
12!
16!
19!
As you step closer, you notice...
It's Maxilla!

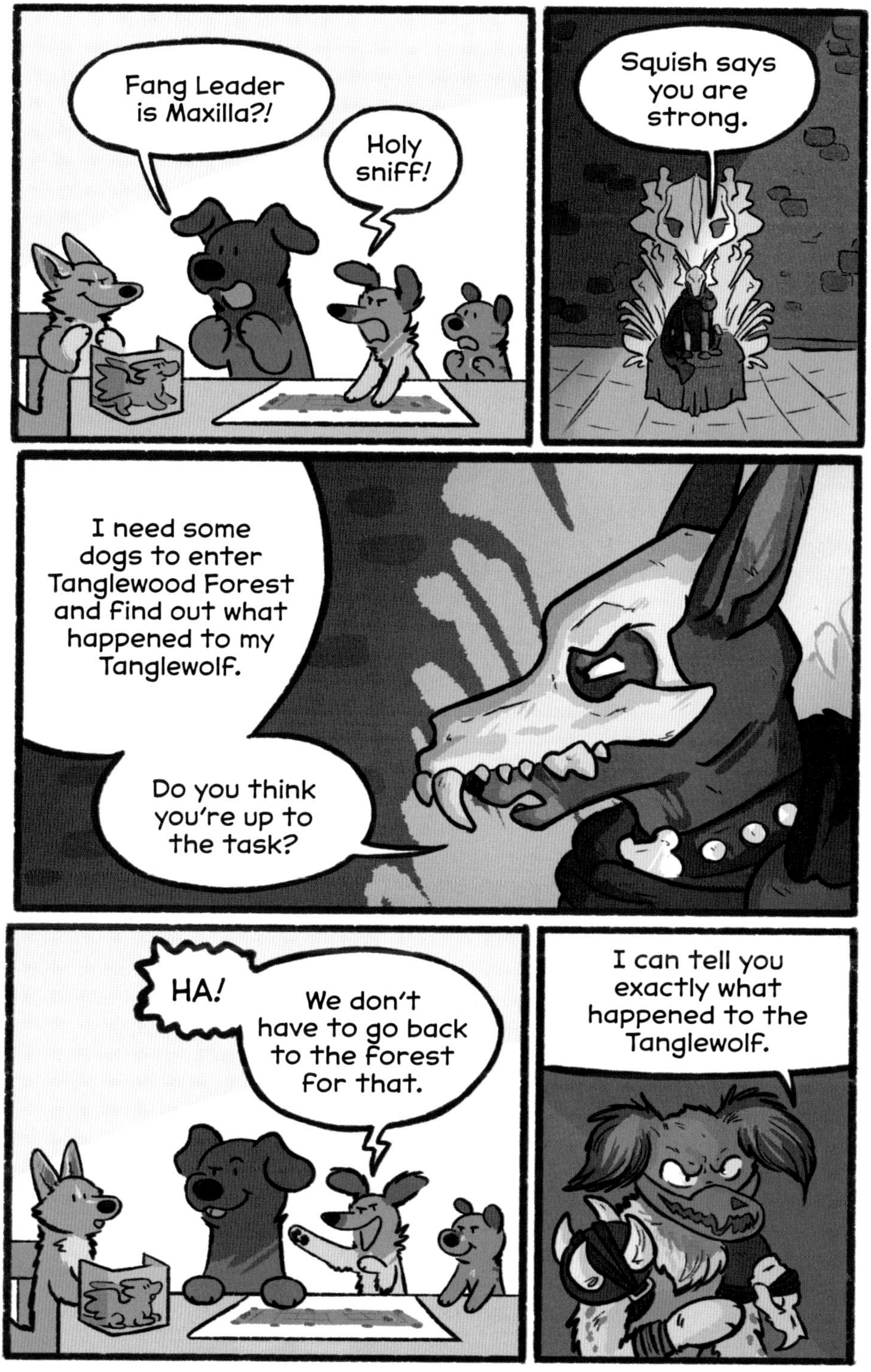
Fang Leader is Maxilla?!
Holy sniff!
Squish says you are strong.
I need some dogs to enter Tanglewood Forest and find out what happened to my Tanglewolf.
Do you think you're up to the task?
HA!
We don't have to go back to the forest for that.
I can tell you exactly what happened to the Tanglewolf.

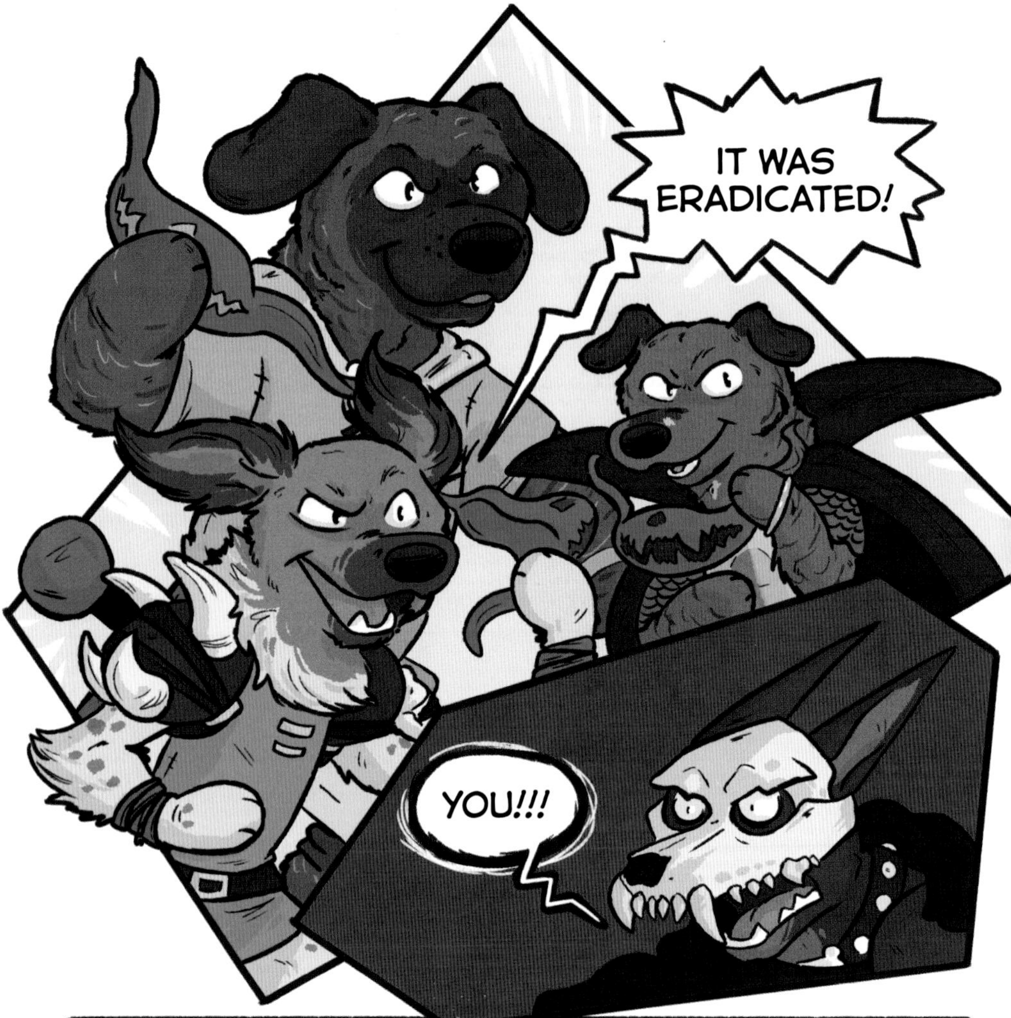
IT WAS ERADICATED!
YOU!!!

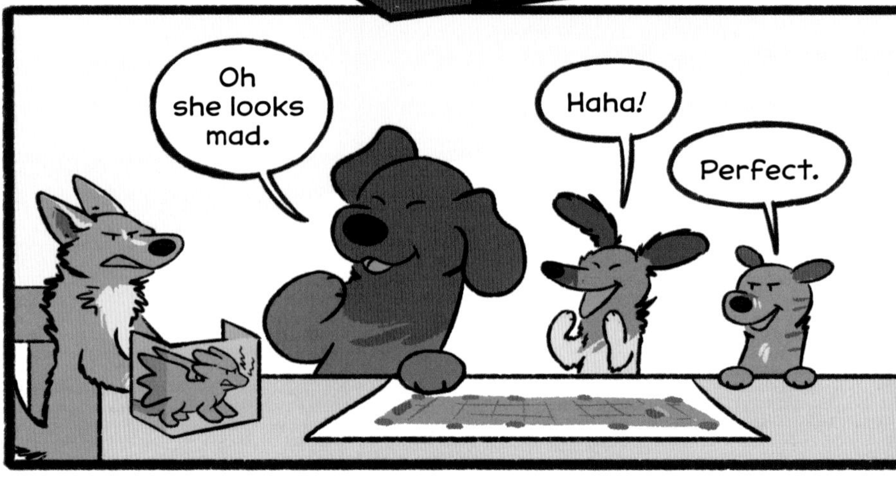
Oh she looks mad.
Haha!
Perfect.

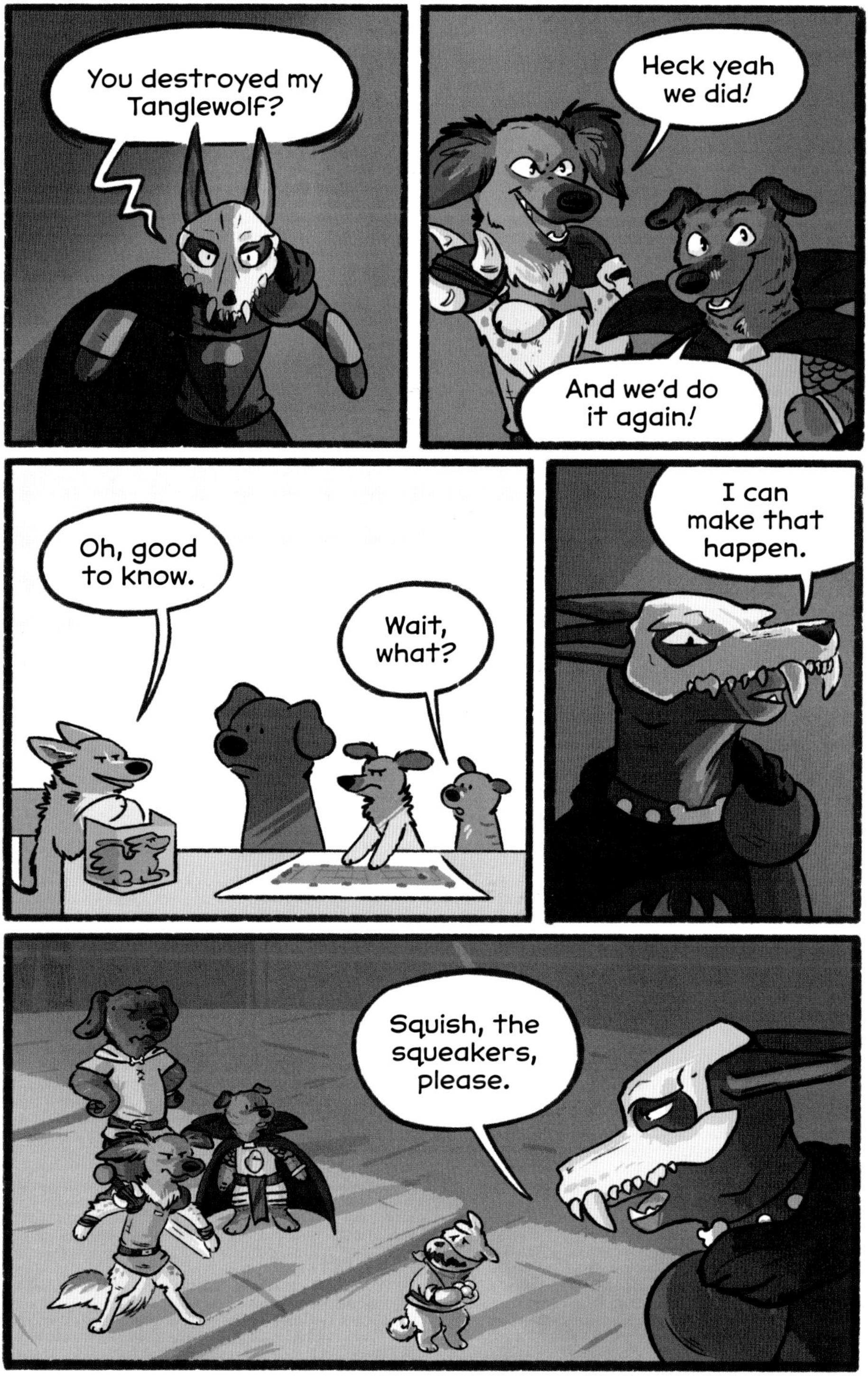
You destroyed my Tanglewolf?
Heck yeah we did!
And we'd do it again!
Oh, good to know.
Wait, what?
I can make that happen.
Squish, the squeakers, please.

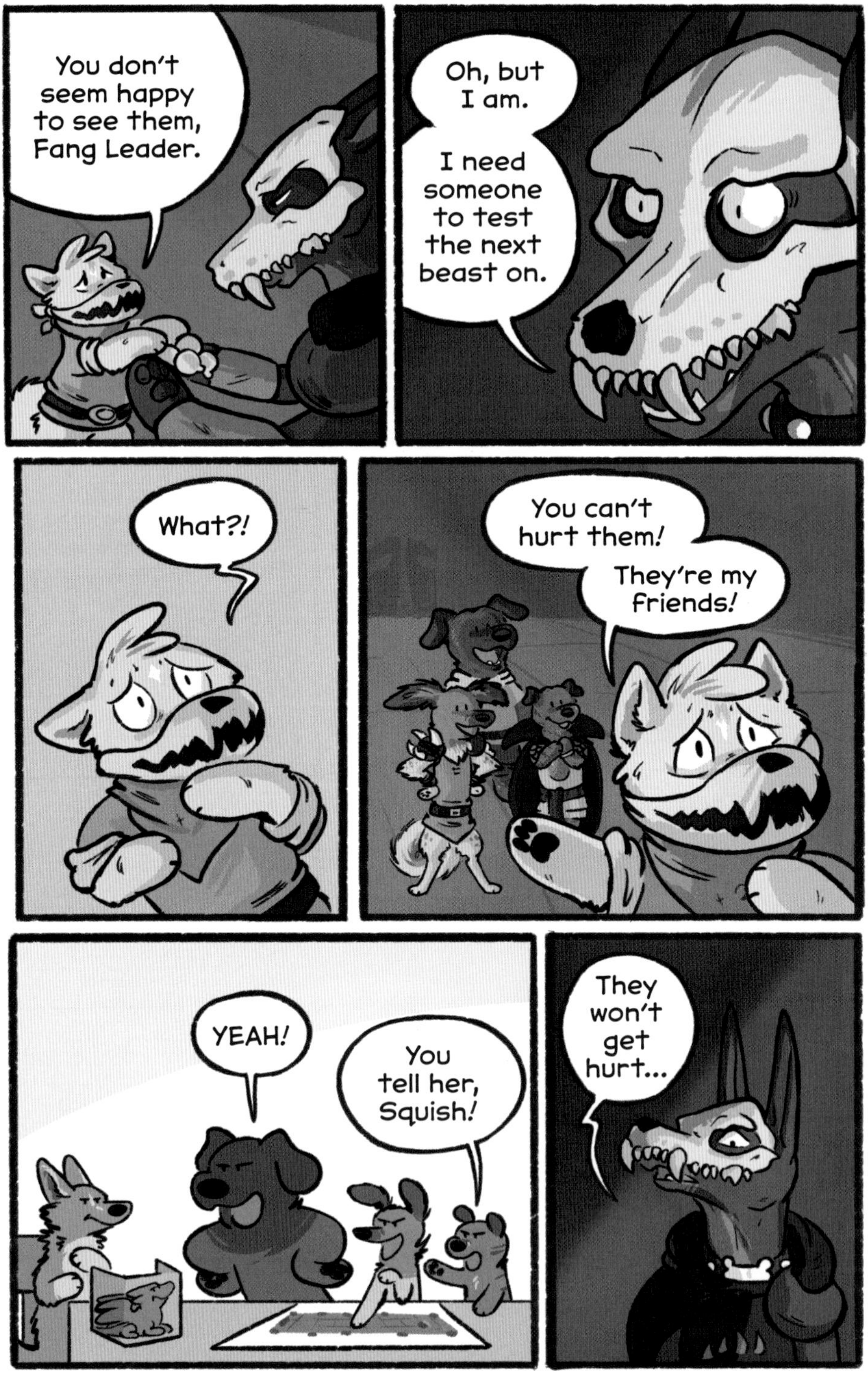
You don't seem happy to see them, Fang Leader.
Oh, but I am.
I need someone to test the next beast on.
What?!
You can't hurt them!
They're my friends!
YEAH!
You tell her, Squish!
They won't get hurt...

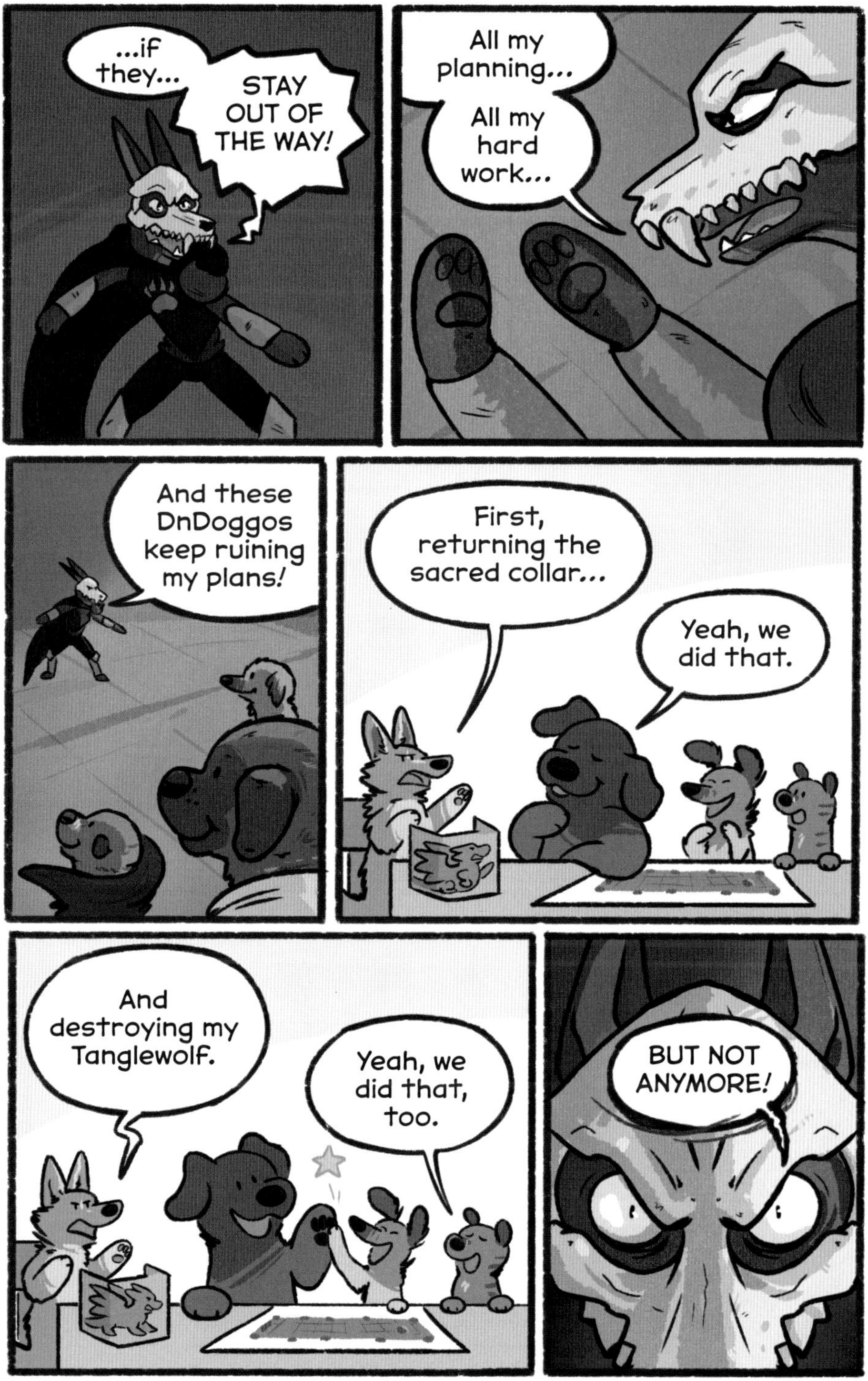
...if they...
STAY OUT OF THE WAY!
All my planning...
All my hard work...
And these DnDoggos keep ruining my plans!
First, returning the sacred collar...
Yeah, we did that.
And destroying my Tanglewolf.
Yeah, we did that, too.
BUT NOT ANYMORE!

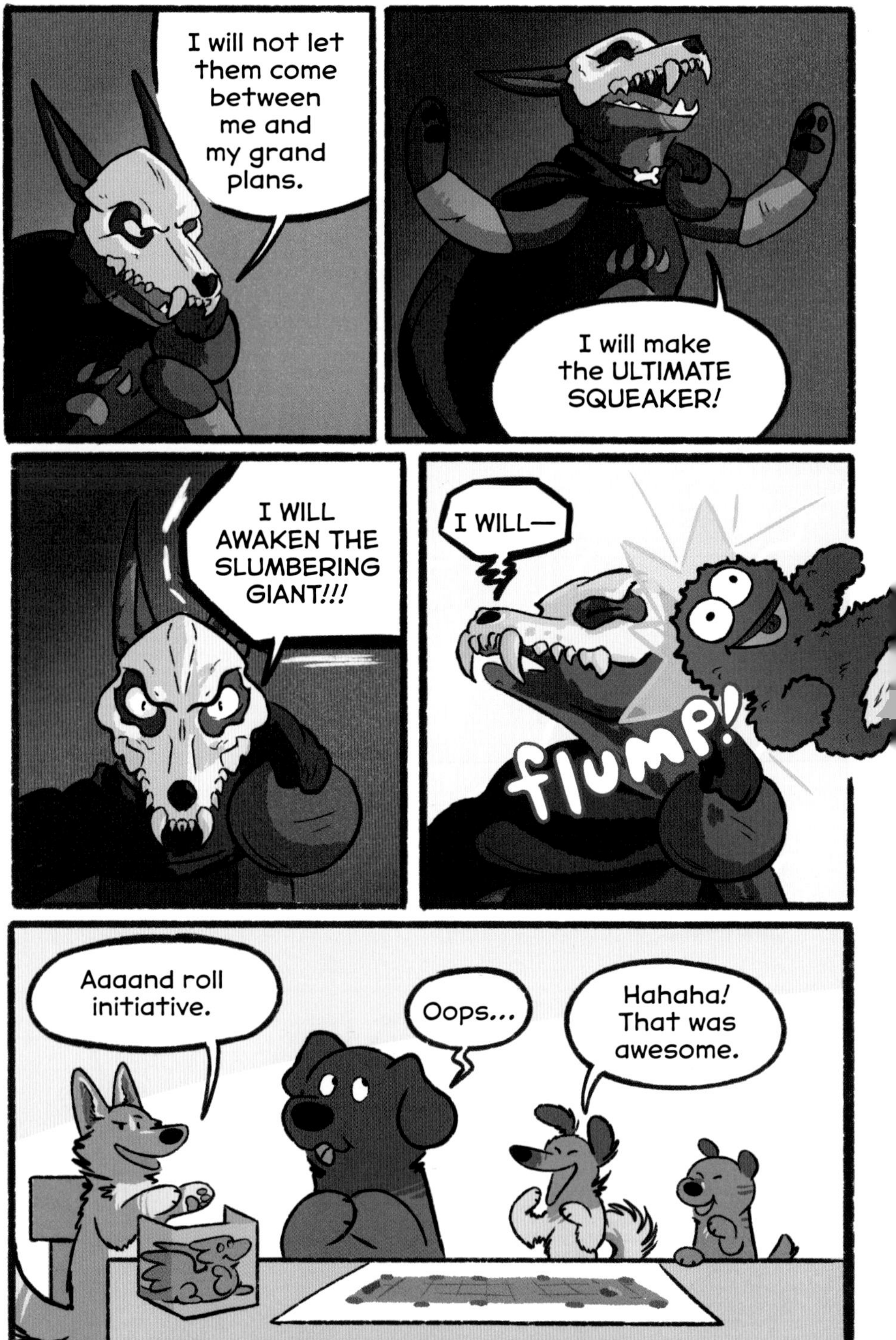
I will not let them come between me and my grand plans.
I will make the ULTIMATE SQUEAKER!
I WILL AWAKEN THE SLUMBERING GIANT!!!
I WILL—
flump!
Aaaand roll initiative.
Oops...
Hahaha! That was awesome.

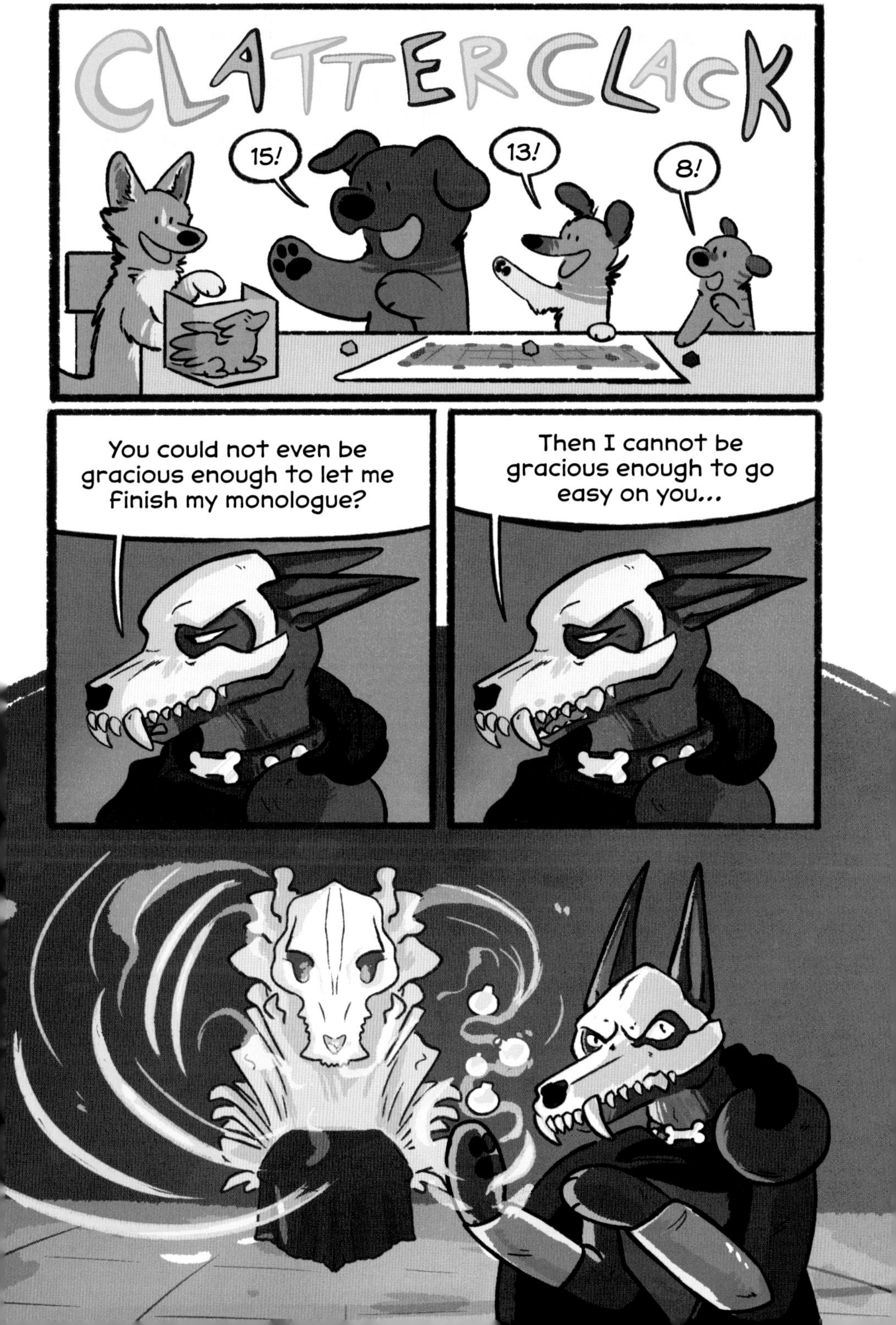
CLATTERCLACK
15!
13!
8!
You could not even be gracious enough to let me finish my monologue?
Then I cannot be gracious enough to go easy on you...

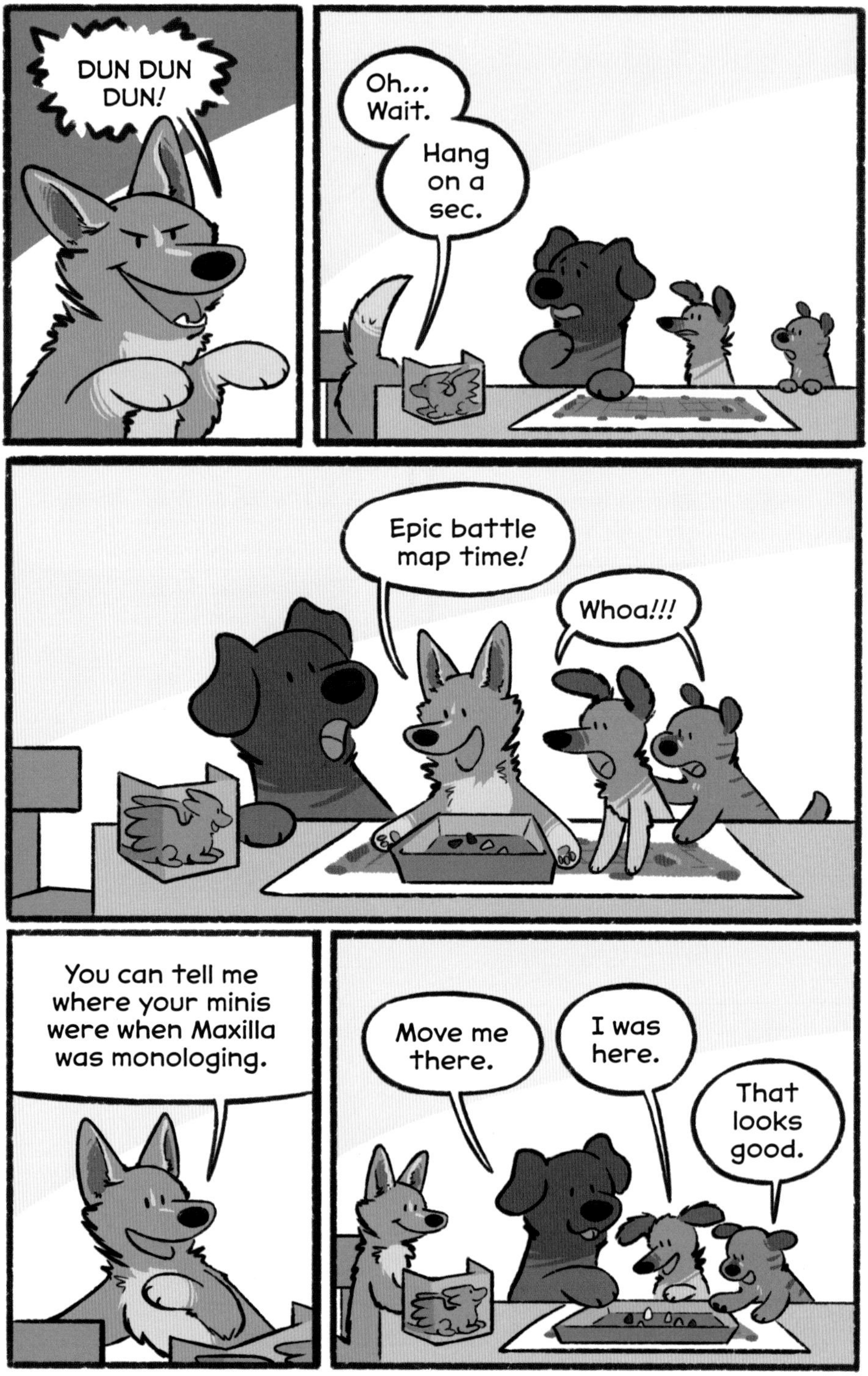
DUN DUN DUN!
Oh... Wait.
Hang on a sec.
Epic battle map time!
Whoa!!!
You can tell me where your minis were when Maxilla was monologing.
Move me there.
I was here.
That looks good.

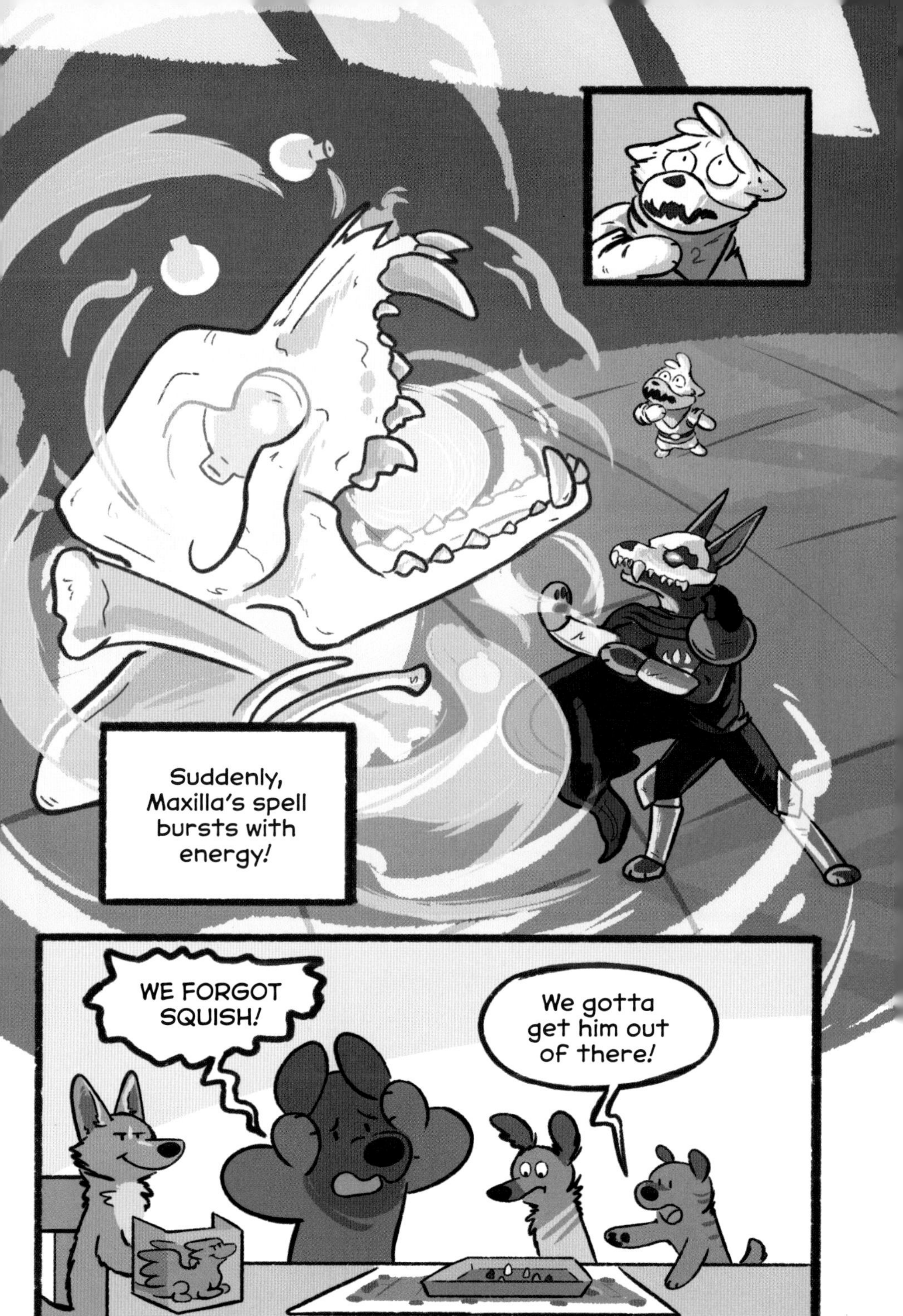
Suddenly, Maxilla's spell bursts with energy!
WE FORGOT SQUISH!
We gotta get him out of there!

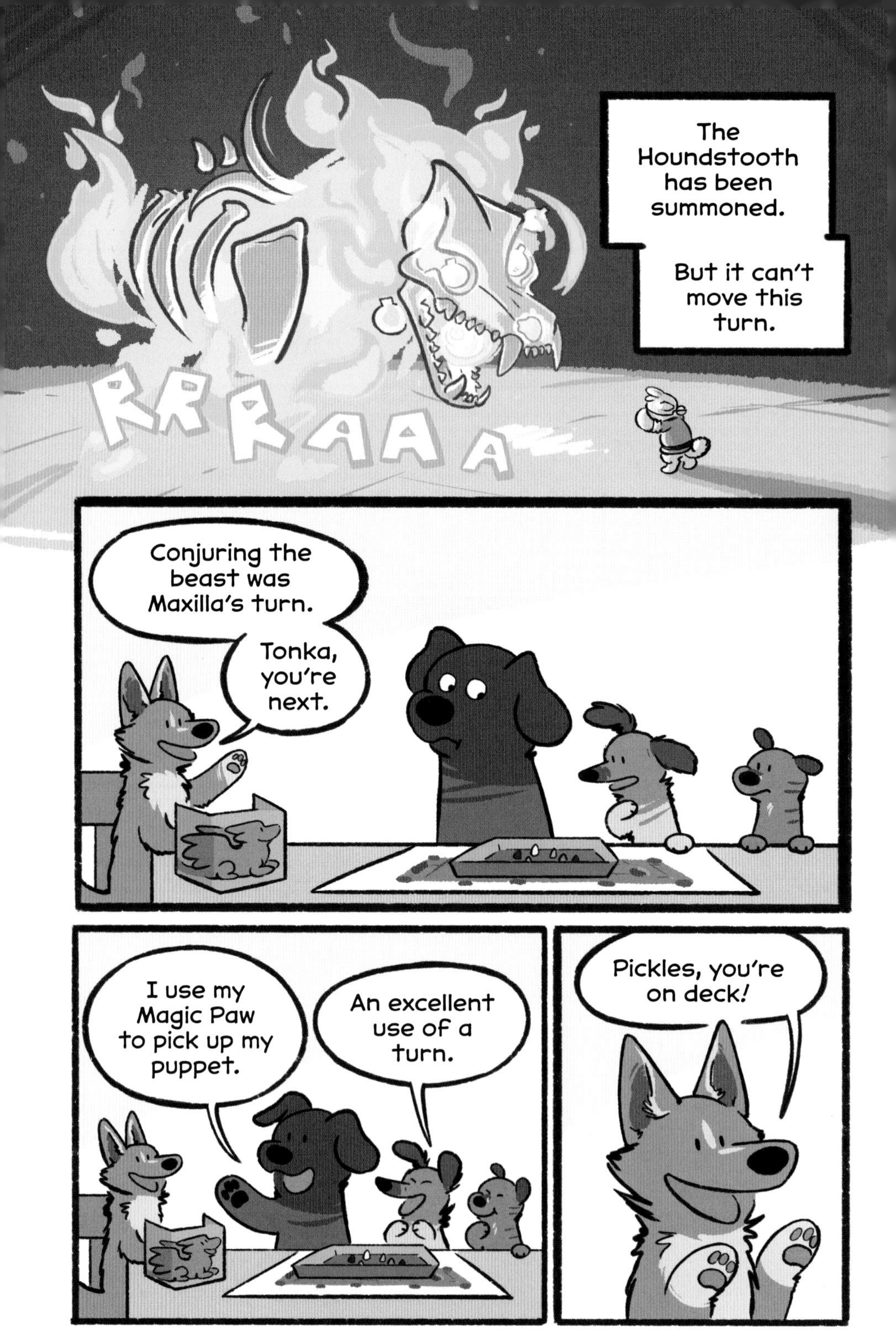
The Houndstooth has been summoned.
But it can't move this turn.
RRRAAAA
Conjuring the beast was Maxilla's turn.
Tonka, you're next.
I use my Magic Paw to pick up my puppet.
An excellent use of a turn.
Pickles, you're on deck!

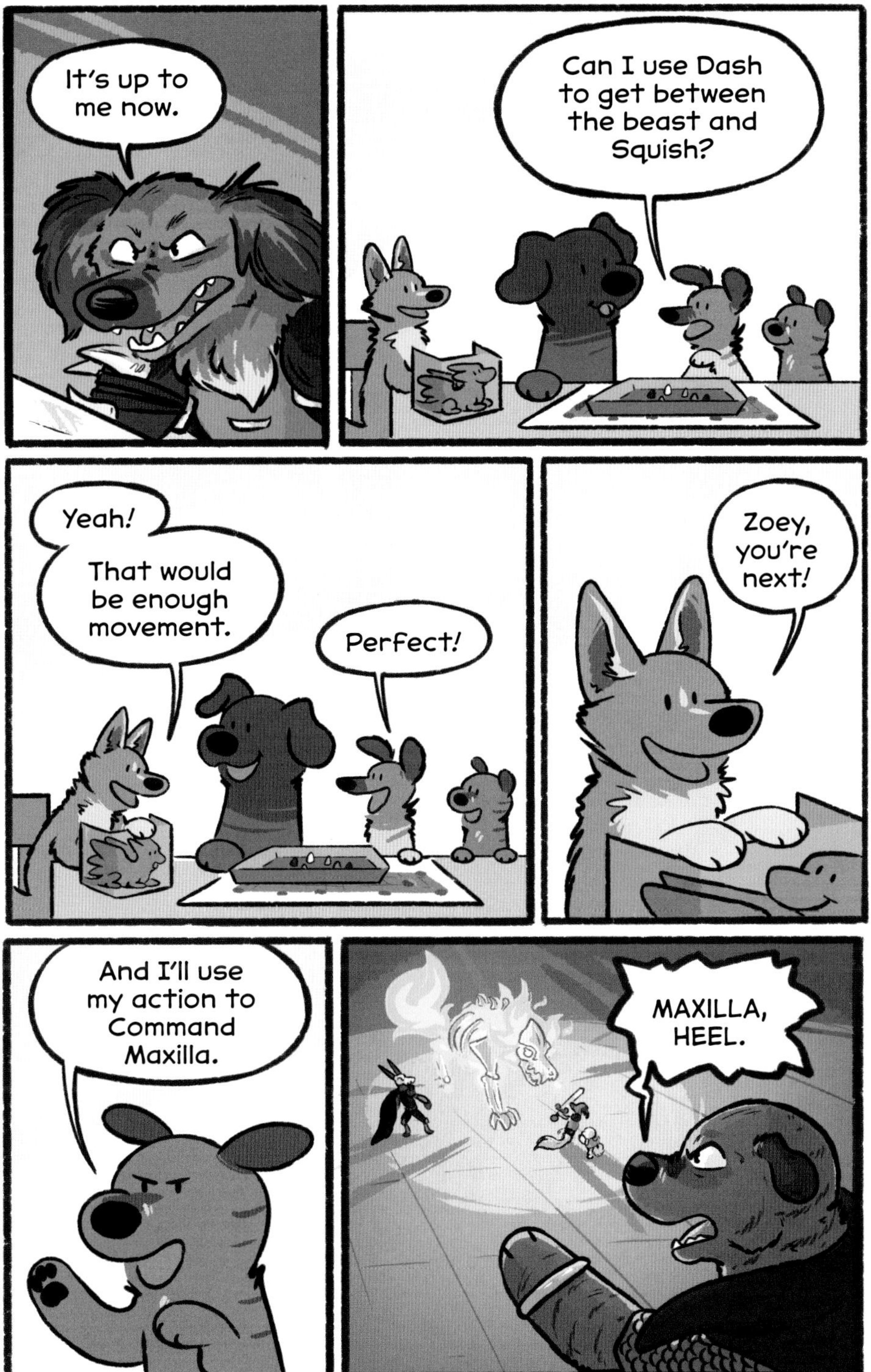
It's up to me now.
Can I use Dash to get between the beast and Squish?
Yeah!
That would be enough movement.
Perfect!
Zoey, you're next!
And I'll use my action to Command Maxilla.
MAXILLA, HEEL.

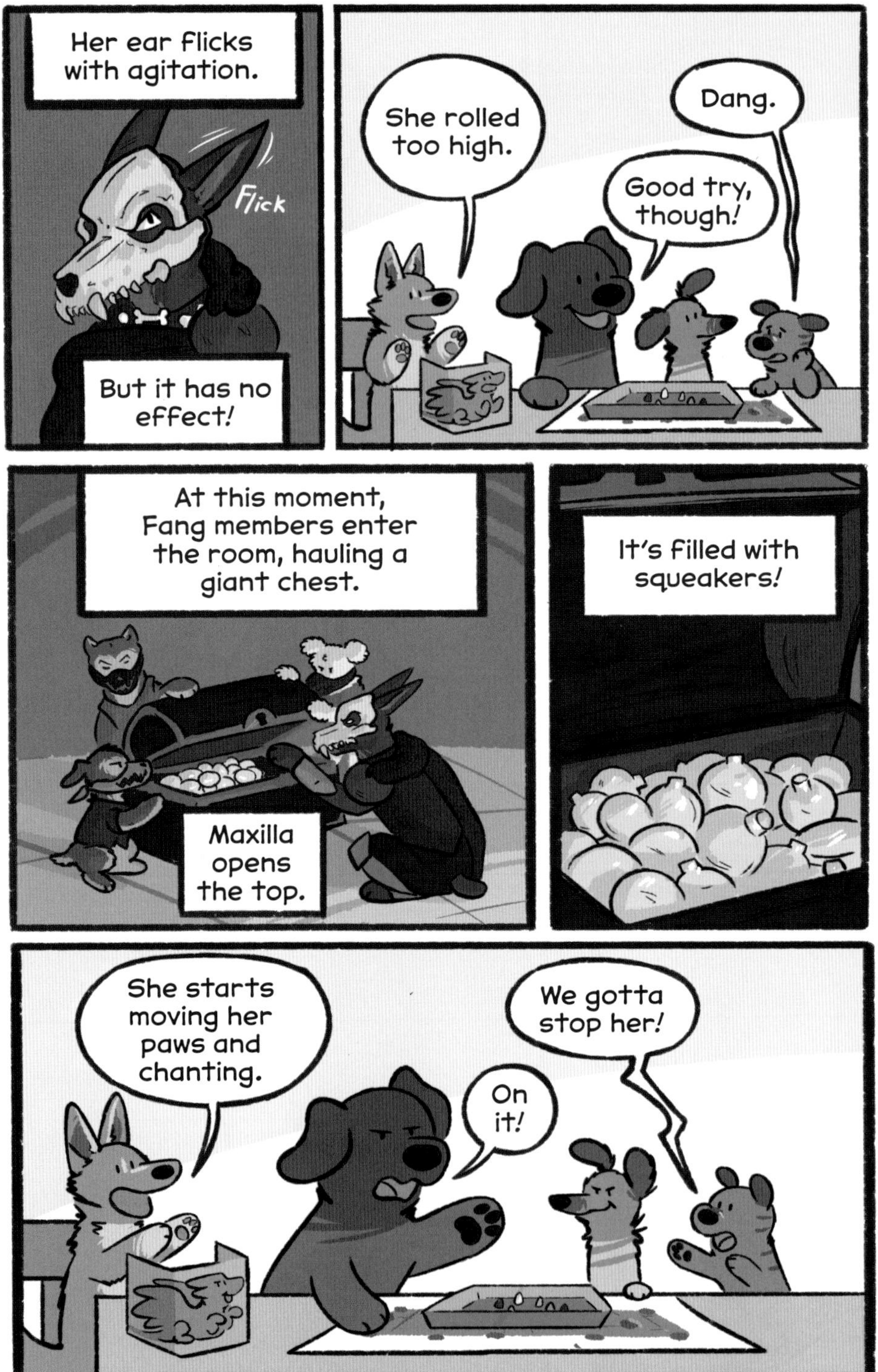
Her ear flicks with agitation.
Flick
But it has no effect!
She rolled too high.
Dang.
Good try, though!
At this moment, Fang members enter the room, hauling a giant chest.
Maxilla opens the top.
It's filled with squeakers!
She starts moving her paws and chanting.
We gotta stop her!
On it!

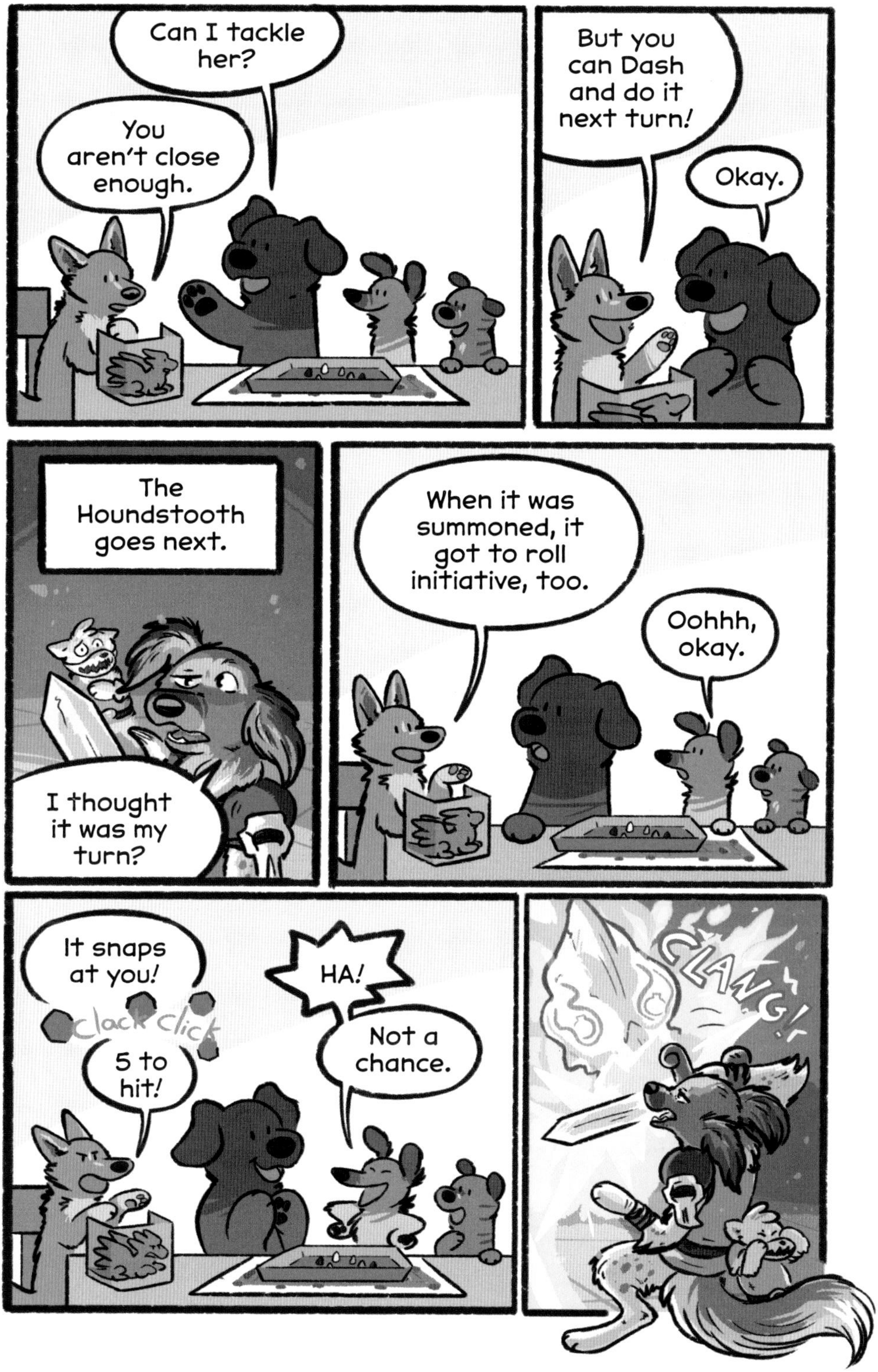
Can I tackle her?
You aren't close enough.
But you can Dash and do it next turn!
Okay.
The Houndstooth goes next.
I thought it was my turn?
When it was summoned, it got to roll initiative, too.
Oohhh, okay.
It snaps at you!
clack click
5 to hit!
HA!
Not a chance.
CLANG!

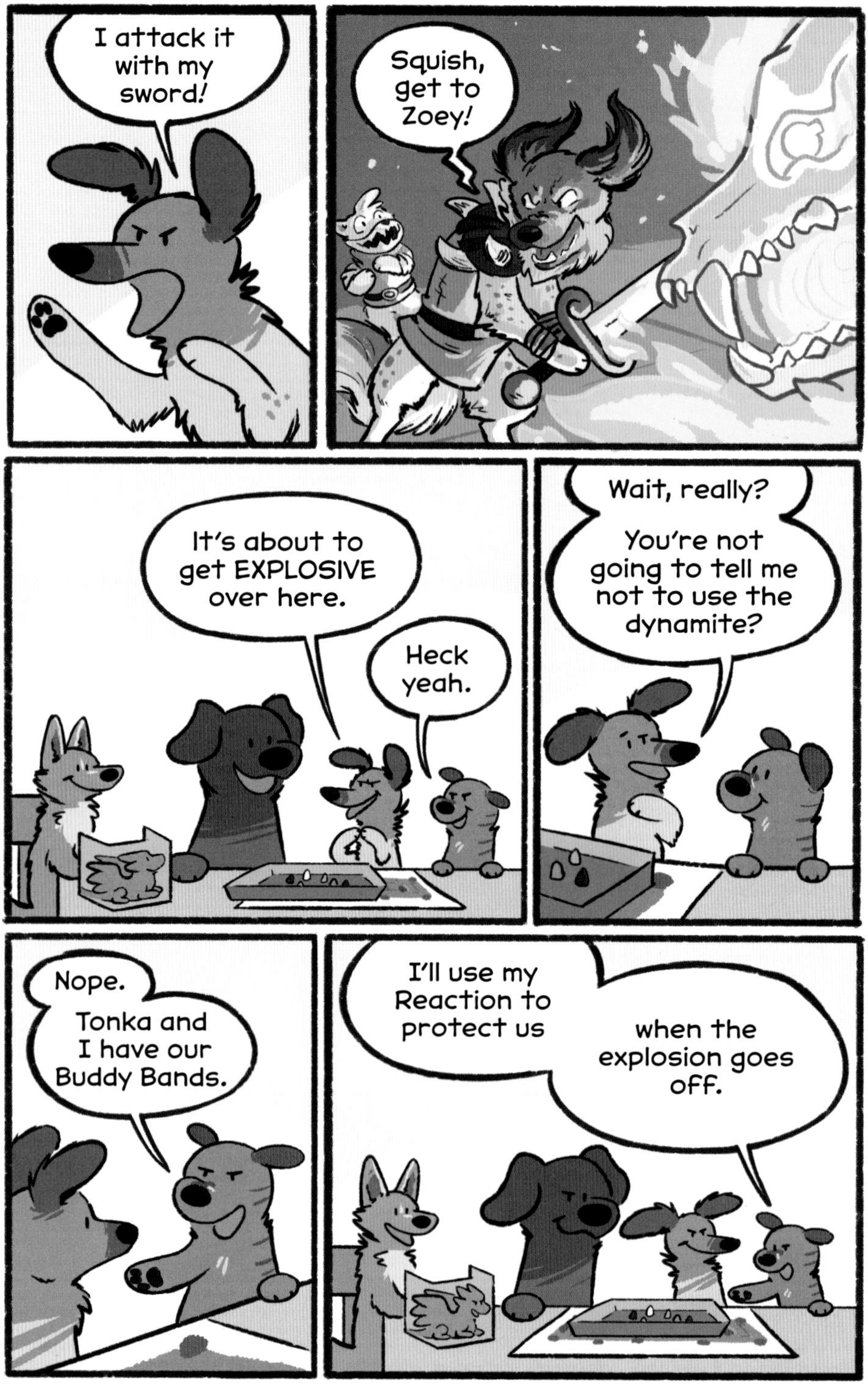
I attack it with my sword!
Squish, get to Zoey!
It's about to get EXPLOSIVE over here.
Heck yeah.
Wait, really?
You're not going to tell me not to use the dynamite?
Nope.
Tonka and I have our Buddy Bands.
I'll use my Reaction to protect us
when the explosion goes off.

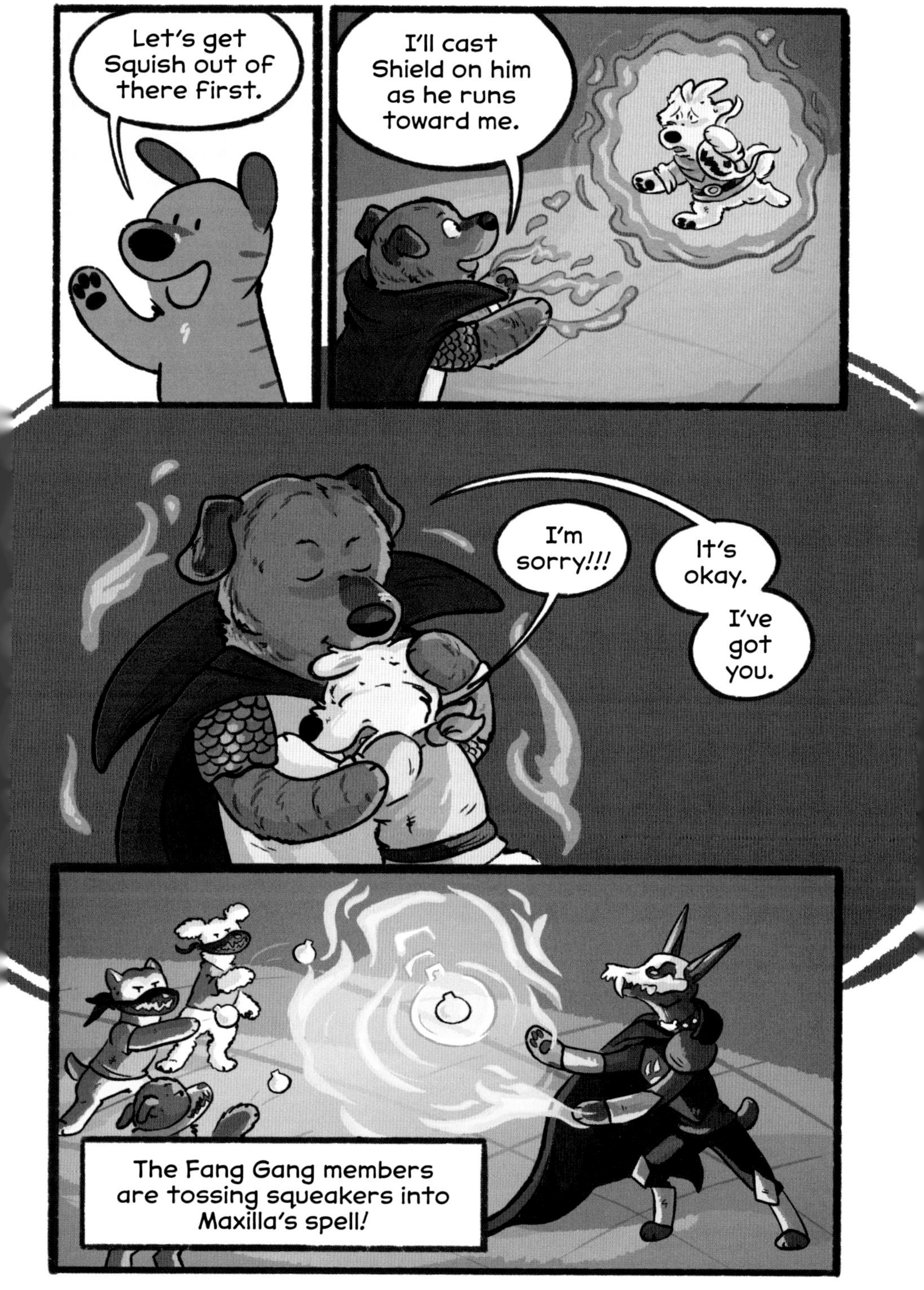
Let's get Squish out of there first.
I'll cast Shield on him as he runs toward me.
I'm sorry!!!
It's okay.
I've got you.
The Fang Gang members are tossing squeakers into Maxilla's spell!

And her spell is growing larger...

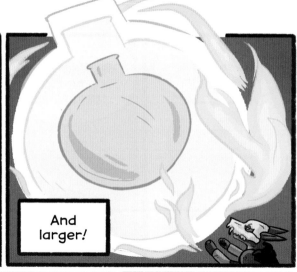

And larger!

I tackle her!

Make an athletics check!

Clickity Clackity

NOOO!

Only a 3...

You can't get to her!

Maxilla! Stop this!

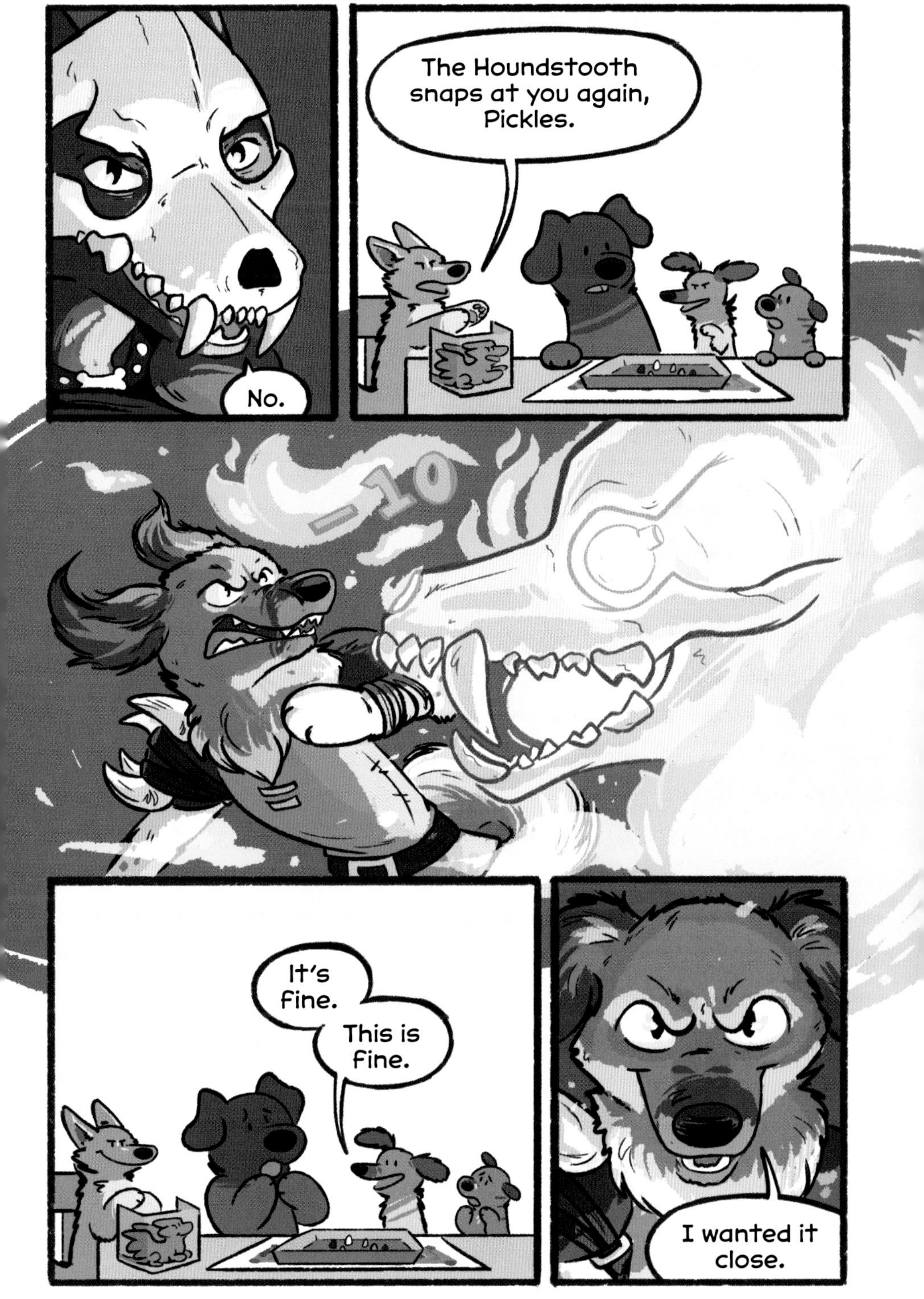
No.
The Houndstooth snaps at you again, Pickles.
-10
It's fine.
This is fine.
I wanted it close.

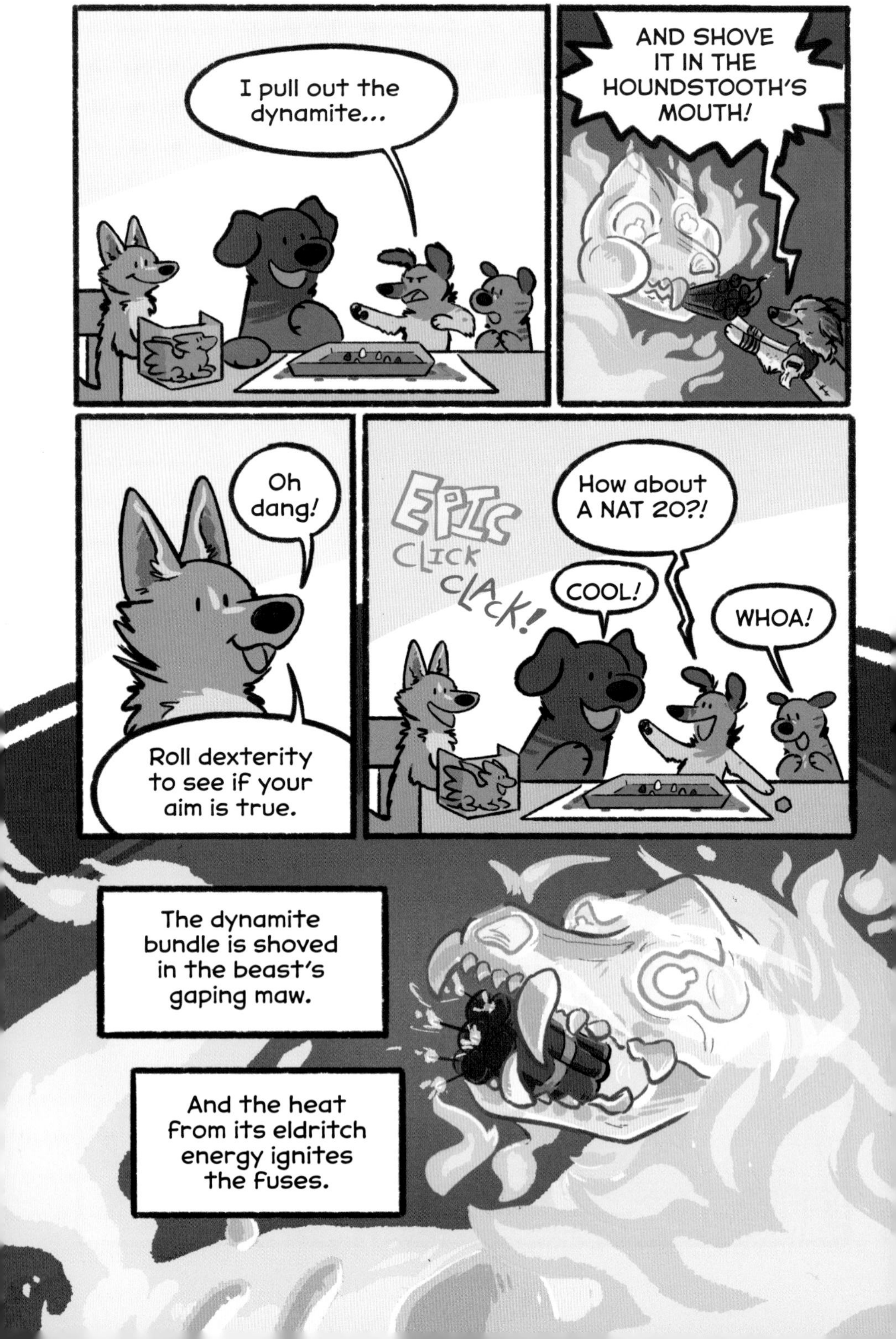
I pull out the dynamite...
AND SHOVE IT IN THE HOUNDSTOOTH'S MOUTH!
Oh dang!
Roll dexterity to see if your aim is true.
EPIC
CLICK
CLACK!
How about A NAT 20?!
COOL!
WHOA!
The dynamite bundle is shoved in the beast's gaping maw.
And the heat from its eldritch energy ignites the fuses.

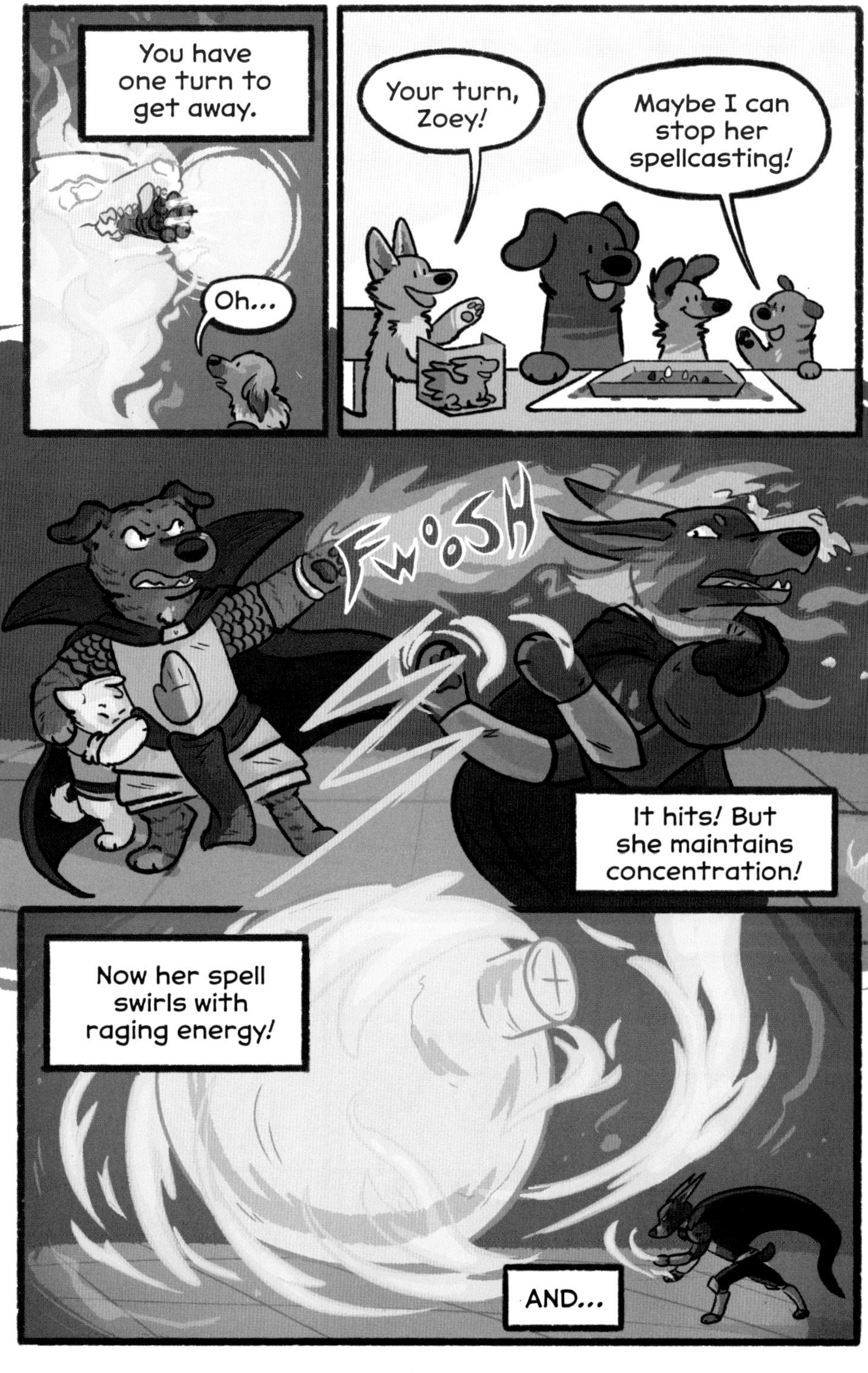
You have one turn to get away.
Oh...
Your turn, Zoey!
Maybe I can stop her spellcasting!
FWOOSH
It hits! But she maintains concentration!
Now her spell swirls with raging energy!
AND...

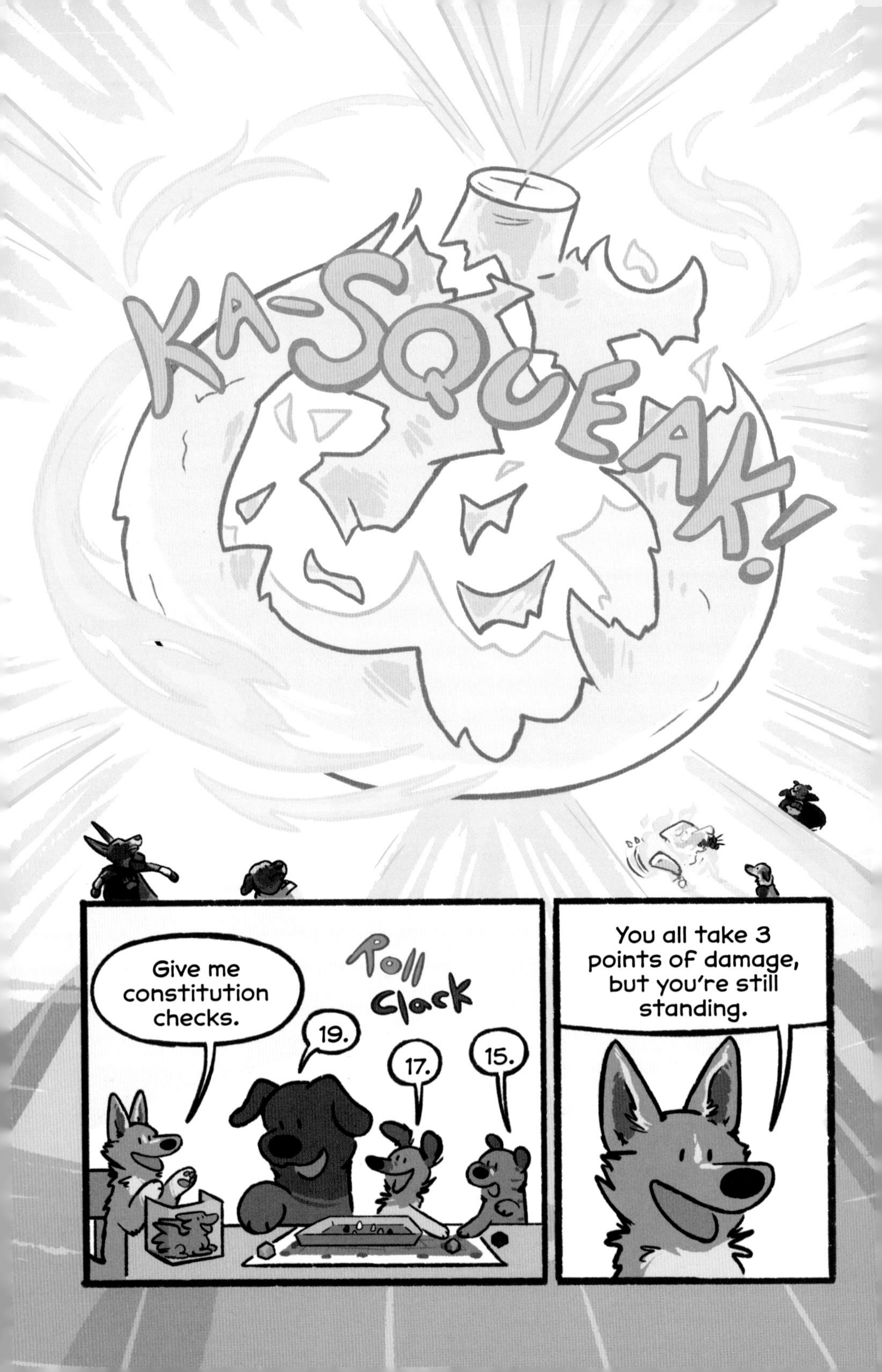
KA-SQUEAK!
Give me constitution checks.
Roll
Clack
19.
17.
15.
You all take 3 points of damage, but you're still standing.

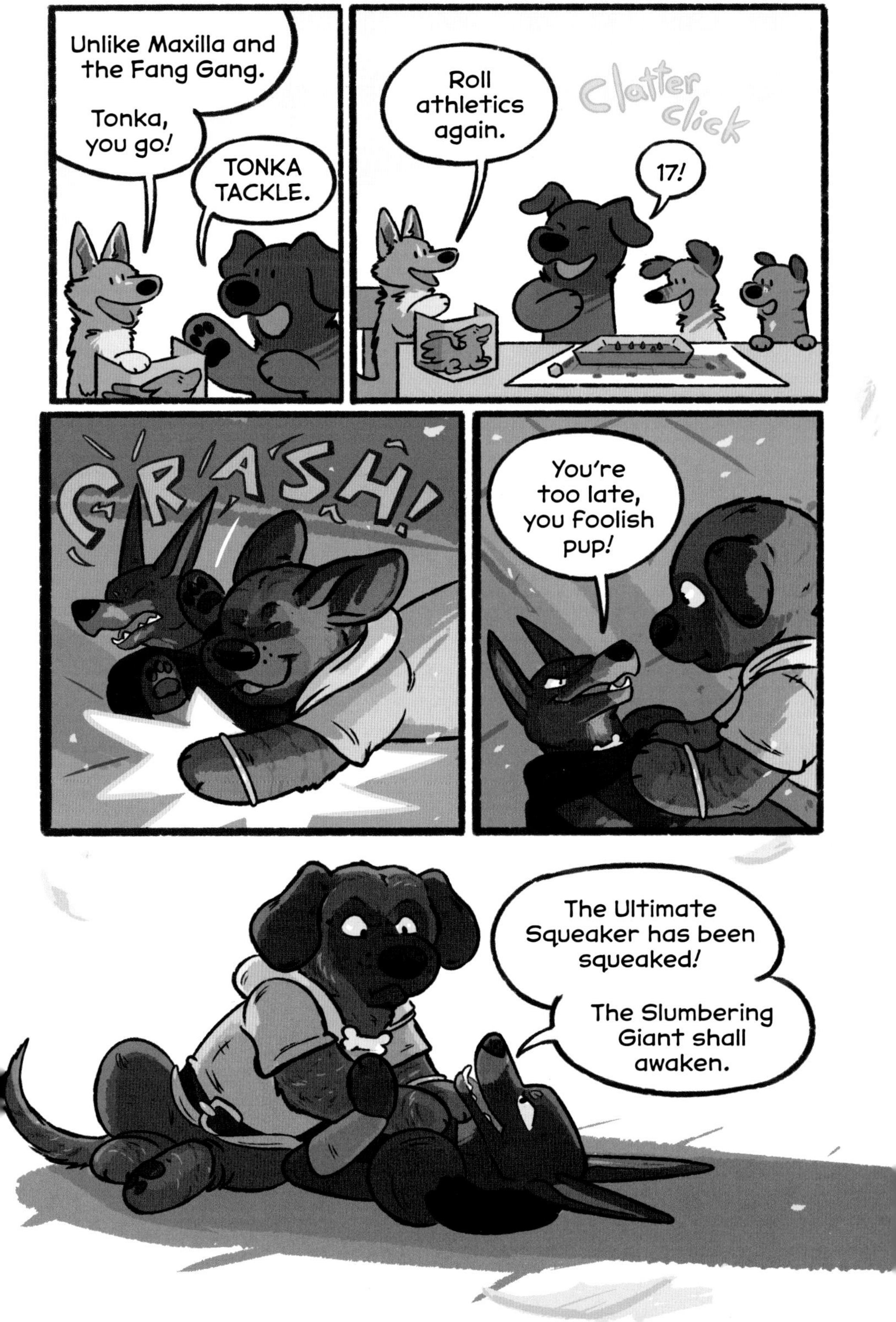
Unlike Maxilla and the Fang Gang.
Tonka, you go!
TONKA TACKLE.
Roll athletics again.
Clatter click
17!
CRASH!
You're too late, you foolish pup!
The Ultimate Squeaker has been squeaked!
The Slumbering Giant shall awaken.

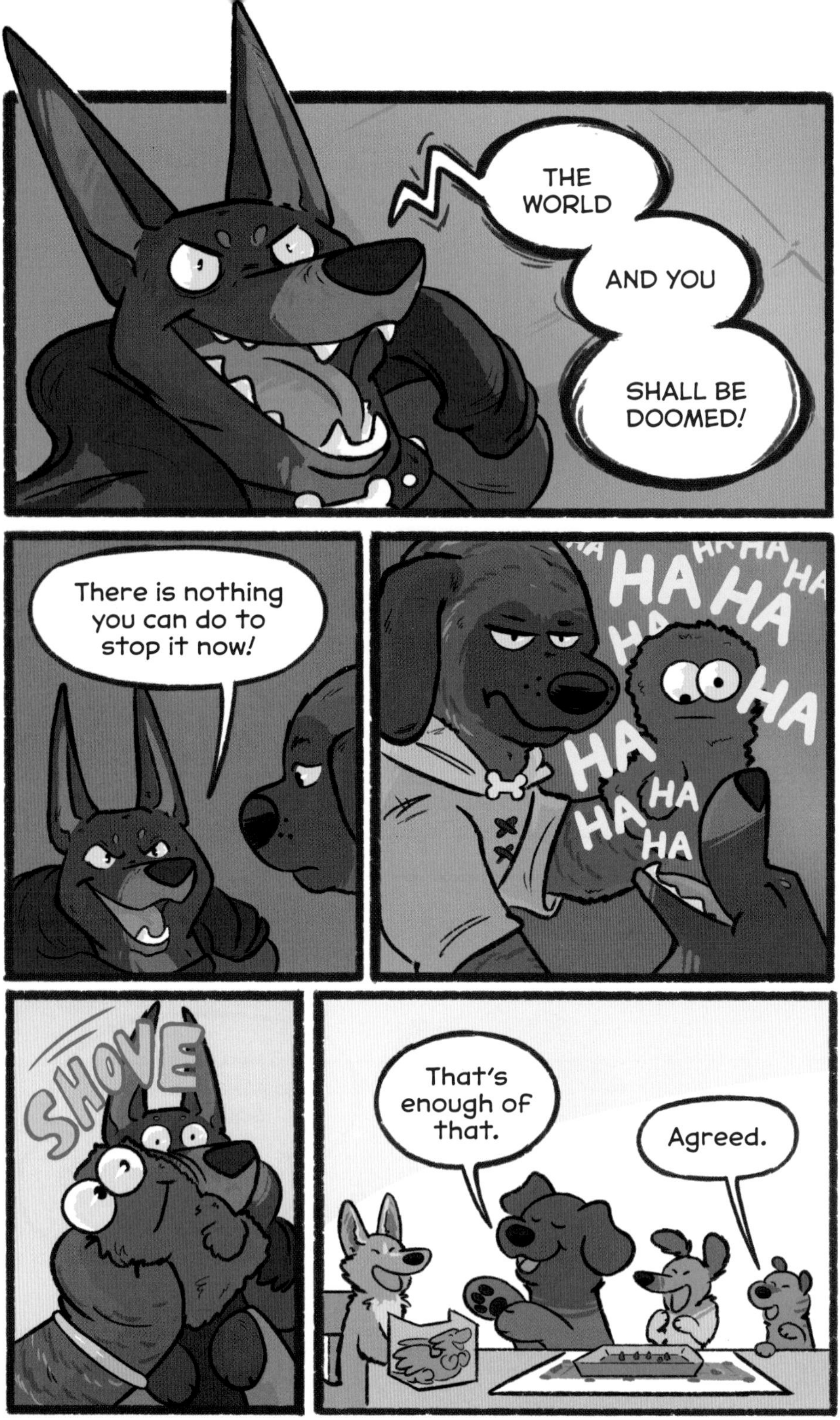
THE WORLD
AND YOU
SHALL BE DOOMED!
There is nothing you can do to stop it now!
HA HA HA HA HA HA HA HA HA HA HA HA
SHOVE
That's enough of that.
Agreed.

Haha! Good choice.

Now the Houndstooth thrashes its head.

But the dynamite is lodged!

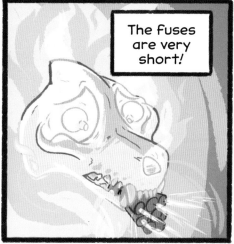

The fuses are very short!

I'm... uh... Gonna go...

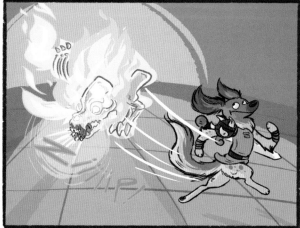

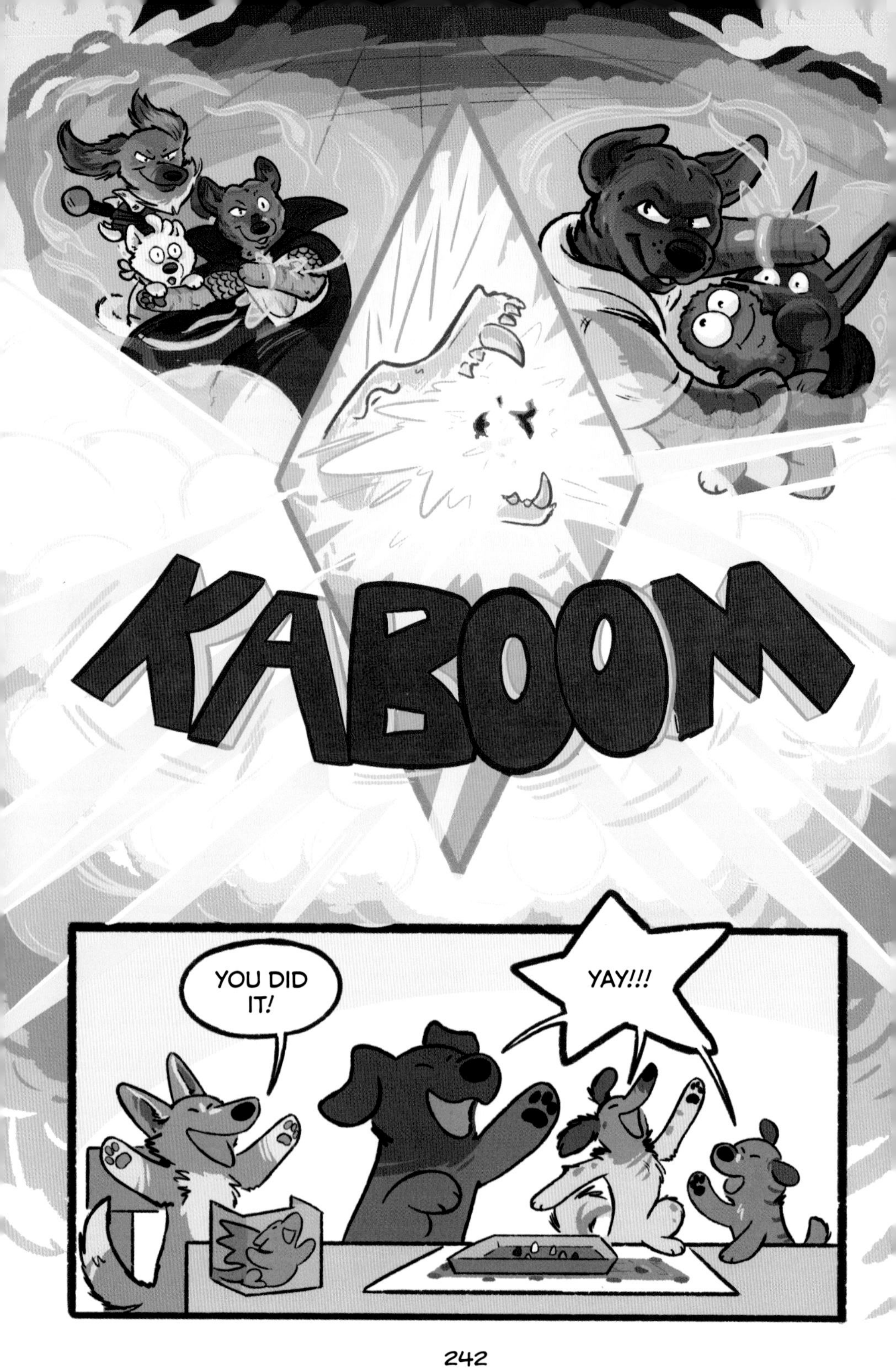
KABOOM
YOU DID IT!
YAY!!!

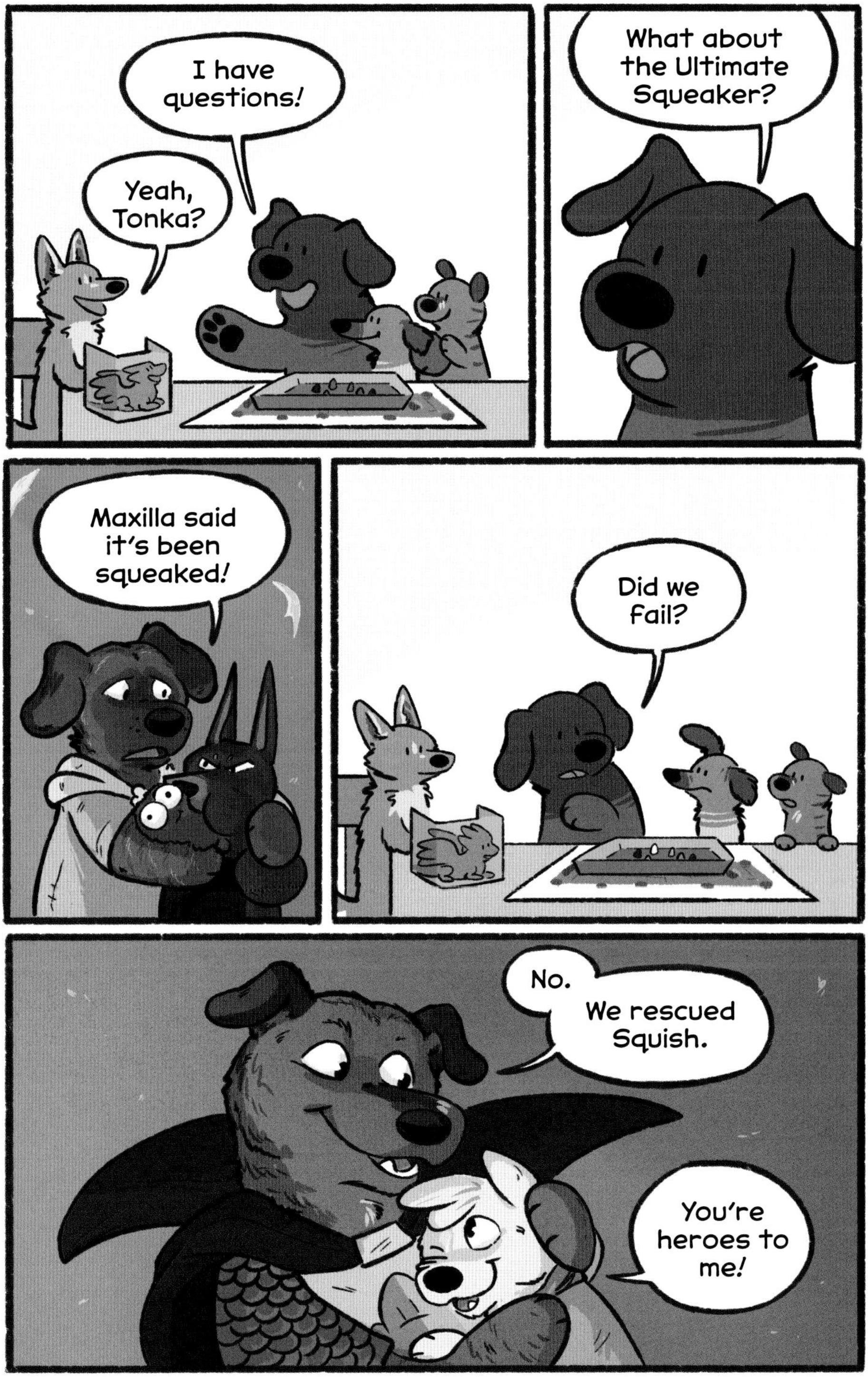
I have questions!
Yeah, Tonka?
What about the Ultimate Squeaker?
Maxilla said it's been squeaked!
Did we fail?
No.
We rescued Squish.
You're heroes to me!

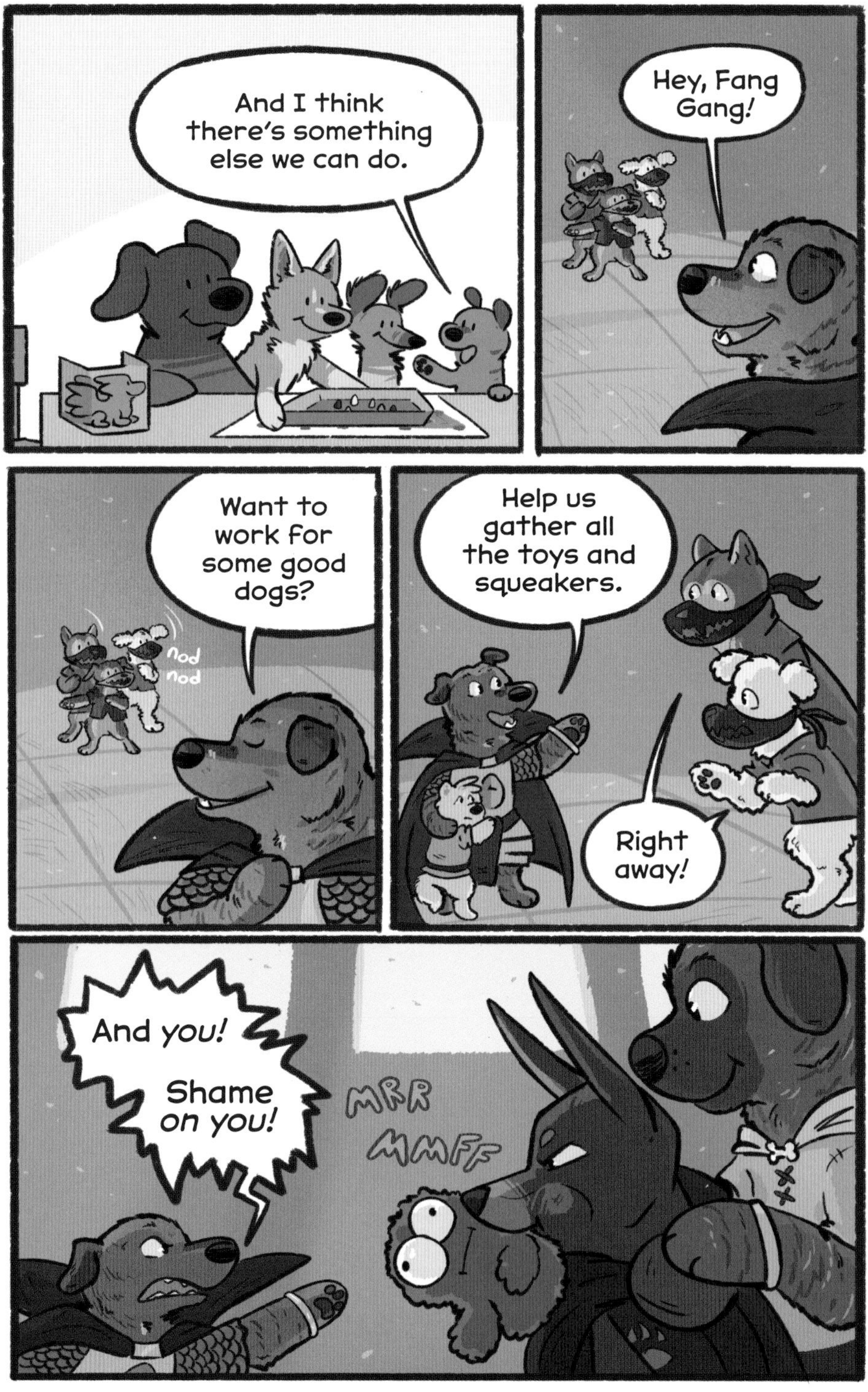

And I think there's something else we can do.
Hey, Fang Gang!
Want to work for some good dogs?
nod nod
Help us gather all the toys and squeakers.
Right away!
And you! Shame on you!
MRR MMFF

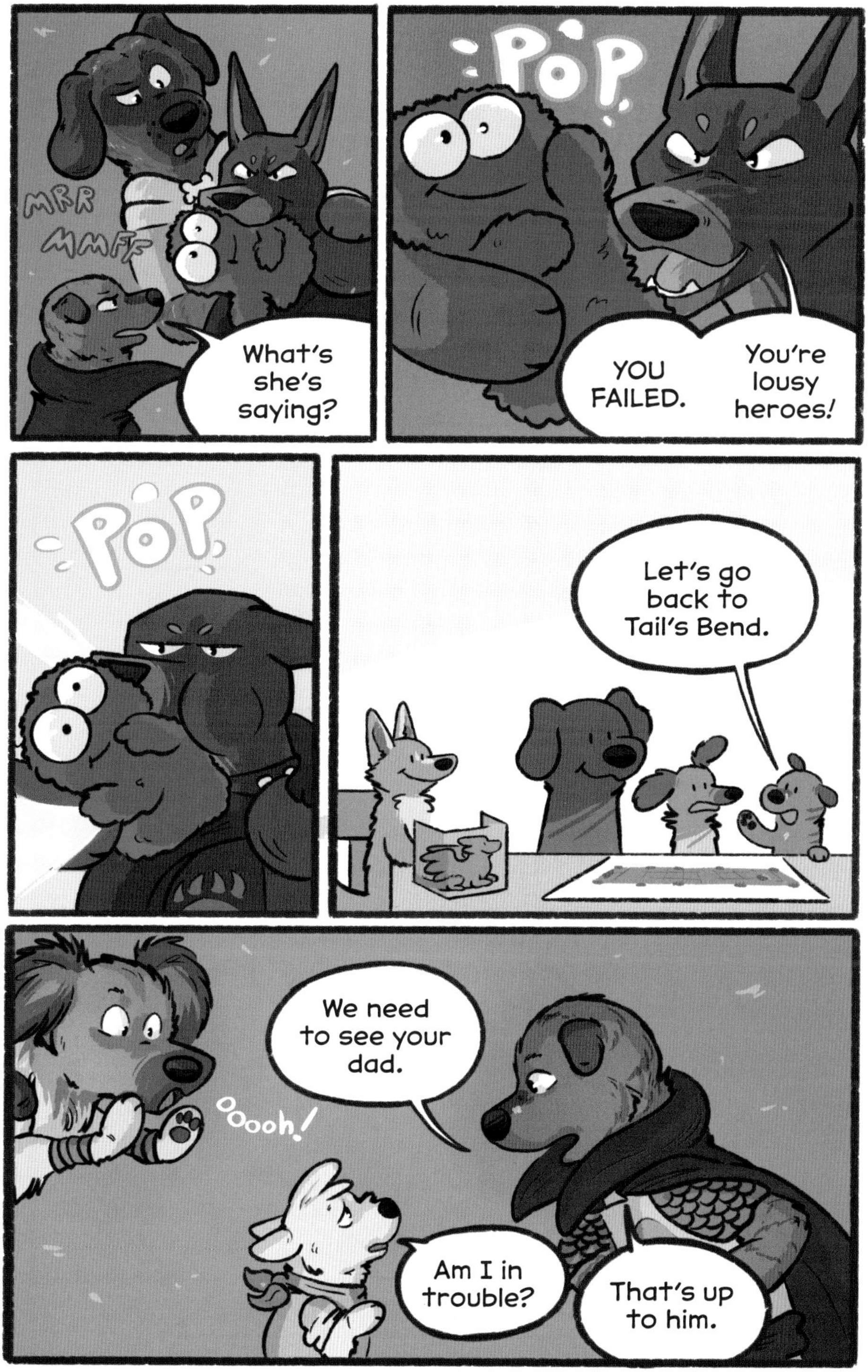
MRR
MMFF
What's she's saying?
POP
YOU FAILED.
You're lousy heroes!
POP
Let's go back to Tail's Bend.
We need to see your dad.
Ooooh!
Am I in trouble?
That's up to him.

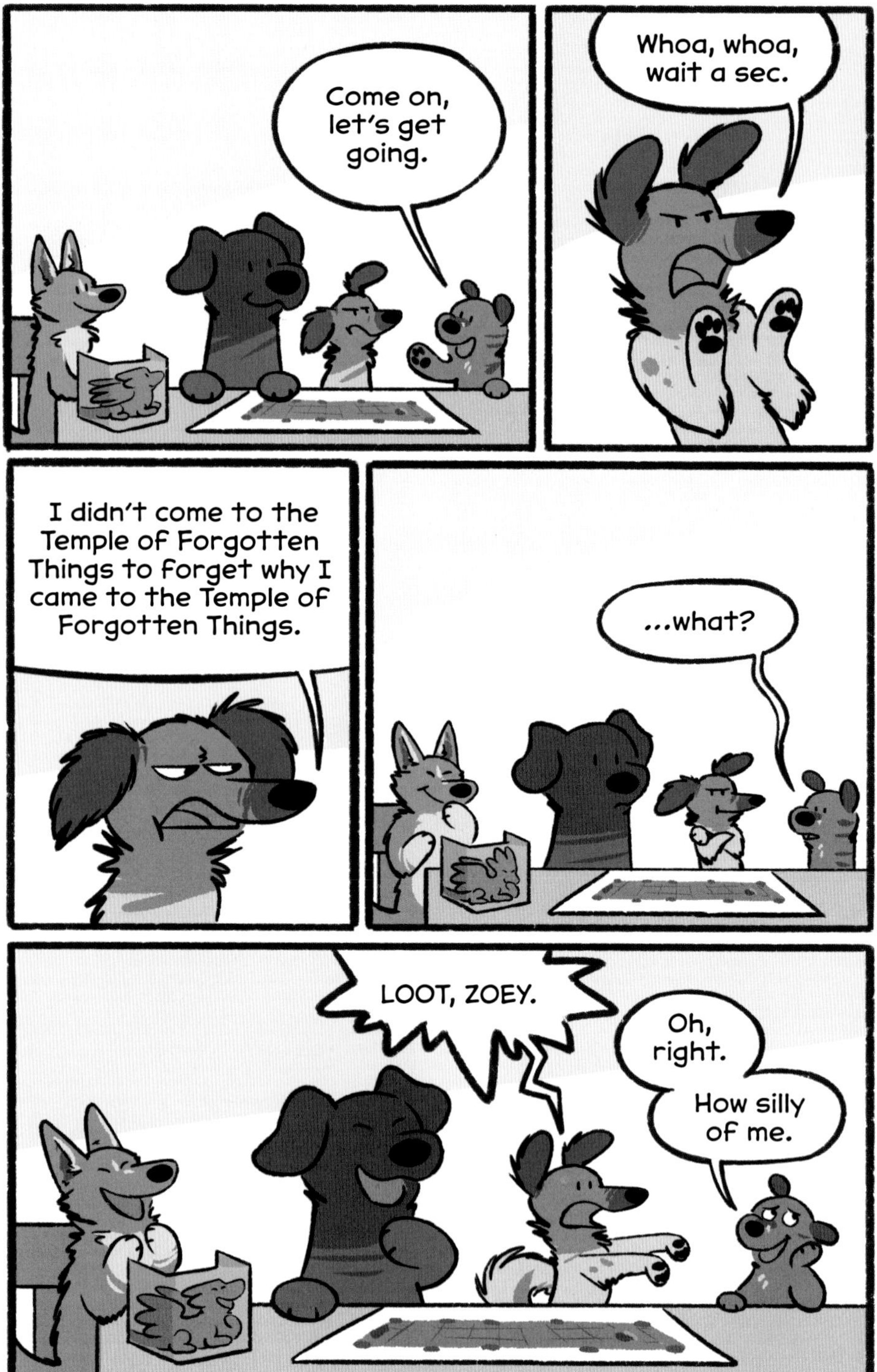
Come on, let's get going.
Whoa, whoa, wait a sec.
I didn't come to the Temple of Forgotten Things to forget why I came to the Temple of Forgotten Things.
...what?
LOOT, ZOEY.
Oh, right.
How silly of me.

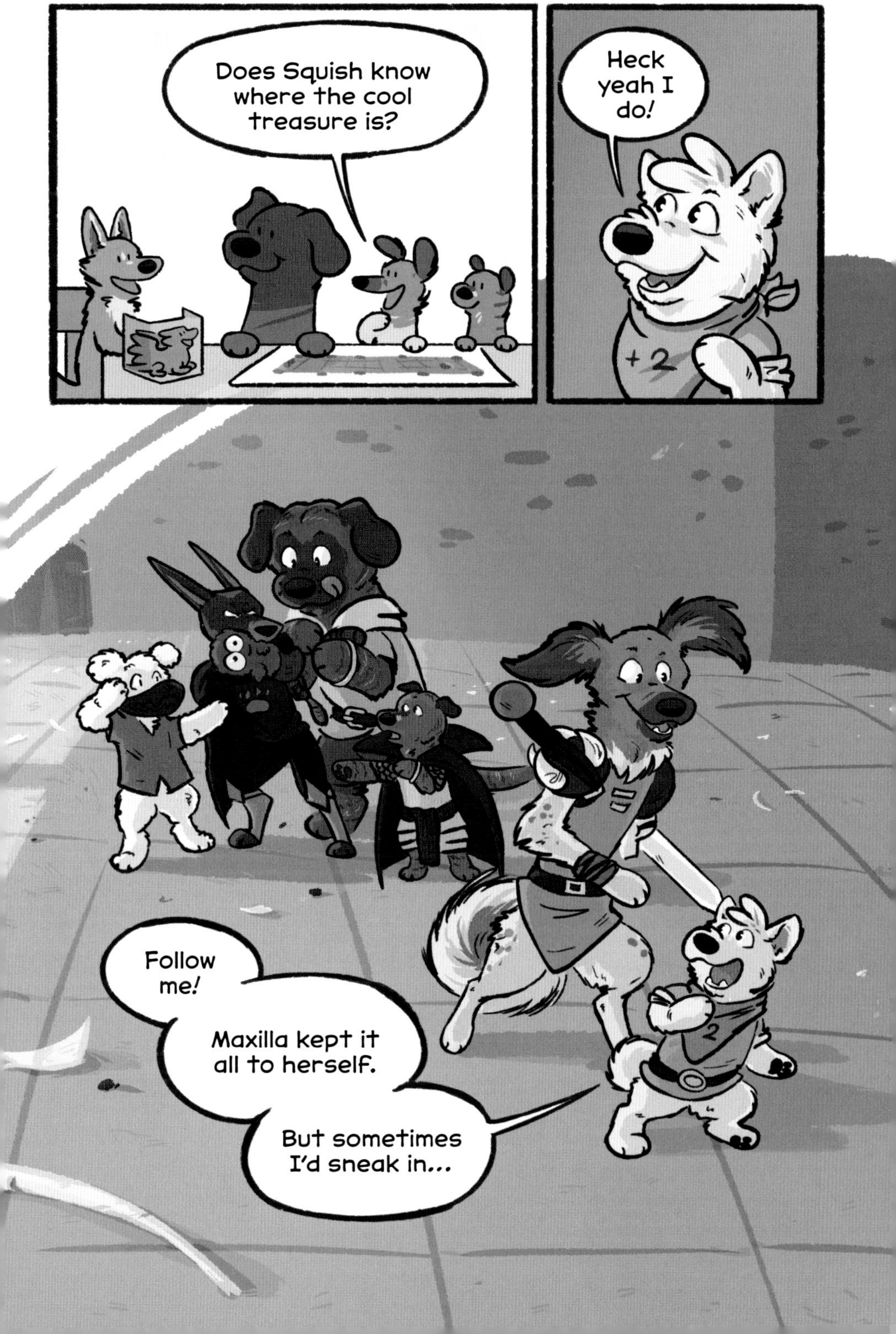
Does Squish know where the cool treasure is?
Heck yeah I do!
+2
Follow me!
Maxilla kept it all to herself.
But sometimes I'd sneak in...

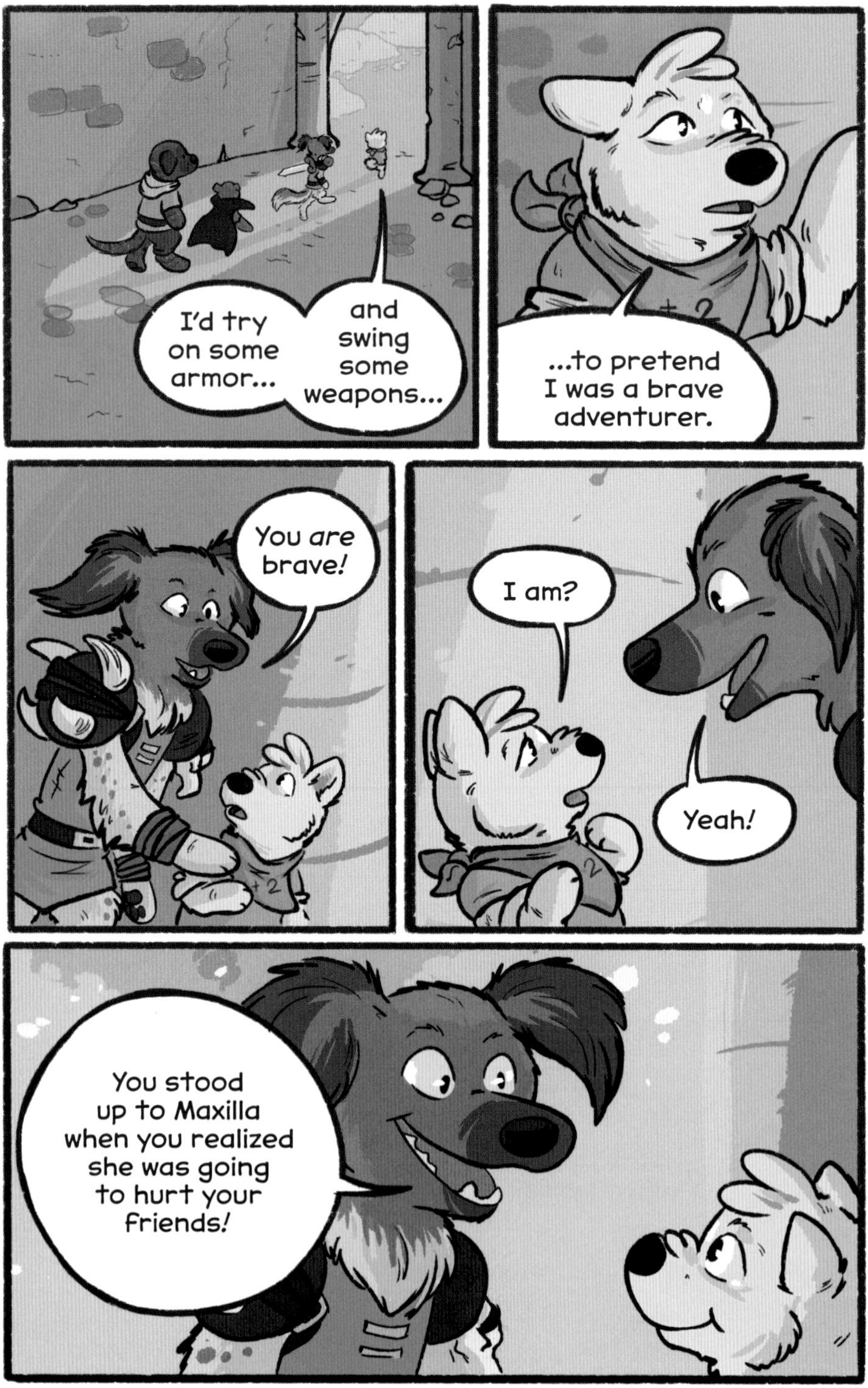
I'd try on some armor...
and swing some weapons...
...to pretend I was a brave adventurer.
You *are* brave!
I am?
Yeah!
You stood up to Maxilla when you realized she was going to hurt your friends!

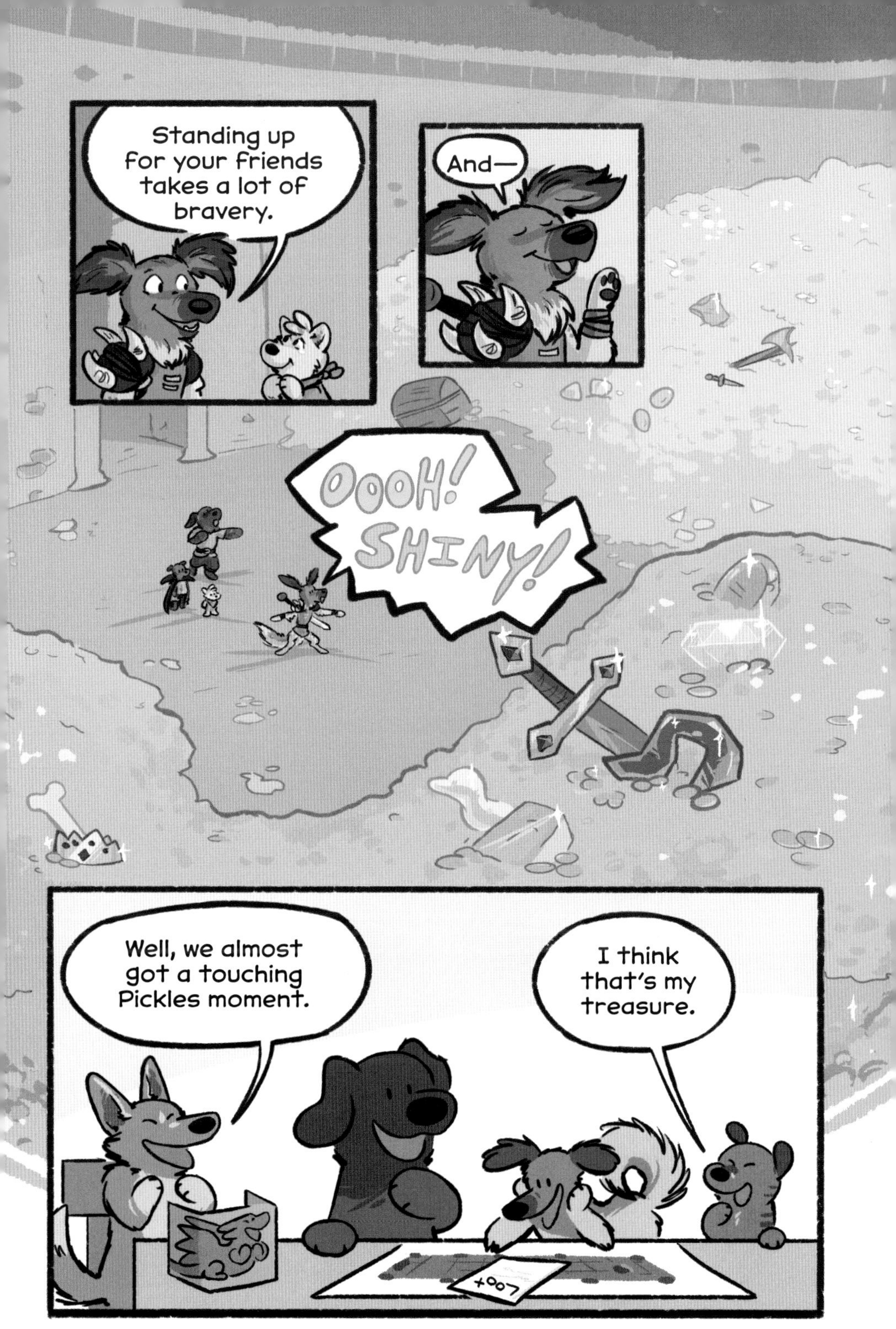
Standing up for your friends takes a lot of bravery.
And—
OOOH! SHINY!
Well, we almost got a touching Pickles moment.
I think that's my treasure.
Loot

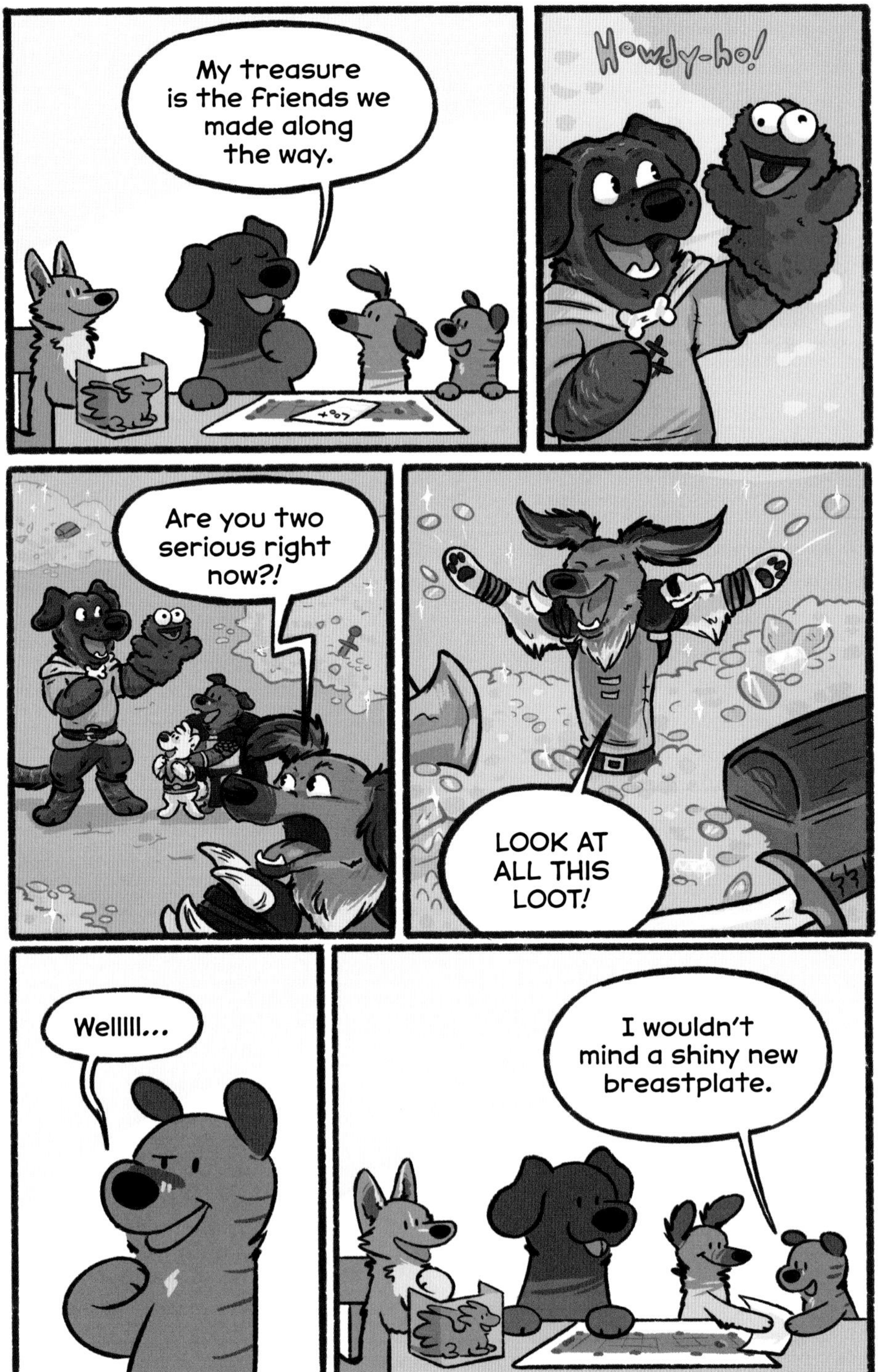
My treasure is the friends we made along the way.
Howdy-ho!
Are you two serious right now?!
LOOK AT ALL THIS LOOT!
Welllll...
I wouldn't mind a shiny new breastplate.

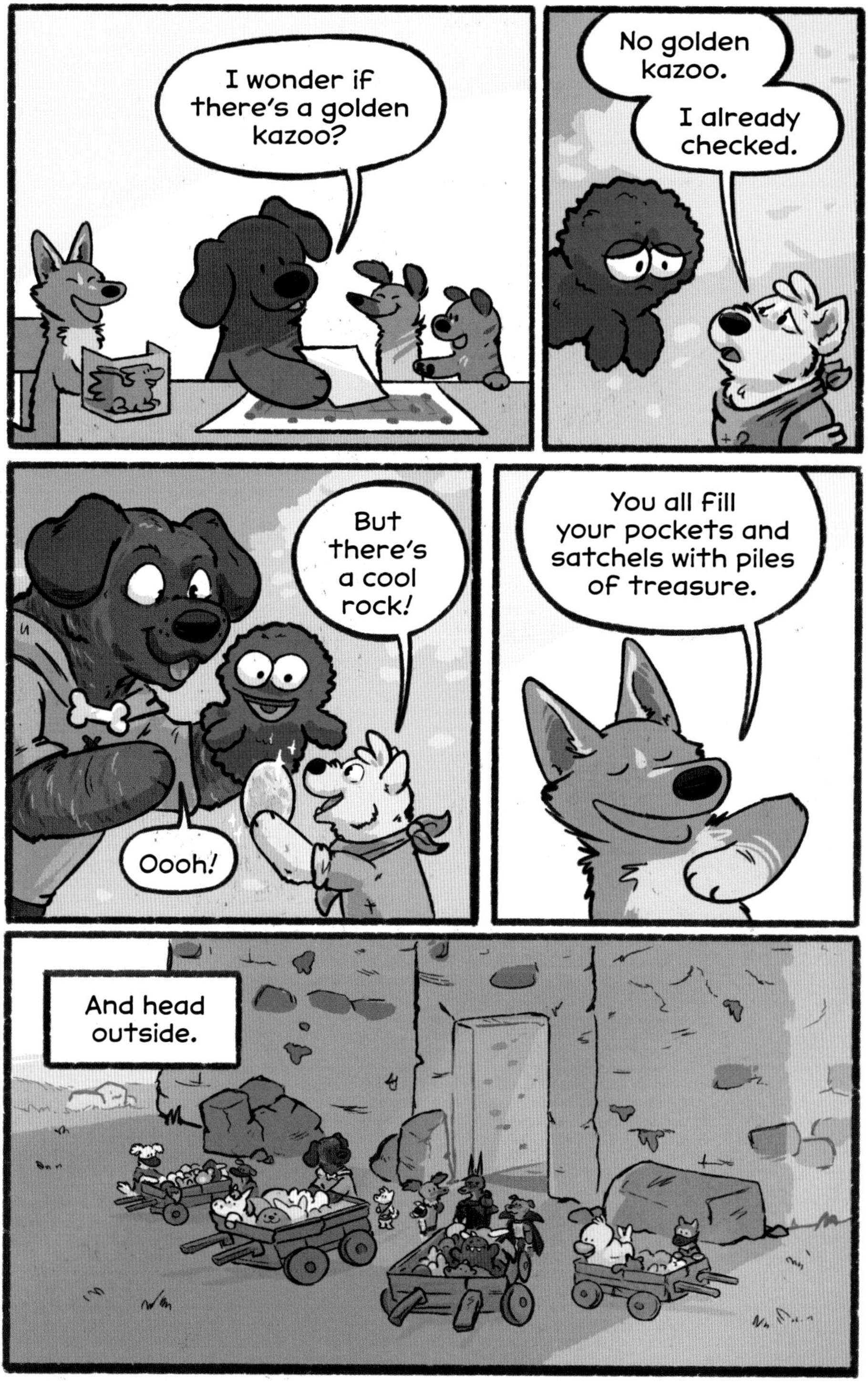
I wonder if there's a golden kazoo?
No golden kazoo.
I already checked.
But there's a cool rock!
Oooh!
You all fill your pockets and satchels with piles of treasure.
And head outside.

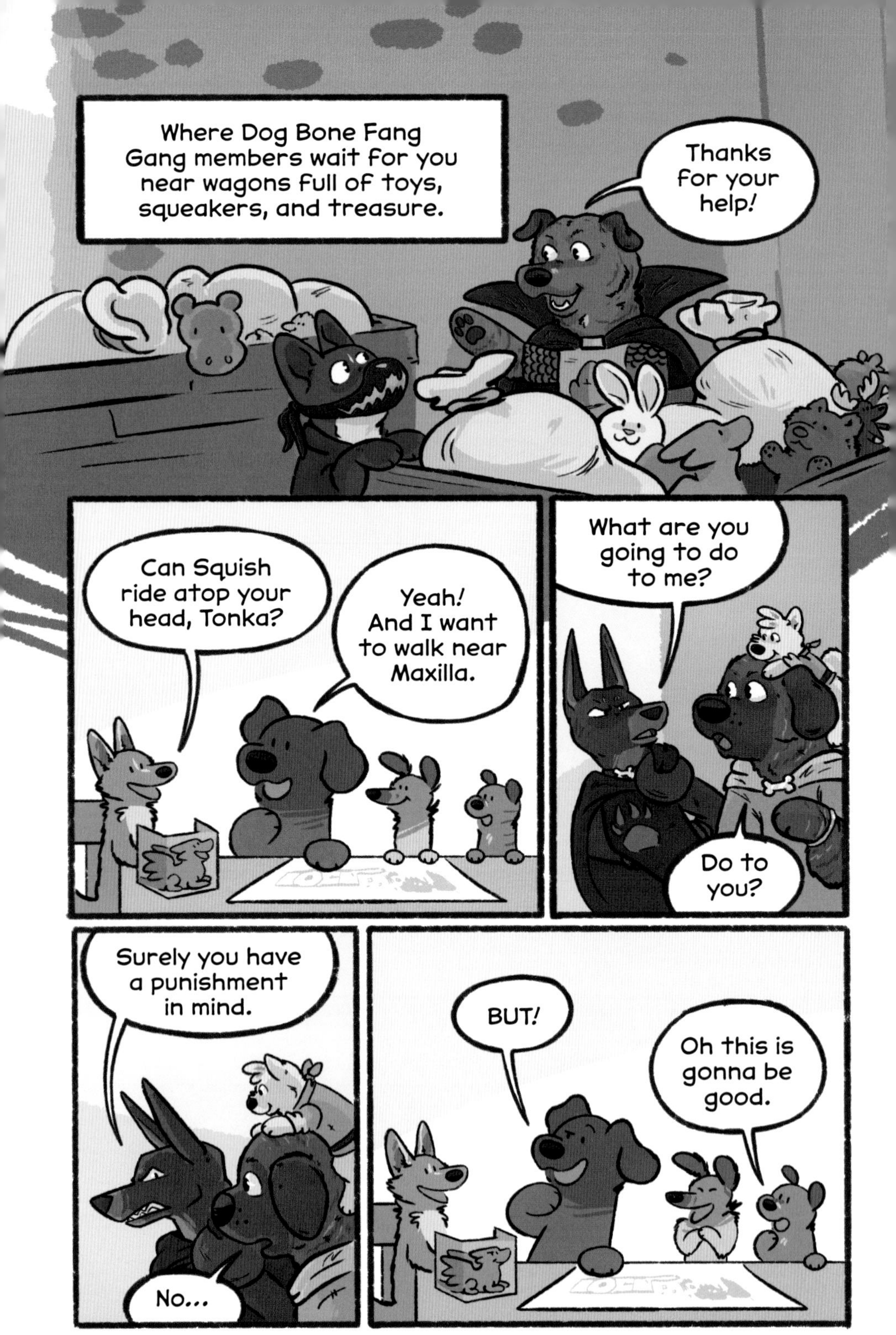
Where Dog Bone Fang Gang members wait for you near wagons full of toys, squeakers, and treasure.
Thanks for your help!
Can Squish ride atop your head, Tonka?
Yeah! And I want to walk near Maxilla.
What are you going to do to me?
Do to you?
Surely you have a punishment in mind.
No...
BUT!
Oh this is gonna be good.

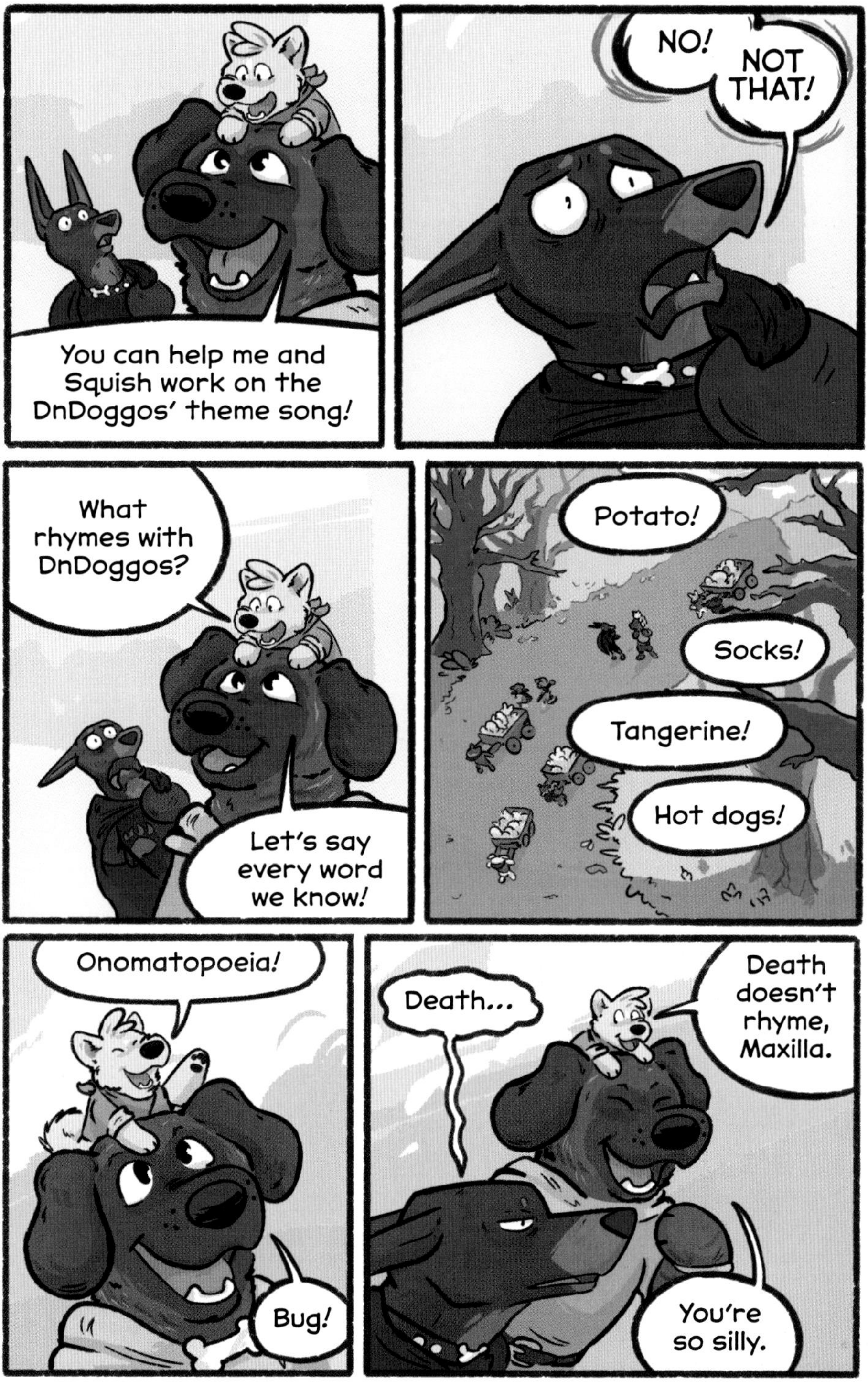
You can help me and Squish work on the DnDoggos' theme song!
NO!
NOT THAT!
What rhymes with DnDoggos?
Let's say every word we know!
Potato!
Socks!
Tangerine!
Hot dogs!
Onomatopoeia!
Bug!
Death...
Death doesn't rhyme, Maxilla.
You're so silly.

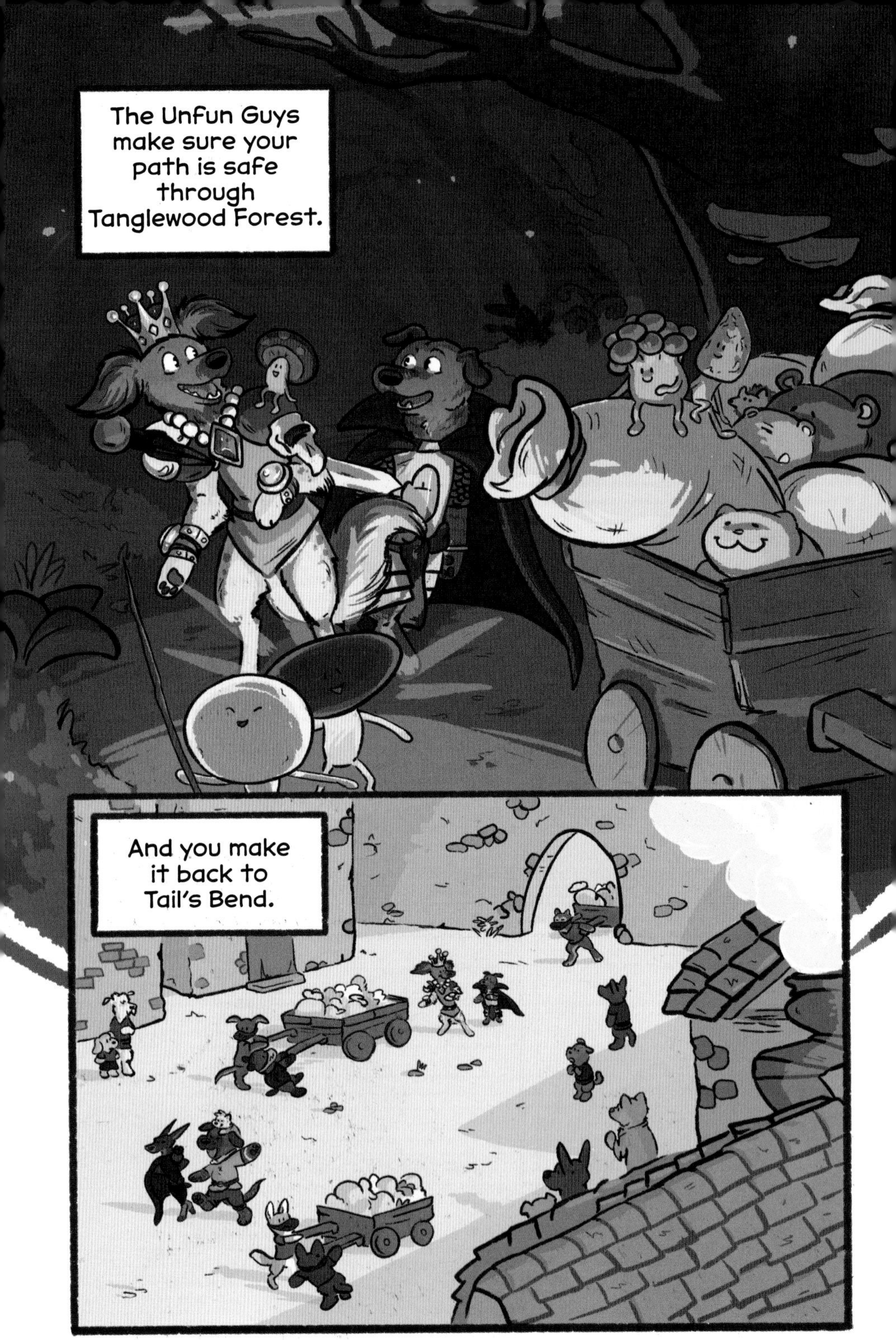
The Unfun Guys make sure your path is safe through Tanglewood Forest.
And you make it back to Tail's Bend.

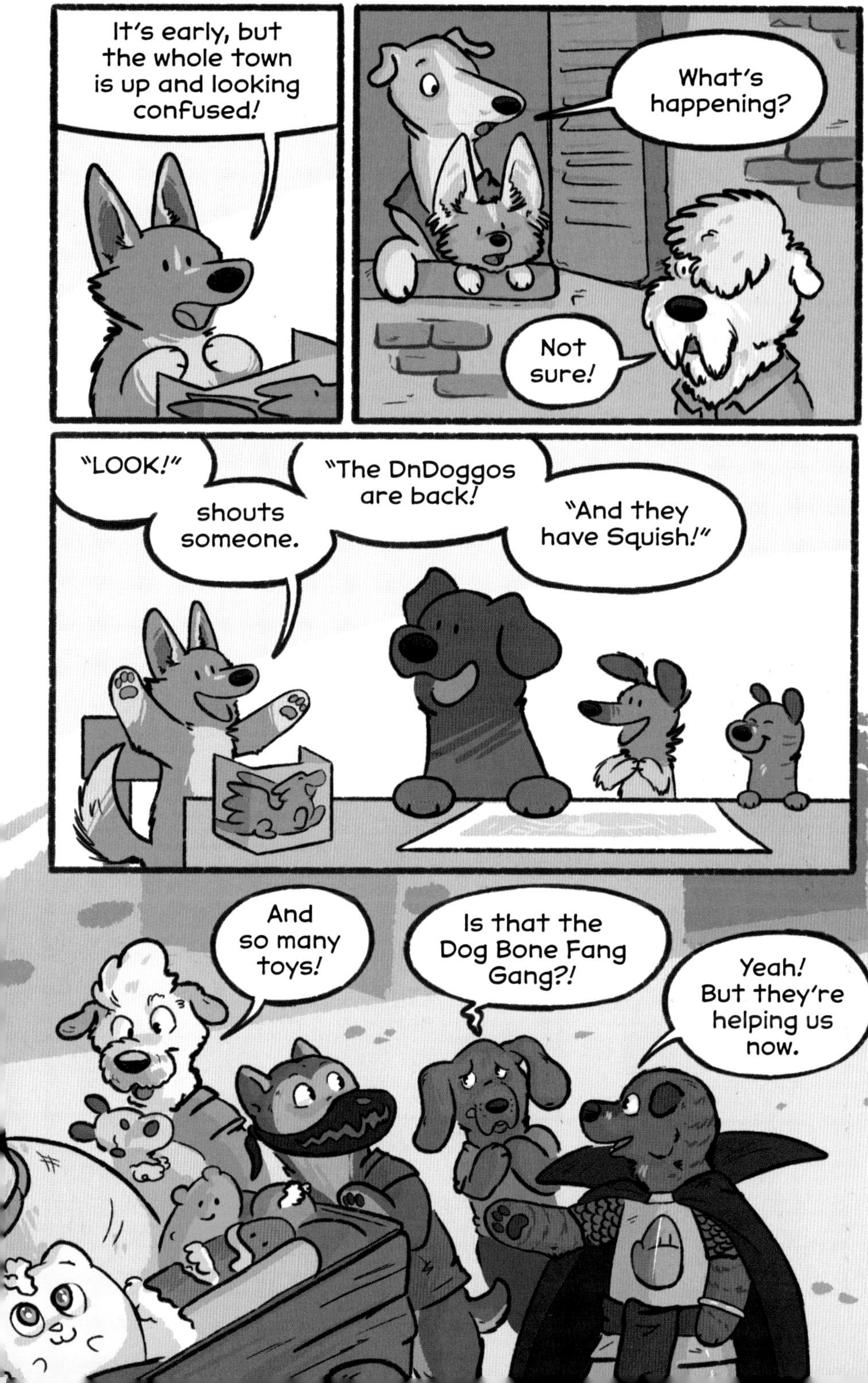

It's early, but the whole town is up and looking confused!
What's happening?
Not sure!
"LOOK!"
shouts someone.
"The DnDoggos are back!
"And they have Squish!"
And so many toys!
Is that the Dog Bone Fang Gang?!
Yeah! But they're helping us now.

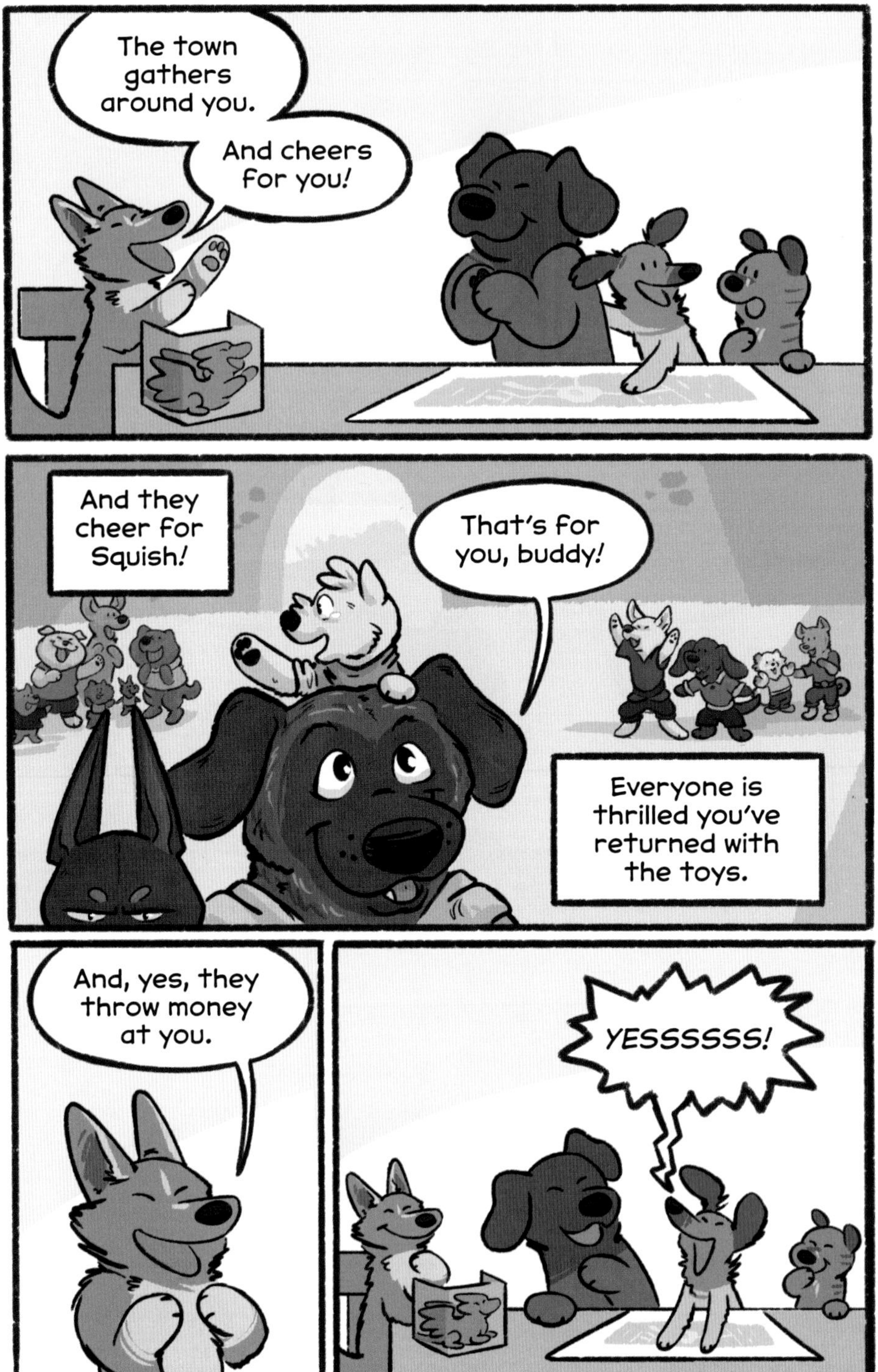
The town gathers around you.
And cheers for you!
And they cheer for Squish!
That's for you, buddy!
Everyone is thrilled you've returned with the toys.
And, yes, they throw money at you.
YESSSSSS!

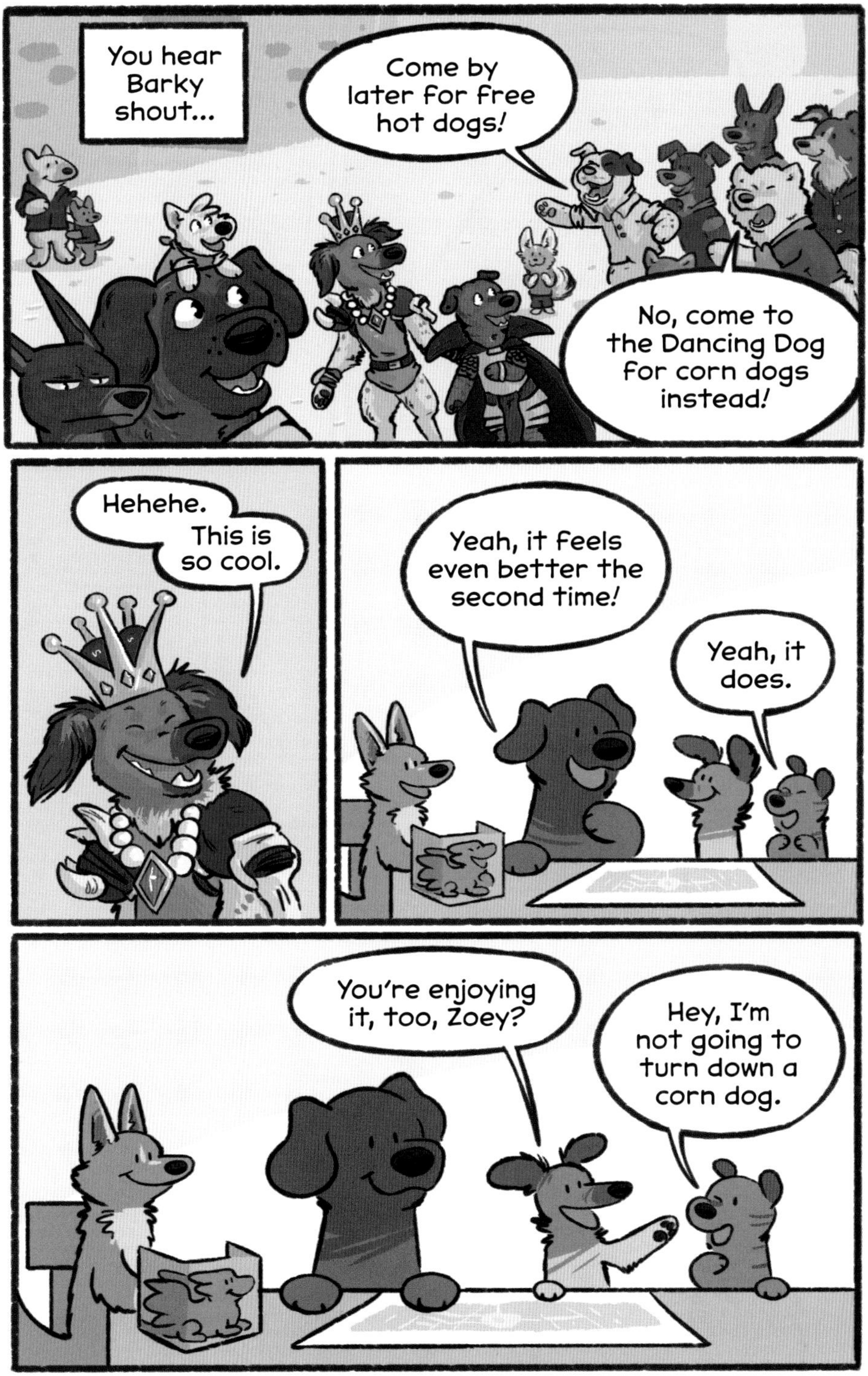
You hear Barky shout...
Come by later for free hot dogs!
No, come to the Dancing Dog for corn dogs instead!
Hehehe.
This is so cool.
Yeah, it feels even better the second time!
Yeah, it does.
You're enjoying it, too, Zoey?
Hey, I'm not going to turn down a corn dog.

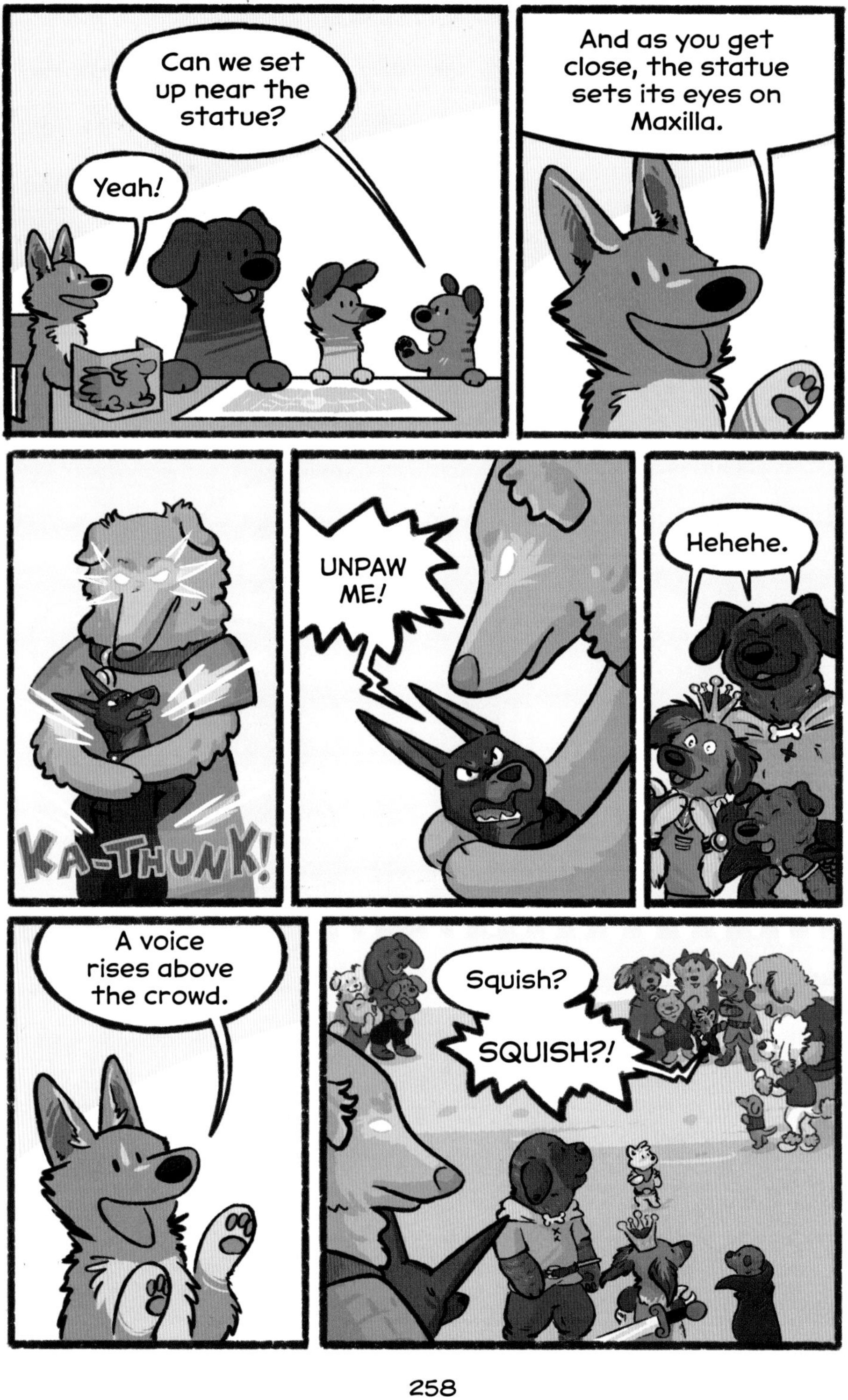
Can we set up near the statue?
Yeah!
And as you get close, the statue sets its eyes on Maxilla.
KA-THUNK!
UNPAW ME!
Hehehe.
A voice rises above the crowd.
Squish?
SQUISH?!

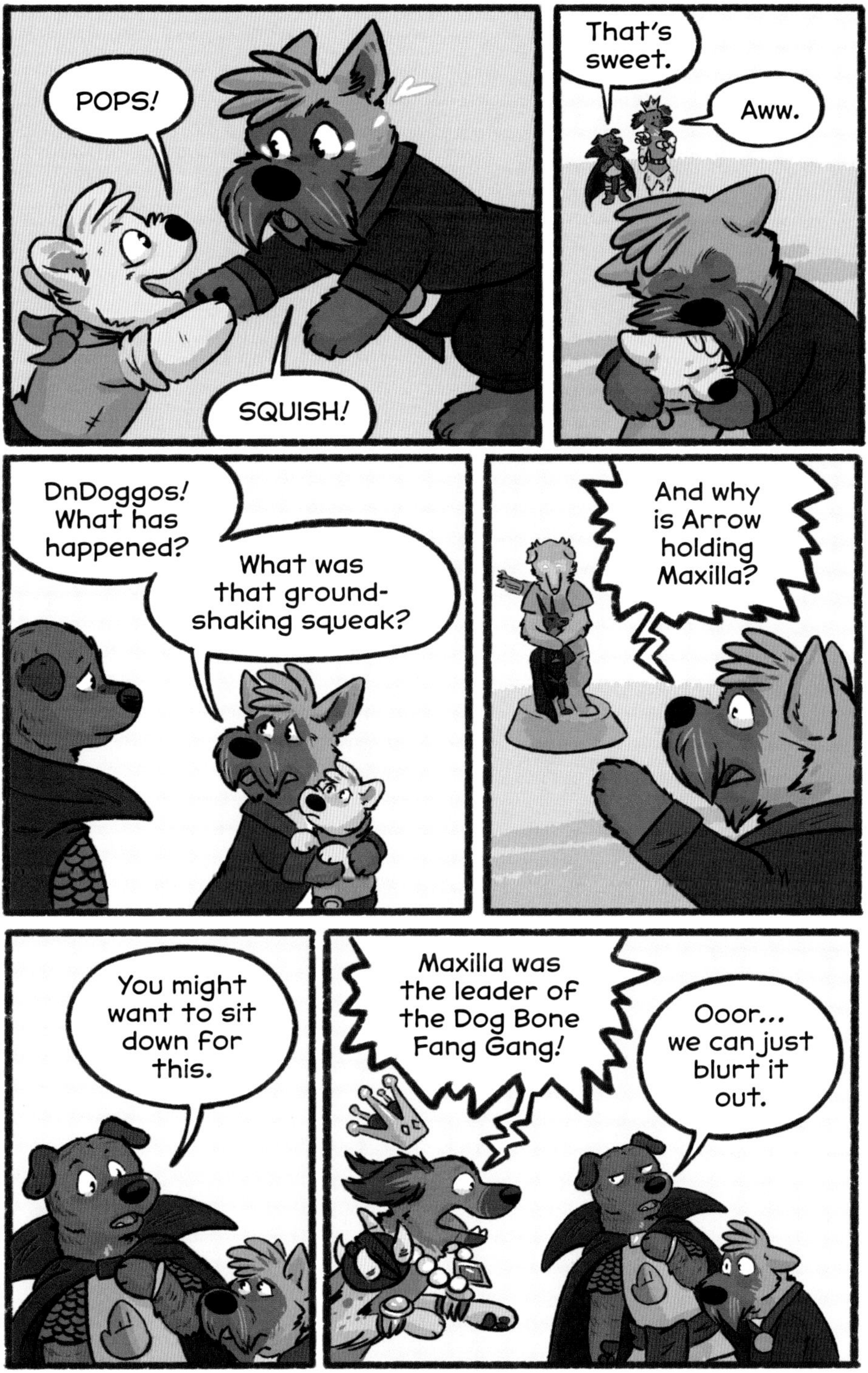
POPS!
SQUISH!
That's sweet.
Aww.
DnDoggos! What has happened?
What was that ground-shaking squeak?
And why is Arrow holding Maxilla?
You might want to sit down for this.
Maxilla was the leader of the Dog Bone Fang Gang!
Ooor... we can just blurt it out.

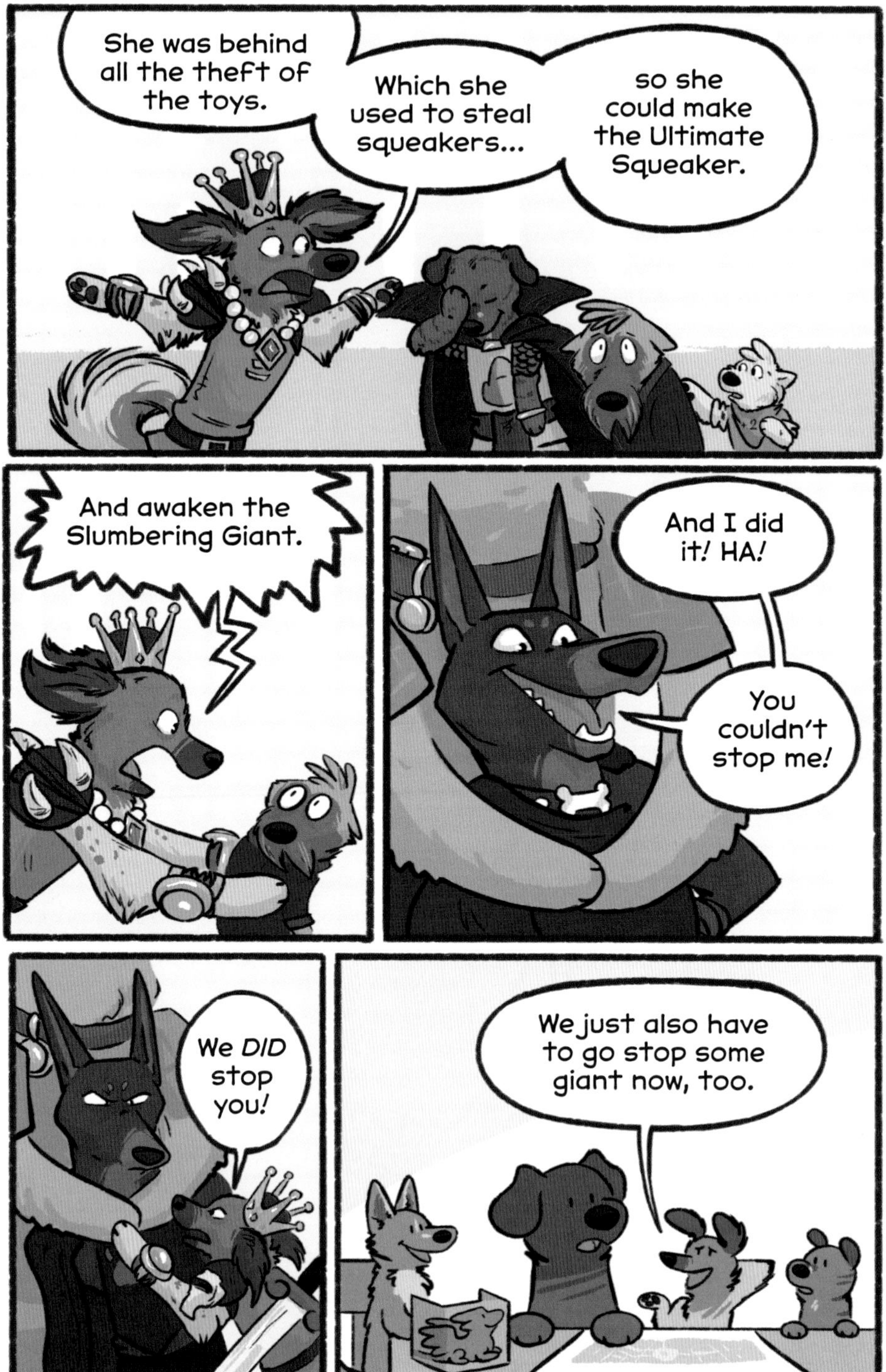
She was behind all the theft of the toys.
Which she used to steal squeakers...
so she could make the Ultimate Squeaker.
And awaken the Slumbering Giant.
And I did it! HA!
You couldn't stop me!
We *DID* stop you!
We just also have to go stop some giant now, too.

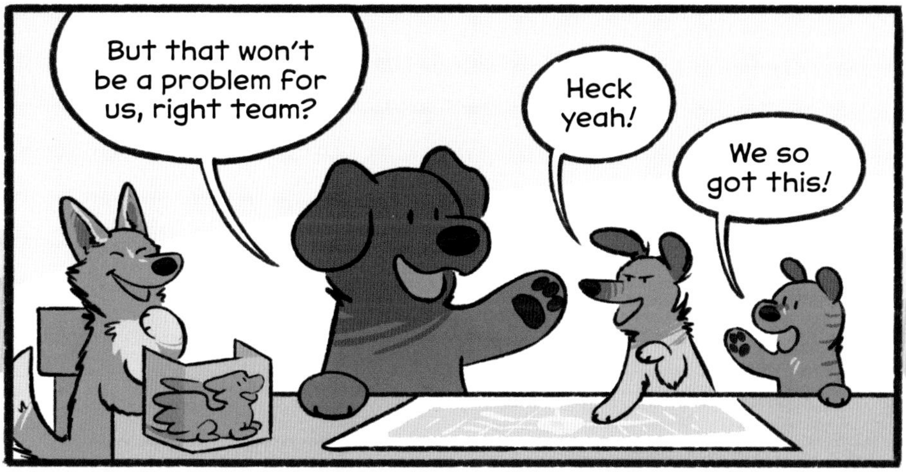
But that won't be a problem for us, right team?
Heck yeah!
We so got this!

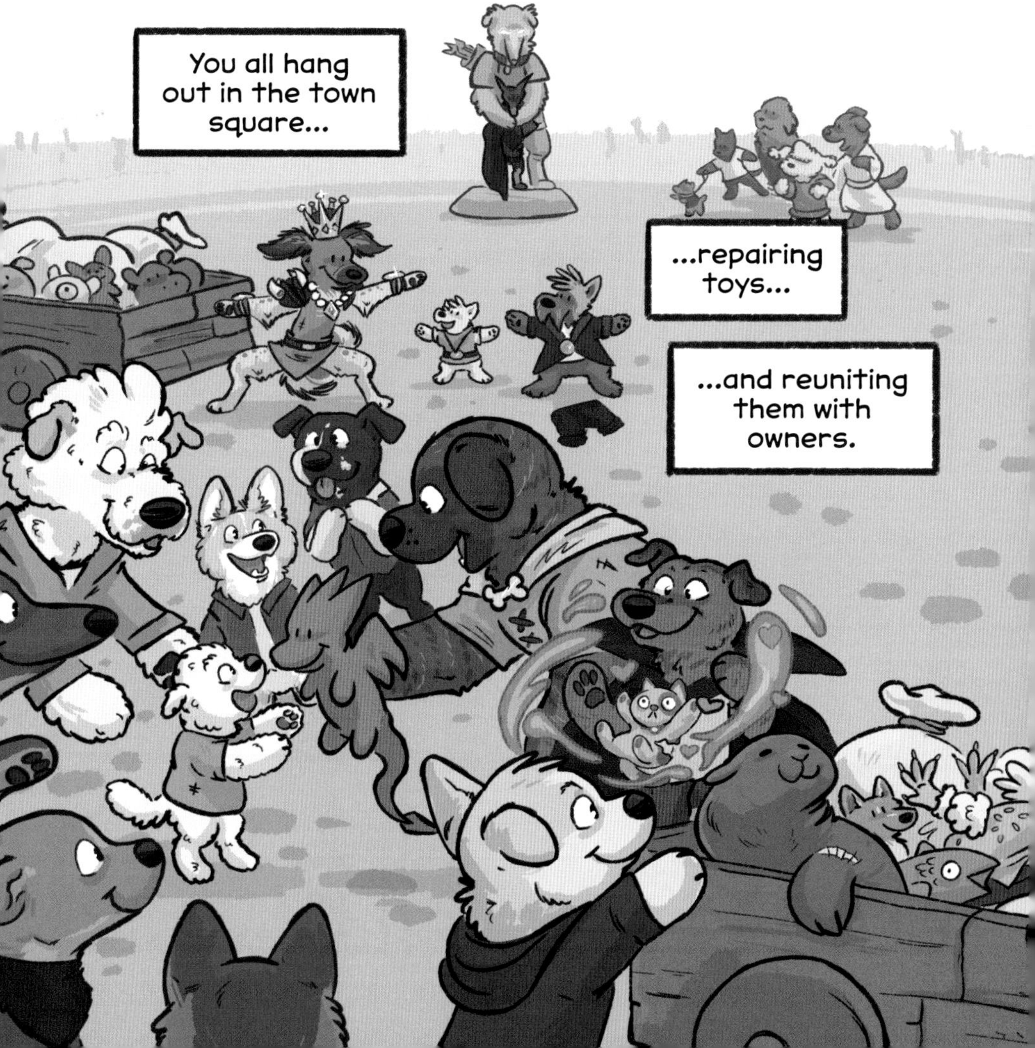
You all hang out in the town square...
...repairing toys...
...and reuniting them with owners.

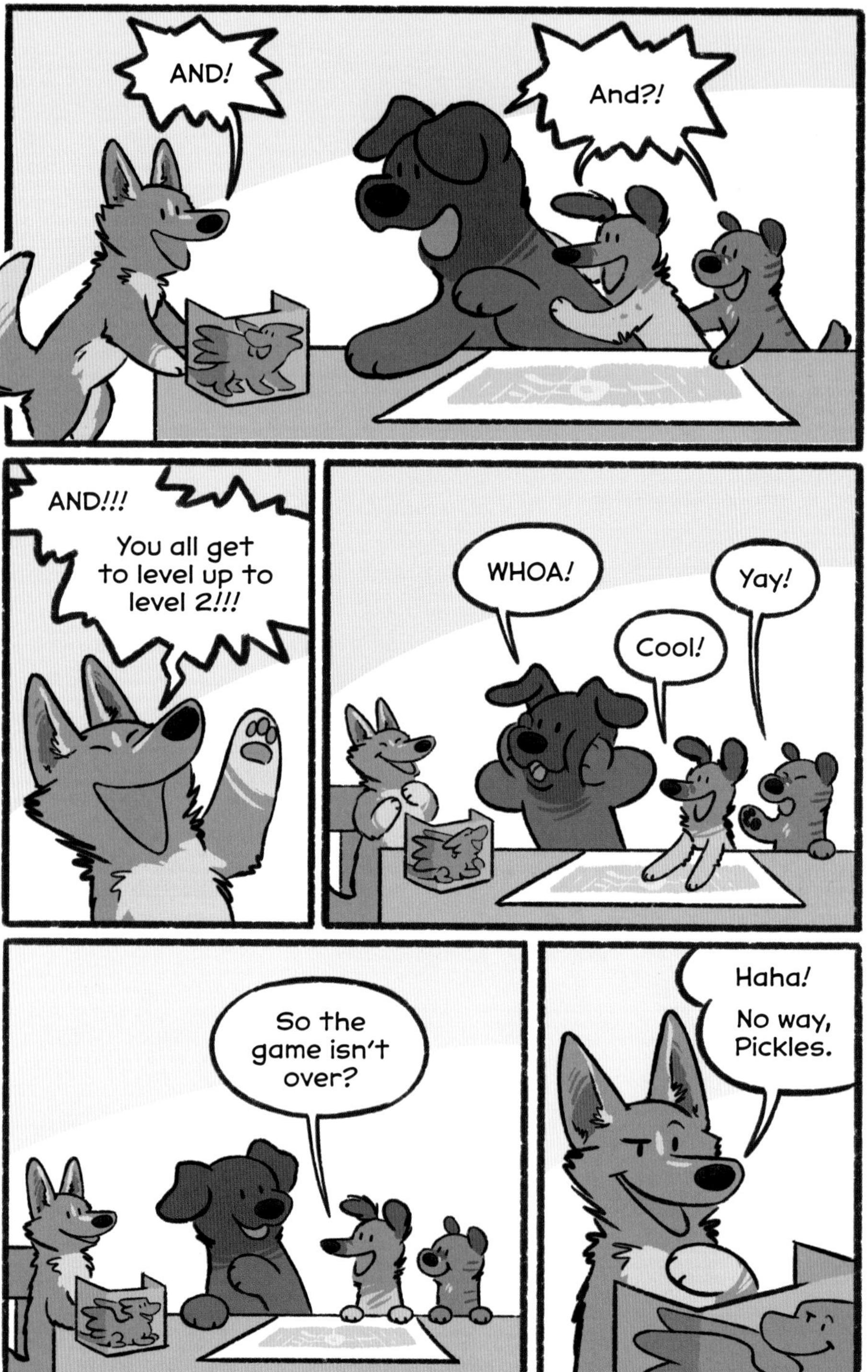
AND!
And?!
AND!!! You all get to level up to level 2!!!
WHOA!
Cool!
Yay!
So the game isn't over?
Haha! No way, Pickles.

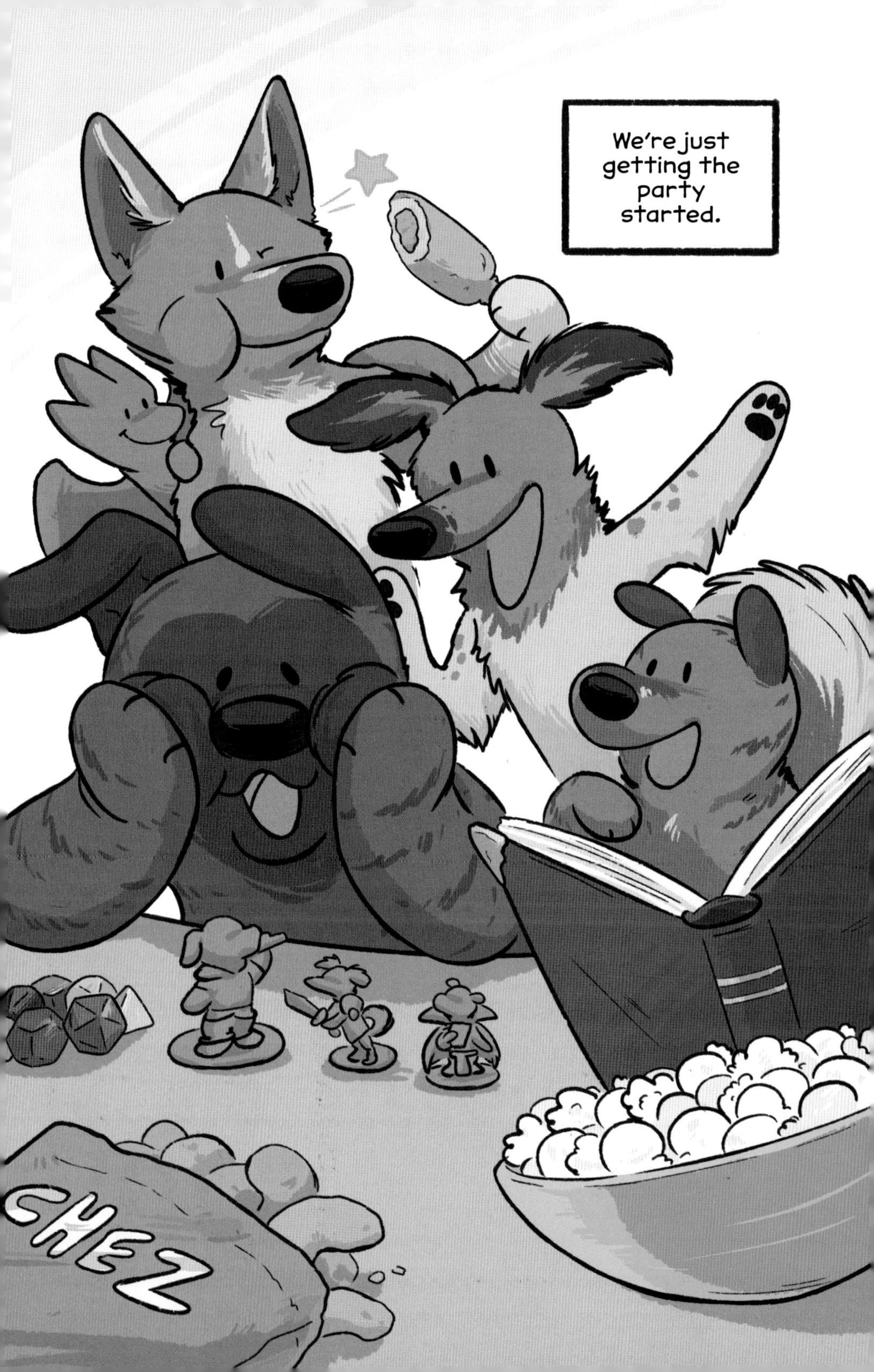
We're just getting the party started.
CHEZ

Magnus's Gaming Tips

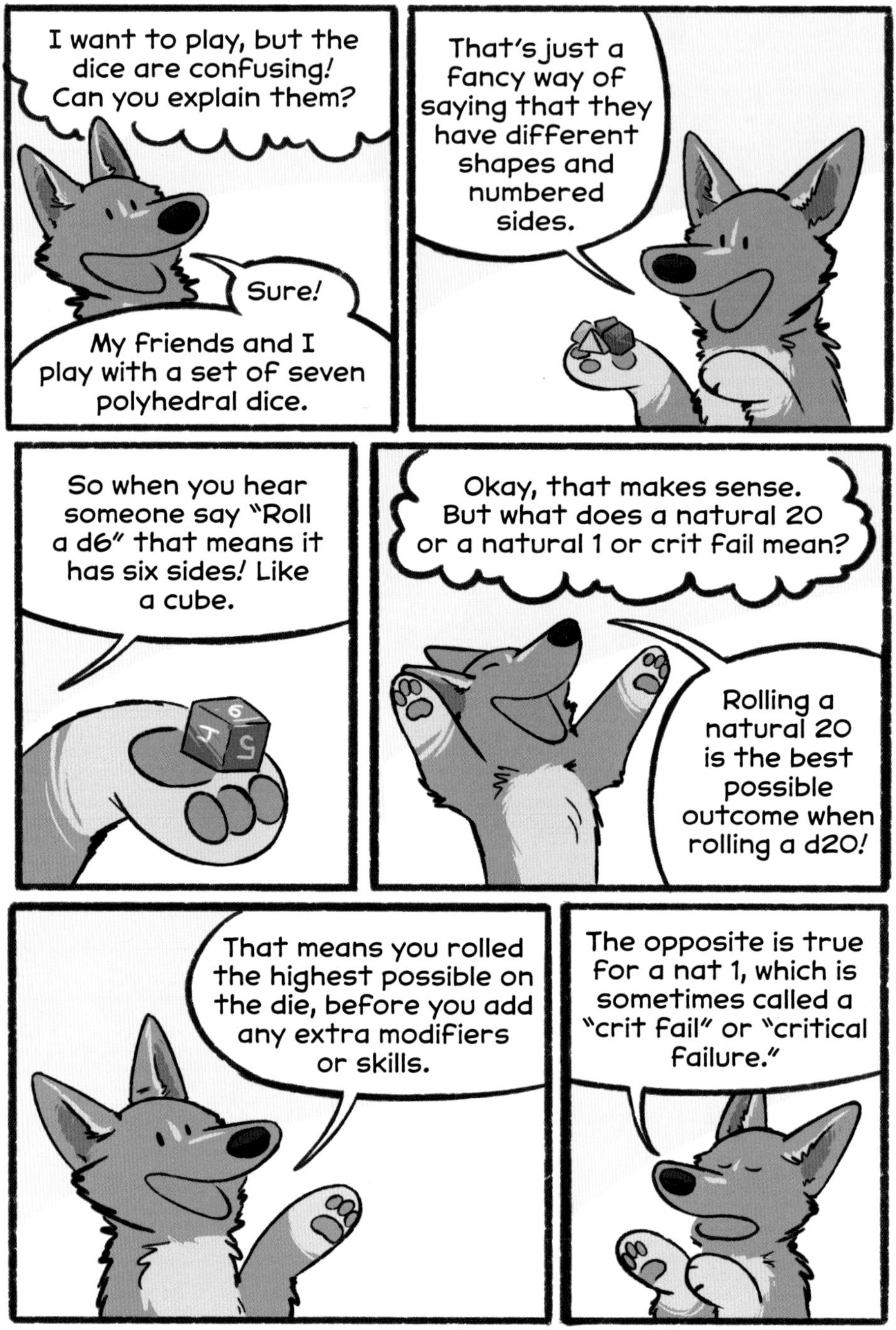
I want to play, but the dice are confusing! Can you explain them?
Sure!
My friends and I play with a set of seven polyhedral dice.
That's just a fancy way of saying that they have different shapes and numbered sides.
So when you hear someone say "Roll a d6" that means it has six sides! Like a cube.
Okay, that makes sense. But what does a natural 20 or a natural 1 or crit fail mean?
Rolling a natural 20 is the best possible outcome when rolling a d20!
That means you rolled the highest possible on the die, before you add any extra modifiers or skills.
The opposite is true for a nat 1, which is sometimes called a "crit fail" or "critical failure."

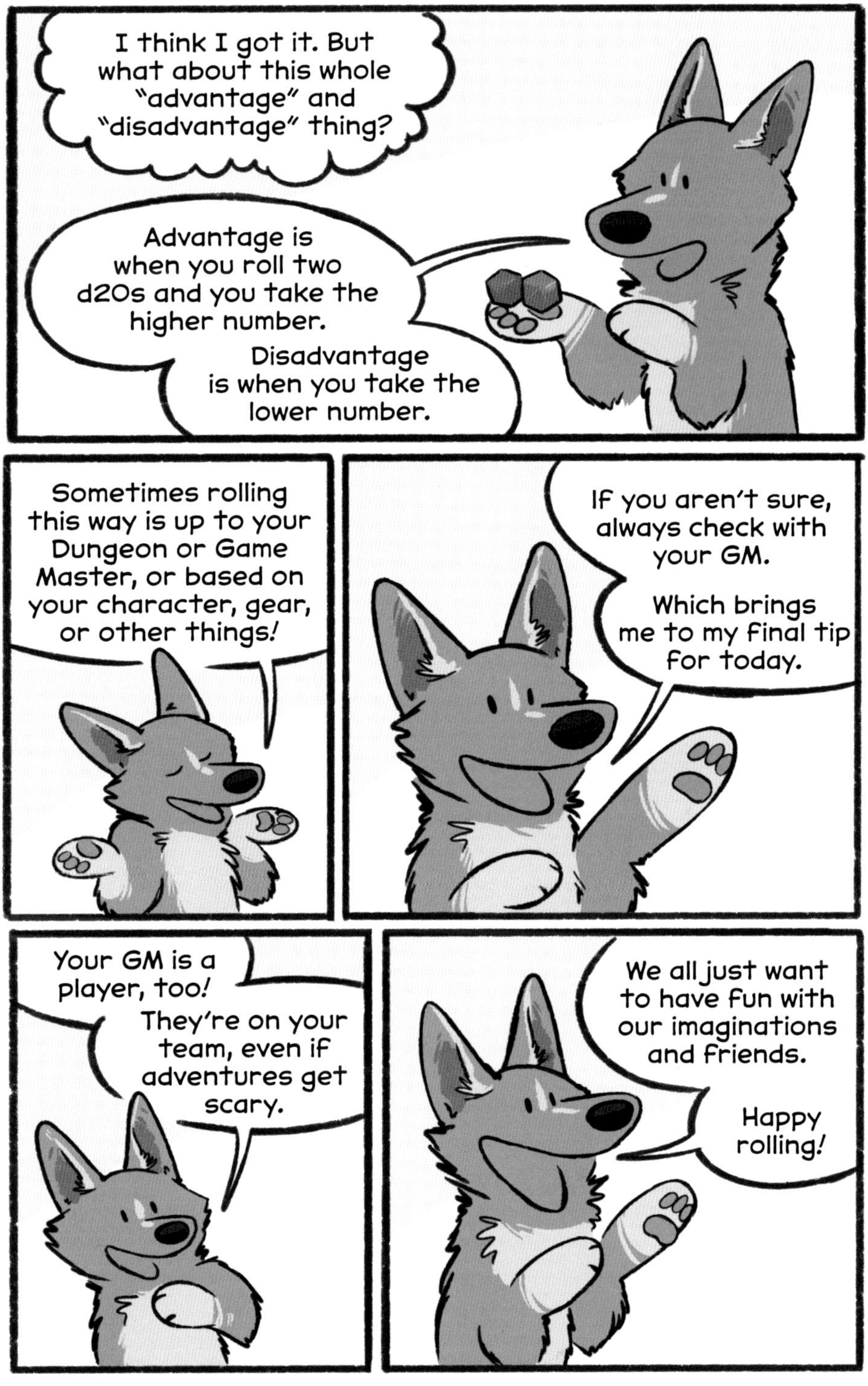

I think I got it. But what about this whole "advantage" and "disadvantage" thing?
Advantage is when you roll two d20s and you take the higher number.
Disadvantage is when you take the lower number.
Sometimes rolling this way is up to your Dungeon or Game Master, or based on your character, gear, or other things!
If you aren't sure, always check with your GM.
Which brings me to my final tip for today.
Your GM is a player, too!
They're on your team, even if adventures get scary.
We all just want to have fun with our imaginations and friends.
Happy rolling!

Scout Underhill started DnDoggos as a webcomic in 2017 when they caught their dogs playing tabletop roleplaying games. Using their newly found internet celebrity status, Magnus and Pickles ~~demanded~~ encouraged Scout to make this book. Scout lives in the woods of Nashville, Tennessee, with their dogs and found family. *DnDoggos: Get the Party Started* is their debut graphic novel. You can see more of their work at dndoggos.com or scoutunderhill.com.

Liana Sposto is an illustrator and cartoonist from Los Angeles, California, where she lives on a sailboat with her husband and a bunch of sea lions. She really loves coloring. You can see more of her work online @lianabnana or at lianasposto.com.

Thank you for reading this Feiwel & Friends book.
The friends who made *DnDoggos: Get the Party Started* possible are:

Jean Feiwel, Publisher
Liz Szabla, VP, Associate Publisher
Rich Deas, Senior Creative Director
Holly West, Senior Editor
Anna Roberto, Executive Editor
Kat Brzozowski, Senior Editor
Dawn Ryan, Executive Managing Editor
Kim Waymer, Senior Production Manager
Emily Settle, Editor
Rachel Diebel, Editor
Foyinsi Adegbonmire, Editor
Brittany Groves, Assistant Editor
Sharismar Rodriguez, Senior Art Director
Lisa Vega, Designer
Avia Perez, Senior Production Editor

Follow us on Facebook or visit us online at mackids.com.
Our books are friends for life.